ERICA JAMES
Three Great Novels

D0890711

Erica James

A Breath of Fresh Air
Time for a Change
Airs & Graces

ORION

Contents

A Breath of Fresh Air

To Edward and Samuel who handled their
mother's tantrums with such patience.
Thanks to Big G. and all my friends who helped
and bullied me through the darkness,
especially Helena, Maureen and Rosemary.

'Man cannot discover new oceans until he has courage to lose sight of the shore.'

Unknown

1

Charlotte had never seen a man cry before, so she wasn't sure how to react to her husband's unexpected display of emotion. Not once had she ever imagined Peter capable of crying; it went against all she had ever known about him.

At a quarter to eight in the morning and while tapping open her boiled egg in their Brussels apartment, Charlotte Lawrence had finally plucked up the courage to ask her husband for a divorce and to put an end, once and for all, to his assumption that because he was fulfilled, so was she. She had told him that life under the corporate umbrella was not sufficient to satisfy both their needs. And then he had cried.

Charlotte passed him the box of tissues and tried to assimilate her own feelings. To her surprise, she felt indifference towards Peter, tinged with a hint of embarrassment. True, a man of the 1990s was allowed to cry – men were now allowed the full gamut of emotions, it was no holds barred, cards on the kitchen table; like women, men had emotions, too. But when it was in their kitchen and over their table, it felt all wrong.

'I'm sorry,' she said, knowing how hollow and inadequate her words sounded. She watched Peter scour his eyes with a tissue, then blow his nose. She looked away, down on to the street below, and wished, as she did every morning she looked out of the window, that she was back in England.

She knew it was pathetic, but she couldn't help it. She was homesick. Oh yes, she'd been given lots of helpful advice, mostly from Peter's father. 'I was a prisoner of war for two and half years and managed to enjoy myself, don't see why you can't just knuckle down to it, girl.' Then of course there was his old favourite: 'Stop feeling so sorry for yourself.'

And in simple justification of their nomadic lifestyle, that in eight years of marriage had taken them from London to Singapore, back to London and then on to Brussels, Peter would say, 'Other wives are happy here.'

'But I'm not other wives!' she would say in desperate retaliation, knowing that Peter had no comprehension of her basic need for the simple things in life: stability, security and a suburban high street of familiar chain stores, not the sophisticated expatriate regime of uncertainty, cocktail parties, language classes and flower arranging.

In a moment of cynicism and real rock-bottom boredom, she too had joined the ranks of the flower arrangers, and then Peter had tried getting her pregnant, believing this to be the answer. But this was one area in Peter's life where he had to admit failure. A genius in the mergers and acquisitions department he was, but with a low sperm count there was little he could do in the baby-making department.

Looking out of the window, Charlotte watched the softly falling snow. She felt as though they were characters acting out their parts in a well-rehearsed performance; a scene which she had produced and directed in her own mind for nearly a year now – except Peter was ad-libbing; he wasn't supposed to cry.

'Why?' he said, bringing her back to the script.

She turned round. 'Because I don't like what you're doing to me.'

He sniffed loudly and she could see he was willing his body to act according to the rules of his straitjacketed upbringing – boys didn't blub at boarding school. 'This is absurd,' he said, at last, and in a firm loud voice that had the effect of disciplining those dark, unexplored territories of his inner self. He picked up his briefcase, once more in control. 'I'll be back late. I'm in Luxembourg all day.'

'But the snow, it's far too dangerous, you can't possibly go all that way . . . and anyway, we need to talk.'

'There's nothing to discuss. The answer is no.'

Lying back in the bath, Charlotte waited for the warmth of the water to ease away the strain of not just the past hour, but the past eight years. It took only a few moments before she realised that she wasn't in need of a soothing balm. She was all right. After nearly a year of waiting for this point in her life, she was actually all right. The truth of her feelings hit her quite forcibly and she let out a sudden laugh. It echoed horribly in the bathroom with its high tiled ceiling. She chewed her lip guiltily.

But what next?

And now the second act in her well-rehearsed performance ran through her mind. This was when she stopped dancing attendance to someone else's tune, this was when she whistled the melody of her own life.

She would go back to England, to Hulme Welford, and move in with her parents until she got herself sorted; it would be hell living with her mother again, but Dad would be sweet.

And work. What about work?

Before she had been moulded into a corporate wife she had run her own business: an upmarket sweater shop. But then Peter had come home one evening with that silly grin on his face and told her his boss had asked him 'to consider Singapore'. Within three months the shop had gone, along with her identity, and she had found herself living a twelve-hour flight away from all that was comforting and familiar.

She knew it would be hard starting over again; finding work was never easy. Wherever they had lived she had tried to find her own niche – even if it had always been taken away from her. After seven months of trying to find work in Singapore, she had eventually managed to get a job within the personnel department of an international chemical company; then when Peter's contract had come to an end they had moved back to London. She had just found herself work there, when Peter announced they were going to Brussels. For the first six months she struggled to learn some basic French and was then offered a temporary part-time job working as a volunteer for a helpline service for the English-speaking community. When this had come to an end though, there had been no more work available, not until she had met Christina.

At half past eleven, Charlotte decided to call round to see her neighbour, Christina. She wanted to share this moment with someone – wanted somebody to tell her how brave she was, that leaving her husband was the right thing to do.

Christina Castelli had moved into the apartment next door and had become Charlotte's only real friend.

'A high-class tart!' Peter had announced, calling in for his clean shirts *en route* for the airport, just as the last of Christina's expensive-looking furniture had been brought up to the sixth floor. 'Perfectly obvious what she is,' he had gone on to say. 'The lift stinks of erotic perfume.'

Charlotte had questioned him on this point; how did he know what erotic perfume smelt like? He had fumbled for an answer and then reaching for his suit-carrier had simply said, 'Be back day after tomorrow, any duty-free you want?'

'Yes,' she had told him, 'some erotic perfume would be nice.'

He hadn't laughed, but then he'd forgotten how. His life had become too serious; too full of live-or-die mergers and acquisitions. He was constantly living on his ability to judge whether a thing was a profit or a loss; it was either black or it was white to Peter. The only grey area in his life was her.

Within a few days of Christina moving in, Charlotte had been forced to admit that Peter may have been right. The *femme fatale* fragrance in the downstairs hall, lift and sixth floor landing seemed now to be accompanied by a steady stream of German eau-de-Cologne. Charlotte never actually saw her neighbour's callers, apart from one man, who by accident got the wrong apartment, and when Charlotte tried to point him in the right direction he shot back into the lift, his face hidden behind a copy of *Le Soir*.

One morning Christina knocked on Charlotte's door and invited her in for a drink.

'You must call me Christina,' she told Charlotte in perfect English, beckoning her towards a cream leather sofa that had more than a hint of Milan to it. 'We have no need to be formal, for I do not think we shall be conducting any business between ourselves. And I may call you . . . ?'

'Charlotte, very plain I'm afraid,' Charlotte said, feeling incredibly plain as she sat next to this catwalk beauty.

Christina laughed, a light tinkling laugh, that Charlotte knew would have the ability to whip the boxer shorts off any man in seconds. 'In that case I shall call you Carlotta – that is your name in Rome, where I come from.'

Charlotte never told Peter about her visits next door, not even when Christina came up with a job for her.

'Carlotta, you and I are alike in many ways,' Christina said one day. 'We both need to be kept busy and I know that behind that beautiful smile of yours you are perfectly miserable, so I have found you work, just two mornings a week for a friend of mine.'

Charlotte looked doubtfully at her. 'What kind of work?'

Christina laughed. 'Do not worry, Carlotta, I am not about to turn you into a . . . now what was the expression I heard Mr Carlotta use, the day I moved in . . . ah yes, a high-class tart. No, I would not suggest such a thing.'

Charlotte's cheeks flushed. 'How did you hear that?'

Christina shrugged her silk-clad shoulders. 'It was a warm day, every window in Brussels was open. Mr Carlotta's voice carried well that afternoon.'

In Christina's company, Peter was never referred to as Peter, instead he had simply become the anonymous Mr Carlotta. Christina had told Charlotte on their first meeting that she never wanted to meet or even know the name of Charlotte's husband. 'After all,' she had said, her full lips turned gently upwards in the most seductive of smiles, 'it might be awkward for us both if it turned out that I already knew your husband.'

'No, Carlotta, you are not to work as a high-class tart, but as a receptionist. There now, I think that would suit you so much more, don't you?'

'But I can't speak French very well, never mind Flemish,' Charlotte said hopelessly, and then added, 'I have tried, I just don't seem to be very good at it.'

'Then I will teach you, I am a good teacher.'

Charlotte suddenly smiled.

'Such a beautiful smile you have, Carlotta, but I am wondering why you are smiling. What is it you think I am good at teaching?'

Looking at the reflection of herself in the hall mirror, Charlotte smiled at the memory of that conversation. She would miss her friendship with Christina when she moved back to England; it would be the only thing from Brussels that she would miss. Just as she was about to pick up her keys and go and see Christina, the door bell rang.

She pulled the door open and saw two Belgian policemen standing in front of her. They started speaking in French and even with her limited knowledge of the language, she was able to understand what they were saying.

Monsieur Peter Lawrence was dead.

2

Shrilling with all the urgency of a telephone, a child's voice invaded the quiet, Edwardian sitting-room of The Gables in Hulme Welford.

'MUMMY!'

Charlotte's younger sister Hilary, who was quite used to her daughter's demanding cry, carried on pouring out cups of tea. Similarly, the Reverend Malcolm Jackson, a robust forty-five-year-old Meatloaf fan and father of three, barely flinched, but not so Iris Braithwaite, a woman who claimed to live on nothing but the remains of her shredded nerves; she jolted vigorously, as though in response to a proffered red-hot poker.

A six-year-old girl, dressed in an assortment of jumble sale goods, appeared at the sitting-room door. With cheap yellow beads bouncing on her chest and over-sized red slingbacks slapping at her heels, she trotted towards her mother.

'Becky,' Hilary said, 'I did tell you not to play with the clothes from the boxes in the hall. Go and take them off, especially those ridiculous shoes, you'll have an accident.'

'Do I have to?'

'Yes you do. Now say hello to Mrs Braithwaite and Malcolm.'

Six-year-old shyness appearing from nowhere rendered the little girl speechless. She played with the biggest of the yellow beads, turning one of her feet inwards. She then remembered what she had wanted her mother for. 'What does bonking mean, Mummy?'

Flanked by an uneasy rattle of china from one side of her and a stifled laugh from the other, Hilary grappled to save the teapot in her hands and to think of a suitable answer. All she could think of was the terrible unfairness of it all.

She had worked so hard today, had tried to make everything just right. It had all fallen apart though, the moment she had opened the fridge door that morning and realised she hadn't got any eggs. The shop in the village had run out of her usual free-range variety and she had been forced to make do with those battery-farmed eggs instead. The sponge, of course, had turned out a disaster and was it any wonder? She had then had to make a back-up batch of scones for her monthly meeting with Malcolm Jackson and Iris Braithwaite – Chairlady of the St John's Replacement Stained Glass Window

Committee. Then, just as she'd got the kitchen cleared up, school had telephoned to say there had been a gas leak and all children were being sent home. And on top of all this her sister Charlotte was arriving in a few hours' time, which meant there had been Ivy Cottage to get ready for her, along with the welcome-home dinner to prepare for that evening. No, life just wasn't being fair with her today.

Then with shame she thought of Charlotte. Life hadn't exactly been fair to her recently.

It was now two and a half months since Peter had died; the funny thing was, it felt longer.

It had been a sad little funeral, on a cold wet day in Aldershot, with their own family far out-numbering Peter's. She had been so sure that Peter's funeral would have been a rather grand affair, had even bought a hat, which thankfully, just at the last minute, she had left behind in the car. In fact there had been few friends present, hardly anyone to mourn comfortingly alongside Charlotte, just a few duty-bound work colleagues; not even Peter's own brother had turned up. She had felt sorry for Peter's parents; sorry, too, that nobody cried, not even Charlotte.

Afterwards they had all tried to talk Charlotte out of returning to Brussels, had tried to get her to leave everything to the company. 'I must go back,' she had said. 'There are things I need to sort out.' She had been adamant. Just as she had been adamant about buying a house in the village. 'I want to be where I grew up,' she had told them on the telephone. 'Hulme Welford is the only place I know as home. It's got to be there.'

Secretly Hilary was looking forward to having her sister to look after, living, as she would be, quite literally on the doorstep. She smiled to herself at the thought of one day taking the credit for getting Charlotte back on her feet. She could almost feel that rosy glow of praise and gratitude, which she knew would be hers within a few months. Yes, she had great plans for her elder sister.

Looking up from the teapot Hilary realised that both Iris Braithwaite and Malcolm Jackson were staring at her, Becky too. Uncharacteristically she chose to ignore her daughter. 'More tea?' she said.

Taking his cue, Malcolm Jackson held out his cup. 'Just a top-up, please.'

Becky was not to be put off. 'But Mummy . . .'

'Have a chocolate biscuit, dear.'

Wide-eyed with delight, Becky took one, thought better, and took another, but then doggedly continued with her line of questioning. 'Philip says he won't give me back my Barbie doll until Ken's finished bonking her. How long do you think that will take, Mummy?'

At the commotion which followed, Becky left her jumble-sale heels behind her and took to her own, whilst Hilary did her best to deal with Iris Braithwaite's tea-soaked tweed skirt and the slice of lemon that had ended up sitting perkily, like a Frenchman's beret, on one of her sensible brown lace-up shoes.

Another cup and saucer was fetched from the kitchen and quickly filled, but conversation, like the tea, was strained, until Iris Braithwaite warmed to her subject: that of the rising sense of apathy in the village. 'It seems to me that people today have lost their sense of generosity,' she said, taking a sip of tea and wincing as she scalded her thin lips. 'Why, I remember a time when we thought nothing of a jumble sale every two months.'

'I think that people are less inclined to throw things away these days,' suggested Malcolm Jackson. 'After all, everyone, in some way, has been affected by . . .'

'It's greed, pure greed,' interrupted Iris. 'People are hoarding things. Greed is such a terrible sin and one to be avoided at all costs.' She punctuated this by reaching for another scone. 'And as the good book says, "Let the wicked fall into their own nets, whilst I pass in safety."'

Malcolm Jackson couldn't resist it and touchéd with 'Ah, but let's not forget "If any one of you is without sin, let him be the first to throw a stone."' His tone was cynical rather than pious and he received a withering look for his trouble.

'We really could do with one more pair of hands for the jumble sale next Saturday,' Hilary said in an effort to steer the conversation back to where it had been before Becky had interrupted. 'We had seven last time, and to be honest we were a bit stretched.'

'What about Charlotte, your sister?' Iris Braithwaite said. 'She could help, she won't have any commitments so soon, will she? Do her good, get her fully integrated into the village again.'

'Oh, I don't think that would be a good idea. Do you?' Hilary asked, turning to the vicar.

'Nonsense,' Iris Braithwaite carried on, ignoring Malcolm's opened mouth. 'She'll need to be busy. When my Sydney died fifteen years ago, the first thing I did was to spring-clean the house and organise the summer fête.' She paused as though reflecting on those halcyon days, then said, 'I don't suppose Charlotte will be bringing any of her deceased husband's clothing back with her, will she? We could make good use of that at the jumble sale.' And casting a meaningful glance over Malcolm Jackson's faded sweatshirt and jeans, she said, 'Perhaps there might even be something suitable for the vicar.'

'I really couldn't say,' Hilary said helplessly, conscious of the sudden sirocco-style exhalation of breath at her side.

It was always the same. Every month, whenever they had to meet to discuss various fund-raising events for St John's, Iris Braithwaite rendered poor Malcolm speechless. Trouble was, Malcolm, being a clergyman, was like the Queen – not allowed to answer back – and she herself, like so many in the village, was just plain terrified of Iris Braithwaite.

'Well,' said Iris, putting her cup down on the tray and then dabbing the corners of her mouth with her napkin, 'I think we've covered everything quite adequately. So, come along, Vicar, it's time we were going. I'm sure Mrs Parker doesn't want us cluttering up her sitting-room a moment longer.'

Dutifully getting his bulky frame to his feet, Malcolm Jackson smiled at Hilary and thanked her for the tea. 'Will you be in church on Sunday?' he added as they moved towards the hall.

'Yes, it's my turn on Sunday School rota – which reminds me, we really could do with a new trainer seat for the toilet. Poor Joel had an accident with the last one.'

'Really, Mrs Parker!' spluttered Iris Braithwaite. 'I'm sure the vicar doesn't want to hear about such trifling matters.'

Oh dear, thought Hilary, another faux pas.

'I doubt whether it seemed a trifling matter to young Joel at the time,' Malcolm said, a smile on his lips. 'No serious damage, I hope?'

'He hurt his bum!' came a loud voice. It was Becky bumping her way down the stairs on her bottom. She was now wearing a pink leotard with grass-stained ballet tights and carrying her treasured Barbie doll in her hands. 'He hurt his willy wobbler as well,' she added for good measure, when she finally bumped to a stop at the foot of the stairs. 'He was such a cry-baby, he cried all during the story of David and Goliath.'

'Thank you, Becky, that's enough,' said Hilary in a tired voice. She pulled open the front door, anxious for the afternoon to come to an end. But Iris was not finished.

'We're a pair of hands short on the church flower rota. Ask Charlotte, it'll give her something to do. Lovely tea by the way, shame about that sponge, though.'

'Have they gone?' It was Philip, a dark-haired ten-year-old boy, calling from the top of the stairs. Satisfied that the coast was clear, he raced downstairs and shot into the sitting-room to gain possession of the remote control of the television before his sister got it.

'What about your homework, Philip?' Hilary asked, fulfilling her son's expectations of her, as she began clearing the wreckage of tea.

'I've done it,' he replied glibly, thereby fulfilling his mother's expectations of him, at the same time waving the remote control device high in the air, just out of his sister's reach.

Out in the kitchen, Hilary fed the dishwasher, cake crumbs and all, mentally going over that evening's meal, and her plan – supper with a few of the neighbours, just to get her sister acclimatised, and, of course, to introduce her to Alex.

If there was one thing Hilary could never be accused of, it was suffering from an over-indulgence of sentimentality, and whilst it was all very sad and tragic that her sister's husband had died so suddenly, she knew that one simply had to carry on. Charlotte would now have to build up her life again, with a little help. She would need company, and preferably the company of a man, and Hilary had just the man in mind.

Alex Hamilton had been in the village for just two weeks now, renting the granny annexe of Charlotte's new house, Ivy Cottage. He was, in Hilary's opinion, quite the most attractive man to have hit Hulme Welford since a few years ago, when a rather notorious snooker player moved into the village, only to move out again rather rapidly when he lost his potting technique, along with his fortune.

There was no doubt in her mind that Alex Hamilton was the tonic Charlotte needed in order to get herself back on her feet again.

Hilary looked up at the clock above the Aga. Charlotte's plane would be arriving within the hour and Hilary knew the traffic would slow her down.

'I can always get a taxi,' her sister had said.

'Nonsense!' had been Hilary's reply.

Now there was a part of her that was regretting this rash offer; she had more than enough to do without getting caught up in Friday night's rush-hour traffic.

Living 'conveniently placed for Manchester airport', as her husband David so liked to describe the village in his estate agency brochures, was the only tangible disadvantage to living in Hulme Welford, as far as Hilary could see. They were situated directly beneath the main flight path and David had to work hard at playing down the noise to prospective purchasers who came into his attractive black and white half-timbered estate agency office in the centre of the village.

In recent years house sales in the area had sky-rocketed, as Hulme Welford, with all its chocolate-box charm, had steadily increased in popularity with the more adventurous members of the Manchester commuter-belt set. When the older and quite dilapidated cottages in the village had been snapped up, small exclusive developments, such as Orchard Way and Pippin Rise, had sprung up like weeds on the perimeter of the village. They provided trouble-free houses for the upwardly mobile; fully centrally heated, double garaged and two bathroomed, gold taps and all. The houses had increased the population of the village, and brought to it an excess of BMWs tearing about the lanes, as well as a universally agreed improvement to the shops. The local infant and junior school had responded with equal expansion and now, with its increased numbers and pulsating PTA, could boast not only good academic results, but a swimming pool as well.

Most of these changes Hilary approved of, especially the pulsating PTA, of which she was currently Secretary. Next year she hoped to be Chairwoman. Just recently though, the idea of joining the Board of Governors for the school had taken root, and the more Hilary thought about it, the more the idea appealed to her. She could even buy one of those smart executive-looking suits to wear for the meetings.

Taking a tray of wine glasses through to the dining-room, Hilary's thoughts about whether to buy a navy-blue or grey suit were interrupted by a pump-action ring at the doorbell. 'Get that, will you, Philip? It'll be Tiffany.'

'Oh Mum, *Grange Hill's* on.'

'Oh, all right, I'll go.' She put the glasses down on the oak table in the hall. 'And Becky, you come out of there, you're too young for *Grange Hill*.'

A shrill wail started up from Becky, followed by a full scale riot, as Philip began thumping his sister to make her be quiet. Unperturbed, Hilary opened the front door.

'Muffin 'ell, what's going on?'

Hearing their babysitter's familiar voice, Becky leapt off her brother and ran out into the hall. Tiffany fascinated her. When she grew up, she wanted to be just like her – black leggings, huge boots, black-rimmed eyes just like a panda and long, long black hair.

'Can I count your rings, Tiffany?'

'Say please.'

'*Please.*'

''Course you can. Let's see how good your maths is today.'

With tongue-poking-out-of-the-mouth concentration, Becky started to count. First on Tiffany's left hand then on her right. 'Four and three, that makes . . . seven,' she announced after careful consideration.

'Who's a clever little madam then. And what *was* you doing to your brother when I came in?'

'*Were*,' corrected Becky.

Hilary smiled. Tiffany's subversive teaching methods with Becky never failed. She and David could shout until they were blue in the face about the correct use of speech and Becky would just throw it back at them.

'Okay if I dash off straight away, Tiffany?' Hilary said. 'I'd like to try and get there early.'

'Yeah sure, no problem.'

'I'll be a couple of hours at most. David might even be back before me, though I doubt it.' She reached for her keys hanging up on the hook by the telephone. 'Oh Lord!' she suddenly cried out. 'I've forgotten to give the children any tea, I've been so busy thinking about tonight and what with Mrs Braithwaite and Reverend Jackson, I've . . .'

'Got any fish fingers in the freezer?'

'Yes, and there's some cake left over from this afternoon. Oh Tiffany, you are wonderful. What would I do without you?'

Tiffany smiled. If only her mother thought the same.

Pushing her trolley of luggage, Charlotte's eyes searched the crowded arrivals hall for her sister's welcoming face, but all she could see were rows of bored-looking men holding drooping placards bearing the names of their charges. There was no sign of Hilary.

Charlotte felt anxious. She wanted to get this bit of the day over with. Knowing her sister's intense desire to do and say all the right things, Charlotte viewed the drive home with a mixture of uneasiness and hostility.

She paused for a moment with her trolley, letting her fellow passengers push ahead of her. She suddenly felt overwhelmed by the juxtaposition of this large, bustling, uncaring crowd around her and the thought of Hilary lavishing well-intended sisterly love on her. Frightened she was about to cry, she reached into her jacket pocket for a tissue. Instead of a tissue, she found the envelope Christina had given to her at the airport in Brussels. She had kept it in her pocket until she was soaring over the Belgian coast with a glass of champagne in her hand. Then she had opened it and read the card with Christina's beautiful words.

'Leave your sadness behind, Carlotta; leave it in Brussels where it can no longer harm you. Take only your beautiful smile with you and offer it to everyone you meet; it will bring you and them such happiness.'

It was the loveliest thing anyone had ever said to her.

And then as if by magic there was Hilary rushing towards her. To Charlotte's surprise, relief flooded through her.

3

'I'm doing a little supper party for you tonight,' Hilary said, stretching her hand out of the car window to insert the parking ticket in the required slit.

'Oh Hilary, not tonight, I can't.'

'Nonsense, you'll be fine,' Hilary said firmly. She hoped to goodness her sister wasn't going to play the grieving widow round the dinner table that night. Moussaka, mirth and a little matchmaking were what she had in mind, not moussaka and misery. 'You know,' she said, choosing her words carefully, 'you know how desperately sad we all are about Peter, but at some stage you have to pick up the pieces of your life again, so it might as well be tonight.' Especially after all the trouble I've gone to, she thought. 'And anyway,' she added with forced brightness, 'it will be a nice way for you to meet Alex.'

The initial flood of relief Charlotte had experienced on seeing her sister's capable face in the crowd had completely flowed out of her. The familiar twinges of irritation that went hand in hand with the sisters' affection for one another were now beginning to surface.

And Charlotte also knew what Hilary was up to. Ever since the contract for Ivy Cottage had been signed and David had found a tenant to live in the granny annexe, Hilary had never stopped mentioning this Alex Hamilton on the telephone: 'Such a nice man . . . very pleasant . . . he'll be no bother to you . . . quite handy really, you know, should you run out of coffee, or anything like that.'

Well, tonight she would meet him, would make up her own mind. In her opinion, Hilary had been watching too many Gold Blend adverts.

She decided to move on to firmer ground. 'How are the children?'

'As wonderful as ever.'

Charlotte grimaced. Wonderful was not the description that instantly sprang to her mind when she thought of her nephew and niece – seismic savages more like it.

'They're really looking forward to seeing you. You'll be a real aunt to them now, living so close.'

'I hadn't thought of it quite like that,' Charlotte said, horrified at the thought. Living opposite her sister had been the only fly in the ointment of her plan to move back to Hulme Welford.

'Philip's just been awarded his thousand-metre swimming badge and Becky has cracked breaststroke. She's a real natural, Mrs Pulman says.'

Charlotte knew it was always best to let her sister ramble on with motherly pride, and over the years she had mastered the art of half listening and oohing and aahing in the appropriate pauses. 'So, who's coming tonight?' she asked, when at last Hilary had run out of glowing reports of her offspring. 'Will it be smart? I haven't brought everything, the rest is following on in the removal van.'

'No, of course it's not posh,' Hilary said, thinking of all the luggage they had just loaded into the back of David's Volvo. 'It's only family and a few neighbours. There'll be you, me, David, Mum and Dad, and Derek and Cindy. Remember I told you about them moving into Rose Cottage just before Peter . . .'

Hilary's unfinished sentence hung stiffly in the air and an awkward silence filled the car.

'Go on,' Charlotte said at last. 'Say it, Hilary, don't be afraid of using the word. *Died.* Peter died. Okay? His car skidded on ice and hit a barrier at a hundred and twenty kilometres an hour. He was killed instantly. Peter's dead. There, I've said it, you try it.'

Hilary found herself unable to respond to what, in her mind, was an appalling outburst of bad taste. Surely even in grief one had to employ a certain amount of dignity? Looking after Charlotte was going to be more difficult than she had supposed. Her eyes firmly fixed on the road ahead, she decided to return to the subject of supper that evening. 'And the only other guest who'll be there is Alex, of course.'

'Of course,' repeated Charlotte, looking out of the window, not trusting herself to look at her sister.

Adopting a cheery voice, Hilary said, 'Have you thought any more about my offer for you to stop the night with us? I just can't bear the idea of you being all alone. You'll be so lonely.'

It was difficult for Charlotte not to laugh out loud. She had spent the last few years of her marriage feeling alone and isolated.

'Stay with us, Charlotte. Come on, why don't you? Just your first night.'

Charlotte considered The Gables for a moment: the noise, the constant bickering, the fighting – and that was just Hilary and David. She smiled to herself, thinking of the calmness and tranquillity she hoped to have at Ivy Cottage. 'It's kind of you to offer,' she said, 'but I'd rather like to get settled in straight away, there's so much to do. I'm quite looking forward to it really.'

'Yes of course, I understand.' She didn't understand at all. How could Charlotte be looking forward to moving into that house all alone?

They entered the village, and as they passed the prettily painted sign that had helped Hulme Welford win the North-West's 'Best Kept Village' title last year, Charlotte began to feel uneasy. Supposing she had made a mistake in coming back? It was a fact of life, one of those clichéd phrases, trotted out with diligent reverence to the worldly wisdom of those unfortunate enough to have tried it for themselves – *you can't go back.*

Only her mother had actually had the courage to say this to her. 'Charlotte, are you sure you're doing the right thing? After all, everyone knows, only a fool tries to turn back the clock.'

'Thank you, Mother,' she had said. 'I can always rely on you for support, can't I?'

'No point in me lying to you, Charlotte, never lied to you before, why should I start now?'

'Because my husband's just died?' Charlotte had replied, knowing how pathetic she was sounding, whining like a small child. 'And it might be nice to be . . .'

'What?' Louise had said, frowning. 'Mollycoddled? You want me to mollycoddle you? You of all people must know I'm not that kind of a mother.'

It was true. Louise Archer had never been the kind of mother to rush to a bleeding knee-cap with a box of plasters, nor soothe an exhausted child with a bedtime story. She had always been busy at some auction or other, or working in her antique shop, buffing up and restoring her 'finds'. From an early age, both Charlotte and Hilary had learnt where the Germoline and aspirins were kept.

They drove along the main street with its plentiful supply of shops; their mother's antique shop, the baker's, butcher's, grocer's, paper shop and Post Office next door, and then the more upmarket chic clothes shop and the kitchen and bathroom shop. It was just after six-thirty and, apart from the paper shop, everything was shut. She spotted David's office. Charlotte could see a light still on. She thought for one awful moment her sister might want to stop the car and take her in to see David. But to her relief Hilary turned left at the church, drove down Daisy Bank and then turned again into Acacia Lane, a leafy cul-de-sac made up of a handful of small terraced cottages and four large houses set well back from the road.

On the right-hand side was The White Cottage. The house was exactly what its name suggested, a neat cottage with a perfect covering of unadorned white rendering. The garden was equally neat with well-dug, weedless flower beds. Daffodils, now well past their best, had been neatly folded with rubber-bands, thwarting any untidiness. This was where Iris Braithwaite lived.

Beyond The White Cottage was Rose Cottage. This came as a complete surprise to Charlotte. Not so long ago Rose Cottage had been a pretty, pale-coloured house. Now it was painted shocking pink, and at the end of the drive was a large sign informing Charlotte it was called 'In The Pink'.

'Derek and Cindy,' Hilary said to Charlotte's look of horror. 'They have a chain of hair salons right across Cheshire and they've turned the house into a sort of health and beauty centre, in record time too. They seem to be doing very well out of it.'

'But it's ghastly. However did they get away with painting it that disgusting colour?'

'Don't ask me. And please, don't ask them. Derek thinks it's quite the thing. By the way, watch out for Derek.'

'Why?'

'Don't be naïve, Charlotte.'

Dropping down into second gear, Hilary turned off the road and carefully drove between two peeling white gates and up a narrow driveway to Ivy Cottage.

Since she'd grown up in Hulme Welford and had made regular visits home throughout her marriage, Charlotte was familiar with every house in the village, except those on the new developments, Orchard Way and Pippin Rise. Ivy Cottage had always been one of her favourites. As a child, she had been fascinated by the house and its occupant, a woman who had been something of a celebrity as a writer of romantic fiction. Blanche Blair had drifted about the village with the glamour one might have expected of a woman of her profession, and she had managed to create an air of mystery around her large Edwardian cottage and beautiful garden. The last years of Blanche Blair's life were spent in a nursing home and the cottage had stood empty. On her death, Ivy Cottage had been snapped up by the Cliffords from Doncaster, who, bringing an elderly mother with them, had the house redesigned to provide an independent granny flat at one end of the house. But the elderly occupant of the granny flat rather ungratefully died and the Cliffords had felt the pull of Doncaster. The house still looked to be one from the outside, but there were two driveways, an original of gravel and one of tarmac.

An abundance of ivy and peeling paint gave the impression that the house and garden were badly in need of work. Yet Charlotte thought it was wonderful. A little sad and drab perhaps, but compared to the elegant, sterile apartment she had left behind in Brussels, with its marble and fake neoclassical gilt work, it was real, and it was hers.

Between them, they took the luggage out of the Volvo and into the house.

'There now,' said Hilary, 'everything's in. Shall I show you round?'

'Haven't you got a meal to prepare?' Charlotte wanted more than anything to be left alone.

Hilary looked at her watch. 'Oh Lord, you're right, I must fly, but are you sure you've got everything you need?'

'I'm fine, really. I'll unpack a few things, have a bath, then be right over.'

'Good idea. I put the immersion heater on for you earlier.'

Charlotte knew she should be grateful to Hilary for thinking of having hot water ready for her, but she felt childishly possessive; it was her house, her immersion heater.

She watched her sister reverse down the drive and turn into her own drive to The Gables. Closing the door behind her, for the second time that day Charlotte felt an overwhelming sense of relief; she had made it this far.

Then for no good reason she could think of, she started to cry.

4

Pound coins chinking in her jacket pocket – the financial rewards of babysitting – Tiffany Rogers sauntered across the road towards In The Pink. She was in no hurry to get home, had even offered to stay on a bit longer to help Mrs Parker set the dining-room table. She was nice, Mrs Parker, though she could do with slowing down a bit; she'd been like a headless chicken just now in the kitchen.

As she walked up the drive, her heavy Doc Martens clomping on the tarmac, Tiffany paused to look at the damage her parents had done to what had once been an ordinary-looking house.

When they had bought Rose Cottage, her parents had taken it in hand, treating it like a client. Only this time they worked in reverse, stretching it to twice its original size by adding two enormous extensions, providing room for a complex of saunas, jacuzzis, gymnasiums, massage rooms and a hair salon. Now Rose Cottage was beyond recognition, smelling permanently of a combination of hospitals, public swimming baths and hairspray.

The walls, which had once been a delicate pastel shade of pink, were now the colour of a vivid Mediterranean geranium. Tiffany knew they stuck out in the village as flagrantly as she herself did.

Coming to Hulme Welford had not been as bad as it might have been; at least she and her brother could stay at the same school, so had kept all their old friends who were now a short bus ride away. Since she was eight years old they had lived in Wilmslow, but then last year Dad had got this idea that the big money lay in buying a large old house and converting it into a health and beauty centre. Tiffany viewed it more as a temple of indulgence for the privileged few and said as much to her parents at every possible opportunity.

Alone in the salon, Cindy Rogers turned off the lights and, carrying her expensive Italian shoes in her hands, made her way along the corridor that separated the work area from the living area of the house. On her feet all day, Cindy knew she should wear flatter shoes, but she also knew that her slim, tanned legs looked even better in a pair of high heels.

She was tired and not looking forward to going out for dinner to the Parkers'. She would have much preferred a good long soak in a lavender-oil-scented bath. Instead she would have to face the ordeal of coping with the excessive amount of food which Hilary would present her with. Eating out always filled Cindy with dread.

She found Tiffany in the kitchen, frying some bacon and making a cup of tea, and at once Cindy felt the familiar surge of disappointment as she looked at her daughter.

She had so badly wanted a daughter. The birth of her first child, Barry, had been a bad enough blow, but nothing had prepared her for Tiffany. The black patent shoes and smocked dresses she had longed to dress her daughter in had been denied her by this wayward, headstrong child. The shopping trips she had envisaged, the shared girl-talk and mutual understanding of all things feminine had been snatched away, right from the moment Tiffany, at the age of four, had stood in the middle of her bedroom and pulled off the beautiful little dress Cindy had just bought for her in Manchester. 'Don't like it,' Tiffany had shouted defiantly, stamping all over the expensive fabric, 'won't wear it, want to be like Barry.' And she had followed this to the letter, fastidiously copying the way her older brother dressed, until she had started menstruating. At that point, she decided to grow her hair. And then, a year ago, on her fourteenth birthday, she had emerged from the bathroom with her long sandy hair completely jet black. From then on, it seemed to Cindy, Tiffany grew each day more and more like Morticia from the Addams family.

Cindy frowned, then immediately relaxed her facial muscles, knowing how damaging it was for the skin. But the strains of her morning argument with Tiffany were still there, hanging in the air of her bleached ash kitchen. Nothing was going to change her mind; Tiffany and her friends were too young to go off for a weekend in the Lake District on their own. Surely her stubborn fifteen-year-old daughter could see that?

It was Tiffany who spoke first. 'Want some tea?'

'No, thanks. Where have you been?' It came out all wrong and she felt her daughter bristle.

'Muffin 'ell, I've been over at Mrs Parker's babysitting. I told you this morning I'd be going there straight after school. You obviously weren't listening.'

They were off again, their mood to one another cold, combative.

'Where's Barry?' Cindy asked, trying to sound conciliatory.

'Up in his room studying.'

'What, already?'

'You should be proud of him. After all, if he does become a surgeon he'll be able to give you the facelift you'll need after all that rubbish you pile on your face.'

Cindy gave up. 'I'm going to have a bath, seeing as you've nothing civil to say to me.'

Tiffany watched her mother go. She hadn't meant to be rude, but her mother's complete misunderstanding of Barry really got to her. Didn't she know how important it was to Barry to get not just good grades in his

A levels, but brilliant grades? Their mother and their father just had no idea of the strain Barry was under.

Derek Rogers was having a sauna. He liked a good sweat before going out. At forty-five, when most of his contemporaries were beginning to look their age and were quite prepared to forget about their bodies, Derek Rogers was obsessed with his.

Physically he was in great shape, but mentally he was not. He was bored, bored to death.

The five salons he and Cindy owned throughout Cheshire practically ran themselves and now that In The Pink was up and running and gaining more clients every day, he felt the need for something more challenging. He was bored with the women of Hulme Welford too. They were no challenge to him. They were all so bored themselves that they leapt at the chance of an added drop of excitement in their lives.

Since the age of sixteen when Derek had discovered he was irresistible to women of any age, and discovered at the same time that he was driven by a compulsive need for a variety of women in his life, he had embarked upon countless affairs, leading up to and during his twenty-two-year-old marriage to Cindy. Affairs to him had never been an added bonus; he needed them like a gambler needs the next roll of the dice. He viewed Cindy as his morning cup of coffee: strong and bitter and always there. He never considered whether he loved her or not, that was irrelevant. She was just there, a part of his life.

Out of the sauna, he rubbed himself down with a towel, pulled on a pair of Paisley boxer shorts then walked through to the gym. A quick ten-minute work-out on the exercise bike and then he would shower and get ready. He was looking forward to this evening. It held the promise of something new. He knew Hilary and David of course, living so close, and he and Cindy had been introduced to Louise and Neville Archer some weeks ago. The two guests he didn't know at all were Alex Hamilton and Charlotte Lawrence. He had noticed that chap Hamilton moving into the granny flat of Ivy Cottage two weeks ago and had seen a lot of books and computer stuff coming out of the back of the removal van, which meant they would have nothing at all in common.

But Charlotte Lawrence, Hilary's sister – now she was a different matter, she intrigued him. He had seen a photograph of her when they had been invited over to the Parkers' for drinks one Sunday lunchtime. Defiant eyes had stared back at him from the framed photograph on the mantelpiece. He had noticed that there was a strong similarity between the two sisters; noticed, too, that while Hilary was a pleasant enough looking woman, Charlotte was the more attractive, more complete somehow – as though the two women had been painted by an artist who had started work enthusiastically on the elder sister, only to run out of paint and motivation by the time he reached the younger woman. Poor Hilary looked like a watered-down version of her sister, Derek thought.

All Derek actually knew about this sister of Hilary's was that her husband had recently died and she was coming to live in Ivy Cottage. He slowed the pedals down on the bike, began to think seriously of the evening ahead and the potential it offered. Should he wear casual – navy chinos and cream polo shirt – or one of his new Italian suits? He favoured casual; the cream shirt would set off his tan better. Looking at his paper-thin wristwatch, he considered a quick five-minute session on the sunbed.

5

Thank heavens for Tiffany, Hilary said to herself for the umpteenth time, as she stepped out of the bath and started rubbing her legs with a towel. During the time in which she had collected Charlotte from the airport, Tiffany had not only cooked the children's tea, cleared up afterwards and then coaxed them up to bed, but she had also found time to read a few chapters of *George's Marvellous Medicine* for them. Tiffany really did have the most fantastic effect on both Becky and Philip.

Hilary bent down and tugged at the bath plug, allowing herself a small smile. There'd be no shower for David when he eventually made it home – she had used up all the hot water and there would be no more until half past six tomorrow morning, which was all down to David's excessive desire to economise. It was one of his most infuriating habits, that and being a lousy host. No doubt he would excel himself tonight, drink too much and forget all about their guests. Well, blast David's economising. As soon as she was dressed she would go downstairs and light a fire in the sitting-room. It was the coldest room in the house with its north-facing position, and even at this time of year it could feel miserably damp.

She went over to the chest of drawers by her side of the bed. Hunting at the back of the drawer, she pulled out a brand new pair of ivory-coloured silk pants and a matching bra. One of her few luxuries in life was buying and hoarding new underwear and saving it for just the right occasion.

Just as she was cutting off the price tags in the bathroom, Hilary heard the familiar noise of her own car coming up the drive. Hurriedly she hid the evidence of her indulgence at the bottom of the bin, pulled on the pants and wriggled into the bra. She was disappointed, though, not to be able to savour the moment alone.

Downstairs the front door banged. This was followed by the sound of David's exploratory footsteps pacing through the hall to the kitchen, the sitting-room, the dining-room, until eventually they could be heard coming up the stairs.

'There you are,' David said, coming into the bedroom, pulling off his silk tie and tossing it on to the bed. 'Mm . . . you look nice.' He eyed her more closely. 'Been shopping?'

She laughed and parried his question. 'You look pleased with yourself.'

'I've every right to be pleased. I've sold three houses today, including that architect-designed monstrosity I thought I'd be stuck with for ever. Could be a sign the recession really is letting up at last.'

'That's wonderful, darling,' Hilary said, opening the wardrobe door and trying to sound more pleased than she was. Ordinarily she would have been delighted for David, but not today, not tonight. For David would be feeling in need of some reward, which would involve an effort on her part – and to be honest she just didn't have the energy this evening after the day she'd had. He would also feel the need to celebrate by drinking too much over dinner, which would mean he'd be as good as useless at helping her with the meal.

'I'll just have a quick shower before the mob turns up,' David said.

'There's no hot water left, sorry.'

'Well in that case,' he came towards her, 'I'll have to do something else to fill in the time. Are you sure these knickers aren't new?'

Irritation flickered through Hilary as David stroked her silky bottom. She felt cheated; the pleasure was supposed to have been all hers, not David's.

Half an hour later, opening the front door to the first arrivals, David found himself poleaxed by a mouthful of Miss Dior and an equal measure of Paco Rabanne. He stood back for air as he let Cindy and Derek in, taking from them a bottle of wine and a box of chocolates.

'Go through,' he said, grimacing behind their backs. 'You know the way.'

In the sitting-room the curtains were already pulled across and a fire was blazing furiously. Minutes earlier, in an effort to save wood, David had flung most of the contents of the kitchen bin on to the gently smouldering logs, and now there was a distinct aroma of burning plastic accompanied by an occasional high-pitched whistling noise. Hilary would give him hell later.

'Do sit down.' David gestured to the chintz-covered sofas. Cindy did as she was told, perching birdlike on the edge of the sofa. Derek made himself at home, taking up pole position by the fire, feet a statutory twelve inches apart, hands pushed down into trouser pockets. After a couple of seconds he started to sniff and looked behind him.

'Think your chimney needs sweeping, David. Bit of a whiff coming from it, isn't there?'

That's rich coming from you, thought David, turning to Cindy. 'So Cindy, what can I get you to drink? No, don't tell me, let me see if I can remember. Gin and tonic?' She shook her head. 'Of course not, glass of white wine, that's got to be it.'

Derek laughed, taking his hands out of his pockets, gold bracelet chinking. 'Must be your other girlfriend. Cindy's practically a teetotal merchant, always has been, always will be, isn't that right, love?'

Cindy laughed politely, but her perfectly made-up lips remained tightly shut.

David laughed too, it was easier that way. He never knew quite what to say to Derek. After all, what sort of man was a hairdresser? But what really went against the grain with him was that Derek had legitimate access to every woman in the village and surrounding area – he was like a doctor, but without the background or ethical code of practice.

'What's that smell?' It was Hilary, her Royal Horticultural Society apron still on, a *hydrangea petiolaris* working its way up her front. Her eyes were trained on the fireplace.

'That's a fine way to greet our guests, darling.' David knew he was on thin ice, so why not go down with the *Titanic*?

'Hello Cindy and Derek,' she said pleasantly. She gave David one of her slightly stern looks, and said, 'Haven't you got the drinks going yet?'

'All in hand, dear, all in hand. Cindy, what would you like?'

'Perrier please.'

'Mine's a gin and tonic,' said Derek.

It would be, David thought, bustling off to the drinks cabinet.

'Hilary, I hope you haven't gone to a lot of trouble,' Cindy said, hoping against all the odds that it might be just a light supper. 'After all, it's only friends and neighbours, like you said.'

'And family,' called out David, trying to decide whether Cindy and Derek came under friends or neighbours, at the same time trying to conceal the bottle of gin which was Sainsbury's and not Gordon's.

'So Hilary,' Derek said, picking up the framed photograph of Charlotte from the mantelpiece, 'tell us what your sister is like.'

Cindy, her perfectly manicured nails digging into the palms of her hands, closed her eyes. Surely he wouldn't? Not with a woman whose husband had so recently died.

6

Charlotte was late. She had spent longer than she intended in the bath, with a large gin and tonic, and when the bath water had gone cold for the second time, she had wrapped her bathrobe around her, topped up her glass and wandered aimlessly about her echoing, unfurnished new home. The removal van from Brussels wasn't due to arrive until Monday morning, so until then all she had was a put-you-up-bed and a couple of chairs which Hilary had loaned her.

Despite this, and despite the dusty wooden floorboards, the naked walls with their ghostly marks where once there had been pictures, Charlotte was delighted with each room she went into; especially the shambling, wooden-constructed conservatory at the back of the house. It was not a neat modern conservatory sold by an aggressive young man on the doorstep, but one built many years ago that recently had fallen into disrepair. Certainly it looked as though the Cliffords had not made it as far as this part of the house in terms of adding their personal touch.

Opening the stiff door, which creaked and groaned for a good rubbing down and some oil and led out on to the garden, Charlotte let in the cool evening air. The air inside was warm and as thick as syrup with flies buzzing wearily against the smeared glass. In this hothouse warmth, Charlotte began to feel lightheaded. Suddenly she had a very real image in her mind of Blanche Blair sitting at her typewriter in the almost tropical atmosphere, conjuring up one of her torrid romances, hearts beating and aflame with desire.

Laughing, she went back into the house. Buoyed up by three large gins, she felt convinced that she had made the right decision in moving back to Hulme Welford. Ivy Cottage, she decided, was going to be the best thing to have happened to her in a long while.

Peter's idea of a home had been an impersonal base that was neat and tidy, without any added complications such as flower beds, leaking gutters and windowsills that needed painting. Each time they had moved, Charlotte had requested they live in a house, but each time Peter had over-ridden her wishes and insisted they rent an apartment. Admittedly, the apartments they had lived in had not been mean and cramped, far from it. The one in Singapore had been ridiculously palatial, even bigger than Brussels, but it had still felt like a prison cell to Charlotte. 'A prison cell!' Peter had shouted indignantly, when Charlotte complained about their latest home. 'Are you mad, Charlotte? Look about you and see how some of the locals live, ask them whether they think we're living in a cell.'

Perhaps, though, it had not been the physical walls of their various homes that had made her feel a captive. It was the mental confines of a marriage going disastrously wrong that had caused her to feel such a prisoner.

Upstairs, in what was to be her bedroom, Charlotte opened a suitcase and pulled out the first dress that came to hand. She tried to gear herself up for the evening ahead. Trouble was, she had no idea how to play her part. Was she to be doleful, demure or stiff upper lippish, displaying shoulders back and best foot forward? It should, of course, all come naturally, but it didn't, because she herself did not know exactly how she felt. With each day that passed she was conscious only of a deepening sense of guilt which most people around her mistook for grief. She had convinced herself that because of her Peter had tried to drive to Luxembourg when he was no longer in control of his emotions and had died as a result. She had told no one of this, not even Christina, and nobody knew what she had told Peter over breakfast. So there was no one to suggest that perhaps her husband – his mind already on his business meeting – had quite simply hit a patch of ice? And why had she told no one? Because then no one would be able to blame her for Peter's death.

Other than this growing, self-imposed culpability, Charlotte had not experienced any great trauma. After all, she had already experienced every level of emotion during the months leading up to that point of no return when she knew that she could not go on pretending. She had cried gulping great tears alone, night after night, lying in a half empty bed. She had cried in the bath, streams of tearful loneliness. She had even wept in the local supermarket, angry tears of frustration over the *pain de blé* when she had finally come to realise that she would never be the wife Peter needed; the kind of wife who didn't mind her husband having an all-consuming mistress – his work.

She shut the front door behind her, and locking it with the unfamiliar key Hilary had given her earlier, Charlotte started to walk down the driveway. But with each step she took away from her new home, her recently gin-induced confidence began to ebb away, until by the time she had reached the gate, she wasn't at all sure she had made the right decision in coming back to live in Hulme Welford, searching, as she was, for the familiar security of what she'd known P.P. – pre-Peter.

She stood on the pavement and looked across to The Gables. She felt like a small child who has just been given its comfort blanket, only to find the silky edging has come away.

Her mother, Louise Archer, opened the door to her. 'Charlotte!' she cried out, as though her elder daughter was the last person on earth she had been expecting to see that evening.

'Mother,' Charlotte replied, finding it difficult to respond in any other way. They almost made contact as they leaned towards each other for a perfunctory kiss.

'Hilary's on the telephone, she won't be long. You look tired.'

'You always say that.'

'Well, isn't that the kind of thing mothers are supposed to say?'

They walked through to the sitting-room, Charlotte following behind her mother.

'Look, everybody, look who's here,' Louise said, in a loud voice. It came out like an over-rehearsed line from a play.

'Charlotte!' Neville Archer said with obvious delight. He levered himself out of a florid armchair and came towards her, spilling a few drops of whisky as he did so. 'How about a hug for your old dad, then? Sorry we weren't there to meet you at the airport – your mother had an auction over at Chester and needed the car.'

Charlotte hugged him warmly. She was always pleased to see her father, with his familiar Toby jug appearance – stout and highly coloured.

'Don't worry,' she said. 'Hilary was there in full control.' Stepping back from him, she said in a voice deliberately aimed at her mother, 'You're looking great, Dad. The new diet's going well, then?'

He smiled at her and at the same time, with great effort, he pulled in his stomach, causing his buttoned cardigan to collapse like a balloon. Lowering his voice so as to exclude everyone else from their conversation, he asked, 'You okay?'

She nodded, grateful for his quiet concern, and said, 'How are the gooseberries?'

He looked worried. 'Not sure, they don't seem as good as last year's.'

Like a number of men and women in the village, Neville Archer spent months preparing for the annual gooseberry-growing contest, but as yet her father's gooseberries had never got anywhere near the weights required to be in the running for a prize. But each year Charlotte hoped that he might be lucky.

She rested a hand on his arm. 'They'll be fine. You'll win something this year, I'm sure of it.'

'Don't, Charlotte, for goodness' sake, just don't start him off about those wretched gooseberries,' Louise said vehemently, shaking her head. 'You know how unbearable he gets on the subject.'

'Talk to you later,' Charlotte whispered to him. Noticing that there were others in the room whom she did not know, Charlotte looked for her sister or David to make the necessary introductions. There was no sign of either. Staring straight at her was an overly tanned, slim woman with a perfect bob of blonde hair, looking for all the world like a candidate for *Come Dancing*.

Cindy, Charlotte decided. And over by the hi-fi, it had to be Derek, a dead ringer for Phil Collins if ever there was one.

'Charlotte, you're here at last.' It was Hilary, coming in with a tray of nibbles, and her choice of words did not go unnoticed by Charlotte. 'Have you been properly introduced? I can't think where David's got to, I only asked him to fetch some logs. That was Alex on the telephone, by the way. Poor man, he just called to say he had been stuck in traffic in Manchester, but would be with us as soon as he'd changed. Cindy, let me introduce my sister.'

Cindy stood up, met Charlotte eye to eye, and was convinced she could smell gin.

There were very few women in the village whom Cindy liked; most of them she considered a threat, with the exception of Hilary. Cindy had decided her neighbour was far too busy coping with her own marriage to stray beyond it and so wouldn't recognise a come-on from Derek, even if he handed her a condom with her name on it. On the other hand, she knew instinctively that this woman, standing in front of her, *was* a threat. Those huge, dusky violet eyes and all that luscious raven-coloured hair would be like a gift from heaven to Derek. And she was free and vulnerable. It certainly didn't take too much effort on Cindy's part to see how Derek could make up his mind to take this woman out of herself; to get her over the death of her husband.

Charlotte sensed Cindy's reluctant hand slip in and out of her own and the brittle smile that went with it. She was aware, too, how simply but effectively Cindy was dressed, unlike herself she now realised. The expensive linen suit she had slung on only minutes earlier should have been ironed, but she had been in too much of a hurry and too lazy to bother.

'You must come and pamper yourself some time,' Cindy was saying. 'Grief can have such a devastating effect on the skin.'

'Yes,' Charlotte said awkwardly, wanting suddenly to step away from Cindy, who with her perfect complexion was probably already sizing up Charlotte's skin as pumice-stone texture.

Almost as though Cindy had been pushed to one side, there was the Phil Collins lookalike standing before Charlotte, cool as you like, a strategically unbuttoned cream polo shirt revealing a sprinkling of fair hairs on a tanned chest. 'Don't be naïve,' Hilary had said earlier in the car. Charlotte smiled to herself, thinking how she might have fun being exactly that.

'Now you do remember, don't you?' said Hilary. 'I told you about Cindy and Derek and In The Pink.'

Charlotte felt the hackles rising. Of course she remembered – she had lost her husband, not her mind. 'No,' she lied for the sheer hell of it, 'no, I don't recall you mentioning a Cindy or a Derek.' She heard her sister's sharp intake of breath.

'Continentals don't go in for much handshaking, do they?' Derek said, moving closer to Charlotte. 'They kiss a lot instead.' Which he promptly did, kissing Charlotte on both cheeks.

'How wonderfully flamboyant,' Louise said, raising her eyebrows.

'Well,' gasped Hilary, slightly flustered, 'that's one way of breaking the ice. Now come on, everyone, sit down, make yourselves at home. Anyone for chicken tikka-flavoured nuts?'

'Somebody mention food? I'm starving.' It was David with a large basket of logs, which he dropped with a crash beside the fireplace. 'Charlotte, you've arrived. Good to see you. Everything all right over the road?'

'Yes thanks, David, just as Hilary said it would be.'

Shaking his hands clean of log dust, he came over and kissed her. 'This isn't on,' he said. 'You're the only one without a drink. Let me get you something.'

'Only a quick one,' chipped in Hilary, who, like Cindy, was sure Charlotte smelled of gin. In answer to the query written on her husband's face, she said, 'We'll be eating soon.'

The doorbell rang.

'I'll get that.' Hilary almost barged past David in her hurry to get to the front door. 'It'll be Alex.'

The rest of the guests sat in awkward silence, listening to the front door being pulled open and the sound of Hilary's voice carrying from the hall. 'Oh Alex, how kind, but you shouldn't have. Really, I don't deserve them.'

You're right, thought Charlotte, you don't deserve them, whatever they are, you scheming little monkey.

The sound of Hilary's voice grew louder until she stood in the doorway, a sparkling smile on her face, a bouquet of gypsophila and pink carnations in one hand and a bottle of wine in the other.

'Sorry I'm late, everybody,' said a voice from behind Hilary. Alex Hamilton made his appearance. 'I hope I haven't kept you all waiting.'

Smooth, thought Charlotte.

'No, no, of course you haven't,' fawned Hilary. 'Think nothing of it. We're just delighted you're here.'

Oh, for goodness' sake, Hilary, stop larding it on, cringed Charlotte, you'll be bobbing and curtsying next. It was quite obvious to Charlotte that this party had very little to do with welcoming her home; this was all about Hilary's honoured guest, Alex Hamilton, and making the right impression on him. While her sister carried on making a fool of herself, Charlotte weighed up the recipient of all this red carpet treatment: about six foot, she reckoned, with fair hair that was showing signs of greying. He was casually dressed in an understated kind of way: striped shirt beneath a pale blue cashmere sweater, jeans and a pair of well-worn Reeboks. He was probably about her age, she decided, mid-thirties.

'Now let me introduce you to everyone.' Hilary was off again and beginning to steer Alex round the room, as though he were a prize bull at an auction. 'And this is my sister, Charlotte,' she said at last.

'Hello,' he said, taking her hand. 'Welcome home to England. What time did you arrive?'

'Er . . .' Charlotte was nonplussed. She wasn't expecting such an ordinary question. For the past two and a half months nearly everyone who talked to her spoke in clichés – *oh it must be so hard, oh poor you, we're thinking of you.* People spent all their time telling her how she must be feeling, or how they felt; nobody actually asked her anything. It seemed as if nothing was expected of her, as though her role as a widow was to be passive. 'Oh, a couple of hours ago,' she answered vaguely, at the same time withdrawing her hand.

'I hope I prove to be a good tenant,' he responded, then, smiling, he placed a hand on his heart and said, 'I promise not to hold any all-night parties or to hang out washing on a Sunday.'

'What a shame,' she said, offering him a small smile. 'I like a good party and it's surprising what you can learn about a person from looking at their washing.'

'Especially their underwear,' cracked Derek.

'Well, yes, I suppose so,' said Hilary, thinking of all hers upstairs. 'Now if you could all go through I'll just put these lovely flowers in water and then follow on in a moment.'

They made their way slowly into the dining-room which, after the warmth of the fire in the sitting-room, felt a little cool. They found themselves confronted with a table laid with rigid military precision: glasses standing to attention, cutlery lined up in ranks, napkins with knife-edge creases and flowery name plates pushed to the front of each place setting . . . and just as Charlotte suspected, she had been positioned next to Alex.

'What an interesting painting, David,' she said. 'Is it new?' And while everyone predictably turned to admire a rather nondescript watercolour above the sideboard, Charlotte switched Alex's name for Derek's.

At the head of the table, Hilary was doing her level best to steer the conversation on a straight course, but somehow it kept slipping away from her. And who, she wanted to know, had ruined her seating plan? Secretly she suspected Derek, all that kissing at the start of the evening. And what did Charlotte think she was doing, whispering and tittering like a schoolgirl, down there with Derek at the other end of the table. Lord knows what Cindy must think. A sideways look told Hilary that Cindy was obviously bored and, by the way she was poking at her chocolate mousse, she was not going to finish it. Hilary felt slighted. Cindy had barely opened her mouth all evening, had only said anything when she was spoken to. Alex, bless him, had tried several times to talk to her, but Mother was making that exceptionally difficult, monopolising the poor man with all her talk of antiques. And Dad, of course, was just being Dad, and for all his scintillating talk, he might have stayed at home. David was predictably drunk now and telling another of his Rotary Club jokes.

'What's the difference between a Skoda and Prince Charles?'

'Not now, David,' she said warningly, knowing the punchline only too well. She got to her feet and started to gather up the dishes. 'Bring these out for me, will you?'

'Right you are, my little sweetie-pie,' he said jumping smartly to his feet and managing to pull part of the tablecloth with him. Glasses crashed against plates and red wine bled on to the white damask cloth.

'Don't worry, everyone,' shrieked Hilary, who seemed to be the only one who was worried, 'a bit of salt rubbed in and a cold soak overnight will do the trick.'

'And that's just for David,' giggled Charlotte.

Everyone laughed and started to clear up the mess, dabbing the table with their napkins, while Hilary disappeared to the kitchen.

'Bit of a boob that, old mate,' said Derek, the only one not bothering to help. 'Though personally, I'm not a boob man.'

Again everyone laughed, except Cindy.

Derek looked up round the table. 'Nothing wrong in that, is there?'

David shook his head and poured himself another glass of wine. Taking the bottle from him, Derek filled his own glass and then Charlotte's. 'Anyone else?' he said holding up the bottle. 'What about you, Alex?'

'No thanks.'

Derek laughed. 'No, not the wine. Are you a boob man?'

'Stop it, Derek,' hissed Cindy.

'No, let the man speak.'

'I prefer the whole body.'

Smooth all right, thought Charlotte.

'Cheese and biscuits,' said Hilary, reappearing with a large plate. 'Cindy, dip in first before it all disappears.'

'No, really I couldn't, that was all quite delicious.'

Liar, thought Hilary, looking disappointed.

'Mother, how about you?'

'Sorry, that moussaka really finished me off.'

David roared with laughter. 'Has that effect on most people.'

'Is that a piece of Cheshire Blue?'

Hilary smiled gratefully at Alex and passed him the plate.

'*Very* smooth,' muttered Charlotte.

'What did you say, Charlotte?' asked her mother.

'I was just saying how smooth this red wine is.'

Hilary looked warily at her sister. She had the most awful feeling that this moment was the lull before the storm. Something terrible was about to happen. 'David,' she said, in an effort to keep the evening on track, 'what about some port?'

Getting slowly and very cautiously to his feet, David reached for a near-empty bottle of port on the sideboard, along with a tray of glasses, and for those who wanted port, he poured it out as sparingly as Communion wine.

Separate conversations began springing up around the table. Charlotte eavesdropped on what was being said.

'. . . you know, Cindy, Tiffany is such a godsend to me,' Hilary was saying. 'I don't know how I ever managed without her. She's wonderful with the children, nothing's too much trouble for her.'

'Really, I find that difficult to believe. At home she's quite difficult.'

'. . . so Alex, you're in computers, are you? I would think that would be extremely tedious. Can you prove to me it isn't?'

'I'm not sure I can, Louise, not right here and now, but I can see why you might think that.'

Alex turned away from Louise and looked down the length of the table and stared Charlotte straight in the eye. 'What plans have you got, Charlotte, now that you're back in England?'

'Plans?' she repeated. He smiled, a smile, she realised to her horror, that was duplicated, as was the cheese in front of her. Hell, she was drunk!

'I just wondered what you might want to do next?' he said, his elbows resting on the table and leaning towards her.

He wasn't going to give up, was he? 'Get a job of course,' she answered brightly.

Her mother laughed derisively. 'It won't be easy, Charlotte,' she said. 'Haven't you heard, there's a recession on and you're not exactly overly qualified, are you, apart from now having a little French under your belt, of course?'

'Thanks,' Charlotte said, picking up her wine glass and tossing back the last mouthful.

'I'm only being realistic,' Louise persisted. 'Firms have been closing down at a terrifying rate all over the country.'

'But not the antiques trade, that right, Mother?'

An uncomfortable hush fell round the table. It was Derek who broke it.

'I'm sure someone like Charlotte won't find any difficulty in getting a job,' he said, leaning into her and refilling her glass. 'Bet you sound dead sexy speaking French.'

Charlotte giggled and Hilary looked up sharply. 'David!' she snapped. 'Coffee!'

Hauling himself out of his chair once more, David looked pie-eyed round the table. 'Coffee for how many?'

'For eight of course,' came Hilary's swift reply, and then, remembering her manners, she looked round the table. 'Unless there are any takers for tea.'

'Better make it for seven,' Louise said tartly. 'Your father's fallen asleep again.'

And looking at her father, Hilary stifled a low groan. What must Alex think of them all?

'So, what kind of job?'

Charlotte silently screamed to herself. Why couldn't that smoothie just shut up and leave her alone? How on earth did she know what sort of work she could get? 'Oh, I don't know, something will turn up,' she murmured, 'and anyway, there's no need for me to get a job immediately. Peter has left me very . . .' Her voice faltered and trailed away.

'A job would keep you busy though, wouldn't it?' said Hilary. 'Keep your mind off things.'

'Why don't you come and work for us?' Derek said, winking at her. 'Classy French-speaking masseuse, that would open up the business, eh Cindy?'

'Shut up, Derek,' Cindy said quietly.

Underneath the tablecloth, Derek placed his hand firmly on Charlotte's left thigh.

Charlotte slowly pushed back her chair and rose unsteadily to her feet. She picked up her glass of wine and brandished it in the air, and in a wavering voice said, 'To Hilary, that was a wonderful lasagne . . . I mean moussaka . . . I'd just like to thank you all for a lovely evening, I haven't had so much fun since . . . well not since I told Peter I didn't . . . Oh I'm sorry, I think I'd better go home.' She banged her glass down on the table and, spilling some of its contents, she slumped slowly down into her chair and started to cry.

A stunned silence followed, then a crescendo of activity with Derek offering to take Charlotte home and Cindy hissing like a swan, saying he'd do nothing of the kind. Hilary told David to get Charlotte out of the dining-room and upstairs before she was sick all over their antique Chinese rug. But Louise surprised them all by saying, 'No, don't be silly, Alex can take her home. He lives nearest, after all.'

'Mother!' cried Hilary, a look of horror on her face. 'Alex can't possibly . . . she must stay here with us.'

'No,' wailed Charlotte. 'Not here. I want to go home.'

'No problem,' Alex said. 'I'll take her back to Ivy Cottage. Could someone find her bag for me, please?' And before Hilary could protest any more, Alex led the snivelling Charlotte towards the hall. 'Goodnight, everyone,' he said. 'Don't worry, she'll feel better after a breath of fresh air.'

7

A cup of coffee in his hand, Alex pushed open the door of his office, or what had once been Mrs Clifford Senior's small dining-room. He could feel the warmth of the early morning sun streaming through the window, even though it was only a quarter past eight. He reached up above his desk and opened one of the windows, looking out at the garden as he did so.

High up in the silver birch tree at the far end he could see two magpies building a new nest. Only yesterday morning these same magpies had been forced to defend their old nest from the onslaught of a large black crow. The noise had been incredible, quite unlike anything Alex had ever heard before, as the birds attempted to protect their home, screeching and squawking, their wings beating furiously, while the crow relentlessly swooped and dived, its wings flapping as menacingly as a vampire's cape. Looking at the two determined birds this morning, Alex wished them well, admiring them for their resilience. He watched them for a while and then sat down at his desk. He took a sip of his coffee, leant back in his chair and wondered how Charlotte was feeling.

After they had crossed the road to Ivy Cottage last night he had walked Charlotte round and round the moonlit garden. At one stage she had even recited the words 'round and round the garden like a teddy bear'. With each circuit completed Charlotte began to lean on him less, until finally she reached the stage when she was completely upright. At that point, coming to a halt in the front garden, Alex took her key from her bag and let them both into the house.

They stumbled around in the dark for a while, because neither of them knew where any of the light switches were. As they crashed about, Charlotte started telling Alex to be quiet. 'Ssh,' she whispered, a finger against her lips. 'You'll wake Peter and he won't like that and then he'll be cross.'

'I'll try to be quiet,' he said in a hushed voice, attempting to placate her.

They found the kitchen and the light switch. But Charlotte immediately turned the light off. 'Look!' she said, smiling and pointing up at the sky through the kitchen window, her eyes wide like those of a small delighted child. 'Isn't it lovely? The moon's shining on us, we don't need a light at all.'

On the draining board stood a kettle, along with a glass, a half empty bottle of gin and two empty tonic bottles. He filled the kettle, plugged it in and then turned round to ask Charlotte where the coffee was. But she was gone.

He went out into the hall and found her coming down the stairs. Her smile, which in the kitchen just now he had decided was quite beautiful, had vanished. 'He's not there,' she said in a small, angry voice.

'Who's not there, Charlotte?'

'Peter.'

This confused discovery on Charlotte's part had the effect of instantly sobering her up. She went into the kitchen, flicked on the light switch and rummaged through the cupboards until she found a small jar of Nescafé. He had left her twenty minutes later.

Alex switched on his computer and prepared himself for a few hours' work, even though it was Saturday. Just this week he had been taken on by a small manufacturing company over in Congleton to install and set up a system encompassing accounting, planning, production and stock control. It was going to be a big job, at least five months' work.

Computers had been Alex's 'thing' since leaving university and it had been generally acknowledged, within his field of expertise, that he was brilliant. Henderson & Wyatt PLC, the huge insurance organisation with a head office in London, had known this only too well, which was why the board of directors were so shocked when Alex, their most experienced IT Project Manager, handed in his notice. Large amounts of money, followed by even larger amounts were offered to keep him. But Alex was adamant. He gave the company six months' notice, and when that was up, he relinquished his company car, sold his flat and put his furniture into store. He then acquired the necessary visas, filled a large backpack and headed east – to Poland, Latvia and Estonia, and for no other reason than that he fancied going there.

Friends and especially family were horrified, and after much exchanging of anxious telephone calls, they decided quite simply that Alex was at 'that age' – Alex Hamilton, they came to the conclusion, was having his mid-life crisis early and was best left alone to get on with it.

His return to Britain coincided exactly with his thirty-sixth birthday. Arriving at Heathrow airport a stone lighter, he had a very firm idea as to just what he was going to do next. He wanted to start up his own consultancy, to be his own boss, to do with his life as he chose. What he wasn't so sure about was just where to do it. He had no desire to live in London again, did not want to pick up his life where he had ceremoniously dumped it eight months previously. From now on he wanted his life to be full of spontaneity, decisions to be made by the hazardous toss of a coin. While still in the confines of the airport, he bought a map of the British Isles, laid it out – Scotland balanced on his backpack and the Home Counties covering the bottom of a sleeping girl – and asked another traveller to point out on the map where he had spent his last British holiday. The man said he had spent a very agreeable few days in Cheshire in the New Year. With a pencil poised over the county of Cheshire, Alex closed his eyes. He brought the pencil down on the village of Hulme Welford – this was to be his new home.

A week later, staying in a smart little bed and breakfast on the outskirts of the village, Alex made his first recce of Hulme Welford. His initial impression, on seeing the black and white half-timbered cottages – some even with thatch – was that he liked what he saw. Strolling into the estate agency in the centre of the village, he was soon on his way to take a look at 1a Ivy Cottage, with a view to renting it.

'As you can see, all the alterations are of a high standard, so you'll have no trouble with the property,' David Parker told him, as they stood in the small empty bedroom looking out over the garden and the open field beyond. A tractor was slowly ploughing ridges with a storm cloud of crows following behind. 'Not a bad view either,' David Parker said, smiling, piling it on a bit more, obviously hoping to clinch the deal there and then in the bedroom.

But Alex didn't need any convincing, his mind was made up. Before stepping foot in the estate agent's office he had already tossed a coin – heads, and he would take the first rented property he saw. It had turned up heads.

They went down the stairs and out through the kitchen door into the garden. Alex stood on the lawn and looked up at the house. 'I'd like to take it, please,' he said. 'But, just as a matter of interest, who will be my landlord?'

'Your landlady actually. My sister-in-law.' Locking up the property and walking back into the village, David Parker explained, briefly, Mrs Lawrence's reasons for moving back to Hulme Welford. 'She needs her family round her,' he added.

Alex hoped that this was indeed the case. Sometimes families were the last thing one needed.

Back in David's office, Alex filled out the necessary forms, giving names and addresses of people whom he hoped would supply him with 'a good character reference'.

'And your line of work, Mr Hamilton?'

'Management Consultant, specialising in Information Technology,' Alex answered, deliberately making himself sound like a contestant on *Mastermind.*

'Right. That sounds . . .'

'Respectable enough?'

The two men smiled, understanding each other perfectly.

'I'll have to check these references – that will take about a week – then I'll have to ask for two months' rent in advance and a deposit of four hundred pounds. Is that all right?'

'No problem. When do you think I can move in?'

David Parker looked at the calendar on his desk. 'Shall we say in two weeks' time, would that suit?'

It had suited very well. For the past fortnight Alex had begun to establish himself in the village. He was made to feel adequately welcome, in a gentle, probing kind of way.

He set out the spreadsheets that he had been working on yesterday morning, flicked a few keys on the PC keyboard and set to. His concentration didn't last long. He looked up and wondered at the sound he'd just heard, a little like a muffled cry, or was it the magpies being assaulted again? He peered out of the window. All was well high up in the silver birch tree. Then followed a sound that was more audible and clearly more recognisable. His landlady was awake and obviously suffering. He got up from his desk and went quickly upstairs to the bathroom, before going next door to see if he could help.

Moussaka second time around was disgusting, especially when it got stuck in the nose. If she lived, Charlotte thought she would never forgive her sister. Clutching her head and stomach both at the same time, she looked down at the kitchen floor. It was not a pretty sight. She had only crawled downstairs to get herself a drink and now she had this awful mess to clear up.

The unfamiliar sound of the doorbell made her jump and was enough to set off a second bout of vomiting. This time she made it to the toilet.

When she staggered back into the kitchen, she thought she must be hallucinating. Alex Hamilton was standing at the kitchen sink, filling a washing-up bowl from the hot tap. She stood open-mouthed, not knowing what to do. She was still dressed in the clothes she had worn last night, and she felt like a pair of old tights just pulled out of the washing machine.

'Ah, there you are,' he said, turning off the hot tap and lifting the bowl out of the sink. 'I thought you might need some help. I did ring the bell but there was no answer, so I came round the back and found your door open. You must be feeling pretty wretched.'

Charlotte's mouth opened even further. Sympathy was the last thing she had expected: mocking contempt, yes; concern, no. She tried to speak but couldn't and instead rushed to the toilet again.

When she reappeared Alex was down on his hands and knees wearing a pair of pink Marigold gloves. She somehow found the energy to laugh.

He looked up. 'What's so funny?'

'I'm sorry, it's just that you look ridiculous in those gloves. I suppose Hilary bought them, she's tried so hard to organise everything for me . . . she means well . . . and I was a perfect cow last night.'

He got to his feet. 'I'm sure she'll forgive you.'

'You know, it would be a lot easier if you could be a complete jerk.'

'Maybe I am,' he said. 'Have you got any disinfectant?'

She felt too weak and too stunned by what was happening to be of any real use. 'Have a look under the sink,' she said, 'Hilary's bound to have put some there.' Thinking about what Alex had said earlier, that he had found the back door open, she wondered how that could have been. Then she remembered. Last night, before going out, she had opened up the conservatory . . . and had forgotten to relock it. But that wasn't all she had forgotten, was it?

'I've never had to admit this before,' Charlotte said nervously, watching

Alex turning out the cupboard under the sink, 'but I have no idea how I got back here last night. I suppose Hilary saw me home.'

Alex twisted off the safety top of a plastic bottle of disinfectant and poured some of the liquid on to the kitchen floor. He turned to face her. 'Don't you remember anything about last night?'

Recoiling from the smell, she said, raising her voice, 'Well, of course I do!' She regretted this, as her head began to pound with the resonance of a kettledrum. 'I just don't remember coming home, that's all.'

'Actually, it wasn't Hilary, it was me.'

'You!'

'For some reason, known only to your mother I think, she suggested I did, not that I minded.'

Charlotte was speechless. What the hell was her mother playing at?

Alex peeled off the rubber gloves and pointed to a glass of murky brown liquid on the table. 'You'd better drink that.'

'What is it?'

'A patented morning-after-the-night-before cure, never fails. I was given it in Poland where they have more than their fair share of hangovers.'

Charlotte picked up the glass reluctantly and sniffed it. 'Smells disgusting,' she said, pulling a face.

'Tastes disgusting as well. But trust me, it works.'

Too weak to argue, Charlotte put the glass to her lips, deciding that if it made her sick, she would at least have the pleasure of making Alex clean up the mess. The thick liquid slipped down her throat, reminding her of the only time she had ever eaten oysters. She shuddered violently and felt ready to pass out.

'I suggest you have a bath now, then go back to bed.'

Charlotte, strangely obedient, did as she was told, until she reached the landing and found herself watching a comparatively unknown man go into the bathroom and start running her a bath. At the sight of Alex bending over the taps and rummaging through her newly placed toiletries, she felt an overpowering sense of intrusion. Peevishly she said, 'I can manage on my own, thank you. You're my tenant, not my husband.'

He looked neither hurt nor offended. Turning off the taps and wiping his hands on his trousers in the absence of a towel, he said, 'Okay, but I'll be next door if you need me.'

8

Iris Braithwaite, armed with a pooper-scooper in one hand and a dog lead in the other, was standing at the end of Charlotte's driveway when she saw Alex Hamilton coming out of the front door of Ivy Cottage.

Hidden by an unruly forsythia bush, and being a founder member of Hulme Welford's Neighbourhood Watch scheme, she had no difficulty in watching Alex unnoticed, as he made his way from one side of the house to the other. She also had little difficulty in piecing together her version of the events of the previous night.

Sin, and sin with a capital S, put all thought of what was on the other end of the dog lead completely out of her mind, until she took a step backwards and found herself slipping on what her eleven-year-old King Charles spaniel Henry had just evacuated. Grasping at a branch of forsythia, Iris Braithwaite managed to remain vertical, thereby keeping intact her highly prized dignity, though not her silk scarf. It floated slowly to the ground and, like part of a magician's act, covered perfectly Henry's squelched offering.

Saturday was Derek and Cindy's busiest day of the week at In The Pink. From the moment they had opened at eight forty-five the salon and gym had been packed. In the back salon, above the sound of the local radio station, Derek could hear Dawn, their beautician, telling a horizontal Mrs Carlton the best way to close up her pores each night before going to bed. Earlier it had been a lesson on the perils of dehydrating the Stratum Corneum by using a defatting something or other. It all sounded pretty convincing stuff, and even if he didn't believe a word of it, the punters did, and that was what counted.

Trying to ignore Dawn's constant stream of prattle, he carried on winding clingfilm around the head of Mrs Jeffs, an attractive bottle blonde from the Orchard Way executive development. She was married to *the* Darren Jeffs, the highly paid key goalscorer for Manchester United – though it was rumoured that Darren was scoring more than goals these days. Until yesterday evening Derek had reckoned Mrs Jeffs was worthy of extra special attention, had thought her to be the most desirable woman in the village.

Now, as Derek looked in the mirror at the sleek face bent over the latest bestseller from Jackie Collins, he viewed her as second rate – he noticed too that she had been reading the same racy page for the past ten minutes.

Overnight he had relegated Mrs Jeffs to the second division, for every bit of him wanted Charlotte Lawrence.

He would have to go carefully with Charlotte, he knew: a grieving widow was a harder prospect than a bored housewife. Last night in bed, after making love to Cindy, he had lain awake thinking of Charlotte: of running his hands through her lovely hair with its natural dark colour; of taking her to that secret place, down in the woods near the mere – where he had intended taking Mrs Jeffs.

'Derek!' It was Cindy standing next to him, a hot brush in one hand and an aerosol of styling mousse in the other. 'I don't know what you're thinking of, but that's quite enough clingfilm for Mrs Jeffs.'

He looked down at the now unwanted Mrs Jeffs, almost hidden beneath a sombrero of transparent plastic. Frankly though, he didn't give a damn. He decided that from now on, if he was going to get anywhere with Charlotte, he would have to be subtle.

Charlotte woke up just after two in the afternoon. She was amazed how well she felt, so well in fact that she wondered whether the hangover, and what had caused it, had all been a terrible dream. But looking at her pile of discarded clothes at the end of the put-you-up, and recognising them by their creases, it hit Charlotte that she had a certain amount of music to face. Earlier, she'd had only a patchy memory of the events of the previous night; now she could remember *everything*. Oh, what a fool she had made of herself, especially all that wandering around the garden with Alex.

Drunk. She closed her eyes and shuddered. She had never been drunk before. Tiddly yes, but not so drunk that she had been sick afterwards.

The most memorable occasion when she'd had too much to drink was when Peter had taken her to meet his parents for the first time. 'I think you should meet my parents,' he had said one night on the phone.

'Why? Am I in for a shock?' she had replied.

Ann and Godfrey were a shock with their puritanical mores. Grace had been barked out at the start of dinner, just as Charlotte had reached for her knife and fork. The first social gaffe of the evening committed she gulped at her wine, saying 'This is lovely.'

'We never touch it ourselves,' Godfrey stated, as upright as a guardsman in his chair.

She tried appealing to Ann. 'Hasn't Peter done well at work this year?'

'We never wanted him to be an accountant.'

Charlotte looked to Peter for his reaction. His face was expressionless, which made him seem so vulnerable. It was then that Charlotte first thought she loved Peter.

At the end of the meal, and having drunk more wine than was good for her, Charlotte committed the final *faux pas*. She reached out for her cup of coffee over the top of a flickering candle and let out a sudden undignified yelp. She dropped the cup, spilling coffee everywhere and saw with horror a flame at the end of her finger – her false nail had caught light. 'I'm so terribly sorry,' she squealed, dousing her finger in the remains of her wine. The hiss was short-lived but not the memory of that evening.

In the car driving back to London, she apologised to Peter. 'I'm sorry. I spoiled everything.'

'Rubbish,' he said, smiling for the first time all night. 'You gave them a good shaking up.'

'I don't think they approved of me.'

'Good. Will you marry me?'

That was the impulsive Peter she had loved, and married three months later.

Charlotte pushed back the duvet and got up. She pulled some clothes out of a suitcase, got dressed and went downstairs to get something to eat. She was starving.

There was a strong smell of disinfectant in the kitchen. She opened every window and door and set about making herself a sandwich and tidying away last night's bottles of gin and tonic. As she leaned against the worktop and bit into the bread and cheese, she began to realise just how much her sister had done for her. The refrigerator and cupboards all seemed to be full of basic food and household requirements. She hadn't noticed any of these things yesterday. How ungrateful she must have seemed.

From now on, she decided, there would be no more wallowing in self-pity, no more blaming herself and then being bloody to everyone else who helped. It was time to move on. What had happened had happened. She hadn't killed Peter, the weather had – all that snow and ice. 'I am not responsible for Peter's death,' she said out loud.

It was time to be strong, to be positive and decisive, but most of all, to be nice. Cynicism had played too great a part in her life recently, so much so that it was possible that she had forgotten what being nice was all about. It certainly wasn't humiliating one's sister at her dinner party; nice wasn't throwing up all over the kitchen floor as a result and then being rude to someone who was trying to help. Even so, that drink had smelt awful. She wouldn't apologise for saying that.

After this self-imposed lecture, Charlotte made herself a cup of tea, stood at one end of the empty kitchen and stared hard at the room. Oblong in shape and bordered with good quality pine cupboards with innocuous cream and blue wall tiles, it offered no obvious horrors. Her pine table and chairs, arriving from Brussels on Monday, would finish it off well, together with a fresh lick of paint and some pretty curtain fabric. Then it would feel like her kitchen. This was what she had wanted for so long – to live in a house that was hers, not an apartment that was rented and had no sense of 'home' or permanence.

She began to feel more cheerful and, rushing upstairs to her bedroom, she unearthed a notepad and pen. She returned to the kitchen, where she started to write out a list. At the top of the list and underlined were the words,

'Apologise to everyone'; next was 'Buy paint', followed by 'Check out curtain fabric', and then, after a moment's pause, she wrote 'Buy a dog'. For years she had wanted a dog, but Peter had always said, 'No, how can we?' Given the circumstances, he was right, of course.

She was just wondering how she would go about buying a dog when the doorbell rang.

Opening the front door, she was surprised to see a large bouquet of red roses proffered by a tanned arm. She couldn't smell the roses but she could smell aftershave and so had a pretty good idea who it was hiding behind one of the brick posts of the porch with his arm extended.

'They're lovely,' she said. 'A shame they're not for me.'

'Oh, but they are,' Derek Rogers said, stepping out from his hiding place. 'They most certainly are for you.' And with one hand placed firmly on her shoulder, he took her inside the house, shutting the door behind them. 'You know, Charlotte, I made myself a promise this morning.'

'That's funny,' Charlotte said, 'so did I.'

'I made a promise to be kind to widows and orphans.'

Charlotte laughed, feeling that perhaps she shouldn't. 'And I've just promised myself to be strong, positive, decisive and nice,' she said.

He smiled. 'Sounds interesting. I hope you're going to be nice to me. You'll need to put those in water.' He handed her the roses. 'This way to the kitchen, is it?'

Why, thought Charlotte, does everyone else seem to think they have a perfect right to gate-crash their way into *my* house? She followed behind, and placing the bouquet in the sink, she put the plug in and turned on the cold tap.

'I think I ought to apologise for last night,' she said above the noise of gushing water. 'I don't normally get drunk.'

'No need to apologise,' he said, stepping towards her. 'I like a woman who can let herself go.'

Turning the tap off, Charlotte took a step back. 'It's just that I wouldn't want you to get the wrong idea about me.'

'And what idea would that be?'

'Well, you know, that I always behave badly.'

He laughed, and moved slightly closer. 'I'd say you behaved beautifully.'

'That's all right then,' she said brightly, remembering last night how she had thought it could be fun to flirt with Derek. She wasn't so sure now. She walked over to the other side of the kitchen.

'So beautifully, in fact, that I spent the entire evening wanting to make love to you, there and then.'

She tried to laugh, to sound blasé, as though she was completely *au fait* with this kind of conversation. 'What, in front of everyone?'

Again, he was moving towards her. 'I think we'd both prefer to do it in private, wouldn't we?'

He's joking, she told herself. He's just trying me out, trying to see whether

I'll fall about shocked. She tried another laugh. He came and stood next to her.

At first she was totally passive when he kissed her, too surprised to know how to react. Then, because she was really rather enjoying it, she responded. It only lasted a split second but it was enough to convince Derek that he was a welcome guest to the rest of her body. 'No,' she said firmly, when his hands strayed from her shoulders and towards her neck.

'No such word,' he whispered.

'How about this?' Charlotte said, coming to her senses. 'Cindy!'

'Cindy doesn't mind.'

'Bloody hell!' Charlotte shouted, pushing him away from her. 'So you think you can add my name to your long list of ego boosts, do you?' She moved back to the sink and, picking up the roses, she thrust their dripping stems at his chest. 'I want to keep my promise, Derek,' she said calmly, 'so will you get out of my house now ... please?'

Iris Braithwaite was doing the rounds distributing the parish magazine. She was just on her way up Charlotte's drive when she heard the sound of the front door being opened and saw Derek Rogers coming out. Iris paused for a moment and turned on her heels, marching off down Acacia Lane to the safety of The White Cottage. 'She's past shame, that Charlotte Lawrence! Her husband's barely cold.' She muttered all the way home in a frenzy of outrage. '*Two* men in one day! I must warn Reverend Jackson, no man is safe. Why the poor man himself might even be in danger.'

9

'Well, you do surprise me,' Louise told Hilary on the telephone. 'I thought you would have raced over the road at the crack of dawn to see how your sister was.'

'Not after her appalling behaviour,' Hilary said emphatically, unaware of her mother's pithy sarcasm.

'Oh don't be such an old woman, Hilary. Charlotte only got drunk. You sound as though she committed mass homicide round the table last night, though to be honest, I can think of one person I would gladly let her murder.'

Finding herself in agreement with her mother for once, Hilary said, 'You're absolutely right, of course – that Derek Rogers is entirely to blame. I did warn Charlotte about him, but you know what she's like, thinks she knows . . .'

'Rubbish! Derek's a dear,' responded Louise, who secretly thought that if Derek hadn't been there last night, they would have all died of boredom. 'I was referring to your father. Dear God, ever since he retired, there's been no keeping him awake. He did the same thing when we were over at the Macmillans' for Easter Sunday.'

Annoyed, Hilary sensed her telephone call being hijacked as she listened to her mother setting off down the familiar track of Dr Neville Archer retired.

For thirty-six years their father had been a GP in Hulme Welford, until last year when he could no longer put off his retirement. Ever since then Louise had complained constantly that their father was at a loose end, permanently moping about and getting under her feet. Hilary could sympathise. She had often thought the same thing about David while on holiday.

Well, that was one thing her sister would be spared. At least Charlotte wouldn't have to put up with Peter getting in the way. Thinking of Charlotte made Hilary remember what she had called her mother for.

'Mother,' she interrupted, 'never mind Dad for the moment. Don't you think you should go and check on Charlotte?'

'Why ever should I?'

'Because, well, she might have thrown up and—'

'What, and choked to death? Goodness, Hilary, you do have a vivid imagination, don't you? Look, it's Saturday afternoon and I've got a shop full of customers. If you're so worried about Charlotte lying in a pool of her own vomit, go and do something about it.'

Hilary put down the receiver with a look of shock on her face. She had forgotten her mother had moved the telephone from her little back office to her desk in the main part of the shop. She cringed at the thought of those customers listening to her mother's one-sided conversation. What must they have thought?

As for going over to see Charlotte, that was quite out of the question. She had no intention of calling on Charlotte, not until her sister had apologised for ruining her dinner party.

In the end, it was Neville – his gooseberries tended to and with time on his hands – who called on Charlotte.

He couldn't be bothered walking to Ivy Cottage even though it was only ten minutes away. He supposed that was what retirement did to you, and he got the car out instead. Turning into Acacia Lane, he hoped that Hilary wouldn't catch sight of him. She would be bound to tell Louise and then he'd never hear the last of it and be restricted to even fewer calories. 'If you're going to lead a completely sedentary life, you must expect to eat less,' Louise had told him the last time he had got the car out for what she called an unnecessary journey. She, of course, cycled energetically everywhere and was the same weight now – as she so liked to tell him – as when she fell pregnant with Charlotte.

'Hello Dad,' Charlotte said, opening the door. 'Come in.'

He stepped inside. 'You look better than I thought you might,' he said.

'Let the side down a bit last night, didn't I?'

He smiled. 'Me too. What a pair we are.'

In the kitchen, Neville couldn't help but notice the opened copy of *Yellow Pages* on the worktop. 'Anything I can help you with?' he said warily. These days he was so used to being told there was nothing for him to do, he hardly dared ask the question.

'There is, as a matter of fact,' she said. 'Have you got a spare hour or so?'

'Yes,' he said, brightening. 'I've got a spare twenty-four, if that's any good to you.'

'Right then,' she said, picking up her bag, 'drive me over to Lower Peover and help me choose a dog.'

Neville followed his daughter out of the house.

He suddenly felt happy. He was going to enjoy having Charlotte around again.

10

Charlotte looked at her watch. It was half past six on Sunday morning. She groaned and tried to ignore the noise coming from downstairs. Surely dogs slept for longer than this? She lay there, listening to the persistent whining for a few moments more, before she gave in, got out of bed and padded downstairs to the kitchen.

Opening the kitchen door, she was all set to be firm, but seeing the small face looking up at her – head slightly tilted – all her strong resolve vanished, and she bent down and scooped the little dog up in her arms.

The dog had looked at her like that yesterday afternoon at the kennels. Mrs Ingram-Walker, whom Charlotte had spoken to on the telephone earlier, had greeted Charlotte and her father at the gate, shouting loudly above the noise of the yapping West Highland White terrier puppies. 'Found us all right, then? Bit off the beaten track really. Still, you managed it, that's the main thing.'

They walked round the kennels, Mrs Ingram-Walker determined to give them an official guided tour, and enthusing every step of the way. The place was certainly impressive, spotlessly clean and festooned with certificates and rosettes for Best Dog and Best Bitch.

'You know what this is all about, don't you, Charlotte?' her father said as they were shown yet another certificate, this time for hygiene. 'This is the sales pitch to justify the huge price she's going to quote you any minute now.'

'That's just the kind of thing Peter would have said,' Charlotte replied tersely.

As they were coming to the end of the tour of puppy pens, Charlotte saw a slightly older-looking Westie on its own. 'Why's that one all alone?' she asked.

'Kept her back from an earlier litter, thought perhaps she might be good enough to run on for breeding. Turned out she's not. Always a problem, that. You get stuck with them then – people want puppies, not a dog at seven months. Still, there we are, she's not a bad bitch though.'

'May I see her?' Charlotte asked, bending down to have a closer look at the shy face, tilted to one side and staring up at her from the back of the pen. Charlotte's mind was already made up. It was this dog or nothing.

Holding the little dog to her, Charlotte looked down at the sheets of newspaper she had laid out on the kitchen floor the night before. Mrs Ingram-Walker had said there would be no need, that the dog was completely toilet-trained, but Charlotte hadn't wanted to take any chances. 'So you really are a good girl then', she said, seeing that all was dry.

She put the dog on the floor and began tidying up the newspapers. As she did so, *Deaths and Funerals* caught her eye. All the recently deceased were women and in their seventies or eighties: Mrs Mary Robinson, Mrs Edith Byron, Miss Alice Hayes, Mrs Annie Tompkins and lastly Miss Mabel Unwin. Charlotte looked up from this last entry and turned to the white dog beside her, who responded with another tilt of its head. 'Yes,' Charlotte smiled. 'I think I've found the perfect name for you – Mabel.'

Breakfast was interrupted by the sound of the doorbell. Mabel, her head down inside a small china bowl of Weetabix, didn't even look up.

'Fine guard dog you're going to be,' Charlotte said, putting her own bowl of cereal down on the worktop. 'You'll be back to Mrs Ingram-Walker if you don't pull your weight round here,' she called over her shoulder as she went out into the hall.

Charlotte opened the door. 'Talking to yourself now,' Louise said, then gave her daughter a hard stare and added, 'or have you got someone here?'

'What, at half past seven in the morning, Mother?'

'Anything's possible.' Louise tucked a thick wad of newspaper under her arm and looked up the stairs to the landing above.

Charlotte stared at her mother, shut the door and then wandered back to the kitchen, shaking her head. 'Is there anything you wanted in particular? I mean, it's lovely to see you, but it is fairly early to be paying social calls, especially for you.'

'Don't worry, I shan't stop for long. Any tea in the pot? Oh, what's that?' She stared down at Mabel.

'She's a breeder's reject,' Charlotte said. 'Can't you tell?'

'It's too early in the morning to play games with me, Charlotte. Who does it belong to?'

'*She*,' Charlotte said with emphasis, 'is mine. I bought her yesterday from a Mrs Ingram-Walker.'

'Are you out of your mind? How are you going to look after it, I mean her, while you're out working?'

'Oh, so suddenly I'm capable of getting a job, am I?'

'Well, that remains to be seen, of course.'

'Don't spoil it for me, Mother,' Charlotte said, handing her a mug of tea. 'I've always wanted a dog, and besides, I need the company.'

Louise put the *Sunday Times* on the worktop behind her and cradled the mug in her hand. 'But you've got Hilary right opposite you, and there's us, no more than a ten-minute walk away.'

'Yes, and you've all got your own lives to lead.' Charlotte thought that right now she'd rather have Mabel than any member of her family, except her father. 'Look,' she said, 'I can't expect you all to revolve around me suddenly. It wouldn't be fair.'

'Well, I suppose you're right.'

'And while we're on the subject of things being right and fair, what on earth were you doing suggesting Alex see me home on Friday night?'

Louise laughed. 'Just a bit of fun, playing Hilary at her own game. You should have seen the look on her face.'

'I can imagine it,' Charlotte said, almost enjoying the thought. 'So what did you come round here for, apart from a cup of tea?'

'Oh yes. To tell you that you must come to church this morning.'

'Why, is there something special on today?'

'No, but I just think you ought to show your face.'

'You've never forced anyone to church before. Why now, and more importantly, why me?'

'Well, Charlotte,' Louise said, putting down her empty mug, 'thing is, you've been found out. I was in the paper shop a few moments ago,' she nodded towards her copy of the *Sunday Times*, by way of supportive evidence, 'and I overheard Iris Braithwaite talking to Mrs Haslip. Apparently it's common knowledge.'

'What is?'

Louise smiled. 'I have to take my hat off to you, Charlotte, you don't do things by halves, do you?'

'Now who's playing games?'

'You are, by the sounds of things. But I'm not sure Hulme Welford is the right place to be playing them. Too small, too parochial – especially for a woman.'

'For heaven's sake, Mother, what are you talking about?'

'Not just me, what everyone's talking about, that not only have you lured your tenant into bed within twenty-four hours of moving into Ivy Cottage, but Derek Rogers as well.'

11

At first Charlotte laughed out loud at her mother's revelation, hot from the lips of Iris Braithwaite. 'But *surely* no one is taking these absurd claims seriously?'

'I think you'll find that most people will be only too keen to believe it, Charlotte.'

'But why?'

'Because it's exciting, it's forbidden, and a woman, at that, is doing it here in Hulme Welford, right under their noses. They want to be shocked.'

'So Derek Rogers could go around seducing everyone and everything, left, right and centre, and that wouldn't be newsworthy, you mean?' Charlotte's voice was beginning to rise.

'Not in the same way. Everyone expects a man like Derek to behave badly, that's entirely within the rules of the game. But you're a widow and expected to behave as such and because you're a woman, you can only play the role of victim. Play it any other way and you're wide open to tabloid sensationalism.'

Charlotte was finding the situation less amusing now. 'But that's ridiculous.'

'I'm sorry, Charlotte,' her mother went on, 'but you've broken the rules and you've been found out.'

'You mean, you actually believe all this nonsense?'

Louise shrugged her shoulders. 'It really doesn't matter what I think, does it?'

'Of course it does.'

'Goodness, I don't understand why you're getting so worked up, you've never been bothered by what anyone thought of you before. Conforming has never been your forte, has it?' She laughed. 'I know you'll hate me for saying this, but there's more of me in you than you'd like to believe.'

Charlotte tried to ignore this last unnerving comment from her mother. 'So, just why are you asking me to go to church this morning?'

'What you get up to in your own home has nothing to do with Iris. She shouldn't be allowed to get away with invading your privacy, or anyone else's for that matter. You've got to fight her.'

Charlotte sighed. Fighting was the last thing she felt like doing at the moment. 'But there's nothing to fight about, none of it's true,' she said in an exasperated voice.

'None of it?' Louise asked, eyeing her daughter speculatively.

'None of it,' Charlotte repeated, looking out of the kitchen window and evading her mother's gaze. Well, there was no need to mention Derek kissing her, was there? And she hadn't kept the roses, she'd given those straight back.

Her mother picked up her *Sunday Times*. 'I must be off. But like I say, just go to church, brazen this out and make sure that as many people as possible, especially Iris, see you there, preferably on your knees. If there's one thing the righteous really like, it's a sinner praying for forgiveness.'

Crashing the breakfast dishes into the sink, Charlotte turned on the hot tap. Water gushed directly on to a cereal spoon, sending up a fountain of water in her face. She wiped herself dry and considered the no-win alternatives: do nothing and everyone would assume her guilty; fight back and everyone would think that the lady doth protest too much.

In front of the altar, a smartly dressed Mrs Haslip was reading out the week's notices. The rest of the congregation was so absorbed in working out how best to avoid being roped in for the jumble sale and the fork supper that nobody noticed Charlotte slipping quietly in at the back and settling herself in an unoccupied pew. So far so good, she told herself, wishing that the real purpose of her visit to St John's was to remain discreet to the point of invisibility, instead of being there to clear her name.

She had made up her mind not to come and to hell with everyone thinking she was man crazy. But then she had thought about Cindy and her children, and the terrible unfairness of the situation had hit her and propelled her out of Ivy Cottage and down Acacia Lane to St John's. She would sort this out, not for her own reputation, or Derek's for that matter, but for that of his family. And of course, there was Alex to think of.

The service was under way now. Charlotte stared at the needlepoint design on the hassock in front of her, and thought of the last time she had been in church. Peter's funeral.

Throughout the funeral service Peter's mother and father had sat motionless, their grief kept well in check until the church service was behind them and the funeral party had moved on to the nearby crematorium, where Ann finally allowed herself a restrained display of emotion, the comfort of her husband's angular shoulder supporting her own. It was as though she was responding to the heat of the flames about to consume her son, letting it thaw her customary coldness to give way, perhaps, to a sense of regret.

When Charlotte looked up she found she was no longer alone in the pew. Malcolm Jackson was well into his stride on the theme of spiritual gifts and he was holding up a small pink wallpaper-covered bin as a visual aid.

Sitting on her right was an earnest-looking tall young man of about eighteen, with a strong athletic build. He was wearing a pair of fashionable tortoiseshell-framed glasses, half obscured by an asymmetrical fringe dangling down on one side of his forehead. Covering the rest of him was a well-worn jogging suit. Charlotte guessed, from his slightly flushed and glistening face, that he had recently been wearing the jogging suit for its originally designed purpose. There was an aroma about him too that corroborated this. She could feel his body heat radiating towards her and she also thought she sensed some hostility. But no. She was just being paranoid. He turned and looked at her. She smiled, but he jerked his head away and gave his attention back to the sermon.

'Gifts come in varying shapes and sizes,' announced Malcolm Jackson. 'This was once a discarded tin of coffee, thrown away from somebody's kitchen cupboard, but with the gift of creativity we now have a wastepaper bin. I want to challenge each and everyone of you. Go home . . .' a slight pause, a smile . . . 'No, not now, but later, and search through your spiritual cupboards and see what God has given you. What has God given you, that you have been ignoring all these years?'

Not daring to think what might lie in her spiritual cupboards, Charlotte surveyed the congregation and the choir. Iris Braithwaite was wearing a wide-brimmed, brown felt hat which managed to ensure that she was the focal point of the choir. Taller than the other ladies, now all on their feet ready to sing, Iris stood at least five inches higher than anyone else. As Mr Phelps from the Post Office pulled out all the stops on the organ and the congregation rose to its feet, Iris, with both her hands crossed in front of her as though guarding her virginity, closed her eyes, opened her mouth and prepared to give everyone the benefit of her deep contralto voice. Within a few words of the opening line of 'Give Me Joy' – far too modern a hymn for Iris's taste, as everyone knew – her eyes shot open at the sound of the happy clappers three rows from the front. She stared hard at the offending couple, but they carried on courageously right to the end of the hymn.

The singing came to an end and the service continued with 'the Peace'. Anarchy seemed to be breaking out in the pews, with people greeting each other as though they were long-lost friends. No one greeted Iris. Charlotte, balking at the idea of being confronted by anyone she knew, turned to her lone companion, hoping to engage him in dull, safe conversation. She was in for a shock.

'You look like you've just been jogging,' she said. How ridiculous she sounded.

Looking down at his clothes, the young man said a little sullenly, 'Do you mind?'

'Of course not, but you'll probably find there'll be those who do mind, and they won't be happy until they see you in a boring grey suit.'

He almost smiled, almost looked her in the eye. 'It's just the only way I can come,' he said, nudging his glasses on to the bridge of his nose.

Charlotte was wondering what he meant by this, when he asked her, 'You're Charlotte Lawrence, aren't you?'

'Yes.'

'Do you know who I am?'

'No.'

And looking her in the eye, he said, 'Have you really been to bed with Derek Rogers?'

'No!' she answered, in a shocked voice. She hadn't been at all prepared for this kind of blatant interrogation, especially from one so young.

Vaguely aware that order had once again been restored, Charlotte turned away from this inquisitive lad and tried to pick up the threads of the service.

'. . . I believe in one God, the Father Almighty . . .'

'Believe me, I haven't,' Charlotte said to the young man, wanting suddenly to defend herself. She slipped down on to her hassock.

'. . . Maker of heaven and earth . . .'

'Do you intend to?'

'. . . And of all things visible and invisible . . .'

'No, certainly not.'

'. . . And in one Lord Jesus Christ . . .'

'Good,' said her companion.

A few minutes after the service had come to an end a sizeable crush had developed in the porch. Charlotte decided to remain in her seat until the worst was over. She was alone again, her strange companion having left. He had made his exit just as silently as he had arrived, leaving seconds before the end of the service. Whilst she hadn't particularly liked his line of questioning, there had been something about him she had liked – his straightforwardness.

She caught sight of her sister hovering by the font, holding what looked like a miniature toilet seat. Charlotte smiled at her, remembering she had yet to apologise. Was it her imagination, or had her sister just ignored her? Confused, she got to her feet and joined the queue for the escape route out, thankful that those around her were completely taken up in their own conversations and didn't seem to be at all worried by what she may or may not have been up to.

From behind her came a voice. 'Charlotte, there you are.' It was her mother, making one of her absurd statements, with her father bringing up the rear. To Charlotte's surprise her mother kissed her. She knew why and was, for once in her life, grateful to her.

The three of them were now level with Malcolm Jackson in the porch and Charlotte began to feel nervous. Had Malcolm heard the gossip? Heavens, he might have been thinking she had been propositioning the young man who sat next to her.

'So good to see you, Charlotte. How are you?' she heard Malcolm say. She nodded mutely, but instead of looking him full in the face, she found her eyes rooted to a small red wine stain on the left cuff of his otherwise immaculate white robe. She wondered if Iris Braithwaite had spotted this during the service and was even now planning a campaign to clean up the vicar of Hulme Welford.

'She's fine,' her mother answered for her. 'We're all rallying round, aren't we, dear, easing your suffering?'

Charlotte looked on bewildered. She had never heard her mother speak like this before. Suddenly, drawn like a magnet to the word suffering, everything seemed wrong. Yesterday she had been happy. This morning, before her mother called in, she had been happy. But it was wrong, very wrong. She had no right to feel anything other than the burden of Peter's death. All that had just passed inside the church, all those words she had listened to and repeated about love and deliverance from evil – she had no right to be there. Not after what she had done to Peter. Panic began to well up inside her. She fought it back, tried to control the monster of guilt within and edged towards the open door and the sunshine waiting outside.

'I shan't pester you, Charlotte,' pursued Malcolm, 'because I'm sure you'll have plenty of offers of help and advice, but if there really is anything I can do for you, you know where I am, though Mrs Braithwaite says I'm the most elusive person she knows. Apparently she was looking for me all yesterday afternoon, had something important to tell me.'

Charlotte forced a smile, wanting more than anything for the conversation to reach its conclusion. At the mention of Iris Braithwaite's name, she changed her mind. 'There is something you can help me with.'

'Yes?' Malcolm looked eagerly sympathetic.

'I just wanted to ask who that young man was, the one sitting next to me at the back of the church?'

'That was Barry. Nice lad, seems to carry the weight of the world on his young shoulders though. He's Derek Rogers' eldest.'

Outside in the sunshine and reeling from the shock of what she had just been told, Charlotte leaned against a large ornate tomb, about the size of a Mini, and tried to take in the fact that she had just been confronted by Barry Rogers. *Have you really been to bed with Derek Rogers?*

'Well,' said her mother, 'that wasn't so bad, was it? We would offer you Sunday lunch, but we're off to a car boot sale which starts in an hour, and I need to get there for the pick of the best pieces before the crowds turn up.'

'Don't worry about me,' Charlotte said in a distracted voice, watching her mother walk away. 'I've got plenty to do.'

'Are you okay, Charlotte?' her father said, walking alongside her. 'Only you look a bit strange.'

'I'm fine,' she lied.

'No, you're not,' he said. 'I can tell, I was a doctor once, you know.'

'Oh Dad, don't be nice to me, not now, you'll make me feel sorry for myself and that would never do. Peter's father always used to say I was full of self-pity.'

'Never mind Peter's father, do you want me to speak to Iris? She's no right spreading lies about the village.'

Charlotte looked up into her father's face and smiled. 'No,' she said, shaking her head, 'but thanks anyway.'

He looked puzzled. 'What for?'

'For believing in me and not what Iris Braithwaite's been saying.'

'Neville, do hurry up,' Louise called out. She was already down at the bottom of the gravel path and pulling open the lych-gate.

For a moment Neville Archer hesitated between his wife and daughter.

'Go on, Dad,' Charlotte said. 'I'm fine, really.'

Alone for no more than a few seconds, Charlotte felt herself the focus of someone's gaze. She looked up and met the icy glare of Iris Braithwaite, who, together with her cronies Mrs Haslip and Mrs Bradley, was encircling Malcolm Jackson in a well-practised pincer movement. A combination of fear and confused guilt told Charlotte to run, but something greater, her anger and her sense of justice, told her that this was the moment to shoot from the hip.

'Hello, Mrs Braithwaite,' she called out, as she made her way back towards the church porch.

In response, the older woman clutched her handbag tightly to her.

'You're just the woman I needed to see,' Charlotte said brightly, now standing directly in front of Iris. Post-service hangers-on, pricking up their ears, turned to watch. They sensed that something cataclysmically more interesting than discussing the vicar's handling of the service was about to happen. Charlotte pushed on. 'I think you have something to say to me, haven't you, Mrs Braithwaite?'

'I certainly have not.'

'Oh, but you have, and not only to me.'

The pearls on Iris's silk-clad chest began to wobble. 'Mrs Lawrence, I assure you, I have absolutely nothing whatsoever to say to you.'

This haughty righteousness was too much for Charlotte. 'Do you really think,' she said in a dangerously menacing voice, 'that I am capable of taking two men, whom I hardly know, into my bed one after the other?'

'I know what I saw,' Iris Braithwaite said, holding her ground and looking for back-up from the two women either side of her, who were beginning ever so slightly to distance themselves from Iris.

'You saw two men leave my house, nothing more, nothing less,' Charlotte asserted. 'I suggest you go and undo all the harm you've done with your vile gossip, and you can start by apologising to Mr and Mrs Rogers and their children.'

Leaving Iris Braithwaite looking like a paralysed rabbit caught in the beam of a car headlight, Charlotte turned and walked away, unaware of the silent applause from those around her who had just witnessed the first ever public dressing-down of Iris Braithwaite.

12

Charlotte felt wretched. Scoring a public victory over Iris Braithwaite should have had her skipping home, happy as a lamb. Instead she was shocked and saddened by what had just happened.

All her life, like so many others in the village, she had viewed Iris Braithwaite as some kind of personal *bête noire*. Iris had ruled the roost of Hulme Welford for as long as Charlotte could remember, her authority never once having been publicly questioned until today. Yet all Charlotte could remember from the short exchange was the terrible look on the older woman's face.

She had noticed that very same look on Peter's face the last time she saw him. She could recall now that look of hurt he was trying so hard to hide from her. So vivid was the picture in her mind that she was back there, in their Brussels apartment, in the kitchen, the smell of coffee, toast, boiled eggs . . . and then her words, words that had stabbed at Peter across the breakfast table: *I want a divorce, Peter.* She thought at first that he had not heard her. Then slowly he put his knife down on the plate in front of him – a blob of butter, half melted, clinging to the serrated edge – and he looked up at her, his lips clamped tightly shut, his eyes never leaving her own. He sat like that for what seemed an age, petrified by his emotionally starved upbringing. Nothing had prepared him for this devastating moment in his life.

Oh God, thought Charlotte, crossing the road, what was happening to her that she could go round hurting people so badly?

Not wanting, just yet, to go back to Ivy Cottage, not with the possibility of being confronted by Hilary, or even Iris Braithwaite, Charlotte turned left and walked down to the main street of the village until she came to Ted Cooper's paper shop.

Behind his back Ted Cooper had always been known as Sleazy Ted. But three years ago, after a lifetime of battling to keep what little greasy hair he had, he'd given up on it and covered the remaining strands with a well-upholstered wig. Then he had become Ted the Toup. Now, after three years of accumulated grime and nicotine, his famous false hair gave the appearance of being fused together into one solid piece.

Charlotte pushed open the door. She saw Ted sitting behind his till. He was leaning back in his chair reading a copy of the *People*. The face of a recently disgraced cricketer stared back at Charlotte. His eyes, beneath his cricket cap, watched her as she approached the counter.

'Hello, love,' Ted said, raising his own eyes over the top of the paper. 'Settling in okay, are you? Making new friends?'

'Not too badly,' Charlotte said, registering the ambiguity of Ted's last question.

''Course, nothing's really changed, has it, from when you left?'

'No, nothing's changed,' she agreed, noticing that Ted's tobacco-stained hands with their effeminately long nails were still the same, as were his cracked and blackened teeth.

She scanned the selection of Sundays on offer. The tabloids seemed to have either a 'distressed' or an 'outraged' Royal on the front page, with the exception of the *People*, who had gone it alone, informing its readership of the lurid sex life of a Northamptonshire top-spinner. The heavy brigade all carried more or less the same photograph of a tired-looking John Major. Having no particular loyalty to any one newspaper, Charlotte picked out the *Independent*, which was the nearest one to her. As she handed over her money she reflected that it seemed a very fitting choice.

Leaving Ted to get back to his reading, she opened the shop door to find herself confronted by a blue anorak and a pink hand-knitted cardigan. Although Charlotte didn't know the couple, she had seen them earlier in church and knew that they had witnessed the exchange between Iris Braithwaite and herself. They smiled at her – a full-blown, obsequious, Cheshire-cat grin. Politely she smiled back, hoping to slide past them and out of the shop. But they were having none of it.

'We'd just like to congratulate you,' the anorak said.

'We certainly would,' the pink cardigan echoed.

'It's about time somebody stood up to her,' the anorak said.

'It certainly is,' the cardigan agreed.

There was a rustle from behind the counter as Ted once again lowered his paper, his attention aroused by something other than bums and boobs. He looked over at them and slithered his way into the conversation with consummate ease. 'Afternoon, Reg, Joan. Congratulations in order, did I hear you say?'

'Didn't she tell you all about it, Ted?' said the anorak, who had now been identified as Reg. Charlotte folded the *Independent* in her hands and looked at the floor.

Reg and Joan closed the door behind them and surged past the displays of greetings cards and racks of magazines in their haste to impart their news to Ted.

'She was very brave,' said Reg.

'Oh, she was, you know,' agreed Joan.

'I really must be going.' Charlotte backed away towards the door. She felt bad enough as it was, without having this misplaced hero-worship to further fuel her considerable guilt.

'She certainly put Iris Braithwaite right on all that nonsense about that hairdresser fellow and her tenant. Of course we didn't believe any of it, not for one moment, did we, Joan?' Turning to reassure their heroine of this fact, Reg and Joan found themselves facing an empty space. They looked about the shop, hoping to unearth Charlotte from behind the rotating rack of thrillers and bodice-rippers. They were disappointed.

Hurrying away from the shop, Charlotte was already turning left into Daisy Bank and making for Acacia Lane. She wanted very much to scream. Coming back to Hulme Welford was supposed to have had a calming influence on her life. It was to have been a return to all that was comfortingly familiar, like the sisterly irritation between herself and Hilary, and the lack of understanding on her mother's part; even the interfering Iris Braithwaite was supposed to have been a necessary part of her rehabilitation. But in less than forty-eight hours she had somehow destroyed the steady equilibrium she had deliberately chosen to return to.

On her first night at Ivy Cottage she had experienced the sensation of having the silky edging torn away from her comfort blanket – now, she had practically unravelled the entire thing.

'And I certainly didn't speak to her, David, not after what she's done,' Hilary said, slamming the dishwasher shut as though underscoring the seriousness of her words, but all it did was make her wince at the sound of crashing crockery within.

'Why are you so cross, Mummy?' said Becky, her head bent over a colouring book on the kitchen table. 'I hope you haven't smashed my Peter Rabbit plate.'

Philip, who was sitting on the back doorstep scraping the mud from yesterday's match off his football boots, laughed and said, 'Serves you right if Mum has, after you deliberately smashed my Manchester City mug.'

Becky threw a yellow crayon at her brother through the open door. In return she got a wedge of dried mud flicked back at her. She set up a high-pitched wail.

'Stop it, you two,' said Hilary, ramming the remains of breakfast down the waste-disposal unit. Turning on the tap, she set off the loud chomping and churning. Above the noise she shouted at David, who was leaning back against the Aga reading the colour supplement. 'I don't know how she had the cheek to even be there.'

'What?' David said without looking up.

'I said . . . Oh, what's the use?' Turning the waste-disposal unit off, Hilary said, her voice still raised, 'If we had the next model up, we wouldn't have this trouble. They're much quieter, the more expensive ones.'

David was lost. 'What on earth are you talking about?' He gathered up the papers and headed off to the sitting-room for some peace and quiet. He knew from experience that it wasn't wise to hang about when Hilary was in one of these moods. Quite frankly, he didn't believe a word of what was being said about Charlotte. He wondered though whether this was because he didn't want to believe it, didn't like to imagine Charlotte capable of such a thing.

Hilary pursed her lips, got hold of a wooden spoon and started to push yet more discarded crusts and congealed cornflakes down the disposal unit.

'Mummy?'

'*Yes*, Becky,' Hilary snapped, before reminding herself that it wasn't her daughter's fault that Charlotte was bringing such shame on the family. 'What is it, dear?'

'Mummy, you know Auntie Charlotte?'

'Yes.' Well, I thought I did, she said to herself.

'Why doesn't Auntie Charlotte wear jim-jams like me?'

'What a strange question. Why do you ask?'

Becky looked up from her colouring book. 'I heard someone at church saying that Auntie Charlotte needs two men in bed with her to keep her warm.'

When Charlotte got home she rushed upstairs and screamed, long and loud, her head inside the airing cupboard where she hoped the sound would be confined. As a form of therapy it fell way short of working. She shut the door and went downstairs to the kitchen where she found Mabel chewing on a squeaky toy bought by Charlotte and her father yesterday, along with tins of food and a lead. Seeing Charlotte, the little dog scuttled over to her. Charlotte smiled and instantly felt better.

She fed Mabel and walked her about the garden wondering what she should do for the rest of the day. She ought to go over and apologise to Hilary but she really couldn't face her sister at the moment. And there was nothing in the house for her to do, not until tomorrow when the removal van would be arriving, and besides it was far too nice a day to be stuck inside.

Seeing the potting shed, with its duck-egg-blue-painted door, Charlotte remembered there was supposed to be some garden furniture stored in there. She went back into the house and found the large, clearly labelled, rusty key.

While she fiddled with the key in the lock to make it work, Charlotte could feel the warmth of the sun on her back. It was quite a suntrap, this corner of the garden, with its overgrown flower beds of London Pride, forget-me-nots and tiny wild purple pansies spilling over on to the path and along the bottom of the brick wall of the potting shed, which was mostly hidden beneath a flourishing wisteria. Against this wall was an assortment of cracked and chipped terracotta pots, some lying haphazardly on their sides. Charlotte thought they looked sad, as if they were still waiting for the Cliffords to come back for them.

Charlotte finally got the key to work. Without any resistance the door swung open. David's particulars of the property had informed Charlotte that not only did Ivy Cottage 'offer a surprisingly capacious potting shed' but that a 'selection of charming, rustic garden furniture could be found within'.

At first glance, this did not seem to be the case. All that Charlotte could discern in the suffused light and cobwebs was that the Cliffords must have forgotten to look in here before they moved. There was an old lawnmower, a collection of brooms in varying degrees of fatigue, a pair of mud-caked gardening gloves adopting a chilling posture on the floor – as though waiting to pounce on their next victim – along with some shears and a trug full of dead-headed roses. It was stiflingly warm, with an oppressive smell of baked soil and fertilizer.

Charlotte stepped inside and realised that the potting shed was much larger than she had at first thought. Beyond the lawnmower she could see a wheelbarrow and what looked like a selection of old garden furniture.

With Mabel trotting behind her, Charlotte carried two white-painted, rickety folding chairs across the lawn, one to sit on and one for her feet. Placing them beside the sprawling fig tree on the left-hand side of the garden, she carefully prised the chairs open. They were filthy, covered with dead insects and patches of flaking paint. She went back into the house and reappeared with a bowl of water and a cloth. A window cracked open behind her and the sound of Bach's Mass in B Minor flooded out, followed by the unmistakable smell of somebody else's lunch being cooked, along with the accompanying clatter of crockery. This reminded Charlotte that not only had she not given a thought to what she was going to eat that day, but that here, clearly, was one of the disadvantages of sharing her house and garden. Should she turn and acknowledge Alex Hamilton, who doubtless was standing in his kitchen watching her, or should she be circumspect and pretend she hadn't heard the window?

She remembered how nice Alex had been to her and that she owed him an apology, so she turned around, ready to give a signal of a peace offering. But there was no sign of him.

She went back to the chairs and started cleaning them. Eventually satisfied that she had done all that she could, she sat down cautiously. The flimsy chair creaked a little, but as it gave no other indication that it was about to collapse, she relaxed into it, clasped her hands at the back of her head, stretched her feet in front of her on the other chair, and turned her attention to the garden.

It was lovely, in need of some work admittedly, but lovely all the same. The lawn was covered with a sprinkling of daisies and dandelions and swept down some hundred feet or so towards a windbreak of high conifers, spruces and silver birches and a variety of rhododendrons on the point of bursting into flower. To her right was a deep, neglected border, and behind this, screening her from In The Pink, was a tall copper beech hedge.

Charlotte couldn't help but think she was going to need something more effective than a beech hedge to keep Derek Rogers out.

To her left, on the other side of the fig tree, was more copper beech hedging, but there was nothing beyond it, only a dense thicket.

She closed her eyes, listening to the tranquil cooing of doves in the trees around her, accompanied by the more fortissimo passages of the Bach that managed to reach this far down the garden. With this peace around her, together with the warmth of the sun, Charlotte soon found herself slipping into sleep.

She started, and sat bolt upright at the sound of barking. Mabel. She had forgotten about Mabel. Where was she? Looking towards the house, she saw the little dog lying on the grass in front of the conservatory being stroked by Alex, who was crouched down beside her.

'Hello,' he said, looking up at Charlotte.

She nodded, got up from her chair and walked over to him.

'I just came out to ask if you'd like to join me for lunch.'

'Oh,' she said, surprised. 'I've just eaten,' she lied.

He looked disappointed, squinting his eyes a little against the sun. 'I thought I'd eat out here. Seemed a good idea, on such a lovely day.'

He was right, Charlotte thought, it was a good idea, and she was starving. Why had she just lied to him?

'Roast beef and Yorkshire pudding,' he said. 'Are you sure you won't join me?'

She pushed her hands down into her trouser pockets. 'Oh, go on then, why not?'

Between them they fished out the cast-iron table from the potting shed and whilst Charlotte cleaned it up, Alex brought out two trays of food, along with a couple of glasses and a bottle of red wine. Mabel danced attendance, getting in their way.

'You knew I was lying, didn't you?' Charlotte said, when at last they sat down.

'Let's call it intuition.' He handed her a knife and a fork. 'I bet you haven't eaten a proper meal since Friday night.'

'Have you been spying on me?' Her voice sounded slightly accusing.

'It's hard not to, living so close.' He passed her a glass of wine and raising his own in the air, said, 'Here's to . . .' he paused, smiled and said decisively, 'here's to a good summer.'

'Yes, a good summer,' Charlotte repeated unconvincingly. She took a sip of her wine.

'Bulgarian, cheap and cheerful,' he said, watching her. 'I'm afraid I don't believe in expensive wines.'

'So what do you believe in, then?' The cynicism in her voice was undisguised.

He placed his glass carefully down on the table. 'Good question, that.'

'I'm sorry, that was uncalled for. I promised myself yesterday I'd stop doing that – being cynical, that is.' She put a piece of fluffy Yorkshire pudding in her mouth and then looked away, down to the silver birches, where she could see a pair of magpies building a nest.

Taking the opportunity to look at Charlotte unobserved, Alex decided that the first thing anyone would notice about Charlotte was her shoulder-length hair; it was so dark and without a hint of grey. She was wearing it, as she had on Friday night, loosely round her face, and it framed a mouth that could be described as large, but for his taste was perfect – full and sensuous – and when she smiled, two dimples appeared. He had noticed this the other night, along with the colour of her eyes that he now realised seemed to change depending on the light. At dinner they had seemed dusky, almost violet; here, sitting in the sun, he was struck by the dazzling gentian-blue colour they had become. He was also aware that she looked worn out. More than this, she looked uncomfortable with herself, there was an awkwardness about her. Was that suppressed anger, he wondered, anger with life for having dealt her such a rough hand? She certainly deserved to feel that way . . . hadn't he himself once?

'Some magpies are building a nest up there in the tallest birch,' he said, 'can you see? Their first nest was in one of the conifers but it got raided by a crow.' He smiled as Charlotte looked at him. 'Life's hard all round, isn't it?' he said softly.

'This is wonderful,' she said, a piece of beef poised on her fork. 'When did you learn to cook like this?'

'A legacy of my student days,' he said, noting the ground on which she wasn't prepared to walk, 'when I lodged with the redoubtable Mrs Holroyd, sadly no longer with us, but out there,' he cast his arm about him as though presenting the world to Charlotte, 'there's a multitude who carry her memory with them. Actually, she was a formidable landlady who taught generations of scruffy students the stuff of life – how to cook, wash and iron.'

Charlotte smiled. 'So where did all this take place, which university? No, don't tell me, let me guess. I'd say you were a Cambridge man.'

He laughed, then took a sip of his wine. 'My parents wanted me to go there, to follow in my father's footsteps and my older brother's. I was even offered a place.'

'So why didn't you go?'

'Lots of eighteen-year-old reasons: I didn't want to conform and I didn't want the hassle and all the pressure, so I opted for Leeds instead.'

'Then what, what did you do next, start a commune out on the Yorkshire moors?'

'Guess what? I conformed. As soon as I graduated, I joined up with Henderson and Wyatt and before I knew where I was, I was a fully paid-up member of everything I had always despised. Disappointing end to an encouraging beginning, wouldn't you say?'

'If it had stopped at that, maybe, but you're here in Hulme Welford. Why?'

Alex told Charlotte how he had ended his career with Henderson & Wyatt, how he had simply sold up and done as he pleased. 'It suddenly became important to me to prove to myself that in the big scheme of things it all meant nothing, all that status, all that supposed power and wealth, it was all a nonsense. I knew perfectly well that my leaving the company meant no real difference in the long term to those individuals concerned. In the short term they were all tripping over themselves to find the right replacement for the dynamic Alex Hamilton, but I bet you now they'll all be saying Alex who? And that's fine, because that's what they would have been saying in the end when I retired with my slippers by the fireside.'

Charlotte frowned. 'It's strange that, isn't it? Most people like to feel that they're important, indispensable even. It's what gives them their sense of identity, their name tag, if you like.'

'It takes courage to be yourself and to know that you're a significant person in your own right, with something worthwhile to offer, without having to acquire all those labels of self-justification.'

Charlotte thought about this for a moment. 'How about marriage,' she said. 'Is that a label you don't need either?'

He looked at her and then placed his knife and fork together on his now empty plate. 'I was very nearly married,' he answered. *Very nearly married* – how glib he sounded, almost as though his time with Lucy hadn't meant anything. Not so long ago he wouldn't have thought it possible to refer to that period in his life without experiencing some degree of pain. Now here he was, living proof of what his friends and family had told him: *Time is the great healer*. It had taken a while, but eventually they had been proved right. 'More wine?' he said.

'Not for me, thank you. After my behaviour at Hilary's I think I'd better be careful. What does "very nearly" mean?'

A blackbird above their heads in the branches of the fig tree began to chirp. Mabel, in response, got to her feet and barked loudly at it. The bird squawked indignantly and flew off.

'She didn't fall for my understated charm and kept turning me down,' Alex said with a light laugh, and changed the subject. 'So tell me, what's St John's like?'

'Better than when I grew up here,' Charlotte replied, acknowledging that, like most people, Alex Hamilton had his own Achilles' heel. 'It's a bit Low Church for Iris Braithwaite's taste though.' Suddenly she was back in the churchyard, seeing the terrible look on Iris's face.

Sitting here in the garden having lunch with Alex, she had managed to forget what had happened earlier that morning. Thinking of it now, she felt the colour drain from her face, wondered whether Alex himself had heard the gossip that must have touched all corners of the village. But if he had, surely he would have mentioned it?

'What's wrong?' he asked.

'I . . .' This was awful. How was she supposed to tell him? She cleared her throat. 'I probably ought to tell you something before you find out from someone else.'

Alex raised his eyebrows. 'What have I missed?'

Charlotte sighed and told Alex what she was supposed to have been up to with him and Derek.

She watched Alex cross one leg over the other and then pull his foot up towards himself. He was trying hard not to smile, she could tell, but she pressed on, telling him about her mother's visit, Derek's son Barry cross-examining her in church, her exchange with Iris Braithwaite and finally the scene at Ted the Toup's.

'So surely that's an end to it,' Alex said, when she had finished. 'Iris Braithwaite apologises and everyone forgets all about it. You've been exonerated.'

She shook her head. 'No I haven't, and I never will be. Don't you see, they all believed I was capable?'

'Well, to a certain extent, we're all capable.'

'And Hilary ignored me in church this morning, snubbed me. There she was standing by the font with some ridiculous toilet seat in her hands and she turned away when I smiled at her. So much for Christian forgiveness!' She lowered her head, her hair cascading over her face, hiding the tears welling up in her eyes.

Alex leaned back in his chair. He looked thoughtfully across at Charlotte. After a moment's quiet, he placed a hand on her shoulder. She jerked her head up, looked at him and then got to her feet.

'I'd better be going. I'm not very good company at the moment, I'm too busy feeling sorry for myself.' She shook her head. 'And do you know, I was feeling sorry for Iris earlier.'

'Now you've really thrown me,' he said, confused. 'Come on, stay a bit longer and explain that one to me.'

She sat down again, surprising herself that she did so, and willingly. 'You know, I challenged Iris this morning because I truly believed it was the right thing to do, like I thought it was the right thing to come back here to Hulme Welford. Now none of it makes sense any more.'

'Tell me,' Alex said, slowly. 'Tell me about your life in Brussels with Peter, what was it like?'

She kicked off her trainers and played her bare feet lightly over the grass. She thought about Alex's question. Nobody had ever really asked her what *her* life had been like. Assumptions had been made – she had been the wife of a 'bright young thing', they had always been going places, geographically as well as figuratively. They had been well off, comfortably placed, a good future ahead of them and she had tried hard to make a life for herself, always adjusting it to suit Peter, until she had realised she could not cope with knowing that her husband loved his work more than her; that she had become an unwelcome interruption to what really excited him. She then saw herself as just another acquisition, picked up by Peter along the way. She was a necessary part of his portrayal of the perfect corporate man, so long as she was prepared to remain a bit player, with hardly any lines to speak.

Waiting in the wings of her mind now was her programmed response to Alex's question – *it was fun, lots to do and see, all that food and culture* – but she found herself looking Alex in the eye and saying, 'It was empty and cold and I hated it.'

13

'Hello, not interrupting, am I?'

David's arrival, crashing into the garden of Ivy Cottage so unexpectedly, blasted away the tableau effect that Charlotte's words had just created in the soft, dappled sunlight beneath the fig tree. His entrance was marked by a confusion of noise and activity, with Mabel barking and the blackbird – who had been frightened away earlier and had since returned – flying off once again to the safety of the beech hedge, squawking noisily as it went.

'Of course you're not interrupting,' Charlotte said, grateful that her brother-in-law had saved her from any further revealing disclosures. What had made her say such a thing? She would have to be careful in future, to ensure no further slip-ups like that, for it would only open up the floodgates of confession. *Why did you hate Brussels so much?* would be the next logical question. *Because my husband stopped needing anything in his life, other than work; because my husband made it impossible for me to love him in the way I wanted to.* Oh no, that line of conversation could only lead in one direction, to that dreaded, final denouement – that she was to blame for Peter's death on that icy road to Luxembourg.

'I'll go and get another chair,' she said.

As he watched his sister-in-law walk away from him, David was reminded of the first time he had seen Charlotte. He had met Hilary in his first year at Oxford Polytechnic and during the Christmas vacation he was invited to stay a few days with Hilary and her family. On New Year's Eve Charlotte had turned up from London in a smart little racing-green MG with a boyfriend called Clive. It had snowed for the best part of the evening, and late that night, coming back from the village after a festive drink to Louise and Neville's half-timbered cottage, Charlotte had started laughing, saying she felt like dancing barefoot in the snow. They thought she was joking, but snatching off her thick overcoat and shoes, she had done just that, cavorting like a nymph in the moonlight. Hilary had, of course, disapproved. 'Oh for goodness' sake, Charlotte, stop showing off.' But he and Clive had watched, mesmerised. As the church bells chimed the passing of another year, they had cheered loudly and kissed one another. He remembered wanting to give Charlotte a long, wet, open-mouthed kiss, but had made do with an impetuous collision of their lips.

Three years later he and Hilary were married. By then he had become like a brother to Charlotte, and kisses were a mere respectable brush of the cheek.

Watching Charlotte now as she walked barefoot across the grass, David wondered whether she had ever, since that night, danced barefoot in the snow again.

Alex looked at Charlotte's retreating figure and wondered at what she had just told him – *It was empty and cold and I hated it.* It was a stark and disturbing image she had given and only a fool would think she was referring to Belgium's low population and inclement weather. But something else was disturbing him.

How about marriage, or is that a label you don't need either? Lucy. Twice now in one day he had been forced to unwrap and touch the memory of her. Sat here in the sun listening to Charlotte he had tried to dismiss Lucy from his mind, to relocate this dislodged memory to the back of his brain where for so long it had been treasured and, like so many treasures, rarely touched. She had been a lively, forceful girl, and so was her memory, even after seven years.

'Alex, if I've told you once, I've told you a hundred times. I'm not going to throw myself away on you, not when there's the hope of marrying someone who doesn't spend his every waking moment in front of a computer.'

'I don't really want to marry you,' he had laughed, catching her hand in his as they walked along the footpath towards the waterfall at Haworth. 'I just want to get you into bed every night, that's all.'

'Well, you do that often enough anyway.'

Kissing her, he had pulled her down amongst the heather and ripening bilberries despite the presence of a coach party of Japanese tourists, their sunhats bobbing, their cameras swinging.

'You're a lout, Alex Hamilton, and I love you!' she had shouted at the top of her voice, just as the last of the tourists had tried to scuttle discreetly by.

There had been other women in his life since Lucy, but without really trying he had succeeded in keeping any subsequent relationship on a purely superficial level.

'Anything to drink, David?' he said abruptly, getting to his feet.

David looked at the bottle of wine on the table. 'A glass of that would be nice, thanks.'

As Alex went into his side of Ivy Cottage to fetch a glass, Charlotte returned with a chair.

'I see you found the garden furniture. It's old, could almost be antique,' David said.

'Very old, I should think,' Charlotte said, giving the chair a rub with the cloth. 'Back to Noah's cruising days I shouldn't wonder.'

Reappearing with another glass, Alex poured the wine. Charlotte refused any more. 'So David, why aren't you over at The Gables, hard at whatever it is fathers do on a Sunday?'

'If you must know, I've had it up to here.' He pointed to his unshaven chin. 'Hilary's got one on her today. I think it's got to do with . . .' He paused and took a fortifying sip of his wine. 'Well, you know, about . . .' Again he paused and nodded his head in the direction of In The Pink and then back at Alex.

Alex smiled. 'But you don't believe any of it, do you, David?'

'Good heavens, no!' David said, stretching his legs out in front of him and resting his glass on his slightly domed stomach.

'Liar,' said Charlotte suddenly. 'You're just as bad as the rest of them.'

'No, really, I don't. It's just, well, you know what it's like, you can't help but fall back on the old maxim, no smoke without fire and all that.'

'So,' Charlotte said, her eyes narrowing slightly, 'Hilary's mad as hell, is she?'

'Tell me about it,' David said, puffing out his cheeks. 'She's in a right lather.'

'Well, the day's not been a complete waste then, has it?'

'Oh that's great, just great,' David said loudly, tossing back a large mouthful of wine. 'This is what I've got to look forward to from now on, is it? You two sisters winding one another up the whole time and yours truly caught in the crossfire?'

'You know who's really caught in the crossfire, don't you?' said Alex, leaning forward in his chair.

Both Charlotte and David looked at him. 'Who?' they said together.

'Cindy, of course. Has anyone been round to see her and tell her the truth?'

Charlotte pulled a face. 'I'm afraid I haven't had the nerve. Do you think I ought to?'

'How about we go together?' Alex said. 'From what I understand of Derek's reputation, she's going to need some pretty good convincing that nothing did actually happen between you two.'

'I'll think about it,' Charlotte said, avoiding Alex's eyes. She had no desire to rush headlong into Cindy.

Apart from Barry, Cindy was alone in the house. She could hear music coming from behind his door: monks singing the same thing, over and over again. Uplifting, Barry had called it the other day, on one of his rare excursions out of his room.

Every day was the same. As soon as Barry got in from school he went straight up to his room, music on, head in a book. And today, Sunday, was no exception. He had been there since he got back from jogging this morning, only coming out briefly for his lunch and hardly saying a word at the table, just forking food into his mouth absentmindedly, keeping his eyes firmly on the book he was reading. Boys she had known at eighteen had never been like Barry. They had been more like Derek, she thought with a rueful smile. But Barry was a strange boy, so quiet, so preoccupied, and recently even more so. She had tried searching his room while he was at school one day, but had come up with nothing. She had hated doing it, but those leaflets from school had told you what to do if you noticed a change in your child's behaviour. She couldn't imagine Barry getting mixed up in anything like that, not drugs. Tiffany, yes. Like a shot. She winced at this unfortunate pun and put the thought of her children aside. She went through to the *en suite* bathroom and looked in the large illuminated mirror above the his-and-hers basins.

She stared critically at her face, then gently smoothed the skin under her right eye with a perfectly manicured forefinger. The shaded hue of the slightly loosening skin beneath her lashes was warning enough that her favourite lemon and apricot eye care pack was needed. *Grief can have a devastating effect on your skin* – the irony of her words to Charlotte on Friday night was not lost on her. But she didn't feel in the mood for an eye care pack, and anyway, it was Sunday. Surely even her skin was allowed a day off?

No, she told herself emphatically, don't let yourself go, don't let it get to you. You've survived countless meaningless affairs before, this is just one more. Let it blow over, let him get her out of his system and then that will be that.

She was very calm, really. She had taught herself to be that. Even when she had heard the juniors in the salon, Tracy and Lorraine, tidying up the linen cupboard late yesterday afternoon, she had stayed calm.

'He's at it again,' Lorraine had sniggered.

'But he's got competition this time, hasn't he?' Tracy had replied. 'That good-looking bloke, just moved in.'

Cindy scraped her hair back into a tight ponytail and secured it with a scrunch band. First she cleansed and toned her skin, then carefully applied the sweet-smelling, creamy paste around her eyes.

With ten minutes to wait for the eye pack to do its work, she walked through to the bedroom to get a magazine. Passing the full-length mirror at the other end of the pale peach room, she caught sight of herself, and for a split second she saw a gaunt, white face that looked nothing like her, but like a hideously deformed old woman. Derek would never love a woman like that, a voice inside her head whispered. She stood looking at this terrifying image and then, slowly, it passed, became the face she was accustomed to seeing and the face she hoped Derek loved . . . in his own way.

She went back into the bathroom with the magazine, sat down on the small cane settee by the bath and started to flick through the pages of life-enhancing recipes for sex and filo pastry, trying desperately not to think of Derek and what he was doing to her.

She didn't hate him for what he did, he couldn't help himself half the time – it was habitual. And for reasons she couldn't make sense of, she loved him, always had, and she knew that this would always be there between them . . . but then, so would all the affairs.

By most people's standards she felt that she was still an attractive woman. Her skin was smooth and firm, her bust hadn't drooped, nor had her buttocks. She worked out, ate the right things, rarely drank alcohol and always kept herself well dressed. And she had never once, in all their years together, refused Derek in bed. So why wasn't that enough for him, what more did he need?

And why did that wretched Charlotte Lawrence have to come and live next door?

14

'I know it's my fault,' Hilary said down the telephone. 'It was stupid of me not to put it on the calendar, but Tiffany can't manage it tonight – apparently it's Barry's birthday – and David's got one of his tedious Rotary evenings, and would you believe it, Mum and Dad are out as well? So I just thought, Charlotte, that maybe, and I do appreciate what a busy day you must have had, but do you think you could babysit for me, tonight?'

Babysit! Charlotte looked at the mayhem all around her in the hall and wondered whether her sister had any idea just how busy a day it had been for her.

At eight-thirty that morning rowdy voices, English and French, had added to the noise of the Belgian removal van as it tried to position itself to reverse up the drive of Ivy Cottage. Having already got the huge pantechnicon tangled up in Hilary's terracotta pots at the end of The Gables' driveway, the driver had then endeavoured to squeeze his load through the metaphorical eye of a needle, bringing with it the lower overhanging branches of a rowan together with a good deal of forsythia.

Charlotte had viewed the approaching removal van with apprehension, knowing that coming towards her, with reversing siren wailing, was the past eight years of her life – approximately thirty-two cubic metres of marital souvenirs. Up until this point, Ivy Cottage had been neutral territory, had been devoid of anything to do with Peter. Now it was about to open its doors and embrace eight years of the man, and Charlotte wasn't sure how she was going to feel about this.

'Any chance of a brew before we get started?' the foreman had said, giving her no further time to be squeamish about what was to be spilled out of the lorry.

Five hours later the team of tea- and coffee-swilling men had filled Ivy Cottage and departed, leaving behind them a house full of randomly emptied boxes. With no one to help sort out the chaos, Charlotte had worked on alone until her father arrived.

'Hello,' he called from the open front door.

'In here,' she called back.

He came hesitantly into the cardboard box havoc of the sitting-room. 'Need any help?'

Charlotte bobbed up from behind the sofa. 'Does a fish need water?'

Together they pushed, lifted, emptied and filled until eventually, exhausted, they retired to the crockery-splattered kitchen for a respite.

'I had no idea you'd be all alone. I thought Hilary would have been here to help you,' Neville said, accepting a mug of tea from Charlotte.

Charlotte slumped down into a chair. 'No, she's off on a school trip with Becky's class. Chester Zoo, I think, back about five.'

'I'm surprised no one else offered to help,' Neville said quietly.

She noticed the inclination of her father's head. 'I heard his car leaving just before eight this morning, Dad, unless of course you were thinking that Derek and Cindy might have liked to help.'

Neville looked deep into his mug of tea. 'Well, I wasn't being specific, I just meant . . .'

'Come on, Dad,' she laughed, 'finish your tea and get off home. I need to take Mabel for a walk.'

Charlotte had just said goodbye to her father, closed the front door and was stepping over boxes of books and piles of unwrapped pictures when Hilary had telephoned.

'I shan't be long, it's a PTA meeting,' Hilary was saying. 'Patricia Longton's away, so I'll be stepping out of my role as Secretary and be acting as Chairwoman for the evening. And anyway, seeing as you've not even seen the children since you moved in, I thought it might be nice for you to have them all to yourself for a while. What do you say?'

Hilary held her breath. She was conscious of the silence at the other end of the telephone. She knew that she was pushing her luck, that she had, since Friday, acted a little harshly towards her sister, as David had gone to great lengths to inform her yesterday when he got back from Ivy Cottage. She had been taking a batch of cup cakes out of the Aga for the school trip when David had breezed in and said, 'Hilary, you're a bloody fool and you're going to have to apologise to Charlotte.'

Concentrating on mixing pink icing in a bowl and searching for the hoard of hundreds and thousands that she kept hidden from Becky, Hilary had let David have his say.

'How you could have thought your own sister capable of such a thing! Hasn't she got enough on her plate without you and all the other old biddies in the village making her out to be some kind of insatiable . . .' She had listened to the silence while he seemingly searched his mind for a suitable word. '. . . Slut!' he said at last.

She had looked up at him at this point. 'David, that's not a nice word.'

'Too bloody right, it isn't.'

'What's a slut, Daddy?'

Together they had spun round to see Becky standing in the doorway, practising a few wobbly demi-pliés. 'Don't stick your bottom out,' Hilary had said quickly, bustling about the kitchen and giving David one of her see-what-you've-done-now looks.

'So what do you say, Charlotte?' Hilary repeated. 'It'll only be a few hours.' She wondered whether she ought to mention anything about letting bygones be bygones: after all, this telephone call was by way of an apology, surely her stubborn sister could see that? Then she heard what she thought sounded like suppressed crying at the other end of the telephone. 'Charlotte,' she said anxiously, 'do you want me to come over?'

'No.'

'But you're upset, you're crying. I'll come over and put the kettle on. I'll make us a nice cup of tea.'

'I wasn't crying.'

'Charlotte, it's all right, really it is, tears are all part of the grieving process, you must . . .'

'I wasn't crying, I was laughing, Hilary.'

'Laughing!' What on earth did her sister have to laugh about, for goodness' sake?

'I had forgotten what a persistent pain you are.'

Hilary sighed with relief. 'So you'll do it. See you in about an hour then.'

Still laughing to herself, Charlotte put down the receiver, located Mabel's lead and then found Mabel, curled up inside a knocked-over packing box.

She locked the front door behind her and set off along the drive. Halfway down she noticed a red Citroën come up the parallel driveway. She saw Alex and because the sunroof was open she could hear the sound of Mozart's Requiem. He waved across the front lawn to her and parked the car.

'How did the unpacking go?' he called out.

'Ongoing,' she said, pulling a face.

He came over. 'Sorry I wasn't around to help. Is there anything I can do now?'

'I've stopped for the day, too exhausted to do any more. But thanks for the offer.'

Bending down to Mabel, who was straining on her lead to reach him, Alex said, 'Have you seen Cindy yet?'

'No,' Charlotte said awkwardly, glad at least to have the perfect excuse. 'I haven't had time today.'

He stood up and looked at her. 'How about now? I could come with you. We ought to put her mind at rest . . . and yours.'

Charlotte looked away, wondered why this man was so concerned about everyone else's feelings.

'What's the problem? Are you worried she's not going to believe us?'

'No, it's not that exactly, it's more . . . oh, I don't know, it sounds silly really, only I don't think Cindy and I are ever going to be the best of friends. I've a feeling she's already condemned me as one of Derek's trophies. Even if I'm found innocent this time, in her eyes it's only a matter of time before I really am guilty.'

Alex shook his head. 'You're right,' he said, 'it does sound silly. Come on, let's just go next door, say what we've got to say and let the poor woman make up her own mind.'

'Do you always bully people like this?'

He smiled. 'Yes, all the time, never stop.'

'Is it possible to see Mrs Rogers please?' Charlotte asked the young receptionist, who immediately pouted her lips in irritation at being delayed at getting off home.

'Have you got an appointment?' she said, pulling on her jacket.

'No, but . . .'

'Well, I'm very sorry but we're just about to close and Mrs Rogers is in a hurry. She needs to get off on time tonight, it's her son's eighteenth . . .'

'Thank you, Tracy, I'm sure I can spare my neighbours a few minutes.' It was Cindy, elegantly poised on cerise high heels and wearing a white uniform which gave her slim arms and legs the appearance of being even more tanned. Her hair, unlike last Friday night, was pinned back and showed off a flawless complexion. She was a walking advertisement for In The Pink, what Charlotte suspected all their customers aspired to.

'We don't actually allow dogs on the premises,' Cindy said looking down at Mabel, 'but Tracy will look after it for you.' Ignoring Tracy's look of annoyance at being delayed even longer, she carried on, 'We'll go through to the office where we won't be disturbed.' She turned and started clicking her way down a corridor. As Charlotte and Alex followed behind, Cindy turned and said, 'Derek's busy with Mrs Jeffs at the moment. She's one of his regulars. She comes in three times a week.'

'Really,' said Charlotte, not missing the point of the statement.

Cindy opened a door. 'Mrs Jeffs' husband plays for Manchester United. Maybe you're a fan of football? I'm not.'

Or of Mrs Jeffs, thought Charlotte looking about her and being surprised by the austerity of the room in which they were standing. What they had seen so far of In The Pink was a frothy concoction of pink frilly blinds and flowery wallpaper; here the walls were a cool grey and the office furniture was uncompromisingly black, modern, angular, and shouted no-nonsense business acumen. Charlotte thought Cindy looked more at home hovering by the large desk than she had in the reception area.

'Please, sit down,' Cindy said. 'Would you like a cup of coffee?'

Nobody sat down. Alex spoke first. 'No thank you, Cindy. We shan't keep you long. Your receptionist told us you were in a rush to get away. All we've come to say is that, well, to try and explain that what . . .'

Cindy smiled for the first time.

Charlotte took over. 'Nothing happened, Cindy. Iris Braithwaite got some silly idea into her head, and went round making a fool of herself and us.'

'I know,' Cindy said softly, though there was little warmth to her voice. This was a new experience for her – one of Derek's women actually protesting her innocence. 'Mrs Braithwaite came to see me last night. She did manage to apologise in the end.'

'I'm so glad it's all been sorted out,' Charlotte said, visibly relaxing.

'Yes,' agreed Cindy, picking up a paperclip from the desk. She turned it over in her hands as though examining it for any possible defects. She looked at Charlotte. 'Except for one thing of course.'

'What's that?' Charlotte said nervously.

'Well, it's only a small thing, but what exactly was my husband doing at your house with a bouquet of roses?'

'I knew it, I just knew it!' Charlotte said, as they walked away from In The Pink. 'I knew this would happen. You see what you've done?'

'Cindy would probably have said that to you anyway. Better it was done there in private. At least nobody else was there to hear her.'

'But what was I supposed to say? How could I have answered her question? Oh yes, Cindy, your husband came to see me with the biggest bunch of red roses I've ever seen and kissed me up against the kitchen sink.'

'She didn't expect an answer. She knows perfectly well what Derek had in mind when he turned up on your doorstep. It was a warning shot she was firing, that was all. She needs to convince herself that she's doing all she can to prevent Derek from hurting her any more.' Alex pushed his hands down inside his trouser pockets. 'So . . . he kissed you, did he?'

Charlotte groaned. 'It was just some stupid kind of grope thing,' she said, exasperated. 'I didn't take much notice of it at the time.'

Alex looked at her and then started to laugh. Charlotte smiled and then she too laughed as she realised how implausible her words had sounded.

Opening Philip's bedroom window, Hilary heard the sound of laughter. She looked across the road and saw Charlotte and Alex walking towards Ivy Cottage. Things were going very nicely.

15

Barry walked blindly behind his sister, allowing her to guide him through the house and out on to the driveway.

'Now stand there,' Tiffany told him, 'and keep your eyes closed, until I tell you to open them.' He felt her hands fumbling at the back of his head, undoing the knot she had tied in the bandana and then he felt the material slip away. 'Open your eyes, now – *surprise!*'

He blinked in the low evening sunlight and then stared unbelievably at a brand new Peugeot 205.

'Well, what do you reckon to that then, Bas?' his father said, leaning against the car. 'Bit of all right I'd say. The most I had at your age was a pushbike.'

'It's great, Dad,' Barry said, still staring at the metallic-grey car. 'I never expected anything like this, I don't know what to say . . . thanks.'

'Nothing like a flash motor to help you pull. You'll have no worries on that score now.'

Barry turned to his mother. 'Thanks,' he said. 'It's a great present.'

'Just make sure you drive carefully,' she said.

'Now all you've got to do is pass your test next week,' said Tiffany, 'and then we can hit the road, just you and me, kid.'

Barry frowned and ran a hand through his hair. 'I might not pass.'

'Muffin 'ell, 'course you will. It's not as if Dad's been teaching you.'

'Less of that,' said Derek. 'Anyway, I don't know about you lot, but my stomach feels like it's been cut off from my throat.' He tossed a key over to Barry. 'Come on, Bas, you can get the feel of it by driving us to the restaurant.'

'We can't possibly go yet,' said Cindy.

'Why ever not?'

'Tiffany can't go looking like that, look at the state of her. They won't let her in the restaurant in those disgusting clothes.'

'Give up, Mum!' shouted Tiffany.

'Don't you dare shout at me for all the neighbours to hear. Just get back in the house and change into something decent.'

Glaring at her mother, Tiffany stood her ground and didn't move.

Barry sensed his mother's anger giving way to bitter disappointment. He felt sorry for her, felt he knew the sense of frustration and disillusionment that filled her life – firstly his father, then himself, and to top it all, Tiffany. It was quite simple really: all his mother had ever wanted in life was a faithful husband and a real daughter.

'Look, Mum,' he said, 'I know it's a pain, but that's how she likes to dress. She's not doing anyone any harm.'

'If you could just quit with all the philosophy crap,' Derek said impatiently, 'we could get a move on.' He shook his head. 'Families, I ask you, who the bloody hell needs them?'

We do, thought Barry, as he walked over to unlock his birthday present.

'I think they must have given me the wrong cassette in the shop,' Derek said, jabbing a finger at the cassette player on the dashboard and ejecting a tape. 'I thought I'd got you the Four Seasons.'

'You have, Dad, it's great, thanks,' Barry said, keeping his eyes firmly on the road.

Derek made a play of reading the label. 'Yep, I knew they'd made a mistake, this isn't Frankie Valli at all. It's that Nigel Kennedy bloke.'

'Muffin 'ell, Dad,' shouted Tiffany from the back of the car, 'you're a plonker, you really are.'

Derek turned round and grinned at Tiffany. 'I can still fool you though, can't I?'

'Idiot!'

'Don't speak to your father like that,' Cindy said.

'Yes,' agreed Derek, smirking, 'it would be nice to see some respect in this family for a change.'

Barry looked in the mirror and caught his sister's expression of explosive retaliation.

'Good evening, sir,' said the *maître d'* at the White Swan. 'I'm sorry but there are no tables free, perhaps you'd care to wait in the bar, I'm sure . . .'

'That's all right, pal, you're new here, aren't you? Rogers is the name. We've got a booking.'

They watched the *maître d'* move off with his air of grandiose superiority to check the list of reservations.

'If you'd like to come this way, Mr Rogers,' the *maître d'* said, sliding back to them, 'your table is over here. You ordered a bottle of champagne on the telephone. Shall I open it right away for you, sir?'

They sat at a fussy blue-and-white-trimmed table and were handed four over-sized menus. Barry watched his father make a great show of tasting the champagne and declaring it adequate. They raised their glasses and set about playing happy families for the evening – an evening which for Barry stretched ominously ahead.

As a family they rarely spent any time together, and on occasions like this when they were forced to act out the part, it was usually a strain. Barry could already see the strain showing on his mother's face. Ever since he could remember, he had sensed a detachment, almost an estrangement, between himself and his mother. For years he hadn't understood what was going on, but more recently he had come to know that no matter what he did, he could not please his mother, could not make her happy. Tiffany had managed it effortlessly when she was small, but then she had grown up, and almost overnight had destroyed the illusion their mother had so carefully created.

'Happy birthday, Bas,' his father said, chinking his fluted glass against Barry's own. 'Now get this down you, and don't worry about driving home, I'll drive.'

'Cheers,' Barry said, taking a small sip. He had no intention of getting drunk. He had far too much work to get through with his exams only a few days away.

'I still don't get it though, Bas. Why the hell didn't you want a night out with your own mates? You could have gone into Manchester, picked up a few girls, had a party? We'd have paid for it, you know.'

Barry shook his head. 'Wasn't what I wanted.'

'And this was?' Tiffany said, looking about her.

'We don't often sit round a table together and talk, do we?' Barry started to say.

'Just as well,' Tiffany interrupted.

'Maybe Barry's right.'

Barry looked at his mother, searching her face for signs of cynicism. He found none. Perhaps tonight he would be able to broach the subject after all.

'Hey, this is all getting a bit serious, isn't it?' Derek said, draining his glass. 'Come on, another glass of champagne.' He reached for the bottle behind him in the wine cooler. At once, a young waiter, about the same age as Barry, appeared at his side and took over. 'Don't worry, pal,' Derek said. 'I wasn't about to get you kicked out of a job.'

'No worries there, mate. They're understaffed as it is. Even if I gobbed in your soup, they couldn't afford to sack me.'

Derek roared. In response, a few heads bobbed up from their plates around the White Swan.

The waiter was just his father's kind of man, Barry thought, someone as brazen as himself with a take-me-as-you-find-me attitude. If he were more like that, Barry knew he would get on better with his father.

'Nice bloke,' Derek said, when they'd ordered their meal. 'Will probably do well in life.'

Tiffany sniffed loudly. 'Hope it's your soup he gobs in, then.'

When they had finished their desserts and coffee and Cindy had gone off to the ladies' room, Barry knew he had lost his opportunity. His father was now regaling the young waiter with his life history – his rags to riches saga. 'You see, lad, your life's all before you. What are you – seventeen?'

'Eighteen,' the waiter replied, stifling a yawn.

'So's my lad, look, the one there sitting like a stuffed Henry. Wouldn't think it was his eighteenth birthday today, would you? He should be out celebrating with his mates, shouldn't he, not stuck here with us? I bet you celebrated.' He poked the young waiter in the ribs and gave him a wink.

The waiter looked at Tiffany. 'Too right I did.'

'I've paid the bill, Derek, it's time we were going.' It was Cindy coming back to the table, looking far from pleased.

Outside in the poorly lit car park Cindy and Barry guided Derek towards the car. 'Now you'd better let me drive, Bas,' Derek said. 'Don't want you losing your licence before you've even got it, do we?'

'He's pathetic, he really is,' Tiffany said with disgust, dragging behind.

'Shut up, Tiffany,' hissed Cindy, 'just remember, he's your father.'

'Oh please, how can I ever forget?'

They drove home, listening to Derek singing 'Ooh What a Night' to Vivaldi's 'L'Autunno'. For Barry, the evening had turned out just as he'd known it would. He had been a fool to think that anyone in his family would be interested in what he had to say. After all, to his father he was nothing more than a 'stuffed Henry' – not a very pleasant revelation that, on his eighteenth birthday. But he was used to it, like he was used to all the jokes and innuendoes. Well, he would just have to wait until the right time presented itself.

16

Hilary had come deliberately early, before Iris Braithwaite and the others arrived to help set up the St John's spring jumble sale. At least this way it gave her a chance to get things done the way she liked, and not the way Iris wanted. It seemed a dreadful shame to Hilary that one woman could so easily put a blight on the community. She knew for a fact that more people would volunteer to help out in the village if Iris Braithwaite wasn't already there on practically every committee. 'Sorry,' people would whisper when asked to help, 'no can do, not with *her* to answer to.'

Hilary hadn't seen or heard from Iris in the past week, which was unusual in the run-up to an event such as today's, but Iris's low profile probably had a lot to do with what Charlotte had said to her last Sunday. Even though Hilary couldn't help but admire her sister, she still felt a pang of jealousy that Charlotte had had the courage to stand up to Iris, and she did not. She wished that she had been there to witness it, instead of rushing off home to clear up the breakfast things and get the Sunday roast in the oven. A shame no one had told her at the time what had taken place; it would have saved an awful lot of misunderstanding between her and Charlotte. Luckily though, Kate Hampton, the PTA Treasurer, had told her about it at their Monday evening meeting. 'Your sister was quite magnificent. There was more drama in that church porch than in a week's worth of *EastEnders*. Perhaps we'll see a few changes round here from now on. Belgium's loss is certainly Hulme Welford's gain. She's become quite the local hero.'

Hilary had tried to clamp down on her disappointment at her sister suddenly getting all the attention. It wasn't quite how she had envisaged things. True she didn't want Charlotte to be miserable, but on the other hand, she didn't want her to come striding back into the village and take over – grieving widows weren't supposed to behave like that. Demure, quietly tearful and in need of a friendly shoulder to lean against was more the mark, surely?

She started setting up the tables, which Brown Owl and her pack of Brownies were supposed to have organised last night, and then she moved on to the boxes of clothes, sorting things out by gender and then by size. She was just holding up a red, lacy G-string – the kind of thing she would never contemplate wearing – and wondering who on earth in the village had donated it, when in walked Iris Braithwaite, followed by Mrs Haslip and Mrs Bradley, each weighed down with several large Tupperware boxes.

'Mrs Parker! I trust you have no intention of offering *that* for sale?'

Hilary flushed. 'Of course not, Mrs Braithwaite. I was just wondering . . .'

'Well don't. Put them, I mean it, in the bin and let's get on, we've lots to do. Mrs Haslip, you get to work in the kitchen, and for heaven's sake make sure the kettles are clean and the coffee urn doesn't have anything untoward inside. I know what those ghastly Cubs are like.'

Philip was a Cub and Hilary wanted very much to rush to his defence. But instead she bent down to the next box of jumble and started sorting through it. It wasn't fair: it was *she* who had done most of the work; it was *her* house that had been used as a collecting point; *their* computer that had prepared all the posters to advertise the event – it was all her time and effort and now, at the very last minute, in came Iris Braithwaite and took command.

It hadn't always been like this. Before she had had the children she had been a teacher, and quite a good one, in her opinion. She knew when it had all changed – it was having the children and being at home. She had read once that each time the afterbirth was ejected from a woman's body, so was a piece of her self-confidence, taking away her sense of freedom and her courage. Hilary didn't normally believe such fanciful theories, but since having the children she had indeed grown afraid of more and more things: heights, flying, deep water – and Iris Braithwaite.

'Now Mrs Parker, I suggest Mrs Bradley helps you so that we ensure no other unsavoury items end up on the tables. Good gracious, just look at the state of this floor. Mrs Haslip, is there a broom in the kitchen? If so, fetch it here this minute.'

As they worked away under Iris's tyrannical directives, Hilary couldn't help but begin to feel a perverse sense of satisfaction. It looked as though Charlotte's brave words after church last week had had no great effect on Iris after all. So much for being the local hero.

At a quarter to eleven Malcolm Jackson, Charlotte, and the other press-ganged helpers turned up, and under Iris's baleful eye stood ready to receive the flood of bargain hunters.

Jumble sales in Hulme Welford were always well attended, and due to the eagerness of the queue outside, the doors were generally opened early. Today was no exception.

'Right, ladies,' announced Iris Braithwaite, 'are you ready?' She stood poised between the locked door and a small table, which had on it an embroidered tablecloth and a battered Quality Street tin ready to receive the twenty pence entrance fee. She turned the key and addressed the crowd. 'Ladies and gentlemen . . .' But her voice was lost as a loud cheer went up and she very sensibly moved back to her Quality Street tin.

Charlotte and Hilary stood together behind the ladies' clothes stall, ready for the onslaught. Charlotte's initial reaction, when her sister had asked her if she would like to help out, had been to say no, but then, why not, she had asked herself, what else had she to do?

It had been a quiet, pleasant week at Ivy Cottage, apart from Hilary popping over every few hours 'just to see how she was getting on'. She had continued with the unpacking and made rather an expensive purchase – a new car. With Peter's words ringing in her ears, she had tried to convince herself that she need not feel guilty about this: '*It's a false economy to buy second-hand,*' he had always said. And as the smartly dressed, Polo-scented salesman in the showroom had said, there was always her own personal safety to consider; statistically she was less likely to break down in a new car than an old one. It still hadn't felt right, though, picking out a car with money she believed did not rightfully belong to her.

The subject of Peter's money was one she tried hard not to think about. If she had gone ahead and divorced him, she would have expected nothing. As it was, he was dead, and because of his well-planned insurance policies, she was now reasonably well off.

'How much is this?'

Charlotte looked at the sharp-faced woman in front of her and at the Marks & Spencer blouse in her hand. 'Forty pence,' she replied.

'Forty pence, luv, you've got to be joking. This is a jumble sale, not bleeding 'arrods!'

Hilary had warned her about the hard-nosed professionals of the jumble sale circuit. She stuck to her guns. 'It's definitely forty pence. It's in very good condition. Look, you can see, it's barely been worn.'

'How do you know that? And anyway, it's only polyester. I mean, it's not silk or anything, is it?'

Charlotte was beginning to enjoy herself. It was good to be arguing on this irrational basis, and over something as trivial as a second-hand blouse. Too much of her married life she had been unable to argue with Peter, who had never liked confrontations. He had always walked away from her whenever she had tried to argue a point.

'Come back and fight with me!' she would shout at him.

'Fight?' he replied once. 'But I'm your husband,' or another time, 'Charlotte, you really do say the strangest of things.' His logic had been irrefutable which had had the effect of suppressing her anger, and in turn had made her angrier still.

'You know how polyester can sometimes bobble up after it's been worn a few times?'

'Yes,' said the woman, screwing her eyes up to look at the cuff Charlotte was showing her.

'Well, look, there's not a bobble in sight.'

'Mm . . .' said the woman, 'perhaps you're right, maybe it's never been worn, but the first time I wear it, it'll probably bobble up something rotten. I'll give you twenty pence.'

'Sorry, it's forty,' Charlotte said firmly, 'and the money does go for a good cause, a replacement stained-glass window in the church.'

'Go on, then, give it here, there's your money, and I'll want a plaque by the side of the bleeding window with my name on it.'

With a triumphant toss of her hand, Charlotte threw the coins into the tin. This was going to be more fun than she had thought.

'However did you manage that?' whispered Hilary at her side. 'I've never been able to hold my ground with that wretched Mrs Barret. Oh look, Malcolm's getting into his stride now.'

Over by the kitchen counter the Reverend Jackson was drumming up interest in the refreshments. 'Teas and coffees now being served, everyone,' he shouted above the din of eager bargain hunters, 'and don't forget the delicious home-made cakes.'

'Hello, you two.'

'Alex!' said Hilary. 'How nice of you to come and support us.'

Charlotte noticed the extra width to Hilary's smile and the hand raised to pat her hair in place.

'How much is this, luv?' It was Mrs Barret again with a navy-blue cardigan in her hand. Charlotte leaned forward, but the old woman said, 'No, I'm not asking you, I'm asking her.' And she thrust the cardigan towards Hilary.

'I see you've already snapped up a few purchases,' Charlotte said, looking at the pile of detective novels in Alex's hands.

'Too good an opportunity to pass by,' he said. 'Five murders for a pound and a book on trees, though I think my ribs have suffered into the bargain.'

'You'll have to get some serious training in before the next jumble sale and wear protective clothing.' Charlotte lowered her voice. 'It's the old women you have to look out for. They're the worst, elbows like skewers.'

'They show no mercy, that's for sure.'

'Come on now, Mrs Lawrence, no shirking. There are customers waiting to be served.' Iris Braithwaite was on the prowl. 'Good to see you participating, Mr Hamilton,' she said. 'May I suggest you try men's clothing just a little further along. There are some rather nice pullovers in your size I think.'

Alex winked at Charlotte and moved off, not to the gentleman's outfitters, but to the miscellaneous junk department.

Charlotte watched him go, at the same time trying to stop the twisted pile of cardigans, blouses and dresses – which seemed to have a life of their own – from falling off the table. She could hear her sister faltering at her side with the indomitable Mrs Barret, who was still haggling.

Smiling to herself, Charlotte observed Alex pick up a revoltingly garish picture of a little boy with a tear trickling down his cheek. To her amazement, he bought it. He started to walk away, but turned back to the table. Something else had caught his eye. Fascinated to see what other rubbish he was about to waste his money on, Charlotte watched him pick up a small spoon. He turned it over in his hands, examined the back of it closely, and then working his fingers down to the bowl he caressed it gently. Charlotte shivered.

'How long do I have to stand here before I'm served?'

'I'm sorry?'

'I want these two skirts, how much?'

'A spoon.'

'I beg your pardon?'

Charlotte flushed deep crimson. 'I mean, a pound. They're fifty pence each.'

The customer handed over her money and moved away. Her place at the table was immediately filled by another. 'Hello Charlotte, heard any good gossip recently?' It was Derek.

'Wouldn't have thought there'd be anything to interest you here,' she said. Looking at Derek's tight faded jeans, pink polo shirt, gold bracelet and cream jacket tossed casually over his shoulder, she added, 'Don't suppose there's anything flash enough.'

He grinned suggestively. 'You'll do for starters.'

Charlotte knew she shouldn't laugh. Men like Derek Rogers needed no encouragement. She tried to sound as businesslike as she could. 'Well, seeing as you've come, you might as well buy something.'

'What a good idea. I could try buying Cindy a present. I hear you came to see her. Did she give you a hard time? She's a real Satan in slingbacks, isn't she?' He put his jacket down on the edge of the adjoining table and started poking around amongst the clothes. 'Oh, what's this I've found?' From the bottom of the pile he pulled out the red lacy G-string. 'Now this is more like it.'

'Oh, go on then, tell me you recognise it,' Charlotte said derisively.

'Now you come to mention it, it does look familiar.' He twanged the garment playfully at her.

At that moment Hilary joined them at the table. 'For goodness' sake!' she said. 'Give that to me, Derek.'

'Certainly not. I want to buy it.'

'Don't be silly. Just give it to me before Iris catches sight of it.'

'Why, is it hers?'

Charlotte burst out laughing. Hilary still looked serious. 'I was supposed to get rid of it, but I forgot. She'll go mad if she sees it.'

'Go on, Derek, hand it over,' Charlotte said, seeing the discomfort on her sister's face. Poor Hilary, she could never see the funny side of things.

'Hand what over?' It was Alex, half hidden behind his ghastly picture.

Derek waved the lacy item in front of him. Alex raised an eyebrow. 'What exotic jumble sales you have in these parts.'

'Hilary won't let me buy it.'

'Perhaps she wants to see the colour of your money first.'

'Well in that case, let me get my wallet.' Derek reached for his jacket and then looked about him. 'It's gone!'

Seeing the G-string abandoned on top of all the jumble, Charlotte made a surreptitious grab for it and passed it to Hilary.

'Come on,' Derek said, his voice beginning to rise, 'a joke's a joke.'

Hilary and Charlotte exchanged worried looks. Rule number one of any jumble sale – *never* put anything down.

'Look. I put my jacket just here. It's cream, it's Armani and it's bloody well gone!'

'Hi Dad, what's all the commotion?'

Derek turned round at the sound of Tiffany's voice, and then fell back against the table, both hands clasped over his gaping mouth. 'Bloody hell, Tiffany!'

Tiffany's hair was immaculately coiffured into an amazing one-foot-high beehive, and it was shocking pink.

'The trouble with you lot is that you can't take a joke!' Tiffany screamed at her parents in their kitchen.

'Some joke,' Cindy said faintly, her face and lips almost as white as her uniform.

'Right now, girl, you can start by telling us what kind of product it was they used, then we can think how to change it.'

'How the hell should I know, Dad? I just asked for it to be pink. Anyway, I've had enough of this, I'm going out.'

'Oh no you're not, young lady,' shouted Derek. 'I don't want people seeing you like that.'

'Not you as well, Dad.'

She slammed the door after her and stamped off down the drive without a clue or care where she was going. Willing back hot angry tears, she muttered to herself, 'Fifteen-year-old girls don't cry.'

'Thirty-six-year-old women do though,' said a voice.

Hilary Parker's sister was standing in front of her.

'Are you okay?'

Tiffany sniffed. 'Don't know,' she said sulkily.

'Your parents giving you a hard time?'

Tiffany sniffed again.

'Why don't you come and have a boring old cup of tea with me. I'm exhausted after all that sales pitch talk down at the hall.'

'You're not going to tell me I've been stupid as well, are you?'

Charlotte laughed. 'Come on, come and tell me what it's like to be a teenager again. I've nearly forgotten what a miserable time it was.'

At Ivy Cottage they were greeted noisily by Mabel at the back door.

'Let her out, will you?' Charlotte said. 'She must be desperate by now. What do you want, tea or coffee or something cold?'

'Coffee please, lots of milk and two sugars.'

'I remember those days.'

Tiffany frowned. 'Why do you make yourself sound older than you really are?'

'Probably because that's the way I feel at the moment. Where do you want to sit, inside or out?'

'The garden would be nice. It looks lovely from my bedroom window.'

They sat on the dry grass beneath the fig tree. With Mabel on her lap, Charlotte kicked off her shoes and looked at Tiffany's heavily clad feet. 'Are those boots as uncomfortable as they look?'

'No, though you have to break them in.' She set to work undoing one of the laces, giving the boot all her concentration. Suddenly she looked up. 'Aren't you going to ask me why I did it?'

Charlotte took a sip of her tea. She looked thoughtfully at this model-thin, fifteen-year-old girl in front of her, with her pale skin, black eyes, dangling earrings and incredible candyfloss hair. 'That depends,' she said at last.

'Depends on what?'

'Depends on whether you really want me to ask you why you did it.'

'I suppose that's it. Mum and Dad didn't even bother to ask me. I really wanted them to ask so that...'

'So that you could have a good go at them?'

Tiffany smiled. 'You see, you do remember what it's like to be a teenager.'

Charlotte lay back on the grass. 'Go on then, tell me all about it.'

With both boots off now, Tiffany rubbed her sweaty white feet, then she too stretched out on the lawn. 'Two reasons really,' she said, looking up at the leaves on the tree above them. 'Firstly I thought it would be a laugh to turn up the same disgusting colour as our house. After all, if they can do it to our home, I can do it to my hair.'

Charlotte smiled, recognising the logic she might well have employed with Peter had he done something so outlandish. 'Go on,' she said. 'What's the other reason?'

'I just wanted to shock the hell out of them!'

Honesty. How refreshing, thought Charlotte. 'Good for you,' she said. 'Though don't quote me on that, will you?'

'Dad's face was good, wasn't it?' Tiffany said, placing a tentative hand on her rigid hair.

'I don't know who was more shocked, Iris or your father.'

'Ma Braithwaite looked great, didn't she?'

'She looked something all right.' Charlotte sat up to finish her tea. 'I don't know your dad well, but I should think that's one of the rare times in his life when he's been left speechless.'

'You're right there. By the way, what happened to his jacket, did you find it?'

'Alex tracked it down. Ted the Toup had bought it from Mrs Bradley and Alex had to barter to get it back again. Ted said he'd paid two pounds for it and that he wouldn't let it go for anything less than three. So tell your father that he owes Alex three pounds.'

Tiffany smirked. 'Dad'll be furious – he paid nearly four hundred for it.'

17

She allowed Alex to lead her upstairs. At the foot of the bed he kissed her, slowly, tentatively, like a faint summer breeze blowing over her. He stood back, held her arms outstretched towards him and entwined his slender fingers through hers. Loving it and loving him, she closed her eyes, capturing the moment for ever, never wanting it to end. She heard a rustle of movement and opening her eyes she found herself staring into the carnal gaze of Derek. His hands reached out for her and pushed her down on to the bed. She turned away and closed her eyes again. She wanted Alex. She called out to him and opened her eyes once more, expectantly. This time, coming towards her was Peter. He lay on top of her and moaned, then she felt his body, hot and wet against her own. He started to scream, violent screams of agonising pain as his body started to open, revealing a shattered ribcage and a pulsating heart. She pushed him away and cried out as she felt herself covered in the wetness of his blood.

Charlotte pushed back the twisted duvet and stumbled to the bathroom. She leaned against the cold sink and stared into the mirror. Covered in sweat, her heart pounding, she ripped off the cotton T-shirt she was wearing and went and stood under the shower, letting the powerful jets of water stab and prick at her. When at last she had stopped shaking, she turned off the water and dried herself roughly with a towel.

In the darkness of the bedroom, she looked at the clock on the bedside table. Half past three, the luminous hands told her.

She opened the window and breathed in the scent of dew-moistened grass and earth. Above her a bulging moon illuminated the garden, picking out in brilliant, magical whiteness the bark of the silver birches at the end of the lawn. It was all so peaceful out there, so undemanding, and it contrasted dramatically with the all-consuming terror she had just experienced.

Resting her elbows on the sill, Charlotte looked down at the tendrils of wisteria trying to reach inside the window. Peter would never have tolerated anything as untidy as wisteria. Peter.

She shuddered. It was the first time since the accident that she'd dreamt of him. She clasped her arms around her body, protecting herself against the thought of that blood. Why had she dreamt of that? It was odd. When she had been taken to identify Peter's body there had been very little blood. She had thought at the time that even in death Peter had been unwilling to give away any of himself. She wasn't proud of that thought now.

She wasn't proud either of the first part of the dream she had just experienced. Just what was happening to her?

She drew the curtains across the window and got back into bed, carefully so as not to disturb Mabel who was curled up, fast asleep, on what had once been Peter's side of the bed.

With a Hulme Welford jumble sale now under his belt, Alex decided it was time to give St John's a try.

He was met at the porch by Mrs Braithwaite and a woman whom he recognised from yesterday in the village hall. Mrs Braithwaite handed him a hymn book and an order of service. 'Glad to see you finally putting in an appearance, Mr Hamilton,' she said.

He gave her a nod of his head.

'Good morning,' said the other woman with contrasting friendliness. She sounded a little breathless. 'I'm Mrs Bradley. I do hope you'll enjoy your visit and come again. It's very old, you know, the church dates back to . . .'

'Really, Mrs Bradley,' interrupted Iris, 'we're working for the Lord, not the National Trust.'

'Thank you,' Alex said. 'I'm sure I'll find it most interesting.'

'Edifying, I should hope, Mr Hamilton. Reverend Jackson's theme today is following God's plan.'

'Ah yes,' said Alex. ' "And he has showered down upon us the richness of his grace – for how well he understands us and knows what is best for us at all times." '

'Quite so,' said Mrs Braithwaite dismissively. 'Now come along, Mr Hamilton, there are other people behind you trying to get in.'

Alex chose to sit where he always did in any church, at the back and in the left-hand pew, and without even looking about him, he bowed his head.

A few moments later when he raised his head he found Charlotte was sitting next to him. She seemed startled when he looked at her. 'I didn't know it was you,' she said, and appeared to back away from him.

'What's wrong?' He noted the deep shadows around her eyes and her pale complexion. 'Am I *persona non grata* all of a sudden?'

She looked down, and he watched her turn her gold wedding band on her finger.

Charlotte felt Alex's gaze and knew she should answer his question. But what could she say? That he was the last person in Hulme Welford she wanted to be sitting next to that morning; that twice in twenty-four hours she had desired him, consciously and subconsciously. 'I'm surprised to see you here this morning, that's all,' she said at last.

'You're not the only one. Mrs Braithwaite has already given me a grilling. A little of that woman certainly goes a long way. Ah, I see we're off.' And picking up his hymn book, he got to his feet as the organ started up jauntily with 'Come Sing the Praise of Jesus'.

They were halfway through the second verse when a third person joined Alex and Charlotte in their pew. It was Barry Rogers. Charlotte recognised the now familiar jogging suit and flushed face, and once again noticed that he was positioned behind the stone pillar. Then, as the service was drawing to a close, he disappeared as furtively as he had arrived, just as he had last week.

'I wonder why?' Charlotte said to Alex after she had explained this to him. 'Why does Barry sneak in and out of church each week? It's a bit odd, don't you think?'

Alex shrugged his shoulders. 'Maybe he's a late riser and has to get away early each time.'

'No, there's more to it than that. I bet you . . .'

'Gambling in the Lord's house, Mrs Lawrence, shame on you.' It was Iris Braithwaite looming large behind them both. 'And Mr Hamilton, I trust the sermon served you well?' Not expecting any kind of reply she was quickly off and moving towards her next prey. 'Now Mrs Haslip, I really must question the suitability of orchids in the altar flowers. Their costliness bothered me throughout the entire service. Reverend Jackson needs serviceable fauna, not exotic frippery.'

'Can't say I'd even noticed the flowers,' Alex said to Charlotte as they inched their way towards Malcolm Jackson.

'All I could think of,' Charlotte said, smiling for the first time. 'Kept thinking, what a lot of exotic frippery about the altar.'

'Hello Charlotte,' Malcolm Jackson's voice cut in. 'Good to see you again. How are things?'

'Fine,' she lied, and parrying with the kind of ease she despised, she said, 'Have you met my tenant, Mr Hamilton?'

'Always good to have new blood sitting in the pews.'

Charlotte flinched.

'Wouldn't be interested in ushering, would you?' Malcolm asked as he shook Alex's hand. 'It would give the congregation someone new to criticise,' he added, laughing.

'Why not?' Alex said.

Malcolm Jackson was amazed, for his sales pitch seldom worked. 'Right you are. I'll call round during the week with a copy of the rota for you.'

'You didn't have to, you know. You could have said no to Malcolm, most people do,' Charlotte told Alex as they waited to cross the road outside the church.

'Well, I'm not most people.'

Charlotte looked at him closely. 'You're not, are you, but then who or what are you?'

'That sounds like the corniest of lines from an old movie.'

'You're right,' she said, 'but the question still stands.'

'Tell you what, let me cut the grass for you this afternoon and then I'll tell you.'

'Okay. How about I do some lunch for us first?' She frowned and looked away from him, staring hard at the ground as they turned into Acacia Lane.

'That would be nice.' Alex was conscious of Charlotte's wariness. 'But only if you really want to.'

She stood still and looked up at him. 'Maybe we shouldn't. I wouldn't want people to ... after all, Peter's only been dead a short while.'

He stared into her eyes which, in the leafy shade of the trees, were that same dusky violet he remembered so well from their first meeting. 'I presume it was only lunch you were offering.'

'For goodness' sake, you're beginning to sound like Derek now,' she snapped back at him.

'That's better, you don't look so ...'

'Go on, what don't I look?'

He hesitated before speaking. It had struck him from the moment he had met Charlotte that there was something wrong about her grief; he didn't know what it was, but knew only that something jarred. He felt at times that he forgot to treat her as a woman who had recently lost the man she loved, because she didn't behave like one. He said, 'I just feel that sometimes you're your real self and at other times it's as if you're trying to become the person you feel others expect you to be.'

'And what might that person be?' Charlotte said coolly.

'The grieving widow,' he said softly, still looking straight at her.

Charlotte said nothing, but walked on ahead, fast. Alex let her go, then, after a moment's thought, he caught her up at the entrance to his part of Ivy Cottage. 'I'm sorry,' he said. 'Perhaps I shouldn't have said that.'

She turned on him and he braced himself for her anger. Instead she looked quite calmly at him. 'Can we carry on with this conversation over lunch?'

'How do you think Charlotte is coping?' Neville Archer asked his wife, as he pulled slowly away at the lights in Wilmslow. He was aware of the impatient Range Rover behind him, practically climbing into the boot of his tired old Volvo, but he would not be hurried. Moving into second gear, he added, 'I mean, really getting on.'

Louise looked up from the Royal Worcester teapot on her lap – the rest of that Sunday morning's car boot sale pickings were in the back of the car, but not this dear little teapot. Despite the small crack in the lid, it was a beauty, a real find. Stroking the spout, she said absentmindedly, 'How do you mean?'

Neville knew his wife wasn't listening. Louise's mind was on, around and inside that piece of china on her lap. Funny that something as small and insignificant as a piece of china should arouse such passion within his wife. Nothing else seemed to.

With him, of course, it was his gooseberries. Now that really was something to get excited about. The endless search to produce the ultimate berry, to nurse it through those first precious days of its infancy, watching it grow, until that exciting, poignant moment when it was time to pick it and give it up to be judged. Rather like children really – nurturing and sheltering them and then giving them up to life. Which reminded him: Charlotte.

'I was just wondering whether we should be doing more for her.' What he really wanted to say, but couldn't, was how inadequate he felt, how helpless he thought himself to be in matters of personal grief. He had been a GP all his working life, had coped admirably with gall bladders, chickenpox, herpes, chest infections and piles, but when it had come to Mrs Jenkins having a breakdown because Mr Jenkins had left her, or when he had had to tell Mr Forbes that his pretty young wife was dying of ovarian cancer, he had been useless, and he'd known it.

For no good reason that he could think of, he was convinced that Charlotte was hiding something. Whether it was from him specifically, or from everyone, he was not sure. Which was why he was now probing his wife. Had Charlotte discussed with her mother something she couldn't possibly tell him? He doubted this. He and Charlotte had always been so close.

'Look out!' Louise's voice crashed unexpectedly into his thoughts. He saw the brake lights of the car in front and pushed down hard on the brake pedal. The Volvo performed a splendid emergency stop, jerking Louise forward in her seat so that her nose almost tipped the glove compartment.

'I don't know what's the matter with you these days,' she said, straightening herself up, at the same time checking her precious teapot. 'You're so . . .'

Neville knew what she was going to say.

' . . . slow!' she said vehemently.

In response, he gripped the steering wheel tighter, his arms at a perfect ten-to-two position. 'You haven't answered my question,' he said holding back the desire to say, and you're so vague these days, you don't listen to a word I say.

'I don't know why you keep harping on about Charlotte. She's old enough to look after herself.'

He indicated to overtake a crawling refuse van, then pulled out. 'Don't you think that's being a little harsh? It was her husband who died, not a family pet. It was hardly an everyday occurrence for her.'

Louise glanced at the driver of the refuse van as they drew level. He gave her a crude wink. She looked away. 'For goodness' sake, Neville, can't you hurry up? And yes, I am well aware of the fact that it was Peter who died and not some nibbling hamster, but this is something Charlotte has got to sort out for herself.'

Neville pushed down hard on the accelerator, imagining for one delicious moment that Louise's cherished little teapot was under the pedal. A smile cracked his face and he pushed down harder. Speeding down the A34 towards Hulme Welford, he made up his mind to ignore his wife. He would go and see Charlotte and get her to talk to him. He would go tomorrow, when Louise was busy at the shop.

18

She was gulping the wine down, much too fast, she always did when she was nervous. But why was she nervous? Alex was the least intimidating man she had ever met.

They had started their meal sitting on Alex's patio, then when the May sun had proved too hot, they had retreated to Charlotte's favourite spot in the garden, to the welcome cool shade offered by the drooping branches of the fig tree. Each having eaten two helpings of spaghetti carbonara mopped up with chunks of garlic bread, they were now sitting back in their chairs, enjoying the feeling that only a pleasantly satisfied stomach can bring. Alex reached out for a grape from the Tuscan pottery bowl on the table between them.

Charlotte tried not to watch him, but she couldn't help it. His hands fascinated her, which was probably one of the reasons why she was drinking too much. Before the spoon incident at the jumble sale she hadn't given Alex's hands a second glance; now they seemed to be constantly on her mind. She shuddered involuntarily and looked down at Mabel at her feet. She lifted the little dog up on to her lap so that she had something to occupy her own hands.

'Are you cold? We could move back into the sun if you want?'

'Sorry? Oh I see, no, no I'm not cold, not at all.'

He smiled. 'Do you want to carry on that conversation now?'

Throughout the meal, they hadn't said a word about what Alex had said to her after church. It hadn't been a matter of skirting round the issue, it just hadn't cropped up. They had talked about all sorts of things: of Alex's love of small silver knick-knacks – hence the spoon; and the game that he and his brother played – who can find the most disgusting birthday present for the other – hence the tearful boy. And then he had told her about the book on trees he had bought.

'Did you know that the name rowan is believed to be derived from the Norse word *runa*?'

'Heavens, is it really?' she had said playfully, pretending to yawn.

'It means charm,' he carried on undeterred. 'Apparently rowan trees were planted outside churchyards and houses to ward off witches.'

Then she had seen the twinkle in his eye.

'I only mention it because I notice there's one at the end of your drive. With a bit of luck it should keep Mrs Braithwaite off your doorstep.'

She had laughed at that and at herself for momentarily accusing Alex of being dull.

But the issue had now been raised. What was she going to do, or say? What on earth had made her think that she could talk to Alex about her failing marriage? Why him? Why not Hilary? Why not her parents? Was it because Alex had never known Peter and she thought he would not sit in judgement of her?

'I . . . I'm not sure, to be honest,' she said. 'I don't think I can. I thought I could, but now I can't.'

He looked at her with a steady gaze, then turned away. 'You have a lovely garden. In London it was something I always wanted.'

'That's stupid,' she said, grateful for the reprieve. 'Why didn't you just buy a house with a garden?'

He leaned back in his chair and glanced up at the drooping wisteria that covered the back of Ivy Cottage. 'Sometimes,' he said slowly, 'dreams are better than reality.' He picked at another grape. 'And anyway, the reality at the time was that I didn't have a free moment to indulge my fantasy. Work was the number one priority then.'

'Peter was like that. He would never admit it though.'

'Most men don't realise they're doing it. It's like falling in love, you don't mean to do it, it just happens. But it must be hard for a wife to accept.'

'It is, or rather, it was,' Charlotte said thoughtfully. 'But somehow you come to terms with the fact that you're no longer your husband's *numero uno*. It hurts though, and there's always a danger that . . .' But her voice trailed away. Should she tell him? Would he understand? Would he understand that eventually being second on the list makes you hate yourself and hate those around you, especially the one you once loved. 'But is work still your number one priority?' she asked, turning the conversation away from herself.

He laughed and rolled a grape between his thumb and forefinger. She wished he wouldn't do that. No she didn't. She wished he'd keep on doing it.

'I think that my very sitting here in my landlady's garden, drinking cheap supermarket Hungarian wine, proves that it isn't that important to me any longer. My eighty-hour weeks have long since gone, but then so has my company car, along with my smart address.'

'So you don't think Acacia Lane is grand enough for you?'

He laughed again and once more stretched forward to pluck a grape. Charlotte watched him carefully remove its small stalk and she shuddered again.

'Come on,' he said, getting to his feet. 'Let's get you back in the sun, you're obviously freezing.'

She tried hard not to laugh, and putting Mabel down on to the grass, she got up and started gathering up the lunch things. 'I've kept my side of the bargain,' she said, 'now it's your turn. The mower's that way.'

'Coo-ee, only me, all right if I come in?' Hilary appeared through the open conservatory door. Stepping into the kitchen, she joined Charlotte at the sink. 'I'm selling tickets for the fork supper next Saturday. I was supposed to be selling them after church this morning, only I couldn't because I wasn't there. I had to take Philip to an away match in Macclesfield – he scored the winning goal. He's really very good, you should come and see him play some time.' She put down her bundle of supper tickets and envelope of money, looked for a tea towel and automatically started drying the plates Charlotte had just washed. 'You've missed a bit,' she said, slipping one of the plates back into the soapy water. 'So, where was I?'

'Selling tickets for the fork supper, I think,' Charlotte said, smiling to herself.

'Oh yes. Well, I've just been trying next door,' she nodded her head towards the kitchen wall that backed on to Alex's part of the house, 'but there was no answer, so I thought that maybe Alex was here with you.'

'Did you now?' Charlotte fixed her attention on the pan she was rinsing under the hot tap.

'This tea towel isn't very clean. Have you got another?'

'In the drawer over there.'

Hilary began rummaging through the chaotically filled drawer. 'Charlotte ...' she said, but got no further as she was interrupted by the sound of a powerful lawnmower starting up. She joined her sister and looked out of the window. 'It's Alex,' Charlotte said unnecessarily, as a lawnmower appeared from behind the potting shed followed by Alex, stripped to the waist and now wearing shorts.

'I can see that,' Hilary said pressing herself hard up against the sink. 'Just look at him.'

'Hilary!'

Hilary slapped a hand over her mouth, as though to prevent any other impure thoughts from slipping out. 'I didn't mean, I only ...'

Charlotte laughed. 'I know exactly what you mean and I happen to agree with you.'

'You do?' Hilary said, her hopes rising. Her sister was falling for Alex after all. Smiling to herself she stared out of the window as Alex pushed the mower towards the bottom of the garden. 'He's well tanned, isn't he?'

Charlotte tilted her head to one side as though looking at Alex's naked back from a better angle. 'Mm ... I suppose he is.'

'Looks good in shorts.' Hilary decided to push the point home. 'Good-looking altogether, wouldn't you say?'

Charlotte was about to respond when Alex reached the far end of the garden, turned the mower round and looked straight up at them. He waved nonchalantly.

They acknowledged him, then moved away from the window. 'Put the kettle on, shall I?' Hilary said, awkwardly.

They sat with their drinks at the table, Hilary just managing to keep one eye on the garden, but Charlotte with her back to it. 'It's a long time since we did any serious ogling, isn't it?' Hilary said.

Charlotte made no response. Hilary decided to be brave. 'You are allowed to, you know ... just because you're a widow, it doesn't mean you're no longer a woman. You're going to have to try and remember what it was like in the old days, before Peter.'

Charlotte reflected on this, taking a sip of her tea. Pre-Peter. In those days Hilary had accused her of having a lascivious nature, but that was only because Hilary had been so taken up with David.

Hilary sensed Charlotte wasn't going to say anything more on the subject. She picked up her bundle of tickets. 'You'll come, won't you?'

Charlotte shook her head. 'I don't think so.'

'Why ever not?' Hilary's disappointment was obvious. She had been so sure that she could lure Charlotte and Alex together for the evening at the village hall.

Charlotte banged her mug down. Splashes of tea spilled over the table. 'I know exactly what you were thinking. One ticket to Alex and one to Charlotte. Do you really think I'm that naïve?'

Charlotte could feel her face colouring, her skin prickling with irrational hot rage. Suddenly she wanted to cry, to cry great sobs of ... she didn't know what. Yes she did. Remorse. Guilt! It was there all the time, baiting her day and night. It had been there when she and Alex had had lunch together. A perfectly innocent lunch, but all the time she had felt it was wrong, wrong to have enjoyed Alex's company. And damn it, she had. She liked being with him. He was nice, amusing, attentive, and what's more she found him attractive. And now here was Hilary egging her on even further. Well, it wouldn't do. She would have to put a stop to it, here and now. It was time for her to take control. There would be no more 'Alex and Charlotte' because then there would be no more guilt ... and no more dreams.

Common sense told her it was too soon. No woman in her right mind would let herself get caught up in another relationship only months after the death of her husband. It was madness. It was disrespectful. Yes. That was it. There had to be a decent period of mourning to be honoured. It was her duty. She may have failed Peter in marriage but she could at least do the right thing in death. She owed him that much. She almost sighed with relief, knowing she had hit upon infallible justification for not getting involved with Alex Hamilton. She had found the right weapon with which to fight off any temptation he offered.

Hilary peered over the top of her mug. She said quietly, 'You could always come on your own.'

'I know that,' Charlotte said calmly. 'Or I could bring a friend with me.'

Hilary looked crestfallen. 'You could.' She decided to force her sister's hand. 'So that's two tickets, then.' She peeled off two orange cards from her bundle. 'That'll be five pounds.'

Charlotte went in search of her bag and wondered at what she had just done. Who on earth could she ask to go with her? She walked back into the kitchen and handed over a five pound note.

'So who are you going to bring?' Hilary said, putting her things together but not daring to look Charlotte in the eye.

For a split second Charlotte hated her sister. 'You'll just have to wait and see.'

Hilary had the grace not to push her sister any more. She headed for the door. 'Tell Alex I'll catch him later, will you? Bye for now.' She left.

Charlotte looked out of the window. Alex was halfway through the lawn now, deep in concentration. He had the look of a man completely at peace with himself.

Charlotte envied him.

Alex switched the engine off and pushed the mower into the potting shed. He noticed Charlotte standing at the kitchen window again. He noticed too the way she instantly turned away the moment she realised he had seen her.

He bent down to the mower and started to clean off some of the stuck-on bits of grass. But his thoughts remained on Charlotte. There were times when he felt sure that there was something she wanted to tell him – maybe not him specifically, just someone. There were other times though when she treated him as if he were Jack the Ripper.

He smiled to himself as he thought of Lucy's words, spoken to him so often: *Alex, I do believe you're a frustrated agony aunt, always trying to sort out other people's problems.*

'There's no need, you know.'

Charlotte was silhouetted in the doorway and Alex knew from the stilted tone of her voice that he had once again taken on the guise of Jack the Ripper.

'I can clean it myself,' she said.

He stood up. Sidestepping the mower, he moved towards her. 'It's no problem,' he said. What had suddenly happened between lunch and now? What had caused her to change? Was it something he had said? 'Perhaps I could become your full-time gardener,' he quipped. 'I could move in here, into the potting shed.'

'And I could be your Lady Chatterley, I suppose.' Her words were heavy with sarcasm.

They stood in silence, each staring at the other, until Charlotte could bear it no more. She felt overwhelmed by the heady earthiness of the stifling shed, together with the sweet smell of fresh grass cuttings and petrol. She stepped back towards the sunshine and fresh air. As she moved Alex picked up his T-shirt which was hanging on the hook on the door. 'I'm sorry I upset you,' he said. 'It was only a joke.'

Charlotte wanted to apologise, but she knew she mustn't. She knew too that standing as she was, barely inches away from Alex and the warmth of his glistening body, she wanted very much to pretend she was Constance Chatterley. She swallowed hard and tried to cling to her objective. 'I've a message for you from Hilary,' she said.

His face was unreadable.

'It's about the fork supper at the village hall next Saturday. Hilary wondered if you'd be wanting a ticket. Of course she realises that you've probably got better things to do on a Saturday night.' She forced herself to add a casual laugh.

Alex managed a laugh as well. 'What, and have Mrs Braithwaite commenting on my absence? No fear. You can tell Hilary I'll have a ticket. In fact, you can tell her I'll have two. I suppose it's okay for me to take a friend along?'

'The more the merrier,' Charlotte said, surprised. 'Actually, I'm taking someone as well.'

Throwing his T-shirt over his shoulder, Alex turned and walked away.

Damn! thought Charlotte, watching him stroll across the lawn. What on earth was she going to do now? Not only was Hilary expecting her to turn up with a man, but Alex was also bringing a partner. Hell!

19

What was happening to her? She never had sugar in her coffee. It was Peter who had sugar.

She had dreamt of him again last night. This time he was lying in a hospital bed, not in a normal ward but in a room that had been made into an office: a fax machine in one corner, an array of potted plants in another, a desk in the middle with Peter's attaché case, and Peter himself, lying on a bed beneath his faithful laptop computer. All this she was seeing through a glass window as she was trying to make an appointment to see her husband. But the attractive nurse was telling her that Mr Lawrence was too busy to see her right now, and could she come back later? 'But he'll be dead later,' she had screamed at the nurse. Then two policemen had led her away, saying they wanted to question her about the death of her husband.

Was she cracking up? Charlotte shook her head. Getting up from the table, she tipped her coffee – Peter's coffee – down the sink. She heard the sound of the letterbox being pushed open and went through to the hall.

She made herself another drink, and taking the letters upstairs to read she found Mabel curled up on the bed. The first letter was from her solicitor, something about investments Peter had made. She put this back in its envelope. The next was a handwritten letter with a Brussels postmark. She knew straight away who it was from. Christina Castelli.

Scanning through the first page Charlotte was not surprised by the lack of 'hope you're settling in' platitudes – that was definitely not Christina's style. Instead it was a full account of a fat German industrialist and an Irish diplomat who had spent an entire evening singing in Gaelic to her. At the bottom of the second page was '. . . and so, Carlotta, I have booked a flight to Manchester and shall come to stay with you next month.' The letter went on to explain the exact date and time that Christina would be arriving, along with '. . . no need to meet me, I shall arrange for a taxi and arrive in time for cocktails.'

Charlotte laughed out loud. 'Cocktails!' she said. 'In Acacia Lane, just imagine.' She laughed again and tried to imagine Christina here in Hulme Welford: Christina and Iris Braithwaite . . . Christina and Derek Rogers! Lying back on the pillow, she reread the letter, squeezing it for more contact with her friend. Her thoughts were interrupted by the shrill ring of the telephone at the side of the bed. She picked up the receiver. 'Hello.'

'Charlotte?'

'Yes.' Her brain automatically ran through a list of possible male callers she might get at eight o'clock in the morning.

'It's me, Jonathan.'

'Jonathan!'

'I'm over in England on Friday, business, Birmingham, okay if I buzz up to see you, Saturday, about lunchtime, a bed for the night wouldn't go amiss?'

Yes, it was Jonathan all right, he always did speak like a telegram. 'Yes of course, I'll look forward to it,' she lied.

'Okay, see you.' The phone clicked and Charlotte was left with a droning sound in her ears and a stupefied expression on her face. She put the receiver down and nudged Mabel. 'So, we're to have the pleasure of Jonathan's company, how fortunate we are. Jonathan, King Kong of Hong Kong. Bet you'll dislike Peter's brother as much as I do.'

In eight years of marriage, Charlotte had only met her brother-in-law on a handful of occasions. The first time was by coincidence, at a party in London, not long after she and Peter had met. At the time she had no idea Peter had a brother, and coming out of their hostess's kitchen with two glasses of wine she had found Peter in the hall, admiring a large painting. Handing him his glass, she had kissed him lightly on the cheek, only to realise he was not Peter, and have it confirmed by the look of wonder on the man's face. Embarrassed, she had simply stood and stared, completely taken aback by the extraordinary likeness between this man and Peter. Peter had then appeared and he too, for a moment, had simply stood and stared.

'Surprise!' the man had said, taking a large mouthful of wine from the glass Charlotte had just given him.

'Another one of your passing-through visits, is it?' Peter said coldly.

'Needs must, when the devil drives. Aren't you going to introduce me?'

Peter turned to face Charlotte, his eyes narrow and dark. 'This is Jonathan, and as you've no doubt worked out for yourself, he's my brother.'

Driving home in the car afterwards, Peter had barely said a word, his tight-lipped expression telling Charlotte all she needed to know – that despite the striking resemblance there was no love between the two brothers.

Another occasion when they had met was in Singapore. It was then that Charlotte began to get a clearer picture of the intense rivalry between the two men. Jonathan was the elder brother by four years and neither of the two seemed able to forget this. 'As older brother, I insist on taking you two out for dinner,' Jonathan had said, when he arrived at their apartment, having just flown in from Hong Kong, where he lived and worked lucrative deals of gigantic proportions.

'I've already booked us a restaurant,' Peter had said, 'where the manager knows me personally.'

And so the evening had continued, with each brother trying to outdo the other, oblivious to Charlotte.

Now, after all these years, Jonathan wanted to come and see her. Why? Was it so that he could have one last shot at Peter – 'You see, little brother, I've got more staying power than you.'

The thought suddenly occurred to Charlotte that she could make good use of Jonathan while he was here.

It was just after twelve o'clock when the doorbell rang and Mabel started to bark.

'Hello.' Neville Archer was standing on the doorstep. He bent down to stroke the little dog. 'Have you got time to see your old dad?'

'Come in,' Charlotte said, kissing his cheek.

He peered into rooms as he walked through to the kitchen. He could see that his daughter had got things more or less straight since Monday when he had helped her with the unpacking. A few pictures were hanging on the walls now, though there were still some propped up on the floor against the wall. Perhaps he should offer to help Charlotte put them up, or would she think he was interfering?

'How about some lunch? I haven't been out to the shops yet but I've got the remains of a bit of Cambozola and some crackers.'

He nodded and sat down at the table. 'Don't tell your mother. I haven't been allowed Cambozola for six months – too many calories.'

They laughed conspiratorially. Neville felt reassured. She was still his ally after all. He waited until Charlotte had sat down with him at the table before embarking on what he had to say. 'Charlotte,' he helped himself to some cheese, 'I know you could tell me to mind my own business, or you could of course throw me out, or simply lie, but just how are you really feeling? I know I'm not much good at this kind of thing, as I'm sure your mother would be the first to agree . . .'

'Has Mother sent you here?' Charlotte wondered at her father's words which had come out like a well-prepared speech.

'No. As a matter of fact, she thinks I've gone to see Ron Wicklow about the gooseberry show.'

'You lied to Mother. Why?'

Neville shrugged. He felt like a small boy caught with apples in his pockets. 'I . . . I was worried about you and wanted to know . . .'

'Oh Dad.' She reached out and touched his arm, finding comfort in the feel of his old tweed jacket – he had always dressed like a country doctor and still did. With a sudden surge of emotion she remembered vividly waiting outside his surgery, as a child, listening to two elderly women discussing her father: 'He's such a dear man, I'd love to take him home and put him on the mantelpiece.'

'I've been worried about you,' Neville pressed on. 'Losing Peter like that, so suddenly, must have been awful. I just want you to know that I'm here if you need me.'

She felt tears welling up, but she battled against them and passed him the plate of crackers. 'We've always been close, haven't we?'

He nodded his head. They were on uncharted territory now and he didn't trust himself to speak.

'We've always sort of known what the other was thinking.'

Again he nodded.

'At the moment though, you couldn't possibly guess what's going on inside my head . . . I wouldn't want you to.'

Still he said nothing, convinced now that there was something his daughter was holding back. If he waited long enough she'd talk to him, it would all come out.

'Do you want some more cheese?' she said, pushing the plate towards him. He shook his head.

'You see, it's not as everyone thinks. Everyone thinks that I . . .' She got up from the table and started fiddling with the kettle.

It was no good. He couldn't take it any longer. He had to say something. 'Charlotte . . .' But he got no further because the telephone rang. Was that relief he saw on his daughter's face as she went out to the hall to answer it?

He watched Charlotte through the open door as she picked up the receiver. 'Hello Mum,' she said. He shook his head and then pretended to hold a gun to his temple. Charlotte tried hard not to smile. 'What, here, you think Dad's here?' She put her hand over the mouthpiece of the receiver and whispered, 'Ron Wicklow's just been on the phone asking for you.'

'Oh heavens,' groaned Neville.

Charlotte packed her father off to meet his fate, cleared up the lunch things and went outside. She collected a few tools and the wheelbarrow from the potting shed, and headed off towards the bottom of the garden.

The flower beds had not been tended in a long while; the death of Mrs Clifford senior must have put the garden very low on the list of priorities for the Clifford family. Death was like that. Or was it? Another person might have absorbed themselves into a regime of digging, weeding and pruning, worked all hours so as not to think of their loss. Perhaps that was what she should do. Throw herself into something, so that she didn't have time to keep blaming herself, would not keep feeling the need to confess. She had almost told her father, had been so close to telling him everything. She dug deep and vigorously into the heavy clay soil. 'Ashes to ashes, dust to dust,' she suddenly said out loud.

Alex put the phone down and made some hurried notes on the pad on his desk – a company over in Knutsford wanted to update their current stock control system.

He looked out of the window. At the bottom of the garden he could see

Charlotte with a fully loaded wheelbarrow. Immediately he was working out what excuse he could use to go and talk to her. He smiled to himself. He was off again.

He went through to his small kitchen and put the kettle on. He would take her a cup of tea.

He made his way down the garden and stood some twelve feet away from where Charlotte was digging. She was talking to herself. No, not talking, it was more like a chant: 'Ashes to ashes, dust to dust,' she was repeating over and over again. He stood still, not knowing what to do. It was obvious she had no idea he was there. He felt like an intruder, and was about to step slowly backwards when from behind him came the sound of yapping. Mabel was scuttling across the lawn.

Charlotte turned round sharply. 'How long have you been there?' Her faced flushed and he noticed a long smudge of earth across her right cheek. He wanted very much to wipe it away for her.

'Thought you'd like a tea break,' he said, ignoring her question.

'Oh, thank you.' She dropped the spade and pulled off her gardening gloves. 'I was miles away, I didn't hear you coming. Have you been working?' Her words were rushed in a conspicuous attempt to overcome her embarrassment. He handed her the mug.

'Yes,' he said, thankful that for the time being he didn't seem to be Jack the Ripper. 'I think I've just gained a new client, over at Knutsford. How long do you think it will take me to get there?'

'Not long,' she said, flicking her hair out of her eyes. 'About thirty minutes. Parking can be a devil though. I should give yourself an extra ten minutes to be on the safe side.'

Glad to be able to talk to her, Alex carried on. 'So what's Knutsford like?'

'Nice, but very twee. Black and white like Hulme Welford, except more upmarket. They've got Mrs Gaskell while all we've got is Iris Braithwaite.'

He laughed.

Charlotte drained her mug and handed it back to him. 'Thank you, I enjoyed that.' He noticed her looking over his shoulder. 'It looks like one of us has a visitor,' she said.

Alex turned and saw Barry Rogers coming towards them.

'Congratulations!' he said. 'I hear you passed your driving test on Wednesday. Well done.'

Barry pushed at his glasses. 'I think I was just lucky.'

'Nonsense,' said Charlotte. 'No such thing as luck.'

'I hope there is. I had my first physics exam this morning.' He pushed his hair back, which like his glasses slipped straight back to its familiar place.

Charlotte groaned. 'How did it go?'

Barry smiled, which had the effect of altering his earnest face completely. 'It was okay actually, easier than I thought it might be.'

'Good for you,' Alex said. 'What else are you doing?'

'Chemistry starts tomorrow, next comes biology and then economics. They're spread out over three and a half weeks.'

Charlotte groaned again. 'You poor boy. But what brings you here? You've not come to me for private tuition I hope?'

As suddenly as the smile had appeared so it vanished. Barry looked awkwardly at them both.

Alex could see how tense he was, and thinking it might be to do with the Charlotte and Derek incident, he said, 'I'll be off then.'

'No, no, don't do that.'

Again a nudge of the glasses and a hand pushing fruitlessly at his hair. 'I'd like to speak to both of you, if that's all right.'

'Sounds ominous,' Charlotte said, leading them towards the chairs which she now kept permanently by the fig tree. 'It hasn't got anything to do with your parents, has it?' she added cautiously.

'No, certainly not, well, not directly anyway. I suppose I should apologise for what I said to you in church that morning. I don't normally go around . . .'

'I'm sure I'd have done the same if I'd been in your shoes.'

'Well,' said Alex, setting the empty mugs down on the table, 'how can we help you?'

'It's a bit difficult.' Barry squeezed his large frame into one of the flimsy chairs. 'I'm not sure where to start, and please don't say at the beginning.'

'I'm tired of clichés myself,' Charlotte smiled. 'Carry on, just as you want.' Her words were warm and sincere and Alex realised that here was the real Charlotte, relaxed and eager to help. Barry posed no threat to her. It was he himself who somehow caused her to smell danger. Why?

'You see, it's true, isn't it?' Barry was saying. 'Most people at some stage in their lives feel something, experience something, that they know will change their lives for ever.' He turned his earnest face up at them both, seeking confirmation of this statement.

Alex nodded and Charlotte leaned forward in her chair, as though willing Barry on.

'Well, I guess I've just reached that point in my life and I'm not sure what to do about it.'

Alex rubbed his chin thoughtfully and for a split second Charlotte's attention was drawn away from Barry and was absorbed in Alex's hands.

'So what you're saying,' Alex said, causing Charlotte to concentrate again, 'is that something has happened to you recently, something that has changed your understanding of your life?'

'Yes, that's exactly it.' Barry looked visibly relieved. 'I felt sure you'd understand. That's why I came to you.'

Charlotte thought about this for a moment. What was it about Alex that had this effect on people? What made people want to confide in him? First her, now Barry. She couldn't understand it, nor this conversation. What were they talking about? Was it a girl? Had Barry fallen in love? She took her courage in both hands. 'So what's her name?'

At first Barry looked confused, then he smiled, again a smile which transformed his serious teenage face into that of a dazzling young man. 'I think, Mrs Lawrence,' he said politely, at the same time making Charlotte feel like Old Mother Hubbard, 'that perhaps I've misled you.'

'Oh,' said Charlotte, 'but I thought . . .' And then another idea came into her head. 'Oh,' she said again, 'you mean it's a . . .'

Alex cut in swiftly. 'I think Barry should spell it out for us.' He looked at Barry and smiled encouragingly.

20

Barry felt better for having talked it through with someone else. Now all he had to do was tell his parents.

It certainly wasn't going to be easy. Bewilderment would come first with his father, then it would be ridicule. Tiffany would be okay. She'd tease him for a while and then get bored with it all. His mother he wasn't so sure about. It was difficult at times to know what she thought.

He could hear his parents down in the kitchen, not talking to one another, just moving about. He decided the time was right, breathed in deeply, got up from his desk and went downstairs.

They started supper in silence. Tiffany's chair was typically empty. Without her, Barry didn't want to say anything. But the longer he waited the more he could feel his nerve going. Perhaps he could tell them tomorrow, after his chemistry exam? He ran his hand nervously through his hair. 'I had my first physics exam this morning,' he said.

His mother looked up from her plate of salad. 'Oh, I'm sorry, I forgot all about that.' She looked genuinely pained at this parental oversight. 'How did it go?'

'Cost of the fees at that school, he'd better have done all right,' his father said, reaching for the jar of mayonnaise. 'Only joking, Bas. How was it?'

'Okay, I think. I was lucky, I'd revised the right bits.'

'You're late,' Cindy said, looking over Barry's shoulder as Tiffany sauntered into the kitchen.

Still cyclamen pink, Tiffany ignored her mother and pulled a face at the sight of the salad on her plate. She sat down and smiled at Barry. 'So, how was it?'

'If you'd been here when you were supposed to be,' Cindy snapped, 'you would have heard.'

Still ignoring her mother, Tiffany said, 'Tell me later, Barry.'

'Actually,' Barry said carefully, putting his knife and fork down on his plate, 'I've got something I want to tell you all.'

His father viewed him speculatively and then a broad smile covered his face, and, brandishing a large radish on the end of his fork, he said, 'You sly old devil, you've gone and got yourself a girl, haven't you? I told you that car would do the trick.'

'Give it a rest, Dad,' Tiffany said. 'Let Barry speak.'

'Watch your step, young lady. You're not so—'

'Look,' Barry interrupted, raising his voice slightly, 'this is hard enough for me to say without you lot arguing as well.'

Cindy looked up sharply. 'Hard enough?' she repeated. 'Why, what have you done?'

'Oh my God,' Derek said slowly looking at his son across the table. 'You've gone and got a girl pregnant, haven't you? All that crap about not being interested in girls and studying like mad was just to fool us. Bloody hell! I'd have expected even you to know about safe sex.'

'What, like you?' Cindy's voice was as brittle as the look she gave her husband.

Barry got up from the table, scraping his chair noisily on the tiled floor. A silence followed as everyone looked up at him. 'Look, Dad,' he said, 'this has absolutely nothing whatsoever to do with a girl.' He had their attention now and so pushed on, trying to gain confidence through momentum. 'I've recently discovered something about myself that I feel I need to share with you, something that may surprise you.' He paused as he sought the right words.

His father threw down his knife and fork on the table. He too stood up and looked Barry straight in the eye. 'Well, you can pack your bags now. You can bugger off somewhere else, anywhere, so long as I don't have to set eyes on you.'

Three pairs of eyes stared at Derek in astonishment. 'Not only,' he said, looking at his wife and then back at Barry, 'not only is he a stuffed Henry, but he's a bloody great screaming poofter.' He turned away from them all. 'I need a beer,' he said, reaching for the fridge.

Cindy's eyes filled with tears as she pushed her plate away and bent her head down over the table. Tiffany got to her feet and stepped towards Barry. She put her arm around him. 'If he goes,' she said dramatically, 'so do I.'

'Good!' shouted Derek, slamming the fridge door shut and yanking at the ring pull on his can of beer. 'Good bloody riddance to the pair of you.'

'But Dad . . .' It was Barry, his voice strangely calm and assured.

'Don't "but Dad" me anything,' Derek rounded on him. 'You've betrayed us all. You filthy . . . homosexual!' He almost spat out the last word.

'But Dad, I'm not a homosexual.'

'Not a homosexual? Then what do you call yourself, got some other bloody fancy name for it, have you?'

'My sexuality doesn't come into this at all,' Barry said.

'Then what the hell does?'

'God does.'

'God!' shouted Derek. 'And just what is that supposed to mean?'

'It means I've become a Christian.'

Frothy bubbles spurted across the kitchen floor as Derek choked on his beer. 'A what?' he gasped.

Barry was fully in control of himself now. 'A Christian, Dad. You know, someone who believes in Jesus Christ as his personal saviour.'

Derek suddenly looked very pale and dazed as he slumped back heavily against the worktop, speechless.

'Muffin 'ell, Barry,' said Tiffany, 'that really has shut Dad up.'

'Perhaps we could all sit down again,' Barry said quietly, aware how drawn his mother looked as she sat completely motionless at the table. Dutifully his father and sister sat down. Feeling better than he had for weeks, Barry picked up his knife and fork and said, 'Anybody want to say anything?'

'So, um . . .' Derek said at last, 'so what exactly does this mean – orange dresses and tambourines?'

Barry laughed and nudged his glasses on his nose. 'Dad, I'm not about to create a Fort Waco here in Acacia Lane.' His words were light, almost flippant, in an attempt to lighten the mood around the table.

'But you haven't been confirmed or anything,' Tiffany said.

'I know. More importantly, I haven't even been baptised.'

'I wanted you both baptised,' Cindy said, her first words in more than ten minutes. 'I wanted you both baptised when you were babies.'

'Only because you wanted a new dress and a party out of it,' Derek fired at her, tossing back the last of his beer.

'I did not!'

'Well, I think it's brilliant,' Tiffany said, sensing a row about to start up again. 'At least now we might get some much needed morality in this house.' She fixed her eyes on her father.

For the first time in his life, Barry saw his father flinch.

By eight o'clock they had finished their meal, which, on reflection, Barry thought, must have seemed like an eternity for his parents, sitting there as though the Archbishop of Canterbury had just dropped in. They both seemed relieved when he said he was going out for a short while.

Barry knocked on Alex's door.

'How bad was it?' Alex led him through to the small uncluttered sitting-room.

'I'm amazed you didn't hear all the shouting. Poor Dad, he thought I was trying to tell him that I was gay.'

'Oh Lord,' Alex said. 'But then, parents have such a tough time of it. I suppose it's only natural they jump to the wrong conclusions, which are usually their worst fears.'

'I hadn't thought of it like that, but you're right. To Dad, sexuality is all.'

'So, what happens next?'

'I go home and get myself ready for my chemistry exam tomorrow morning.'

21

'Left you nicely, didn't he?'

Charlotte swallowed hard, not for the first time in the two hours since her brother-in-law had turned up, driving an oversized hired Mercedes and carrying his Ralph Lauren garment bag and matching leather briefcase.

She looked across the sitting-room at Jonathan in his expensive, crisp suit, his long legs sticking out from the sofa, and felt repelled by his air of being entirely at ease, wherever he was. But what had really taken her by surprise was the shock of being with such a tangible reminder of Peter. She hadn't prepared herself for that, hadn't thought how disturbing it could feel to be face to face with a man who looked so similar to her dead husband. Even the way Jonathan picked minuscule specks of fluff off his jacket sleeve put her in mind of Peter.

'Lucky old you.'

Charlotte looked up at Jonathan. 'Lucky old me,' she repeated. 'How's that exactly?'

Jonathan crossed his legs. 'All that money Peter must have left you.'

Charlotte got up from her chair, trying to keep a rein on her anger. How typical, how bloody typical that Jonathan should show no sign of missing his own brother, but only show a keen interest in how well off Peter had left his widow. And why? Why the hell should Jonathan care about how much money she had, when he himself had bank accounts scattered far and wide? Did he feel cheated? She breathed in deeply, determined to stay calm. She had to keep Jonathan sweet until tomorrow morning, then she could tell him what she really thought of him. If she blew it now, she would lose her 'date' for the evening down at the village hall.

'Nice place you've got yourself, Charlotte. An expensive but worthwhile investment, I shouldn't wonder.'

She nodded. How dare he! How dare he talk to her like this. What right did he have to make these assumptions? Or was she angry because it was almost as though Jonathan knew the truth: that Peter's death had left her better off – in all ways. She looked out of the window trying to take her mind off this dreadful man sitting a few feet away from her. 'I can't dispute that Peter has left me comfortably off, so I suppose, as you say, I am indeed lucky.' She turned to face Jonathan once more. 'But you know, there's more to life than how much money is involved. Wasn't it John Ruskin who said "The only wealth is life itself"?'

He smiled, like a weasel. 'Helps though.'

Charlotte pushed her nails hard into the palm of her hand. 'Coffee?'

'Black, no sugar.'

She escaped to the kitchen and vented her anger by rattling mugs and spoons until she realised that she was no longer alone. Jonathan was standing in the doorway. He came towards her. She suddenly felt uncomfortable.

'You'll soon marry again of course, won't you?' he said.

She could feel his hot breath on her neck and moving away from him she wondered at this statement. The very idea was preposterous. Why would she want to replace one man with another, who in the end would probably do exactly as Peter had done – turn her into second best. No. The answer was no. She would not marry again.

She looked out of the window and saw Alex walk across the lawn in front of his part of the house. He was carrying a glass of beer in one hand and a book in the other. She watched him settle himself down on the grass. Why wasn't that man ever at work? she thought angrily to herself. She turned round sharply to face Jonathan.

'No, I have no intention of remarrying,' she said, smiling sweetly up at him. 'Just in case that was a proposal from you, Jonathan.'

Derek switched off the lights in the salon. It had been a busy Saturday and they had finished late, leaving him no time for a session in the gym and a sauna before going out for the evening. A village hall jamboree was far from his idea of a good night out, but it would do no harm for the business for him and Cindy to be seen socially in the village. And of course, there was always the prospect that Charlotte would be there.

He hadn't seen Charlotte since that farce of a jumble sale last Saturday and what with the ridiculous number of problems at the Wilmslow and Altrincham salons, he hadn't had any free time during the week to slip next door. What really bothered him, though, was that her tenant might be doing more than his fair share of '*slipping next door*'.

Going up the stairs in the main part of the house, Derek could hear Tiffany's hi-fi playing loudly in her bedroom – The Doors, yet more revival music. A spark of annoyance flickered within him as he stood and listened to 'Come on Baby Light my Fire'. He hated nostalgia. It served no purpose other than to remind him he was getting older.

He moved further along the landing and paused outside Bas's room. Silence. Probably down on his knees, Derek thought caustically. Immediately he regretted this thought. He didn't know why, but he did, and that disturbed him. He never regretted anything. He remained standing outside his son's room, half tempted to go in. But what would he say? What could he say? He shook his head. Just what was happening to his family? He didn't understand any of it. Tiffany running around like a liquorice allsort and now

Bas turning into some bloody kind of monk! Brother Bas! He shook his head again, it was all beyond him. Religion was for weirdos, for those cranks and loonies too weak to get through life without some kind of mental crutch. So where did Bas fit in?

'Hello Dad.'

Derek started and turned round to see Barry standing behind him. 'Bas,' he said, feeling unaccountably pleased to see his son, all six foot two of him and looking anything but a crank or a loony. 'I thought you were in your room.'

'No, I've been down at the village hall helping to get things ready for tonight. I went to see Malcolm Jackson earlier and he kind of roped me in.'

Derek looked uneasy.

'I went to see him about being baptised. He said he could do a service later in the summer.'

'I see,' was all Derek could think to say. He could sense that his son had something else to tell him. He watched him push his glasses up on to the bridge of his nose.

'Dad, I'd like you and Mum to be there, Tiffany too.'

Derek gaped. 'Oh no, I don't think . . . I mean, we can't . . . not Tiffany, not the way she looks.'

'Dad, it really doesn't matter what she looks like. But you don't have to come if you don't want to. I . . . I don't want to cmbarrass you. I understand.'

Derek looked at his son. All at once he felt like the biggest shit that had ever walked the earth. Unable to meet his son's gaze, he pushed his hands deep into his pockets and looked down at his shoes. At last he raised his head. 'Okay, if you want us there, we'll be there. But you'll look a right prat in a christening gown. I'll buy you a decent suit.'

'Thanks, Dad, that's great.'

They stood facing each other, suddenly not knowing what else to say, with the noise of thumping music invading the silence between them.

The moment was broken by the sound of a door opening followed by Tiffany. 'You look dead serious,' she shouted above the music. 'Been arguing again?'

Derek and Barry exchanged looks and both laughed.

'What's got into you two?' Tiffany said.

Inexplicably, Derek felt an unfamiliar rush of warmth run through him for his children. Wondering where Cindy had got to, he said, 'Where's your mother?'

'She was having a lie-down earlier, said she had a headache,' Tiffany answered.

'Well, you can turn that bloody din off then,' Derek said. 'How do you expect her to rest with all that noise going on?'

Baffled, Barry and Tiffany looked at each other. Consideration – from their father?

*

'Oh Lord, where have I put it?'

'Put what?' David asked Hilary, as she pushed past him like an express train.

'The key,' Hilary shouted. 'The key for the hall, for tonight.'

David always knew when his wife was panicking. She seemed to grow six inches taller and her nostrils flared imperceptibly. Experience had taught him that in these situations there was usually very little he could do. Years ago he had been stupid enough to think that it was his job to take control of the situation, but now he knew better. He stood back patiently watching, while Hilary gave the oak chest of drawers on her side of the bed a ruthless body search.

'I had it earlier when I came back after setting up all the tables,' she said.

David cleared his throat and decided to risk it. 'What did you have on this afternoon?'

'Oh don't be so stupid, David. Of course I've already thought of that. I'm not that daft.' She let out a cry of frustration as she slumped down on to the bed, sitting heavily on the dress she had just spent ten minutes ironing. 'I was so looking forward to tonight,' she moaned. 'I thought for once I had it all carefully organised: the tickets, the food, the drinks. Everything. And now I've gone and lost the wretched key and no one will be able to get into the hall. What *will* everyone think of me?'

David took a cautious step towards the bed. 'Can't we borrow Brown Owl's key?'

Hilary sniffed dismissively. 'No. She's gone rambling in the Peak District this weekend.' She reached for a tissue and blew her nose. 'I've got exactly one hour to find this key,' she said, determination rising in her voice, 'and find it I will.'

Knowing there was nothing he could say or do, David sat down on the small boudoir chair in the corner of the bedroom, at the same time being careful to move to one side Hilary's jeans. He remembered having seen her wearing them earlier. Wouldn't do any harm to check, he thought. Fumbling furtively so as not to alert Hilary that he had doubted her, he searched all the pockets. To his relief he touched cold metal, but there was something with it, something lacy. 'Hilary,' he said, 'what's this?'

'For goodness' sake, David, don't bother me now,' she replied tersely, rushing past him and heading full tilt for the *en suite* bathroom.

He followed her in and closed the door behind him. 'I've got something for you.' He held up a large key and waved it in front of her.

'David, you wonderful man! Where was it?'

'Your jeans.'

She looked puzzled, at the same time seeming to shrink back to her normal size. 'But I checked the pockets,' she said, 'truly I did.'

'The back pockets?'

She shook her head and reached out for the key. But David snapped his hand away. 'Not so fast.' With his other hand he dangled something red and lacy in front of her. 'What's this, darling?' he said. 'Something you've been hiding from me?'

Flushing as red as the G-string in David's hands, Hilary blurted out, 'It's not mine. I found it at the jumble sale. Derek Rogers wanted it and I wouldn't let him.'

David laughed. 'Well that wasn't very sporting of you, was it?'

'You don't understand.' She was flustered. 'Iris told me to get rid of it and I forgot and somehow it ended up on the table with all the other clothes and I . . .'

David looked at his wife. 'Ah, and there was I thinking you'd got me something special.' He pulled Hilary to him and kissed her, leaving her in no doubt what was in his mind.

'The children,' she said.

'They're watching the telly.'

'We haven't got long . . . Tiffany will be . . .'

He kissed her again. 'I'm claiming my reward for finding the key.'

22

For the third time in five minutes, Charlotte looked at the broken lock on the bathroom door. Jonathan was taking a shower in the guest bathroom, but there was something about the way her brother-in-law had been acting during the day that had seriously unnerved her. In the eight years she had been married to Peter, Jonathan had never once paid her the slightest bit of attention; now suddenly he seemed overly attentive.

Sitting in the bath, she wished fervently that she was one of those glamorous women you see on television who always have froth-filled baths, so that if a surprise guest just happens to drop in only a pair of perfectly tanned shoulders peep seductively above the bubbles. As it was, her own stark, white nakedness was all too apparent in the clear bathwater.

She lay back and tried to relax, wondering how to control the events of an evening that seemed to stretch dauntingly ahead of her. She had finally dared to ask Jonathan – while sitting out in the garden – if he would mind taking her to the fork supper. From the look on his face, at first she thought he was going to turn her down. Then he had smiled and said, 'How quaint. What time?'

Resting one foot on the hot tap, Charlotte considered her objective for the evening: to throw her sister off the scent and to convince Alex she was in no need of his attentions. To this end, she would have to achieve the impossible – to appear thoroughly at ease with Jonathan at the supper and to remain at his side throughout the entire evening. Tonight, she had to be seen as a woman who needed no outside help in re-establishing her life.

She closed her eyes and doused her face with the strawberry-shaped sponge. She shook the water off her face and tried harder to relax. Smiling was supposed to be helpful here. It struck her that it might be a good idea to practise thinking of Jonathan and smiling at the same time – after all, she would have to do plenty of that at the village hall this evening. She parted her lips and grinned inanely. She caught sight of herself at the end of the bath in the reflection of one of the shiny chrome taps. The distorted convex image made her smile more naturally. She covered the tap with her foot and thought how tonight she was going to prove to herself that she could handle not only Jonathan, but all the rest of them who seemed so intent on organising her life. She breathed out deeply, having convinced herself that all would be well.

Then all hell broke loose.

'God dammit, what the bloody hell's been going on here? I leave my room for ten minutes . . .'

Charlotte sat up at the sound of Jonathan's angry voice on the landing. She heard barking followed by a sound that had her springing out of the bath and reaching for a towel. It was Mabel, yelping.

She threw open the bathroom door. There was Jonathan, a towel around his waist, holding up in one hand a mangy-looking tie, and in the other hand Mabel, grasped firmly by the scruff of her neck, eyes bulging, teeth bared.

Charlotte acted without thinking. She kicked Jonathan in the shin, twice, and then she reached out for the little dog. Hugging the whimpering animal to her, she pushed past Jonathan and slammed her bedroom door shut. Only then, as she sat down on the bed to look at Mabel, did she realise that her towel had gone.

'Now remember, Neville, avoid all the dishes with mayonnaise.'

'Yes dear.'

'Did you remember to lock the back door?'

'Yes.'

'I hope Malcolm doesn't make a long speech like he did last year. I seem to remember hearing your stomach rumbling throughout most of it. Just look at that.' Her hands full of quiches, Louise nodded towards David's Volvo. 'You'd think they'd have walked, wouldn't you? Did I tell you that Hilary said Charlotte would be coming tonight? Apparently she's bringing a friend. I wonder who. I mean, she doesn't really know anyone here, does she? Neville, are you listening to me?'

'What?'

'Oh never mind. But remember what I said about the mayonnaise.'

'Mrs Parker, the music is far too loud, turn it down. If I've told you once, I've told you a hundred times, my shattered nerves just won't take that kind of volume.'

'But I don't know how to, Mrs Braithwaite. There are so many switches and dials.'

'Well, don't just stand there in the way. Let me through.'

Easing herself out of the small boxed-in area that contained Malcolm Jackson's state-of-the-art CD player and amplifier, Hilary escaped to the safety of the kitchen at the back of the hall. Within seconds the sound of Mantovani – Iris's own personal choice – was blaring through the hall. Then there was nothing, just an awkward silence, leaving people stuck mid-air in unfinished sentences.

'Mrs Braithwaite, allow me,' said a worried Malcolm Jackson moving swiftly across the wooden floor to ensure that no further harm came to his most prized possession. 'This knob here, the one marked volume, you have to make sure that the needles are both synchronised, that way you avoid overloading the . . .'

'Quite so, I'm sure, Vicar. But I can't stand around here all evening discussing synchronised needles. I have work to do in the kitchen.'

Malcolm sighed with relief and moved off to greet more of his parishioners at the door. 'Ah, Louise and Neville, good to see you.'

'Hello Malcolm,' Louise said. 'Excuse me if I don't hang around. I must get these quiches on the tables.'

'Evening Malcolm,' Neville said as the two men shook hands. 'Anything I can do?'

'That's kind, but I think everything's under control now. Between your daughter and Mrs Braithwaite, we all seem to be more or less whipped into shape.'

'That's our Hilary for you.' Neville moved off to get himself a drink. He could see his son-in-law behind the drinks table, acting as barman. He joined the queue. 'Need any help?' he called out above the rumblings of conversation ahead of him.

'No thanks,' David called back. 'I think I can manage.'

Eventually it was Neville's turn.

'What can I get you? I've got red wine, white wine, some dreadful non-alcohol stuff, lager, beer, orange juice, Seven-Up, or mineral water?'

'I'll have some red wine, please. Are you sure I can't help you?'

David smiled. 'No, that's all right. You go off and enjoy yourself.'

Seeing the queue of people waiting behind him to be served, Neville paid for his drink and wandered away. He stood beneath a curling photograph of the Queen and tried hard not to allow his sense of isolation overwhelm him. He was no good in a large gathering such as this, unable to march in step with the rest of the parade. He looked at his watch and wondered where Charlotte was.

Alex and his guest entered the hall and were greeted by Malcolm Jackson. 'Ah, I see you've brought some liquid refreshment. Put it on the table at the back there where David Parker looks like he's being mobbed.'

Pushing through the crowd of villagers, most of whom he had never seen before, Alex guided his guest through to the bar. 'David,' he said, 'these bottles any use to you?'

'Hello Alex. Yes, they'll do nicely, thanks.' David took the two bottles of white wine from Alex and added them to his stockpile. 'Hilary mentioned you might be coming,' he said. 'And with a friend.'

David's eager eyes rested predictably on his guest's face, so Alex made the necessary introductions. 'David, this is Heather; Heather, this is David, one of my neighbours and my landlady's brother-in-law.'

'You're not from around here, are you?' David said. 'I'm sure I would have remembered you if I'd seen you before.'

Alex smiled to himself at this hackneyed line which David had delivered with true conviction. For indisputably it was true. With her young, willowy figure, powder-blue eyes and curly blonde hair, Heather fitted neatly into that category of female that was all things to most men. He had met her only a few days ago in Knutsford, where she worked as a receptionist at the company which had approached him earlier in the week about some consultancy work. While handing in his visitor's badge on his way out of the building he'd asked her out for lunch. They had eaten in a crowded wine bar in King Street and he had let her do most of the talking, while he sat and questioned his motives for being there at all. He had never once used a girl before and yet here he was doing exactly that. And all because of Charlotte.

When he had told Charlotte he would be taking a friend to the fork supper he had said it as a knee-jerk reaction to her sudden change in mood towards him. That evening, though, he had regretted his words. But following their conversation in the garden with Barry later that week when he had seen how relaxed she was in somebody else's company, the thought had occurred to him that if he backed off she might feel more comfortable in his presence. He had reasoned that if he was to take someone else to the supper, there was a chance he would still be able to enjoy Charlotte's company without causing her to feel threatened in any way. The one question in all of this he hadn't asked himself was why he was prepared to go to such lengths to be with Charlotte.

By the end of the meal his plan was fixed. 'A fork supper,' Heather had repeated. 'I've never been to one of those. What should I wear?'

'Casual,' he had answered, feeling almost sorry for her. A nightclub in Manchester was probably more what she was used to.

'What can I get you?' David asked Heather.

'I'd love a 20-20.'

'Ah,' David said, looking at his supply of bottles. He didn't have a clue what he'd just been asked for. 'Try again.'

'Malibu and Coke?'

'How about a glass of white wine?'

'And a beer for me please.' Alex looked around him. So this was a village hall fork supper. He'd never been to such an event before. It was busier than he had imagined it would be, with people appearing to enjoy themselves – more than he thought might be the case. He tried to pick out a few familiar faces. There was Hilary over by the kitchen hatch looking flushed and agitated; Louise Archer chatting to a middle-aged woman whom he didn't know; Ted the Toup being told in no uncertain terms by Iris Braithwaite not to smoke and Neville Archer standing on his own looking up at a gaudy photograph of the Queen. 'Come on,' Alex said, taking their drinks from David and leading Heather by the arm. 'Let me introduce you to my landlady's father.'

They inched their way through the crowd. 'Hello Neville.'

He swung round. 'Good to see you again, Alex.'

'This is Heather.' Alex hesitated before adding, 'A friend.' They shook hands. 'No sign of Charlotte, then?' Alex said lightly, looking up at the Queen.

'No. And to be honest, I could do with her here. I'm not much good in these situations. Never know what to say to people. I find it difficult to make small talk with those I've seen without their clothes on.'

Alex laughed. Seeing the look of surprise on Heather's face, he said, 'Neville's a doctor.'

'*Was* a doctor,' Neville corrected him. 'Now I'm just a . . .'

'Just a what?' It was Louise, with a handful of peanuts.

'Nothing, dear,' Neville said, looking longingly at the nuts.

Louise turned to Alex. 'How are you, Alex? I hear you've taken up gardening.'

'Are you ready, Jonathan? It's time we were going.'

The question, called through the guest-room door, sounded ludicrous. But Charlotte could think of nothing else to say to this man for whom she cared so little and whom she had just physically assaulted, not to mention cavorted naked in front of.

The door opened and she offered a smile. 'Look, Jonathan . . .' she started to say.

'Thirty-six pounds, that tie,' he said.

She breathed in deeply. 'I can write you out a cheque if you like, or perhaps you would prefer cash?'

He ignored her and turned back into the bedroom.

He reached for the jacket which completed his dark navy Yves Saint Laurent suit. He looked at himself in the full-length wardrobe mirror before stooping to pick up a towel from the floor. He handed it to her. 'Yours, I believe?'

She coloured and took it from him. 'Thank you.'

His garment bag lay packed on top of the bed. He picked it up. 'A hotel for the night is the best thing.'

'No,' she said, 'don't do that.'

He looked at her closely.

'There's no need, Jonathan,' she said, and biting back every instinct within her, she added, 'I'm sorry, I shouldn't have kicked you like that. I don't know what came over me.'

He continued to stare at her in silence, as though assessing her, and then suddenly his face broke into that familiar weasel-like smile. With a patronising shake of his head he said, 'God, Charlotte, you're going to need a man in your life again, and soon.'

She didn't trust herself to say anything to this preposterous remark, so she turned away and moved towards the stairs. 'We'd better go,' she said. And with each step she took, she prayed, Please God, just get me through this evening.

It was still light as they walked the short distance to the village hall, Jonathan being careful just where he placed his expensive shoes. They were silent until they had almost reached the hall, when Charlotte, conscious that Jonathan looked dressed more for dinner at the Ritz than a village beanfeast, said, 'You'll find it all terribly simple, Jonathan, not at all what you're used to.'

He said nothing.

She laughed brightly and slipped her arm through his. He looked taken aback. Her public performance had begun.

Inside the hall, Charlotte saw Alex straight away, and knew too that he had seen her. Automatically she smiled up at Jonathan. 'Come on,' she said, 'I need to ... I mean ... I want to introduce you to someone.'

For a moment, the two couples stood facing each other, like four advancing pawns on a chess board. 'Hello Charlotte,' Alex said. She nodded back at him and placed her hand on Jonathan's arm. 'I'd like you to meet Jonathan. He's stopping the weekend with me.' Was it her imagination, or did she detect a slight lift of the eyebrow?

'Hello,' Alex said, taking in the contrast between his own jeans and plaid shirt and the immaculate suit in front of him.

'And you are?' Jonathan enquired.

Alex couldn't help himself. 'Alex Hamilton. I live with Charlotte.' He felt Heather stiffen at his side, saw the horrified expression on Charlotte's face, but most of all, the look of surprise on her companion's.

Charlotte laughed, a little too loudly. 'What Mr Hamilton is trying to say is that he's my temporary tenant in the granny annexe.' She emphasised the word 'temporary' and threw Alex a wait-till-I-get-you-home look.

'But you can't be his landlady?'

Charlotte looked at Heather, twenty-two at the most, she reckoned, and with a waist to match. 'Why ever not?' she asked.

Heather looked at Alex accusingly. 'You told me your landlady was bad-tempered and rude. I was expecting someone much older.'

Alex felt Charlotte's eyes blazing at him. He laughed awkwardly. 'No, no, that was Iris Braithwaite I was describing.'

'So,' said Jonathan, obviously bored with the conversation, 'what are you in?'

That did it. Now Alex knew for certain that he didn't like this so-called friend of Charlotte's. 'The village hall actually,' he replied. 'Can I get you and Charlotte a drink?' Alex noticed Charlotte biting her lower lip. Was that a slight smile she was trying to hold back?

'I'll get them,' Charlotte said. 'White wine do you?'

'A well-chilled Chardonnay would be out of the question, I suppose?'

Alex tried not to laugh and followed quickly behind Charlotte as she moved off to the bar. 'I'll give you a hand,' he said.

'There's no need,' she hissed back at him. 'I can manage.'

'Of course you can,' Alex said, as they joined the queue. 'I know that. Who's your friend?'

She smiled. 'Oh, we go way back.'

Alex pushed his hands into his pockets. 'Nice suit he's got on.'

'And what's that supposed to mean?'

'Nothing, nothing at all,' he said innocently. 'Nice suit in the right place, that is.'

'As a matter of fact he's just flown in from Hong Kong and that's all he had with him.'

'Oh,' Alex said, nodding his head in an exaggerated fashion, 'that explains it.'

'So what time do you have to get your little friend home?'

'*Touché.*'

They took the glasses of wine back to where they had been standing, only to find that both Jonathan and Heather had disappeared. 'Ah well,' Alex said, 'that just leaves you and me.'

'So it does.' Charlotte looked anxiously round the hall for Jonathan.

'And what was all that about me being a temporary tenant?' Alex said.

'Well, you are. You'll be wanting to buy your own house soon, won't you?'

Alex frowned. That of course had been the original plan, but now he wasn't so sure.

'And how dare you describe me as being bad-tempered.'

'And rude,' he added helpfully.

'I've a good mind to evict you.'

'Hello you two.' It was Hilary. 'Having a good time? Don't tell me your dates have stood you up, then?'

Charlotte glared at her sister.

'We seem to have lost them,' Alex said. 'They're here somewhere.'

'What do they look like? I might have seen them.'

'His,' Charlotte said, 'looks as though she ought to be home in bed by now.'

'And hers looks like he's lost his briefcase.'

'Oh well,' Hilary said brightly, not really listening, 'I'm sure they'll pop up. We're just about to serve the food, but whatever you do, don't touch Iris's lentil dip. I was on the loo for days after it last year. Oh look, Derek and Cindy at last.'

Following behind Cindy was Derek, pushing an ostentatious hostess trolley. 'Coming through,' Derek yelled, scattering people in his wake as he steered the trolley at full speed through the crowded hall.

'I'd better go and see what they've brought,' Hilary said. 'It looks a lot, whatever it is.'

Left alone again, Alex said, 'Your father was looking for you earlier. He's a nice man. I like him.'

Charlotte smiled. 'I'm still going to evict you though.'

'Come on, let's get some food. I'm starving. You can serve me notice while I'm eating.'

'I think, everybody,' Malcolm Jackson shouted, turning the music down, at the same time halting the raised cutlery over the bowls of rice salads and quiches, 'that we should now take this opportunity to bow our heads and give thanks . . .'

From nowhere, a loud scream filled the obediently drawn silence. Alex saw Hilary slump against Louise, who in turn gasped loudly. Wide-eyed and staring, both women looked as though they had been turned to stone. He followed their gaze and found himself looking at Charlotte's friend Jonathan, standing next to Heather.

'Damn!'

He turned to Charlotte at his side.

'Damn,' she said again.

'For goodness' sake Charlotte, why on earth didn't you tell us?'

'Yes, Mother's right, why didn't you?' Hilary said, as they stood in the hall kitchen. 'He's family, after all.'

Charlotte bristled. 'No, he's not. None of you know him, and anyway, you wouldn't want to know him, he's a pig.'

'Charlotte!' Hilary remonstrated with predictable horror. 'He's Peter's brother.'

Charlotte pursed her lips.

'Well,' said Neville, feeling he ought to contribute to the conversation in some way. 'He's certainly the spitting image of Peter, isn't he?'

Hilary shook her head. 'I couldn't believe it when I saw him. I was so convinced it was Peter . . . a ghost . . .' Her voice trailed away. 'I feel a bit of a fool now.'

'Seeing as we've all recovered from the shock,' said Louise, 'I suggest we all go out there and at least introduce ourselves to Peter's brother.' She threw Charlotte one more reproving look and led the way, followed by Hilary, then Neville and finally Charlotte, who dragged disconsolately behind. Her plan had misfired because she had failed to take into account the simple fact that anyone who had known Peter would be struck by Jonathan's likeness. But she hadn't thought that anyone would go so far as to think he was Peter's ghost. Silly Hilary. And how typical of her to jump to such a ridiculous conclusion.

She chewed unhappily on her lower lip, knowing she had made rather an idiot of herself. How on earth had she thought she could get away with such a half-baked scheme? Convincing Alex that Jonathan was an old flame from way back was one thing, but thinking she could fool her family was another.

In the main part of the hall the other party-goers seemed to have forgotten about the commotion. Frank Sinatra had replaced Mantovani and the general ambience indicated that everyone was having a jolly good time.

'Suddenly I don't feel hungry,' Charlotte said despondently to her father.

'Come on, you'd better try something. Tell me which dishes have got mayonnaise in them. I want to try them all.'

Over at the bar, David was pouring out a glass of wine for Derek.

'You mean Charlotte's husband looked just like that jerk in the suit?'

David tried not to smile as he handed Derek his drink. 'Pretty much like him. But how about the blonde piece? She came with Alex, but seems to have abandoned him now.'

Derek laughed. He looked about the hall, trying to track down Alex. He found him eventually, balancing a plate of rice and an empty glass in one hand and a fork in the other, listening attentively to Iris Braithwaite. 'Looks like our Alex prefers older birds,' Derek said. He took a gulp of his wine. 'That's disgusting,' he shuddered, 'like gnat's pee. What the hell is it?'

David looked at the bottle. 'I'm sorry. I've given you the non-alcoholic wine by mistake. Iris Braithwaite insisted we have some, says alcohol is the way to hell.'

'Well, don't just stand there, give me a one-way ticket,' he said. 'No, on second thoughts, make that two tickets to hell.' And taking the glasses from David, he sauntered in the direction of Alex and Iris Braithwaite.

'Evening, Mrs Braithwaite,' he said sidling up to her. He nodded to Alex. 'Thought you'd like a drink.' He handed her a glass. 'I must say, this non-alcoholic wine is very good. I could become quite an addict.'

Alex looked at Derek, wondering if he'd heard right.

'I'm pleased to hear that,' Iris said. 'Alcohol is the way to—'

'Hell,' Derek finished for her. 'That's so true, Mrs Braithwaite.'

Again, Alex wondered if he'd heard correctly. 'Well, if you'll excuse me, I'll just go and help myself to some more food.'

'Try some of my lentil dip. There's lots left,' Iris said after him. She raised her glass and drank from it. She winced, drawing in her lips like a cat's bottom.

'Quite dry, isn't it?' Derek said smiling. 'It's an acquired taste.'

Helping himself to a slice of spinach quiche, Alex found himself standing next to Cindy. 'Hello,' he said. 'I've just left Derek extolling the merits of alcohol-free wine to Iris Braithwaite.'

She looked at him as though he were mad. 'I doubt that somehow.'

'I should go easy on that lentil dip,' he said. 'Hilary told me earlier it has rather a lethal effect the next day. How's Barry?'

'Barry? He's fine, why?'

'I was thinking about his exams. He seems a bright lad, he should do well. I expect you'll miss him when he goes off to university?'

Cindy picked up a stuffed tomato which she added to her sparsely filled plate. 'I suppose I will. Though to be honest with you, even when he's at home, we hardly ever see him. Just shuts himself away in his room mostly.'

Moving away from the tables of food, they located a couple of chairs and sat down. Over on the other side of the hall, Alex could see Derek at the bar again. He watched with interest as Derek carried two full glasses of wine in Mrs Braithwaite's direction. He turned back to face Cindy and was surprised to see her with her hand over her mouth. Her eyes were watering. 'Lentil dip?' he asked.

At about half past ten, when Charlotte was helping her sister to make sixty-two cups of coffee, she realised that something was wrong. Iris Braithwaite had a distinct pink edge to her. An election-winning Margaret Thatcher sprang to mind as Charlotte watched Iris bobbing about the hall, talking animatedly to everyone as though they had just returned her to high office. Even her handbag was swinging from her arm *à la* Maggie. Charlotte decided to go and investigate.

Armed with a cup of coffee, she caught up with Iris as she laid a hand on Alex's shoulder. 'Mrs Braithwaite, cup of coffee?'

Iris spun round at the sound of Charlotte's voice. 'Certainly not,' she announced. 'I want some more of that delicious alcohol-free wine that nice Mr Rogers has been giving me. Kindly fetch me some while I talk to your lovely young man.'

Charlotte took a discreet sniff at Iris's powdered face. She looked at Alex and mouthed the incongruous words, 'I think she's drunk.'

Alex thought fast. 'There's none left, Mrs Braithwaite,' he said.

'What!' shrieked Iris, causing those around to look at them. Alex and Charlotte moved closer to Iris, trying to shield her from view.

But Iris was having none of it. 'I want a drink,' she said like a determined four-year-old. 'Where's Mr Rogers?' And turning away from them, she hurried off to look for Derek. Charlotte and Alex saw her track him down by Malcolm Jackson's hi-fi, sorting through the selection of CDs and cassettes. He seemed alarmed at her approaching figure and quickly moved away.

'Oh, oh, you naughty man,' giggled Iris, increasing her step. 'Running away from me, are you?'

Derek looked genuinely horrified and sped off. Then disaster struck. Iris, in her haste to catch up with Derek, tripped over an electricity cable running from the hi-fi to the main power socket. She reached out to hold on to something secure, only to plunge the hall into complete darkness by pulling the fuse box off the wall.

Amongst the general crashing about that followed – the screams of mock horror, the giggling, the sonorous tones of the vicar requesting everyone to remain calm and one ridiculous voice calling out 'Let there be light' – there was one very loud crash, accompanied by an even louder cry and an expression that was quite out of place at a church fund-raising event.

Neville, who had been hiding out in the kitchen at the time of the black-out, managed to find a box of candles and some matches on a shelf above the coffee urn. It wasn't long before a procession of candle bearers, somewhat akin to acolytes, miraculously emerged from the kitchen and streamed out into the main body of the hall. And a voice, presumably the same one that had said 'Let there be light', called out, 'And then there was light.'

The air of wreckage everywhere was surprising. Chairs had been knocked over, along with one of the tables that had been heavily laden with rice salads. In the flickering candlelight, the floor looked as though it was covered with a thousand stunned maggots. A ripped curtain, complete with track, lay in a bedraggled heap on the floor.

'I think I've broken something!' came a cry from the semi-darkness. Recognising her husband's voice, Cindy carefully made her way over to Derek, lying sprawled out on his side. She bent towards him, then stood up again. 'What's that all over your back, Derek?'

'I think it's dog crap!' he shouted, wincing with pain. 'I bloody well slipped on it.'

Somebody laughed. 'I think you'll find that's Mrs Braithwaite's lentil dip.'

23

'Start spreading the news, I'm leaving today . . .'

'Please, Mrs Braithwaite, be quiet, someone will hear you,' Charlotte pleaded with the older woman who was held firmly between Alex and herself as they slowly made their way, in the dark, from the village hall towards Acacia Lane.

But Iris was not to be put off. ' . . . I want to be a part of it, New York, New York . . .'

'Come on, Mrs Braithwaite,' coaxed Alex, 'we're taking you home.'

Iris beamed back at him, and then kissing him on the cheek continued with ' . . . These vagabond shoes are longing to stray right through the very heart of it, New York, New York . . .'

Charlotte started to laugh. Iris at that moment slipped away from Charlotte's grip and swung round to face Alex, and staring him in the eye she sang at him, her deep contralto voice wobbling just slightly off key, her pronunciation, though, surprisingly clear for one so drunk, ' . . . I want to wake up in a city that doesn't sleep and find I'm king of the hill, top of the heap . . .' And in a moment of inspiration, Alex threw his arms round Iris and started to tango with her, skilfully edging her towards The White Cottage.

Charlotte followed behind as best she could. Tears were rolling down her cheeks, she was helpless with laughter. 'I don't think I can take much more of this,' she groaned, bent double and with her legs crossed. 'I think I'm going to wet myself.'

'Well, before you do, see if you can find her key,' Alex called over his shoulder as they approached Iris's gate. 'It's probably in her handbag.'

Charlotte reached forward but Iris pushed open the gate and, dragging Alex behind her as though *she* were leading the way home, she marched him up the path. She rummaged in her handbag and pulled out her door key. She snapped the bag shut and promptly pushed the key through the letter box. She turned and looked at them both, her eyes wide with surprise. 'The keyhole's grown,' she said, and rocking from side to side as if on a tilting ship, she sang out, ' . . . I'll make a brand new start of it in old New York and if I can make it there I can make it anywhere . . .'

'Now what do we do?' Charlotte said. 'Break a window?'

'Certainly not, Mrs Lawrence,' said Iris sharply, breaking off from her singing, 'not when there's a perfectly good key hidden in the back garden.'

'Come on,' Alex said 'let's go a-hunting.'

Iris was off again. 'A-hunting we shall go, a-hunting we shall go . . .' she sang as she led the way, almost breaking into a jaunty little skip as she cornered the house.

'Mind my pelargoniums, Mr Hamilton, I believe you're perry close to them, I mean, peril, peril, perilously close to them. Who's that hiding in the dark?'

'It's me, Mrs Braithwaite, Charlotte Lawrence.'

'Well, what on earth are you doing in my herb garden at this time of night?

'Mrs Braithwaite,' Alex interceded patiently, 'can you find the key?'

'Well of course I can, young man, but you'll have to close your eyes while I get it, and you, Mrs Lawrence, you too.'

Amazingly Iris not only found the key, but managed to insert it into the lock and open the back door. They stepped into the kitchen, Alex fumbling blindly for a light switch. He found it at last and steered Iris towards the hall. Charlotte said, 'I'll get her up to bed, you make her some coffee.'

'I'd better find her a bucket, or something,' Alex said. 'She's likely to be as sick as a dog at some stage in the night.'

'Did somebody mention my dog? Where is Henry?'

Alex and Charlotte looked at each other. It was a good question. Where was Iris's spaniel? Surely he should have barked the house down by now with all the din they had just been making outside in the garden.

'Come on, Henry,' Iris cooed, 'come to Mummy.'

'Get her upstairs,' Alex said. 'I'll look for him.'

'Let's look upstairs for Henry, shall we, Mrs Braithwaite?' Charlotte said, taking her by the hand. 'I expect he's waiting for you up there.'

Iris looked pleased. 'Henry,' she called out with each stumbling step, 'Henry, Mummy's coming.'

Alex found Henry in the sitting-room, curled up in his basket. He knew straight away that the dog wasn't asleep. He was dead.

'Oh my darling Henry,' wailed Iris. 'He was my only real friend, the only one who truly loved me . . . even Sidney didn't really love me. Poor little Henry, he was only eleven years old, he should have lived until he was at least fourteen. Why has he died?' Her grief was enormous, she was inconsolable.

'I wish Henry hadn't chosen tonight to snuff it,' Charlotte whispered downstairs in the kitchen, when they had at last got Iris off to bed. 'For just a few moments Iris seemed . . . well, sort of happier than I've ever seen her. It seems like a particularly cheap and nasty trick on God's part, don't you think?'

Alex shook his head. 'I'll dig a hole in the garden tomorrow for him. I suppose that's what she'll want.'

'Alex?' Charlotte suddenly said. 'Why are we here?'

'What, you mean planet earth and all that?'

'No. I mean, why did *we* get Iris out of the village hall and bring her home?'

'You mean why didn't we just abandon her to the public humiliation that everyone thinks she probably deserves?'

'Yes, that exactly.'

'Because we're nice people, I suppose.'

'Are we?'

Alex laughed. 'Charlotte, I'm too tired for this, go home. I'll stay on here in case Mrs Braithwaite is ill in the night.'

Charlotte looked hard at Alex. 'What is it with you and vomiting women?' she said. 'Anyway, shouldn't you go and see what's happened to your little bit of moorland Heather?'

He laughed again. 'I don't think I'll bother. I expect she's being well looked after by your ... by Jonathan ... do you mind?'

Charlotte shook her head. 'No.' She decided to come clean. 'I guess you got the gist of all that fuss earlier in the evening, didn't you?'

'That Jonathan is Peter's brother? Yes, I did. Does he look very much like Peter?'

'The first time I met him, I thought he was Peter.'

'But that must be so ...' he paused, making sure he used the right word, 'difficult for you.' He knew from experience how painful it was to be physically reminded of someone you'd loved and lost.

Charlotte picked up the mugs on the green Formica-topped table and carried them to the sink. 'I didn't think it would be, but you're right. It was quite a shock seeing him coming up the drive this morning.' She rinsed the mugs out, and then turning round, she found Alex standing behind her. Only that afternoon, Jonathan had been standing behind her in much the same way, and only a couple of weeks ago, so had Derek.

She looked up into Alex's face. Blue eyes. She hadn't noticed their colour before, nor that there was a small white scar just below his left eyebrow. His lips were parted and she felt he was about to say something. Her heart began to beat faster.

'Charlotte—'

'No, please don't say anything.' And with the slightest of movements she leaned towards him, knowing what it would mean, knowing also it was what she wanted. He reached out to her and the touch of his fingers against her cheek made her turn and kiss his hand. He kissed her and she held him tightly, frightened he might stop, thinking only how much she wanted him.

But from upstairs came an unmistakable sound.

'Another time perhaps,' Alex said calmly, looking into her eyes and tracing the outline of her cheek with his hand.

Charlotte swayed slightly. She felt anything but calm. She swallowed back her disappointment and followed Alex out of the kitchen.

*

It was three o'clock in the morning when they finally settled Iris Braithwaite. They collapsed on the sofa in the sitting-room – Henry and his basket having been moved to the dining-room as his makeshift chapel of rest.

Charlotte said, 'You know, I don't understand how all this happened. How on earth did Iris end up drunk? She never drinks alcohol.'

'I think you'll find that Derek had a lot to do with it,' Alex said, yawning and putting his arm around Charlotte.

She kicked off her shoes, tucked her feet under her and snuggled up to him. 'How stupid I've been. Of course, that's what Iris said, didn't she? She wanted some more of that lovely non-alcoholic wine Mr Rogers had been giving her. Poor Iris. She's lost her dignity, her reputation and her little Henry all in one night.'

She looked up at Alex. His eyes were closed. She didn't know whether she was feeling lightheaded from being so tired or was still reeling from the shock of what she had instigated in the kitchen, but she was aware of an added frisson of pleasure and expectancy running through her. 'Alex?'

'Yes.'

'What would have happened in the kitchen, if Iris hadn't . . . ?'

He opened his eyes. 'You mean, would I have made love to you there and then on the kitchen table?'

'I didn't mean . . . well yes, okay then, is that what you would have done?'

'No, Charlotte. I wouldn't have made love to you.'

She sat up straight. 'Why?' She felt affronted. 'Why not?' she repeated.

'Come on, Charlotte, it's late. Can't we talk about this tomorrow?'

'No. I want an answer. Would you now, for instance?'

He looked at her, confused. 'Am I dreaming this conversation, or have I missed a huge chunk of it?'

She moved away from him and went and sat in one of the armchairs. 'It seems Iris is not the only one to have made a fool of herself tonight.'

24

Derek lay awake in the strange bed. The injection he'd been given had wiped out the excruciating pain, but not his anger and the humiliation he had felt lying on the village hall floor. He shuddered at the memory of all that revolting muck he had lain in – nobody was ever going to convince him that it was something edible he had slipped on. Thank God there had been a 'doctor in the house'. Neville Archer had never struck him as a particularly competent man before, but he had certainly shown his mettle, clearing away all those gawping onlookers and sending someone off to call for an ambulance.

A broken leg was his reward for showing up at the village hall jamboree, but that wasn't all – that fool of an ambulance man had ripped his trousers! Eighty quid those trousers had cost him last month. Fine bloody evening it had turned out to be and not even a moment of it spent with Charlotte. And where was she when he was lying on the floor in agony? Bloody scarpered with that Alex, that's where. He'd seen them leaving together.

And now here he was alone, three-thirty in the morning and surrounded by stale bodies in striped flannelette. Thank heavens he'd had the presence of mind to make Cindy pick up a pair of decent boxer shorts on the way to the hospital. He eased himself upright and craned his neck forward to see if any of the nurses were about. Ah yes. There she was, sitting at her illuminated desk, the pretty young blonde one, Nurse Wilkins, who earlier had helped him into bed. She was bent over a book with her hands around a mug in front of her.

Derek pressed the green button just above his plastic jug of water. 'Nurse,' he called out. Hurried squeaking steps sounded out across the thick linoleum floor.

'Yes, Mr Rogers, what is it?'

'Hello,' he said brightly, as though she were a wine bar waitress coming to take his order.

'Ssh . . . you'll wake the others. Now what's the matter?' Though young and recently qualified, Nurse Wilkins was already astute enough to know what her newest patient was up to.

'Come and sit here,' Derek said, patting the side of his bed, 'and I'll tell you.'

Nurse Wilkins smiled and turned to go, but Derek let out a loud groan, which had her instantly bending over him, giving him a closer inspection.

'That's better,' he said. 'Come and talk to me, I'm lonely.'

'It's very late, Mr Rogers, you should get some sleep.'

A smile spread across Derek's face. 'I can't. I'm not used to sleeping on my own.'

'Somehow that doesn't surprise me,' Nurse Wilkins said, contemplating her healthy-looking patient, with his bare tanned chest and roving eyes.

'So, now that I've thoroughly captivated you, tell me your name. Mine's Derek.'

'It's Rosemary and I really should be getting back to my desk now.'

Satisfied that he had made a sufficient enough impression, Derek said, 'I'll see you in the morning, then, before I'm wheeled away to meet my fate on the operating table.'

'Sorry. Tomorrow you'll be in the capable hands of Nurse Baker. You'll like Nurse Baker.'

'I will?'

'Nurse Baker's very nice, very accommodating. Goodnight.'

'Goodnight Rosemary.' At last Derek was beginning to feel the onset of sleep as the lingering humiliation he had experienced earlier began to fade.

'I tell you I'm right,' Hilary said. It was ten minutes past eight the next morning and she was looking out of the bedroom window across the road towards Ivy Cottage. 'Charlotte didn't go home last night, none of the curtains have been drawn and that Mercedes has gone as well.'

'What?' David said, peering out from beneath the corner of the frilled duvet cover, which had wrapped itself around his head making him look as though he was wearing a baby's bonnet.

Hilary appeared from behind the curtain. 'Come on, David, it's perfectly obvious what happened.'

David tried hard to think. It was Sunday morning, the one day of the week when he was sure of a lie-in; most Saturdays he was in the office persuading people to buy their dream house – nightmares, more like it, as some of them discovered. Nightmares, that rang a bell. Yes, last night, chaos down at the village hall. He turned over, pushed his head under the pillow and thought about Derek Rogers lying there on the floor. While Neville had been sorting Derek out, he had made himself scarce and hidden in the kitchen so that no one would see him laughing.

It had been a funny old night, one way and another. That business with Charlotte and Peter's brother had triggered events. Fancy Charlotte not telling any of them Jonathan was coming. On the other hand he was a complete jerk – bit like Peter really – maybe that was why she had kept him quiet.

He certainly had a condescending way with him, David thought. 'Real estate,' Jonathan had said, shaking his head dismissively, when David had introduced himself after the furore of Peter's 'resurrection' had calmed down. 'What's your turnover?' he had gone on to ask. Mind your own business, David had wanted to tell him, but instead he had plucked an astronomical figure out of the air and then quadrupled it. Even that had been pushed aside as Jonathan went on to explain in detail why, in general, the British made such lousy businessmen. 'No balls,' seemed to be the long and short of it.

Finally he had been rescued by Neville appearing at his side, and he had escaped to man the bar once more. Then later on he had hardly been able to believe his eyes as he watched Old Ma Braithwaite chase Derek round the hall, until they were all plunged into complete darkness, only to discover, when some candles had been found, Derek lying on the floor clutching his leg.

As though picking up on his thoughts, Hilary said, 'Funny that when the ambulance came there was no sign of Charlotte or Alex. That's why I'm so sure—'

'You can't be sure of anything, Hilary,' David said grumpily from beneath the pillow, 'but wherever Charlotte is, I hope she's getting more sleep than I am.'

Giving up on David, Hilary got dressed and went downstairs, to find Philip and Becky in their pyjamas at opposite ends of the sofa, imbibing their weekend diet of brain-wasting pre-breakfast television. 'How long have you been down here?' she asked.

'Only ten minutes,' Philip said, never taking his eyes off the screen.

Becky unplugged her thumb from her mouth. 'We've seen *Sonic the Hedgehog, Disney Club* and *Scooby-Doo.*'

'That's an awful lot just in ten minutes.'

Philip scowled at his sister. 'Bigmouth,' he said. 'When's breakfast, Mum?'

'When you're both dressed you can get your own. I'm popping over the road to see Auntie Charlotte. I'll be back in a moment and then it won't be long before we're due at church.'

'Ooh, can I come?' Becky asked, bouncing off the sofa. 'I want to see her little dog. She didn't bring it when she came to babysit.'

'No,' Hilary said. She wanted to go and snoop about in private, to prove to herself that she was right and that Charlotte had spent the night with Alex. But then a thought struck her. Supposing her sister was there after all? If she took Becky with her at least she had a perfect excuse for calling so early – to see if Charlotte would let Becky play with Mabel. She smiled at her daughter. 'All right then, but hurry up and get yourself dressed. I'll wait for you in the kitchen.'

As they crossed the road, Becky ran on ahead to ring the door bell. To her dismay she found she was too small to reach the button. While she waited for her mother to come up the drive she pushed open the brass letter box and peered inside. Mabel came yapping towards her. Becky poked a small finger in, then seeing that Mabel could jump quite high, she withdrew it quickly with a high-pitched squeal.

Hilary pressed the door bell, which in turn brought on a further burst of yapping. Hilary looked pleased. Here of course was her excuse – she had been worried about Charlotte's dog, she had heard it barking.

'Do you think Auntie Charlotte's still in bed, Mummy?'

'Quite likely,' she said and brought out a bunch of keys from her pocket.

'Will one of our keys work in Auntie Charlotte's keyhole?'

'Ssh,' Hilary said, turning the key in the lock, suddenly realising that if her sister was with Alex, they were, after all, only next door. 'No,' she whispered in answer to Becky's question. 'This is an Ivy Cottage key.'

'Did she give it to you?'

'Yes,' lied Hilary. She knew her sister would never get around to giving her a spare key, so she had taken the precaution of having an extra key cut, just in case ... just in case of an emergency such as rescuing a small dog, she thought, absolving herself of any accusation Charlotte might throw at her.

'Shouldn't we come back later if she's still in bed, Mummy?'

'Just be quiet, Becky.'

Hilary pushed against the door and was immediately confronted with Mabel dancing excitedly around her feet. 'You play with Mabel while I nip up and see Auntie Charlotte.'

She went slowly up the stairs, calling Charlotte's name quietly as she went, then crept along the landing, checking the bedrooms. All were empty. With a smile on her face she went back down the stairs. As she reached the bottom step she heard Becky say, 'Oh, you naughty little dog. Look at all the puddles and splatter-pies you've made.'

Hilary grimaced at the scene in the kitchen. She stepped cautiously across the floor as though tiptoeing through a minefield. She made it to the back door and let in some much needed fresh air, then opened the cupboard under the sink where only a couple of weeks ago she had put a selection of cleaning fluids.

'Let me help you, Mummy,' said Becky, bored with Mabel and liking the look of one of the aerosol cleaners. She made a grab for it.

'Watch where you put your feet!' shouted Hilary. But it was too late. Becky skidded on a wet patch, sending her legs in different directions, until she lost her balance altogether and ended up sitting down with a bump in one of Mabel's puddles. She started to wail.

Sensing some excitement after a night on her own, Mabel pattered across the floor and climbed on top of Becky.

'Get away,' Becky squealed, 'get away from me, it's all your fault.'

Mistaking Becky's pushing for playfulness, Mabel sank her teeth into the sleeve of Becky's sweatshirt and with her tail waving in the air like a high-speed windscreen wiper, she started to pull, shaking her head from side to side and giving off an occasional growl. Becky pulled sharply in the opposite direction and tipped backwards with Mabel still attached. Hilary made a desperate attempt to prevent her daughter's fall but she wasn't fast enough. She watched helplessly as Becky's head landed in the inevitable with a soft splat.

Hilary and Becky retreated from the mayhem of Ivy Cottage to the relative quiet and hygiene of The Gables. Becky was hysterical by now and Hilary was only seconds away from slapping her daughter as she stripped off Becky's sodden leggings and sweatshirt. She was throwing the clothes in the washing machine, when David appeared in the kitchen.

'What the hell's going on?' he shouted above the noise of Becky's screaming.

'Daddy!' she shouted. 'I fell in Mabel's—'

'We had a little accident,' Hilary said, trying to sound quite calm, knowing that David would never understand what she had been doing over the road at Ivy Cottage.

'I'm never, never, ever going over to Auntie Charlotte's again,' whimpered Becky.

David looked at Hilary and noticed that she was looking anywhere but at him. 'What were you doing over at Charlotte's? I seem to remember you saying something earlier about knowing that she wasn't there.'

'I was worried about her dog, if you must know.'

David laughed, not with humour. 'You were snooping, weren't you?' Not expecting an answer, he turned to go, but then looked back at his wife. 'Well, was she there or not?'

25

When Charlotte woke up in Iris's sitting-room, she was stiff and cold. Alex was still asleep on the sofa. Seeing him she remembered how angry she had felt last night, not so much with Alex, but with herself.

After all her resolute determination not to get involved with Alex, she had allowed herself to do a complete U-turn. Kissing him and being in his arms had made her want him more than she would have imagined possible. Had the circumstances been right last night she knew she would have made love with Alex. But then later he had made it only too clear that he wasn't interested. She had fallen asleep stinging with hurt pride and the decision firmly resolved in her mind that it was not going to happen again. His rejection had, once and for all, established their relationship. From now on he was merely her tenant.

She drew the heavy velvet curtains and looked out over Iris's front garden, trying to decide what she was going to say to Alex. When she turned round he was sitting upright and rubbing his face. 'Good morning,' he said.

She walked over to the fireplace and rested one hand on the mantelpiece. 'Alex . . .'

'You're not going to give me a lecture on snoring, are you?'

'Alex,' she started again, conscious that the tone of her voice was at odds with his. 'What happened last night was . . .'

He looked at her for a moment, then stood up. 'Charlotte. Do I take it you're referring, and stop me if I'm wrong, to us kissing each other last night? Because if you are, I have to tell you, from where I was standing it was pretty enjoyable. I don't know what went through your head afterwards, but I was left with the distinct impression that yet again I had done something wrong. For the life of me I can't think what.'

'That's rich. It was you who said . . .'

'Said what?'

'Oh nothing. Forget it.'

'No, go on. Tell me.'

'You said you didn't want to make . . .' she moved away from the mantelpiece, over to the window, 'so on the basis of that it would be better all round if . . .'

'My God, I don't believe it, you think . . .'

'Alex, will you let me finish? I acted without thinking last night.' She took a deep breath. 'I can't handle being on this emotional roller coaster any more, so I would prefer it if we got things sorted out between us. You're my tenant. Let's just keep our relationship on that level from now on.'

'This is ridiculous. I only meant . . .'

'Please, Alex.'

He shrugged his shoulders. 'You don't give me much choice, do you?'

Alex pushed hard on the spade, forcing it down into the soil as he began digging Henry's grave. Charlotte bloody Lawrence! What was she doing to him? *She* was tired of being on an emotional roller coaster? Well, so was he for that matter. Enough was enough. But how could she be so dense? He hadn't meant that he didn't want to make love to her. He'd said those words, yes, but only because he didn't want her to think he would take advantage of her when she was still so vulnerable. Why couldn't she see that? He pushed on the spade again. And who in their right mind would want to make love in Iris Braithwaite's kitchen? Instantly some of his anger vanished at the thought of Iris catching him with his trousers down.

Charlotte watched Alex in the garden, to convince herself that she could now regard him quite dispassionately. She found she could, and picking up the kettle from the cooker, she filled it at the enamel sink. She placed it on the gas ring and struck a match. Last night she had done exactly the same, but then she hadn't noticed her surroundings. This morning though, with the early morning sunlight pouring in through the spotlessly clean window, the kitchen was picked out in detail like a 1950s film set. Everything about it was cluttered and unfitted, with bulky appliances which Charlotte could remember from her own childhood along with the same green and cream colour scheme – where others had moved on, Iris had not.

As she waited for the kettle to boil, Charlotte picked up the mugs she had rinsed out last night and looked around for some tea. There was no sign of a tea caddy on the green Formica worktop between the cooker and sink, so she slid back one of the plastic doors on the freestanding unit. Coffee, but still no tea. She noticed a door off the kitchen and pulled it open. As she'd thought, it was a larder. She was instantly reminded of her grandmother. Granny Archer had been a notorious hoarder. From the looks of things, so was Iris Braithwaite.

On the highest shelf Charlotte could see a tin of Bird's Custard Powder, and she knew that if she were to look inside, the ancient-looking tin would be half empty just like Granny Archer's, and its contents rock hard. Her eyes roaming the shelves, Charlotte counted ten rusting tins of evaporated milk, eight polythene-wrapped bags of sugar, four packs of Bisto, numerous jars of fish paste, rows of tinned pears and peach slices, and half a dozen bottles of gravy browning. The kettle began to whistle. Charlotte went to turn off the gas and then returned to the larder to continue her hunt. Surely amongst this hoard of goodies there had to be at least one packet of tea?

On the lowest shelf, crammed with tins of Campbell's soup and pilchards in tomato sauce, Charlotte saw an old Cadbury's tin commemorating the Queen's Coronation. She remembered Granny Archer's identical tin – Hilary had it now and kept old buttons in it. Out of curiosity, she took it down from the shelf and carefully prised the lid off. She wasn't expecting tea bags, but she was surprised to find a selection of used birthday-cake candles, along with some small plastic cake decorations. Iris had never had any children. She noticed that all the cake decorations were a variation on the same theme – a dog holding up a paw, a dog curled up in a basket and a dog with a bone in its mouth. Moving these objects to one side of the tin, Charlotte caught sight of a faded, stained envelope at the bottom. Ashamed of her nosiness but unable to stop herself, she opened the envelope and pulled out a set of photographs. Each photograph showed Iris's dog sitting in front of a decorated cake with writing in shaky blue icing that read 'Happy Birthday Henry'. Charlotte counted the photographs. There were exactly eleven.

'Damn!' she said out loud, and screwing up her eyes in a futile attempt not to cry, she pushed the tin back on the shelf and closed the larder door behind her. As she wiped away her tears with the palms of her hands, Alex came into the kitchen.

'You all right?' he asked.

She told him about the tin and the photographs of Henry. 'It's silly, isn't it?' she said. 'But it's always the trivia in life that gets to you. I saw poor Henry quite dead last night and that didn't upset me, but put a collection of sentimental plastic bits and pieces in front of me and I'm a hopeless wreck. Why do you suppose that is?' She paused, but not long enough for Alex to answer her. She went on, her words hurried and full of restrained emotion, 'Do you know, when I was told Peter was dead . . . I didn't cry . . . Can you believe it? I didn't cry, not one tear.' She bit her lower lip, clenched her fists, held her breath, all to keep her body in check, to stop it trembling and betraying her completely, but no matter how hard she tried she could not hold back the tears.

'Charlotte,' Alex said, 'you must—'

'No,' she said without looking at him. 'Don't. Just leave me . . .'

'I have only vague memories of last night . . .'

They both spun round to see Iris Braithwaite, looking pale and gaunt, framed in the doorway. She was wearing a dressing-gown and somehow managed to appear strangely majestic.

'. . . but I remember enough,' she carried on, 'to have woken up with the distinct impression that for some unaccountable reason I behaved very badly. I would prefer it if you never mentioned or referred to the event again. And now . . .' she hesitated slightly, as her voice began to waver, 'I would appreciate, Mr Hamilton, you taking Mrs Lawrence home, who, for her own reasons, seems to be quite overwrought. I would very much like to be alone with my poor Henry now. Thank you for being so kind as to dig a hole for me. I watched you from my window. You made a good choice, beneath the magnolia tree ... it was planted the same year Henry came to live ...'

Unable to continue, she went back upstairs.

They left The White Cottage in silence. Aware now that his role had been so clearly defined, Alex knew he had no right to intrude upon Charlotte's unhappiness. But he couldn't help wondering how much longer she would be able to fight back the need to free herself from the prison of her own making. For that was what it was, and he knew all about self-imprisonment. Standing in Iris's kitchen he had seen the pain in Charlotte's tormented face, and had recognised it as the same pain he himself had once experienced. Guilt. As surely as Charlotte was a willing prisoner of her guilt over Peter's death, so he too had been held captive after Lucy's death.

'I feel so angry,' Charlotte said, suddenly coming to a stop.

He looked at her, but she was turned away from him, staring up the drive of In The Pink. 'It's all *his* fault. How *dare* he come here with all his flash charm and ruin Iris's life. He's got no right hurting people like that.' She turned on Alex, her face flushed with angry indignation. 'I've got a good mind to go and have it out with him. Coming?'

Halfway up the drive, they were met by Barry jogging towards them.

'Is your father up?' Charlotte demanded.

Barry looked startled. 'I'm sorry?' he said, pushing a nervous hand through his hair.

'I asked if that rotten stinking father of yours was up yet? Probably enjoying a good laugh, is he?'

'Dad isn't at home, he's ...'

'Out ruining somebody else's life, no doubt,' Charlotte said hotly.

'Look, Charlotte,' Alex intervened, knowing that Charlotte was taking out her frustration on the nearest person to hand, 'this has got nothing to do with Barry. Leave it till later, when Derek's back from wherever he is.' He tried to lead Charlotte away, but she was firmly rooted to the ground.

'Actually Dad won't be home until he's been discharged from hospital.'

'Ah, somebody got to him before me, did they?'

'Hold on a moment, Charlotte,' Alex said, placing a hand on her arm. 'Why, what's happened?' he asked Barry.

Slowly, Barry's earnest face cracked into a cautious smile. 'Dad broke his leg down at the village hall last night. I thought you were there. Surely you saw what happened?'

Two blank faces stared back at Barry. 'We left early,' Alex volunteered.

'Apparently the power went off and Dad slipped and ...'

'And broke his leg,' finished Charlotte. 'Well thank goodness there's still a spark of justice in the world.'

'I'm going to see him later, do you want me to pass on a message?'

'No need. I think I'll go and see him in person.'

*

When Charlotte got back to Ivy Cottage she was horrified and shocked – horrified at the state of the kitchen and shocked that she could have forgotten poor Mabel so completely.

After cleaning up, feeding Mabel and generally making a fuss of her, Charlotte decided to take the dog for a walk down by the mere. She set off down Acacia Lane and turned left on to the footpath between In The Pink and The White Cottage. She peered through the neatly trimmed privet hedge to see if Mrs Braithwaite was about. There was no sign of her so Charlotte pressed on, down the hill, towards the mere.

It was a beautiful morning with clear blue skies. While Mabel scampered on ahead, snuffling around in amongst the fir trees, Charlotte followed slowly behind, enjoying the moment of freedom. Freedom. It seemed she had been searching for this commodity all her life. Was this the only way to experience it? To be utterly alone? For it seemed to Charlotte, standing there in the clearing, overlooking the still water and breathing in the sweet smell of pine, that whenever people were involved, restrictions were applied and demands made. In her experience even the nicest of people pushed others about for their own purposes.

Calling Mabel to heel and turning for home, Charlotte thought of poor Iris again. She wondered how she must be feeling right now. All at once the anger she had felt standing there on the driveway of In The Pink came flooding back. Derek!

Charlotte lied to the nurse, saying she was 'family', then walked through the ward towards Derek's bed at the far end. It was seven-thirty and the ward was packed with evening visitors.

'Charlotte!' he called out, seeing her. Huddled visitors and patients all looked up as she made her way past them. 'My mistress,' Derek said loudly, with a big grin on his face.

'Shut up, Derek,' she said, when at last she stood over him.

'What, no kiss, not even a peck on the cheek?'

She glared at him. 'Not after what you've done.' Her voice was raised and unmistakably angry and everyone else in the ward was making a poor job of pretending not to be listening.

'After what I've done? What on earth are you talking about? Here I am, recovering from major surgery, and you accuse me . . .'

'I said shut up, Derek. I don't know how that family of yours puts up with you.'

'Must be my magnetic . . .'

'I said shut . . .'

'All right, all right, you've used that line,' Derek said, frowning. 'And anyway, you sure you're not muddling me up with somebody else? I'm Derek Rogers, he of the compound fracture fame.' He pointed to the end of the bed. 'They've put a pin in my tibia-whatsit or something or other. I've been very brave. Surely I deserve just a little sympathy from you? One kiss would do it.'

'You're despicable. What you did last night was pathetic.'

'Charlotte, a guy can't help breaking his leg . . .'

'Not that. What you did to poor Mrs Braithwaite, that was such . . .'

'A laugh, I thought,' Derek said smiling. 'Got her a touch frisky, didn't it, relaxed the old bird a bit?'

'You've ruined her!' Charlotte shouted. 'And you don't give a damn, do you?'

'Oh come on, Charlotte,' Derek retorted with equal volume, 'don't exaggerate. You talk as though I'd raped her.'

An audible gasp rippled round the rest of the ward.

'Well, you might just as well have done. She's lost all her dignity and reputation in one go. She'll be the laughing stock of the village.'

'Rubbish! She was that already and why the hell are you so defensive on her behalf? I would have thought after what she'd done to you, you would have been pleased with what I did, grateful even.'

'You . . . you don't understand, do you?' It was hopeless. Charlotte turned her back on Derek and rushed out of the ward, goggled-eyed faces following her as she went.

'Too bloody right I don't!' Derek threw after her, and then, as all faces turned back to look at him, he shouted angrily, 'Oh, sod off, the lot of you!'

What a day! Derek thought to himself, reaching for his jug of water – a day that had begun with Nurse Baker, of whom he had had high hopes, who had turned out to be a mustachioed, red-haired Cliff Baker and was probably as bent as a Uri Geller fork. He took a gulp of his water and looked up to see Cindy and Barry coming towards him.

'What did Charlotte want?' Cindy asked sharply, as she stood at the end of his bed. 'We passed her on the stairs. She looked upset.'

'If you must know, she's just been giving me a right mouthful and I don't mean we were snogging. Ask this nosy lot here,' he said, gesturing with his hand towards the rest of the ward, who were all, once again, not so discreetly tuning in.

Barry looked down at his father. 'Alex said you got Mrs Braithwaite drunk last night. Is that true?'

'Isn't anyone at all interested in how my operation went? I reckon I'm bloody lucky to be alive.'

'Well, is it true?'

'Of course I didn't,' Derek said, turning away from his son and looking out of the window. In the car park below, he could see Charlotte getting into her car. He watched her slam the door shut and then slump over the steering wheel, her hands covering her face.

'Dad?'

Derek turned and faced Barry. 'Okay,' he said irritably, 'so what if I did?'

'You stupid bloody fool,' Cindy said with undisguised contempt.

'I thought it would be a laugh.'

'Alex says Mrs Braithwaite's dog died last night,' Barry said.

'Oh Alex says this and Alex says that,' shouted Derek. 'I'm sick of that man.' Heads again turned their way.

Cindy suddenly smiled. Jealousy! How wonderful that at last her husband should have come to know that most self-destructive of emotions. 'Well, we're all sick of you,' she said, and walked away, her head held high as all eyes followed her down the ward.

Derek looked at his son. 'Are you leaving as well?'

Barry nudged his glasses. 'Not if you don't want me to.'

They stared at each other. Then Barry walked slowly round the bed and sat in the chair between the window and his father.

'Been a bit of a plonker, haven't I, Bas?'

'You could say that, Dad.'

26

My dear Carlotta, I am so very sorry, but I shall not be able to come and visit you this month. I have to be in Rome for a funeral. I think it will be quite a party! Forgive me for disappointing you. Love, Christina.

'No!' said Charlotte out loud, looking down at the letter in her hand which had just arrived by that morning's second post. 'No, I won't forgive you. I want you here with me.'

Charlotte had found Hulme Welford strangely quiet for the past five weeks. Flaming June had been and gone and for once had lived up to its name, being hot and dry, but July so far had been a wash-out, forcing people to stay indoors, abandoning their gardens to the daily downpour of torrential rain, which left delphiniums battered and cheap barbecues to fill up with water and rust.

Charlotte had put her time to good use, though, spending most days up a ladder with a paintbrush in her hand. She had even taught herself to stencil and had festooned the kitchen walls with wisteria and the bathroom with ivy, echoing exactly the exterior of the house. She was really quite pleased with her efforts at decorating. But she didn't feel pleased now. She had been looking forward to Christina coming to stay, had even decorated a bedroom specially for her. There was so much she wanted to talk to Christina about. What with all the rain and being cooped up inside the house, she felt as though she hadn't talked properly with anyone for weeks.

Everyone, it seemed, was busy. There was Dad with his gooseberries – trying to protect them from all the rain – and Mum with her shop and the passing holiday trade; even Alex, who previously had seemed always to be around, had been absent recently. Charlotte had missed their chats in the garden. Occasionally she would hear music coming through the wall, but Alex was a good tenant and the music was always to her liking, and never intrusive. She sometimes heard him going out early in the morning and not returning until late. Some nights, he didn't come home at all. She wondered what he did then. Was he with Heather? Perhaps not, not after Jonathan.

The last she had seen of Jonathan had been when she had got back from the hospital after giving Derek a piece of her mind and found him waiting for her on the doorstep. 'I need my things,' he had said, with not a hint as to where or what he had been doing since the previous evening. And then he had gone, accelerating smoothly down Acacia Lane in his hired Mercedes.

She had seen hardly anything of Hilary either. Her sister had been busy organising just about every end-of-term social activity for children and parents alike, at the same time getting ready for their annual camping holiday. Only two days ago Hilary had sat in the conservatory with Charlotte, the rain coming down like stair rods on the glass roof above their heads, and had said, very smugly Charlotte thought, 'Well, at least we'll be able to rely on the weather in Haute Provence.' They had set off yesterday morning, the Volvo weighed down with patched canvas, Marmite, Ribena, mosquito repellant, water-purifying tablets, factor twenty sun cream, as well as several bagfuls of pre-holiday tension. They were supposed to leave at the crack of dawn according to David's itinerary, but at nine o'clock he was still sitting in the car, revving the engine and waiting for Becky, who that morning had started complaining of an upset tummy, to get off the toilet.

She heard Mabel scratching at the conservatory door and went to let her in. The little dog was drenched. Charlotte picked up a towel and rubbed her down. The doorbell rang.

'Hello Tiffany,' Charlotte said, opening the door.

'You okay for a visitor?'

'Yes, of course, come in. I was just about to indulge in some comfort eating. Fancy joining me?'

They sat in the kitchen, Charlotte loading crumpets under the grill and Tiffany absentmindedly carving patterns in the butter. With her head bent over the table, Charlotte could see that Tiffany's own natural colour was showing through the defiant puce of the rest of her hair. She was no longer wearing the elaborate beehive, but a plait, which hung down her back like a stick of rock. Not for the first time Charlotte wondered how on earth Tiffany had got away with it at school. Didn't teenagers get expelled for such things?

'The house seems so empty without Barry,' Tiffany said, looking up at Charlotte. 'It's dead boring not having him around. I know he's quiet and all that, but at least, when he's there, I can ...'

'Annoy him?'

Tiffany laughed. 'Isn't that what brothers are for?'

'Sisters too,' Charlotte said with a smile.

'You know, I don't think Dad can work Barry out. He's paid for us both to have a dead expensive education, expecting at least one of us to end up as a smart something or other, you know, an accountant or a barrister, something boring like that. Dad thinks you've got to spend money to make money.' She laughed scornfully and plunged the knife deep into the butter. 'And Barry's gone off to do charity work in an orphanage in Romania for the summer. Ironic or what?'

'Have you heard from him yet?' Charlotte asked, setting a plate of hot crumpets down on the table.

'Yes, we got a letter yesterday. He's been sprayed for fleas and lice and is helping to install twelve new toilets.'

'Well, at least he's doing something positive,' Charlotte said, sitting down and passing Tiffany a knife and a plate.

'Meaning I'm not, I suppose.'

Charlotte shook her head. 'No,' she said emphatically. 'Meaning *I'm* not.'

'Do something, then.'

'Like what?'

'Hang on,' Tiffany said, balancing a thick slab of butter on a crumpet, 'isn't that supposed to be my line? I'm the awkward teenager, you're supposed to be the one with all the answers.' She took a huge bite of the buttery crumpet, and with her mouth full, said, 'Why don't you just get a job?'

Charlotte looked up from her plate. 'I know that's the answer. The trouble is I haven't got a clue what I really want to do.'

'There must be hundreds of things you could have a go at. I'll prove it to you. Got a newspaper?'

Charlotte went through to the sitting-room and came back with a copy of the *Chronicle*.

'Right,' said Tiffany, taking it from her and laying the relevant pages out on the table. ' "Receptionist required, must be smart in appearance." ' She looked at Charlotte in her jeans, paint-splattered sweatshirt and hair scraped back in a rubber band. 'Well, we'd have to get Mum and Dad to tidy you up a bit.' She continued with the advertisement. ' "Must have excellent communication skills and knowledge of Monarch system." ' She lifted her head. 'What's a Monarch system?'

Charlotte shrugged. 'A computer for Royals? Helps them to foul up perhaps.'

'Okay then,' Tiffany grinned, returning to the paper. 'How about "Efficient organiser and administrator, must be confident and discreet and able to act under pressure." '

Charlotte gave a short derisive laugh. 'I think I've got enough pressure in my life just at the moment.'

Undaunted, Tiffany carried on. 'Well, that rules out secretarial and administrative. How about domestic? Some poshy over in Prestbury wants a housekeeper. You've only got to be conscientious and like children.'

'Grilled or fried?' laughed Charlotte.

'You're not taking this seriously at all, are you?' Tiffany said, throwing the paper on the floor.

'Let's forget about me. How's your dad's leg?'

'Covered in kisses,' Tiffany said in disgust. 'Every woman who comes into the place wants to sign her name on his plaster. By the way, did you know he tried to apologise to Mrs Braithwaite?'

'No, I didn't,' answered Charlotte, wondering what crass things Derek might have said.

'She wouldn't even speak to him, just slammed the door in his face. He said she looked awful, well, worse than she normally does.'

Charlotte frowned. She had been worried about Mrs Braithwaite for some time now. Ever since that dreadful night at the village hall and Henry's death it was as though Mrs Braithwaite had disappeared from the village. Nobody seemed to have spoken with her; nobody knew whether she was hiding her grief or her embarrassment, or even both. 'When was that exactly, when did your father see her?'

Tiffany thought for a moment. 'Ages ago, I think, before all this rain started anyway. Why?'

'I don't know, I just feel uneasy about Mrs Braithwaite. Even Hilary, before she left for France yesterday, said she hadn't seen her about, and Hilary usually sees most things going on in Hulme Welford.'

'Surely someone must have seen her down at the shops.'

'Apparently not.'

'What's she eating, then?'

Charlotte thought of all the jars of paste and tins of pilchards in Iris Braithwaite's larder and feared the worst.

In his study at the Vicarage, Malcolm Jackson pulled the telephone towards him and dialled a number from his parish address book. He waited and waited. At last he heard Neville Archer's voice.

'Hello Neville, it's Malcolm. You all right? You sound out of breath.'

'I'm fine. I was in the garden.'

'What, in this weather?'

'Especially in this weather. I was making sure I'd got enough rhubarb leaves covering the gooseberries. It's only a couple of weeks to go until the big day.'

A smile flickered over Malcolm's face. 'Oh yes, of course, the gooseberry show. I'd forgotten about that. How are they doing?'

'Best not say, not over the telephone, careless words, etc.'

They both laughed. Gooseberry growers were notorious for their rivalry and secrecy, and sabotage was not unheard of.

'So what can I do for you, Malcolm?'

'Actually, Neville, do you think you could leave the gooseberries for a short while and bob round? There's something I'd like you to do for me.'

Neville approached The White Cottage in the drizzling rain, taking each step with increasing trepidation. 'She might listen to you, Neville,' Malcolm had said. 'For so long in her life you've been a figure of standing in the village. You were her doctor for goodness knows how long, she's more likely to listen to you than anyone else. She's got to realise that we all care about her, that she can't hide in her house for ever, for whatever reason. She's got to come out.'

On the doorstep, Neville didn't feel a figure of any standing whatsoever.

He lifted the brass knocker and brought it down sharply. He counted to twenty and knocked again, and then again. He bent down, pushed open the letter box and peered inside. 'Mrs Braithwaite,' he called out nervously. 'Are you there, Mrs Braithwaite?'

Why nervously? What was he afraid of? Afraid that they, that he, had left it too late, that Iris was lying on the floor . . . dead?

Why did he imagine Iris lying dead *on the floor*. Why be so dramatic? Why not just imagine her in her favourite comfy armchair? Not every old person living alone had to die on the floor. Stop being so useless, Neville Archer! he told himself. Get on and do something! Smash a window, do something heroic for once in your life. But be careful, let the gas out before you go in. Gas? Who mentioned gas? He breathed in deeply, then exhaled slowly. One more time and then I'll call the police, he told himself. 'Mrs Braithwaite,' he shouted through the letter box again, 'it's me, Dr Archer.'

'I can see that perfectly well, Dr Archer.'

Neville spun round at the sound of Iris Braithwaite's voice.

'Though why you should be shouting through my letter box for all the neighbours to hear, I really cannot think.'

'Mrs Braithwaite!' he said, revelling in the fact that Iris was looking wonderfully alive and not gasping her last in front of the gas cooker.

'Perhaps you would be so good as to help me with my case. It's heavy and I've just walked with it from the bus stop.'

'You've been away, then?' Neville said, watching Iris unlock the front door.

'My word, Dr Archer, retirement has done nothing to weaken your diagnostic powers, has it? Well of course I have, you don't think I've been shopping with a suitcase, do you?'

'It's just that we were all so . . .' Neville hesitated.

'Come on, Dr Archer, in with that case, if you please, and what were you all?'

'Pleased to see you back,' Neville said smiling.

In the hall Iris freed herself from her raincoat and stared at Neville. 'Well, that's very civil of you.' Then removing her plastic rain-hood and patting her hair into place, she said, 'Now don't let me keep you. I'm sure you must have plenty to do.'

'Yes,' he answered, edging towards the door. 'Been anywhere nice?' he ventured, realising that Iris was exhibiting a tan that could not possibly have been acquired anywhere in the North of England during the past few weeks.

'Yes, as a matter of fact, somewhere very nice. Goodbye.'

27

When, three weeks later, the removal of his plaster cast coincided with two days of continuous sunshine, Derek decided to hold an impromptu barbecue. It was early Sunday morning and he sent Tiffany off to invite the neighbours. He told her to ask Louise and Neville. 'And you'd better ask Old Ma Braithwaite,' he added, 'and that vicar bloke.'

'The vicar?' Tiffany said, astonished. 'Why him?'

'I want to see what kind of man is going to baptise my son. I want to know whether he's into choirboys or not.'

Both the vicar and Iris Braithwaite sent their apologies, or rather Malcolm Jackson did. Iris informed Tiffany she would rather sup with the Devil. Undaunted, at one o'clock, resplendent in knee-length shorts, espadrilles, sunglasses, and with his hands stuffed inside the mouths of a pair of crocodile oven gloves, Derek greeted the rest of his guests, as well as their plates of microwave-defrosted meat and freezer-chilled bottles of wine. He was an incongruous sight with one evenly tanned leg and an elastic support stocking covering the lower part of his other leg which was white and scrawny. He was leaning on a walking stick, but mostly he used this to direct operations.

'Meat over there,' he said, pointing with the stick to the hostess trolley they had all seen at the fork supper, 'and booze over here, where I can reach it easily. A guy can only hobble so far. Tiffany, go and tell your mother to bring out that sangria I made earlier.'

Alex felt Charlotte wince at his side. They had arrived at the same time, though not together. He hadn't seen her to talk to in ages. Their landlady–tenant relationship had consisted of fleeting glimpses of each other, and that was all. Earlier in the summer their lives had been unexpectedly thrust together, but after that morning in Iris's kitchen they had gone their separate ways; and if he was truthful with himself, despite missing her company, life had been a lot more straightforward since then.

Standing slightly apart from the rest of the group, which numbered Louise and Neville and Hilary and David, along with their children, Alex turned to Charlotte. 'Good thing Mrs Braithwaite isn't here,' he said.

She responded with only a slight smile, though enough, he noticed, to set off those two dimples either side of her mouth. He couldn't read her eyes, for they were hidden behind dark glasses.

'Anyone found out where she went on holiday?' he asked.

'No,' she answered. 'Apparently she's been quite secretive about it, hasn't told a soul where she went. Dad reckons it's the first holiday she's had since she brought Henry home as a puppy.'

Alex looked directly at Charlotte, and – conscious that he was shifting a gear or two – said, 'To be honest, I'm surprised to see you here. Aren't you still angry with Derek?'

Charlotte returned Alex's unwavering gaze for a moment, then looked away towards Derek, who was prodding indiscriminately at the fake hot coals of his gas-fired barbecue. At the same time he was chatting to her mother and leaning on his stick. 'It's hard to stay mad with such a fool,' she said.

'And are you still mad with me?' he ventured.

'No,' she said.

He noticed there was no hesitation in her reply. 'Friends, then?'

She nodded. 'Friends.'

'Fancy a stroll?'

'Yes, if it means getting out of having to drink Derek's lethal sangria.'

They wandered down to the bottom of the garden, away from the smoke and the sound of Becky and Philip starting to argue, and Hilary and David telling Neville, yet again, about their eighteen hours of hell on the French roads coming back from Haute Provence.

'How have you been?' Alex asked, as they sat on a white-painted wrought-iron garden seat, overlooking a small pond with a spouting cherub and an ugly-looking ornamental toad.

'Quiet, but busy,' she answered. 'In fact I've struck up quite a relationship with Mr Dulux. How about you, you don't seem to have been around as much?'

'I've been busy with several . . .'

'You're not going back to your eighty-hour weeks, are you?'

'Would you be disappointed in me if I was?'

'Yes,' she said, 'I would. I had high hopes for you, Alex. I thought you were a real nineties man.'

Was it his imagination or was she more at ease, not just with him, but with herself? 'Oh don't worry about me, I'm way ahead in the emancipation of men stakes. I already organise my work schedule around *Neighbours* and *Home and Away*.'

'Now you have disappointed me. I had you down as an Anne and Nick fan.' She pushed her sunglasses up over her head and closed her eyes. 'After all that rain this is wonderful. I feel as if I'm on holiday.'

'Do you think you'll go away this summer?'

'I shouldn't think so,' she said. 'I know it sounds like I'm being a bit of a wimp but I don't much fancy a holiday alone. And before you say anything,

I'm too old for Club Eighteen and too young for a bowling holiday in Bournemouth with a bevy of grey-haired grannies. I'd rather stay at home.'

An idea occurred to Alex. 'Charlotte?' he said. 'Do you trust me?'

'What an extraordinary question,' she said, reminded of the morning she had discovered Alex cleaning her kitchen floor when he had given her that hangover cure. 'Trust me,' he had said then. 'Why, what have you done?'

'It's not so much what I've done, as what I'm about to suggest.'

Charlotte opened her eyes. She fixed her attention on a blackbird some six feet away, basking in the sunshine, its feathers so plumped up it looked like a sooty powder puff. 'Go on,' she said.

'I'm going to stay with some friends next week, over in Yorkshire. I've known them since we were at university together.'

'That's nice. I hope you have a lovely time.'

'Why don't you come with me? It might be fun for you to get away for a few days.' Was he pushing it? Was he already putting their re-established friendship in jeopardy?

She kept her eyes on the blackbird. Recently her life had begun to show signs of becoming trouble-free, with each day gently easing itself into the next. She had even started to feel better, the dreams had stopped and she couldn't remember the last time she had cried. Would going away with Alex complicate things again? But surely they were both over all that nonsense now. 'I don't know what to say,' she said at last.

'I am only offering you a few days in Yorkshire.'

'I know that. If I thought it was anything else I wouldn't be considering the idea.'

'Say yes, then, and before Long John Silver gets bored with his alfresco Keith Floyd impersonation and comes yo-ho-ho-ing down here to rout us out.'

She laughed.

'Hey you two,' shouted Derek, right on cue, 'quit your canoodling in my bushes. I've got a lovely steak for you, Charlotte. Alex, I'm sorry but your burger's burnt.'

'Subtle, isn't he?' Alex said, as they began walking back to the house. They hadn't got as far as the patio when Tiffany called from the kitchen French window.

'Dad, there's a man on the phone for you.'

'Well bring it out here. What's the point in having a mobile phone if it's stuck in the kitchen the whole time? You don't expect me to be Linford Christie with this leg, do you?'

Coming out into the garden and rolling her black-lined eyes, Tiffany slapped the phone down into her father's hand. He poked her with his stick.

'Hello,' he said, 'Derek Rogers here . . . yes, that's right . . . what, what kind of . . . what do you mean you don't know . . . what kind of agency are you . . . you send my son . . . too right I'm worried, pal!'

Derek pushed the aerial in and tossed the phone on to the pink-frilled hammock behind him.

'What is it, Dad?' asked Tiffany, seeing the look on her father's face.

'You'd better go and tell your mother. Bas is being flown home from Romania ... he's ill, caught some ... they don't know what. He'll be at Manchester, about six.'

'He'll be fine,' Hilary said brightly, looking inanely about her. 'It'll just be some kind of tummy bug, you know what these foreign places are like. Last year in the Dordogne we ...'

'They've arranged for an ambulance to be there at the airport,' Derek said flatly.

Nobody said anything else.

They were met at the airport by a small nervous man in baggy trousers and a creased shirt. 'Mr and Mrs Rogers? I'm from Aid Now and I'd ...'

'I don't give a shit about you,' Derek shouted, pointing an accusing finger at the man, 'so shut up until you're spoken to.'

An airport official escorted the tense group to a private lounge. 'We'll let you know the minute the plane lands,' he said. 'I'm afraid you won't be able to see your son straight away. We have a medical team on standby ... we need to know whether he's infectious.'

When the man left them, Cindy began to cry and Tiffany put her arm round her mother's shoulders. She was shocked to feel how thin and insubstantial her mother really was – her mother, who had always seemed to be rock solid, fighting Tiffany every step of each day.

Derek breathed in deeply, and stood and glowered over the man in baggy trousers.

They saw the plane land and then watched in helpless disbelief through the triple-glazed window as a stretcher was carried down the steps of the aircraft and was pushed into the awaiting ambulance.

At the hospital Cindy looked through yet another glass window at her son. 'I can't believe this,' she said, 'I can't believe he's going to die.'

'He's not,' Tiffany almost growled. 'He's bloody well not going to die.'

Derek turned away from the sight of his son, twitching spasmodically, suffering God knows what. It was too much for him. 'I'm going to look for that doctor. It's been long enough for them to know something by now.'

Before he even got to the door it was opened by the young doctor they had spoken to earlier, a man who looked as though he would be more at home on a rugby pitch than in an intensive-care ward. He came into the room, filling the small space. 'We've performed the lumbar puncture,' he said briskly, 'and it's as we thought: your son has meningitis. I think you should prepare yourselves for a long haul.' He turned away from them and looked through the glass at Barry and two nurses who were hovering over him. 'I have to tell you, the delirium may well wear off quite soon, but there's a strong possibility that he could lose consciousness.'

'Will he . . . ?'

The young doctor looked kindly at Cindy. 'We know exactly how to treat your son, Mrs Rogers, it's more a question of timing. If we can treat the illness in the early stages, there's a good chance of a full recovery, but . . .'

'What you mean,' Derek said, cutting in, 'is that we might be too late in Bas's case.'

'Dad,' shouted Tiffany, 'stop it!'

'I'm sure you'd like to see your son now,' the doctor said simply. 'First though, I'll show you where you can wash and put on some gowns.'

They stood at the foot of the bed, staring down at Barry's restless body. Tiffany was the first to move forward. 'Oh Barry,' she cried, bending over his flushed, sweating face. 'Barry, what have you done?'

Slowly, as though using all his strength, Barry opened his eyes. Tiffany could see he was trying to focus on her. 'Tiffany?' he said faintly.

'Yes,' she said, 'it's . . .' Then, moving away from the bed, she began to cry quietly.

Cindy came forward, her hand covering her trembling lips. Behind her, Derek leaned over towards his son, and swallowing hard, he said, 'So Bas, it's your turn to be a bit of a plonker, is it?'

Barry's eyes closed.

They took it in turns to stay awake by Barry's side throughout the night, even though a nurse was constantly monitoring his progress. Each watched helplessly as Barry's restless, fevered body thrashed from side to side. A drip was in place, its plastic bag of liquid vanishing steadfastly into Barry's arm.

At about four in the morning, as Derek felt himself falling into a much needed sleep, he was brought up with the strongest of feelings that something was wrong. His son wasn't moving. 'Bas!' he cried, convinced that Barry was no longer breathing. There was no sign of the nurse, so he stumbled out of the room, forgetting his stick and trying to ignore the pain shooting through his leg. 'Help! Somebody come quickly,' he shouted down the empty corridor. At once Tiffany and Cindy were at his side, along with the nurse. 'He's not moving . . . I think he's . . .'

The nurse pushed past him and went to Barry. 'He's unconscious,' she said, hurrying out of the room. 'I'll fetch Dr Bawton.'

Alone again, Cindy sat by her son. She reached out her hand and eased back his damp hair. It was such a simple gesture, but that lock of hair was such an integral part of her son's make-up. She felt Tiffany and Derek moving behind her. 'I want him baptised,' she said quietly. 'He's to be baptised, just as he wanted.'

Exhaustion, fear and bewilderment made Derek unusually quiet. He greeted Malcolm Jackson in the waiting-room with nothing more than a nod, taking him through to Cindy and Tiffany and Bas. What was there to say anyway? He listened to the vicar talking about Barry's courage and about pulling through and then about them joining him in a moment of prayer.

'I usually like to kneel,' Malcolm Jackson said, 'but if you'd feel more comfortable standing, that's fine.'

Derek watched the others to see what they would do. They knelt, and so he got awkwardly down on one knee. He couldn't concentrate on anything that was being said. He could only think how scared and isolated he felt, kneeling alone on his side of Bas's bed. More than anything he wanted to run away from this room, to be outside in the sunshine, in their garden, where only yesterday they had been drinking sangria and burning cheap steak. Oh God, he wasn't strong enough to cope with this.

At last it was over and they were getting to their feet. Derek limped over to the window and looked out over the car park. In the background he could hear more kind words being said. Then he lost it. Something deep inside him exploded and, bringing his fist down on the windowsill, he shouted, 'What's the bloody sense in all this?'

28

'This doesn't feel at all right,' Charlotte said, as the Elton John cassette came to an end. Alex looked across at her briefly, wanting to keep his eyes on the motorway ahead. They were on the M62, just passing Hollingworth Lake, and for most of the journey neither of them had spoken much. He wondered whether Charlotte was beginning to regret coming.

He didn't know which had most surprised him; his impulsiveness while sat in Derek and Cindy's garden, or Charlotte's agreement to come away with him, and without any real persuasion on his part. All he could be sure of was that the anticipation he had experienced over the past few days at the prospect of spending some time with Charlotte had made him face up to how he really felt towards her. When they had first met at Hilary's, he had been intrigued by her. Intrigued because she had seemed determined from the word go not to like him. She had been on the attack as soon as Hilary had introduced them, and had been in that position ever since . . . until now possibly. When she had told him Derek had kissed her he had realised then that what he felt for her was more than just passing curiosity. Imagining Derek kissing Charlotte had not set him off down the path of jealousy as he might have supposed, but had made him want to protect her from any further advances from Derek . . . or any other kind of roué for that matter. From that moment on he had wanted Charlotte for himself, and the whole of her, not just the fragments she was prepared to share. During their brief time apart he had almost convinced himself that his feelings for her had changed. But they hadn't. He still wanted Charlotte, and now that he had somehow gained her trust, he didn't want to risk losing it.

'I said this doesn't feel right,' Charlotte repeated, looking pointedly at Alex.

'I'm sorry,' he said. 'I was miles away.' He pulled out into the fast lane and overtook a shirt-sleeved man in a Cavalier, his jacket hanging limply behind him on the specially designed hook. 'So what exactly doesn't feel right?'

'Oh, I don't know . . .'

'Come on, you can do better than that.'

'It feels . . .' She looked out of the window, realising that at some stage during the journey, the landscape had changed – ribbons of dry-stone wall had replaced the familiar hawthorn hedges of her native Cheshire. 'I feel bad about Barry. It's as though we don't care by coming away.'

'I know what you mean, but Barry could be in a coma for ages. Somehow life has . . .'

'Oh please no, not that old number,' Charlotte said. 'You're beginning to sound like Hilary.'

Her defiance made him want to smile; it was one of her traits he had missed these past few weeks. 'I called in at the hospital last night,' he said. 'Cindy was on her own. She looked worn out.'

'I know. Tiffany burst into tears when I went and poor Derek couldn't even talk to me.'

They drove on in silence, until Alex indicated to come off the motorway. 'Nearly there,' he said.

Charlotte tried to block out her anxiety for Barry. Instead she began to wonder what Alex's friends would be like. He had barely said a word about Sally and Stephen, other than to say that he was sure she would like them and that they had a five-year-old son called Mark. She stole a quick glance at Alex, thinking how little she really knew about him. It wasn't so much that he was a secretive man, it was more that he seemed to prefer encouraging others to talk about themselves. Initially this had disturbed her – he had probed a little too deeply for her liking. Then he had frightened her, or rather her own response to Alex had made her scared of him. She hadn't expected to feel such a physical attraction to another man so soon after Peter's death. It had taken her completely unawares and she had found herself out of her depth, floundering through her inability to cope with her confused emotions. It had been her misreading of the situation that had led to all the problems, she could see that; she had simply read too much into Alex's relationship with her and had over-reacted. Thank goodness she had come to her senses and she could now enjoy Alex's friendship on a more down-to-earth level. He was good company and made her laugh, and since their truce he had stopped probing. Which was why she had decided to accept his invitation. A few days away from Hulme Welford might even help her to start thinking more clearly about what she was going to do with her life. She had spent long enough licking her wounds; it was time to think of the future.

'You're quiet. You okay?'

'These friends of yours,' she said, 'what are they like? Green wellies and Labradors?'

Alex laughed. He slowed the car down, eased it round a sharp corner and then turned through a gate that led into a small cobbled courtyard. Turning the engine off, he said, 'Do I look like the sort of man who has friends out of a Jilly Cooper novel?'

Charlotte gazed up at the house in front of them. It was lovely, possibly more than a century old. Its original light stone was now, in parts, blackened with age and dotted with small, staring, mullioned windows. Around the front door was an assortment of stone-coloured tubs, but not one was filled with the usual summer array of geraniums and lobelia. Instead, the pots were home to burgeoning tomato plants.

She got out of the car and instantly the front door opened and out came a petite blonde girl in jeans and an oversized T-shirt. Her hair was tied up on top of her head in a loose knot, and wisps of it framed a pretty face that was almost angelic in appearance. Charlotte thought she looked about nineteen and that she couldn't possibly have been at university the same time as Alex.

The girl rushed to Alex's side of the car and kissed him delightedly. Their pleasure at seeing one another was obvious, especially when Alex picked her up and swung her round.

'Stop it, Alex,' she called out, 'and let me say hello to Charlotte.'

Alex did as he was told and introduced them.

'Come on in. Don't bother about your luggage, Alex can see to that later. Can't you?' Sally said, looking over her shoulder as she steered Charlotte inside. 'I've just pulled some scones out of the oven, would you like one? I've even got some cream.'

She took them through to a large welcoming kitchen – welcoming because of the smell of baking and the fact that it was so colourful and looked as though it had evolved through use rather than careful planning. There was a large dresser painted royal blue, which dominated the room. It was packed with books rather than artfully placed pieces of china. In the centre of the stone-flagged floor was a table which held a further assortment of books and the floury remains of a baking session. The walls were covered in wrinkled pieces of artwork. Charlotte presumed the artist himself was the small blond-haired boy at the far end of the kitchen sitting with his back to her. Like Becky and Philip, he was engrossed in watching the television in front of him, but unlike Becky and Philip, the sound of the television was not at blaring pitch.

'I'll just go up and tell Stephen you've arrived,' Sally said, darting out of the room.

Charlotte watched Alex walk over to Mark. He said nothing until he was directly in front of the child. When the boy saw Alex he leapt excitedly to his feet. Alex gathered him up in his arms and brought him over to Charlotte. 'Mark, this is my friend Charlotte.' His voice was strangely slow.

'Hello,' she said, a little shyly and somewhat surprised at how gorgeous this particular child was. But there again, the only children she even vaguely knew were Philip, with his belligerent face, and Becky with her many pouting madam expressions.

An open smiling face looked at her with undisguised curiosity, but soon turned back to Alex. 'Uncle Lex,' Mark said, slowly and in a distorted voice, 'play monsters?'

Alex smiled and then put him down on the floor. 'Later, Mark,' he said slowly. 'Let me say hello to your father first.' Satisfied, Mark went back to the television and Alex joined Charlotte.

'Is he deaf?' she asked in a low voice.

'Yes. So there's no need to whisper. But isn't he great?'

'God, life's a bitch, isn't it?'

'I wouldn't say that.'

'Stephen!' The two men hugged each other with unrestrained affection, Charlotte noticed, and in a way so few men feel able to do. Alex introduced Charlotte.

Stephen smiled at her as he shook her hand. He was slightly taller than Alex and almost as blond as his pretty wife. It wasn't hard to see how between them they had created such a beautiful child.

'I hope my coming hasn't put you to any extra trouble,' Charlotte said, wanting to sound genuine but suspecting she sounded terribly trite.

'Not a bit of it,' Sally said, coming into the kitchen. 'Stephen, why don't you take Charlotte into the sitting-room and Alex can help me get some tea together.'

Leading the way but still within earshot of his wife, Stephen said, 'Round here we call Sally the Ayatollah. We pray to her at least six times a day.' A pair of rolled-up children's socks came flying through the door and hit him on the back of his neck.

He took Charlotte into a large square room with deep mullioned windows which overlooked the garden and a vast landscape of open moorland beyond. Late afternoon sunlight filtered through the windows giving a brilliant, almost theatrical light to the room. Like the kitchen, this room was no slave to fashion either, but held an eclectic assortment of homely-looking armchairs and tables, with a patchwork of paintings on the walls ranging from bucolic landscapes to a stunning watercolour portrait of Mark. There was a silver-framed photograph on a windowsill that caught Charlotte's eye. It was of Stephen and Sally on their wedding day and Alex was there too, with his arm round . . . a girl who looked just like Sally.

Stephen gestured to a squashy armchair for Charlotte. He sat down opposite her. 'You've caught us on a good day,' he said. 'The sun has barely shown itself all week. With a bit of luck, you and Alex might even be able to go on some decent walks. He has warned you about his passion for walking, hasn't he?'

'No, he's kept quiet about that.'

'Hold on, Stephen,' Alex said, coming into the room with a large tea tray, 'you're not giving away all my secrets, are you?'

'I wouldn't dream of it,' Stephen said.

Later that evening, while Stephen and Alex were both upstairs putting Mark to bed and Charlotte was helping to prepare supper, Sally caught her off guard. 'Alex told us your husband died earlier this year . . . in a car crash, he said.'

Charlotte concentrated hard on scraping the potato in her hand. 'Yes,' she said, simply. She felt annoyed at this untimely reminder of Peter. The day had been going so well. 'So what else did he tell you about me?' The thought occurred to her that perhaps Alex had asked Sally to do his probing for him.

Sally stopped what she was doing. She put the vegetable knife down on the chopping board. 'I'm sorry,' she said, 'I shouldn't have said anything. Here, have some wine and you can tell me to mind my own business.'

Grateful for Sally's change of tack, Charlotte took the glass from her. She remembered the silver-framed photograph she had seen earlier and asked, 'Is that your sister in the wedding photo of you and Stephen, in the sitting-room?'

'Yes, my twin sister Lucy,' Sally replied, bending down to the oven and sliding a large casserole in. 'She died seven years ago.'

Her voice was matter of fact, in a way Charlotte felt sure hers would never be when talking about Peter's death. 'It's my turn to be sorry now,' she said.

'Don't be. It doesn't hurt any more to talk about her. You're not intruding on my grief . . . like I just did with you. It was crass of me. I should have realised it would be too soon for you to talk about your husband with somebody you hardly know.'

Was that another attempt to get her to open up, Charlotte wondered? She chose to ignore it. 'Was it a sudden death?'

'No. Leukaemia. It took her sixteen months to die . . . it was a long and painful time for us all . . . especially for Alex.' She saw the look on Charlotte's face. 'You did know that he and Lucy were . . .'

'No,' Charlotte said, her heart suddenly heavy with sadness for Alex. Why had he never said anything? Was it possible he was still in love with the memory of Lucy?

'You know, Lucy and I could never fool Alex,' Sally said, adopting a more cheerful voice. 'We led all our boyfriends a merry old dance. We'd swap dates and they'd never know. We even fooled poor Stephen. But Alex was the only one who could separate us. I used to joke that it was his sixth sense. Once he threatened to put us both over his knee if he ever suspected we were trying it on with him.'

'And did you?'

Sally laughed. 'Lucy was all set to give it a go but I chickened out. Believe it or not, I was the more timid of the two of us.'

'You must miss her. How did you come to terms with losing someone you were so close to?'

'This might seem strange but I don't think in terms of having lost her completely. Maybe because we were twins I feel a bit of Lucy is still with me.'

'And Alex, how did he . . . ?'

'It was so much harder for Alex. When Lucy died it was as though she took away his future. He had spent so long determined he was going to live the rest of his life with her. I had Stephen. But Alex had no one. He was alone and has been ever since.'

29

As they were finishing breakfast the next morning, the telephone rang. Stephen went to answer it in his study. He came back after a couple of minutes. 'Sorry,' he said, picking up the remains of his toast, 'but I'm going to have to leave you. One of the surgeons has gone down with tonsillitis, so bang goes a rare day off.' He turned to Sally. 'I'll give you a ring when I think I'll be able to get away.'

'You didn't tell me Stephen was a surgeon,' Charlotte said, when Sally and Mark had gone to the front door to wave goodbye to him.

'I didn't think we needed to pin identity labels on everyone,' Alex said, getting up from the table and starting to clear away the dishes.

Charlotte laughed. 'What a horrid, nasty man you are.'

At Sally's insistence, Alex and Charlotte were sent out on a walk. Mark's disappointed face peered from the doorway as they set off.

They turned left at the gate and set off along the open moorland road. At a fork in the road Alex chose the right one and led Charlotte uphill until they came to a footpath, which took them to a small craggy outcrop. A dozen or so frightened rabbits scampered away at the sound of encroaching footsteps, their lean bodies slithering into crevices hidden deep in the rocks. A bird flew overhead and Charlotte watched Alex raise his head, shading his eyes against the sun. 'A curlew,' he said, coming to a stop.

'I'll take your word for it,' she answered, her eyes remaining on Alex. Since her conversation with Sally last night she had been unable to stop herself thinking of Lucy and the devastating effect her death must have had on Alex. But the most persistent thought running through her mind was what it must have been like for Lucy to be loved in such a way. Plainly Alex had adored her.

From where they stood, they had a clear uninterrupted view of a landscape of endless moorland. The purple heather was at its best, with a summer fragrance that carried lightly on the wind. Charlotte sat down on one of the rocks, letting the moment last. The sprawling landscape held a quietness that right now she needed. There was a timeless quality about it that meant just here, just now, she was held in its reassuring vacuum. 'Thank you,' she said, looking up at Alex.

'What for?' He joined her on an adjacent rock.

'For this, for bringing me here.'

'It was a risk though, wasn't it?'

She smiled. 'I hadn't got you down as a gambling man.'

'Full of surprises, me.'

'Mm . . . you're right, you are.' Charlotte decided it was now or never. She wanted Alex to tell her about Lucy. She knew if she didn't hear the words from him she would never be able to rid herself of the memory of what Sally had told her last night – *He was alone and has been ever since.* 'Sally told me about her sister dying.'

There was no shocked response from him, as she might have thought. 'Did she tell you about Lucy and me?'

'A little. She mentioned . . .'

'Come on.' He stood up and took her hand, pulling her towards him. 'Let's walk and I'll tell you about my dark and murky past.'

They left the crags behind them and followed the footpath out across the purple heather. 'The four of us were all at university together,' Alex told her. 'We were a mixed bag to say the least. There was me, a complete freak as far as computers were concerned, and Stephen studying medicine. We were in our third year and both lodging with Mrs Holroyd. Remember, I told you about her? Then along came Sally and Lucy, into the house next door. They were both studying psychology – they really were identical, in everything. There were times when Stephen couldn't even . . .'

'Yes, Sally told me how he had trouble telling them apart, but that you always could.'

'Don't ask me how, I just knew.'

'I'm sorry, I interrupted. Carry on.'

'It wasn't long before I knew that I wanted to marry Lucy. I asked her several times and each time she turned me down, but refused to give a reason. Then we graduated and both ended up in London, independently of each other, but friends, close friends. I was working with Henderson and Wyatt and in a better position to ask Lucy to marry me, so I asked her one more time. Over dinner in her flat she told me she would never marry anybody and she explained why. She had this recurring dream – she'd had it since she was a child – that she was going to die before the age of thirty. She didn't want anyone to be saddled with that kind of heartbreak . . . she was so certain she was going to die.'

'But that's awful. Surely you must have convinced her otherwise.'

He shook his head. 'I managed to persuade her to live with me, and then, two years later, she was diagnosed as having leukaemia. She carried on working for as long as she could but she spent more and more time in hospital, until the doctors said there was nothing else they could do. She pleaded with me to bring her up here to Yorkshire to be with Sally and Stephen. They'd settled here by then. They nursed her to the end. Sally gave up her lecturing job at Leeds and I tried to spend as much time as I could helping . . . and just being there with Lucy. We all became very close during that time. I suppose the textbooks would call it a bonding experience.'

When he didn't carry on, Charlotte reached out to him. She touched his arm with her hand. 'Oh Alex. How *did* you cope, when you loved her so much?'

'I . . .' He looked down at his arm and without thinking he picked up Charlotte's hand, turned it over and pressed her palm to his lips, closing his eyes momentarily. 'It was Sally who held me . . . held us all together.' He lowered Charlotte's hand, but kept it at his side. 'She's incredibly strong. Nothing ever fazes her, not even after Mark was born and she and Stephen realised he was deaf.'

'Yes, I could see when she talked to me last night that there was a lot more to her than her youthful good looks.' But Charlotte wasn't only thinking of Sally's strength of character and courage, but of the determined love Alex once had for another woman. To be loved like that . . .

'Shall we go back to the crags now? There's something I'd like to show you.'

They stood where they had been an hour earlier. Small puffy white clouds had bubbled up and were hanging listlessly in the blue sky; the persistent cry of curlews overhead provided the only sound to penetrate the emptiness of the landscape.

'What did you want to show me?'

Alex guided her round to the back of a massive rock, weathered smooth by wind and time. 'Stand just there,' he said, 'about four feet away from the rock, and tell me what you can see.'

She laughed, feeling slightly silly, but did as he asked. 'Nothing in particular, just a large dark stone.' She turned to face him. 'Is that it?'

'Charlotte – I asked you this before – do you trust me?'

'For goodness' sake, Alex, what is all this?'

He took a step closer to her. 'That large dark stone, as you call it, represents Peter.'

She stepped away from him and pushed her hands down deep into the pockets of her jeans. She felt cross with Alex for reminding her of her failed marriage. And anyway, she had all that under control now. She had already begun to close that particular box in her life. 'I thought I was supposed to come here to get away from my problems.'

Why had he started this? What was he doing risking everything with her all over again? But Alex's instinct told him that something was stopping Charlotte from putting Peter to rest, and he suspected he knew what it was. 'I think it's time you started facing up to the main problem in your life,' he said.

'Oh yes,' she said, scathing sarcasm ringing in her voice. 'And what would that be, Mr Know-it-all?'

'I'm only guessing, but for some reason I think you're blaming yourself for what happened to Peter. Am I right?'

'That's rubbish,' she shouted defiantly. 'And what gives *you* the right to make assumptions like that?' She started to walk away from him. She was furious. Why couldn't he leave her be? They had been happy a few moments ago. Why did he have to keep spoiling things?

'Because,' Alex called out, catching up with her, 'when Lucy finally died . . . I felt such relief that it was all over. Suddenly I was free of the daily burden of grief that I'd experienced for two years. But that feeling of freedom soon passed and guilt took a hold of me and I nearly screwed up completely. I think guilt is your problem and, believe me, I know about it.' He was almost shouting at her now. He hadn't meant to, but he wanted to convince Charlotte that she was not alone.

She faced him. 'So what happened to you?'

'I pushed myself harder and harder at work, got more and more run down. Then Stephen came to stay. He saw the mess I was in and insisted I came back here to rest. One day Sally brought me to this very place and stood me behind that rock. She asked me what I could see and my answer was more or less what you just said, except I emphasised the darkness . . . for me the whole world had been eclipsed by what I was doing to myself.'

Charlotte swallowed hard. 'What did Sally say next?'

Alex led Charlotte back to the rock. When she was standing where she had stood a few moments ago, he said, 'Step back six paces and tell me what you can see now.'

She wanted to shout, oh stop all this nonsense, it's so facile, but instead she said, 'I can see . . . how much do you want me to tell you?'

'Everything you see.'

'Blue sky, white clouds, a bird flying, dry-stone walls, grass, some sheep, small houses over there, a church.' Without looking at Alex, she said, 'Is that where Lucy is buried?'

'Yes, but don't change the subject. Do you want to know what Sally said next?'

'Okay.'

'She told me it was time to step back from my boulder of guilt and take a look at the world behind it.'

'That's very interesting,' she said, 'but I'm over Peter's death, and I certainly don't have a problem with guilt.' She gave the rock a vicious kick and once again started to walk away.

But Alex was ready for her. He placed a firm hand on her shoulder and pulled her round to face him. 'Charlotte,' he said gently, 'stop pretending. Try talking to someone about it. Surely you must have a friend you could talk to.'

'No,' she answered. 'We were on the move so much I didn't make many close friends. Anyway, they're too busy, too wrapped up in their own lives and marriages to listen to me . . . apart from that, they all think that Peter and I . . .'

'Peter and you what?'

She remained silent, turned her face away from him.

And then he knew, understood at last what Charlotte's real pain was about. How stupid he had been! He had wondered at the time about those words she had uttered in the garden at Ivy Cottage, about her life in Belgium – *It was empty and cold and I hated it.* But that wasn't about her life in Belgium at all, that was her life with Peter. He said, 'So they all think that you and Peter had the perfect marriage? That you of all people couldn't possibly have stopped loving your husband. Is that it, Charlotte? Charlotte, talk to me.'

'Yes!' She yelled back at him. 'Yes, yes! Only hours before Peter died I'd asked him for a divorce . . . there, you're the first person I've told. Are you satisfied now?' Her words were angry and filled with pain as though they had been extracted from her under torture. And then suddenly her anger subsided and she fell against Alex and allowed him to lead her back to the rocks. There they sat, her shaking body held tightly against his own, while she sobbed and sobbed.

'I killed him, didn't I?' Charlotte said, when at last she had calmed down and had managed to tell Alex what had happened that snowy February morning and what had led to it. 'I upset him and he was in no state to drive. I shouldn't have let him go . . . I should have . . .'

Still with his arms round her, Alex said, 'But it was Peter who chose to walk out of the apartment that morning, it was Peter who was behind the wheel of his car, not you.'

She pulled away from him and shook her head. 'But Alex, if I hadn't said anything, Peter would still be alive today. I'm sure of it.'

'Would he, though? He would still have driven on that same road, he would have been just as determined to get to his meeting in Luxembourg . . . would have encountered that same patch of ice.'

'Yes, but that conversation did take place and it must have affected the way he drove.'

'Look, Charlotte, you have to come to terms with the fact that we can't control other people's reactions, it's just not possible. What happened to Peter happened because he chose to make that journey.'

He took her hand in his and squeezed it gently. She sighed and leaned against him again. They sat in silence for a while, until Alex placed a hand under her chin. 'Okay now?' he said in a low voice.

'Yes.' She lifted her head. Her eyes fixed on him were heavy with sadness and wonder. His heart twisted with compassion and he stroked the stray wisps of hair away from her face. Her eyes closed at his touch. He kissed first one eye, then the other, and then he kissed her on the lips, tentatively at first, but when she responded with an eagerness that matched his own, he cradled her head and tilted her back on to the flat surface of the rock. The touch and feel of her body clinging to him filled him with desire. Then in the distance he heard voices, children's voices. He tried to ignore the noise, hoping he was imagining it, but Charlotte's body was shaking. He looked down into her face, concerned. But she was laughing, her eyes wide open and reflecting the blue sky above. 'God, you're beautiful,' he said. 'Do you suppose we're always going to be interrupted?' He sat up and pulled her towards him as the voices came nearer.

She sprang to her feet, still laughing as a Scout troop weighed down with enormous backpacks passed by. 'We'll have to see, won't we?' she said.

They headed for home, hand in hand.

That evening, Charlotte and Sally were left alone while Stephen and Alex disappeared off to the pub for a pint of beer. It was a warm evening and they sat out in the garden with a bottle of Chianti and a large bag of peas to shell for supper. Charlotte began to tell Sally some of what happened on her walk with Alex that morning.

Looking up from the bowl of peas on her lap, Sally said, 'Why do you think you and Peter got married in the first place?'

'I think he only asked me to marry him because his parents didn't approve of me. They thought I was just a shop girl. The fact that it was my own shop was immaterial to them. I wasn't good enough for their son and Peter wanted to get his own back. In fact I don't think he would have married anyone who his parents actually did approve of.'

'So why did you accept?'

'Because . . . oh dear, this is going to sound pathetic, but I truly believed I could undo all the harm of Peter's upbringing.'

'Saint Charlotte the Saviour, eh?'

'That's not nice,' Charlotte said, but she smiled all the same.

'So, you married and then found you didn't have the necessary saintly qualities. But what made you want to take that final step to end your marriage?'

Charlotte snapped open a pea pod and popped out the peas. She put one in her mouth. 'It was when I knew that Peter was always going to put work first, that he didn't need a wife, simply someone permanently on hand to massage his ego. Then I knew I couldn't carry on as we were. Selfishly, I suppose, I wanted more . . . I wanted to be loved.'

'Nothing particularly selfish in that.'

'Okay then, you might be able to convince me that I shouldn't feel guilty about wanting to be loved, but how about the fact that I'm responsible for Peter's death?'

Sally put her bowl of peas down on the grass and picked up her wine glass. 'You're *not* responsible for Peter's death. It's possible that you want to believe you're to blame, and then not forgive yourself for it, because you want to keep punishing yourself. It can be an insidious self-defence mechanism against grief. Focusing on the injustice means that you can't forgive yourself, can't grieve properly. Does that make any sense, ring any bells?'

Charlotte leaned back in her chair. 'Oh yes,' she said. 'Yes, it certainly does.'

'More Chianti?'

'Mm . . . please.'

As Charlotte reached forward with her glass Sally said, 'Now, what are you going to do about Alex? You do realise, don't you, that you're the first woman he's allowed himself to fall in love with since Lucy?'

30

They drove back to Hulme Welford after breakfast the following day. Mark was disappointed that Alex wasn't staying longer. 'Come again,' he shouted as Alex started up the engine. And while Stephen said goodbye to Alex, Sally came round to Charlotte's side of the car.

'Now remember,' she said, 'stop being so hard on yourself.'

Charlotte leaned out of the car and gave Sally a kiss on the cheek. 'Thanks for everything.'

Once they had left the Pennines behind them and they were skirting round north Manchester, Charlotte realised that she was going home reluctantly. She had hoped her time away from Hulme Welford would give her the opportunity to think more clearly about her future. It hadn't. Her disclosure to Alex had left her battered and bruised, but it had made her see that she had been kidding herself that she was getting over Peter. Sally was right: she hadn't allowed herself to grieve for Peter, she had been too frightened of the consequences.

And Alex. What was she to do about him? Again she could no longer ignore what had been staring her in the face all these weeks. But love? Perhaps Sally was wrong. Maybe Alex might never be able to love another woman. Could anyone ever replace Lucy? Could she . . . did she want to?

With so much of the past hanging over her, Charlotte knew there was a lot she had to consider before she could even contemplate the future. She had to speak to Alex, and soon, but she didn't know where to start.

'You've got something to say, haven't you?'

She looked across at Alex. 'Sally mentioned you had a sixth sense.'

'That's great coming from her. I've never known anyone more perceptive.'

You're the first woman he's allowed himself to fall in love with . . . 'And is she always right?'

'Usually. But I'm an amateur compared to her. I only know when you've got something important to say because you frown slightly and you get three lines, just here.' He took his eyes off the motorway briefly and placed a finger on her forehead.

Her stomach lurched as he touched her. 'You're right though,' she said, watching his hand move back to the steering wheel, 'I do have something I want to say.'

'Go on, then.'

'No, not now. Later. I need to think first.'

'How about tonight, then? I'll cook us a meal, and you can talk.'

'I don't . . .'

'Look,' he said patiently, 'I want to call on Cindy and Derek and then perhaps go and see Barry in hospital. Do you want to come with me? We could talk afterwards.'

'You're very sure Barry's still alive, aren't you?'

He moved his hand from the wheel and rested it on her knee. 'If there's one thing my time with Lucy taught me, it was never to give up hope.'

'But she *died*, Alex,' Charlotte said, mystified.

'Yes, but *I* didn't . . . I thought my life would end when hers did, but it didn't.'

They tried calling at In The Pink later that afternoon and found the whole place shut. They drove on to the hospital where, at Barry's door, they were greeted by Tiffany. 'Come in. We were just talking about you two.'

'You were?' Alex smiled and walked over to the bed. 'Hello Barry, how's it going?'

'Surprisingly good, considering. Just tired, mainly.'

Charlotte couldn't believe what she was seeing. There was Barry, sitting up in bed wearing his familiar glasses, with a book lying open at his side. He looked pale and tired, and was still attached to a drip, but there was no sign of death about him, nor that there ever had been. She was so pleased! She went straight up to Barry and gave him a kiss, and then, sensing his embarrassment at her unexpected display of euphoria, she said, 'We've all been so worried about you.'

'Sorry to have been a nuisance,' he said, pushing his glasses up on his nose.

'Muffin 'ell, will you listen to him!' Tiffany shouted. 'Get him to tell you his exam results, they came this morning.'

'No, Tiffany, they don't want to know about that.'

''Course they do.' She turned to Alex and Charlotte. 'They're brill. Pure genius, this lad.'

Barry picked up the piece of paper by the side of his bed and passed it to Alex.

'A for physics,' Alex read out, 'A for chemistry, A for biology and, wait for it, A for economics. I'll say one thing for you, Barry, you're consistent. Well done!'

'Yes,' agreed Charlotte. 'Congratulations! I used to hate people like you at school. Your parents must be delighted, and I don't just mean with your exam results.'

'Dad's been a real head-case,' Tiffany said. 'He was here on his own when Barry came round on Tuesday.' She laughed. 'I'm not sure Dad's the first person I'd want to see after being in a coma!'

'Don't be so hard on him,' Barry said.

'What?' she cried. 'After the things he's said to you?'

'It's just his way.'

'So where are your parents?' Alex asked. 'We called in at your place, but there was no sign of anyone there.'

'The salon and everything's been shut since Barry's been here, but Mum and Dad are somewhere in the hospital. They went off to find the doctor to see about Barry coming home. We're hoping it'll be in a few days, or rather Dad is – he won't want to be paying for this private room for too long, will he? So anyway, you two been away or what?'

'Stop being so nosy, Tiffany,' Barry said.

Alex laughed. 'So that's what you were talking about when we arrived.' Worried that Barry was more tired than he was letting on, he added, 'We'd better be going, don't want to wear out the patient.'

'We reckon you've been away, *together*,' Tiffany persisted.

'Correction,' said Barry. 'That's what my sister thinks. Honestly, Tiffany, you get more like Dad every day.'

'Bloody well don't!'

Charlotte looked at Alex and realised that he was leaving it up to her to decide what to say. 'You're absolutely right, Tiffany. Alex took me to see some friends of his.'

Tiffany was triumphant. 'Told you,' she said, looking at her brother.

'You know,' Alex said, in the car on the way home, 'I don't think I can take the suspense any longer. Do you want to tell me now what it is that's on your mind?' Since their drive back from Yorkshire, he had been conscious of Charlotte's preoccupation with her own thoughts and he suspected that it had something to do with what she wanted to talk to him about. He sensed it wasn't good.

'Yes, perhaps you're right,' Charlotte answered distantly, 'now is probably as good as later. I just want to say how grateful I am for these past few days. You were right about many things, especially my liking Stephen and Sally.'

'So, why is it I detect an unspoken "but" in what you've just said?'

'Alex, both you and Sally made me see that I haven't really begun to get over Peter . . . Sally also said . . .' Charlotte paused, unsure just how to carry on. In her mind, she had worked out exactly what to say to him; it had sounded perfectly reasonable when she had gone over it earlier, but now she didn't feel so convinced. Sitting close to Alex in the car, watching his hands on the steering wheel, she was reminded of their time at the crags, when his hands had caressed her with such tenderness. The memory was so provocative she could almost feel the weight of his body against her own, could remember exactly the sensation of his mouth on hers. She shifted awkwardly in her seat.

'She told you I loved you, didn't she?' Alex said, bringing the car to a stop at a red traffic light. He turned and looked at her.

'Yes, she did.'

'So where does that leave us?'

'Oh Alex, I don't know. I feel so confused. I don't want to lie to you, it wouldn't be fair. I just don't think I'm capable of loving anyone, not after . . .'

'But you might feel differently in time.'

'Please, please don't push me.'

The traffic lights turned to amber, then green, and they completed the rest of the journey in silence.

Sat in his office, Alex was strangely calm. Surely he hadn't really hoped for more. He had been a fool to think that anyone who had gone through what Charlotte had would be inclined to take up with another man so soon. He had to give her space, so that she could get over Peter's death properly. She may not have loved him when he died, but she still had to go through some sort of grieving process for the man she had been married to for eight years; a process which, up until now, she had avoided.

Patience. That's what was called for. Let's face it, he had been patient with Lucy for all those years. He stared into the VDU screen in front of him, its blank whiteness waiting expectantly for him to fill it. He switched it off. Why, he wondered, did he fall for women who were determined to keep him at arm's length? Why couldn't he be satisfied with the Heathers of this world?

31

When Barry was discharged from hospital, he was welcomed home by the residents of Acacia Lane. Even Iris Braithwaite surprised everyone by calling round. 'A pot of honey for your son, Mrs Rogers. I recommend two spoonfuls a days, soon have him back on his feet.' Then Charlotte herself received a surprise.

She had just got back from the supermarket and emptied the car, when she looked out of the kitchen window and saw Alex sitting in the garden talking to an extraordinarily glamorous woman. It was a while before Charlotte realised who it was, because initially the combination of this particular woman sitting in this particular rickety old garden chair beneath her fig tree threw her completely.

'Christina!' she shouted, rushing outside. 'What on earth are you doing here?'

'Carlotta, my darling,' Christina said, rising elegantly from the old chair, 'I have been waiting here for you, so long.' She wrapped her graceful arms around Charlotte and kissed her several times. Then, standing back, she gave Charlotte a long hard stare. 'You still look dreadful, but slightly better than when you lived in Brussels. Carlotta, why are you looking like that, as though you weren't expecting me?'

'That's because I wasn't expecting you.'

'Did you not receive my letter, telling you I was coming?'

Charlotte shook her head. 'Sorry, no letter.'

'Oh, that is too bad. Then there is nothing else for it. I shall leave you to recover from your shock and return tomorrow. Perhaps that would suit you better?' She offered Alex one of her most seductive smiles. 'I am sure Mr Hamilton here would provide me with a bed for the night.'

Alex smiled, until Charlotte threw him a keep-out-of-this look. 'Don't be so silly, Christina,' she said. 'I'm delighted you're here. It's just that there's nothing ready for you and the house is such a mess.'

Christina shrugged her shoulders dismissively. 'What else do I need? I have your company and your nice Mr Hamilton to amuse me.' She laid a perfectly manicured hand on his arm. 'Oh yes, I have everything I could possibly desire.' She seemed to add an extra emphasis to the word desire. Charlotte began to feel uneasy.

'And why, Carlotta, have you never written to me of your charming neighbour? If I had been you I would have written of little else.'

Trying hard not to laugh, Alex got to his feet. 'I think I'd better leave you to it. I have some work I need to get on with.'

Christina looked up at him. 'I am so sorry to have kept you. But Carlotta darling, could we not invite Mr Hamilton for dinner?'

'I'm sure,' Charlotte said firmly, giving Alex a warning glance, 'that Mr Hamilton has far too much work to do to spare us any of his valuable time.'

'I have?' asked Alex.

'You have,' Charlotte repeated. 'You've probably got enough to keep you busy for days.'

'Oh, stacks to do,' Alex said, making a move towards his part of the house. 'I shan't surface for weeks probably. Goodbye.'

'Well,' Christina said, in a voice designed to carry, 'what a most desirable man and those gorgeous blue eyes. Have you slept with him?'

'Christina!' cried Charlotte in a shocked voice, watching Alex as he disappeared inside. Had he heard?

'What, what have I said? He's young, he's handsome, he's amusing and he's living in your house with you. Why in heaven's name do you not sleep with him?'

That, thought Charlotte, is the million-dollar question.

Charlotte unpacked the shopping and stuffed the empty carrier bags into the bin, ignoring Hilary's imaginary voice in her head reminding her of the recycling banks in the village. What on earth was she going to give Christina for supper that night? She pulled open the fridge, knelt down and stared at all the food she had just bought. She waited for inspiration to come, but it was no good – she had only chosen convenience foods in the supermarket. They would have to go out to eat. She'd drive them over to Knutsford; plenty of upmarket restaurants there to impress Christina with.

Charlotte opened a can of dog food for Mabel and was putting the dish down on the floor by the back door when a cloud of expensive perfume came into the kitchen, followed by Christina. She was dressed in a close-fitting, red and white striped dress, which would have made anyone else look like a stick of candy, but on Christina looked stunning.

Mabel obviously thought so too. Giving her dish of food not a second glance, she pattered across the kitchen floor, looked up at Christina and rolled over on to her back, her paws hanging limply in the air.

'Oh, what a perfectly splendid little *bambino*,' Christina cried. She bent down to Mabel and rubbed her tummy. 'Carlotta, you have much to tell me, I think. Why don't you take me out to one of your famous pubs for supper?'

Charlotte laughed. 'I don't think the Spinner is quite ready for you, Christina.'

'But I am ready for the Spinner. Come on, Carlotta, where is your sense of fun? Let me get you out of those drab clothes and into something to set the Spinner on fire.'

It was impossible not to catch Christina's infectious humour and it made Charlotte realise that up until that point she had acted quite churlishly towards her friend. She wondered why. Was it because Christina had flirted so outrageously with Alex in the garden?

They opened the wardrobe doors in Charlotte's bedroom and got to work. 'Too dull,' Christina said, as Charlotte took out a smart pair of fawn-coloured trousers. 'Too morbid,' she sighed in response to a black pair. 'Come on, Carlotta, go for lightness, lightness of heart and spirit. Oh, I can see I came just in time to save you from dying of dullness. Ah here, wear this.'

Charlotte looked doubtfully at the strapless cream dress in Christina's hands. She hadn't worn it since last summer, when she had gone with Peter to Nice, he to give a presentation at the company conference and she to sit next to him at the dinner afterwards and bask gratefully in his reflected glory. After the meal the chairman had stood up and thanked all his hard-working colleagues for their unstinting loyalty to the company, telling them to keep up the good work. Not a word did he say to those wives present who had given up so much of themselves to travel with their husbands so that they could feel fulfilled; not a word of thanks to those wives who had given up their own careers and possibly their children to boarding school for the sake of continuity in their education. When the last of the liqueurs had been tossed back and the cigars stubbed out, Charlotte had tried to tempt Peter into a walk along the beach, but he had refused, preferring instead the company of his overhead slides for another presentation he had to give the following morning. And so, beneath the midnight sky, her shoes in her hands, Charlotte had walked along the water's edge alone.

'Okay,' she said. 'I'll wear it.'

She slipped into the dress and sat on a stool in the bathroom to let Christina see to the rest of her. First her friend wove her hair into a French plait. Then came her face. Looking with disgust at Charlotte's haphazard collection of make-up, Christina fetched her own. When she declared that she was finished, Charlotte looked apprehensively into the mirror. She was delighted. The shadows under her eyes had magically disappeared and somehow Christina had managed, with a few simple strokes of powder, mascara and lipstick, to give her a facelift. She looked good and she felt wonderful.

'And now,' Christina said, 'you must wear my perfume. We must not clash, we must not compete with each other.' She sprayed Charlotte liberally. 'There now, you are ready, and I think it would be nice for us to have a chaperon for the evening.'

'No,' Charlotte said vehemently. 'Alex is busy.'

Christina laughed. 'What a charming idea. But no, I was thinking of your little *bambino*. This is strictly a girls' night out.'

When they strolled arm in arm down Acacia Lane Charlotte was aware of a strange feeling bubbling up inside her. It wasn't until they got as far as the village hall that she recognised what the strange feeling was. She felt incredibly sexy. Tottering along on her high heels, wearing her girlfriend's lipstick and feeling as radiant as a star, she was nineteen again. With sadness, she knew she had never felt like that with Peter. How out of touch with her emotions she had become . . . until now. She caught her breath. Oh Alex. There it was. The truth, at last. Alex had unwittingly frightened her because he had made her come to know what she had been missing all these years and as hard as she had tried to resist him it had only made things worse, had made her want him all the more.

They made a predictably striking entrance at the Spinner, causing heads to turn and Ted the Toup to lose contact with the cigarette drooping out of his mouth; it plopped and fizzed into his beer. While Charlotte herself wasn't entirely comfortable with the position of centre stage, she knew Christina was perfectly at ease. For Christina there was no other position.

Hoping there would be fewer people outside, Charlotte led the way through the noisy public bar and out to the garden. They sat in the evening sun at a large wooden table with two benches either side, and the landlord came out personally to serve them. He took their order with a flourish of efficiency that would have even impressed Iris Braithwaite.

'Now Carlotta,' Christina said, when they were alone, 'how have you been? Your letters tell me nothing about you, only about your sister and your parents, oh, and a Mrs Britwit.'

'Mrs Braithwaite,' Charlotte corrected, with a smile.

'Now, tell me about yourself. Are you happy?'

'I'm happier.'

Christina shook her head. 'That is not good enough. Let me ask you this: would you rather be back in Brussels in that miserable apartment with that miserable husband of yours?'

'Christina, you can't ask things like that.'

'But I just have.'

'Well, no. No, I wouldn't want to be back there.'

'Good, so we have progress; now all you have to do is forgive yourself.'

Charlotte looked up sharply. This was exactly what Sally had told her. Was there a conspiracy? 'Why do you say that?'

'Because it's true. I was there with you in Brussels, I saw how unhappy you were. I knew why too. I knew that you felt guilty because you could not make yourself fit your husband's requirements. Few wives truly can. I knew too that you did not love Mr Carlotta . . . and that Mr Carlotta did not love you. So simple really. Nobody's fault, so nobody to blame, just forgive and—'

'But you can't forget,' Charlotte interrupted.

'No, I was not going to say forget, I was going to say *move on*. You should be a Catholic like me: you get forgiven every week and you move on.'

Charlotte laughed and then she frowned. 'Would you like to hear a confession?'

'Why not?'

'Remember the morning Peter died?'

'Yes, I remember it well, all that snow.'

'While we were having breakfast I asked Peter for a divorce.'

Christina looked across the table at her friend. She took Charlotte's hand. 'Oh my poor little Carlotta, so that is why you are still sad, I see now. But why did you not tell me?'

'Because . . .'

'Because you are so very English.'

'And you are not, if you don't mind me saying,' said the landlord of the Spinner as he put their tray of food down on the table.

'My dear man,' smiled Christina, 'how clever of you. What gave me away?'

The man beamed. 'Oh you know, little things.' He passed them their chicken and chips. 'The drinks are on the house,' he added, almost bowing as he made his exit.

'Tell me, Carlotta, here is a phrase I do not know – the drinks are on the house. What does it mean?'

Charlotte laughed. 'It means they're free, because the landlord of the Spinner has fallen in love with you, Christina.'

'That is good, we shall come here tomorrow, I think,' she said, spearing a huge chip with her fork. 'And why have you not fallen in love with Mr Hamilton?'

Sprinkling salt on to her meal and then some vinegar, Charlotte said. 'To be honest, Christina, I think I probably could fall in love with him.'

'That is very good.'

'No, it's not good. I don't want to fall in love with him, or anyone else for that matter. Not at the moment.'

'Oh Carlotta, you make your life so very difficult.' She speared another chip. 'Delicious,' she said, putting it to her lips and managing to make it look like an erotic act. 'Now I will tell you all about my friend Henri the Diplomat. He's so beautiful and with legs to die for.'

Glad the pressure was off her, Charlotte said, 'You must be missing him.'

'I had thought I might, but that was before I met your delightful Mr Hamilton.'

Charlotte laughed. But Christina looked serious. 'Why are you laughing? What is so funny?'

'Come on, Christina, Alex is too nice to be added to your list of . . .' She paused, list of what? What did one call Christina's men friends? Were they clients or lovers? She settled for the latter. '. . . Lovers.'

'I think a little souvenir of England to take home might be nice though.'

Charlotte looked shocked. 'But you can't . . .'

Christina smiled. 'Oh, but I think I will. After all, you do not seem to want him, do you?'

32

'Just thought I'd pop round,' said Hilary coming through the open conservatory door. 'Heard you'd got a friend staying.'

I bet you did, thought Charlotte, knowing that last night's visit to the Spinner would have the village spinning on its axis in a tizzy of excitement and curiosity for days to come. And all because Christina had insisted, in a loud voice, that the Spinner wasn't the real thing. 'How can it be so, there is no piano, there is no one singing?' Hearing this, the landlord had fetched his son's keyboard down from upstairs and called upon Mr Phelps, the church organist, to come out of the snug and put his hands to good use. With everyone gathered round him ready to sing, including Christina and Charlotte, Mr Phelps rose to the occasion and surprised them all by revealing his true musical bent, which was honky-tonk. He opened up with 'Down at the Old Bull and Bush' and then moved through a repertoire that included 'We'll Meet Again', 'I'm Getting Married in the Morning', and because he knew Christina came from somewhere across the Channel he played '*Viva España*' again and again, until Ted the Toup demanded 'The Birdy Song'.

'I heard there was a bit of a party down at the Spinner last night.' Hilary already knew all the details of last night's goings-on. Ted had been only too willing to impart his news when she had gone to pick up her copy of *Hello!*

'I danced with a fancy foreign piece last night,' he had told her with relish. 'She's a friend of your sister's from abroad, you know, got a real body on her, too.'

'So where is she, this friend of yours?' Hilary pursued.

'She's not here,' Charlotte said, scrubbing hard at a particularly stubborn stain on the cooker hob she was cleaning.

'Oh, you mean she's gone home already?' Hilary was unable to keep the disappointment out of her voice. She had rushed straight from Ted the Toup's to Charlotte's in the hope of meeting this incredible creature, who had apparently enslaved both Ted and the landlord of the Spinner in one fell swoop.

'She's out with Alex,' Charlotte answered through clenched teeth. 'He's taken her to see the Italian Gardens at Tatton.'

Hilary was shocked. She had thought that things were more or less in the bag, ever since Tiffany had told her Charlotte and Alex had been away together. But if Ted's description of this woman was anything to go by, then Alex was in serious danger. 'Why on earth didn't you go with them?'

'Because I had a headache,' Charlotte snapped back, 'and I didn't feel like it.' Reluctant as she was to admit it, this was not the truth. Over breakfast Christina had suggested they go out for the day, suggesting also, 'We could take your lovely Mr Hamilton with us?'

'Look, Christina,' Charlotte had said on the edge of losing her temper, 'let's just get this clear. Alex Hamilton is not my lovely anything, okay?'

'Okay, okay, but let's invite him anyway . . . I think I would very much like him to be my lovely something for the day.'

Before Charlotte could stop her, Christina was next door inviting Alex to accompany them on an outing. Even worse, Alex proposed a trip to Tatton to show Christina the Italian Gardens. At the last moment, in a desperate attempt to sabotage things, Charlotte feigned a headache – a headache that had all the potential of a full-blown migraine.

'My poor Carlotta,' Christina sympathised, 'you must rest, you must stay out of the sun. I will put you to bed and there you will stay. But we cannot possibly disappoint Mr Hamilton. I shall try my best to amuse him in your absence.' She settled Charlotte in bed, pulled the curtains across and ignored her protestations of suddenly feeling so much better. 'No, no, you are only trying to be brave,' Christina insisted, shutting the bedroom door softly behind her and then the front door with a resounding bang.

'What time did they go out?' Hilary asked. 'And when are they due back?'

'What is this, Hilary, the Hulme Welford Inquisition?'

'I only asked.' Hilary decided she had better change the subject. 'What are you wearing to Barry's confirmation tomorrow?'

Charlotte moved over to the sink and rinsed out the cloth she had been using to clean the cooker. 'I really don't know. I haven't thought that far ahead.'

No, thought Hilary, I'm not surprised, not with Alex being seduced in amongst the topiary, right now this minute. 'Shall I help you choose something?'

'No!' shouted Charlotte. 'No, and I just wish everyone would leave me alone.'

Hilary tactfully withdrew to The Gables. Her only hope was that if her sister was ruffled by the fact that Alex was out with Christina, then all was not completely lost.

It was nearly ten o'clock that evening when Charlotte heard Alex's car pulling up on the drive, followed by the sound of Christina's light tinkling laughter. But it was well past midnight before Christina came and rang the door bell.

Charlotte let her friend in and tried to show indifference to Christina's profuse apologies for being so late. 'Carlotta, forgive me, please. I have never known the time to fly so fast.'

'Goodness, is that the time already?' Charlotte responded. 'I had no idea it was so late. I've been reading.'

Christina dropped gracefully on to the sofa and looked about her, to where her friend must have been sitting. The armchair with its squashed cushion was surrounded by a trail of late-night snacking debris – an empty coffee cup, a plate with the remains of some crackers and an empty packet of crisps. No sign of a book.

'I was reading upstairs,' lied Charlotte, knowing the conclusion Christina must have reached. Then, looking her friend in the eye, she said, 'What have you been up to all day and all evening?'

Christina laughed, eased off her shoes and stretched out her long painted toes, managing to make them perform a neat Mexican wave. Charlotte wondered whether those artful little piggies had just been caressed by Alex's hands. But the thought of Alex's hands, which she had so coveted, caught her off guard and exposed the depth of her anger.

'So come on, Christina,' she demanded, 'what have you done to Alex?'

Again that light tinkling laugh. 'Carlotta, please, do you have to be so blunt?'

'Ah! That's rich coming from you. What was it you said yesterday in the garden and quite loud enough for Alex to hear – "Have you slept with him?" Well, if that wasn't being blunt, I don't know what is.'

Christina stretched back lazily on the sofa. The smile was still in place, but her eyes were not looking so kindly. 'Tell me, Carlotta,' she said, 'what exactly is it you want to know? Whether I have been making love to your adorable Mr Hamilton, the lovely Alex, with his so, *so* blue eyes? By the way, have you ever noticed his hands, he has the most creative hands?' She noticed Charlotte's face blanch. 'Well, Carlotta, is that it, is that what you want to know?'

'Yes,' cried Charlotte, pacing the room, 'yes it bloody well is!'

Christina sighed and got up from the sofa. Carrying her shoes, she made for the door. 'I think I shall go to bed now, I am so very tired ... but Carlotta, I think you already know the answer to your question, don't you? Goodnight.'

33

Tiffany came into the kitchen brushing her long pink hair with a heavily matted brush that had never been near the salon sterilising unit. She took one look at Barry and whistled. 'You look a bit of all right. Shame you're my brother!'

'For God's sake!' rebuked Derek, coming in behind her. 'Do you have to be so vulgar? This is Bas's bloody confirmation, not an episode of *Blind Date*.' He turned to his son. 'She's right though, Bas. That suit looks great on you. Makes you look quite a chip off the old block.'

Tiffany cringed. 'Let's hope not.'

Barry ran his hand through his hair, nudged his glasses, then fiddled with the knot of his new tie. Picking up on his son's nervousness, Derek said, 'Where's your mum? It's about time to get this show on the road, isn't it?' He looked up at the kitchen clock and then at his wristwatch, remembering that this was how he had felt twenty-two years ago, standing in his parents' tiny kitchen, before driving off to the church in his father's light green Zephyr to marry Cindy. God, how he had wanted to get all the churchy business over and done with, so that he could get on to the reception afterwards and pour a beer down his throat. He began strumming his fingers on the worktop.

'For goodness' sake, Dad, calm down,' Tiffany said, tossing her hairbrush on to the table. She bent down to tie up a purple ribbon she had threaded through the lace-holes of one of her boots. The other boot wore an orange ribbon and both laces matched perfectly the tie-dye baby-doll smock she wore over aubergine-coloured Lycra leggings. Straightening up, she added, 'Mum was outside ordering the caterers about in the marquee the last time I saw her.'

'Well go and give her a shout, will you? Tell her it's time to hit Westminster Abbey.' He watched his daughter go clomping off, then called after her, 'And tell her nicely. I don't want you rattling her today. Nervous, Bas?' he said, when Tiffany had gone.

Barry smiled. 'A bit.'

'Jesus, so am I! Sorry, shouldn't have said that, should I?'

'What?'

'You know, the Jesus bit.'

Barry laughed. 'Relax, Dad, it's me who's getting confirmed, not you.'

Derek looked hard at his son and felt real pride. Bas hadn't put the weight back on that he'd lost and his face still showed signs of fatigue, but despite this, Derek found himself having to admit that Bas was better looking than he himself had ever been. A damned sight smarter as well. Ever since that dreadful phone call, the day of the barbecue, he had felt differently towards Bas. Strange, too, that since that day he hadn't made any further attempts on Charlotte; he had left the gate to that particular field wide open for Alex. God, he hoped he wasn't going through some kind of midlife crisis.

He glanced across the kitchen at Bas again, seeing him no longer as some young kid who embarrassed him, but as a man ... as a friend even. He cleared his throat. 'Look, Bas,' he started to say, 'things haven't always been ...' He paused, frightened of making a complete fool of himself.

'What, Dad, what's up?'

Derek paced over to the French windows and looked out at the garden where there seemed to be dozens of people milling about, some with chairs, some with covered trays and some with bottles of wine. He ran his tongue over his lips, wanting more than anything a drink.

'What's wrong, Dad?'

He turned round to face his son. 'I just wanted to say ... well, the thing is ... I don't want to let you down today.'

'You won't.'

'But I have already. I mean, all these years I've been a ... I've been a right bastard to you, haven't I?'

'Dad ...'

'You see, Bas, I've never really understood you ... Jesus, Bas, I've always been scared of you.'

'Scared!' Barry repeated, taken aback at this revelation. 'How do you mean?'

'It's no good, I need a drink,' Derek said, striding across the kitchen and pulling open the fridge. He offered a can of lager to Barry.

'No thanks.'

Derek hesitated, his hand poised over the ring pull, his dry throat gasping to be satiated, but his brain calling for restraint. 'Perhaps you're right,' he said, 'perhaps I shouldn't either. Don't want the old biddies at St John's keeling over from the fumes of probably the best lager in the world, do we?'

Barry watched his father move away from the fridge. 'Why are you frightened of me, Dad?'

Derek swallowed hard and pushed his hands down into his trouser pockets. 'Because you're so bloody clever! You've always managed to make me feel such a prat.'

Barry looked shocked. 'I never meant to.'

Derek shook his head. 'I know, Bas, and let's face it, I don't need anyone's help to make me look an idiot. I do a pretty good job of it on my own.'

'Dad, I ...'

'Yeah, well, keep it to yourself,' Derek said, his face breaking into a sudden smile as he heard the sound of his wife's voice coming towards the kitchen. 'Don't want everyone knowing I've been baring my soul to you, do we?'

Cindy stood still for a moment and stared at Barry. 'You look wonderful,' she said with a faint tremor to her voice.

Barry didn't know what to say; first a confession from his father and now, after all these years, for the first time in his life, he had pleased his mother.

Derek followed behind his family as they walked up the aisle towards their reserved pew. He tried not to look about him, tried hard to fix his eyes on the chequered floor ahead, but he found it impossible. He hadn't expected the church to be so full. He knew that Bas had invited a few friends, but he hadn't said half the school was coming. And wasn't that Mr Knox, the headmaster, sitting next to Louise Archer?

'Okay, Dad?' Barry whispered, as they sat down.

'Yes,' Derek rasped back, 'I'm fine.' No I'm not, he thought, panic-stricken and looking anxiously about the church. He caught sight of Iris Braithwaite beneath a stern black hat and felt the comforting urge to crack a joke. He turned to nudge Bas and found he wasn't there. Oh God, he said under his breath, seeing his son on his knees beside him. Was that really necessary? He waited for what seemed for ever before Bas surfaced. 'That better?' he asked.

At the end of the service, Charlotte tried to bundle Christina out of the church as quickly as she could. She had no intention of letting her friend stir up as much interest at St John's as she had in the Spinner.

'Oh Carlotta, such a handsome young man, that Barry is,' Christina said, as they passed through the lych-gate. 'No wonder you wanted to come back to Hulme Welford. How is it that there are so many gorgeous men in such a tiny village?'

'Good grief, Christina!' Charlotte said bad-temperedly. 'Isn't one conquest in the village enough for you?' She had barely opened her mouth to Christina all morning; breakfast had been distinctly chilly, just two cereal bowls and a jug of cold milk between them.

'Carlotta, you are very cross with me, aren't you?'

'Cross, me? Why on earth should I be cross with you?'

Christina laughed. 'Oh, there's Alex.'

Charlotte turned and saw Alex coming up behind them as they were about to cross the road. Her mood wasn't improved by the wide smile on his face. 'Saw you sitting at the back of the church,' he said, drawing level.

'We were lucky to get a seat,' Charlotte said tersely. 'Madam here was so exhausted from your exploits in the Italian Gardens yesterday that she overslept.'

Christina rolled her eyes at Alex. 'I think our poor Carlotta still has her headache, she is in such a bad mood.'

'Oh rubbish!' Charlotte said, stepping off the pavement and causing a

Lycra-clad cyclist to swerve out into the middle of the road. He threw his fist at her along with a few choice expressions.

'Neville, have you gone completely mad?' Louise raised her voice above the sound of Abba's 'Dancing Queen'. 'There's more than a thousand calories on your plate.'

'Yes dear, I know,' Neville answered, licking his lips in eager anticipation of sinking his teeth into the chicken drumstick on his plate, along with the large dollop of avocado dip, a couple of miniature sausage rolls and a slice of salmon and cream cheese roulade, 'and that's nothing compared to the calories I shall be consuming when it's pud time,' he added with a glint in his eye. 'Tiffany told me there's trifle, crème brûlée and strawberries and cream.'

Louise raised her eyebrows. 'I don't know what's got into you. Ever since you won that prize yesterday you've been quite unbearable. It was only second prize. Anyone would think you'd won the wretched cup.'

Neville beamed, took a large bite out of his chicken drumstick and chewed with lip-smacking delight. 'Time to circulate, I think. I should get yourself some lunch. Derek and Cindy have done Barry proud.' Leaving his wife floundering – for the first time in their marriage – Neville saw Charlotte and her famous friend sunning themselves on a bright pink swinging seat. He pulled in his stomach and strolled over.

'Hello, Dad,' Charlotte said, helping herself to a sausage roll from his plate. 'Mum know you've got all that?'

'Indeed she does.'

Something in her father's voice made Charlotte look at him more closely. 'You're looking very pleased with yourself. What have you been up to?'

He smiled broadly and cleared his throat as though preparing to make an important announcement. 'I won second prize yesterday at the gooseberry show: thirty-five pennyweights and sixteen grains with my Edith Cavell.'

Charlotte's mouth fell open. She was mortified. 'Dad, I was going to be there.' She looked sideways at her friend. 'But I forgot all about it, what with Christina turning up so unexpectedly.'

With perfect timing, Christina held out her hand to Neville. 'My dear man, I am so sorry to have kept Carlotta from you, do forgive me.'

Neville chuckled like a schoolboy. 'Think nothing of it.'

Christina patted the space between herself and Charlotte. 'Now sit here with us and tell me about this wonderful prize you have won. But first, what is a gooseberry show and who is Edith Cavell?'

Charlotte got up from her seat. 'Go on, Dad,' she said, 'don't hold back. This is your big opportunity. Tell Christina all about it while I go and get us some wine.'

She wandered over to the yellow and white striped marquee and saw Barry coming towards her, carrying a tray of glasses. 'Hello,' he said. Behind him a small, attractive girl appeared. She had a mop of curly red hair, which gave her an Orphan Annie appearance. She too was carrying a tray of drinks. 'I'll go on ahead and give these to the others,' she said, offering Barry a dazzling smile.

'Okay. I'll be there in a moment.'

'Nice girl,' Charlotte said, watching Orphan Annie make her way to the bottom of the garden where all the younger members of the party were congregated.

Barry nudged his glasses. 'She is, isn't she? Going to Leeds as well.'

'Really,' she said with a smile. 'Medicine?'

'No. Theology.'

'You do surprise me.' She turned to look up at the house as the sound of 'Sultans of Swing' came to a finish and 'Like a Bat out of Hell' started up.

'Dad loves this,' Barry said.

'And so does Malcolm Jackson, by the looks of things,' Charlotte replied, watching what was taking place on the patio.

Cindy's carefully placed tubs of pink geraniums had been moved out of the way and Malcolm – now in mufti – together with Derek, was giving Meatloaf a fair run for his money. They were each holding a stick of celery and singing into the leafy end as though it were a microphone, the volume of their voices matching that of the hi-fi system.

Charlotte and Barry looked at one another and began to laugh. Then Barry handed her the tray of drinks and, grabbing a baguette from a passing waitress, he went up to join his father and the vicar. But when Barry approached the patio Derek seemed to falter, losing his place. He watched his son take up the baguette and start to sing. He put his arm round Barry and they sang together.

Most of the guests started clapping and cheering, and Barry's school-friends, hearing the noise, came up from the bottom of the garden to see what was happening. They soon joined in with the cheering, and a few went on to the patio to give their voices an airing and to pluck a few imaginary guitars.

Coming out of the marquee with her hands full of dirty plates, Cindy took in the scene. Charlotte watched her anxiously. Cindy's eyes filled with tears and she began to cry. Charlotte ditched Barry's tray of drinks on a nearby table, took the pile of crockery from Cindy and hugged her.

'Oh God,' Cindy cried, 'why has it taken eighteen years for this moment? Why are families so horrible to each other?' She sniffed loudly and then pulled away from Charlotte. 'I'm sorry,' she said, patting her perfect hair into place, 'this is absurd.'

Charlotte stiffened. Peter had said exactly the same the morning he had died, the morning he had revealed to Charlotte that he was emotionally fragile after all, just like any other human being. Poor Cindy. Why couldn't she just throw away that self-protective mask she wore and let people see her for what she really was? But of course it wasn't that easy, was it? Wasn't that what she herself had been doing all the time she had been back in Hulme Welford, hiding behind her precious mask of widowhood?

They watched the show on the patio come to an end and joined in with the applause.

'Muffin 'ell!' shouted Tiffany, coming towards them with Becky on her back. 'Were they embarrassing or what?'

'I thought they were good,' Cindy said, reaching for the pile of plates Charlotte had taken from her. 'I'll go and put these in the dishwasher.' She walked towards the house.

'What's up with Mum?' Tiffany shifted Becky to a more comfortable position on her back.

'I think she's happy.'

'Happy? Mum? Never. Come on, Becky, let's go and find you something to eat.'

Remembering she was supposed to have been fetching some drinks, Charlotte followed Tiffany into the marquee and was knocked back by the mélange of canvas-induced heat, the scent of crushed grass and the not-so-sweet smell of fifty-seven varieties of overstretched deodorant. On one side of the marquee tables covered in yellow cloths held an assortment of buffet food and on the other side stood white-dressed tables laden with shining glasses and bottles of wine, mineral water and beer. Charlotte helped herself to three glasses of wine and, wanting to get out of the oppressive heat as fast as possible, she turned to go but crashed into another guest. She jerked at the splash of cold wine against her chest. She looked up to see Alex.

'I'm sorry, Charlotte,' he said.

She glared at him, and for a moment, neither seemed to know what to say next.

'Mrs Lawrence,' boomed Iris Braithwaite, who knew exactly what to say. 'Just look at the state of you. What kind of a confirmation party is this? First Reverend Jackson makes a fool of himself out there in the garden and now you, in here, revealing ... revealing all!'

Charlotte followed Iris's pointed stare and saw to her horror that the top of her white shift dress was practically transparent. She wasn't wearing a bra and the material was clinging mercilessly to her breasts. She plucked frantically at the thin fabric, trying to pull it away from her nipples. Looking up, she saw that Alex was smiling.

'How dare you!' she shouted angrily. She crashed the now half-empty glasses on the table behind her and turned and slapped Alex hard on the cheek.

'Mrs Lawrence!' roared Iris. But she got no further as she watched in horror Alex seize Charlotte and kiss her full on the lips.

'Mr Hamilton!' Iris almost pleaded, looking about her for back-up. But none was in the offing and the only voice to be heard was, 'Ooh look, Mummy, Auntie Charlotte's bonking that man who lives next door to her.'

'How dare you!' Charlotte repeated as Alex dragged her out of the marquee and towards the bottom of the garden. 'How bloody dare you do this to me . . . and in front of everyone.'

'Oh, come on,' he said, rounding on her, 'that's not what this is all about.'

'And what's that supposed to mean?'

'You know perfectly well what I'm talking about. You're as angry as hell with me, aren't you?'

'Yes . . . I mean no. What am I supposed to be angry with you about, apart from drenching me and making me look a fool?'

'You're angry because you think I slept with Christina. Isn't that right?'

She gave a loud derisive laugh. 'What you get up to in the privacy of your own rented house has got nothing to do with me.'

'Admit it, you're jealous.'

'I am *not*!' she exclaimed contemptuously, raising her hand once more to slap him.

'Charlotte,' he said, catching hold of her wrist, 'do as you're told for once and listen to me, *please*.'

She snatched her arm away from him. 'Okay then, I'm listening.'

He placed his hand under her elbow and marched her to the seat they had shared once before, overlooking the small pond. The cherub was still spouting and the ornamental toad looked just as ugly.

'I'm sorry for what just happened, Charlotte. I shouldn't have done that. But haven't you any idea how incredible you looked, standing there . . .'

'Don't be ridiculous.' She crossed her arms in front of her.

'What in heaven's name do I have to do to make you understand what you mean to me? Tell me and I'll do it.'

She said nothing, her mouth tightly shut.

'Charlotte, I think you ought to know that I've simply no intention of letting you go. You should know me well enough by now to realise I don't give up easily. And as to last night . . .' He lifted his hand to stop her outburst. 'Please, just hear me out. I've asked you several times before if you trusted me, right?'

'Yes,' she said, heavy irony in her voice, 'you have.'

'Have I blown it now?'

'Well, what do you think? Christina's my friend.'

'Would it have been okay with Heather, then?'

'No! I mean yes . . . oh Alex. For God's sake stop it, please.'

'Charlotte,' he said, 'nothing happened last night. It was an idea I should never have agreed to.'

'Whose idea?'

'Christina's.'

'I might have known. And what was this *idea* supposed to achieve?'

'To make you jealous,' he said, shamefaced. 'I'm sorry. It was a rotten thing to do to you. I never wanted to hurt you. And now I have and I hate myself for it. You'd think at my age I'd be past playing juvenile games like that, wouldn't you?'

Charlotte thought for a moment, taking Alex's words in. Jealous. Of course she had been jealous. Christina's plan had worked perfectly. She had lain awake all last night picturing Christina and Alex in bed; the images of them together had tortured her hour after hour in the dark until finally dawn had filtered through the curtains, allowing her a couple of hours of precious sleep. 'Well, it worked, didn't it?' she said, looking straight ahead of her. 'I *was* jealous.'

Alex sighed. 'I've made a right bloody mess of things, haven't I?' He took her hand and raised it to his lips. 'Do you think you could forgive me?'

'You know, I told Christina the other night that I probably could fall in love with you . . .'

'Charlotte . . .'

'No, let me finish. It's just that I'm terrified of discovering that it's me . . . that I'm not capable of making a relationship work . . . I'm petrified of taking the risk, of hurting you.'

'Try me. I'm pretty tough.'

'There's something else I'm scared of: Lucy.'

'Lucy? My God, you don't think I'm still in love with . . .'

'It's possible, isn't it?'

He put his hands on her shoulders. She tried to turn away from him, but he held her firmly and forced her to meet his gaze. 'We all have a past,' he said slowly, 'and Lucy is mine. When she died I truly thought there'd never be anyone else in my life. But now there is. You. I just wish you could understand what that means to me.' He clasped her face in his hands and kissed her. 'Charlotte, I love *you*.'

She felt her throat tighten with emotion. She tried to swallow, but found she couldn't. 'Alex, I could never . . . I couldn't cope with being second best again.'

'Peter was a fool,' Alex said sharply. 'He didn't deserve you. And anyway, can't you see that I love you because you're not second best? Charlotte, you're special. You're bloody wonderful!' He kissed her again. 'If I had my way I'd spend the rest of my days making you feel unimaginably special.'

'Oh you sweet-talker,' she said, managing a smile.

'Don't look at me like that, Charlotte. I don't know which is more devastating, your smile or the sight of you in that wet dress.'

Charlotte cleared her throat and changed the subject. She said, 'If you weren't making mad passionate love with Christina till gone midnight, what were you doing?'

'Talking. She's a great listener, a vital ingredient in her line of work.'

'She told you what she does for a living?' Charlotte was shocked.

'Yes.'

'Were you surprised?'

'I don't know really.'

Charlotte laughed, kicked off her shoes and stretched out her toes in the warm sun. She closed her eyes. Suddenly she felt unbelievably happy.

'You have lovely feet.' He picked one up and manoeuvred it into his lap. He began to stroke her ankle.

'Alex,' she said warningly.

'A shame your dress has nearly dried out.'

Charlotte looked at him. 'You don't give up, do you?'

'No,' he said, 'I don't. And I won't.'

34

The airport was full of eager travellers brandishing passports and pushing overloaded trolleys of luggage or wheeling tombstone-sized cases on small squeaky wheels. Standing in the departure hall waiting for Christina's plane to be called, Charlotte felt reluctant to part with her friend. There was so much to be said, especially since yesterday, when Alex had told her the truth about the night before. She had hoped they might have had a chance to talk after Barry's party, but it hadn't broken up until nearly two in the morning, with Derek and Malcolm Jackson forming a cabaret act. Poor Iris was the only guest to leave early. She went home to The White Cottage next door and pointedly banged all her windows shut.

'Now Carlotta, my dearest friend,' Christina said, bringing Charlotte's thoughts back to the crowded airport, 'promise me one thing, that you will try to be honest with yourself.'

'Are any of us?' Charlotte said, shaking her head.

Christina smiled. 'You know, it takes courage, real courage to know another person, but it is a supreme act of heroism to know oneself and one's own darkness – remember that, Carlotta. Remember also that you are now brave enough to stop being evasive with yourself or anybody else. You must believe that.'

Charlotte reached out to her friend and hugged her. 'I wish you weren't leaving today. Can't you stay a few more days?'

'No, Carlotta, my plane will be called in a few moments, and anyway, I want to get back to my wonderful Henri. He will be waiting for me and I have a feeling that I do not want to keep him waiting for too long. He is quite a catch, you know, I think I may marry him.'

'Somehow I can't imagine you married.'

Christina feigned a look of shock. 'You want me to remain the old maid, as you call it?'

'You could never be that, Christina. But what does Henri think of your . . . your work, your profession?'

'He thinks it is a very good one. Why?' asked Christina, a mischievous smile on her lips.

'Oh,' Charlotte said. 'He won't want you to give it up, then, if you marry him?'

'I don't think so. Do you think I should?'

Charlotte wasn't sure what to say. This was an area of their friendship that had been discreetly tucked under the carpet, or perhaps under the bedclothes.

'Carlotta, you haven't answered my question.'

She felt she was being pushed into a corner. 'It's just that, well, you know, I wouldn't have thought that what you do – entertaining men, I mean – and being a diplomat's wife would be terribly compatible.'

Christina's beautiful eyes opened wide and she laughed. 'Oh my darling Carlotta, at last you have been honest with me.'

Charlotte looked confused.

'All this time,' continued Christina, 'you really did think I was a prostitute, or as Mr Carlotta called me, a high-class tart.'

'You mean . . . ? But what about all those men who kept calling on you?'

'Of course I had men visiting me. I'm a sex therapist.'

'A what?'

'Surely I don't have to explain . . .'

'No. No, I didn't mean that.' Charlotte was stunned. How could she have got it so wrong? 'I just meant . . . Oh, Christina, I made such an awful assumption. A sex therapist. You!'

'Yes, me,' Christina said. 'You know, there are a lot of sexual problems in Brussels, so many men who have the big work drive at the expense of the sex drive.'

'But there was no sign on your door, no office, no surgery, or whatever it is you need.' Part of Charlotte still needed convincing.

'One has to be discreet, my clients have to be treated with sensitivity. A large sign saying "This way for all those who can't get it up" would not do.'

'But even inside your apartment, it looked quite normal, not like . . .'

'Ah, you did not see the whole of my apartment, but then so often, we only scan the surface of life, only perceive what we are prepared to let ourselves see . . . for instance, you view Alex as another Peter.'

Charlotte frowned.

'There, I'm right, aren't I? You think Alex will hurt you in the same way Peter hurt you. But he really loves you, Carlotta, and for all the right reasons. Now they have called my plane, I must go, Henri awaits.'

They hugged each other again. Christina kissed Charlotte flamboyantly. 'Forgive me for trying to make you jealous, Carlotta,' she said. 'Forgive Alex too.' Then she walked towards the passport control booth and turned round for a final wave.

Ivy Cottage felt uncomfortably quiet when Charlotte got back from the airport. She wandered about the kitchen, absentmindedly picking things up, then putting them down. She made herself a drink, but left it untouched. She went into the conservatory and flicked through a magazine. Bored and restless, she tossed it on the table and went outside. She sat beneath the fig tree and looked up at the house. She saw Alex staring down at her from what she guessed was his bedroom window. She held his gaze. Her throat went dry and she felt her heart beat faster.

She walked purposefully across the lawn and pushed open the back door. She had never been inside Alex's part of Ivy Cottage before. She found him at the foot of the stairs, his hand on the banister. He looked as though he was waiting for her, as if he had known she would come. She went to him, and without speaking she kissed him. He covered her face with kisses and then her neck, whispering her name, over and over. Breathless with what she knew was relief, she moved away from him, to the first step of the stairs. He followed her up.

In the gathering twilight Hilary tugged at the weeds in amongst the fading nemesia in the front garden. The summer would soon be over, she reflected; new school uniforms to buy and label, and autumn term PTA functions to start thinking about.

From across the road she heard the sound of barking followed by laughter. She peeped over the low wall she was hidden behind. She saw Mabel first, then Charlotte and Alex, arm in arm. When they reached the end of the drive she saw Alex whisper something in Charlotte's ear and heard her sister laugh again. Hilary crouched a little lower behind the wall as in fascinated delight she watched Charlotte kiss Alex. Not just a peck, but a full-blown belter of a kiss, their hands and arms all over the place. Heavens! gawped Hilary, goggle-eyed. And to think it was all down to her.

Iris Braithwaite stood poised over her tomato plants, a green plastic watering can in her hand. In the dwindling light she peered through the privet hedge, hearing the sound of voices coming towards her along the footpath.

'If you ask me,' she said in a loud voice, 'it's time you got yourselves married. At least that way we'd all be spared scenes of depravity such as we witnessed yesterday afternoon.'

'I beg your pardon, Mrs Braithwaite,' said Charlotte, facing Iris through the hedge.

'It's what I should have done after Sidney died. I've regretted it ever since.' Her voice sounded out of character; wistfully pensive. 'Of course now I've left it too late. Who would want an old thing like me?'

'I'm so sorry, Iris,' Charlotte said, risking the uncustomary familiarity of using Mrs Braithwaite's Christian name, albeit through the safety of the hedge. 'I had no idea. You've always given the impression . . .'

'That's as may be, but don't ever quote me as having said it. I shall deny it of course. Goodnight, Mrs Lawrence, you too, Mr Hamilton.'

With the smooth, darkening water of the mere behind them Charlotte rested her head against Alex's chest, his arms around her shoulders.

'I'm exhausted,' she said.

'Me too.'

She gave him a playful punch. 'I wasn't talking about this afternoon.'

'Oh,' he said.

'It's been an exhausting summer.'

'That's because you spent most of it fighting me.'

'Only because . . .'

He kissed her. 'I think I've found the only way to keep you quiet.'

'No. There is another way.'

He caught the look in her eye and laughed. 'You do realise, don't you, that I won't let you end up like Iris Braithwaite, blue rinse and sensible lace-up shoes?'

'Well, that's a relief.'

'Charlotte?'

'Be quiet, Alex, and take me home, please.'

'Your place or mine?'

'Alex!'

Time for a Change

To Edward and Samuel
who said it would be all right

Thanks to everyone who helped me through *Time for a Change.* To Big G for making it happen. To Helena for the gossip and inspiration. To Maureen for the laughs and kind words of encouragement. To Miranda and Adrian for the quality bed and breakfast facilities. To John and Eirian for the long, long phone calls. To Jonathan and Victoria at Curtis Brown.

And lastly, but by no means least, thanks to Jane and Sarah at Orion who know how to make a girl feel great.

'*Change is not made without inconvenience,
even from worse to better.*'
Richard Hooker 1554–1600

'*The mind is its own place, and in itself
Can make a heav'n of hell, a hell of heav'n.*'
Paradise Lost
John Milton 1608–74

1

Hilary Parker was a Monday-morning kind of person, but there was something not quite right about this particular Monday morning.

Usually she liked nothing better than to answer Terry Wogan back while bustling about her large cluttered kitchen, organising breakfast with one hand and sorting out her daughter's lunch-box and her son's chaotically filled sports bag with the other. She believed in taking the start of any day firmly by the horns and meeting it head on. Today, though, Hilary had the uneasy feeling that something was wrong.

She popped a couple of tea-bags into the Welsh-dresser-shaped teapot and swept aside the thought that a potential disaster was hanging over her.

Breakfast dealt with, she watched David make his escape to his estate-agency office in the centre of the village and then she began the ritual of shouting at the children to make them get a move on while she filled the washing machine and added a few last-minute thoughts to her shopping list. Eventually, when Becky had found her gloves – not the plain blue hand-me-downs from Philip, but the cream pair with the fluffy bits at the wrists – they set off to wait for the bus to take Philip to his new school. One child down and one to go, Hilary took her seven-year-old daughter's hand and crossed the road to join the posse of frazzled mothers heading for the local primary school.

It wasn't until Hilary had reached home and drawn breath as she stood over the washing machine waiting for it to finish its last spin cycle that she could no longer avoid the unconscious thought that was battling its way through the Monday-morning rush-hour traffic of her mind. Had she forgotten to do something?

She bent down to the machine and looked through the glass port-hole. She caught strobe-like flashes of Becky's pink pyjamas being chased by a pair of Philip's rugby shorts. The machine finally shuddered to a halt and she waited impatiently before the door-release button would work. She debated whether to go and clear the breakfast things from the kitchen table but the nagging worry wouldn't leave her. Was she supposed to have telephoned somebody? Was it some PTA matter? Georgia D'Arcy could be quite sharp if she felt people weren't pulling their weight.

She pressed the button and started hauling out the clothes. First came

Philip's determined shorts, followed by a tangled ball of leggings, socks and pyjamas. She tugged hard at the bulky mound until it finally burst free – pulling washing out through that black rubber ring always reminded Hilary of childbirth, especially Philip's difficult breech birth.

No. It wasn't something she hadn't done. It was David. Something *he* had done.

She moved the basket of wet clothes to one side and refilled the machine, pushing David's work shirts into the gaping hole; something that never failed to give her pleasure. Ever since they had been married and she had washed and ironed David's shirts she had enjoyed the smell of maleness from his clothes. She picked up the last of the shirts, the one he had worn last night for a Rotary Club dinner.

Last night. That was it. David had been talking in his sleep.

Then suddenly there it was: the nagging subconscious knowledge that had been with her throughout the darkness of night to the break of day was finally free and she heard David's words as clearly as if he were crouched on the floor next to her and reciting them: '*Catherine . . . Hilary must never find out . . . she'd never forgive me . . . the children.*'

She gasped and crushed the shirt to her face, but something hard in the folds of the fabric scraped against her cheek. She pulled out a small restaurant card together with a bill. The strip of paper had yesterday's date on it and showed it was a meal for two.

But David had said he was going to a specially arranged Rotary Club dinner . . . '*Catherine . . . Hilary must never find out.*'

Well, she had. She bloody well had!

Hilary turned the key in the ignition of her car. 'It can't be true, it just can't be. Not David!' She pressed hard on the accelerator and launched her Renault Clio out of the drive. She hurtled noisily down Acacia Lane, ignoring the look of outrage on the face of Iris Braithwaite, who was already hard at work sweeping the autumn leaves from the baize-green lawn of The White Cottage, and drove through the village, past the row of shops including David's black and white half-timbered office and reached the supermarket in less than ten minutes. She bolted into the first available space in the car park.

Inside the store and propped up by a trolley, Hilary gripped her shopping list. Fruit, vegetables, she muttered. Fruit, vegetables. How could he? How could he have an— She scrunched up her shopping list unable to utter, even in her head, the unthinkable. Anger and bewilderment threatened to overwhelm her and she made for the neatly constructed pyramids of fruit, which normally appealed to her sense of everything being well ordered and exactly placed. 'A home for everything,' she always told the children. David wasn't tidy, though. Ties strewn all over the bedroom, trousers left on the . . . Her throat tightened and her legs went wobbly. She felt sick.

Concentrate, she told herself. The shopping. She ripped off a plastic bag and with shaking hands she picked an apple from the top of the pyramid of

Granny Smiths. She carefully selected another three but as she reached for a fifth her hand knocked against the pile and she watched in helpless horror as she set off a shiny green avalanche; apples cascaded on to the floor, bumping against her legs as they fell.

'No!' she cried out. 'No. Stop it.' Tears streaming down her cheeks she fled, aware of people staring at her as she skittered up the next aisle. She raced alongside the shelves throwing things into the trolley: baked beans, sweetcorn, flour, rice.

Why had she come? What was she doing here in the supermarket? She had just discovered her husband was having an affair and she was doing the weekly shop. Was she mad?

On autopilot she reached the aisles of frozen food. Pizzas, garlic bread, peas. Stir-fry vegetables, where were they? It was Monday. She always did stir-fry vegetables for David on a Monday evening. She leaned over the freezer, pushing the packets of frozen broccoli and cauliflower aside in her determination to find what she was looking for. 'Where are they? They must be here.'

'Hilary?'

She jerked upright and found herself face to face with her neighbour Cindy Rogers, who together with her husband Derek ran In the Pink, the thriving health and beauty centre in Acacia Lane. As ever Cindy's hair and make-up were immaculate. Hilary felt Cindy's critical eyes sweep over her. 'Hello, Cindy,' she said. Her voice sounded breathless and overly cheery.

'You okay?'

'Of course I am . . .' *Catherine . . . Hilary must never find out . . .* 'I'm fine, why wouldn't I be?'

Cindy was convinced Hilary looked far from well. It was obvious that the Princess of Hulme Welford – as Derek called their neighbour – had been crying. She said nothing and reached into the freezer for a packet of peas. If Hilary was upset and didn't want to share it, then that was her business and Cindy certainly wasn't going to get involved in someone else's problems if she could help it.

'I'm fine, really,' Hilary repeated, 'just a bit of a cold, that's all. It's always the same – soon as the children go back to school after the summer holidays it's an endless stream of colds and runny noses' . . . *she'd never forgive me . . .* 'run down a bit I suppose if I'm honest.' The flow of words came to an end and she stood staring blankly at Cindy.

'How's David?' Cindy asked. It was all she could think of to say.

'David? Oh, he's fine. Busy, working all hours, you know what it's like.' He had, hadn't he? He'd been coming home later and later just recently. And there'd been all those phone calls in his study with the door shut. Oh, it was all so obvious! How could she have been so blind and not seen the signs? Her lip trembled.

Cindy didn't know what to do. She hated being confronted with emotion of any kind. She'd spent a lifetime keeping hers in check and she expected others to do the same. 'I must get a move on,' she said. 'I only slipped out for some—'

'Yes, of course, don't let me keep you, I know how busy you are.'

'I'll see you, then, Hilary. Why don't you call me some time? Treat yourself to a facial.' Heaven only knows she could do with it.

'Yes, perhaps I will.' What, at their prices? Hilary watched Cindy push her trolley further up the line of freezer compartments. But suddenly she felt frightened at being left alone. Cindy might be an ice maiden but her company right now seemed infinitely better than her own. 'Cindy,' she called out. 'I just wondered . . .'

'Yes?'

Something in Cindy's manner was so cold, so matter-of-fact, it prompted a mirrored reaction from herself. 'I've just discovered David's having an affair,' she said. She saw Cindy's hand tighten on her trolley, her long pearly pink nails curling round the metal handle. 'I . . . I don't know what to do,' she added, her voice now wavering and not at all stoic as she had intended.

'Come on,' Cindy said, 'I'll take you home.'

They abandoned their shopping, left Hilary's car in the car park and drove back to The Gables in Cindy's brand new Celica.

'I'm all right. Really I am,' Hilary said, sniffing loudly as they got out of the car.

'Don't be ridiculous,' Cindy threw at her. 'You feel awful. You feel like your world's just come to an end. I should know.' She glanced over the road towards In the Pink. 'Just remember who I'm married to.'

Cindy made Hilary sit in a chair next to the Aga. She filled the kettle and to her shame found herself cringing at the state of Hilary's kitchen. While her own kitchen was spotless and devoid of clutter, Hilary's worktops were lined with rows of brightly coloured tins, above which were intricately carved shelves weighed down with a hundred and one cookery books. Did anyone really cook that much? She herself ate little more than a lightly dressed salad each night. She reached out for one of the brightly coloured tins, hoping it contained coffee. It was tea and behind it was a faint tidemark of dust. She pulled a face, wondering how long it was since there had been the merest hint of Jif behind the tins. Weeks possibly. Months more like it. But whatever else had been going on at The Gables just recently it certainly wasn't any cleaning, not to her way of thinking anyway.

She poured out the tea into two mugs with pictures of huge pigs on tiny legs. 'Here you are,' she said to Hilary, who was now sitting at the kitchen table, her elbows resting amongst the breakfast things. There were toast crumbs and splashes of milk everywhere. A blob of orange marmalade was clinging to the side of the jar. Cindy had to fight the urge to gather up all the offending mess and put the kitchen straight. It would be a far easier task than trying to reassure Hilary that everything would be all right. In her experience, once a man had one affair it didn't stop there.

Hilary sniffed. Cindy glanced round the kitchen for a box of tissues. All she could see was some kitchen roll on one of those green cast-iron posts. She tore off a square and handed it to Hilary.

'Cindy, I'm so sorry to land you with all this . . . I didn't mean for you to . . .' She sniffed again.

Blow it, for goodness' sake, Cindy thought.

'Look,' Hilary said. She pushed a small piece of paper across the table towards Cindy.

Cindy read the restaurant bill. It was familiar enough. 'Could it have been an ordinary business dinner?' she responded. She had asked herself the same question twenty-two years ago, a year after her first wedding anniversary.

'No,' Hilary whispered. 'He told me he was going to a Rotary Club dinner. He lied to me, Cindy. He's been coming home so late these past few weeks, and he talked in his sleep last night. Her name's Catherine . . . How could he, how—' She began to cry.

Cindy didn't want Hilary to cry but she had no idea how to stop her. She sipped her tea and tried hard not to think of the grotesque pig in her hand. Instead she thought of herself twenty-two years ago: first she had found a restaurant receipt, then a letter and then the phone calls had started. She had tried to ignore it, just as her mother had advised her. 'Let him get it out of his system. It'll blow over.' And it had. Until the next gust of wind had brought with it another black cloud almost a year later.

Another sniff from Hilary made Cindy put down her mug with a bang. 'So what do you want to do, Hilary?'

'Do? What do you mean?'

'You either confront David with this,' she waved the small piece of paper in the air, 'and risk losing everything, or you pretend you never found it.'

'Pretend I never found it!' Hilary shouted, her bloodshot eyes wide in bewilderment. 'How can I do that? I mean, he's been . . . he's been . . .' Her voice trailed away.

Cindy leaned forward. 'It just happens in some marriages. Particularly in mine.'

'Oh, God, Cindy. I'm sorry. I've been so insensitive to you, haven't I?'

Cindy nearly smiled. She knew only too well that in the nineteen months they'd been living in the village of Hulme Welford it had become common knowledge what sort of a man Derek Rogers was. It was also generally accepted that Cindy knew exactly what was going on but chose to turn a blind eye to his infidelity and, more importantly, nobody spoke to her about it. Though recently she had become increasingly concerned about Derek's behaviour, but for the life of her she could not work out exactly what was wrong. It was odd that he had taken to reading all those strange books – that really was out of character. It was the first time she had known him to sit still long enough to get through anything more detailed than the front page of the *Daily Mail*. She was concerned that Derek was dissatisfied with his life. Perhaps even the affairs had begun to pall for him. So what was next?

'You have to decide what it is you want, Hilary,' she said at last. 'I presume you do love David.'

'How could you ask such a question?'

'I'm sorry, but it would make things easier if you didn't.'

'Don't you love Derek, then?' Hilary asked, hardly daring to ask Cindy such a personal question. Before today their conversations had always been impersonal and along the lines of 'Tea or coffee?' and now here they were discussing adultery and whether or not they loved their husbands.

'Goodness knows why, but yes, I do love Derek,' Cindy said simply. 'That's why I know it would be a lot easier if love didn't come into it. It's easier to be objective then.'

Hilary raised her tea to her lips. It was cold. She put it down. 'I can't believe we're sitting here and being so rational. I mean, aren't you at all shocked by what David's doing?'

'That's hardly the point, is it? The point is, what are *you* going to do?'

Hilary started to cry again. 'I don't know,' she squalled. 'I just don't know.'

'Do you want me to make a suggestion?'

'Please,' Hilary said, lifting her eyes from the screwed-up piece of kitchen roll in her hands. 'I need all the help I can get. I don't want to lose him, Cindy. He's the only man I've ever loved.'

'Right, then. The first thing is that you mustn't tell anyone. The fewer the people who know the better. From now on you've got to pretend, just as I said earlier, that you never found that receipt or heard David talking in his sleep. Hilary, you're going to have to fight for your husband.'

'Like you have for Derek?'

'Yes,' Cindy said grimly. 'Like I have for Derek.' She got up from her chair and took the mugs to the sink. 'By the way. Do you know who this Catherine might be?'

'Yes,' Hilary said softly. 'She's his new secretary.' Her body shook and she covered her face with her hands and sobbed.

Men, thought Cindy. Consistent if nothing else.

2

'Okay, folks. Let's cut the waffle and get straight on. We've got a hell of a lot to cover tonight and I don't know about you but I'm knackered.'

Hilary saw the raised eyebrows along the front row of chairs which testified to the fact that this was not the usual way to open a St John's Infant and Junior School PTA meeting. There had been murmurs and more vocal expressions of dissent at the start of term when the outgoing chairwoman Patricia Longton had been replaced by Georgia D'Arcy, whose eager supporters were presently occupying the back row of seats in 2A's classroom, while Patricia and company were at the front where they felt they could be most intimidating. They had no idea what the members of the opposing camp were mouthing behind their backs.

Hilary did a quick head-count. Numbers were abnormally high. She suspected it had something to do with the free drinks on offer that evening – another change from the norm. She jotted the number down, disappointed that yet again she had been asked to remain as secretary – it was always the job nobody else wanted. She had hoped to step into Patricia's shoes herself but had withdrawn her name from the selection procedure when she found out she was up against the formidable Ms Georgia D'Arcy who had been well backed by the hairy-armpit brigade, as David called the more maverick and Bohemian inclined mothers of the school – 'Hippie by nature and hippy in size,' he would laugh.

'First on the agenda,' Georgia D'Arcy announced, 'is to thank all those present and note those absent.' She gave a deep laugh, which belied her bone thin appearance and put paid to David's hip theory. 'Jobs will, of course, be allocated to those not here to defend themselves.' There was raucous laughter from the back row, while Patricia and Co., scandalised, exchanged sideways glances, uncrossed and recrossed their legs, knowing that this jibe was aimed at one of their number – Kate Hampton, the PTA treasurer.

Hilary wrote down 'thanks' and wished she was at home. She was exhausted. It had been a long day since her discovery that morning that David was having an affair. She hadn't eaten a thing, had felt too sick even to consider food. It was as though a pneumatic drill was at work inside her and one minute she was hot, the next cold.

Cindy had told her to expect this. 'You'll lose weight as well,' she had gone on to say. So that was the secret to Cindy's enviable sylph-like figure, Hilary had thought cynically. 'You must keep yourself busy,' Cindy had instructed, as they drove back to the supermarket to pick up her car. 'Or otherwise you'll find yourself thinking of *them.*'

'But what else can I think of?' Hilary had wailed in return.

'Your children, for a start.'

After Cindy had left her she had tried to keep herself busy. But it was hopeless. All she could think of was David's betrayal. So wantonly had he destroyed all that was important to her. She had tried to occupy herself by switching on the television but had ended up mindlessly channel-hopping between *The Rockford Files*, a programme on flamenco dancing, an old movie with Bette Davis and horse-racing from Newmarket until it was time to go and collect Becky. They had walked back from school and, turning into the tree-lined cul-de-sac of Acacia Lane, they had made slow progress as Becky kicked her way through the drifts of fallen leaves in the gutter. 'Ooh, what's this?' she had said, her voice ringing with seven-year-old delight as she bent down. It was a dead mouse. 'Why's it so flat?'

'Because it's dead.'

'Will I be flat like that when I'm dead?'

'No, dear,' Hilary said, taking hold of Becky's hand.

'But why—?'

'Because it's been run over lots of times,' Hilary answered, feeling a bit flat herself.

She had been looking forward to Becky's company, hoping that her daughter's usual demanding behaviour would occupy her. It hadn't. Instead she found she was irritated by Becky's incessant chatter.

'Are you listening to me, Mummy?' Becky had asked in the kitchen where they usually sat with a cup of tea and a biscuit discussing what kind of day Becky had been subjected to.

'Of course, darling,' Hilary had replied.

'Fibber.'

'I'm not lying.'

'Yes, you are. I can tell.'

'Well, what were you saying? Tell me again.'

Becky pouted. 'No.'

Hilary had wanted to cry then. Had wanted to put her arms around her small daughter and talk woman to woman with her. But she couldn't. She'd have to wait at least ten years before she could do that.

Philip's first words when they went to pick him up from school after his rugby practice were: 'You been crying, Mum?'

Strange that her eleven-year-old son should have noticed her red eyes and not Becky. But that was Becky all over.

Tea-time had passed without event, until David had telephoned. Philip took the call. 'Dad'll be late,' he had shouted from the hall. 'He's got an appointment to keep.'

She had cried again, upstairs and alone. Then she had phoned Cindy's daughter Tiffany to see if she could babysit that evening. 'Sorry it's such short notice, I just can't keep up with David,' she had said brightly to Tiffany when she arrived to take charge of the children . . .

'I'd like that going on record.'

'Hilary, you are getting all this down, aren't you?'

Hilary lifted her head and wondered what on earth she was doing at a PTA meeting when her life was falling apart. 'Carry on as normal,' Cindy had told her. But not a word had she said about how one went about acting normally when all Hilary felt like doing was throwing herself on the floor and screaming like a baby.

'Hilary?' Georgia D'Arcy was frowning at her, one eyebrow quizzically arched beneath an urchin short fringe which had the colour and shine of a perfectly plump aubergine. Two fob-watch-sized ear-rings dangled either side of her sharp little face. She wore no make-up but her complexion was nut-brown, corroborating the fact that she worked outside each and every day. Since her husband Rory had left her two years ago the inhabitants of Hulme Welford had watched Georgia singlehandedly build up and run Hulme View Nursery on the edge of the village. She was not a woman who suffered fools and Hilary was a little in awe of her. 'I'm sorry,' Hilary said, 'what did you say?'

Georgia caught sight of Hilary's blank note-pad. She cleared her throat and waved to one of the mothers in the back row. 'Crack open those bottles of wine, will you, Cas, and pass some cups round while I have a chat with Hilary.'

Hilary heard muttering from the front row. 'Wine? We've never had wine before.'

'Right, chuck,' Georgia said, turning back to Hilary. 'What's up?'

Hilary's mouth opened but no words came out. She shut her mouth and tried hard to keep her lips from trembling.

'Come on, Hilary. I've watched you do this job standing on your head for the past three years. Granted I've seen you get flustered, but never incapable. Is it me? Can't you work with me? Because if so—'

'No. I mean, no, it's not that.'

Georgia smiled. 'Good. I know I put certain backs up, like the frosty five there,' she inclined her head towards Patricia and company, 'but I'd hate to think I was that bloody obnoxious. I had hoped that you and I could get along. Perhaps some wine will help.' She got up from her chair and went across to where Cas Mitchell and Jo Shaughnessy were handing out plastic cups. Hilary noticed that the 'frosty five' were huddled together and guzzling their wine enthusiastically.

'Here,' Georgia said, coming back. 'Take a big mouthful. I'm not going to pry. It's none of my business what's given you a face like an empty coal scuttle, but I guarantee there's a man in there somewhere prodding you where it hurts.'

Hilary tried to protest but Georgia ignored her. 'Sod the lot of them, I say. If it'll help I'll take notes as we go along.' She drained her plastic cup, faced everyone and instantly called the meeting back to order.

Hilary felt herself relax for the first time that day. How good it was for somebody else to take charge. She had been grateful to Cindy earlier that morning for being there when she needed somebody in whom to confide, especially with her own experiences to tell, but she hadn't made Hilary feel any better. In fact, she had made her feel worse. Listening to Cindy had filled her with fear, as if all that lay in store for Hilary was a life stretching ahead as dauntingly as a life prison sentence. But Georgia was different. Somehow, in those few no-nonsense words Georgia had just uttered she had lifted some of the awful responsibility of the day off Hilary's shoulders. She felt enormously grateful to Georgia.

3

Cindy came out of the *en suite* bathroom, a thick peach towel swathed around her slender body. She was surprised to see Derek sitting up in bed reading. He slapped the book shut when he saw she was there.

Just over an hour ago she had left him downstairs in the office. 'Paperwork,' he had said to her when she had looked in on him before coming upstairs for a bath.

'Everything's all right, isn't it?' she had asked. It was more by way of making conversation than worrying about the state of the business. All their married life Cindy had kept a firm hand and a weather eye on all the financial elements of the six salons they owned, as well as In the Pink. There was nothing that could get past her. But the persistent thought that had kept running through her mind these past few weeks was the possibility that Derek was sorting out their finances before leaving her. Since this morning when she had witnessed Hilary's shock she had felt it was an omen that she, too, was about to discover something unpleasant.

'Good book?' she asked, pulling a silk nightgown out of the stencilled chest of drawers by her side of the bed.

'Not bad,' he answered, his face noncommittal. He dropped the book face down on to the floor.

'You've been doing a lot of that lately,' Cindy said, her back to Derek. She let the towel fall away from her and slipped the nightgown over her head.

'A lot of what?'

She caught the defensiveness in his voice, and to avoid any kind of confrontation that might lead to him declaring his hand, she said, 'Have you seen much of David recently?'

'Are you going to stand there all night giving me the third degree or are you getting in?' He pulled back her corner of the duvet and patted the bed.

She climbed in and sat stiffly beside him, taken aback by this simple act of courtesy . . . Helping her into bed? What was it she had heard once? A man about to leave his wife behaves out of character, starts doing all he can to please her before dealing the final blow. Scared, she said, 'Well, have you?'

'Have I what?'

'Seen much of David recently.'

He shook his head. 'Same as usual, I suppose.' He took off his paper-thin wristwatch and gold bracelet and placed them by the bedside lamp. 'What's all this anyway? What's the sudden interest in David?'

'Oh, nothing,' Cindy said, turning out her light. She lay back and waited for Derek to do the same. She had the feeling, though, that he wasn't about to. She was right.

'Cindy?'

'I'm tired, Derek. Can it wait?'

'I'm tired as well.'

'Then switch off your light.'

'Not that kind of tired.'

She sat up. Well, if this was it, if he was about to tell her he wanted a divorce, she might just as well pay attention and listen to him.

'Are you happy, Cindy?'

'Happy?' This was new. He'd never asked her that before.

'Because,' Derek said, facing her, 'I'm not.' He smiled.

Oh, God. How could he? How could he smile like that? Was it supposed to soften the blow? She clenched her fists under the duvet and braced herself for what she had feared all her married life.

'I've been thinking about us.'

'Yes.'

'I think it's time for a change.' He kicked back the duvet and suddenly leapt to his feet. He pulled on his towelling robe and started to pace the bedroom floor, backwards and forwards at the end of the brass bed.

'What kind of change?' she asked.

'Life-enhancing!' he shouted, throwing his arms up in the air. He stared at her, wide-eyed. 'Tell me, Cindy, how long have we been in the beauty business?' He didn't wait for her reply. 'Too long is the answer.' He came round to her side of the bed and sat down. She moved her legs away from him.

He grabbed her hands and held them tightly. 'I've had this idea. I've been working on it for weeks now. I want to turn In the Pink into a sanctuary of spiritual exploration, where the hopeless can find hope, where . . .' He looked about him as though seeking inspiration from the walls of their bedroom. 'Where the unsure can find themselves. And let's face it, there's plenty of people like that here in Hulme Welford. What do you think?'

'You're hurting my hands,' Cindy whispered.

'I'm sorry,' he said, letting go. 'Don't know my own strength. But what do you say to my idea?'

Cindy was speechless. She was so relieved that Derek wasn't about to leave her that she knew at that precise moment she would agree to anything he wanted to do. She hadn't been so relieved since the day just over a year ago when she had realised that Hilary's sister Charlotte Lawrence was in love with her tenant Alex Hamilton. Prior to that day she had been convinced that Charlotte would be yet another woman to come between Derek and herself. But it was clear to Cindy, as it was to everyone in the village, that Charlotte and Alex were very much in love, and even Derek himself had made it obvious that he was no longer interested and had backed off.

'I don't know what to think, Derek,' she said finally.

He kissed her, excitedly. 'That's the whole point. Too many people out there don't know how or what to think. We're going to help change all that.'

'A sanctuary of what did you say?'

'We'll run courses on inner healing, assertiveness, there'll be journeys of self-discovery—'

'There won't be any chanting, will there?'

'Chanting?'

'I've seen things like that on the television. People sitting on cushions, their eyes rolling and rubbish coming out of their mouths. It's so embarrassing.'

He laughed. 'Cindy, Cindy, this is me, Derek. Would I be that stupid?' He mentally ruled out that particular course he'd been reading up on. 'Come on, I feel like celebrating. Let's go down and open a bottle.' He kissed her again and ran his hand the length of her arm. 'Then we'll come back up and I'll take you on a journey of self-discovery.'

'I haven't said yes yet,' Cindy said, getting out of bed.

'You will, though. I just know it.'

Cindy had a feeling he was right.

4

Becky looked pleased with herself, which Hilary knew meant one thing and one thing only: Becky had got one over her brother. For most of her young daughter's life Hilary had generally taken her side in any sibling fracas, but more recently her loyalty had been pushed to its limits and Philip had started to gain more of her respect and sympathy.

She handed Becky the packet of breakfast cereal and scanned her daughter's face for any tell-tale signs of guilt. She found none, only a look of undisguised glee.

She lifted the kettle from the Aga and made the tea, setting the pot down on the table. She then switched on the radio. 'Are we downhearted?' asked Terry Wogan from beside the bread bin. Yesterday the self-effacing Irishman had posed the same question and she had smiled back at him. Today she had nothing to smile about. She *was* downhearted.

When she had got home last night after the PTA meeting she had gone straight upstairs, calling to David in the sitting-room that she had a headache and was going to bed.

She had pretended to be asleep when he had joined her. She had lain silently beside him, her body tense with fear and anger, trying hard not to think of him as he lay on the other side of the bed; a chasm of duplicity between them. And as the night hours had slowly passed she had punished herself again and again wondering how many times David had done *it* with *her*? And was *it* better with Catherine? Of course it was, she had told herself angrily while tiptoeing to the toilet at three in the morning, why else would he be having an affair? Illicit sex early in the evening was always more fun than a tired ten-minute domestic session slotted in between Jeremy Paxman's *Newsnight* and setting the alarm clock.

Eventually, worn down by such torturous thoughts, she had given up the fight and had slept, but now it was breakfast time and any minute David would be out of the shower and downstairs. How would she cope? She would have to look at him, speak, even. She could avoid him no longer. There could be no escape.

'Mummy?'

'Mm . . .'

'What do you get if you hang—?'

'Please, Becky, not now.' Hilary could hear footsteps on the stairs. She pushed four slices of bread into the toaster.

'Daddy, what do you get if you hang Pamela Anderson upside down?'

'Shut up, Becky,' Philip said, coming into the kitchen behind his father. He knew he shouldn't have told his sister that joke. She was always getting him into trouble with her big mouth. 'Mum, these pants you got me, they're too small.'

Hilary looked at Philip. She could see David out of the corner of her eye. He was pouring himself a mug of tea. 'I only bought them at the start of term,' she said. 'They can't be too small.'

'Well, they are,' Philip said sullenly. He sat down. Hilary noticed him wriggling. She noticed too that David seemed to be moving uncomfortably in his chair. He looked shifty. Guilty. How long had he been doing that?

'Any toast?' he asked, barely lifting his eyes from the level of his mug.

'Coming,' she replied. She filled the toast rack and sat down.

'Flora?'

She looked up at David and moved towards the fridge. 'Flora,' she repeated slowly, taking off the lid and dropping the plastic tub on to the table. The china and cutlery rattled and a small yellow dollop of sunflower spread leapt out of the carton and landed on David's forehead. For a few moments nobody spoke, then Becky's shrill laughter, accompanied by the eight o'clock pips on the radio, filled the kitchen. Hilary didn't know what to do. The atmosphere was awful. She watched David take out his handkerchief from his trouser pocket and wipe his forehead. He didn't look at her and he wasn't smiling. 'Here,' she said, offering him the dishcloth. 'Wipe up your tea.' Then, sensing Philip wriggling next to her, she vented her anger on him. 'For goodness' sake, keep still!' she shouted.

Philip sprang from his seat. 'I can't,' he shouted back. 'It's these pants. I told you, they're too small.'

'And I told you they can't be.'

'Mummy's right,' Becky said slyly, her mouth a dark cavernous hole of Coco Pops. She started to laugh again and getting up from her chair she began pirouetting about the kitchen. 'Itchy bum, itchy bum!' she chanted delightedly.

Hilary looked from Philip to Becky. 'What have you done?' she demanded.

Philip's face darkened and he rushed from the room. 'Itchy bum!' Becky yelled one more time after him.

'Becky!'

Becky came to a balletic stop, her feet in a perfect first position. She looked like a penguin. 'I put itching powder in his pants,' she confessed with a giggle. Her words were said with immense pride and satisfaction. She looked like a smug penguin now.

For the first time ever, Hilary slapped her daughter, hard, on the legs and then she too left the kitchen.

*

Hilary couldn't bear to see the expression of humiliation on Philip's face as he climbed on to the school bus. His sister's antics would be with him for the rest of the day, a day that Hilary knew would be bad enough for him anyway. The transition from the village primary to senior school had not been an easy one for him. He had won a scholarship to the same school Tiffany attended and which her brother Barry had recently left with his string of grade A A-levels. He was now studying medicine at Leeds, and while Derek was vocally proud of his son, Cindy was more reluctant to sing his praises. It never ceased to amaze Hilary that Derek and Cindy could have produced two such unlikely children – Tiffany, possibly every mother's nightmare and Barry, every mother's dream son-in-law. On the other hand, she herself had produced Becky.

'Come on, Mummy. We'll be late. I want to get to school before Sarah Jenkins today.'

There was no contrition in Becky. No sense of remorse for what she had done to her brother. Not even any hurt pride or anger for having had her legs smacked. Life was just one series of practical jokes as far as Becky was concerned. It made Hilary even angrier, this blatant cavalier attitude to life that Becky had. It made her want to lash out at her daughter. Life wasn't one big bloody joke. Life was hard, tough, and just now hers was tumbling down around her. She stuffed her fists inside her coat pocket. She had always prided herself that while most of her friends gaily slapped their children for their wrong-doings, she had not. 'A mother who resorts to violence has lost the respect of her children and the right to their love,' she had said, on so many occasions. She could remember telling her own mother this after she had caught Louise smacking Becky for smashing a small china dog in her antique shop. Her mother had responded with, 'Don't you know anything, Hilary? You slap the respect into them.' And now here she was, twice in one day wanting to unleash an extraordinary amount of violence on her young daughter. She knew, though, that it had nothing to do with disciplining Becky and all to do with her anger and frustration at what David was doing to her and what he was apparently prepared to keep on doing.

They walked away from the bus stop and crossed the road towards the church. At the school gate Becky skipped away, leaving Hilary standing empty-handed. She felt relieved, rid of Becky and the threat of causing her any real physical harm. She turned to hurry off, not wanting to get caught by Patricia or any of the other mothers and be sucked into the early-morning school-gate gossiping session.

'Hilary, I was hoping I'd catch you.' It was Georgia D'Arcy striding purposefully behind her. She was wearing a mustard-coloured beret pulled down over her head and a bulky scarf wrapped loosely around her thin neck. She wore no coat, despite the sharp October wind that morning, just a striped woollen jumper and a pair of khaki dungarees.

'I'm sorry,' Hilary said automatically, 'I haven't had a chance to write up the minutes yet.'

'To hell with those. The meeting was only last night.'

Only last night. It felt an age away.

'Why don't you come for lunch? I usually break about twelve thirty. The nursery's as dead as the grave then.'

'Oh, I couldn't. I've got—'

'Suit yourself,' Georgia said, already moving towards her mud-splattered Jeep. She looked back over her shoulder. 'But if you change your mind, you know where I am.'

While Hilary cleared up the debris of breakfast she had the strongest of desires to smash everything within sight. She was shocked. She was not a violent woman, not one of those drama queens given over to fits of plate-smashing pique. But now she crashed and slammed her way about the kitchen until at last everything was put away. Then she found one of David's whisky tumblers in the sink. He usually had a glass of whisky when he came in from work each evening and never once did he wash the glass or put it in the dishwasher, he just dumped it in the sink each night. She picked it up and turned it round in her hand. She wanted to smash the glass, wanted the satisfaction of throwing it hard against the wall. But she thought of the shards all over the kitchen and knew she couldn't do it. How about outside? Against the garage wall, perhaps? No. There would still be all that mess to clear up afterwards; slivers of lethal glass everywhere. Surely there had to be some way of satisfying her craving to destroy something of David's that wouldn't involve her in clearing up any mess.

Yes, of course there was. She laughed. My God! She could laugh at a time like this. Was she going completely round the bend? She opened the glass display cupboard above the worktop at the far end of the kitchen. There were twelve tumblers in it, all expensive cut glass, which David's mother had given him over the years. In the drawer below Hilary found a plastic carrier bag and started filling it.

She drove to the local council tip, negotiating the bumps and bends in the road with infinite care – she didn't want to waste her precious cargo and be cheated out of her moment of revenge.

She drew up alongside one of the huge metal containers and put on her sunglasses from the glove compartment. On the back seat she saw one of Philip's old Manchester City caps. She grabbed it and forced it on her head.

She carried the glass-filled bag under one arm and made her way up the metal steps to the container. After a quick surreptitious glance to check that she was completely alone, she pulled one of the tumblers out of the bag and threw it. It was a lousy shot. A timorous effort that had the glass landing comfortably on a discarded piece of Axminster. It hadn't even broken. She felt no satisfaction. She picked out another tumbler and this time extended her arm for greater leverage. The tumbler crashed noisily against the sides of the container and Hilary felt the smash deep inside her. Thoughts of a broken heart flickered through her mind, but she dispelled this poetic image instantly by reaching into the bag for another glass. She threw it, followed by a fourth and a fifth. She was well into her stride now, remembering how at school she had been rather good at rounders; the best fielder, she had been called, noted for the quality of her over-arm throw; she had even won a small medal. 'Bastard!' she shouted, as the sixth glass shot into the air.

'Deceitful bastard!' she hurled after the seventh.

'Having fun?'

Shocked, she spun round and nearly toppled off the narrow gangplank and into the container. A strong arm caught her and held her firmly. 'Steady on. You don't look ready for the rubbish heap yet.'

'Somebody obviously thinks I am,' she muttered, without looking up. She clutched the half-empty bag to her, rigid with embarrassment and the realisation that she had been so engrossed in exacting what now seemed her petty revenge on David that she had been oblivious to everything around her, even the sound of an approaching car.

She moved to get past the man but found his hand was still on her arm. She slowly lifted her head, mortified that he must have heard all the terrible expletives she'd just uttered.

He released her and bent down to a cardboard box of junk at his feet and because there wasn't room on the gangplank for Hilary to squeeze past she was forced to stay where she was. She watched him drop his box into the container. A gust of wind snatched at a small wodge of photographs and they flew up into the air then fluttered momentarily in the breeze before settling like butterflies on an old mattress, its springs bursting through the stained and ripped fabric.

'No point in hanging on to the past,' he said, as though addressing the mattress. 'It only makes us cling on to what we once thought was important.' He turned and gave her an uncomfortably direct stare.

Hilary was glad of the sunglasses she was wearing, but not of the hat – it probably made her look like an eccentric old bat.

'Go on, then, throw the rest of them away, don't mind me.'

She suddenly remembered the bag in her hands. 'I don't need to,' she said, knowing that her voice didn't ring true.

'Perhaps you should, though.' And without another word he left her and walked back to where his car was parked just behind hers.

She watched him go. His hair was dark and slightly curly, streaked with grey and much too long, she decided. His plum-coloured jacket and black polo-neck struck her as being of good quality and quite fashionable but his moss green trousers were rumpled and baggy with creases at the knees. He looked vaguely arty or perhaps academic, or how those types were so often portrayed on the telly.

He drove away leaving her alone with her bag of whisky tumblers. She tried throwing the eighth glass, but she felt no anger, no excitement at what she was doing. She had run out of adrenaline and the moment had passed. She dropped the carrier bag on top of the mattress displacing the rubbish the man had just left behind him. A wedding photograph showed itself fleetingly before it coyly slipped under cover beneath an unwanted pushchair.

Hilary got into her car and drove home, disappointed and annoyed that the interfering man with his direct stare and untidy trousers had spoilt things for her.

5

'Good God, Hilary, you look awful!'

'And what, in the name of all that is wonderful, is that disgusting smell?'

Hilary looked first at her mother then at Iris Braithwaite, whose nose was twitching like that of a cartoon mouse catching a whiff of cheese on the air. 'Must be *eau de* tip,' Hilary said, surprising herself with the unexpected sharpness of her wit. She tried to squeeze past Iris and her mother who was scrutinising her so intently that she was inadvertently blocking the path of a man behind her, pinning him against the racks of greeting cards with her shopping basket.

'Oh-the-what?' Iris demanded, her nose still taking in the air.

'I think my daughter was trying, in her oh-so-clever way, to tell us she's just been to the council tip,' Louise Archer said, shifting her basket from one hand to the other. Seizing his moment, the man behind her made his escape.

'Never go there myself,' Iris said. 'I have a perfectly good working compost heap at the end of my garden. Grass cuttings in one, peelings in another and leaves . . . Hold it right there, young man.'

The escapee froze, his hand hovering over the door handle.

'It's you, isn't it?'

He looked at Iris. 'Sorry?'

'Dog mess. Check your shoes, young man, and watch where you're walking in future.'

He fled.

'Now, as I was saying, I always put my leaves in a separate area. Laurel leaves never rot down. Remember that.'

Oh, shove your leaves, Louise thought, as Iris moved away. I want to know why Hilary's looking as threadbare as an old rug. 'Join you for lunch, Hilary?' she said, curious rather than concerned, because nothing ever went wrong in her younger daughter's life. She watched Hilary straightening the magazines; a crooked *Bella* here and a slipped *Hello!* there. You always were a fidgety little madam, Louise reflected. 'Lunch, then – what do you say?'

'*Orgasms for the Woman in a Hurry*', Hilary read to herself from the cover of *Cosmopolitan* as she jerked it upright, trying hard to concentrate on anything but her mother. She couldn't bear the thought of Louise knowing that she had failed in her marriage. Oh, God. It was such basic stuff. She was ashamed that she had failed to please her man. She pulled out the magazine and pretended to flick through it, while all the time thinking of a way in which she could avoid having lunch with her mother and end up spilling the beans.

'Hilary, in my opinion if you haven't learned about multiple orgasms by now it's much too late. Now do you or do you not want me to join you for lunch?'

'Multiple what?' exploded Iris Braithwaite, from the revolving rack of tights.

'Multiple orgasms, Mrs Braithwaite,' called out Ted the Toup helpfully from behind his counter. His hands covered in newspaper print, he was putting the finishing touches to his display of confectionery.

Iris gripped the ends of her headscarf as though protecting herself from a high wind. 'All I came in for was a pair of tights. I did not think I would be subjected to the smell and language of the gutter.' She slapped a packet of tights on the counter.

Ted the Toup's face cracked into a nicotine-tinted smile. 'Three pounds fifty, love.'

'Don't you love me anything, you charlatan!' Iris roared. 'Three pounds fifty, indeed. Last week I only paid—'

'Ah, well, these ones you've picked out are special, like.'

'I should say they are at that price. Explain yourself.'

Ted leaned forward, his patched elbows resting on the counter. 'Peephole gusset,' he said confidentially.

Iris gasped and shrank back from Ted's leering face.

He picked up the packet of tights and began reading from the label, curling his tongue round the words as though giving them extra meaning, ' "Glamorous and fashionably hygienic, to leave you cool and sensual—" '

'Stop!'

'You haven't heard the best bit. It says here—'

'Outrageous,' fired back Iris, breathless with shock. 'Absolutely outrageous.' She turned on her heel and pushed past Hilary and Louise. She gave Ted one last look of disgust before slamming the shop door behind her.

'What about you, ladies?' Ted tried gamely.

'Not now, Ted,' Louise said, amused. She had other fish to fry. She took Hilary by the arm and led her outside.

In the chill, leaf-swirling wind Hilary felt like a small child who had just been dragged out of a sweetshop before having the chance to spend her pocket money. She said, 'But I didn't get my magazine, Mother.'

'Never mind your magazine, Hilary. Just what the heck is going on? You look dreadful. Come on, out with it.' Stern words had always worked with Hilary when she was little; they would have her trembling into submission in no time at all.

'Why aren't you at your shop, Mother?'

Louise frowned, annoyed that she didn't seem to be getting through to

Hilary. Normally her daughter was a giver of information, painfully honest and unable to avoid answering a direct question, and here she was parrying with all the ease of a well-seasoned, tabloid-hounded politician. 'It's Tuesday, Hilary,' she said. 'I never open the shop on a Tuesday. It's my day off, you know that. Would you like to join me for lunch?'

'Lunch?' Hilary tried to appear thoughtful, as though giving the invitation all her consideration. Inside she was panicking. If her mother got her round the lunch table she would never be able to withstand her lightbulb-in-the-eye interrogation tactics. 'Oh, yes,' she suddenly said, inspiration dawning.

'Krakatoa erupts,' Louise said scornfully. 'I'm getting through at last. Shall I come to you, or shall—'

'Sorry,' Hilary said, sounding as genuine as she could, 'but I'm having lunch with Georgia D'Arcy.' She edged towards the door of the newsagent. 'I really must get her a box of chocolates.' And before her mother could say another word she shot back inside the shop.

Louise was put out. She decided to pay a call on her elder daughter, Charlotte, to see if she knew what was going on. She wheeled her bicycle along the pavement, passing the row of shops until she came to the end of the road where the expensive kitchen and bathroom shop had been in business, selling Jacuzzi baths and rainforest-free mahogany units at vastly over-inflated prices – until last winter, that was, when the market for conscience-clear goods at unrealistic prices had slipped down the plug-hole, as David had joked when he'd put the leasehold of the premises on the market. 'It's impossible to be truly environmentally friendly and make money,' he'd said. A few days later they had all been surprised when Charlotte had pulled out her cheque book and announced she would like to take on the lease and run her own business again. 'Another attempt at turning back the clock, Charlotte?' Louise had said to her daughter.

Charlotte had had her own shop years ago, before her marriage to Peter. As sons-in-law went Peter hadn't been a bad effort; not the worst but certainly not the best. Louise herself didn't like men who had too high an opinion of themselves and Peter had definitely thought a little too well of himself for her liking, though since his death she was conscious that he had gone up in her estimation. Death did that, she supposed, softened and smoothed the bits that had previously irritated and snagged on one's nerves.

She propped her bicycle against the plate-glass window of Charlotte's shop and thought of Alex, who was shaping up into a much better proposition. She opened the door.

'Hello, Mother.'

'Surprised you've not got yourself one of those twee tinkly little bells for the door.'

'What, and go completely round the bend?' Charlotte replied, wanting to add, *like you.*

'Of course, you wouldn't catch me dead with one,' Louise continued, coming further into the shop. 'I've come in for some of those dried flowers,' she said, deciding to take the devious route for what she really wanted, 'the dusky pink ones that look like they were used in Miss Havisham's wedding bouquet.'

'Sorry, I've sold out of those. And, anyway, I told you last week I wasn't going to let you have any more, not after Mrs Braithwaite told me you were selling them on at double the price.'

Louise smiled. 'That's the antique trade for you.' She rested her heavy basket on the corner of the stripped pine table which Charlotte used as a counter. She watched her daughter arranging some large china ducks, their long necks straining over the wooden shelf, black beady eyes staring dumbly at the floor. She was reminded of Hilary's expression just now at Ted the Toup's.

'Anything else I can help you with, Mother?'

Louise wasn't going to be rushed. 'Set a date for the wedding yet?' She knew that would annoy Charlotte and set up a suitable smoke-screen for the real question she wanted to ask. If Charlotte did know what was wrong with her sister and was under orders to keep quiet, Louise knew it would be a waste of time coming out directly with 'What do you know about Hilary?' Charlotte would only dig in her heels and refuse to tell her. Her elder daughter had always played it close to the chest and it had irritated the hell out of her.

Charlotte swung round. 'No, not yet, but I'll stick an invitation in the post for you, just as soon as we know ourselves.'

'You've lost one husband, Charlotte, you don't want to let Alex slip through your hands. Husbands aren't like buses, they don't come along in threes.'

Charlotte returned her attention to the necky ducks. 'If he's that slippery a customer, I'm not so sure he's worth keeping.'

'And if you're going to bore me with your enigmatic routine, Charlotte, I'll be off.' She picked up her shopping basket and said casually, 'Seen much of Hilary recently?'

'No. Why?'

Louise decided to offer a snippet of information. 'I've just seen her in Ted's. She really doesn't look at all well.'

Charlotte was suspicious. Her mother rarely noticed what was wrong with anyone, and if she did, she never commented on it. 'Perhaps she's got a cold. You know what a terror Becky is for bringing germs home from school.'

Louise knew only too well what a terror her granddaughter was, and not just where germs were concerned. She said goodbye and left.

Charlotte stood in the window and watched her mother cycle across the main road, past the church and towards Pippin Rise, the new development which had been built almost on the doorstep of her parents' black and white thatched cottage.

Even when Louise had disappeared out of sight, Charlotte remained where she was. Why had her mother asked about Hilary? And why did she have to keep bringing up the subject of marriage? That was the third time in as many weeks. It really was none of her business, but all the same, she hugged the thought to herself that only that morning before she'd left to open up the shop she and Alex had been discussing what they were going to do.

He had been Charlotte's tenant, and technically he still was, but now he used the granny annexe of Ivy Cottage solely as his office. Since last Christmas when he had moved in with her, Charlotte had lost count of the number of times he had proposed. He had been so patient, never once giving her an ultimatum, and not once had he made her feel guilty for her indecision. But last week she had finally said yes to the idea of marriage. He had been delighted, had wanted to rush her down to St John's there and then. 'No!' she had cried, as he'd swung her round.

'Now don't give me any of that,' he'd shouted. 'You can't change your mind. I clearly heard you say yes.'

'I mean yes, I'll marry you, but no, not straight away. Let me get used to the idea.'

He had bought her a ring the very next day. It was beautiful and, looking at it now on her finger, she felt so sure she was doing the right thing. Her hesitation in marrying Alex was nothing to do with him, but all to do with herself. The latter years of her seven-year marriage to Peter had had a disastrous effect on her self-confidence, and the circumstances surrounding his sudden death in a car crash had compounded her already low sense of self-worth to the extent of making her think she wasn't capable of making a relationship work.

A cold draught blew in at her feet through the badly fitting door and she moved over to the counter where Mabel, her West Highland White terrier, was curled up in her basket in front of a small fan heater which was gently humming to itself. She smiled, reminded of Alex. He had been humming this morning in the shower and she had thrown a wet sponge at him for his choice of song – 'I'm Getting Married in the Morning'.

'Don't waste your breath,' she had said, laughing at him, loving him for his ability always to make her feel *something*. But to surprise him, just as she was leaving the house she had promised she would make up her mind by that evening as to when they would get married. He had telephoned her three times already that morning. She shook her head and suddenly thought how happy it would make not just herself but her sister to see her and Alex married. How busily Hilary had schemed all last summer to get the pair of them together but, then, she always had been such a shocking schemer.

Charlotte's thoughts strayed from her sister to their mother. It was so unlike Louise to notice anything amiss with either Hilary or herself, and yet she had been very specific: 'She really doesn't look at all well.'

Charlotte bent down to a box under the pine table and opened it up. It was full of the dusky pink roses Louise had asked for. She filled a large wicker basket with them and decided to call in at The Gables on her way home later that afternoon.

6

Hilary parked in the gravelled area alongside a row of large greenhouses; they were constructed of plastic sheeting and, as she got out of her car, a gust of wind rippled their sagging sides, making them flap and snap like sails in a boatyard.

She was nervous. It had been all very well using Georgia D'Arcy as an excuse for avoiding her mother but the trouble was, as she'd known the moment she'd uttered the words, she was then committed to following through. She had never been able to lie to her mother and, having told Louise she was seeing Georgia, there was nothing else for it but to do exactly that or the inevitable would happen – her mother would find out she had lied.

She had fibbed once to her mother when she was ten years old. It had been her birthday, and while Louise had been busy in the kitchen preparing for the party and putting the finishing touches to her birthday cake Hilary had been in the sitting room, playing with one of her presents, a plastic dolls' house, which for months she had longed for and had been promised. She had been delighted with the gift, so much so that she had hopped and skipped around it. But disaster had struck. She had slipped and kicked it with her black patent-leather party shoe. Quick as a flash she had carried the dolls' house to her mother in the kitchen and said – with real tears welling up in her eyes – 'Mummy, look, there's a crack in one of the walls. It must have been like this when you bought it.' The next day, she and the dolls' house were taken to the toy shop in Macclesfield where Louise had made the purchase. Hilary had stood there, mortified, in front of the little bald man who, from behind his counter, was being pebble-dashed with a vitriolic attack on shoddy shop practice. When the man tried to defend himself, Louise, with a curious smile on her lips, had said very quietly, 'On one side of this counter stands a liar.' Unable to cope with ten-year-old guilt and feeling sorry for the poor pink-headed man, Hilary had piped up with, 'It's me. I'm the liar.'

In the car going home she had cried and her mother had said, 'I knew all along you were lying, Hilary. I hope I've taught you a valuable lesson today. Lies always have repercussions.'

She glanced at her watch, it was just before twelve thirty. Probably Georgia

219

wouldn't be over at her bungalow yet. Through the smeared window of a small battered caravan beneath an oak tree Hilary saw Georgia's bereted head bobbing to and fro as she talked into a mobile phone. When Georgia caught sight of Hilary she beckoned her over.

It was three years now since Georgia and Rory had moved into the village with their young daughter Chloe. Shortly before this Rory had lost his job with a local pharmaceutical company and had decided to use his redundancy money to start up his own landscaping business, but within a short space of time things started going wrong and gossip began flying round Hulme Welford. The most credible rumour Hilary heard was that Rory had started to drink more than was good for him and the offers of work had dwindled away to nothing. Not long after this Georgia had thrown out her husband and instigated divorce proceedings. Rory had been a good-looking man, full of bonhomie, and had been generally well liked in the village, so not surprisingly Georgia was cast as the villain of the piece. 'A woman should stand by her man,' was the commonly shared view and voiced principally by Patricia Longton. And Georgia had not. She had kicked a man when he was down.

Before yesterday Hilary would have agreed with these smug sentiments. But now she wasn't so sure. Based on what she had unearthed in her own marriage in the past twenty-four hours, what did any of them know of Georgia's and what had gone on before? How easily they had taken sides, because they had all been fortunate enough to have the safety net of a trouble-free marriage.

But that had all changed now.

She remembered how David had come home one evening and said, 'Poor old Rory's ended up with nothing and that hard piece of an ex-wife of his has just been into the office today and bought a two-acre parcel of land up at Hulme View.' Even Hilary had known that Rory had ended up with a whole load more than nothing – namely, most of their savings, what was left of them. In order to buy the land for the nursery Georgia had sold the house, which she'd been awarded as part of her settlement, and she and Chloe had lived in a draughty old caravan while she got the nursery business up and running, working and saving like mad to have a small bungalow built for the two of them.

'Come in,' Georgia mouthed as Hilary peered into the caravan. She stood awkwardly amongst the piles of paperwork, seed catalogues and ripped-open bags of potting compost and bone meal. Georgia pointed to a bench seat and after Hilary had brushed off a sprinkling of white powder, which she then identified as mildew, she sat down and tried her best to pretend she wasn't listening to Georgia's one-sided conversation.

'I don't give a damn about your mother's plastic hip. I ordered that forest bark two months ago ... Well, don't complain to me. I didn't vote this bloody government in ... I'll expect you tomorrow, or I'll come over and do your mother's hip for her.'

'Hi,' Georgia said, facing Hilary and slipping the phone into the pocket on the front of her dungarees. 'Come on, let's go over to the house. It's freezing in here.'

Hilary was glad to get out of the caravan. The confined space, together with its damp coldness, was having a depressing effect on her. How on earth had Georgia and Chloe stuck living in it? She followed Georgia down the rusting metal steps, across the gravel car park to a muddy path that led to the recently built bungalow, which in Hilary's mind sparkled like an oasis in this jumbled mess of dirt and toil. She imagined the house to be warm, clean and inviting.

Georgia unlocked the front door and kicked off her mud-caked boots. 'I didn't think you'd come,' she said. 'Throw your coat over the back of that chair and come on through to the kitchen.'

Hilary's oasis image was fast disappearing as she watched Georgia washing her hands at the sink amongst an enormous pile of dirty pots and pans. The kitchen was almost as untidy as the caravan, but at least it was warm and there was the tantalising smell of garlic and herbs, which certainly had the edge on bone meal.

'I'm not going to apologise for the state of the place,' Georgia said, as she bent down to open the oven. 'I know it's a mess, but Chloe comes first, the nursery next and the dust and mess a poor last.'

'It's not a mess at all,' Hilary said, politely turning away from the sight of Georgia's and Chloe's underwear drying on the radiator. To her shame she found herself thinking how much more acceptable washing was hanging from the ceiling on one of those smart Edwardian clothes-dryers.

'That's a load of crap, Hilary, and you know it.' Georgia slammed the oven door shut. 'Now what have you got there?'

Hilary looked down at her hands, suddenly remembering what she was holding. 'They're for you. Chocolates. I thought you'd like them.' She offered them to Georgia and found herself holding her breath. *Déjà vu.* She breathed out. No, it wasn't *déjà vu* at all. It was the past, something that had happened a long time ago, when she had moved on to grammar school, joining Charlotte who was already there in her third year. In her first term she had developed a monumental crush on a girl in the fifth form and after days of plucking up courage she had approached Naomi Scott with a box of chocolates that had cost her several weeks' pocket money. 'I thought you'd like them,' she had said. Naomi, beautiful as well as clever, had taken the box and walked away without even thanking her. Later that day Hilary heard Naomi laughing about her with her friends. She had cried that night in bed, trying to come to terms with her first lesson in rejection.

And now something very real and intense inside her was making her hope that Georgia might be her friend, that she wouldn't reject her.

'How bloody daft and lovely of you,' Georgia said, taking the box and placing it beside a pile of ironing. 'I can't remember the last time anyone gave me chocolates.'

*

Lunch was better than Hilary had expected. She hadn't thought a radical like Georgia would be able to do anything creative in the kitchen. She didn't know which most surprised her, that there was meat on the table and not beans and pulses, or that she had actually managed to eat any of it. It was her first meal since yesterday morning.

'We must leave enough for Chloe's tea,' Georgia instructed, scooping out a second portion for Hilary, 'or I'll be in the doghouse for days.'

Hilary could think of nothing more unlikely.

'So, Hilary, what gives in Acacia Lane?'

'Gives?'

Georgia smiled. 'What's going on at The Gables that's made you take up a wild invitation for lunch with a heretic like me?' Georgia watched Hilary closely as she finished chewing what was in her mouth. She was aware she had just put Hilary on the spot, and even more aware that she was making her guest nervous. She was often told she made people feel uncomfortable. It was her honesty, she supposed. People didn't usually appreciate such directness. But life was too short to waste time beating about the bush.

'Nothing,' Hilary said at last. 'Why ever would you think there was?'

'In my experience, there's always something going on at home. When there isn't, that's the time to worry.'

Hilary felt torn. Something made her want to confide in Georgia, but Cindy's words telling her to keep quiet were rattling around inside her head. 'How long is it since you've been on your own?' she asked, already knowing the answer, but finding herself wanting to hear it from Georgia herself.

So that's it, thought Georgia. Our old friend matrimonial trouble giving Hilary grief. Wasn't it always?

'Two marvellous years,' she answered, resting her elbows on the table and her chin on her roughened and scratched knuckles. A moment passed, then she threw back her head and laughed, her long ear-rings dancing against her slender neck. 'Okay, then, I admit it. One exhausting year preceded by one year of sheer hell.'

'Why did—?'

'Why did I throw him out? Is that what you want to know?'

Hilary nodded and lowered her eyes, unable to meet Georgia's gaze.

'Ever since Rory had been made redundant he'd been knocking about with another woman. Coming here to Hulme Welford was supposed to have been a new start but I soon found out that he was still seeing her. And why did our marriage go wrong in the first place, is probably your next question. The answer to that is easy. Like so many men, Rory couldn't handle the dent that redundancy had made in his self-esteem. And yeah, sure, I'm fully aware that Rory is by no means the first man to seek out somebody else to bolster up his deflated ego.'

'So where is he now?'

'God knows. We've not seen hide nor hair of him for over six months. But

Chloe and I are just fine without him. At least now I don't have to spend half my time mothering an overgrown schoolkid who still needs to be told what a good boy he is. Men just never grow out of needing a mother figure to tell little Johnny, or little Rory . . .' she hesitated before adding one other name '. . . or little David, what a good boy he is. When they come home from work, their briefcases bulging with the flimsy achievements of the day, they're only after one thing, and that's to be told what clever boys they are. Do you see what I mean?'

'I think so, but—'

'It's all sick. If they think they're not getting enough praise at home they simply look elsewhere.'

'Why did you mention David's name just now?' Hilary said quietly. 'He isn't like that.'

'You sure?'

Hilary thought for a moment. She tried to think of an average evening spent at The Gables: David would come home from work, pour himself a glass of whisky and stand in front of the Aga – getting in her way – and proceed to tell her about the latest house he'd sold or been offered to sell. And she, while getting the supper ready and supervising Philip's homework, would nod and say things like, 'That's nice, dear.' She swallowed hard. Maybe Georgia was right: perhaps David had simply found somebody who would listen more attentively; somebody who would ask all the pertinent questions that she was too tired or bored even to consider.

She put down her knife and fork and looked up at Georgia. For a split second Cindy's words from yesterday went quiet inside her head and she seized her opportunity, wanting Georgia to know . . . wanting Georgia to help her. 'David's having an affair,' she heard herself say. 'Oh, God. This is like something out of a Joanna Trollope novel.'

'Get out of here. This is an Aga-free zone, I'll have you know.'

'Please don't joke with me,' Hilary said, her stomach beginning to churn, her throat tightening with the effort of holding back the tears.

'I'm sorry. So what are we going to do about it?'

'We?'

'Good grief, Hilary. You don't think I'm going to let you go through this alone, do you? Hey, come on. Don't go all trembly on me.'

'I can't help it,' Hilary whispered, tears filling her eyes and trickling down her pale cheeks. 'I can't help it. You're so much nicer than Naomi Scott.'

Georgia didn't have a clue what Hilary was talking about, but she got up from her chair and went to her. She knelt down and put her arms round Hilary's shaking shoulders.

The comfort of Georgia's slight body against her own made Hilary lean into her and she cried all the more.

7

'So, Dad, let me get this straight. You want to give up the world of curling tongs and mud packs for the world of emotional cripples looking up their bums?' Tiffany let out a loud laugh. 'This I have to see!'

Derek looked across the office desk at his seventeen-year-old daughter. He had just told Tiffany about his plans for changing In the Pink into a centre of self-discovery and he knew, as any parent knows, that his teenage daughter was probably his biggest critic. Part of him, the old Derek, wanted to shout at Tiffany for her insolence and tell her not to be so bloody rude, but the new Derek was struggling to remain a paragon of selfless patience and understanding. There was no room for outbursts of indignation and anger in the new world he wanted to create. 'Prejudice against any new idea does, of course, betray an underlying sense of inadequacy and inferiority,' he said smoothly, pleased with himself for being able to quote so easily from the book he'd been reading earlier in the salon while Mrs Jeffs was at the back wash.

Tiffany laughed again. 'Muffin 'ell, Dad. What's got into you? You've not been the same since Barry had his born-again experience.'

Derek shuffled some papers in front of him. He kept his eyes down, finding Tiffany's words uncomfortably near the truth, but he'd be damned if he ever let on. All that talk from Bas of a living Christ had brought him up short and left him feeling embarrassed but strangely curious. Sure, it was all gobbledegook, but for the life of him he couldn't work out how a smart bloke like Bas could get caught up in it. But that wasn't really what had got to him. What had was Bas being flown home from Romania with meningitis. That was when things had got to him. He'd always kept his distance with Bas because secretly he'd been afraid of him. Bas was so effortlessly more intelligent than he was, but seeing his son helpless in that hospital bed, not knowing whether he was going to live or die, had made him feel so useless, had made him face up to how badly he'd let his son down. That was the moment when something – something he didn't really understand – had touched him on the shoulder and said, 'Get a grip, Derek old mate. There's more to life than touching up Mrs Jeffs' roots every three weeks.'

But it wasn't until he'd been listening to some of his customers discussing how they had to get home early that afternoon because they wanted to catch the latest daytime discussion show on the telly that an inkling of an idea had begun to take root in his mind.

The following day he'd set the video to record the programme and later that night, when both Cindy and Tiffany were asleep in bed, he'd secretly watched a dozen or so Americans laying out their neuroses in front of a live audience along with countless numbers of viewers. An expert in an absurd waistcoat with an equally absurd name – Dr L. S. Nutter III – was there on hand to help these troubled people work through their phobias and self-doubts. He'd been gobsmacked. It was incredible. And rewinding the tape he'd watched the bit again where a grossly overweight man had stood up and said, 'Help me! I'm terrified of my left hand.' He had gone on to explain in detail that ever since the age of thirteen he'd been unable to bring himself to use it. Dr L. S. Nutter III had suggested that the man was, in fact, lying and that what he was really saying was, 'Hey, look at me, I'm into self-abuse and what about it?' The fat man had leapt out of his chair and grabbed Nutter by the throat, but the doctor, cool as you like, had merely said, 'The truth has cured you. You see that hand you're about to hit me with? It's your left one!' The fat man had broken down and cried like a baby and the audience had gone wild, clapping and stamping their feet. They'd witnessed not only real live drama but a miracle. It was heady stuff.

'Just wait till I tell Barry.'

Derek dropped the papers he'd been shifting around on the desk. 'No. I'd rather you didn't.'

Tiffany stared at him, her eyes dark and critical – a reflection of her mother's. He had a pretty good idea what she was thinking and he didn't want to hear it. He got up from his chair and went over to the filing cabinet behind the desk. He opened one of the drawers. 'I want to be the one to tell Bas,' he said casually, his back to Tiffany.

'Suit yourself.'

He heard her open the door and when he turned round she was gone. Well, that wasn't so bad, he told himself.

'Classic mid-life crisis behaviour, I reckon,' Tiffany said, her head suddenly appearing round the door. She was grinning at him.

'Out!' he shouted.

Damn silly thing to say. Of course he wasn't going through a mid-life crisis. Good God, anyone would think he was behaving like those stressed-out executives you read about, who for no apparent reason give up their smart company cars and take to growing turnips in Wales. He wasn't like that. All he was doing was reviewing the schedule. It was time for a change. Surely that wasn't such a big deal. And there were market trends to take into account. It didn't pay to play the same game for too long, not when there were so many other opportunities out there to grab hold of.

There was still the question as to how he was going to tell Bas. The last thing he wanted was Tiffany running off to the phone and smirking into it that their father was going doo-lally. He hoped Bas would be pleased, even proud of him. It was important to him now that he had his son's approval.

'Life. Bloody old life,' he said out loud. 'What's a simple guy supposed to make of it?'

Tiffany gave a quick knock on the conservatory door. There was no response so she knocked again. She hoped Charlotte and Alex were in. She liked coming next door to Ivy Cottage where she was never treated as an awkward teenager. Instead Charlotte and Alex treated her as an awkward adult. She often came round to them when she wanted to get away from In the Pink – at least here she could escape the sight of all those gullible over-dressed women pandering to their vanity. Sad. Woefully sad the whole lot of them. Didn't they know that there were millions starving all over the world while they tried to sweat a few pounds off their wobbly bums and chins? Disgusting.

She knocked at the door again then turned the handle. 'Charlotte,' she called out. 'It's me, Tiffany.'

'Hello, you Tiffany,' said Alex, from the kitchen. 'Charlotte's upstairs having a bath. Anything I can help you with?'

Tiffany rolled her eyes and pouted. 'I need some help with my biology homework,' she said, sounding and wiggling her hips like Marilyn Monroe. It was a ritual she and Alex went through occasionally – she parodying the dumb blonde and he the lecherous older man.

'Ah-ah! And would I be right in thinking it was to do with the reproductive organs?'

She rolled her eyes again. 'You've found me out. How about we try psychology, then?'

Alex sidled up to Tiffany. 'Miss Vogers,' he said, 'I know your problems only too vell. You are mad for zee right man in your life. Am I correct?'

'Oh, oh,' squeaked Tiffany, sounding more like Betty Boop. 'Take me, Doctor, take—'

'Just watch yourself, Dr Kildare!'

It was Charlotte, standing in the doorway wearing Alex's bathrobe and a towel round her head. She was smiling. 'Honestly, I leave you to tidy up the kitchen and then find you seducing our next-door neighbour's daughter. Is it your age? Or am I making your tea too strong?'

Alex put his arm round Charlotte and kissed her.

Tiffany coughed loudly. 'If you could stop thinking about sex for a few moments, you two, I've got some news.'

Alex could feel the warmth of Charlotte's naked body through the towelling robe and suddenly sex was very much on his mind. 'Well, don't let us keep you, Tiffany,' he said.

'Don't be so rude,' Charlotte said, pushing him away.

'That's all right. I've heard about men like him. Anyway, do you want to hear my news, or what? Dad's having a mid-life crisis. The full works. He's chucking in exploiting women under the guise of health and beauty and setting himself up as a manager of some kind of therapy clinic. Never mind In the Pink, this'll be In the Stink if you ask me.'

'You mean no more Don Juan of the curlers?' Alex laughed.

'No more Lothario wielding his scissors?' Charlotte said, amazed.

'He's not been the same since Barry was ill. I've seen him mooching about the salon. He's obviously bored with the whole scene.'

'Perhaps he thinks he'll make more money out of therapy. Your dad's no fool.'

'You could be right, Charlotte,' Tiffany said. 'On the other hand, maybe he's worked out he can get to women more successfully by curing their emotional problems.'

'Talking of which,' Alex said, 'time you were going. I want to talk to my future wife about her emotional problems.'

'Future wife, eh? When, how and why?'

'That's what I want to talk to her about, little Miss Nosy Parker. So on your way.'

'I'm going, I'm going,' Tiffany said good-humouredly. 'I'm due at Hilary's in a few minutes to babysit.'

As Tiffany closed the door behind her, Charlotte frowned.

'Oh no you don't,' Alex said. 'Don't go pretending you're suddenly ill in an attempt to get out of our conversation.' He picked her up and carried her through to the sitting-room where earlier he'd lit a fire. Mabel was stretched out in front of it on the rug. He set Charlotte down on the sofa and knelt beside her.

'What a suspicious nature you have, Alex. As a matter of fact I've just remembered I was supposed to go and see Hilary myself.'

'Hilary can wait. I can't.'

She raised an eyebrow and reached out to him.

'No,' he said firmly. 'I'm withholding my body until you've given me a date, time and place.'

She laughed. 'Ssh, you're embarrassing Mabel.'

He kissed her, then stood up. 'I'll get you a glass of wine, then I'll have your answer.'

When he came back into the room, Charlotte was sitting in front of the log fire; she'd removed the towel from her head and was running a hand through her long dark hair. She looked up as he stood over her.

'What do you think about Christmas?' she said.

'I rather thought we'd have it here again, like last year.' He put another log on the fire and nudged it into place with his foot.

'I didn't mean that.'

'You mean . . .'

'Christmas Eve falls on a Saturday this year. I've phoned Malcolm and he says he can fit us in. What do you think?'

'I think I've just stopped withholding my body.'

*

'Où est Paul?'

How should I know? Hilary thought angrily to herself. Carry on as normal had been Cindy's advice and, God help her, she was doing her best. Tuesday night was David's squash night and her French evening class at Becky's school, and unbelievably, here she was – but was David really playing squash?

'Hilary, où est Paul?'

She looked down at her textbook and studied the drawings. 'Il est encore au lit,' she answered. Typical. Half past eleven in the morning and the stupid man was still in bed.

'Pourquoi?'

The classroom door opened.

'Bonsoir! Sorry I'm late.'

Everyone looked up, including Martina their French teacher. 'Hello,' she said, from the desk on which she was perched and uncrossing her legs. 'Are you sure you've got the right room?'

'I hope so. French, intermediate? My name's Nick Bradshaw. I should be on your list.'

While Martina flicked through the names on her register, Hilary bent her head and tried to sink as low as she could into the small primary-school chair. Her only hope was that he wouldn't recognise her without her sunglasses and ridiculous hat.

'You *are* late, aren't you?' Martina said, looking up from her file.

'About three weeks late, I make it.'

She laughed. 'Find a seat and we'll chat at the end of the session. If you sit at the back with Hilary you can partner her in the conversational work in a moment. Hilary, would you mind sharing your book?'

Hilary mumbled a yes and without looking up she slid it across the small desk.

'D'accord. Paul, il est encore au lit. Pourquoi? Patricia?'

'Parce qu'il est fatigué.' Hilary heard Patricia's reply, quick as a flash.

'Hi,' Nick Bradshaw said, squeezing himself into the chair next to her.

She managed a nod.

'Et Maman, où est-ce qu'elle est?'

'Where all good mothers are,' Nick Bradshaw whispered, 'at the tip throwing away expensive cut glass.'

Hilary froze. Out of the corner of her eye she could see he was smiling at her. He was making fun of her.

At the front of the classroom Martina closed her textbook. 'Okay,' she said, 'conversation work now. Pair off and choose one of the following subjects.' She started writing on the blackboard: Shopping, Gardening or Discussing a Book or a Film.

'What shall we pick?'

'You choose,' Hilary murmured, her head still bent over the textbook.

'How about some small-talk instead?'

Oh, please, the smaller the better. 'Oui,' she said.

He laughed. 'Très bien. Bonsoir, je m'appelle Nick.'

At last she looked him full in the face and flinched slightly under the same direct stare he'd offered her at the tip. He seemed older than she'd remembered him; somewhere in his early forties. His face had that rumpled kind of look that she supposed some women found attractive. She decided it matched his trousers – a quick glance downwards told her he was wearing the same pair as this morning. When she didn't say anything, he said, 'Hilary *qui*?'

'Hilary Parker,' she said reluctantly.

'Et qui est le bâtard?'

Who is the bastard? Oh my God! He *had* heard her this morning. She turned away, the colour instantly draining from her face.

'Votre mari peut-être?'

What was he, some kind of mind-reader? 'My husband? Of course not,' she said loudly.

'En français, Hilary.'

'I'm sorry, Martina,' Hilary said, suddenly gathering up her book and getting to her feet. 'I'm not feeling well. I'd better get off home.'

'Okay, everyone. Time's up anyway. Now remember, there's no lesson next week, it's half-term break, so that means you have two weeks in which to do your homework. I want you to prepare a talk on your last holiday. Hilary, you do look rather pale, do you want me to give you a lift home?'

'No. I'll be fine once I'm outside. It must be the heating in here.' She struggled into her coat.

'What, no hat?'

Hilary flashed an angry look at Nick. 'Why don't you mind your own business?' she said. Then, astonished at what she'd just said, she hurried out of the classroom. But Patricia was there, barring her way at the door.

'Martina's right, Hilary, you do look pale. You do know there's diarrhoea doing the rounds at school, don't you?'

'Then you'd best get out of my way,' Hilary snapped.

Outside in the corridor, as she hurried past the frieze of autumn artwork displayed on the walls, Hilary wondered what was happening to her. She was never bad-tempered with other people. Patience was her middle name and here she was sounding off at anyone who spoke to her. Bloody David! It was all his fault. Because he had changed, she was changing. She didn't like it. She wanted him to be the same old David and herself to be the same old Hilary.

She scurried across the floodlit playground and paused at the school gate to catch her breath. How long was she supposed to keep this charade going? How had Cindy managed it all these years? From behind her she heard the sound of footsteps.

'I'm sorry about that, back there,' a voice called out. And before she was able to push open the gate Nick Bradshaw was next to her standing in the light cast from the street-lamp above them. 'I have a habit of wading in, I can't be bothered with mincing about. Getting to the nub of things is what I like to do, it's what I'm paid to do.'

'I'm sorry too,' she responded, deciding that David wouldn't change her completely. She would still remember her manners. 'I shouldn't have bitten your head off like that.'

'I probably deserved it. Fancy a drink?'

The rest of the group were now coming towards them across the tarmac. Hilary could see Patricia walking alongside Martina. Bet she was teacher's pet at school, she thought. 'A drink?' she repeated, suddenly registering what this practically unknown man had asked her. How ridiculous. She was a married woman, a mother of two young children being asked out for a drink! The very idea.

'From the look on your face I'll take that as a no.'

'I really must be going,' she said, flustered. 'I've a babysitter waiting, PTA minutes to type up and—'

'And a husband.' He smiled. 'No worries. I'll see you in two weeks.' He held the gate for her. 'Don't forget your homework.'

8

When Hilary let herself in there was no sign of David, or of the children. Tiffany was lying on the sofa reading a book. She moved her long legs and made room for Hilary.

'I hope that's homework,' Hilary said, betraying her years as a teacher. She knew that Tiffany's mock exams were fast approaching, and although it was obvious that Tiffany was a bright and able student, she was also aware how easy it was for her to get sidetracked. In the short time that the Rogers family had been living in Acacia Lane Hilary had not only witnessed Tiffany trying to come through her adolescence by battling with her parents over her individuality – whether it was dressing herself from top to toe in black or dyeing her hair bright pink – she had also watched her go through her vegetarian phase, her custodians-of-the-earth phase and more recently her singlehanded attempt at shaming the residents of Hulme Welford into donating money for the homeless by sitting in a cardboard box outside Ted the Toup's shop one wet Saturday afternoon. Cindy and Derek had been away that particular weekend, had been blissfully ignorant of Tiffany's plan and had missed the sight of their daughter drenched and shivering, her hand outstretched, and the opportunity to try to stop her. But Hilary suspected that even if they had known about the collapsible cardboard box Tiffany had stashed away under her bed, Cindy and Derek would have been powerless to prevent their daughter's protest – like herself, they must have long since arrived at the unpalatable truth that there was nothing they could do to dissuade their youngest child from pursuing her chosen line of action.

'Background reading for Jane Austen,' Tiffany replied, waving the cover of *Emma* in front of Hilary. 'Bit of a spoilt madam, isn't she? Always poking her nose into everybody else's business and all the time she hasn't got a clue what's going on right under her own smug nose.'

'I think you'll find things change for her later,' Hilary said thoughtfully, struggling to recall her own A-level studies.

'Yea, well, she deserves the fall that's coming to her, if you ask me.'

'Children okay?' Hilary asked, suddenly feeling uncomfortable with the conversation.

'Philip was his usual quiet self and Becky got worked up over something and nothing.'

'Mm . . .' Hilary said, distracted. Her mind was still on *Emma*. At the door she paid Tiffany and said goodbye, then went back into the sitting-room where she looked along the shelves of the bookcase to the right of the fireplace. There, on the highest shelf, she found what she was looking for. She blew away the dust and opened the book at chapter one.

Emma Woodhouse, handsome, clever, and rich, with a comfortable home and happy disposition, seemed to unite some of the best blessings of existence, and had lived nearly twenty-one years in the world with very little to distress or vex her.

Apart from the age and perhaps the *handsome* and *clever* references it could be herself. Hadn't she always thought she'd lived a charmed life with David? All these years she had been so complacently happy with her lot . . . and now there was the risk that she was about to lose everything.

She put the book back in its place on the top shelf then caught her reflection in the mirror above the fireplace. She looked tired, dull even, but surely not so awful that David had stopped loving her? When had it all gone wrong? She thought back over the past year or so, searching her mind for some tell-tale sign that would explain David's indifference to her. She could find none, but she could hear Charlotte's voice telling her how bossy she was. And, yes, deep down she knew her sister was right, but that wasn't such a crime, it was just her way, and anyway everybody had their little foibles. But Charlotte had also implied that she had a habit of interfering and David himself had accused her of the same thing last year. 'Stop meddling in other people's lives,' he'd said, 'especially your sister's.' She had been stung by his words – after all, she'd only been helping Charlotte to get over Peter's death by nudging her in Alex's direction. What harm had she done? And were these crimes justification for a husband to cause untold harm to his family by having an affair? Tiffany had just condemned *Emma* by saying she deserved the fall that was coming to her – would people say that about herself, she wondered.

The phone rang.

'It's me.'

'Where are you?'

'Still at the squash club.'

Hilary pushed the receiver closer to her ear, trying to make out the sound of squash balls being whacked against a wall – she wanted to believe David, truly she did.

'I'll be a bit later than usual. There's a free court so I'm having another game . . . Hilary, you still there?'

She slammed down the phone and was still crying when she heard somebody at the front door.

'Cindy!' She had never known Cindy to go calling, not even during the day, let alone at night.

'When Tiffany came home, I thought I'd see how you were.'

'As you can see, not very well,' Hilary answered, making no attempt to wipe away her tears.

'Would you rather I left you alone?' Cindy said awkwardly.

'No, no. Please come in, I was just going to make myself a drink.'

Cindy followed Hilary into the kitchen and while Hilary made some coffee, she took off her coat and started to clear away what was obviously the remains of tea. 'You should get Tiffany to tidy up for you while she babysits,' she said.

'I couldn't do that,' Hilary snivelled, 'she's got her homework to do.' She blew her nose, loudly and messily, knowing she looked awful; she always did whenever she cried. At the first sign of a tear her eyes would swell and redden, almost to the same shade as the rubber gloves Cindy was now pulling on. What on earth was Cindy doing? She sensed Cindy didn't approve of tears, which made her want to cry even more. Disapproval was almost as bad as rejection.

As she watched Cindy wring out the dishcloth she realised that the other woman made her feel ashamed and inadequate. Georgia hadn't made her feel like that. Georgia had been warm and comforting, which had surprised Hilary. She hadn't expected kindness from such a tough woman.

Cindy had now moved on to wiping the work surfaces. Hilary felt a stab of anger towards this woman who was so calm, so cool, and who had probably never cried in her life. 'Cindy,' she said, trying to sound assertive, 'you don't have to do that. Come and have your coffee.'

'It's no trouble,' Cindy answered, moving back to the sink and spraying some Mr Muscle behind the mixer taps. She rubbed hard then, satisfied that the worst of the tears were over, she peeled off the gloves, sat opposite Hilary and thought, Thank God I never fell apart like this. She felt proud of herself that during all the years of putting up with Derek's dalliances she had held herself together as well as their family.

She had called on Hilary to see how she was and to escape Derek's endless talk of his latest brainchild. She was finding it hard to be as motivated as he was about the whole idea, but in a funny kind of way it pleased her to see Derek so enthusiastic about something. Just after Barry's confirmation last summer Derek had seemed more content than she'd ever known him, but more recently he had become distant and distracted. She hoped that the transformation of their business would be the answer to whatever had been causing him to wander listlessly about the salon. Perhaps, finally, he was about to find his true vocation. It might even stop him from straying, give him a sense of fulfilment. She was beginning to sound like him now, as though quoting from one of his wretched books.

A sniff from the other side of the table reminded her of Hilary.

'I don't think I can carry on much longer pretending nothing's happened,' Hilary said flatly.

'Why don't you come over to me tomorrow and I'll give you a facial?'

'Georgia D'Arcy says I should confront David.' She paused. 'Actually, Georgia said I should confront the sodding bastard.' She gave a queer little laugh. 'I don't normally go in for profanity, but since yesterday I seem to have done little else.'

Cindy examined one of her long, varnished nails. It was chipped. She must have knocked it just now. She said coolly, 'Well, Georgia D'Arcy would say that, wouldn't she?'

Hilary looked up sharply. 'What do you mean?'

'And just where did it get her when she confronted her husband? Living in a caravan and working all hours just to scratch a living together. Is that what you want, Hilary?' She cast her eyes round the cluttered but comfortable Aga-warmed kitchen. 'You'd lose all this. You know that, don't you?'

Hilary began to cry again. 'She doesn't live in a caravan any more and at least she has her dignity.'

'And I haven't?' suggested Cindy.

'I . . . I didn't say that. All I meant was—'

'I know what you meant, Hilary, but are you strong enough to do what Georgia did?'

'Georgia says that a woman is like a tea-bag and it's only when she's in hot water that she knows how strong she is.'

Cindy's usually brittle features softened. 'I like that,' she said, smiling.

'I don't think I have the same kind of strength you have, Cindy. I'm not at all stoic like you.'

Stoic? Strength? Cindy had never thought of it like that. She had merely taken it for granted that she would hold things together.

Hilary sniffed. 'Georgia says—'

Cindy raised her hand. 'Okay. I think I've heard enough from Ms D'Arcy. As far as I can see, you've a choice to make, Hilary. Either you play it my way and hope David tires of this one-off thing—'

'If it is a one-off—'

'Or you confront him and risk losing your husband because you've forced him into making the wrong choice. It's up to you.'

Not long after Cindy had left, Hilary went upstairs to check on the children. She stood in Philip's bedroom at the end of his bed. She watched him turn over in his sleep. He was restless, the duvet tossed aside, his pillow hanging over the edge of the bed. She moved forward and stooped to rearrange the duvet, remembering how when Philip had been a baby she would put him in his cot on his side at bedtime and in the morning he'd be in exactly the same position – the sheets barely wrinkled, the blanket undisturbed. So when had he changed? And when had he started biting his fingernails, she wondered, catching sight of one of his hands in the strip of light from the landing as it streaked through the doorway and across his bed? Poor Philip, she suddenly thought, what was troubling him?

And how on earth could she confront David when it might threaten her children's security?

9

It was Saturday morning when Charlotte remembered she still hadn't called on her sister to see how she was. But as she unlocked the door of her shop she decided that if anything had been seriously wrong, Hilary would have come to see her.

Not so long ago Hilary had practically been a permanent resident at Ivy Cottage, continually popping over the road with some spurious reason for visiting when all the time she had been checking up on Charlotte and Alex.

Their relationship had been what Charlotte had supposed was a fairly typical one between sisters. As children they had been the best of friends one moment and sworn enemies the next. Best friends had consisted of sleeping together in the same bedroom, playing T. Rex records until gone midnight and then tuning in to Radio Luxembourg. Enemies had consisted of Charlotte defacing one of Hilary's treasured David Cassidy posters and Hilary jamming her up against the wall and beating her about the head with the lid of a biscuit tin. Thinking about it, it was the only time Charlotte could recall her sister losing control. On the whole, and especially so nowadays, Hilary had always been a control freak; worrying and herding those around her like the most persistent of sheepdogs.

There had, of course, been the one-way rivalry between them. Hilary had desperately wanted to be the older sister and had fought sneakily as well as blatantly to usurp Charlotte's role; a role for which Charlotte had never given tuppence. She knew that, after Peter's death, Hilary had relished her role as sister of mercy to the rescue and had played the part with supreme heavy-handedness.

Charlotte opened the small safe at the back of the shop and then put the float into the till. At nine o'clock she switched on the lights and waited for her first customer of the day, knowing that trade wouldn't really get going until gone nine thirty, and now that the weather was turning nasty perhaps it would be even later. She was enjoying running her own business again, even if her mother had greeted her decision to take on the lease with her usual scorn. 'Just don't be muscling in on my patch,' Louise had said. 'Only room for one antique shop in the village.' Charlotte knew that her mother was as mad as hell that by somebody else's bad luck she had acquired one of the largest shops in the village with its spacious double frontage – Louise had only the one cramped window. Dad had been great and helped her and Alex redecorate the place after Jim Lloyd had cleared the last of his bathroom fittings from the shop.

She had decided against going back into clothes retailing, which she had done in London, all those years ago, before Peter had forced her to sell up and move abroad. What Hulme Welford needed, she had concluded, was a shop selling quality gifts, along with a cheaper line in Third-World goods for the caring nineties consumer.

Filling a basket with a new batch of friendship bands – ready for the pocket-money spenders – Charlotte thought of the look that she would put on Hilary's face when she told her she and Alex had at last fixed a date for the wedding. The only downside was that Hilary might dive in, take over and organise a monumental bunfight. The last thing Charlotte wanted was her sister hijacking her wedding.

The shop door opened and Charlotte lifted her head to greet her first customer. It was Hilary with the niece from hell, Becky. 'Hello,' Charlotte said, trying to keep the shock out of her voice. Her sister looked dreadful. She was so pale.

'Hello, Auntie Charlotte,' piped up Becky, making a beeline for the shelves of china candlesticks.

Charlotte watched Becky start to move the expensive pieces of Italian chinaware as though she were playing chess, while at the same time she was conscious of Hilary drifting towards the counter, her hands playing nervously over the pile of paper bags next to the till.

'You're out and about early,' Charlotte said, troubled that for the first time in her life she was experiencing the sensation of feeling sorry for her sister.

'I'm selling tickets for the school fireworks party. Do you want some for you and Alex?' Hilary replied, without looking at Charlotte. Her voice was flat and mechanical, and unmistakably wrong to Charlotte's well-trained ear. Even though Hilary believed herself the most circumspect woman alive, Charlotte knew otherwise. Her sister had never been able to hide anything – secrets had always burst out of her with rocket-like propulsion and her face was as easy to read as a book.

'I'll get my bag,' Charlotte said.

When she returned from the small back office, she found her sister looking at a handmade Advent calendar. Charlotte noticed that Hilary's hands were shaking. 'What is it, Hilary?'

Without turning round, Hilary said, 'I was just thinking of Christmases when we were little. It was always Dad who made it happen, wasn't it? I'd never thought of that before.'

'Dad did the presents, but it was you who made everything else happen, bossing everybody about like a good 'un.'

'I wasn't that bossy,' Hilary retaliated.

Charlotte frowned. Hilary, bossy – the two were synonymous, everybody knew that. 'How much are the tickets?' she asked, moving on to safer ground.

'Two pounds fifty each. There's a free drink thrown in.'

A sudden crash from Becky made them both turn.

'I haven't broken anything,' Becky said brightly.

'For heaven's sake,' shouted Hilary, 'can't you be more careful?'

Charlotte was taken aback. She'd never heard Hilary admonish her daughter like this before. It had always been Charlotte's privately held opinion that if Hilary had been firmer with Becky from the word go, she wouldn't be such a pain now. 'Hilary,' Charlotte said, quietly, 'what's up?'

Hilary glanced away, but not before Charlotte had seen her lips trembling and her eyes filling with tears.

'Has something happened?'

Hilary shook her head.

'Please, Hilary. If I can help.' She placed a tentative hand on her sister's arm. 'What is it?'

'I'm not supposed to tell anyone,' Hilary blurted out. It sounded ridiculous.

'For God's sake, why?'

'I . . .' Hilary finally met her sister's gaze and disintegrated beneath it. 'It's David . . .' She looked over to where Becky was still playing chess. 'An affair,' she whispered, 'he's having an affair.'

'No! Not David, I don't believe it.'

The door flew open, followed by a dramatic blast of wind which brought with it a flurry of leaves and Iris Braithwaite.

'Mrs Lawrence, a word, if you please.'

'Can it wait, Mrs Braithwaite?' Charlotte asked, her eyes never once leaving her sister's face.

Iris rattled the door shut and approached Charlotte and Hilary. She had with her a pen on a long piece of string attached to a black clipboard. 'I'm on a mission of merchandise cleansing,' she boomed, 'so no, it cannot wait. And waiting, I might say, Mrs Lawrence, is the very kind of attitude that has got us where we are. The day has come—'

'Mrs Braithwaite—'

'I haven't finished, Mrs Lawrence. The day has come for us to rid Hulme Welford of everything unsavoury and of an ambiguous nature.' Her eyes swept accusingly round the shelves of Charlotte's shop.

'What on earth are you talking about, Mrs Braithwaite?' Charlotte asked.

'A smut-free zone is what I'm talking about and I'm not at all sure I like your tone of—'

'A what zone?' Hilary interrupted, speaking for the first time.

Iris approached the counter and banged down her clipboard. She gave Charlotte a handwritten poster. 'Make Hulme Welford a Smut-free Zone' it declared in large letters. 'In the window, if you please, Mrs Lawrence, and if you'd like to sign my petition I'll be on my way. You too, Mrs Parker.'

Charlotte read aloud from the piece of paper: '"I the undersigned agree to the closure of Ted Cooper's newsagent's and will not tolerate the selling of undesirable items in any other retail establishment in Hulme Welford.'"

'Undesirable items?' Charlotte repeated.

'Pornographic!' exclaimed Iris, so vigorously that her brown cowpat of a hat with a little stalk sticking up from it nearly slipped off her head.

'But he's always sold smutty magazines.'

'I'm not referring to those.' Iris shuddered. 'It's pornographic items of clothing he's moved on to. He'll be turning the premises into a sex shop next. Hulme Welford will soon become the Soho of the North if we don't stop him.'

Charlotte wanted to laugh, but Iris's highly censorious manner was verging on the manic and it was possible that an unchecked snigger might tip the old woman over the edge.

'What exactly is Ted selling?' she asked patiently.

'Tights with . . . tights without a . . .' Iris cleared her throat and began again. 'No gusset,' she hissed. '"Peephole", he called them.'

'Peep-bo!' sang out Becky, her head appearing over the top of a display rack of cotton throw-overs. 'What's a sex shop?'

It was complete chaos. They would never be ready in time, and just how on earth had she let Derek talk her into this?

Cindy looked at what, until a few days ago, had been the reception desk in the foyer – it was now pushed against the door waiting to be thrown away. According to Derek they weren't going to have a desk. Apparently such a solid block would act as both a mental and physical barrier, making a them-and-us situation. 'We are to meld as one,' he had explained last night, while watching Cindy stack the dishwasher after she'd got back from seeing Hilary. Tiffany had walked in at that point looking for food and had muttered something about melding her father together.

'And what exactly are we calling ourselves?' Cindy had asked.

'Don't tempt me,' Tiffany had sniggered, her head inside the fridge.

Derek had looked pleased with himself. 'All in the Mind. What do you reckon?'

'I should think it bloody well is all in your mind!' Tiffany had shrieked, her raucous laughter telling Derek exactly what she thought. Cindy had wanted to laugh, too, but had refrained from joining in with her daughter's ridicule.

Cindy was struck now as she had been last night that this was a new and strange phenomenon – Tiffany and herself in agreement. For years it had been open warfare between the two and over the slightest of issues, mainly her daughter's appearance. But recently the friction had eased. It was as if all Tiffany's energy was being channelled into the superhuman feat of her becoming a woman, leaving her little or no strength to be so antagonistic – though there had been that recent incident with the cardboard box outside Ted Cooper's.

Earlier in the year, she and Derek had breathed a sigh of relief when

Tiffany had at last thrown away her wrung-out dishcloth look in favour of the more stylish and flattering clothes she spent her Saturday afternoons unearthing in the charity shops in Congleton. She still wore predominantly black but gone were the heavy eye make-up and dyed black hair: instead she'd let her own sandy colour grow through and had actually allowed her father to restyle it, asking him to cut ten inches off the length, keeping it bulky on the top but graduated into the nape of her neck. It made her look older but at the same time more vulnerable.

Tiffany's appearance might have softened over the last year but Cindy knew, better than anyone, that her tongue had not. That was still as sharp as ever, but instead of being directed at her, it was now aimed mostly at Derek.

Funny thing was, Derek seemed reluctant or perhaps unable to fight back with his daughter. Was this because he no longer saw Tiffany as a child, but more as a woman? Derek had never been able to resist the charm of any woman, no matter what kind of charm she exuded. In many ways Tiffany was just as much a challenge to win over as any of his past conquests. It was also true that since Barry had gone to university the atmosphere in the house had changed. Derek as the sole man was up against two women, who were showing all the signs of joining forces.

Cindy smiled to herself as she heard the sound of a radio playing loudly from somewhere in the salon. Bob Dylan was singing 'The Times They Are A-Changin''. And weren't they just?

She looked out of the large window on to the front garden and the parking area filled with builders' and decorators' vans. At the end of the drive two men were hard at work removing the old In the Pink sign and replacing it with a new one. She supposed that it was only a matter of time before the colour of the house was changed. Cindy had been well aware that when the first coat of pink paint had been brushed on to the walls there had been shock waves of disapproval in the village. She had asked Derek to show restraint but he had ignored her. 'Cindy,' he'd said, 'this is to be the pinnacle of our career in the health and beauty industry, we've got to go for it.'

So, Cindy thought wryly, as she watched the two men at the end of the drive, if the pinnacle of their career was in the process of being dismantled, what was next? Her life before had been predictably unsure, but she had successfully walked the tightrope of their precarious marriage in the knowledge that beneath her was the safety of the business. It had been the one certainty in her life and had provided the reassurance – the only tangible reassurance – upon which she had been able to rely. But what was she sure of now? What was her role to be at All in the Mind? Not so long ago, Tiffany, in one of her bitchier pre-menstrual moods, had described her as being good only for plucking and pruning. Had her daughter been right? After all, she was no counsellor, no mind-bender, as Tiffany described the people who were going to be taking the places of Tracy and Lorraine, along with all the other members of staff who had grumbled to hell and back at being made redundant. Their grievances had soon been mollified by the generous financial packages Cindy had offered.

Last night she had asked Derek what her role was to be. Plumping up the cushion in his armchair he had said, 'We'll all find our own niche, given time.'

'Niche?' she had repeated. 'I'm not sure I want a niche, Derek. I want something I know I can do. Something real.'

He'd smiled. 'Finding our own personal niche is the challenge we're all seeking in this life.'

She'd switched on the television at that point and settled down to watch a videoed episode of *Coronation Street* – something she could understand. Her husband was now communicating in a language she didn't recognise, but at least the goings-on of the Street were familiar territory.

'Cindy! There you are, I've been looking all over for you. I'd like you to meet Rosie Williams. She's to be our marriage guidance expert.'

A bit late for that, thought Cindy, as she turned round to face a statuesque young woman at Derek's side. She took in the soft brown eyes flecked with green, the smart suit and the long, long legs encased in the sheerest of tights. One hand held a briefcase and the other was extended towards her.

'Your husband has just confirmed my position.'

'Has he, indeed?' Cindy was nettled, not just by this woman with her smooth poise and well educated voice but by Derek. 'I had no idea he was interviewing this morning. I thought *we* were doing that *together*, this afternoon.'

Derek laughed awkwardly and Rosie raised a surprisingly large hand in the air. 'And there we have it,' she said, in a tone of voice that smacked of teacher-knows-best. 'Communication. That's the name of the game, isn't it? It's the basis of every sound, rock-solid marriage.' She put down her case and drew a square in the air with her two forefingers. 'See?' she said. 'The lines meet head on. There are no crossed wires.'

'That's the stuff,' Derek said enthusiastically.

God help us, thought Cindy.

'I'll see you to your car,' Derek said, filling in Cindy's obvious silence. He steered Rosie Williams towards the door. 'Mind how you go, don't want you breaking your neck on all this rubbish before you've even started work with us.' He picked his way over a large blue tool-box and a coil of electric cable with a drill attached at one end.

'Nothing is rubbish,' Rosie said meaningfully. 'Everything and everyone has a purpose. Thrilled to have met you, Cindy. Byee.'

'Goodbye, Miss Williams, or is it Mrs?' Cindy asked, her voice just as meaningful.

'Oh, definitely Miss.'

Perfectly qualified, then, to guide others through the misfortunes of marriage. Cindy watched their first recruit follow Derek out of the door and down the steps to the parking area. 'Late twenties perhaps, and about as many brain cells,' she muttered. She turned away and tried hard not to think of leopards and spots.

10

Thank God, Hilary thought from her front pew.

Thank God it wasn't her turn on the Sunday School rota. And thank God Malcolm Jackson was a devil for rambling sermons and she could sit here in peace for a whole hour and thirty minutes. No Becky – she was tormenting some other unfortunate volunteer. And no Philip either – he was playing in a school rugby match with David standing on the touchline . . . Please, God, let David freeze to death.

She could hardly believe it was a whole week since she'd discovered David's affair and it was a reflection on her own life that up until now she'd had no idea what despair and misery were really about. How glib adultery was made to look on television. How poignant it was in novels, and how glamorously sensational in the tabloids. Never was it portrayed as it was. It was terrifying. Terrifying and bewildering, so much so you could barely eat, sleep or even think properly.

Yesterday Charlotte had suggested she go to the doctor. 'You're obviously worn out, Hilary,' she'd said, when Iris Braithwaite had finally left them in the shop. 'Are you eating? And what about sleep?'

Sleeping and eating were the least of her concerns right now. Coping was uppermost in her mind and it seemed to her that that alone was taking up all her energy. David, blast him, had even had the nerve to say, 'What's wrong, Hilary? You don't look right.' She had nearly confronted him then, had so very nearly thrown the whole damn thing at him and shouted, 'Of course I'm not looking right, and is it any wonder knowing that your every spare moment is spent with that . . .?' But she hadn't. She had kept quiet and carried on ironing his shirt, banging the iron down on the cuff, wishing his arm was still in it.

And each day it took all her powers of self-restraint not to march straight into David's office in the village and have it out with that wretched Catherine. How could she do it? How could one woman treat another so badly? It was beyond her. A part of her didn't want to confront Catherine. It was almost as though her subconscious was saying, 'If you leave well alone, then it's more likely that none of this is really happening.'

Like Cindy, Charlotte had urged her not to have it out with Catherine. 'You're blameless in all of this, Hilary,' she had said. 'Keep it that way. If you see her you'll lose your temper. Just don't do anything you'll regret. Would you like Alex to talk to David?'

'No!'

'But he might be able to get David to see what he's doing, what he's risking.'

'I don't want David to find out that I know—'

'Why in heaven's name not?'

'Oh, Charlotte, you just don't understand. Just think yourself lucky that Peter died.'

Their conversation had ended at that point with a sudden rush of customers coming into the shop and Hilary and Becky setting off for home.

Now, in St John's, Hilary felt appalled at what she'd said to her sister . . . *think yourself lucky that Peter died.* What a dreadful thing to say. She tried to concentrate on the sound of Malcolm Jackson's voice telling her, along with all the other sinners assembled in St John's that morning, that she was saved, and wasn't that wonderful.

But all Hilary could think of was how wonderful it would be to be saved from having to go back to The Gables when this service came to an end, and how wonderful it would be to be saved from pretending that everything was fine. Everything was not fine. Far from it. David, her husband, a man whom she had trusted with her life all their marriage, had betrayed her in the worst possible way, and what, she demanded, looking up at the stained-glass window above the altar, was God doing about it? Never mind all this stuff about saving sinners. How about some old-fashioned retribution? In her opinion a dose of Old Testament wrath was called for. A thunderbolt or two wouldn't go amiss, especially in the direction of the trollop who had thrown herself at David.

Aware that all behind her were now on their feet, hymn books open, Hilary stood up. Still thinking of this other woman in David's life she clenched her hymn book as though she were grasping Catherine bloody Renshaw around the neck while she sang with the rest of the congregation, ' "Your hands swift to welcome, your arms to embrace." '

As usual coffee was being served at the back of the church by Iris Braithwaite along with Mrs Bradley and Mrs Haslip. Alex nudged Charlotte. 'There go the Golden Girls,' he whispered.

'Why don't you make Mrs Bradley's day by chatting her up over the coffee urn?' Charlotte replied. 'You love it when she goes all breathless over you.'

'I'd rather you were breathless—'

'That's as may be but I need a word with Hilary.'

Charlotte found Hilary at the foot of the altar, not deep in supplication, as her position suggested, but fiddling with the large arrangement of autumn flowers. Since yesterday morning Charlotte hadn't had an opportunity to talk to Hilary about what she'd told her in the shop – after all, she could hardly have gone over to The Gables with David there. She still couldn't come to terms with what her brother-in-law was up to. She bent down and touched her sister lightly on the shoulder. Hilary almost leapt in response, pushing Charlotte up against the altar and sending the eucharistic tackle crashing.

'Charlotte! I'm so sorry, I had no idea you were there.' Hilary was flustered.

Charlotte tidied up the mess and led her sister to a pew.

'Please don't be nice to me,' Hilary suddenly said. 'I . . . I really couldn't bear that.'

'Okay,' Charlotte agreed, remembering how difficult she had found coping with sympathy offered to her after Peter's death. 'I'll do my normal horrid-sister routine, shall I?' She was conscious that, whether Hilary liked it or not, she was going to have to let her, Charlotte, be the older sister for once.

Hilary sniffed. 'All right,' she said, staring straight ahead of her, her hands twisting the stalk of a dying chrysanthemum she had just pulled out of the altar flowers. She suddenly faced Charlotte. 'You haven't told anyone, have you?'

Charlotte shook her head. 'Nobody.'

'What about Alex?'

'Hilary, you made me promise not to tell anyone. Now stop worrying about that and tell me when you found out about David.'

'On Monday.'

All that time ago and her sister hadn't come to her. 'How? How did you find out?'

Hilary told her.

'But are you sure? I mean—'

'Good God, Charlotte, of course I'm sure. You always did treat me like a fool. I never could—'

'Shut up, Hilary,' Charlotte said sternly. 'This is no time for one of our squabbles.'

'I wasn't squabbling, I was merely—'

'Never mind that. What are you going to do?'

'Cindy says I should pretend it isn't happening and Georgia D'Arcy says I should confront David.'

'Who else knows about this?' Charlotte asked, surprised at how hurt she felt that Hilary hadn't come to her for help. But then she herself, when her own marriage had been falling apart, hadn't turned to her sister or any member of her family for advice and support. Even now Hilary had no idea that she had asked Peter for a divorce the morning he had died.

'Nobody else,' Hilary replied, 'just Cindy and Georgia.'

'So you've told me what they think you should do, but not what you want to do.'

'It's obvious, isn't it? I've got to try and ignore what's happening.'

After a moment's quiet Charlotte said, 'If it's worth anything I agree with Georgia. Until you and David talk this through you're not going to be able to—'

'But don't you see? I could risk losing him if I do that.'

'You risk losing him anyway,' Charlotte said softly.

Hilary swallowed. 'There's less danger this way.'

'But, Hilary, you never could keep a secret, or lie convincingly. You've got to say something to David, or you'll end up making yourself ill.'

'I've got Philip and Becky to think of, they need their father. I'll do it for them.'

'And you truly believe staying silent will—'

'It's worked for Cindy. Why not for me?'

Charlotte covered her sister's hands. Poor Hilary. Poor Hilary trying to be so brave. 'Because you're not Cindy and you're not used to living with all this bloody chaos.'

'Auntie Charlotte, that's not nice,' Becky said, squeezing into the pew. 'Jesus won't have you in heaven if you go round saying bloody all the time. Ooh!' she squeaked, and quickly slapped a hand over her mouth. 'Now Jesus won't want me to sit by his throne either.' Her eyes swivelled in their sockets as though expecting to see the Messiah himself lurking behind one of the pillars.

Charlotte watched Hilary hug her daughter to her. What a mess indeed, she thought, raising her eyes to the vaulted ceiling above. Sorry, Jesus, but throne or no throne, it's a bloody fine old mess down here.

11

Monday morning, the first day of half-term. David had already left for work, the children were downstairs, plugged into the cartoons so thoughtfully programmed for the school holidays, and Hilary was in the shower. She was crying and washing away David's semen. How could he have made love to her? How could she have let him?

The questions had ricocheted around inside her head all night. She had no answer for why David should want to have sex with her, when he was obviously satisfying himself elsewhere, but she knew well enough why she had offered herself to him. It was all part of the charade: letting him, encouraging him even to make love with her might make everything all right. Allowing him to join their bodies as one would perhaps magically hold their marriage together – might even make him give Catherine up. In the moment he had reached out to Hilary in bed last night she had known that her decision to follow Cindy's example was the right one. She would do exactly as Cindy had done all these years. It was a small sacrifice to ensure their family stayed together.

She turned off the shower and reached for a towel. She wrapped it round her and walked over to the basin. Wiping the steam away from the mirror she looked at her wet face. Tears or shower water? Who would know? Who would even care? She felt herself succumbing to that one single emotion she despised in others – self-pity. She had never once pitied herself and something deep within her was telling her to pull herself together. 'Right,' she said aloud, 'you may cry in the shower, but nowhere else. You are going to be strong. You are going to smarten yourself up and show David you're worth a hundred Catherines – bet she can't make flapjacks like you!' She gave a brave little laugh, but immediately felt the onset of tears again. She quickly leapt back into the shower so as not to break her first resolve of the day.

At half past ten Hilary left Philip in charge of Becky while they watched a video and she went across the road to see Cindy. Cindy, Hilary had decided, was going to be instrumental in her plan to win back her husband.

She stood for a moment at the end of the drive of In the Pink, except it wasn't any more. Gone was the puce board and in its place was a discreet dark blue sign with stylish Gothic letters in gold: All in the Mind, it read. How long had that been there? Was she in such a state that she'd lost touch

with what was going on around her? She walked past the caravan of builders'
and decorators' vehicles and found the front door wide open. Loud music,
accompanied by the sound of an electric drill, blasted out at her, along with
the smell of paint. A man in overalls with a woolly hat pulled down over his
head was kneeling on the floor painting a skirting board.

'They're busy,' he shouted at her, pausing briefly with his paintbrush,
'interviewing.'

'Oh,' Hilary said, her disappointment obvious.

''Bout another ten minutes, I should think. They said they'd be free at
quarter to.'

'I'll wait, then,' she said, knowing that if she went back to The Gables now,
she might never pluck up the courage to come back to see Cindy.

'Suit yourself. There's a chair in one of them back rooms.'

She picked her way carefully over the dust sheets, minding the haphazardly
placed tools and off-cuts of wood. The hair salon had undergone a dramatic
change. The back washes and mirrors had all gone, so had the chairs and
shiny floor. Now all there was was a large empty room with an oatmeal-
coloured carpet, the smell of which testified to it being new and only recently
laid. Behind the door was a small stool and on this was a stack of glossy
pamphlets. Hilary helped herself to one. On the front cover was a picture of
Derek and Cindy with the words All in the Mind emblazoned above them.
She turned the first page and started to read about Derek and Cindy's new
venture:

> Join us at our sanctuary of inner spiritual exploration and hope. Come on
> a voyage of discovery to experience your hidden depths. Let us help you to
> find the real you so that you can reach your full potential. Marital
> problems a speciality at All in the Mind.

In the background all went quiet as the sound of the drill stopped. 'Brew up,'
shouted a man's voice. Then Hilary heard Derek. She replaced the pamphlet
on top of the pile and went out to the reception area.

'Hello, Hilary,' said Derek, 'you anxious to get your name down for one of
our classes? Positive thinking, assertiveness or how to pep up your marriage?
Take your pick.'

'Goodness. What would I want with all that?' Hilary said, her cheeks
reddening. 'I've only come over to see Cindy.'

'She'll be out in a moment. She's just showing one of our new members of
staff round the place.' He looked about him. 'What do you reckon, then? Bit
of a change, isn't it? Might even put sleepy old Hulme Welford on the map.'

'Lovely,' she responded, trying her best to sound enthusiastic.

'Marriage will be the thing, mark my words,' Derek continued, rubbing his
hands together. 'Always marital problems going on, especially in a place like
this.'

'Really,' Hilary said quietly. 'What makes you think that?'

He grinned and slipped his arm round Hilary's waist. 'Now I know what you're thinking. That's rich coming from old Derek, but believe me, I'm a reformed character. I—'

'And what could that possibly mean, I wonder?'

'Ah, Cindy my pet,' Derek said, swinging round to face his wife.

Hilary tried to manoeuvre herself away from Derek's arm, but he didn't seem at all inclined to let her go. At Cindy's side stood someone she recognised only too well. Nick Bradshaw. He smiled at her and she wished even more that Derek would remove his arm.

'What do you make of the set-up, Nick?' asked Derek. 'Glad to be in on the ground floor, I should think.'

'I'm impressed. You've thought it all out very well.' His words were aimed at Derek but his eyes were on Hilary. She felt uncomfortable beneath his now familiar gaze and wanted very much to wriggle out of Derek's grasp and away from this man's direct way of looking at her.

'Sorry,' Derek said suddenly. 'Forgetting my manners. Let me introduce Hilary Parker, she lives over the road and is one of our most industrious neighbours, organises us all like you'd never believe.'

'We've met already . . .'

Oh, please don't mention the tip, thought Hilary, not that.

'. . . at, of all places, the local tip,' Nick said, with a light, easy laugh.

Derek gave Hilary a squeeze with his arm. 'Well, you are a dark horse, Hilary,' he said, 'but I can think of more salubrious venues for a secret assignation.'

'Don't judge everyone by your own standards, Derek,' Cindy said coolly.

'I was only throwing away some rubbish, that was all,' Hilary said, flustered.

'Aha,' Derek said, remembering Rosie's words of a few days ago. 'There's no such thing as rubbish. Everything and everyone has a purpose.'

Cindy shook her head and Nick Bradshaw gave his new employer a polite smile.

'Nick's going to be head of stress and positive thinking here at All in the Mind,' Derek went on. 'Perhaps you should book your David in for a course. He's looking a bit frazzled these days. Been burning the candle at both ends, has he?'

'Derek!' snapped Cindy. 'I'm sure that what David is or is not doing is none of our concern. Mr Bradshaw, I'll show you out. Hilary, I presume it was me you wanted to see. I'll be back in a few minutes. Derek, go and put the kettle on.'

'*Ja, mein Kapitän!*' Derek said, letting go of Hilary and clicking his heels together.

12

It was nearly half past three when Neville Archer remembered he hadn't been out to the shops. He threw a last handful of leaves on to the bonfire, picked up his rake and lumbered up the path to the back porch of the black and white timbered cottage.

He slipped off his gardening boots and padded through to the kitchen where he'd left his shoes over an hour ago. From the window he could see a thin trail of smoke threading its way upwards in the still, damp afternoon air. He knew he shouldn't leave the bonfire unattended but Louise would play up worse than a child if she came back from the shop and found no supper to eat, which right now far outweighed the potential risk of their thatch catching fire. But gradually the thought of explaining the remains of their burnt-out cottage to Louise took root in his mind and had him reaching under the sink for a plastic bucket. He carried it, slopping, down the garden path and doused the fire.

Back inside he grabbed his keys from the hook above the boiler, put on his overcoat and banged the front door shut after him. He left his Volvo in the car park behind the doctors' surgery, where he hoped that neither his wife nor Hilary would catch sight of it. 'Not too old to learn to ride a bike,' Louise would, no doubt, jibe at him for his laziness. He crossed the road and delved in his coat pocket for his shopping list. He tutted. He'd left it behind on the kitchen table. With a surge of regret he remembered how easy and straightforward his days as a GP had been – diagnosing and prescribing had been simplicity itself compared to the haphazard way he led his life now.

Now that he had been retired for some time the tasks of cooking and shopping had fallen into his lap. Not that he minded. But Louise seemed to take great delight in making things more complicated than they needed to be. Instead of writing a clear and easy-to-read message on the wipe-board on the kitchen wall as a reminder of something they had run out of, she would leave him cryptic notes lying about the house, yellow rectangles of paper with messages such as, 'We need some cuts grease to the squeak' – that was washing-up liquid – and 'some squeezably soft', toilet paper.

She was going through a phase of avid television viewing and she plundered the adverts each evening not only for new slogans to add to her collection of obscure names for household products, but for new and faster ways of eating. No longer was she obsessed with trimming him down to what she felt was a better weight. Now she had a thing about convenience foods. 'That looks easy enough,' she'd say, in response to a parsley-garnished meal-for-two emerging from a gleaming microwave. 'Even you could manage that, Neville.'

In defiance he'd taken to watching a cookery programme just before the lunchtime news. Last week he'd jotted down the recipe and served up beef and orange stir-fry for supper the following evening. He had thought it a culinary triumph and later that night had caught Louise hunting in the kitchen bin for the packaging.

Today on the television that nice blonde girl with the lisp had been making carrot soup. It had looked easy enough to him, just a matter of putting all the ingredients into a blender and Bob's your uncle – if only he could remember all the ingredients.

There was nobody in the grocer's when he pushed open the door. Joan Carter, whom he'd diagnosed three years ago as having angina, served him.

'Carrot soup? Well, you'll be wanting some carrots, then, won't you?' she said, putting some muddy ones on to the scales. 'A couple of pounds should do it.'

'I need an onion as well.'

'Spanish or home-grown?'

'You've got me there,' Neville said, trying to remember what the girl with the lisp had said above the noise of the blender.

'I've no truck with all this Euro nonsense,' Joan said. 'Have home-grown. How about some coriander?'

'Curry what?'

'Coriander. It's a herb. Here.' She handed him a bunch. 'You chop it up and sprinkle it over the food. It's all the rage, but give it a while and we'll soon be back to parsley. Probably them that knows best will find coriander's bad for you and say it's poisonous.'

Neville thought of Louise and nearly asked for two bunches.

Outside on the street again, he walked along the row of shops until he came to Charlotte's. She was busy stacking a set of shelves with Christmas ornaments. It didn't feel two minutes since Charlotte had stood on a chair helping him to decorate the Christmas tree each year; he passing the glass ornaments up to her while she, with infinite care, placed things in order of colour and size. 'No, not there,' she would say to herself, 'that bauble needs more space.'

'Hello, Dad,' she said, turning round to face him, 'and, yes, before you say anything I know I'm early with the decorations, but what the heck? Can you pass me that box from the counter?'

He handed it to her. 'I can't stop for long. I just thought I'd call in to see how you are.'

'I'm fine.'

'And Alex?'

Charlotte smiled. 'He's fine as well. How about you?'

'Fine.'

'Good,' Charlotte said mischievously, 'it's good that we're all fine.'

Neville picked up one of the large glass ornaments and turned it round in his hand. He could see his face looking back at him, all bulging eyes and bulbous nose. 'Any sign of . . . well, you know?'

'Oh, Dad. Stop beating about the bush. Come right out and ask me.'

'Ask you what?' Neville said, putting the ornament back on the shelf.

'When Alex and I are getting married.'

Neville looked away, embarrassed. 'I'm not being nosy, Charlotte.'

She gave him a hug and breathed in the smoky smell of burning leaves from his clothes. 'I know you're not and as a matter of fact I'd like you to do something for me. Are you free on Christmas Eve?'

'I should think so. You know me, more time on my hands than I know what to do with.'

'Well, put it in your diary. You're coming on a walk with me.'

'I am? Not some ghastly rambling event, is it? That's more your mother's line of country.'

'Up the aisle of St John's. Let's see if we can get it right this time, shall we?'

Neville looked affectionately at his favourite daughter. Last year Charlotte had told him the truth about her marriage to Peter. At first he had been shocked, not so much because Charlotte's life with Peter had worked out the way it had but for the pain she had gone through alone after Peter's death – until, that was, Alex had come on the scene.

'I've a feeling Alex will make you a good husband,' he said simply. 'Peter was all right, but he wasn't really . . .'

'He just wasn't the right man for me, Dad.'

'And you're absolutely sure Alex is?'

'I'm as sure as I can be.'

'Shall I tell your mother you've set a date?'

'Why not? She'll have to be told sooner or later.'

'You'll be making Hilary's day. She's convinced it's down to her that the two of you got together. Flushed with this victory under her belt, who knows who else will come in for her Cupid's arrow?'

Poor Hilary, thought Charlotte. The last thing she needed to think about at the moment was a wedding, never mind Cupid's arrow. She was wondering whether she ought to say anything to her father when the door opened and in walked David's secretary, Catherine Renshaw.

Too thin, was the first thought that came into Charlotte's head. Too thin, with much too much of the little-girl-lost look about her.

David's previous secretary had left to have a baby last year and Catherine had been the replacement. Then, a little over five months ago, David had reported to them all one night over dinner at The Gables that Catherine had been in tears in the office that day. 'That wretch of a husband has simply upped sticks and walked out. What kind of a man does that? Of course I've said I'll help all I can. Probably a pay rise would be a good idea.'

A pity David couldn't have stuck with just adding a few extra pounds to his secretary's salary, Charlotte thought angrily, watching Catherine in her smart woollen jacket move about the shop. She came to a stop at the shelf of silver frames and took off her leather gloves. Must have been a damn good pay rise, Charlotte thought bitterly, thinking how simple it was for a man like David to fall so helplessly for the oldest trick in the book, that of providing his strong manly shoulder to the tearful woman who seemingly has no one else to turn to.

'I'd better be off,' Neville said. 'I'm making carrot soup for your mother's tea.'

'Lucky old Mum,' Charlotte said, opening the door for her father.

She returned to displaying and pricing yet more Christmas decorations, while all the time keeping a watchful eye on her only customer. She felt fiercely protective towards her sister and wanted very much to lay into this smart piece of work who was doing her best to destroy another person's life.

'Do you have this in a smaller size?'

What, to match your brain? 'No, that's the smallest I have.' Charlotte kept her eyes on the frame in Catherine Renshaw's hands, not trusting herself to look her in the eye without revealing her anger. She was only too thankful that although this woman worked for her brother-in-law, there had been no previous social contact between them in the village, so no bright chit-chat was expected of her. She could remain aloof and sacrifice a sale if need be.

'Oh, that's a real shame. I suppose I could always have this one and put a mount in.'

'You could,' Charlotte replied airily.

'Except I don't really like mounted photographs.'

And I don't like you, so why don't you push off and leave my brother-in-law alone? 'Not working today?'

'Yes, but I've just slipped out. It's so quiet at the moment. No one likes to put their house on the market at this time of the year.'

'That's funny. David seems to have been pretty busy just recently. Hilary was only telling me the other day how he's always so late coming home these days.' She gave Catherine a long, hard stare, deciding to make her understand that nobody messed with the Archer sisters.

'I don't think I'll bother today.'

'Bother?'

'With the frame. I think I'll sleep on it.'

'Okay.' And make sure it's alone!

13

'What do you think?'

Cindy didn't answer. All her working life she'd been asked to transform women into something they weren't meant to be. She had lost count of how many women had asked her to turn them into the Princess of Wales – with or without the marriage problems. Years ago, of course, there had been a run on young girls wanting the Kylie Minogue or Madonna look, but the older women usually went for television presenters. Jill Dando was popular at the moment with the every-hair-in-place look, along with that wine expert now turned antiques buff. Judy Finnigan and Anne Diamond continued to have a steady following for the stay-at-home-mum look, but Gaby Roslin and Anthea Turner, with the more tousled appearance, were definitely number one for the wannabes.

'Well?'

'Hilary, are you sure this is a good idea?'

'I wouldn't be here if I didn't think it was,' Hilary answered with more assurance than she felt. She'd have preferred to be at home in the kitchen baking parkin and wrapping potatoes in foil ready for tonight's PTA bonfire party as in previous years, not sitting here in Cindy's pristine bathroom. It had seemed such a good idea on Monday when she'd called in and asked Cindy to do her hair later in the week for her – but, then, she hadn't let on to what she had in mind.

Cindy looked again at the picture Hilary had given her. It was a cutting from the *Radio Times* and Anthea Turner stared back, eyes twinkling, mouth grinning, skin perfection itself. Cindy gave Hilary's face in the mirror a professional appraisal: eyes red, mouth sloping, complexion mottled. She would have to lie, she decided, like she had to all those other women. So why, then, was she hesitating? Because . . . because Hilary was depending on her. Poor Hilary was hoping that this was all it would take to save her marriage. And it wasn't the first time she'd been asked to perform this miracle.

'Wouldn't you rather stick to your own hair colour?' Cindy suggested. 'This will be such a dramatic change.'

'I want it just like that,' Hilary replied, pointing at the picture in Cindy's hand. Her voice was raised and bordering on the petulant. 'I want my hair and make-up exactly like that. David likes Anthea Turner. He never used to miss her on a Saturday night. He once said he'd rather win a night out with Anthea than the lottery.' Hilary almost snatched the piece of paper out of Cindy's hands. She looked at it closely. When she'd been younger she'd always had her hair lightened, but since she'd had the children she hadn't bothered. At odd times over the years David had hinted at her having her hair like she'd worn it when they'd first met. 'Why?' she'd once asked him. 'Don't you like me as I am now?'

'Please, Cindy,' she said, 'can't we try it? What have I got to lose? It shouldn't be that difficult. After all, she's about my age, isn't she?'

True, thought Cindy, but sadly that's the only similarity. 'I'm sorry, Hilary, but I'm not a miracle worker.'

'Then I'm sorry to have taken up so much of your time,' Hilary said, getting up from the chair and mustering what little dignity she had left.

Years of professionalism hit Cindy smack in the face – she'd never yet lost a customer. 'I'm sorry, Hilary. I didn't mean that the way it sounded. Sit down and I'll explain.'

Under the slight persuasive pressure of Cindy's hands on her shoulders, Hilary sat down.

'I was going to say that I'm not a miracle worker in as much as I can't turn you into a replica of Anthea Turner. Your bone structure's completely different for a start and your hair—'

'How about as near as you can?'

Cindy smiled. 'So long as you accept the limitations I'm working with.'

Hilary nodded.

'Okay. Let's get started. It's going to take a few hours. I'll do the cut first, then put the highlights through and after I've blow-dried your hair and done your make-up we're going into Manchester.'

'Manchester?'

'Clothes, Hilary. We're going shopping.'

'But I can't, the children—'

'Tiffany won't mind babysitting for a few more hours. She needs the money.'

Manchester was busier than they had expected and when they had managed to find a space on the third level of the multi-storey car park Hilary and Cindy joined the warm buzz of shoppers inside Kendal's.

'These are much too expensive,' Hilary protested, after Cindy had guided her towards an area of spaciously displayed suits and separates. 'I can't possibly afford these prices.'

'It's your marriage we're trying to save, not your money,' Cindy said impatiently.

'But you know how stingy David is. He's only one step away from recycling the toilet paper. It won't just be my marriage I'm trying to save when he sees the bank statement, it'll be my neck. Can't we go downstairs? The clothes are cheaper – I mean, more reasonable – there.'

Resigned, Cindy headed towards the escalator. Hilary followed quickly behind and they climbed aboard. Half-way down Hilary caught sight of herself in the mirror that lined the wall to her right. She felt a slight quickening in her stomach at the thought of surprising David when he came home from work that night. She felt so sure that her new hairstyle and make-over would bring him to his senses, would make him appreciate what he already had.

When Cindy had turned the chair round and Hilary had seen her hair for the first time, several shades lighter than her own natural mouse, it had been a shock. It certainly was a startling transformation, that and the effect of Cindy's cleverly applied make-up techniques. The initial shock now dealt with, Hilary was delighted with her new look and she smiled back at her reflection, confident that she had found the answer. *She would have her man.*

They stepped off the escalator and made for the racks of colour co-ordinated clothes. Hilary's eyes lit up at the sight of a display of red polo-neck sweaters. On the front of each jumper was a Scottie dog wearing a large tartan bow.

'No!' Cindy said adamantly.

'What do you mean?' Hilary said, already searching the rail for a size twelve.

'Tat!'

Hilary looked hurt. 'But they're so cute.'

'Look, Hilary. Cute is not going to woo David away from what's keeping him late at the office.'

'But I've always worn—'

'They're awful and I'm not letting you buy one. Not after all the trouble I've gone to. Believe me, Anthea wouldn't be seen dead in one. Now come on.'

Hilary raised her eyebrows. She'd had no idea Cindy could be like this – and Charlotte thought *she* was bossy!

An hour and a half later Cindy sank gratefully into a chair in the Venetian Restaurant on the fourth floor of the department store. She slipped her heels out of her shoes and moved her feet around, easing away the strain of supervising Hilary's new wardrobe. She poured out two cups of tea from the china pot and saw Hilary coming towards her, squeezing her way through the crowded restaurant. She looked hot and flustered, her hair showing signs of beginning to flop. More mousse needed, Cindy told herself. She would have to tell Hilary.

'Sorry I've been so long. The queue for the loo was horrendous. I thought I'd never get in.' She plonked herself down and stowed all her carrier bags on a ledge behind her. 'Oh, lovely, a cup of tea.'

'I got you a cake as well.' Cindy pushed the plate towards Hilary.

Hilary was touched. 'Thank you,' she said. 'And thanks also for, well, you know . . . I'm sure it's going to work.' She looked at Cindy expectantly, hoping for her agreement.

Cindy didn't say anything. She opened her napkin and placed it on her lap. She knew the words Hilary wanted to hear – *Don't worry, this will put an end to David's adultery* – but she couldn't say them. She sipped her tea, feeling surprisingly sorry for Hilary and remembering how years ago when she had stumbled on Derek's second affair she had confided in Angela, her closest friend. Angela had been so helpful, had let Cindy cry on her shoulder and had even said all the right things, that everything would be all right. A week later she had discovered that it was Angela with whom Derek was sleeping. She had never trusted another woman since, which was, perhaps, why she had relied so heavily on the potential Tiffany had offered. She had hoped that Tiffany would become the close female confidante that she had so badly needed, someone who would never betray her. Poor Tiffany, Cindy thought, no wonder she had bucked from such an early age at her attempts to make her an ally. She had probably felt used and put upon.

But, now, here she was, helping another woman to cope with her husband's adultery. Why? What did she feel towards Hilary, with whom she had nothing in common, other than their unfaithful husbands?

Cindy's silence was making Hilary feel uncomfortable. She could sense some of her new-found hope slipping away from her. 'Cindy, you don't think I look like mutton dressed . . .?'

Cindy placed her cup on the saucer and, meeting Hilary's anxious eyes, it came to her that it wasn't just pity she felt towards Hilary, she actually quite liked her. Since living in Hulme Welford she had viewed Hilary as nothing more than a neighbour – a rather interfering neighbour at times – but more importantly she had seen her as safe, someone who wouldn't interest Derek and pose a threat. Now she saw her not only as neutral territory but as someone she could trust. Suddenly she wanted Hilary to be able to trust her.

'I'm not going to lie to you,' Cindy said, 'but I really do believe that what you've done today will make you feel better about yourself. It'll give you more confidence, which in my opinion is the most important aspect of trying out a new image.'

'You're right,' Hilary said, stirring her tea thoughtfully. 'You're absolutely right. And I'm going to go home and show David that I'm the best thing since sliced bread.' She took a long sip of her tea, then said, 'Cindy, can I say something?'

'Go on,' Cindy said warily.

'Since you've lived in the village you've always kept yourself to yourself and I think that's a waste, because until today I hadn't appreciated what a strong and considerate person you are. You don't mind me saying that, do you?'

Cindy slipped her shoes back on to her feet. For the first time since Angela's betrayal, she had allowed herself to make a friend. 'No,' she said quietly, 'I don't mind at all.'

Hilary sensed Cindy wasn't going to say any more on the subject and because she never felt comfortable with pregnant pauses in conversations she said the first thing that came into her head. 'That Nick Bradshaw character you've just taken on, what's he like?'

'That remains to be seen,' Cindy answered, forever cautious. 'He's certainly got all the right credentials and at least he . . .' Her voice trailed away.

'At least he's what?' Hilary asked, curious.

'I was going to say at least he's a man and not another woman roaming around the place.'

'Oh,' Hilary said, disappointed. For some reason she had hoped Cindy was going to embark on some long, elaborate story about this man, who from nowhere had suddenly appeared in Hulme Welford. 'Is he married?' she found herself asking.

'Has been, I think.'

Come on, Hilary thought, what kind of an interview session was it? 'How old is he and where does he live, in Hulme Welford?'

'Forty-four, I think, and not in the village, though off-hand I can't remember exactly where. Why all the questions?'

'No reason,' Hilary answered, annoyed with herself for having even thought of the wretched man. But then he had, in fact, provided her with a few short moments during which she had thought of something other than the pain David was inflicting on her. Maybe he wasn't all bad.

14

'Bloody hell!' David stood in the kitchen doorway, his briefcase in one hand, the evening paper in the other, his mouth wide open. 'What have you done?'

'Don't you like it?' Hilary asked, as she passed him a glass of whisky and offered him a smile, both of which she'd prepared in advance.

'It's . . . so different.' He took a gulp of whisky and continued to stare.

'Cindy did it for me. I fancied a change,' Hilary said, as casually as she could manage. Earlier, in the bedroom, she had stood in front of the mirror and practised what she was going to say to David. *I fancied a change* was supposed to have been accompanied by a sultry stare and a nonchalant flick of her hair while leaning back against the worktop, a vision of sexual enticement. But, from the way David was staring at her, she had the feeling that she looked about as alluring as one of those models from a fifties knitting pattern.

'You remind me of someone,' David said, putting down his briefcase and loosening his tie.

Self-conscious, Hilary turned her back on him and straightened the tea towel on the Aga rail.

'Damned if I can think who.'

'But you like it, don't you?' Oh, God, she was almost pleading with him. It wasn't supposed to have been like this at all. Why couldn't she be more confident?

'Hope Cindy gave you a bargain rate.'

Hilary whipped the towel off the rail and twisted it in her hands. 'No, she didn't,' she almost shouted, turning round and facing him. 'Cindy did it for free, if you must know, as a friend.'

David smiled. 'Clever old you. What do the children think?'

Bugger the children! Hilary wanted to scream, I haven't gone to all this trouble to please Philip and Becky. When she'd arrived home from Manchester their reaction had been predictably derisive, with Becky shouting out the most painful comments. 'Mum looks like that woman on the telly.'

'Which one?' Hilary had asked hopefully.

'That one in the film we saw. Mrs Doubtfire!' She had then collapsed in exaggerated laughter on the floor in Philip's bedroom.

Philip had been comparatively less hurtful in his condemnation. 'It makes you look ... well ... kind of too young.'

'Too young?' she had repeated. 'What's wrong with that?'

Barely taking his eyes off the computer screen, he had gone on to say, 'Well, you're old, Mum, aren't you? And now you don't look right. You look wrong. I can't explain it any better.'

Tiffany had been sweet, though, but then Hilary had just been handing over her babysitting money. 'You look great,' she had said, eyeing Hilary up and down, taking in the new clothes Cindy had insisted she change into before dropping her off at The Gables. 'You've got less of the Marks and Spencer about you now.'

Under David's critical eye Hilary could feel her cheeks reddening despite the foundation and blusher Cindy had applied. 'Becky laughed, if you must know,' she said.

David gave a loud snort of appreciative laughter.

Hilary glared at him, knowing that all the anger she had been working so hard to keep in check since she had discovered David's unfaithfulness was no longer in check. She took the glass from David's hand and tipped the last quarter of an inch of whisky over his head, then calmly handed it back to him.

'What the hell—?'

'Yes, David,' she said, over her shoulder, as she walked away from him. 'What the hell indeed?'

'The flames of hell will be hotter still for some of those in this village,' declared Iris Braithwaite, as she and Charlotte backed away from the twenty-foot-high bonfire – all that was left of poor old Guy Fawkes was a pair of charred safety shoes, which were more than living up to the manufacturer's claims.

In the darkness and flickering orange light Iris's face had taken on the guise of a luminous Hallowe'en pumpkin. She looked dangerously menacing and, assuming that the older woman was referring to Charlotte and Alex's impure state, Charlotte prepared herself for the onslaught of a homily on the avoidance of sin. Instead, and above the crackle of burning garden refuse and wooden pallets, Iris hissed just two words, 'Ted Cooper.'

Charlotte relaxed and unclenched her gloved hands. At least she was off the hook. 'Ted Cooper?' she asked innocently. 'What's he been up to?'

'Been up to?' repeated Iris. 'Been up to, Mrs Lawrence? The man's a monster. A sexual fiend, peddling ...' She paused for breath.

'Peddling what, Mrs Braithwaite?' Charlotte said, hoping the laughter rising within her could be staved off just a few minutes longer.

Iris fixed her with a long, hard stare. 'I notice you did not put my poster in your window as I asked.'

Charlotte stamped her feet on the iron hard ground; her face was hot and flushed from the heat of the bonfire, but her feet were frozen. 'I can't see what Ted's done wrong,' she said. 'You can buy those sorts of tights in most department stores. They're quite respectable, in fact women who suffer from thrush wear—'

'I'll thank you not to go into details, Mrs Lawrence. But I take it, then, that you have not been in for a newspaper today?'

'No. No, I haven't.'

'I suggest you get down from your high and mighty position on the fence, Mrs Lawrence, and see for yourself what's going on here in Hulme Welford. It's quite apparent that Ted Cooper is not going to stop at the one lewd item of merchandise in his shop. He's added to his stock and it's the fault of people like you who don't care a fig. I hope your conscience allows you to enjoy yourself here tonight. Goodnight.'

Charlotte watched Iris Braithwaite disappear into the crowd. Added to his stock, she reflected. What on earth had Ted the Toup placed on his shelves that was giving Iris such apoplexy?

From the other side of the bonfire she saw Derek Rogers in a smart blue and cream skiing jacket and matching band round his head. He was waving to her through the smoke and flames. She waved back and he started making his way through the throng of over-excited children waving sparklers in the air and overwrought parents trying to prevent a replay of last night's television programme, 999.

Derek would be bound to know of any dodgy goings-on in the village, Charlotte decided. After all, he had been the main perpetrator of most things newsworthy since his arrival in Acacia Lane.

'Charlotte, where's that man of yours?' Derek greeted her, kissing her on the cheek. 'Abandoned you already, has he?'

'He's gone for some mulled wine.'

'Now, what's this I hear about you finally succumbing to his charms? I hope I'm invited. I'd love to be the one at the back of St John's with a just cause or impediment.'

'Well, you've certainly got an impediment,' Charlotte said, with a laugh.

'Oh, Charlotte, how did I ever let you slip through my fingers?'

'Derek,' Charlotte said firmly, 'I was never even there in your hands.'

He grinned. 'I distinctly recall a moment when I had you up against the kitchen sink in what the romantic novelist would describe as a passionate embrace.'

'Rubbish. You kissed me and tried to stick your hand down my blouse, in what a pubescent *Just Seventeen* reader would describe as a grope.'

'Yeah, well, call it what you want, but the old Derek Rogers School of Charm never fails. I still got you to kiss me.' And, as though to prove his point, he leaned into her and kissed her on the lips.

'Having trouble with your balance?' asked Alex, coming up behind Derek. 'Or are you still testing the water?' He handed Charlotte a polystyrene cup of mulled wine and placed a proprietorial arm around her shoulder. 'Oh and,

Derek, if you're going to make a habit of kissing Charlotte, perhaps you could go easy on the aftershave. Less obvious that way.'

'Hey, you've got me all wrong,' Derek said, putting up his hands in a gesture of innocence. 'I was merely congratulating Charlotte on her good fortune. The best man obviously won.'

'Oh, shut up, Derek,' Charlotte laughed, 'and tell us how All in the Mind is shaping up.'

For a few minutes Derek had wandered back into the territory of his old self. He hastily switched to the new-style Derek – this New Man thing was going to be harder work than he'd supposed. 'We open next week,' he said, adopting what was fast becoming his welcome-to-the-fold voice. ' "Spiritual Journey" is fully booked. So is "Reaching Your Full Potential".'

'How about the marriage seminars you were advertising in the *Chronicle* this week?' asked Alex. 'Many takers?'

'Little disappointing there. I feel people are reluctant to step forward to the altar on that particular subject. They're frightened to admit to problems going on in the jolly-rogering department. So often marital problems are caused by sexual inadequacy and people just don't want to admit to it. But you, Alex, you wouldn't have any qualms about coming to our "Screw Your Inhibitions to the Bedpost" seminars if you weren't all that our lovely Charlotte was in need of, would you now?'

Alex smiled. 'Maybe people just can't equate All in the Mind with the man who probably thinks *The Man Who Mistook His Wife For a Hat* is a Les Dawson joke book.'

Charlotte gave Alex a dig in the ribs, but Derek looked at him as if he'd just flown in from Mars.

'Ever thought of some kind of therapy, Alex? Perhaps you should book in to see our Nick Bradshaw. He's head of stress and would be great at getting to the bottom of all your funny little quirks. He's here tonight as my guest with Rosie Williams. I'll introduce you. He'll have you sorted out in no time.'

'If Alex has got any funny little quirks, I'll be the one to minister to him.' Charlotte laughed, then changed the subject. 'Tell me what you know about Ted the Toup. What's he doing to give Iris such palpitations?'

'Come off it! The Pope would give old Ma Braithwaite palpitations, never mind Ted's range of intimate items of clothing.'

'His what?'

Derek gave Charlotte a wink. 'Best get yourself down there and order your trousseau. You might even pick up a little something in the way of posing accessories for your man here.'

'For goodness' sake, talk sense. What exactly is he selling?'

'It's perfectly harmless stuff, just a little erotica to pick up with your daily tabloid – you know the kind of thing.'

Charlotte and Alex waited expectantly. 'Come on then, what?' Alex said at last.

'Well, he's moved up the body, doing a line in lingerie. Basic kind of things, mostly cheap imports from the sweatshops of our Far Eastern friends – nothing that I would buy for Cindy, of course.'

'But why?'

'Cindy prefers pure silk, not—'

'No,' Charlotte said, exasperated. 'Why's Ted doing this?'

'You can't knock a man for extending his business, Charlotte.'

'Cods!' she retorted. 'Why smutty underwear? Why not birdseed?'

'Obvious, I suppose,' Alex said. 'After Mrs Braithwaite's petition he's coming back guns blazing.'

Charlotte shook her head and, as the first of the rockets was let off on the far side of the school playing field, she thought of the fireworks about to explode in the village, and of Iris Braithwaite putting on her boxing gloves for possibly the fight of her life.

As the fireworks exploded high above her head, Hilary caught sight of David and Catherine Renshaw standing together. Catherine's face was turned upwards, her lips parted in the obligatory *aah* position as diamonds of white magnesium light speckled the windless night sky forming, for a few magical seconds, a perfectly shaped dandelion.

Hilary's first thought was to run; to run all the way back to the safety of The Gables. Her second inclination was to ram the hot dog in her hand down that *aah*-shaped mouth.

She did neither, hearing the sound of her name spoken at her side.

'*Bonsoir,* Hilary.' It was Nick Bradshaw. 'Go easy on that hot dog you're squeezing the life out of it.'

Hilary grimaced at the sight of mustard and ketchup oozing all over her hands. The twisted bread roll and sausage looked disgusting. She threw it on the grass.

'Here.' Nick offered her a tissue from his coat pocket.

'Thank you,' she mumbled.

'I nearly didn't recognise you.'

She looked puzzled.

'Your hair. You've changed the colour and the style. It looks good.'

She turned away self-consciously.

'Ah,' he said.

'What do you mean, *ah*?' she said, meeting his gaze.

'You've forgotten how to receive a compliment, haven't you? Especially from a man you hardly know, whose motives could be considered at best dubious and at worst manipulative.'

'Good Lord. How ridiculous.'

Overhead another firework illuminated the smoke-filled sky and Nick's face suddenly seemed much too close. She took a small step away from him.

'Do I make you feel uneasy, Hilary?'

'You say the most absurd things. Or is that what you're paid to do?'

He laughed. 'More or less, but if it makes people understand that bit more about themselves then I can justify it. That throttled frankfurter, anyone I know?'

Hilary caught her breath. 'I shouldn't think so. And, anyway, why should it be *anyone*?'

'Just wondered whether it had anything to do with those glasses you were smashing the other day and the rich vocabulary you were trying out.'

Hilary had had enough. Everything was going wrong. Her new image had done nothing to bring David to his senses, in fact almost the reverse. On the way here he'd even questioned her on how much money she'd spent in Manchester with Cindy and then he'd gone on to ask her where she'd put his special whisky tumblers – without looking at him she'd made up some stupid story about having an accident when cleaning out the cupboard – and now here he was enjoying the fireworks with his mistress. And here she was, stuck with this wretched man and his smart-alec questions, poking his nose in where it just wasn't wanted. 'Why can't you mind your own business?' she responded hotly.

'Ouch!' Nick said. 'That's the second time you've said that. But well done. Keep going and I might eventually get the message that you don't like me.'

Hilary turned her back on him and watched Patricia Longton's husband light the fuse for the mounted display of fireworks. The first to go was a Catherine wheel. In the hushed, expectant silence Hilary suddenly laughed.

'Want to share the joke?' Nick whispered in her ear.

'Definitely not,' she said, trying to stifle yet more laughter at the image so clearly forming in her mind's eye – that of David's mistress impaled on a spike and spinning round and round before being tossed into orbit, never to be seen again.

'Enjoying yourself, Hilary?'

'David!' She decided to test him. 'Where have you been?'

'Just over there.' He pointed to where Catherine was talking to someone Hilary didn't recognise. 'I'm surprised you didn't see me.'

How brazen he was!

'I'm afraid I'm probably to blame,' Nick said, 'I've been talking too much.'

'This is Nick Bradshaw, David. He's starting at All in the Mind next week.'

David gave a short, loud laugh. 'You need your own head tested getting in with Derek on this latest harebrained scheme of his.'

'David!'

'It's all a load of tosh, isn't it?' David carried on, ignoring Hilary's admonishment. 'Just another way to exploit bored housewives. I guarantee you won't find any decent hard-working bloke skulking there on a couch having his innermost thoughts paraded in front of him. What do you call it? Ah, yes, getting in touch with oneself.'

'That's quite a commonly held view. But usually voiced by those with something to hide. Tell me, David, what are you most afraid of?'

'What's this? A free therapy session?' David said aggressively. 'I'm not that stupid. Next you'll be pulling out the ink blots and trying to draw out the feminine side of me.'

'David, stop being so rude.'

A firework screeched overhead, zigzagging its way high into the sky. In the sudden burst of silvery light Hilary saw both men clearly illuminated in front of her. In David's face she was struck by the hardness of his features, lips tightly drawn in a rigid line, which seemed to her in that moment to betray his dislike of their marriage. If there had been any trace of doubt in her mind that David was innocent of the crime he had allegedly committed, his face now confirmed his guilt. She felt sick, consumed with pain, as if her insides had just been ripped out. She turned to Nick and in his face saw all that she so badly wanted to see in David's face – warmth and understanding, kindness and humour. It was all there . . . *but in the wrong man.*

'I apologise for my apparent rudeness, which my wife has been only too quick to point out,' David said stiffly, when the sky darkened once more. 'I just wanted you to know that you're banging on the wrong door as far as I'm concerned.'

'You're probably right,' Nick said lightly. 'But at some time in our lives we all need a guiding hand. When we're up against the wall there's no better time to explore the dark nooks and crannies of our minds.'

'And what's that supposed to mean? Are you trying to tell me—'

'All I'm saying is that by having the opportunity to examine ourselves we can so often change our attitude or improve on our situation, not just for the benefit of ourselves but more importantly for those around us.'

'Mm . . .' David said. 'I suppose there could be an element of truth in what you say.' He turned to Hilary. 'You've got no complaints with me, though, have you?'

Hilary wanted to pick up the squashed hot dog from the grass beneath her feet and shove it down David's throat. No complaints! Not much she hadn't. She was only having to share her husband with another woman. 'Well, David, there are times when I feel you could—'

'There you are!' David rounded on Nick. 'You see what you've done. You've filled her head with silly nonsense about me not making the grade in some way.'

'And is that what you're afraid of, David?' Nick said quietly. 'Not making the grade?'

For a moment David seemed unable to speak. His anger was almost palpable. Then, as though fighting the urge to take Nick by the throat, he said, 'That's a load of crap. And if you want somebody to analyse try Hilary. Ask her why the new hairdo and why earlier this evening she poured whisky over me.' He walked away, his shoulders hunched, his hands thrust deep inside his coat pockets.

Hilary gasped.

'Interesting man, your husband.'

'Oh, shut up, can't you!'

15

'Bloody marvellous!' Georgia shouted at the top of her voice as she threw down the *Chronicle* on top of the paperwork spread over the small table in the caravan. Gordon, who was leaning on a broom outside, gave her a quizzical look. She went to the door and called him over. 'Come and see this.'

Gordon left his broom propped against a greenhouse, grateful for the opportunity to get out of the cold for a few minutes. He pulled off his gloves and climbed into the caravan. 'What's up? Not that git of an ex-husband of yours making a nuisance of himself again, is it?'

Georgia shook her head. Ever since she'd taken Gordon on as her right-hand boot – as he described himself – he had referred to Rory in this way, which was how he also referred to his previous employer. Several years ago, and at the age of sixty, local cutbacks in the National Health Service had forced him out of his post as a hospital porter. Then, having watched the work going on over the road from his cottage, he had called in one morning to ask Georgia if there were any jobs going. At first she'd turned him down for the simple reason that she didn't have the money to pay any wages. But within four months she was knocking on his door in a position to offer him part-time work. 'It's not much,' she'd told him.

'He'll take it,' his wife Winnie had said. 'I want him out from under my feet. He's always talking through Jimmy Young's programme on the radio. It's the medical bits he hates, embarrasses him summat rotten. If he starts giving you any nonsense just start talking prostate trouble. Lord knows how he lasted all those years in the hospital.'

Georgia had taken an instant liking to Winnie – who turned out to be a willing babysitter for Chloe – and Gordon, who more than proved his worth around the nursery.

She showed him the paper. He let out a long whistle. 'Skin and hair'll soon be flying, then, won't it?'

A black and white picture of fury stared back at them from the front page. Iris Braithwaite was photographed outside Ted the Toup's and the headline read, 'Hulme Welford's very own Mary Whitehouse'. The journalist had then gone on to report on Mrs Braithwaite's campaign to clean up the village of Hulme Welford. 'We must all fight this evil sin and do our public duty,' she was quoted as saying. The paper's editor had added to the article by inviting readers to write in with their comments on the debate 'To Censor or Not to Censor' – a debate which no doubt he clearly hoped would run and run and increase his circulation figures.

'I've said it once and I'll say it again,' Georgia said. 'It's bloody marvellous. Good for old Ma Braithwaite.'

'That's as may be,' Gordon said, pulling on his gloves to go back out into the cold. 'But, like as not, she'll bring trouble on herself and others.'

'How very profound of you, Gordon. You been listening to *Thought for the Day* again?'

From the doorway of the caravan she watched Gordon pick up his broom and start sweeping the leaves covering the path leading to one of the greenhouses. The newspaper was still in her hands and, catching sight of Mrs Braithwaite again, she made up her mind to go and see her.

'Gordon,' she called out, 'I'm going early to pick up Chloe, there's something I need to do. Hold the fort, will you?'

Georgia parked outside The White Cottage in Acacia Lane and as she walked up the garden path she tried hard not to be too disdainful of the overly ordered front garden. There was not a stray leaf in sight, not an overlooked bedding plant left there by chance from the summer. All was crisp and dreadfully bare.

She banged the brass knocker, loudly and eagerly: she had much to say to Mrs Braithwaite. She knew that most people in the village were scared of her, intimidated by her overbearing manner. Georgia had always privately admired the way she handled herself. Before she'd encountered the older woman she had never come across anyone more single-minded than herself – a criticism Rory had levelled at her on more than one occasion.

But she was used to criticism, having put up with a bellyful since she'd got rid of Rory and his endless stream of excuses. She knew only too well what people like Patricia Longton had to say about her: What kind of a woman kicks out her daughter's father? She could have retaliated with the truth – which was, quite simply, that Rory couldn't be trusted to part his own hair, never mind run a business – but she'd chosen instead to thumb her nose at anyone who dared to point the finger of accusation in her direction. She knew, though, that despite themselves people had come to respect her for having got the nursery up and running. Where Rory had failed, she had succeeded. In her opinion people generally preferred success stories to depressing tales of failure.

She rapped the door knocker again.

'Whoever it is out there, kindly show some manners and have the goodness to wait a few moments.'

Georgia smiled and listened to the lock being turned.

'Oh, it's you, Mrs D'Arcy,' Iris said, surprised. 'What can I do for you?'

'It's *Ms* D'Arcy,' Georgia said firmly. 'I've come to see you about Ted

Cooper.' Georgia felt the older woman's suspicious eyes weighing her up. She decided to take the initiative. 'May I come in?'

Iris pursed her lips at such forwardness. 'I'm a busy woman, Mrs D'Arcy.' She began to nudge the door closed.

'And so am I,' Georgia parried. 'I don't have much free time but I've come especially to see you.'

The older woman seemed to consider this for a few seconds before saying, 'I can spare you a few minutes, no more,' holding the door fully open, and grudgingly allowing Georgia over the threshold. But almost immediately she shouted, 'Boots! Off with those muddy boots, if you please. I've had this carpet twenty-two years and I'm not about to have it ruined.'

She left Georgia to take off the offending articles and went through to the kitchen. 'I presume you do drink tea, Mrs D'Arcy,' she called out, 'or is that too conventional for you?'

'Tea will be fine and it's Ms D'Arcy. I was Mrs Maddox, but now that I'm divorced I've reverted back to my maiden name, okay? Perhaps Georgia would be easier for you to remember?'

Iris's head appeared abruptly at the kitchen door. 'Are you trying to imply I'm not capable of remembering a simple thing like a name? I'm not senile, young lady, if that's what you think.'

'Not at all, Mrs Braithwaite,' Georgia said, amused.

'Then I suggest you sit down in the sitting-room and I'll join you there in a moment.'

Georgia went where she was told but prowled round the tidy room. It was almost as bare and clinical as the front garden, devoid of all the personal mementoes that usually cluttered up one's life. The thought occurred to Georgia that maybe this was deliberate. Perhaps Mrs Braithwaite didn't want the waters of the present muddied with reminders of the past because, as Georgia herself had come to know, retrospection of any kind led only to regret.

She sat in a high-backed winged chair and warmed her feet by the coal fire. It was two thirty on a Tuesday afternoon and here she was, lazing in an armchair feeling absurdly decadent, as if she was bunking off school. She almost wanted to laugh, but then her mood changed and she found herself feeling sorry for herself, that such a simple thing was now a complete luxury to her. She sat up straight and snatched her feet away from the fireside. Self-pity was such a wasted emotion and she couldn't afford to waste anything.

'I dare say you could manage a slice of Genoa cake,' Iris said, coming in with a tea-tray complete with a paper doily. 'You look like you could do with feeding up.'

'Please don't go spoiling me,' Georgia said briskly. A little too briskly. Iris's eyes shot up from the tea-tray.

'I've never spoilt anyone in my life,' she said firmly, handing Georgia a cup and saucer. 'I was merely making an observation,' she continued. 'In my opinion you look no more than two-penn'orth of copper. You clearly work too hard and give yourself little or no time at all in which to eat. Though I dare say you would disagree with me and tell me to mind my own business.' She passed a large slice of cake to Georgia, along with a napkin, and in a less strident tone added, 'It can't be easy for you, though, doing all that you do alone.'

'Thank you,' Georgia muttered awkwardly. This was an area of her life on which she preferred not to dwell. There was nothing, absolutely nothing, to be gained in self-pitying explorations of the soul. If she did that she might lose the motivation to get out of bed in the morning. As it was, it was struggle enough summoning up the energy to face each day.

'So, what is it you want to discuss with me?' Iris asked, filling in the silence. 'I suppose you've come here to tell me not to be such a stupid interfering old woman. Is that it?'

'Quite the reverse, Mrs Braithwaite,' Georgia said, glad to be moving the conversation on to less personal ground. 'I've come to congratulate you and to offer my services.'

It was Iris's turn to be taken aback. 'You want to offer your help in ridding Hulme Welford of the likes of Ted Cooper? Go on.'

Georgia leaned forward in her seat. 'Yes,' she said, nodding, her long ear-rings swinging precariously 'There's no room for disgusting old men like him in this world.'

'How right you are Mrs . . . Ms D'Arcy. And how refreshing to hear such a plainly spoken view on this contemptible issue. I had thought that people like yourself were full of rampant liberalism, promoting the ethos that anything goes.'

'I believe in absolute equality, Mrs Braithwaite, which means the exploitation of women has to be stopped. Do you see what I mean?'

'Good Lord, young lady. Please don't lecture me.'

'I'm sorry,' Georgia said, biting into her slice of cake. When she'd finished her mouthful she said, 'So what's the next step in your campaign?'

'I'm hoping that this newspaper article will shame the grubby little man into disbanding his ghastly scheme.'

Georgia shook her head, her ear-rings swinging again. 'No chance!' she said, with such vehemence that Iris clattered her cup on its saucer. 'I don't believe that will happen. The newspaper story will just antagonise the man. We're going to have to come up with further retaliation. We've got to produce a barrage of disapproval at what he's doing.'

'You've obviously given this some thought. And just what do you have in mind exactly?'

A slow smile spread over Georgia's face. 'Another cup of tea, Mrs Braithwaite, and I'll gladly tell you.'

Iris filled Georgia's cup, but when she handed it back Georgia nearly dropped the green Beryl-ware china as she heard the unexpected words, 'Perhaps you'd like to call me Iris.'

*

The three thirty school-gate gathering was buzzing with the news.

Patricia Longton pulled Hilary into the fold with evangelical zeal. 'I'm thinking of putting an opposing petition together,' she said. 'It's all perfectly innocent what Ted's selling. You'll sign of course, won't you, Hilary?'

Hilary shivered inside her coat and wondered why Patricia never did up the zip on her smelly old waxed jacket.

'I'm sure we can rely on Hilary's support,' Kate Hampton chimed in. 'After all, she's always been one of the girls.'

'*Les girls*, that's us.' Patricia laughed.

Hilary didn't feel at all one of the girls, not after Patricia's comments this morning at the gate. She'd spent a good fifteen minutes tearing apart the organisation of the school bonfire party. 'Fancy not having enough hot dogs,' she'd opened up with. 'Not a hint of a relish to be had and as for having sparklers for all the children, well, let's just say it was a miracle we didn't have any serious casualties. *She* won't last long, take my word for it. And you know what people are saying about *her*, don't you?'

Out of habit Hilary had given the necessary tilt of the head thereby giving Patricia the green light to continue with her axegrinding.

'They say that Rory had other women because ...' here Patricia had paused for dramatic emphasis, turning her head from left to right, 'because she's a lesbian. I should keep your distance, if I were you. Just think what David would say if there were rumours that you, well, you know what I mean. People might not want to buy their home from a man whose wife ... I'm sure I don't have to spell it out for you, Hilary.'

It was all right, of course, for an estate agent to be bonking his secretary, Hilary had muttered all the way home, after managing to escape Patricia's vile tongue, but heaven forbid that his wife should have a friendship with another woman whose sexuality was in question. And how dare Patricia say such awful things about Georgia, especially when Georgia had been so kind to her? Stupid, smug Patricia was probably just jealous that she had found a new friend.

'French class tonight, Hilary,' Patricia said, bringing Hilary back to that afternoon's gossip session. 'Done your homework?'

Damn! She hadn't. 'Plenty of time yet,' she said airily.

'Hope you're not going to keep that nice Nick Bradshaw all to yourself this evening. I'd rather like to do some conversational work with him myself.' She gave Kate Hampton a wink.

'You're welcome to him,' Hilary replied.

'A lover's tiff already?' Kate chirped. 'How much to keep it quiet from David?'

Oh, the irony, thought Hilary. With relief she saw Patricia's infamously uncontrollable sons coming across the playground.

'See you all,' Patricia called as she led away the two small boys, who lagged behind her throwing leaves at the passing cars.

Kate Hampton's pony-mad daughter Victoria was next to appear in the throng of children, and when she left Hilary felt herself relax. *Les girls*, indeed. *Les bitches*, more like it. And to think she used to consider them friends.

'Hello, Hilary.'

'Georgia,' Hilary said brightly.

'I don't know what I've done to deserve a smile like that, but thanks all the same.'

'Would you like to come back for a cup of tea and some cake?' Hilary asked, not sure whether she was responding to Georgia's undernourished appearance – she was wrapped in a duffel coat and looking even more urchin-like today – or more to spite Patricia.

'Must be my lucky day for tea and cake. Are you sure? Don't you have Philip to pick up?'

'He's got a play rehearsal tonight. I don't have to collect him until six.'

'Okay, then, but only for a short while. I've left Gordon in charge. And I ought to warn you about Chloe. No time, here she comes.'

A girl in a bulky duffel coat not much smaller than Georgia's was striding across the playground. And, also like Georgia, her hair was cut short framing a small pixie face. All that was missing to complete the similarity was a pair of dangling ear-rings.

In the distance was Becky, skipping happily along in a world of her own, her plaited hair bouncing on her shoulders, her pink lunch-box swinging in her hand.

'Okay, chuck?' Georgia said to her daughter.

'Another day of the same old female repression,' Chloe announced mournfully. 'Mrs Arnold is insisting I play Mary in the nativity play. I told her I wanted to be Joseph, that I know my way round a hammer and saw better than a baby's bum.'

Georgia smiled. 'Hilary's invited us for a cup of tea, that all right with you?'

'Fine.'

'Mummy, Mummy! Guess what?' Becky said breathlessly as she joined them. 'I'm going to be an angel in the nativity play. You'll need to get me loads of tinsel for my halo and wings, some white tights and a huge white sheet.'

Chloe gave a contemptuous grunt.

Hilary set the tea-things on the pine table in the kitchen. She was fussing, she knew, over-compensating for ten-year-old Chloe's disapproval of everything Becky said and did. But Becky couldn't help being a typical girl, it was just the way she was. She had always wanted long hair and to play with dolls.

'You've had your hair done,' Georgia said, helping to pass plates of cake around the table.

Hilary sensed yet more disapproval. 'I fancied something different,' she said defensively, convinced that Georgia had guessed at the reason behind the sudden change in her appearance. 'Do you want Ribena or orange squash, Chloe?'

Chloe pulled a face. 'I'd prefer tea, please. Black, no sugar.'

Becky was impressed. She sometimes had tea but it was always milky with a tiny bit of sugar, if she was lucky. Black without sugar was dead grown-up. 'I'll have the same,' she said, looking at her mother.

Eyebrows raised, Hilary fetched two more mugs and exchanged a knowing look with Georgia.

When tea was over Chloe reluctantly agreed to go upstairs to see Becky's bedroom.

'Poor Chloe,' Hilary said, after the girls had left the kitchen, 'she's so very grown-up and modern, Becky's the complete opposite.'

'No worries. Chloe will soon have her whipped into shape. Now tell me about this new look of yours. Has it worked?'

Embarrassed, Hilary started to clear away the mugs and plates.

'Leave all that,' Georgia said, sharply. 'Sit down, stop fidgeting and talk to me. Did the rat even notice the trouble you'd gone to?'

'Oh, he noticed all right,' Hilary said. She slipped into her chair. 'I think for the first time in his life he was stuck for words.' She chewed on her lower lip. 'Then he laughed . . . Oh, Georgia, he laughed at me. He's probably been having a good laugh with her as well.'

'Best not think of that,' Georgia said softly.

'I only did it because I know how much he likes Anthea Turner on the telly. It's pathetic, isn't it? I got Cindy to do it for me . . . She didn't want to, but I made her do it, so that I . . .'

'So that you could please David?'

'Yes.'

Georgia leaned back in her chair and shook her head. 'Believe me, it doesn't work. I tried it for years with Rory. Whatever you offer to some men, it's just not enough.'

Neither spoke for a few minutes, the ticking of the clock above the Aga the only sound between the two women, that and the occasional thud from Becky's room above them.

At last Hilary looked up. She was shocked to find Georgia staring straight at her, as if she had been doing so for some time. Something in her face reminded Hilary of being back at school with Naomi Scott. How she had wanted Naomi to look at her in the way Georgia—

Suddenly she recalled Patricia's whispered words at the school gate: '*They say she's a . . .*'

Hilary swallowed hard, horrified. What was she doing? What kind of situation was developing between her and Georgia?

'Poor you,' she heard Georgia say. Then a hand reached out across the table towards her.

Panic-stricken she leapt to her feet. 'I've got to prepare the vegetables for supper,' she squeaked. 'And then I'll have to collect Philip.'

Georgia frowned. 'I thought you said he didn't finish until six. It's not even half past four.'

'I lied . . . I mean I forgot the play rehearsal isn't tonight, it's tomorrow.' She started clattering the plates into a pile and making for the dishwasher. 'I'm like that these days. Forget things all the time, must be hormones or something. Senile, even. Yes, that's it. I'm probably going senile. Not at all the kind of person you'd like as a friend.'

Georgia laughed and got up from her chair. She walked towards Hilary, her hands outstretched.

Oh my God, Hilary thought. She's going to kiss me. Help! Somebody help me.

Help came at once in the form of two loud rings on the doorbell.

16

Never in all her life had Hilary been so pleased to see a man. And Nick Bradshaw, all six foot of him, corduroys and plum-coloured wool jacket and scarf tied loosely round his neck standing on the doorstep, was a gift from heaven.

'Come in, come in,' she said, pulling him over the threshold. 'Tea! I'm sure you'd love a cup, wouldn't you?'

Nick was bemused. He had called on the off-chance of apologising to Hilary for what he'd said to David at the bonfire party last week and had expected little more than a frosty welcome. 'Thank you,' he said, 'so long as you're sure it's no trouble.'

'No trouble at all,' Hilary burbled, leading the way to the kitchen.

'I thought you were in a hurry to collect Philip?' Georgia said coldly, staring straight at Hilary. She was leaning against the Aga, her legs crossed at the ankles and her arms folded over her small breasts.

Nick looked from one woman to the other. He sensed he had come in on the middle of something. He also sensed hostility emanating from the woman by the Aga. 'Hi,' he said, offering a smile and a handshake. Just as he had expected, both were treated to a dismissive shrug by a pair of fragile-looking shoulders.

'I'll be off, then,' Georgia said, picking up her duffel coat from the back of a chair. 'I'll call Chloe down while you see to your *guest*.'

'Don't go,' Hilary said.

Alert to the falseness in Hilary's voice, Nick watched her closely. Relief was written all over her face. Intrigued, he turned to the other woman. 'Please don't leave on my account.'

'I wouldn't do anything on your account,' came the quick-fire put-down.

He listened to the politely said goodbyes in the hall and the sound of the front door shutting.

'Sorry about that,' Hilary said, coming back into the kitchen. 'Georgia's on the PTA with me. I barely know her, really, in fact I'd go so far as to say—'

'It's okay, you don't have to explain your friends to me. I was over the road with Derek and Cindy and thought I'd call by to apologise for the other night.'

'Oh,' she said, surprised.

'Any chance of that cup of tea?' He removed his scarf and took Georgia's place against the Aga. 'Or was that just a ruse to get rid of your unwanted visitor?'

Hilary was beginning to feel tired of having to keep up with so many different conversations. Her life never used to be like this. The most taxing word game she'd ever played before was second-guessing Becky. Fed up, she filled the kettle.

'I'm sorry I pushed your husband the way I did. Some might say I was behaving in an unprofessional manner, but I'm afraid I don't go in for the conventional tried and tested views a lot of the time. Do you forgive me?'

'If it makes you feel better, yes,' she answered wearily, staring out at the back garden. It was dark outside and something must have set off the security light: the lawn and flower beds were brilliantly illuminated – she could see a cat disappearing into the laurel bushes at the far end of the garden.

'I would rather it made you feel better.'

'Sorry?'

'You look tired, Hilary.'

'I am,' she said flatly. She made him a mug of tea and wondered why she felt so uncomfortable when he called her by her name.

'Do you think your husband will accept my apology?'

Hilary thought how defensively aggressive David had suddenly become and of his many prejudices; his condemnation of the two and a half million unemployed in the country, his dislike of change and his reluctance to part with any money, and now his obvious cynicism towards the world of therapy, something she'd been unaware of until now. 'I shouldn't think so for one minute,' she said.

When Nick didn't say anything but watched her over the top of his mug, she felt even more uncomfortable and compelled to say something herself. 'Do you counsel people on their marriages?'

'I have done in the past,' he said slowly, 'but that won't be what I'll be doing at All in the Mind.'

'But you could offer help, for instance, to a friend of mine who was having difficulties?' What on earth was she doing? Of course he'd see through what she was saying. Why couldn't she just shut up, let him drink his tea then get him out of the house?

'I'd like to think that if anyone needed advice they would feel able to ask me straight out for help. You included, Hilary.'

There he went again. Why did he have to keep calling her by her name? She decided not to say anything further. She'd let him do all the talking.

'Are you and David—'

The door opened and banged noisily against a cupboard. Becky appeared with her arms full of Barbie dolls and accessories. 'Chloe says I must chuck these out. Oh, who are you?' She gave Nick an accusing stare.

'Oh, he's just a man,' Hilary said quickly, grateful for once for her daughter's habit of barging into conversations.

Becky gave a shrill laugh and squeezed her eyes tightly shut. She looked constipated, but Hilary knew better: some newly learned piece of knowledge was about to be given an airing.

'Chloe says that when God made man she was only joking.'

It was pitch black and Philip was alone. All the others had gone, picked up by their mothers or fathers. He peered into the darkness of the badly lit school driveway, hoping to see his mother's Renault Clio. Some of the mothers drove to school in sports cars, most drove estates or Shoguns. It would be nice if Mum had a flashier car. In the mornings he came to school by bus, which was okay, but because there were so many activities to do after school it usually meant that he was picked up by Mum in the afternoon.

Most of his friends from junior school had gone on to the High, but he'd won a scholarship to the same school that Tiffany went to. He could remember the look on his dad's face when the letter had come in the post. Yeah, that had been great. He and Mum had bought him a computer for doing so well in his exam. It was hard being at St Hugh's, though, more difficult than he'd thought it was going to be. Some of the masters seemed to enjoy making him get upset when he couldn't do the work. He cringed at how he'd wet himself on his first day. Bloody hell! Eleven years old and he'd wet himself. Bloody, bloody hell!

He looked at his watch. Where was she? He hoped she was okay. He'd heard her crying last week and just the other day. Why? What did she have to be sad about?

Batesy said his mother was like that last year. But, then, she'd had something to cry about. Batesy's dad had left home last year just before Christmas; brought them all presents, Batesy said, then disappeared off with another woman on Boxing Day.

Philip chewed what was left of his bitten thumbnail. His dad wasn't going to leave, so Mum wouldn't be crying for that reason, would she? Stuff Batesy! Batesy's dad probably left home because Batesy was such an idiot. He wasn't an idiot, he'd won a scholarship. So that was okay then.

But where was Mum?

'Still here, Philip?'

'Yes, sir.'

'Why don't you come into the warm and wait?'

'I'm all right, sir. I'm sure my mother will be here soon.'

'Suit yourself.'

He watched Mr Wells, the Latin master, disappear into the school building. Mr Wells was okay. He was one of the nicer teachers. It was Mr Wells who had caught those boys the other day. Tiffany had warned him that there were bullies in the school. She'd even said that she'd sort them out if he needed help. Flipping heck, no girl was ever going to sort out his problems. Anyway, if those boys tried it on again, he'd be ready for them.

He looked at his watch. In the distance he heard the sound of a car and saw two headlights coming towards him. He held his breath. Please let it be Mum. The car drew level and he caught sight of Becky sticking her tongue out at him. He let out his breath in one long deep sigh.

'How are you getting on with *Emma*?' Hilary asked Tiffany, watching her drop her large bag of schoolwork on to the floor in the sitting-room.

'That geek Mr Elton has just tried it on with her. He's really got the hots for her, hasn't he? Serves her right, if you ask me. I can't understand what George Knightley sees in Emma – you'd think he could do better for himself.'

'Well, I'd better leave you to it,' Hilary said, gathering up her own schoolwork. 'Becky's in her room having a sort-out and Philip's on his computer. I've left some cake for you and there's plenty of biscuits in the cupboard.'

'Thanks, have fun with your French.'

Hilary banged the door shut after her and turned up her coat against the wind as she walked the short distance to school. Have fun, Tiffany had said. How could she? Not only was that wretched Nick Bradshaw going to be there but she hadn't done her homework. A sudden gust of wind cut through her coat and she shivered. And on top of that Patricia would be gloating like mad that she'd done hers.

The day had rushed past her in such a flurry of activity that she'd barely had time to think of David. Even when he'd got in from work she'd been so preoccupied, thinking about Georgia and Nick, that she hadn't thought twice about what David might or might not have been up to at the office or, indeed, whether he would be going anywhere near the squash club that evening. Thinking about it now, he had seemed distracted at the supper table and hadn't even said anything when the children had started bickering. Philip had started to tell one of his jokes and Becky had looked him in the eye and said, '*You're* just a boy.'

''Course I am. So?' he had answered.

'My new friend Chloe says that boys don't grow as fast as girls, so you know what that means, don't you? It means I'm probably more intelligent than you.'

'Let's see *you* get a scholarship, then!'

Even when Becky had flounced out of the kitchen with her nose high in the air like Miss Piggy and had then bumped into the door and started wailing like a siren, David had seemed oblivious to it all and had got up from the table saying he'd better hurry or he'd be late for his game of squash.

It started to rain just as Hilary crossed the main road opposite St John's. She quickened her pace and shuddered as a drop of water trickled down her neck. By the time she reached the school gate the rain had turned to hail. She bolted across the playground, head down, at the same time trying to shelter her textbook by tucking it close to her chest. At the main entrance door she stepped inside and gasped for air, shaking her wet and bedraggled hair. As she walked along the echoing corridor she could hear Martina's voice giving out instructions for the lesson.

Damn! She was late.

Then behind her she heard the sound of the door crashing shut, followed by hurried footsteps.

'Glad I'm not the only one who's late.'

Without turning round she knew who it was. Subconsciously she slowed her step. Some mad part of her wanted to be able to enter the classroom with Nick – That'd show Patricia, she thought.

Nick held the door open for her and she went in. 'Hello, Martina,' she said brightly, 'sorry I'm late.'

'Me too,' Nick said.

'Make them stand in the corner,' Patricia said, 'but not together.'

'Shame,' laughed Nick, making his way to the back of the classroom where he'd sat previously. Hilary immediately started for a free chair next to an elderly woman who had never once, in Hilary's knowledge, opened her mouth during any of the lessons.

'Hilary, would you mind sharing with Nick again?' Martina asked. 'I haven't managed to get a book for him yet. We're on page thirty-one: "*Dans la Chambre à Coucher*".'

Hilary heard a snigger from the front row – Patricia. Reluctantly she sat next to Nick.

'Sorry to get you lumbered with me again,' he said. Then, in a quieter voice, he added, 'Thanks for the tea earlier, by the way.'

After Becky had made her dramatic entrance into the kitchen, Hilary had been surprised at how Nick had treated Becky. He'd bent down to her and thoughtfully examined one of the Barbie dolls destined for the bin. He'd shaken his head and tutted loudly. 'Dolls, instruments of oppression without a doubt. I'd get rid of the whole lot of them if I were you.' Then he'd stood up and, with his back to Becky, he'd winked at Hilary and smiled. 'Time I was going. Looks like you've a revolution on your hands, I'll leave you to it.'

'Hilary. Qu'est-ce qu'il y a dans l'armoire?'

Hilary studied the picture. *Armoire*. What on earth was an *armoire*? 'Um . . . le lit?' she said hopefully.

Patricia laughed. 'It'd be a pretty big wardrobe!'

'Quelle chatte!' Nick whispered at Hilary's side. 'Me-ow!'

'Non, Hilary, le lit est sur le plancher. Qu'est-ce qu'il y a dans l'armoire?'

Hilary hesitated. What was the wretched word for clothes?

'Vêtements,' whispered Nick.

'I knew that,' she hissed at him. 'I don't need any help. Vêtements,' she said out loud.

'Bien, et maintenant vos devoirs. Patricia?'

'Oui, Martina. Mes vacances en Florida.'

Hilary closed her eyes and groaned quietly to herself. She'd heard it all before at the school gate. Patricia and family at Manchester airport. Patricia and family miraculously upgraded. Patricia and family at Kennedy Space Center. Patricia and family at Universal Studios. She felt a nudge at her elbow and opened her eyes to see a scrap of paper on the desk in front of her. On it was written, *You thinking what I'm thinking?*

She nearly laughed – nearly risked one of Patricia's disapproving looks. She turned the piece of paper over and wrote, *I doubt it.*

He passed her another note: *Do you think you could chance just one drink with me when we've finished here tonight?*

Certainly not. I'm married! she scribbled in large letters.

'Does that mean you never get thirsty?' he whispered.

She laughed. Patricia huffed in her direction. 'Quand nous sommes arrivés . . .' she repeated for Hilary's benefit.

Good grief, thought Hilary, we haven't even got to the bit where the hotel porter got the brand-new Samsonite luggage mixed up with some inferior cases.

At this rate maybe she'd need a drink by the end of the class.

17

'Come on, stop fussing. They'll be fine.'

Hilary heard David leave the room and go downstairs. She thought how easy it was for men to switch off their emotions, even when it came to their children.

Very carefully, Hilary sat on the edge of Becky's bed – she was fast asleep and looking her most benign. Hilary kissed her lightly on the cheek and breathed in the smell of her newly washed hair. It made her want to take off her coat and nestle down beside Becky. She didn't want to go out. She didn't want an evening with David, pretending to all those at Derek and Cindy's launch party that their life was just fine. Her life was far from fine and she felt like shouting it out to everyone that night that David was an adulterous, selfish swine.

She kissed Becky once more as if for luck, then went across the landing to Philip's room where she could hear the low throb-throb of Oasis's latest CD. Philip was bent over his desk staring at a book.

'How's the homework going?' she asked.

'The Crusades,' he answered, without looking up. 'It says here they boiled babies alive and then ate them. You don't suppose we could do the same with Becky, do you?'

'Philip!'

'Only joking.'

'And I only came in to say goodbye. You're sure you'll be all right?'

'I'll be fine, Mum, honestly.'

'I'll keep popping back every thirty minutes.'

'You're only going over the road. I'll be okay.'

'You won't go watching anything unsuitable on the television, will you?'

'Mum!'

She gave him a quick kiss on the top of his head, so quick he didn't have time to duck out of the way.

Philip waited for the sound of the front door to shut. Then, reaching across his desk, he parted the bedroom curtains with the end of his pencil and peered through the inch gap. He watched his parents cross the road but flicked away his pencil when he saw his mother glance back up at the house.

Had she seen him? He hoped not. He didn't want her thinking he was scared of being on his own.

He wasn't scared.

Like he wasn't scared of those idiots in the changing rooms at school. Batesy was pathetic to have given in to them. He shouldn't have done that, not when they'd promised each other they'd stick together.

He chewed his little finger and returned his attention to the gruesome pictures of severed heads and blood-tipped spears in his history book, convinced that what the Crusaders had experienced was nothing compared to what he was going through.

When at last there was nothing left of his fingernail he slapped the book shut, threw himself on his bed and buried his head under the pillow to block out the thought of Batesy's betrayal and how alone he felt.

It was almost freezing, just as the weather forecast had predicted, and their breath formed gauzy clouds in the still night air. Alex wrapped his arm round Charlotte. 'Shall we make a run for it?' he asked, as they set off down the drive of Ivy Cottage.

'What, in these heels?'

'Well, I'm not carrying you. I'm saving all my energy for the honeymoon. There are certain obligations a man's got to fulfil on his wedding night.'

Charlotte laughed. 'You've still not told me where we're going.'

'And nor shall I.'

As they turned into Derek and Cindy's drive Charlotte stopped and faced Alex. 'What, not even if . . .' She buried her face in his neck and whispered in his ear. He laughed out loud and kissed her.

'Well really!' reprimanded Iris Braithwaite, appearing from nowhere in the darkness with a puff of dragon-like steam coming out of her mouth.

Ignoring the ticking off and taking in Iris's voluminous fur coat Alex said, 'You're looking very fetching tonight, Mrs Braithwaite.'

'Don't waste your flattery on me, young man. Save it for Mrs Lawrence. It might help you to get her to the altar quicker.'

'Hadn't you heard, Mrs Braithwaite? We've already set a date for the wedding,' Charlotte said, as they fell in step up the floodlit driveway of All in the Mind.

Iris gave her a reproachful glance. 'Yes, I had heard talk, but not having seen hide nor hair of an invitation I dismissed it as nothing more than idle gossip.'

'Alex, you surely didn't forget Mrs Braithwaite's invitation?'

'Silly me,' he said, squeezing Charlotte's hand. 'I must say, I'm surprised to see you here tonight,' he said to Iris. 'You're not exactly one of Derek's greatest fans, are you?'

'I'm here in an official capacity. In a small community such as ours it pays to keep one's finger on the pulse.' And coming to Derek and Cindy's front door she raised her hand and gave the bell a long, hard prod.

Tiffany greeted them.

'Love the dress,' Charlotte said, kissing Tiffany. 'Very vampish.'

Tiffany smiled, one hand fiddling with a wispy tendril of hair hanging in front of her right ear and the other playing with a black velvet choker at her throat.

'You'll catch your death of cold, young lady,' declared Iris, casting a disapproving eye over Tiffany's *décolletage*. It was encouragement enough for Tiffany to lower both her hands and push out her chest.

'Attagirl,' whispered Alex, coming forward to kiss her. 'Take no notice, you look great – especially without the Doc Martens.'

'I'm into glamour these days,' she purred provocatively, and kicked him with an elegant black suede shoe with a three-inch heel. 'Give me your coats and I'll throw them on the bed upstairs.'

'You'll do no such thing with mine,' Iris said. 'I've had this coat since nineteen fifty-seven.'

'Too late to give it back to the poor animal who lost it in the first place, then.'

'I beg your pardon, young lady. I'll have it—'

'Stuffed?' said Tiffany, under her breath.

'Hung up, if you don't mind.'

'Go through and help yourselves to a drink,' Tiffany said to Charlotte and Alex. 'Barry's here somewhere. He's come home for the weekend specially for Dad's big night.'

The sitting-room was packed and guests had spilled out into the conservatory. Both rooms were decorated with navy blue and gold swags with matching balloons with the words All in the Mind printed on them. Music was playing but was only just discernible above the noisy hubbub of voices.

'There's Dad,' Charlotte said straight away, seeing her father standing alone. He was giving all his interest to a large ornately framed photographic portrait of the Rogers family. She and Alex grabbed a couple of glasses of champagne from a passing waiter and headed over towards Neville.

'Charlotte. You've rescued me at last. What took you so long? I've been waiting ages for you. You know how I hate parties.'

'I'm partly to blame,' Alex said. 'Mrs Braithwaite caught us kissing.'

'Not enough of it going on, in my opinion.' Neville laughed.

'Not enough of what going on?'

'Kissing,' Charlotte said with a wink, making room for Derek to join them. He was dressed in cream trousers with a dark navy-blue T-shirt with the words All in the Mind scrolled across his chest in gold letters.

'You really must stop all this sexual harassment, Charlotte. After all, I am a married man.'

'And since when has that ever stopped you?' Cindy said, coming over with a tray of bite-sized vol-au-vents. She, too, was wearing cream trousers and a top just like Derek's.

'So how are all the alterations going?' Alex asked.

'Fine, just fine,' Derek answered. 'The only job pending is to repaint the outside of the house. I know you'll all be disappointed, but I'm afraid it's time to say goodbye to Windolene Cottage. Anyway, how do you like the T-shirts? Good bit of advertising, eh? I'm thinking of selling them to the punters ... I mean, clients.'

'I feel like having one with Losing my Mind on it,' Cindy muttered.

'Hey! I like that.' Derek laughed. 'Catchy slogan, "Losing your mind? Then come to All in the Mind". You're a genius, Cindy. Perhaps we could get it put to music and have it as a jingle on local radio.'

Cindy groaned – he was probably serious.

'Well, I think we ought to drink to your new venture,' Charlotte said, raising her glass. 'To All in the Mind. May it be all in the bank as well.'

'Oh, Charlotte,' Derek said, shaking his head. 'No, no, no. This isn't about making money. This is a window of opportunity to save lost souls.'

'I thought that was my department,' Malcolm Jackson called over, from where he was talking to Louise.

Derek grinned. 'The ones we can't help I promise to send on to you.'

'Very generous of you,' Malcolm said. 'Any chance of a repeat perform-ance of Barry's confirmation party tonight? Music's a bit on the dull side so far.'

Cindy looked away guiltily. As a precautionary measure she had hidden some of Derek's favourite CDs, knowing what the outcome of the evening would be if he and Malcolm got together over Meatloaf's *Bat Out of Hell*. She had never forgotten the sight of Derek and Barry singing together at his confirmation party over a year ago. She had been moved to tears that it had taken eighteen years for father and son to reach a point where they could enjoy each other's company.

'Hey up, Cindy's off in a dream,' Derek quipped.

'I'm sorry,' she said quickly, 'I was thinking of Barry.'

'Where is he?' Charlotte asked. 'Tiffany said he was home for the weekend.'

'He was just finishing off some work the last time I saw him,' Cindy answered.

'Nothing changes, then,' Alex said.

'*Au contraire*,' Derek said enigmatically. He pointed to his chest. '*Au contraire.*'

Hilary wanted to go home. She'd had enough of listening to David talking about the state of the property market. But, most of all, she'd had enough of watching David lie his great big fat head off. He was a liar, a cheat, a betrayer of trust, a complete and utter double-crosser – all the right credentials, some might say, for a good estate agent.

Disconsolately she wandered away from David, who didn't even notice she'd gone – he merely closed up the gap she'd created by moving one step to the right within the circle and waving his arms about more expansively as he spoke.

'You look glum.'

Automatically she forced a smile to her lips, even before she'd registered who was talking to her. It was Nick Bradshaw and, like Derek and Cindy, he was wearing one of the specially designed T-shirts. She decided, though, that she liked him better in a polo-neck sweater and jacket.

'How did you enjoy hearing about Florida in such detail the other night?' she asked, finding herself slipping into conversation with him more easily than she had previously.

'I feel like I've been there,' he answered.

'Me too. Many times.'

'Tell me, Hilary, you were almost tempted, weren't you, to have a drink with me after the class?'

How arrogant of him. 'Not for a single moment,' she replied.

As she'd walked home afterwards she'd asked herself the question over and over again: Why not? Why not go to the pub with him for a drink? If he'd been a woman she wouldn't have thought twice about going home to David and saying she'd been for a drink with one of the girls from the group.

'I wouldn't have tried anything, if that's what you were worried about.'

'Well, of course, you wouldn't,' she said quickly, 'I know that.'

He stared at her. 'Why?'

'Why what?'

He smiled. 'Why are you so sure I wouldn't make a pass at you?'

'Because . . . because you just wouldn't, not with somebody like me. Men make passes at women like my sister Charlotte. Look, there she is, over by the fireplace talking to Derek, and that's Alex next to her. They're getting married next month.'

'She's an attractive woman,' Nick said, glancing across the room. He turned his attention back to Hilary. 'And would I be right in thinking that you're the younger sister?'

Hilary frowned. 'Yes, but what's that got to do with anything?'

'Quite a lot I should think. When was the last time you read *The Ugly Duckling* to Becky?'

She opened her mouth to reply, then snapped it shut.

'Think about it, Hilary.'

'Stop teasing me,' she said, in a small voice.

'I'm not, I assure you.'

A loud laugh coming from David made Hilary frown again. Anger flared within her.

'Your husband's enjoying himself tonight,' Nick said, watching her closely.

'And why shouldn't he?' she said crossly.

'More to the point, why aren't you?'

'Says who?'

'Hilary, how long do you think you can live like this?'

She stared at him, suddenly scared. 'Like what?' she asked, hesitantly.

'Pretending. Pretending that whatever it is in your life causing you pain isn't happening.'

'Heavens, Mr Bradshaw. Whatever makes you say something as ridiculous as that?'

'Don't Mr Bradshaw me, Hilary. Just stop lying, not only to other people but to yourself. Face up to what David is doing to you.'

Hilary felt sick. The noise of so many voices, together with the sound of the Gypsy Kings, began to pound inside her head. In front of her Nick's face filled her vision and she swayed slightly. She felt his hand on her arm. She jerked away. 'I need to check on my children,' she said, pushing past him.

When she was outside she breathed in deeply, wanting the icy air to cut through her, wanting everything that was hurting inside her to be cut clean away.

'You okay?'

Damn. It was him. 'Yes,' she lied, and started to walk away from the house. But she heard his footsteps coming up behind her. She had no idea what to say, so she said nothing and let him follow her across the road to The Gables.

The children were both fast asleep and when she came downstairs she found Nick in the kitchen. He handed her a glass of water. She took it gratefully and sat down. 'Must have been all that champagne,' she said, avoiding his eyes. 'It suddenly made me feel sick.'

'How long has this been going on?'

She gripped the glass in her hands, unable to speak.

He sat down opposite her. 'Hilary, I'm pushing you, I know. Something tells me that things are not right between you and David and it won't be long before everyone else starts noticing it. And what will you do then?'

She ignored his question.

'Look,' he carried on, 'people don't have to go around in pain, and that includes you. If you had a broken arm and I was a doctor you'd let me help you, wouldn't you?'

She nodded.

'You've potentially got a broken marriage on your hands, so why not let me help you?'

'I have nothing of the sort,' she said adamantly. Broken marriage – how awful that sounded, how statistical! 'And how dare you suggest David doesn't love me? Why on earth wouldn't he? Now please—'

'I didn't say that, Hilary.'

'Oh, stop it, stop it! You're too clever for me. You're trying to trip me up. All these ghastly word games I keep getting caught up in. If you want to help, just leave me alone and stop trying to make me say things I don't mean.'

A few minutes later she heard the front door close quietly.

'Oh, come off it. What harm is he doing?'

'Muffin 'ell, Dad! You've got to be joking.' Tiffany looked around the group for support. Charlotte was the first to speak.

'Tiffany's right,' she said. 'Ted's gone too far.'

Derek laughed. 'Didn't have you down as a prude, Charlotte.'

'Far from it,' added David, tottering towards Charlotte.

She pushed him away in disgust, thinking how pathetic he was at that moment, her drunk, adulterous brother-in-law.

'And you, Mr Hamilton,' Iris said, poking Alex's shoulder with her finger. 'Where do you stand on this issue? Should we, in your opinion, be subjected to this filth Mr Cooper seems intent on peddling right here under our noses?'

Alex took a long, deliberate sip of his wine. 'No,' he said at last, 'no, I don't believe we should, I think—'

'Thank you, Mr Hamilton,' Iris said, pleased, and turning her attention to Derek, she said, 'I think you'll find yourself outnumbered, Mr Rogers.'

'How about we widen the net?' Derek said.

'Certainly,' Iris replied, sure of her ground.

Derek went out to the conservatory and asked Nick and Rosie to join them.

'Now, Nick,' he said genially, his hand on Nick's shoulder, 'you're a man of the world, liberal and broad-minded, wouldn't you say?'

'I'd like to think so, yes.'

'Now I know you don't live here in Hulme Welford, but I'm sure you're aware of some ill-feeling in the village regarding our local newsagent selling something a little more exotic than the usual newspapers and sweets.' He gave his nose a tap and added, 'And I'm not talking mangoes, Nick.'

Nick ran his hand over his chin and looked at the expectant faces all around him. 'All things considered, I don't think it's appropriate for a village newsagent to be selling the things Ted Cooper is.' Then, shrugging his shoulders, he went on, 'Call me old-fashioned, but if I wanted to go and buy some seductive lingerie for a special person, then I'd rather go to a shop which specialises in such things, not a paper shop run by a man who doesn't know a camisole top from a filter-tip cigarette.'

'I've heard all I need to hear,' Iris announced, allowing herself a small triumphant smile. 'I congratulate you, Mr Rogers, on your choice of personnel. Mr Bradshaw has a refined quality about him which I admire and I would strongly recommend you to take note of it.' She acknowledged Nick with a nod, then turned away and went in search of something to eat.

'Hear, hear!' laughed Tiffany. She was delighted with Nick's response to her father and offered Nick one of her most beguiling smiles. Charlotte nudged Alex and whispered, 'I think you've just been usurped.'

'I don't agree with you, Nick,' Rosie Williams said serenely, her long fingers steepled together in front of her, just below her nose, as though deep in an act of worship. 'What are you all afraid of?' she asked, facing them all, one by one. 'Why are you so hung up about sex, because that's what this is about, isn't it?'

'I agree,' said Derek. 'Our old friend sex, once again, pulling back its foreskin and penetrating the bashful.' Everyone cringed at this graphic metaphor, but undeterred, Derek carried on. 'Sex,' he said loudly, 'the Englishman's—'

'Achilles' heel?' suggested Rosie, helpfully.

'Cock-up!' finished Derek.

They laughed but all fell silent when Iris rejoined the group with a plate of food. In the ensuing quiet a voice said, 'Hilary likes underwear.'

Surprised, they all looked at David, who seemed to stagger under the sudden focus of attention.

'She's got drawers full of the stuff. She thinks I don't know. She buys it and then hides it. What do you make of that?' His eyes swept round the hushed and embarrassed group. When he saw Nick Bradshaw he repeated the question. 'What do you make of that, then?'

'I think you've had too much to drink,' Nick said politely.

'No, I haven't,' David answered, his voice slightly raised. 'Now answer my question, Mr Damn-Know-It-All-Psycho . . . Psycho-bloody-Expert.'

'Come on, David,' Charlotte urged. 'Leave it be and go home before you make a fool of yourself.'

He shrugged her hand away from his arm and moved nearer to Nick.

Derek tried to intervene. 'Let me get you another drink, old mate. Come out to the kitchen.'

'Another drink, I should think *not*!' declared Iris. 'He should be horsewhipped for his appalling behaviour, besmirching his wife's good name in public.'

'I want an answer,' David demanded, continuing to hold his ground.

'Okay,' Nick said calmly. 'Perhaps your wife feels the need to fill a void created by someone she loves.' He met David's angry gaze and didn't flinch, not until David landed a fist in his jaw and sent him sprawling across the room.

18

Hilary gave the visiting curate from Knutsford a cursory glance then ran her tongue over the top row of her teeth. She had been up early this morning after waking from one of her recurring dreams – the teeth dream. Ever since she'd sat her O-level exams and in subsequent periods of stress she'd had the same dream of her teeth crumbling and falling out. Apparently it was a sure sign of anxiety.

Last night she hadn't bothered going back to the party after Nick had left The Gables, and, convinced that David wouldn't even miss her, she had gone upstairs to bed. He'd come home just over an hour later and when he'd flopped on to the bed fully dressed she had pretended to be asleep. He had fallen into a heavy stupor almost immediately, leaving her wide awake and thinking what nonsense the phrase 'no peace for the wicked' was.

She had left him half an hour ago, still asleep but now under the duvet. The children had been in one of their lazy moods and, feeling the need to be alone, she had willingly left them with a video to watch and made her escape to St John's.

'And now let us confess our sins to Almighty God,' the visiting curate said, his arms outstretched and his voice resonating with a touch too much of the dramatics. Hilary lowered her head along with the rest of the congregation. But I haven't sinned, she thought, lifting her head. I haven't done anything wrong. It's David who's sinning like mad. Indignation bit deep as she stared at the robed man in front of her. How dare this silly young curate with his newly acquired theological-school piety tell her how bad she was. If he wanted a real sinner he should go and knock David up and make him confess. Why was it always the innocent who were called to ask for forgiveness?

To the right of the curate in the choir stalls, Hilary noticed Iris Braithwaite. She had one beady eye open and it was directed at Hilary. Hilary bent her head and snapped her own eyes shut, blocking out that dreadful face; not so much the beady eye but the shocking and improbable smile the woman had just given her – shocking because Hilary recognised it as a smile of sympathy. Did it mean . . . that Mrs Braithwaite knew about David's affair?

Had Charlotte told her? Surely not. Cindy, then? Even more unlikely.

Perhaps David and Catherine had been seen together and the pot of gossip was already beginning to bubble.

Oh, God! she started to pray, don't let everyone start talking about me. I'm sorry if I've ever gossiped in the past. Sorry that I might have said the odd unkind word about anyone. I'll never do it again. Just please don't let people talk about me – give them somebody else to gossip about.

Audience participation had never gone down well at St John's and this morning was no exception. The inexperienced curate had now taken up residence in the pulpit and was on to his sermon, and it was falling flat. Hilary felt almost sorry for the man. Perhaps over in Knutsford this kind of thing went down well, but here in Hulme Welford they didn't take kindly to being asked daft questions. One or two rebel members of the congregation were deliberately calling out the wrong answers. What awful stories would go back to Knutsford, she wondered. That they were all as thick as two short planks in Hulme Welford? Undaunted, he continued to take them by the hand through Isaiah's condemnation of sin, fully determined to get his message across.

'Would anyone care to share with us,' the curate offered up, his eyes scanning the congregation, 'what they think the great prophet would have said if he had been approached by one of his contemporaries and asked, "What's the matter, Isaiah?"'

'That's obvious,' somebody called out from the back.

The curate's relief was obvious too, that somebody was actually listening to him. 'Yes?' he said eagerly.

'He'd say, one eye's higher than the other! Boom, boom!'

Guffaws of laughter reverberated around the church and even the young man in the pulpit had the grace to concede a small smile. If he had started out that morning believing himself to be of the Laurence Olivier school of liturgy he was now heading for the club circuit, where he'd be lucky to finish his act.

But, true to his profession, he carried on valiantly. 'Don't think for one moment that I'm scaremongering,' he said, beginning to raise his voice and alerting everyone to the fact that that was exactly his intention, 'but there's real evil going on out there. We live in a fallen world. Society is falling apart. Businesses are falling apart. Marriages are—'

Stop! Hilary wanted to shout back. Stop it. I don't want to hear any of this. Don't you understand, you silly fool of a man, we don't want to hear this kind of thing. Hulme Welford's a nice place in which to live. We lead nice, comfortable lives where not very much happens. We don't want people like you coming here and telling us how awful the rest of the world is. Leave us alone. I want to be happy. I don't want to be miserable and dream of my teeth falling out.

'I sense real pain here in this church,' the curate said, theatrically, at the same time pointing his finger round the congregation.

'Yes, and I'm looking at it right now,' someone muttered behind Hilary.

*

Over coffee it seemed that part of Hilary's prayers had been answered. Almost everybody was talking about the sermon they'd just been forced to endure and agreeing that Malcolm Jackson had had no business going away to visit his elderly mother in Lincolnshire without checking the suitability of his locum.

Reluctant to go home, Hilary busied herself with collecting stray pew bibles.

'There you are, Hilary,' her mother said, handing her a bible. 'Wasn't that just the most banal sermon you've ever heard? How's David after last night?'

'What do you mean?' Hilary said warily.

Louise smiled. 'Exactly what I said.'

'He was asleep when I left him.'

'I bet he was. Sleeping it off, more like it.'

'Are you trying to tell me something, Mother?'

'I hope you gave him hell and didn't fuss over him with any sympathy.'

'Sympathy?' she repeated. 'Whatever for?' There were times when Hilary felt sure that Louise lived in a different world.

'Come on, Hilary, loyalty only needs to go so far. It's very admirable that you should want to stand by your husband, especially after the things he said about you, but so many people heard and saw what he did last night that you're going to have to face up to what happened.'

'Mother, I have no idea what you're talking about. I left the party early. Just what did David—'

'Don't start bleating, Hilary,' Louise said, deciding that her daughter really didn't have a clue what she was referring to. 'David hit somebody last night. To the ground, in fact.'

'I don't believe you,' Hilary said, astonished.

'Close your mouth, Hilary, or we'll all fall in. If you don't believe me, ask your sister. She'll tell you exactly what we all saw with our very own eyes. David punched a man to the floor, right there in front of everyone.'

'Who?'

'That new fellow, just started at Derek and Cindy's—'

'Nick Bradshaw?'

'Yes. That's right. You know him, then?'

Something in Louise's voice made Hilary feel guilty. Ridiculous. She had nothing to feel guilty about. 'He's in my French class,' she said. 'But why did David hit him?'

'I rather think David had enjoyed too much of Derek and Cindy's champagne and started talking. Well, more like shooting his mouth off, really. You know the way he is when he's had too much to drink.'

'Can you get to the point, Mother?'

'Okay, seeing as you've asked. But I'm warning you, you won't like it. David said something about you of rather an intimate nature and then asked Nick whatever-his-name-is to comment. He wouldn't – obviously more of a gentleman than your David – and that seemed to make David fly off the handle and he forced Nick to answer his question. When Nick did, David punched him in the face.' Louise laughed. 'You've got to hand it to Derek. Whenever he's at a party something always happens. Remember at your welcome home party for Charlotte and how drunk—'

'What did he say?' Hilary demanded, more concerned with what David had said about her than her mother's admiration for Derek's effect on any social gathering.

'What? When Nick was lying on the floor?'

'No. About me?'

Louise tried her best to keep a straight face. 'Something about you having a penchant for drawers full of lingerie.'

Hilary's face coloured. How could he! 'So what did Nick say that made David hit him?'

'David wanted this penchant of yours psychoanalysed by Nick. He refused at first. Then, when pushed, and you know how pushy David can be at the end of a good evening, he said that maybe you were filling a void created by someone you loved.'

'What rubbish!'

'If you say so, Hilary. By the way, is it possible David's suffering from some sort of stress? It might explain his bizarre behaviour. Maybe you should book him into All in the Mind. Leave that little thought with you. Must dash. See you.'

Stress! What a joke, thought Hilary, watching her mother hurry away to shake hands with the curate.

'Mother looks as if she'd like to take him by the scruff of the neck, doesn't she?'

'Charlotte!' Hilary exclaimed, seeing her sister at her side. 'Don't say anything to me, just take me back to Ivy Cottage, please. I don't want to go home today. I've had enough.'

Outside St John's the cold air hit them full in the face and, buttoning their coats, Charlotte, Alex and Hilary walked in silence down the gravel path, through the lych-gate and out on to the main road. There they caught up with Iris Braithwaite, who was staring straight ahead of her and clutching her handbag as though it were a shield.

Charlotte followed her gaze. 'What on earth's going on?'

The main street of the village was lined on both sides with cars parked bumper to bumper, and outside Ted the Toup's was a queue of men waiting to go in.

'Armageddon,' replied Iris, her face like thunder. 'I warned you.'

They crossed the road, Iris leading the way. She accosted a youth just getting out of a rust-pocked Ford Fiesta. He wore a cap back to front and a thick unbuttoned check shirt over a T-shirt with the words *Stay Cool* written on it. He gave Iris a scornful look and said, 'You'll catch myxomatosis in that fur coat.'

'I beg—'

'Forget it,' he answered, and sauntered away to join the queue outside Ted's.

Hilary and Alex went over and peered inside the shop. It was full and Ted was up to his armpits in red and black lace. Hilary thought of what her mother had just told her and turned away.

'Come on, Mrs Braithwaite,' Charlotte said, when Alex and Hilary came back. 'Let's go home.'

'Outrageous. Outrageous. I shall personally see that that disgusting Ted Cooper is hounded out of the village.'

They left Iris marching up her own drive and walked on to Ivy Cottage, where they were greeted by Mabel as Charlotte let them in through the conservatory.

'Go into the sitting-room, Hilary,' Charlotte said. 'We banked the fire up before we went out and it should be nice and warm in there for you.'

When they were alone Alex turned to Charlotte. 'What's wrong with Hilary?' he whispered. 'She's not herself at all.'

'It's nothing,' she said, remembering her promise to Hilary.

'Charlotte?'

Oh, what was the point? The way things were going it wouldn't be long before others found out what was happening. And who knows, Alex might be able to help.

'It's David,' she replied. 'He's having an affair with his secretary.'

'Bloody hell! Since when?'

'I haven't a clue,' she said, shaking her head. 'And I doubt whether Hilary has either. So far David doesn't know that Hilary has sussed him. She thinks if she stays quiet she'll ride out the storm while David comes to his senses and gets over his mid-life crisis, or whatever it is that makes a man jeopardise everything he once held precious.'

'But that takes all the coolness and determination of . . .'

'Of somebody like Cindy,' Charlotte said, reaching into the fridge for a bottle of wine. 'That's why Hilary's in the mess she is. She's too impulsive to play the hard, confident wife willing to preserve her marriage.' She took three glasses from the cupboard and handed Alex the bottle of wine. 'Come on,' she said, 'I'm going to get my sister to loosen up and then hopefully talk some sense into her.'

'What about David? Won't he wonder where Hilary is?'

'Stuff David! Let him wonder.'

19

As Georgia drove along Acacia Lane she thought how it was that a good cause never failed to bond a group of people together, even the most diverse characters. In her experience it was usually a transient yoke of loyalty but one that was guaranteed to bring out the gung-ho spirit in all concerned.

'You sure we've got enough stuff?'

'Plenty,' Georgia answered, looking at Tiffany in the mirror. Next to Tiffany was Chloe, her small face hidden by a balaclava and on whose lap was a large cardboard box with the lid firmly down. Georgia hadn't questioned her daughter on the contents of the box as they'd rushed out of the house after Iris's call, but she'd noticed when locking the back door that the cat-litter tray was suspiciously empty. Tiffany's box, on the other hand, had a far less sinister look about it and contained an innocent collection of hair products.

In the front passenger seat, as rigid as a corpse, and about as white, was Iris Braithwaite, nursing a box of the remains of a Chinese takeaway from Georgia and Chloe's supper last night, half a dozen eggs, some overripe tomatoes along with what Iris had personally contributed, a quantity of rotting vegetable peelings. It was to be real chemical warfare.

They hadn't had much time to put together their weapons – Iris had only called her fifteen minutes ago.

'Ms D'Arcy,' she'd commanded down the phone, 'I would greatly value your assistance. Now!'

Chloe had jumped at the chance to join in with the action. 'Time to nuke the oppressors!' she'd shouted, climbing into the Jeep. They'd left Gordon holding the fort with a bemused look on his face.

It was while they were parked outside Iris's house that Tiffany had appeared. Tiffany had babysat once or twice for Georgia on the few occasions Winnie had been busy and, seeing her coming out of the drive of All in the Mind, Chloe had leaned out of the window and waved to her, shouting, 'We're going to have some fun down at Ted the Toup's. Want to come?'

They turned right at the end of Acacia Lane and drove along the main street of the village. Georgia could see a small line of parked cars and a tall thin man standing outside the newsagent's. She felt a rush of adrenaline.

'There's one!' shrieked Chloe. 'Open the sun roof, Mum, quick.'

Georgia slid back the glass panel. 'Ready everybody?' she said, smiling. 'How about you, Iris?'

'Ready,' the older woman replied. 'Let's not defer a moment longer.'

Both Tiffany and Chloe were already preparing to take aim, and as Georgia slowed the Jeep, the first dollop of grey, clinging ammunition was fired through the air. It caught a man full in the face just as he was coming out of the shop. His stunned pebble-dashed expression was only clearly revealed when he wiped away the sticky stones. He looked upwards, as if expecting to see a bird of enormous proportions flying overhead. The tall thin man next to him started to laugh until he caught a chest-load of shrapnel. In disbelief he, too, lifted his head skywards.

Chloe squealed excitedly, exposing her ten-year-old self in a rare moment of giddy delight.

'Talk about thick,' Tiffany shouted, aiming a plastic bottle of shampoo and firing out globs of orange gunk. Even she was surprised at what an effective cannon she had in her hands. She squeezed again on the bottle and a large jelly-like blob landed exquisitely on the crown of a bald-headed victim also standing in the doorway of the shop.

Seeing that Ted's customers had now found the source of the missiles, Georgia pushed her foot down hard on the accelerator and sped off to the other end of the village. They hovered outside Patricia Longton's double-fronted cottage.

'Close that box, Chloe!' shouted Georgia. 'The smell's disgusting.'

'An inspired idea, though,' Iris said in congratulation, turning round to Chloe, whose eyes were shining brilliantly through the holes in her balaclava.

'It's your turn now, Mrs Braithwaite,' Chloe said. 'You'll get them from your side of the car as we go past.'

'Ready for round two?' asked Georgia, revving the engine.

'Drive on,' instructed Iris, pulling on a pair of rubber gloves and delving into the box on her lap.

Still dusting themselves down, the three men didn't hear the sound of the approaching Jeep, not until it was once again alongside them, broadside fashion, with what looked like Queen Boadicea leaning out of the passenger window firing off a round of beansprouts and chewed spare ribs. Slimy, curled-up potato peelings that had taken on the appearance of slugs followed, hotly pursued by eggs which Tiffany hurled, yelling, 'Surface-to-air missiles.'

'Myxomatosis, indeed,' Iris called, taking aim with a tomato.

Georgia reckoned that the onslaught had by now girded the collective loins of their victims, so she pressed on the accelerator pedal again, but the engine stalled. 'Shit!' She turned the key. Nothing. She caught the expression on Iris's face beside her and the sound of angry voices from the pavement. She tried the key again, promising the Jeep unswerving loyalty in the future if only it would start. It did, and as the engine roared into life, she gripped the steering wheel and pushed her foot to the floor. They rocketed away, just as the group of men began to move towards them. Georgia gave them a glance in her mirror and grinned at the sight of the man – the one who had been the first on the receiving end of the ballistic cat litter – losing his balance on the mucus-like mixture of shampoo and raw eggs. She watched him land on his backside with a bump.

The bald man with the skullcap of protein-enriched shampoo was now also sporting a medal of beansprouts on his right shoulder. He threw his hands in the air. 'Sodding hell! I only came here for a present for my wife.' Bewildered, he wiped away the beansprouts and wandered back to the safety of his car. He'd stick to catalogues in the future, he decided, less bother that way.

At the nursery, Georgia brought the Jeep to an exhilarating halt, sending up a cloud of dust behind them.

'Mission accomplished,' she said, snatching on the handbrake.

'I'll say it is,' agreed Tiffany, grinning broadly and pulling off one of her father's skiing hats.

'Iris?' Georgia asked cautiously. 'You okay?'

The older woman was staring straight ahead through the windscreen. She was motionless and still bearing the same cadaverous pallor she had worn earlier. The only colour in her face came from her eyes, which were as dark and as shiny as those of a bird.

'Iris?'

She turned to face Georgia. 'I heard you the first time,' she said, carefully peeling off her rubber gloves as though they were expensive kid leather.

'I need to wash my hands,' Chloe said, opening the door and getting out.

'I bet you do,' Georgia said, cuffing her daughter lightly round the ears. 'Take Mrs Braithwaite and Tiffany over to the house while I check that Gordon's okay. I'll be with you in a minute.'

Chloe led the way, and once she'd washed her hands, she went outside leaving Tiffany and Iris alone.

Tiffany threw herself on to the sofa and fiddled with the fringe of the throw-over on it. She watched Iris Braithwaite, who was standing perfectly still at the window, and began to wonder how she had ended up spending part of her Sunday afternoon lobbing rubbish out of a sun-roof with, of all people, old Ma Braithwaite. She herself was a known trouble-maker in the village, but what the hell would people start saying about Mrs Braithwaite when they found out that she had been part of the attack on Ted the Toup's shop?

'Gordon seems to have managed pretty well without me,' Georgia said, joining them. 'Won't you sit down, Iris?'

Iris threw a disdainful look at the only free chair with its threadbare arms and collection of brightly coloured cushions. She remained standing. She was still deathly pale.

'You okay?' Georgia asked, concerned. Since her afternoon-tea session with Iris some days ago she had surprised herself at how often she had thought of her, surprised, too, that she found herself caring about Iris. Sure, she was nosy, bossy, interfering and as dogmatic as hell, but the old girl had spirit in spades, which was more than you could say for most of the people in Hulme Welford. It amused her to know that she felt a curious sense of empathy with Iris. She hadn't yet worked out why. 'No regrets, I hope?'

The loose skin under Iris's chin wobbled, reminding Georgia of a turkey, and suddenly laughter filled the room. 'Good Lord, why on earth would I regret anything? I've just had the time of my life!'

'I wondered if you thought we'd gone too far,' Georgia replied, relieved. How could she have doubted Iris's nerve?

'Too far? We've barely begun. Our cause has a long way to go yet, young lady, if we're to beat our old enemy Beelzebub. St Paul himself told Timothy that they had to fight the good fight.'

'Good for you,' Georgia said, not sure that she wanted the likes of St Paul brought into it – he'd had some pretty weird ideas about the role of women. 'I can see you would have been one of the first to have been tied to the railings.'

'That's as may be, but I certainly would not have been so stupid as to throw myself under a galloping horse.'

'I wouldn't half mind pushing Ted the Toup under one, though,' Tiffany said, with a giggle.

Ted pulled at the blind on the shop door. He was knackered, like he'd just been knocked flat and run over by a steamroller. The shop had never been so busy. Stroke of luck, that publicity in the paper – it had attracted no end of people. A shame he hadn't had enough stock. Thongs were obviously the thing and he'd looked bloody stupid turning all those customers away empty-handed.

And as for that trouble outside, well, he knew who was behind that. Stupid old woman. Just what was wrong in selling some saucy kit anyway? Plenty of the usual customers had been in and made a few purchases during the week, like that Mr Longton. He'd come in yesterday to pay his paper bill and had left with a nice pair of knickers for his wife.

Providing a service, that was what he was doing.

He opened the till and began to count that day's takings.

20

Charlotte was surprised at the depth of contempt she felt for David as he stood at the door. She had always got on well with her brother-in-law. In fact, there had been times in the past when they had turned to each other for help, especially when Hilary had what David would call 'one on her'.

'I'm sorry,' she said, standing two steps higher than David, her arms folded in front of her – an assertiveness technique Peter had learned on one of his many management courses and had come home and tried on her. 'Hilary's lying down. She's probably asleep by now.'

'But why?'

'I told you, she's got a headache.'

'Yes, but why here? Why didn't she come home and go to bed?'

Charlotte gave an exaggerated roll of her eyes. 'Come off it, David. You know jolly well you and the children wouldn't have given her a moment's peace. As soon as she'd walked through the door it would have been, "What time's lunch?" "Where are my football boots?" '

'Odd,' he grunted. 'Bloody odd I call it when a wife doesn't come home from church and goes to bed in another person's house. How do I know she's even here? She's been acting pretty strangely these past few weeks.'

Charlotte tried to lighten the mood with a laugh. 'So I'm just another person, am I?'

He scraped at some loose paint on the door frame with his fingernail. 'I should have known you moving back here would mean trouble.'

Again she laughed. 'You know what sisters are like.' She started to close the door. 'I'll let her home when I'm convinced she's fully rested. In the meantime, why not make some lunch for you and the children? I expect they're hungry by now.' She closed the door and listened to the sound of David's angry footsteps fading away.

'Was he very annoyed?' Hilary asked, when Charlotte returned to the sitting-room.

'Not really, just confused. I told him to go home and make some lunch.'

'Talking of which,' Alex said, 'I'll do us some omelettes, shall I?'

'I couldn't eat a thing,' Hilary said morosely, staring into the fire.

'Nonsense,' Charlotte threw back, knowing at once how like her sister she was sounding – not the poor confused version sitting before her now but the

297

strident, bossy Hilary, who had always turned any monumental crisis into an everyday occurrence with a hearty let's-roll-up-our-sleeves attitude. She would have been great in the war.

Alex laid a gentle hand on Hilary's arm. 'You'll feel better for some food inside you.'

They watched him leave the room. With tears in her eyes, Hilary said, 'You *will* marry him, won't you, Charlotte?'

Charlotte came and sat on the floor in front of Hilary's chair. 'Of course I will. You know as well as I do, the wheels are already in motion for our big day.'

'But you might get cold feet between now and then.'

Charlotte thought back to her wedding day with Peter, remembering how she had stood at the altar fighting against the nagging doubt that she shouldn't have been there. She shook her head. 'No cold feet this time.'

Hilary lifted her eyes. 'This time,' she repeated. 'What do you mean?'

'Oh, Hilary, it's a long story, and one I'll save for another day. Talk to me about David.'

'How's the dress coming on?'

Charlotte could have shouted at her sister for her persistent prevarication, but she knew it would get her nowhere. Right now, bullying was not the answer. She would have to cajole her. She reached for the bottle of wine and refilled Hilary's glass, inwardly cringing at the thought of Becky following her up the aisle on Christmas Eve. She must have been mad to have given in to her niece's pleading a few weeks ago. 'I've never been asked to be a bridesmaid before,' she'd said, 'please let me do it.' I'm not surprised, Charlotte had wanted to say. Who, in their right mind, would want to court disaster in such a deliberate fashion on such an important day? Goodness knows why, but she had finally said yes.

'It was good of Dad to suggest having the reception at their place,' Hilary said. 'I had no idea he was becoming such an expert in the kitchen.'

Charlotte frowned. And that was another act of reckless foolishness on her part. Who knows what on earth they'd get to eat? Dad might have developed a new hobby out of watching cookery programmes on the telly, but doing the buffet for her wedding reception was surely way beyond his capabilities. She suddenly smiled to herself – he'd never yet let her down, had he?

'David's not much cop in the kitchen,' Hilary said quietly. In the background they could hear Alex whistling to himself as he prepared their lunch. 'In fact, I don't think he's much cop at anything any more.'

'Oh, Hilary. This is all such a mess. What can we do to help you?'

'We?' Hilary repeated.

'I ... I told Alex just now when we were in the kitchen,' Charlotte confessed.

Hilary covered her face with her hands. She started to sob. 'Not *another* person who knows what a failure I am. I can't bear it. Oh, Charlotte, how could you?'

Charlotte let her sister cry.

'How could you? How could you?' Hilary repeated over and over, rocking herself backwards and forwards in the armchair. 'I don't want anyone to know. I feel so disloyal towards David. It's as though I'm telling tales out of school.'

'And where's David's loyalty in all of this?' Alex asked, coming back into the room with a large tray.

Charlotte stood up and took one of the plates and handed it to Hilary. 'Alex is right,' she said. 'Why should you be so hung up on being loyal when David clearly doesn't give a damn?'

Hilary gave a loud sniff and looked down at the omelette on her lap. She should have been at home cooking roast pork, roast potatoes, sage and onion stuffing, apple sauce, parsnip chips – David always had to have parsnips – she shouldn't be here at all. What were they doing over the road? How were they managing without her? Just what kind of a mother was she to let her family go without their Sunday lunch? And who was Charlotte to say whether David gave a damn or not? 'He does love me,' she said defiantly. 'I know he does.'

'You may well be right,' Alex said, sitting down next to Charlotte on the sofa, 'but the problem still remains. How are you going to cope with David loving you and perhaps thinking he loves another?'

She prodded uninterestedly at her omelette. 'I don't know, but if Cindy's managed it all her marriage, then so can I.'

'But you're not Cindy,' Charlotte said.

'Then maybe I should become more like her.'

'That,' Alex said softly, 'would be a great shame. For what would happen to the real Hilary?'

'Is he always like this?' Hilary asked Charlotte.

Her sister smiled. 'From the moment I met him. Don't you remember him bullying me round your dinner table that night?'

Hilary managed a smile, remembering vividly the time to which her sister was referring. 'I was so very proud and sure of myself that night . . . Now look at me.'

'You like to be in control, Hilary, don't you?' Alex said, unexpectedly.

'Yes,' she answered, not looking at him. 'I like to know what's happening, when and how. There's nothing wrong in that, is there?'

'Not at all. So, who at the moment would you say is in control? You or David?'

Hilary pushed her untouched meal away from her. She reached for the box of tissues. 'I . . . I don't know. And I don't know why that question should upset me so much.'

I do, thought Charlotte. All those years in her own empty marriage with Peter she had kidded herself that she was in control of her life. She had convinced herself that as long as she was in charge she could control the amount of pain she was experiencing. But it was all a lie. Peter had been the one in charge of her emotions. She had been at his mercy, waiting for him to pull on the strings of her heart – today would be an okay day, or today would be a day of despair. She had even stopped trusting her own judgement because she'd been so busy trying to control her surroundings in the belief that that would prevent anything from hurting her. She had lived like that for too long – lying to Peter, but worst of all, lying to herself. Just as Hilary was now doing and was prepared to go on doing for as long as it would take. 'Answer Alex's question, Hilary,' she said. 'Think hard and answer truthfully. Which one of you is in control?'

Hilary shook her head. 'David,' she said. 'Bloody David is and I hate him for it.' She bit her lip. 'No!' she cried out. 'I don't hate him. I love him. I do honestly. Oh, God, I sound quite mad.'

'Not mad,' Alex said, 'but hurt and confused.'

In the silence that followed, Charlotte got up and threw another log on the fire. The light outside was already fading. She switched on the lamps, casting the room in a gentle roseate glow, then drew the curtains.

Hilary watched her sister moving about. She felt like a young, cosseted child, sitting here in Charlotte's warm and comfortable sitting-room. Compared to The Gables it was a sanctuary of peace and quiet. Lucky Charlotte, she thought with envy, conscious that, for the first time in her married life, she wanted something her sister had.

Ever since she'd met David her world had revolved around his and while Charlotte had bounced from one precarious relationship to another, in her late teens and early twenties, she and David had lived in each other's pockets, planning with meticulous care each stage of their lives – careers, marriage and children. Everything had been so straightforward, so well controlled . . . until now. The rigid timetable that had given her such security and comfort had suddenly been taken away from her, and in contrast it was Charlotte who was now cocooned by love and the stability of a settled existence.

That's what I want, she whined to herself, in the voice Becky usually used when she wanted something her brother had.

Just after six o'clock there was a knock at the back door. It was Philip.

'I'm afraid your mum's still asleep,' Charlotte said, quite truthfully, for Hilary was indeed now asleep by the fire.

'Oh,' he said, disappointed.

'Did your father send you over?' she asked suspiciously.

Philip shook his head.

Charlotte was no expert when it came to children, but this one looked upset. 'You okay?'

He wobbled his head in no particular direction.

She wasn't sure how to proceed with her unsmiling nephew – a nephew with whom she had never really had much contact. And now here he was in her kitchen, a picture of misery. What was she to do? 'How's school?' she tried.

'Okay.' Philip knew the score. All grown-ups asked about school.

'Made many friends?'

'A few. There's Batesy. He's okay ...' But he didn't want to think of Batesy. 'Is Mum all right?'

'She's fine. She's just worn out,' Charlotte replied, genuinely surprised at the concern in Philip's voice. It showed in his eyes as well. 'She'll be home soon. Don't worry.'

He shrugged and turned away, his head bent and his feet dragging disconsolately.

Charlotte watched him go out into the dark. Poor Philip, she thought. She had never seen a more miserable-looking child.

21

Cindy missed the smell of In the Pink – shampoo and hair spray in the salon, water-treatment chemicals in the Jacuzzi, the combination of perspiration and deodorant in the gym, even the smell of towels in the tumble-dryer.

All in the Mind smelled of new carpets and barely dry paint, with the occasional waft of essential oils. Cindy had insisted they kept on their aromatherapist, and with Hazel now reinstalled in her newly decorated room, the familiar smell of lavender oil and rosemary acted as a welcome balm against the insanity of Derek's latest idea on this their opening day.

So far they had got off to a good start. The classes were fully booked, just as Derek had predicted. Even when Cindy had helped to fill out the booking forms for people to sign up for their chosen seminars she had refused to believe that All in the Mind could possibly work – now, of course, she consoled herself with the thought that it couldn't possibly last.

For the life of her she couldn't understand what made anyone want to sit in a room full of strangers and bare their souls. Why couldn't they simply learn to keep their mouths shut and be quiet about their problems? Constantly talking about the problem served no purpose, in her opinion. Worse still, she had come across those who had merely exploited the role of a counsellor and got their wrong-doings sanctioned by continuous rationalisation of their appalling behaviour.

Just as well she'd never found the need to go running off to some counsellor every time Derek had hurt her. If she'd done that she wouldn't have had time in her life to do anything else. Though what any counsellor would make of Derek was anybody's guess.

Sitting in the office, she started writing out a cheque for the exorbitant decorator's bill. She slipped the cheque into an envelope and sealed it up, then drummed her long fingernails on the desk and sighed.

She was bored. In the days of In the Pink her time had been crammed with appointments with her regular customers. Now she had nothing to do. So much for finding a niche, as Derek had claimed she would.

She got up from the desk and opened the door on to the corridor. All was quiet. Not a sound of a hair-dryer or the local radio station, not even the whirr of the washing machine. The place felt dead. She breathed in deeply, catching the smell of gloss paint. It reminded her of when she and Derek decorated their first salon. It was over in Northwich, a tiny box of a place squeezed in between a down-at-heel ironmonger's and a flower shop – Derek had always been next door buying her flowers from the old woman, whom he had said looked like the flower-seller in Trumpton. Their first day, all those years ago, had given them both such a thrill. Derek, with his Kevin Keegan hairstyle, had rushed about the salon chatting up the clients seeking customer loyalty, while she, too, had enjoyed herself achieving her ambition of running her own business. But she had been happy enough just seeing Derek so pleased with life.

So why wasn't she happy today, then? It was obvious to everyone that Derek was over the moon with their new venture, as Tiffany had pointed out at breakfast before she'd set off for school. 'Dad looks like he's died and gone to heaven,' she'd said.

'A man needs to be fulfilled to really know himself in order to be happy,' he'd said, his mouth poised over a croissant.

Typically Tiffany had laughed at her father and taken the croissant from his hand. But not so typically she'd squeezed Cindy's arm and said, 'Best of luck, I think you're going to need it.'

Cindy went back into the office. It wasn't luck she needed, it was something to do. And what was frightening her most was that she suspected she was no longer required. Had Derek done this deliberately? Had he planned to squeeze her out of the business ... and his life?

She went over to the bookcase beside the filing cabinet and idly read some of the titles of Derek's recently purchased books – *The Search for Self-Awareness*, *Journey into the Unknown* and lastly *Are You in Control?*. She picked this one off the shelf and started to flick through it.

'Hope you don't mind, Nick, old mate,' Derek said, coming into the largest of the seminar rooms. 'Just thought I'd sit in at the back and see how it all hangs together.'

The group of women looked up eagerly. They had been sufficiently encouraged with Nick to think the two-day course their managing director had sent them on wasn't going to be a total waste of time, and now they had the added bonus of a Phil Collins lookalike.

'I don't normally allow onlookers,' Nick said firmly. He was sitting in a chair in the gap of the horseshoe of occupied chairs around him, one leg crossed over the other, his hands clasped behind his head – he knew better than anyone how important body language was, and watching Derek stroll to the back of the room he could see quite plainly that his employer gave off an undisguised air of confidence.

'Shan't make a noise,' Derek said, smiling round at the group. 'Forget I ever came in.'

'We'd rather not,' one of the women said provocatively, and then laughed coarsely. Her personnel department colleagues joined in with her and instantly the atmosphere of the room turned into a girls' night out.

Derek smiled back at the ringleader, enjoying being the focus of attention at the same time as wanting to get his hands on her hair and tone down all those over-bleached highlights – he realised too late that he should have been looking for the woman within.

'So,' Nick said loudly, leaning forward and clapping his hands together sharply. Instantly the group was back with him. 'Reaching your full potential is what we're about this afternoon, as indeed we will be tomorrow. What I hope to show you is the unlearning of unconscious responses which you learned as children. By unlocking this particular door you'll discover just how much potential there is deep inside each and every one of you. This will be the first step to freeing yourselves of the mental as well as the physical stress we are all likely to experience at various stages in not only our working life but our private life. Everyone with me so far?'

The woman with the highlights looked over at Derek. 'Certainly am,' she said.

The phrase 'money for old rope' was dangerously close to the tip of Derek's tongue as he left Nick to wind up his mid-afternoon session, but the new Derek made him swallow this unworthy thought clean away.

He pushed open the office door, hoping to find Cindy, but there was no sign of her. He felt disappointed. He wanted to talk to her about how well the day was going. This therapy game was going to be easier than he'd thought. All those years he'd been messing about with the outside of people's heads when all the time the inside was a whole lot more straightforward. Why he hadn't cottoned on to the therapy industry before he didn't know.

He sat back in his chair and put his feet up on the desk. He had Bas to thank for this, of course. Good old Bas. A rush of fatherly pride crept over him. God, he was proud of Bas. Medical school. Just think of it, a son of his a doctor one day, maybe even a surgeon. And wasn't he practically in the medical world himself now? He smiled. No more feeling inferior to his son. Those days were gone. At last he was on an equal footing with Bas.

He looked at the diary planner on the wall and saw that Rosie was about to start her six-week seminar on 'Marriage, Sex and Happiness – They Needn't Be Incompatible'. He decided to go and have a nosy.

Rosie welcomed him with a broad smile, unlike Nick, Derek reflected. 'Mind if I sit in on this?' he asked.

'No free-wheelers,' she answered, crisply.

Derek wondered if she was as brusque in bed. 'Now, darling,' he mimicked in his head, 'left a bit . . . right a bit . . . Here, let me do it!'

'Mr Rogers?'

'Sorry,' he said. Not only was Rosie looking at him but so were her clients – a lacklustre group of two couples. 'Miles away,' he apologised again.

'If you stay, Mr Rogers, you'll have to join in with the session.'

'Oh . . . perhaps not, then.' He moved towards the door.

'Not frightened, are you?'

He recognised the challenge in her voice. 'Group sex? Nothing like it!' he shot back, and promptly sat next to a poker-thin woman in a flowery pinafore dress with eyes like gobstoppers. Her husband, the other side of her, was a Mr Comb-Over wearing a jumper that was home-made and looked far too small – to the point of asphyxiation. The old Derek thought they would both be better off for a damn good shop in Wilmslow to smarten themselves up and if that failed they should shoot each other and put everyone else out of their misery at having to look at them. But the new Derek considered how many sessions of positive stroking it would take to lick them into shape and give them both a new lease of life.

'Can we get on?' asked a large burly woman with nipples protruding like shuttlecocks through her turtle-neck sweater – she had more facial hair than Derek had ever seen in his entire career. 'Take the Braun to her!' Derek wanted to shout across the room. 'Somebody hold her down and I'll do it.' He tried hard to see her as a whole and complete person but all he could think of were those two enormous nipples and a beard which would have given ZZ Top a scare. 'We've already lost five minutes,' she continued, 'and I've come here expecting value for money because, since poor Alan's depression, we don't get out much.'

I'd have depression if Cindy had whiskers like that, thought Derek, contemplating *poor Alan* beside the incredible bearded woman. *Poor Alan* was wearing what looked suspiciously like Crimplene trousers, which were hitched up almost to his knees as he sat, straight-backed and embarrassed, trying to lose himself in the mind-bending business of pushing back his cuticles.

'Marriage,' struck up Rosie, her hands steepled in front of her, 'designed in heaven but lived out in hell. Does that mean anything to anyone?'

Nobody spoke, but the man in Crimplene hitched up his trousers a notch.

Tiffany saw Nick before he saw her. She flicked her hair back from her face, except for one tendril which she twisted round her finger. Despite the cold wind she unbuttoned her school-regulation duffel coat and walked nonchalantly up the drive. 'Hi,' she said, as he opened his car door.

'Hello,' he called back. 'Good day at school?'

She tried to think of something clever to say. 'It's a means to an end,' she said, with a long, bored sigh.

Nick smiled. She reminded him of his youngest daughter, who had recently left home to go off to university – all that reluctant enthusiasm for life stored up in such a delightful package.

'So how was your first day?' she asked, coming round to his side of the car and leaning against it.

'Your father's pleased with the way it went.'

Tiffany flicked at her hair. 'You mean nobody accused him of being a bungling quack?'

'No,' Nick answered, with a laugh.

'What about a bonehead? Somebody must have said that?'

He shook his head.

'A bogus—'

'Now why exactly would you think anyone would want to say those things about your father?'

'Because he is all those things! Therapy indeed!' She suddenly saw her mistake. 'I mean, he doesn't know the first thing about what makes people tick.' She tilted her head and smiled. 'But I'm sure you know what you're doing.'

'Quick on your feet, aren't you, Tiffany?' he said good humouredly.

Glad to have recovered the situation so easily, but cross with herself for having wasted valuable talking time discussing her father, she said, 'How's your jaw?'

'Not a mark on me,' he answered, giving his chin a rub.

'Do you always go around making such provocative comments?'

He laughed. 'It never fails to invoke the right response.'

'And getting David Parker to thump you was what you wanted?'

'Ah. As you said a few moments ago, it was a means to an end.' He threw his briefcase on to the back seat of his car and stooped to get inside.

'I'll see you, then,' Tiffany said.

He heard the expectant tone in her voice. 'I should think so,' he replied, putting the key in the ignition.

As he indicated to turn left at the end of the drive – conscious that Tiffany was still watching him – he saw Hilary's car coming towards him. He flashed his lights at her in the dark, she came alongside him, and as they both wound down their windows he heard her young daughter say clearly, 'Here's Mummy's boyfriend,' followed by a loud ssh.

'How's things?' he asked.

Awful, Hilary wanted to say, I've had about as much as I can take. But instead she said, 'Busy. I've got a hundred and one things to start doing for the PTA Christmas Fayre.'

He looked thoughtfully at her. It never ceased to amaze him how adept human beings were at pretending.

'I heard about you and David . . .' she started to say.

But sensing that she didn't want to say anything more with the children in the car he shook his head and said, 'No worries. He's obviously got a lot on his mind at the moment.' He saw her grip the steering wheel, her knuckles turn white and, reaching inside his jacket pocket, he took out a card with his name and telephone number on it. He handed it to her. 'Ring me if you need to.'

'I'm never going to get married,' Becky declared, when Nick had driven off.

'Why's that, dear?' Hilary asked, as she parked outside The Gables. She brushed away an unchecked tear rolling down her cheek.

'I'm going to live on the moon with lots of other women and we'll talk about important things like making the men stay at home to look after the babies. Chloe says that way there won't be any wars because the men will all be too busy and exhausted to fight one another.'

'It's a commune, you idiot,' Philip said scornfully.

'Okay, then, a commune. But, Mummy, do you think Daddy's busy enough?'

Nick stopped his car one more time on Acacia Lane or, rather, Iris Braithwaite brought him to an abrupt halt by staging what looked like a stick-up in the dark alongside the entrance to The White Cottage. He quickly wound down his window. 'What's the problem?' he called out.

She lowered her arms and came round to his side of the car. 'I wonder, Mr Bradshaw, if you could possibly help me.'

'Of course. What can I do? You've not locked yourself out, have you?'

'I may be many things, Mr Bradshaw, but careless is not one of them. Now if you'd just wait there for a few moments, I've got something which I'd like you to deliver to a friend for me. Not being able to drive can be such a nuisance at times.'

Nick watched Iris march back up her driveway and disappear into her cottage. Within seconds she reappeared carrying two large biscuit tins.

'I'm so pleased to have caught you,' she said, passing him the tins through the car window and offering him a smile. 'I had meant to call round and see you during the day at All in the Mind, but then who knows what I may have burst in on. So very kind of you to do this for me. I knew you were a decent and honourable man when I met you at the Rogers's party and you showed yourself to be a willing supporter of my campaign here in Hulme Welford. I'm most grateful to you. Goodnight.'

'But, Mrs Braithwaite,' Nick replied, nonplussed, 'where exactly am I taking these?'

She let out an unexpected laugh. 'Oh, didn't I say? I am sorry. If you could just see your way to dropping them off at Ms D'Arcy's. I believe you live only a short distance from her.'

'Do I?'

'She runs Hulme View Nursery, just off—'

He nodded. 'Yes, I know where it is. I had no idea it was her place and, to be honest, I'm not so sure she'll be all that delighted at seeing me.'

'Nonsense, Mr Bradshaw. She must get very lonely stuck out there with only her young daughter. She'll enjoy your company. Now hurry along, I've kept you long enough. Tell Ms D'Arcy those scones are best eaten tonight but the cake will last a few days.'

Driving out of the village Nick smiled to himself. He had the distinct feeling he was being manipulated. But from what he knew of Iris Braithwaite and from what Derek had told him of the woman, she was the last person in the world to try her hand at matchmaking. More likely she possessed a perverse sense of humour.

The main entrance to Hulme View Nursery was barred by a large, padlocked metal gate and Nick was forced to leave his car on the road and walk across the gravel car park, which he entered through a small wooden gate hanging off its hinges. His shoes crunched noisily in the dark and twice he nearly stumbled into the bushes, tripping over goodness knows what.

'Hell!' He righted himself a third time, only just managing to keep a hold of Iris's tins. He pushed on a few more steps, finding himself on what he hoped was a path. A security light flashed in his eyes, momentarily blinding him, then ahead of him a door opened spilling out yet more light from a small squat building.

'I can't afford double glazing or a time-share . . . Oh, it's *you*, what do you want?'

'Mrs Braithwaite asked me to drop these off for you,' he answered, when he reached Georgia D'Arcy, who was leaning against the door frame.

She looked at him suspiciously, then at the tins in his hands. 'What's in them?'

'Testicles. Mashed up and trodden underfoot.'

She tried hard not to smile. 'Are you trying to tell me something?'

'No, I'm simply the errand boy trying to make a delivery.' He pushed the tins at her. 'And I've been told to tell you to eat the cake tonight and . . . No, wait a minute, that's not right. You've to eat the scones tonight and keep the cake.'

Georgia laughed. 'The sly old bird.'

'Sorry?'

'Don't worry about it. And don't worry about me being polite and asking you in and you having to put up with thirty minutes of deadly conversation.'

'I wouldn't dream of putting you to all that trouble,' he answered smoothly, already turning to go. 'Goodnight.'

'Who was that, Mum?' asked Chloe, as she came out of the bathroom and into the hall.

Georgia closed the front door. 'Just somebody Mrs Braithwaite conned into acting as a delivery boy.' She opened one of the tins and smiled. 'Silly old woman thinks I don't eat enough.'

Chloe picked out a scone. 'Mmm, yum. Have we got any jam?'

'Not sure. Have a look while I ring and thank her.'

Georgia left Chloe rummaging in the kitchen cupboards and went into the sitting room to look for the telephone book. She then picked up her mobile phone.

'Iris?'

'This is Mrs Braithwaite speaking.'

'It's Georgia, just ringing to say—'

'Ah, so Mr Bradshaw found you all right. He's a pleasant enough man, wouldn't you say?'

So she was right.

As improbable an idea as it was, Georgia was left in no doubt that it wasn't just her weight that Iris was concerned about. So why not tell her to mind her own business? Iris had no right to go poking her nose into her life. She was fine just as she was. The last thing she needed right now was a stupid man mucking up her life again.

'Ms D'Arcy, are you still there, I was just saying what a pleasant—'

'I heard you, Iris, and I wish you'd stop . . .'

'Yes?'

'I wish you'd stop . . .' She took a deep breath. 'You really must stop calling me Ms D'Arcy all the time. I told you before, call me Georgia, okay?'

Soft! She was going bloody soft in the head! Heaven help her.

22

'Dinner?' repeated David. He lowered his *National Geographic* magazine. 'Why?'

'Does there have to be a why?' asked Hilary. 'I thought it would be nice to eat out tomorrow night. We haven't for ages.'

'I suppose so, if you really want to.'

'I do,' Hilary said firmly. The book she'd got out of the library said it was essential to keep a marriage alive by finding time to be alone with one's partner – *just the two of you*, the author of the book had stressed, *to enable each to focus on the other.*

It was a week now since Derek and Cindy's party, and while David had played down the Nick Bradshaw incident, laughing it off by attributing his loss of temper to high spirits and a misunderstanding between him and Nick, Hilary was aware that others were not so keen to accept this explanation.

At the school gate Patricia had given Hilary one of her notorious reassuring squeezes of the arm. 'Is he under a lot of pressure, your David? He's not being violent at home, is he?'

And as if it wasn't bad enough knowing that everybody knew that David had punched someone to the ground there was the small matter of his having made it public knowledge that she . . . that she liked to buy underwear and save it for a special occasion. It was only an innocent treat she allowed herself now and again and David had somehow managed to turn it into something vulgar and shamefully sordid. She hadn't had the nerve to confront him over it, for fear of her anger and humiliation being unleashed at what he'd done, which would quite likely lead to her revealing that she knew about his affair.

But at least the Ted the Toup fracas of last Sunday afternoon had taken the heat off her and provided a diversion for the likes of Patricia. A picture in the *Chronicle* of Ted, standing outside his shop with the caption 'Ted Terrorised by Tomato-throwing Tearaways', had gone a long way to fuel the argument in the village as to whether Ted Cooper was right in what he was doing. There was no disagreement as to who was responsible for the attack, though. It was generally accepted that Georgia D'Arcy and her Jeep had been involved, but as to her accomplices, no one could come up with any names.

'She was outside my house for a bit,' Patricia had told Hilary, again at the school gate. 'I saw her face quite clearly, but the others were dressed up like bandits. Probably a load of her *friends*. They do things like that, you know. I'm just so grateful we haven't got any trees in the village that need knocking down or she and her friends would be up them like a shot! But I'm sure that on my evidence alone Ted Cooper could prosecute. Only I won't say anything, because what would happen to poor little Chloe if her mother went to prison?'

It seemed strange to Hilary that the whole point of what Georgia had done, if indeed Georgia had been responsible for taking up a stance against Ted the Toup, was being lost. The actual protest was being buried beneath the trivia of whether or not the protesters had any right to do what they had done.

Personally Hilary thought Ted deserved what he got, but David had read the local paper on Wednesday evening and said, 'They want a damn good sorting out!'

'I suppose you mean by having a decent man in their lives?' she had thrown back at him.

He hadn't caught the irony in her voice. 'Yes,' he'd said, 'I suppose I do mean that. After all, look at you, Hilary. You don't go around indiscriminately throwing eggs and tomatoes at strange men, do you? And why not? Because you've always had me in your life.'

'I think they were most discriminate,' she'd replied in a low voice, appalled at David's arrogance. 'But haven't you forgotten how I poured whisky over you a couple of weeks ago, or doesn't that count?'

His answer had been lost in the kerfuffle of Becky crashing into the kitchen with yet more toys destined for the dustbin.

'I think it would be a good idea for us to go out,' Hilary pursued, as she watched David pick up the remote control for the television.

'Okay,' he said, tuning into Trevor McDonald and *News at Ten*. 'How about we go to Tony Farrand's place over at Knutsford? The children like it there.'

'The children?' Hilary repeated, crestfallen. 'I thought we'd go alone.'

'No. Let's take them – that way we don't have to bother with a babysitter.'

No, we don't, thought Hilary. And you can hide behind Philip and Becky all evening and not speak to me. She got up from the sofa and went out to the kitchen where she had a pile of ironing to get through. She switched on the iron and picked up one of Philip's school shirts from the wicker laundry basket. The phone rang. She waited for David to answer it. After six rings she went through to the hall herself.

'Hello, is that Hilary – Hilary Archer as was?'

'Yes,' she answered, cautiously.

'Hi, this is Lesley Blake, or you might remember me more as Skinny Lesley or Lesley the Rake. I found your parents in the phone book, gave them a ring just now and your mother gave me your number.'

The voice at the other end of the phone rattled on while Hilary collected her thoughts. Lesley Blake, she said to herself several times before she heard the words *school reunion* mentioned.

'I thought it was time for a reunion,' Skinny Lesley was saying, 'especially when I heard how poor old Richard was killed in that plane crash in Scotland. Definitely time to gather everyone together before any more of us snuff it. I've had such a job tracking everyone down. You'll come, won't you?'

Hilary gripped the receiver in her hand. A school reunion was the last thing she needed right now. All those clever people brought together to outdo one another and what did she have to boast? A failing marriage. That was all. 'It's lovely to hear from you,' she said briskly, trying to imagine Skinny Lesley as an adult, 'but no, I shan't be able to make it. I'm so busy these days.'

'But I haven't even told you when it is.'

'Oh.'

'You always did jump to conclusions, Hilary. Remember how you caught me at school with my hands full of Wagon Wheels and you thought I'd stolen them from the tuck shop and reported me?' Skinny Lesley laughed.

Hilary squeezed her eyes shut. 'When is the reunion?' she asked politely.

'The eighth of December. Say you'll come. Everyone else will be there. Even Johnboy Malone has said he'll turn up. You'll never guess who he married. That stuck-up Naomi Scott! Can you believe it? And he was so sweet on you, Hilary.'

No. Hilary couldn't believe it. And neither could she believe this conversation.

'I'll send you a letter with all the details of the hows, whys and whens. I shan't ask you now what you've been up to these past eighteen years, you can tell me on the eighth. See you.'

The phone clicked and Hilary went back to the kitchen to stand over the ironing board and Philip's school shirt. Skinny Lesley, Johnboy Malone and Naomi Scott all appeared in front of her. She slammed the iron down on top of them.

Star Struck was packed. It always was, and not just because the restaurant had such a good reputation for its menu. It was also renowned for its entertaining owner, Tony Farrand, who behaved like an eccentric showman – because that was what he was or, at least, what he had once been back in the seventies when, for a few short years, he had been very much the current flavour and had hosted not only his own comedy show, but *Star Struck*, a celebrity-quiz panel show. His act had been ostentatious and exuberant and had gone down well in the glittering seventies but the eighties audience had required something a little more succinct and sophisticated. His popularity had waned and brought him to the north-west of England, where house prices were lower than in the south and his style could be put to good use in the restaurant trade.

When he greeted Hilary and David at the door he was dressed in a flamboyant suit that had more than a touch of the Liberaces about it. Sparkling like a Christmas tree, he took Becky by the hand and led them to a central aisle table. He offered her a kiss and Hilary was amused to see how readily Becky accepted this, for all her recently acquired feminist tendencies. Philip was given a cigar, which was immediately snatched away, and when Tony blew into it a daisy popped out of the end.

Next Tony kissed Hilary's hand but thumbed his nose at David. Watch yourself, Hilary thought, as she sat down, or he might punch you in the face.

Menus were handed round the table, along with a bottle of Calpol for the children. 'Oh, so you're not ill?' he said, seeing the bemused look on Becky's face. 'Okay, then, I'll bring you something else.' He returned with two glasses of lemonade and said, 'These are on the house . . . my house. You're paying my mortgage!' He laughed and left them alone.

Hilary suddenly felt scared. Having Tony around had offered her a kind of protection. In his crazy way he made life seem sane and infinitely more bearable. She peeped over the top of her menu at David and caught him pushing back the cuff on his jacket to look at his watch.

'In a hurry?' she asked.

He ignored her, or perhaps he hadn't heard her above the loud music – she still wanted to give him the benefit of the doubt.

Next to David Becky was crumbling a breadstick into her mouth, while Philip was swinging on the back two legs of his chair reading his menu.

'What do you fancy?' she asked him.

'The ravioli with ricotta cheese, please,' he answered, tossing the menu on to the table and bringing his chair down with a sudden bump.

'Not the Bolognese? You usually have that when we come here,' Hilary said.

'I had it at school for lunch yesterday.'

'How is school?' David asked, finally joining in with the conversation.

Philip looked at his father. 'I hate it!' he wanted to shout at him. 'And it's all your bloody fault I'm there!' It was true, it had been Dad who'd suggested he sat the scholarship exam and Dad who'd promised him a computer if he passed. Well, he had passed and he had got a computer but he was getting hell kicked out of him into the bargain. He reached under the table and rubbed his bruised shin. Yesterday he'd been pushed over. Then he'd had his briefcase taken and his work thrown around the classroom and all because he wouldn't give in and hand over any money. But at least Batesy had helped to pick everything up. 'Just do as they say and they'll leave you alone. It's easier that way,' he'd whispered. The hell he would!

'It's okay,' Philip said at last.

'What about Latin and classical studies? You didn't think you'd enjoy those, did you?'

Philip stared at his father again and shrugged his shoulders. 'It's not so bad. Yesterday was a bit tedious – we were learning about love.'

'Yuck,' Becky said, pulling a face. Hilary reached for a packet of breadsticks and started fumbling with the wrapper.

'Oh, yes,' David said. 'And what earth-shattering conclusions did you learned youngsters reach? Not to have anything to do with it, I expect.' He gave a short laugh which, to Hilary's ears, sounded pompous. Had he always laughed like that? Did other people find him pompous?

Philip ignored his father's question. 'There are three types of love,' he said, '*eros*, *agape* and one other that I can't remember. Sir says that *eros* is the kind of love that makes you do stupid things like Romeo and Juliet did, and *agape* is the unconditional love, which according to sir goes on for ever. How do you love Mum, Dad, in the *eros* way or *agape*?'

David shifted awkwardly in his chair. 'The most I learned in Latin at school about love was *amo, amas, amat*, never mind all this guppy stuff.'

'*Agape*,' Philip corrected.

'I want a pizza,' Becky announced, banging her menu down on the table and knocking over a tiny vase with its single red carnation. Water flooded across the paper tablecloth.

'Ah!' shouted Tony, appearing from nowhere to mop up the damage. 'An extra ten pounds on the bill. That was holy water I brought back from the Vatican after cooking dinner for the *Papa*. You don't believe me, eh? I'll ring him up and ask him to tell you it's the truth.' He grabbed a large pepper-mill from a passing waiter. 'Hello,' he said, talking into it as though it was a telephone. 'Hey, Papa, you tell the girl here about the holy water.' He passed the pepper-mill to Becky, who slowly raised it to her left ear but when she saw the look on Philip's face she flung it back at Tony.

'Silly man,' she said, embarrassed.

He took their order and, once again, Hilary felt the strain of being left to their own devices.

'I want the loo,' Becky said loudly above the sound of Wet Wet Wet – her boredom threshold nearing zero.

'You only want to play with the soap dispenser,' Philip accused her.

'I do not. I'm bursting and I'll prove it if—'

'Hurry up and go,' interrupted Hilary, who knew better than anyone to call her daughter's bluff.

'I'll go as well,' Philip said.

Just you and me, then, David, Hilary thought, watching David's turned-away face as Becky and Philip left the table. Speak to me! Say something nice. Give me some hope . . . just a hint of hope that you do still love me.

He said nothing to her unspoken questions and his silence made her want to run away and cry. She felt unimaginably sorry for herself and blew her nose in an effort to hold back the tears. Oh, God, don't let me fall apart now, not in front of all these people. 'I think I'd better go and check on Becky,' she said, getting to her feet and stumbling away.

She met Philip and Becky coming down the narrow staircase on their way back to their table. Inside the ladies' there was soap everywhere. Without thinking she started to clean up the washbasins, throwing paper towels – which she suspected Becky had been using as water bombs – into the bin.

While Wet Wet Wet sang 'Put the Light On' through the restaurant sound system she tried to stem the flow of tears threatening to stream down her cheeks. Why doesn't he love me? she asked herself, looking in the mirror as she wiped away yet more soap. What's wrong with me? Why am I not enough for him? Nick obviously thinks I'm all right.

Horrified, she stared at her reflection in the mirror. Where had that thought come from? And why had Nick Bradshaw appeared in her life the moment she had discovered David's unfaithfulness? Thoughts of guardian angels crept into her mind. Had he come into her life to help her? *Ring me if you need to.* His echoing words seemed to join forces with those of Marti Pellow. '. . . put a little light in her darkest day . . . ring me.'

Her meal was waiting for her when she got back to the table.

'We didn't wait,' David said, forking up a pasta bow and staring at a young waitress with a skirt no bigger than a napkin at the top of her long, slender legs.

When had he started doing that, Hilary wondered. He never used to eye up other women, let alone a girl young enough to be his daughter. So when had he got so bored with her and changed? Or was it she who had changed? Had he always been like this and she was only now waking up to him and his irritating habits?

'I need the loo again,' Becky said, having picked over her pizza and lined the edge of her plate with little bits of onion.

Oh, if life was as easy as playing around with a soap dispenser every time you got bored, thought Hilary, watching Becky disappear once more.

Playing around – she glanced across the table to David. He met her stare.

'You're not eating,' he said, pointing with his knife at her untouched plate.

'I'm not hungry,' she said faintly.

He rolled his eyes. 'A waste of an evening and more money down the drain!'

'More money?' she repeated. 'What do you mean?'

'New hairdo, new clothes, a meal out, and all for what, I ask you?'

That was it! He'd gone too far now. Her mind was made up.

Ring me if you need to.

She would! She would ring Nick. That would show David!

'Does that mean another lemonade's out of the question?' Philip asked, awkwardly.

'You'd better ask Scrooge here,' Hilary replied, unable to keep the anger and sarcasm out of her voice. Obviously running a mistress as well as a family was proving a more expensive proposition for David than he had thought.

23

Hilary was up before anyone else. It was still pitch black outside and in the light cast from a couple of underlighters in the Aga alcove she stirred a pot of porridge.

She hadn't eaten a thing at the restaurant last night and had woken up at five o'clock almost sick with hunger. Knowing that she couldn't lie there a moment longer next to David's restless body, tossing and turning, she'd come downstairs in search of something to eat.

As she stirred the bubbling pan she found the smell of warm milk comforting and reassuring. In those first few days after finding out about David and Catherine she had cooked mechanically and without enjoyment. It had all taken too much effort. Then last week she had thrown herself into spending hours filling the freezer and cake tins with what she had felt sure would lure David back to the safety of The Gables, tempting him with his favourite Delia Smith sticky toffee puddings and gingerbread. She had done it because she recalled that earlier in the year David had said that Catherine was a lousy cook. At the time it had never occurred to Hilary to ask him how he knew this. Had she simply told him in the office one day or had he discovered for himself that she was disastrous in the kitchen but dynamite in bed?

Now, though, as she scooped out some porridge into a bowl she didn't give a fig about finding the way back to David's heart through his stomach. She made herself a pot of tea, opened the fridge for a bottle of milk and found a half-empty pot of double cream. She poured it over the bowl and then added a sprinkling of brown sugar, followed by some more and then a dollop of honey. She contemplated some maple syrup, but decided against it. That was going too far.

To hell with that, she thought, this was no time for propriety. She squeezed the plastic bottle over the bowl and it fired off a loud raspberry.

And with years of everything-in-moderation out of the window, Hilary raised the first wicked spoonful to her lips and wondered if this was how Eve had felt. Had she got up early one morning and wandered into the garden and done the unthinkable because Adam had pushed her beyond what she could bear – just as David was doing with her? She swallowed another spoonful of porridge and pushed this thought aside, preferring instead to equate herself with Goldilocks – Goldilocks hadn't meant any harm, had she? She helped herself to some more cream and thought of her resolution, made last night at the restaurant – the moment when she had decided to take control.

As she'd lain awake in the early hours listening to David's unsteady breathing and occasional bursts of muttered words in his sleep she had thought not just of Nick Bradshaw but of Johnboy Malone.

Skinny Lesley had been right: Johnboy had been sweet on her all those years ago. And at teacher-training there had been that rugby player with arms like bolsters who had always been knocking on her door wanting to have coffee with her – much to David's annoyance. She had been attractive once, hadn't she? So when had that all changed? When had she become so sexless? Was it during pregnancy? Or had it happened during those matter-of-fact years of leaky breasts, disgusting nappies, prize-winning moments of potty training and heroic sleepless nights? She had no idea. She got up from the table, went over to the dishwasher and placed her empty bowl on the top rack. In pursuit of yet more self-indulgence she opened one of the high cupboards where she kept a secret supply of goodies – deliberately stored there out of Becky's reach. She pulled down a packet of chocolate biscuits, sat at the table again and started flicking through her latest copy of *Hello!* Chocolate and the rich and famous with their beautiful designer homes and clothes – was there ever a better combination for inspiring and encouraging a search for something more exciting in one's own drab life?

When she had finished reading about the latest society goings-on in London she moved on to *Cheshire Life* and this month's feature article on the north-west's most wealthy and eligible men. 'Thirty-nine and how many millions?' she said out loud, looking at a photo of the handsome owner of a well-known chain of sportswear shops. She wondered whether the magazine would ever do an article on Derek and Cindy's latest enterprise. In her mind's eye she pictured the two of them smiling into the camera lens and appearing, to all intents and purposes, the perfect couple, with their long marriage and business partnership behind them and their new venture launching them into the future.

How many lies did they all cover up? Was everyone out there pretending to live lives that in truth they found unbearable at times? Was the answer simply to make the best of a bad job and get what satisfaction one could?

She picked up another chocolate biscuit and chewed it thoughtfully.

'Nick?' she whispered into the phone five minutes later.

'Yes . . . Hilary?'

'I'm sorry it's so early, but you said if I needed help you'd—'

'I can be ready in ten minutes. Where do you want to meet?'

'I don't know,' she said, suddenly unsure.

'Come here, then, and we'll talk. That is what you want, isn't it, Hilary?'

She nodded dumbly into the phone and listened to him giving her directions to where he lived.

'Who were you on the phone to?' David asked, when she went upstairs to get dressed and found him awake in bed.

'Georgia D'Arcy,' she lied.

'What on earth do you want with that man-hater at this time of day?' He yawned.

'PTA stuff,' she answered, from the depths of the wardrobe. 'I need to go through a few of the arrangements for the end-of-term Christmas Fayre. I'm going to see her now.'

'What, this early? And, anyway, won't she be sharpening her claws in that nursery of hers?'

'She's capable of doing more than one thing at a time. Perhaps you could haul yourself out of bed and take the children to church this morning.'

David groaned. 'God won't miss them just one Sunday.'

'They missed last week so they really should go today,' she said, wanting her children to be in the safe hands of God for the next few hours. She selected one of the outfits Cindy had helped her buy in Manchester and sped off to the bathroom to get dressed. The thought of dressing for duplicity in front of David was too much. She slipped into the softly pleated trousers Cindy had chosen in preference to the crisp navy ones she had wanted, then pulled the pale pink angora sweater over her head. She brushed her hair away from her face and tried to apply some make-up. She managed some blusher and lipstick but her hands were trembling so much she had to give up on the mascara. She didn't look at all like Anthea Turner any more but she gave herself six out of ten for effort.

She closed the front door, climbed into her car and reversed out of the drive. She didn't look back at the house for fear of catching sight of the children peering out of a window at her. This, she told herself sternly, had nothing to do with the children. This was between her and David.

At the end of Acacia Lane she stopped the car and reached into her handbag for her small bottle of Anaïs Anaïs. She sprayed her neck and wrists liberally, then had to wind down the window for air. She coughed and spluttered, trying to catch her breath, and nearly jumped out of her skin at the sound of tapping and Iris Braithwaite's face appearing through the open window.

'You're surely not driving to early-morning communion, Mrs Parker.'

'Heavens, no,' squeaked Hilary.

'So where are you off to at this time of day, and all dressed up?'

Only Mrs Braithwaite could be so direct. Nerves and guilt rendered Hilary's reply almost inaudible.

'I beg your pardon, Mrs Parker.'

'PTA ... Georgia D'Arcy,' she managed more intelligibly.

Mrs Braithwaite's powdery face broke into an unexpected smile. 'Hulme

Welford would be a far better place if we had more people like that young woman living here. And how's that ill-mannered husband of yours? Brawling in public and over what, one asks oneself? Where was his sense of decency and respect when he took it upon himself to besmirch your name?'

'I really must be getting on,' Hilary said boldly, and ignoring the other woman's questions she pressed lightly on the accelerator pedal and tweaked the engine.

As she turned the corner on to the main street of the village Hilary had the uncomfortable feeling that Mrs Braithwaite was still standing in the middle of Acacia Lane staring suspiciously after her and putting two and two together. The older woman's appearance had acted like a spectre at the feast, intruding in an area where Hilary wanted no reminders of everyday life. As she drove out of the village she struggled to reinstate the picture of the world she had created in her mind while reading about the Earl of Whatsit and his beautiful new girlfriend on holiday in the Maldives.

Nick's house was not far from Philip's new school, and as the fields and recently cut hedges of the familiar lanes slipped by she watched the sky on the horizon release its hold on the last remnants of night, finally giving way to morning strands of pink and gentian blue.

She saw the sign for the trout farm Nick had described and slowed down to third gear on the bend in the road as he'd instructed. His small end-of-terrace cottage was set back from the road and a plume of smoke was rising from the chimney. She felt her body go taut with nervous expectation.

She parked the car on the verge, switched off the engine, gathered up her bag, locked the car door and breathed in deeply. High up in the oak trees she heard the loud cawing of crows – or were they rooks? Dear God! She could think of things like that when she was about to embark on ... She cleared her throat, tucked her bag under her arm and went up to the door, which was at the side of the cottage. It opened before she had even raised her hand to the knocker.

'I've made us some coffee,' he said, as she stepped inside. He took her coat and hung it on the back of the kitchen door alongside an overcoat she recognised from bonfire night. 'Have you eaten?'

She nodded and looked awkwardly about the tiny kitchen; there was an empty wine bottle on the floor along with a brown carrier bag of foil cartons with the remains of some pilau rice clinging to the edges. 'You're not very tidy, are you?'

He passed her a mug of coffee. 'And you're making small-talk.'

She turned away and stared out of the leaded window which overlooked the road. She wondered if anyone would recognise her car.

'We all do it,' he said.

'Do what?' she said, facing him again.

'Avoid saying what we really want to say. Come through to the other room. It's just as untidy but at least it's warm. I lit a fire as soon as I put the phone down.'

'I'm sorry to have put you to all this trouble. Oh,' she said, standing in the middle of the sitting room, 'you're right, this is as untidy.'

He laughed, gathered up a pile of books and files from an armchair by the fire, and flung the heap on to the floor where another stack of books teetered with intent. 'I'm disappointing you, aren't I?'

'How long have you lived here?' she asked, sitting cautiously in the chair he'd cleared. She half expected it to collapse beneath her. The fabric was wearing through on the arms and she played with a loose thread that stood proud from a faded dianthus.

'About three years. And if you want a life résumé before you're going to talk properly to me I'll give it to you.'

'I didn't mean to sound—'

'Relax and listen for a change. I get the impression you don't do a lot of listening, Hilary. You make a lot of assumptions, don't you?'

She said nothing. It wasn't turning out exactly how she'd imagined it would. Surely this wasn't how the Earl had wooed the lovely Annabel.

'I'm forty-eight years old. I used to be a lecturer in organisational behaviour, then when my second marriage hit the skids five years ago I took a long hard look at myself and found I didn't much like what was there. I decided to make the switch from always talking to occasionally listening, which is what I want to do with you.' He moved away from his position by the fire and sat in the chair opposite her. 'Are you ready to talk to me now?'

Would tears work? she thought. If she started to cry, would he take her in his arms and . . .?

'David doesn't love me,' she said. 'He barely looks at me these days, let alone talks to me. He's . . . he's having an affair and I feel . . .'

She heard him move towards her, then felt his hand on hers.

'You feel hurt,' he said, taking her untouched mug of coffee away from her. 'You feel betrayed and rejected. You feel spread all over the floor and about as worthless as you can get . . . and you want someone to put you back together again and make everything better.'

'Yes,' she whispered. Now hurry up and kiss me.

He did.

24

Nick was surprisingly gentle with her, unlike David who had always treated her as though she were a rag doll. 'Don't push me about,' she had told him on their second date, when he had pressed her against the door of her room in the college hall of residence.

As Nick tilted his head to one side she wondered if she was going about things the right way – it was so long ago since she'd been in this situation. Would it be better if she was to open her mouth wider? And what about her hands? Should she be doing something with them?

One of Nick's hands was stroking the nape of her neck. She felt wobbly inside and even more conscious of his lips, so warm and soft against her own.

Just as she closed her eyes Nick pulled away. 'Tell me, Hilary,' he said, 'has that made you feel better? Did it stop you thinking of David for a few moments?'

'Yes,' she lied, 'completely.'

He gazed at her steadily and she sat waiting for him to say or do something else – she wanted him to stroke her neck again. He stood up abruptly and went and stood by the mantelpiece in front of the fire.

'It's only a short-term answer, Hilary,' he said firmly, his arms crossed in front of him. Suddenly he looked like a stern headmaster. 'And how about the guilt? Could you cope with that?'

Kiss me again and I'll see, she wanted to say flippantly, high on the thrill of having kissed another man – she had actually kissed another man! 'David's managing pretty well,' she said.

'But is he? He's obviously under an enormous strain at the moment, living his double life. How much longer do you think he can go on as he is?'

'Why is everyone so concerned about the strain David's under? What about the strain he's put on my life? This is no picnic for me I can assure you.'

He smiled, and came and sat next to her again. 'I know,' he said gently, no longer a stern headmaster. 'But having an affair with the first available man is not the answer.'

'So why did you kiss me?' she asked. 'Were you making fun of me?'

'I kissed you because I knew that was what you wanted.'

'I . . . I didn't,' she stammered.

'And I wanted to prove to you that it's not the answer. Tell me, Hilary, has your marriage made you happy?'

'I—'

'Or have you assumed you were happy – have marriage, have happiness? Can you remember the last time you were heart-stoppingly tickled pink with the love you feel towards David?'

She lowered her eyes and fiddled with her sapphire engagement ring. 'It's not like that,' she said at last. 'You just muddle along. Nobody can be expected to dance around the supermarket on a Monday morning in a state of euphoria after more than a decade of marriage. Life simply has a habit of getting in the way.'

'What a sad world we live in where our expectations become so dulled by routine. Hilary, when will you, and everyone like you, understand that this is not a dress rehearsal? This is it. You have to live life to the full.'

'I suppose that's what David's doing,' she said in a small voice, pulling absentmindedly at the thread on the arm of the chair.

'It could be. Though ask yourself this. Does he seem happier because of what he's doing?'

Hilary thought of David's miserable face, his thin lips drawn in a tight line and his apparent ambivalence to their life together. 'No,' she said, 'he doesn't look like a man who's enjoying himself.'

'Because he's feeling guilty. He knows what he's doing is going to hurt you and the children, if he's found out. Like so many seeking a quick fix he's not thought this through. He should have looked carefully at his life to find the reason he felt the urge to stray.'

'Perhaps it's all my fault. Maybe because of the way I am I've made him have an affair. If I had been more—'

'It's a possibility. But in reality quite often it's not what's happening around the home that causes a partner to be unfaithful. I'm not making excuses or trying to justify what David's done but I guarantee that the reason for his infidelity lies deep within his own make-up, not yours. As Thoreau said, "The mass of men lead quiet lives of desperation."'

Hilary looked up sharply. 'Why's it always the men having such a hard time?'

He smiled. 'Don't take things so literally. And, as I just said, I'm not making excuses for David but what I am trying to say is that we all react to a given situation and our response determines the consequences.' He stared hard at her. 'David chose to have an affair . . . just as you chose to come here today.'

She turned away.

'Did you really expect me to whisk you upstairs and bed you?'

She continued to stare into the fire, watching the flames lick at the loose bark on a log in the grate. 'You make it sound so sordid.'

He laughed lightly. 'The state of my sheets, it would have been.'

She tried to laugh as well but it came out more like a whimper. 'I've made a complete fool of myself, haven't I?'

'Not at all. You've done what so many people do in your situation.'

'Predictable as well as foolish. I'm sorry to be so boring.'

'Stop giving yourself such a hard time, Hilary. You're an attractive, intelligent woman with everything going for you—'

'Please, don't say any more or you'll start me crying.'

He put his arm round her shoulders and kissed her forehead. 'Go ahead. Feel free. But go easy on that armchair or it'll be shredded by the time you leave.'

She looked down at the thread of cotton in her fingers: it was twice its original length and there was now a hole in the middle of the dianthus. 'I'm sorry—'

'Would you stop apologising and listen to what else I've got to say? You've got some very difficult decisions ahead of you and only you can make them. You can talk it through with me, if you like, or any amount of your friends and family, but ultimately you're the one who is going to have to live with whatever is decided, so it's only right it should be you who reaches a decision. Remember, nothing is by chance. We each make a choice to determine our future. And the priority in your immediate future is telling David that you know about his affair. When are you going to tell him?'

'Not yet. Not with my sister's wedding and Christmas coming up so soon. I'll talk to him in the New Year.'

'And will you be ready for his response if he says he wants to leave you?'

'I feel like he's left me already. At least then the awful pretending will be over.'

On her way home Hilary called at Hulme View Nursery, so at least her alibi would have some weight should David have any suspicions that she hadn't been telling the truth. She hadn't seen Georgia since that dreadful scene in the kitchen when she'd invited her back for tea and Nick had turned up unexpectedly. How horribly complicated her life had become. Would it ever be the way it used to be?

The nursery was busy with Sunday browsers selecting trays of winter-flowering pansies and heathers. Hilary found Georgia pushing a large muddy trolley of potted five-foot-high conifers.

'Hello, stranger,' Georgia said, coming to a stop. She started to unload the trolley. 'I'd ask you to help,' she said, as she lifted the first of the tall conifers, 'only you're done up like a lardy cake. I suppose you've been to church, have you?'

Hilary nodded.

'I didn't think the devout still thought God loved them more when they were decked out in their finery.'

'They don't!' Hilary retorted. Dear God, she was fed up with all these sharp-witted people around her.

'I'm sorry,' Georgia said, settling the conifer next to a row of small laurel bushes. 'That was rude of me. The unconverted don't have the right to knock the few who do believe. What can I do you for?'

Hilary hesitated. She was doing a lot of that, these days. She never used to. She'd always known exactly what she wanted to do and say. 'PTA,' she blurted out. 'I thought we could go through some of the Christmas Fayre arrangements.'

Georgia frowned. She reached for another conifer but then changed her mind. She pushed back the sleeve of her donkey jacket. A quarter to eleven. She returned her attention to Hilary. 'Have I got this right? I'm making the assumption that you've been to church this morning and that you've left early to come here and talk to me about the fayre. How am I doing?'

Hilary looked awkwardly at her feet. 'It just crossed my mind—'

'To dip out of the Eucharist and dash along here. Well, that seems eminently feasible. I wish all the members of the PTA were as diligent as you. Just fancy, there you were, down on your knees, and suddenly you thought of me, or perhaps it was the hand of God intervening, "P-T-A," his sepulchral voice boomed through the vaulted ceiling.'

'Hardly anybody gets down on their knees at St John's,' Hilary said, petulantly.

'You speak for yourself,' Georgia said, struggling with another conifer. 'I'm frequently on mine.'

Hilary felt tired and out of her depth.

Georgia looked at Hilary's miserable and confused face. 'Oh, shit,' she said, 'I'm sorry. I'm premenstrual and feeling as bloated as the *Hindenburg* and about as volatile. Forgive me?'

Hilary nodded. 'And I'm sorry I lied to you.'

Georgia smiled. 'You mean, no PTA talk? You do surprise me. Come on, let's go over to the caravan and you can tell me what you've really come for.'

'But what about your customers?'

'Gordon's here today. He's taking care of them, leaving me to clear a space ready for the order of rooted Christmas trees coming in tomorrow.'

'I don't want to keep you from your work, I can easily—'

'Give it a rest, Hilary.'

The caravan felt only marginally warmer than it was outside. Georgia switched on a small heater, which whirred noisily. 'Fancy a coffee? I've got some in a Thermos here.'

Hilary shook her head.

'Suit yourself.' Georgia poured some for herself. She cradled her half-mittened fingers around the plastic cup. 'So what's been going on at The Gables since I saw you last? Which reminds me, you were acting very strangely that day. I could have sworn you were suddenly frightened of me.'

Hilary picked up a packet of lupin seeds and tipped it upside down. She listened to the seeds trickling from one end to the other.

Georgia laughed. 'And if I didn't know better I'd say that witch Patricia Longton put some silly idea into your head.'

'Goodness, of course not,' Hilary said, too quickly.

'Stupid bitch has always thought I was gay ever since I kicked Rory out. Well, to put the record straight, I'm not. Look at me when I'm talking to you, Hilary. I'm not some sex-starved lesbian about to take advantage of a vulnerable woman. Okay?'

'Okay,' Hilary repeated quickly. Heavens, what a morning it was turning into!

'Not that there's anything wrong in being gay, some of my closest friends are. But that's beside the point. Get on and tell me what you came here for.'

Hilary had had no intention of telling Georgia about Nick Bradshaw when she'd driven through the nursery gates, but now that their friendship was back on a more reassuring level she decided she wanted to confide in her. She explained about wanting to use Georgia as an alibi and why, then went on to tell her partly what had happened at Nick's.

'Bloody hell, Hilary! You mean you let that wily bastard get his tongue down your throat?'

Hilary frowned. 'I only let him kiss me,' she said defensively.

'Crap! *You* kissed him.'

The two women looked at each other in silence. Hilary was disappointed. She had made Georgia angry and she didn't want that. Then she saw her friend's face soften with a smile. 'Well, you've learned two important things this morning, Hilary. One is that you don't have to worry about me leaping on you and the other is that you've proved to yourself that if you wanted to dip your toes into the shark-infested waters of catching yourself a man, you could. So where exactly does that leave you?'

'Lord only knows. Probably going clean round the bend.'

25

She was mad. Stark raving bonkers mad. She looked again at the clock on the dashboard. Five to eight – nearly half an hour late. What had made her agree to Skinny Lesley's invitation? Worse still, what had actually made her stick to it when she could have so easily backed out at the last minute claiming a headache? Nobody would have been the wiser.

It had been Charlotte who had insisted she go. 'It'll be a laugh, Hilary,' she'd said that afternoon at the shop.

'And how would you know?' she had thrown back at her sister. 'You've never been to one of these dos.'

'Only because nobody's bothered to go to the trouble to organise one for my year.'

'Well, I wish Skinny Lesley hadn't bothered. What on earth am I supposed to say to all those people I haven't seen for nearly twenty years?'

'I'm sure you'll think of something,' Charlotte had said, adding, 'strange, isn't it, that we haven't seen much of anyone from our schooldays?'

As Hilary flicked her headlights to full beam on the unlit stretch of dual carriageway she wondered about what her sister had said. Charlotte was right, it was strange. Their old school wasn't exactly a million miles from Hulme Welford but it was in a different county, chosen specifically by their mother for its vigorous hard-work ethic and long hours – it had been the only day school within a twenty-mile radius that had insisted on compulsory Saturday-morning attendance, something that had fitted in perfectly with Louise's work commitments at her antique shop and their father's surgery hours and house calls in the village.

But, then, perhaps it wasn't so much the geography of the school's location that had meant there had been no contact between the classmates once they'd left. Maybe it was simply that most people had moved away at the first possible opportunity and that it was only she who had unimagina- tively moved back after going away to teacher-training. After a moment's reflection, she consoled herself with the thought that, years later, Charlotte was equally dull.

She turned left at the roundabout and there it was. School. Not that there was anything about the Victorian Gothic edifice in front of her that filled her with dread: she had enjoyed the period in her life that the building represented. School had been fun. All that structure and work to get on with, it had suited her just fine. But what *did* fill her with dread was facing everybody tonight, and them all guessing, one by one, that her marriage was on the rocks.

The car park – which had once been the netball courts – was almost full of sleekly moulded cars: Mercedes, BMWs, Audis, Volvos, a couple of Jaguars and every conceivable variety of four-wheel-drive vehicle, shining examples of success and affluence. Hadn't they all done well? she thought cynically.

She parked her Clio alongside a smart little midnight blue BMW Coupé. She had planned to drive David's Volvo, but only that afternoon he'd booked it in for a service. The garage had telephoned later saying they'd found a fault on one of the wheel-bearings and that it would be at least Tuesday before they'd be able to fix it. So much for turning up in style.

She pulled on the handbrake, released her seat-belt and jerked the mirror towards her to examine her make-up. She bared her teeth, checking for any wayward smears of lipstick.

The main entrance door was decorated with a couple of balloons, one of which was already showing signs of deflating and wrinkling – not unlike herself, Hilary thought, as she pushed against the glass-panelled door. The foyer was empty, save for a massive Christmas tree covered with art-department-generated decorations and flickering lights. The door to the main hall, which had been used for gym and morning assemblies, was wide open and through it she could see a crowd of animated faces. Automatically she put on her best smile, hoping it would conceal the look of failure on her own face.

'Not so fast. You need a badge before you can go a step further.'

Standing to attention behind a table and holding a clipboard and a pen was ... Skinny Lesley?

'Hilary, it's you!' whooped an amazingly large Skinny Lesley.

'Lesley!'

'You look great, Hilary, and you've not changed a bit.'

'Neither have you.'

'Oh, come on! I've put on four stone since those days – gained one for each child I've produced and one for luck.' She let out a loud laugh and smacked a name badge on Hilary's shoulder. Hilary staggered slightly under the force of Skinny Lesley's hand. 'Now the procedure is this. First question is, do you still live in the area, followed by, are you married and how many children have you got? Bar's over there in the corner. I'll catch up with you later when I'm off duty.'

Hilary turned from Skinny Lesley's bristling efficiency and straight away saw Carrie Maxwell standing alone, an empty wine glass in her hand – heavens, she'd been a terror with a hockey-stick in her hands. She went over to her. 'Hello, Carrie.'

'Hilary!' Carrie's delight was obvious. 'Just look at you! Apart from the colour of your hair, you're exactly the same.'

'Except I don't wear tank tops any more,' Hilary said, with a smile, finding some of her nervousness beginning to slip away.

'My eldest daughter does, though. You should see her, flares and platforms, the whole performance all over again.'

Hilary laughed and took a quick glance round the hall. 'Isn't this whole thing bizarre? How many have you stayed in touch with?'

'Nobody. I moved away after A-levels and never came back. I live in Kent now.'

'Married?' Hilary ventured.

'Hell, no! The rat deserted years ago.'

'Oh, I'm sorry.'

'And you?'

'Hilary Archer! I don't believe it!'

They both turned to see Johnboy Malone advancing towards them. 'I don't believe it!' he repeated, *à la* Victor Meldrew – he even had the same cropped thinning hair.

'Hello, Johnboy,' Hilary said, quietly.

'No, no, no. That won't do at all. You've got to get into the part, Hilary. The men slap and punch one another and you girls are supposed to throw your heads back and squeal loudly with your arms either side of you waving like a mad thing. Here, hold my glass and I'll show you.'

'You're such an exhibitionist, John,' came a deep, sexy voice from behind him. It was Naomi Scott.

Hilary gulped unthinkingly from Johnboy's wine glass – Naomi Scott, dark-haired, dark-eyed and looking as fabulous as a model, dressed in an Audrey Hepburn tailored black suit with a small shiny handbag, no bigger than a handkerchief, hanging from her wrist. She was utterly gorgeous – and didn't she know it? Hilary watched, fascinated, as Naomi placed a hand of red-painted nails on Johnboy's shoulder.

'Introduce me,' Naomi purred in Johnboy's ear, then, looking at Hilary and Carrie beneath her long lashes, she said, 'I shouldn't really even be here, not being in your year group, but John never goes anywhere without me, these days.'

'I vaguely remember you,' Hilary said crisply. She was furious that this smouldering beauty couldn't even remember who she was. 'You're four years older than the rest of us, aren't you?' she carried on and, fired up with resentment, she pointed to the name badge on her left shoulder and added, 'You must have forgotten your glasses.'

'I'm dying for a drink,' Naomi said uninterestedly, after giving Hilary a vacant stare. She unwrapped herself from Johnboy and walked away.

'I don't remember you being such a tiger, Hilary,' Johnboy said, with a laugh. 'How about a kiss for old times' sake?' He leaned towards her and kissed her cheek. 'Can I have my glass back now?'

Hilary handed it to him. She suddenly felt very bold. There had been more than a hint of malice in the words she had just spoken to Naomi Scott and she knew that not only had she meant every ounce of it but that the poignant humiliation she had recently recalled over that wretched box of chocolates and what she had once felt for Naomi Scott had magically vanished.

'I'll get you a glass of wine while I leave Johnboy to chat you up like in the old days,' Carrie said, already moving off.

'You look well,' Hilary said awkwardly, when they were alone and she had the opportunity to take in Johnboy's expensive wool blazer and silk tie.

'Thank you. Though I can't say that stockbroking has done anything for my hair.' He ran his hand through what little he had. 'I like your hair short, by the way. You always wore it long, though I don't remember you being so fair.'

She smiled self-consciously. 'A bottle job.'

'Aha. To cover up the grey?'

'Certainly not!'

'Naomi does it all the time. But she'd bloody kill me if she knew I'd told you.'

Hilary wanted to hug Johnboy. What other spectres from her past would he put to rest for her tonight, she wondered.

'So how about you, Hilary? What have you been up to since 'seventy-eight?'

'Nothing very exciting, I'm afraid. Teaching, marriage and children.'

'I always had you down as a career girl. When the rest of us were larking about you were there handing in the longest essays known to mankind. I dread to think how many times you saved my skin by letting me read through your work so that I could at least have a clue what the teachers were expecting me to write about. God, but you were sweet.'

'How long have you been married to Naomi?' Hilary asked, revelling in Johnboy's flattery. He hadn't changed.

'Only a year.'

'Is that all?'

'I kept putting marriage off then, purely by chance, along came Naomi. We met on a skiing holiday last year in Wengen.'

Hilary was just imagining the beautiful Naomi on skis – as quick and as sleek as a snake – when Johnboy said, 'We're not suited, I know it. I can see it in people's eyes every time they look at us. I'm her third husband.'

Hilary gawped. 'Third?' she murmured. She felt extraordinarily sorry for Johnboy. And was there nobody here tonight who had experienced a normal happy marriage?

'What's your husband like, Hilary?'

'He's an estate agent—'

Johnboy threw back his head and laughed. 'Are you telling me he's a dishonest, underhanded so-and-so?'

Hilary bit her lip, then remembered her lipstick.

But Johnboy had caught the change of expression on her face. 'I'm sorry,' he said. 'In poor taste, I assume.'

She didn't know what to say but was glad to see Carrie coming towards them with two glasses of wine.

'Sorry I've been so long, I've been talking to Craig Montana – just discovered he only lives a short distance away from me. Not married either.' She handed Hilary her glass. 'Mind if I get back to him?'

They watched Carrie disappear.

'Children?'

Hilary turned back to Johnboy. 'Sorry?'

'You said you had children. How many?'

'Two. Philip and Becky.'

'That's nice. And is Becky like her mother?'

'Lord, I hope not. Or, rather, I hope no one thinks she takes after me. She can be very difficult at times.'

'Substitute challenging for difficult,' Johnboy said, quietly. He leaned into Hilary. 'That's what I say to myself about Naomi at times.'

'I hope you're not trying out the my-wife-doesn't-understand-me routine,' Hilary said with a giggle, enjoying the close proximity of Johnboy and the expensive smell of him.

'As if I would,' he said, with a twinkle in his eye. 'But, then, you always were an expert at keeping me at arm's length.'

Hilary blushed. Right now she'd switch that particular skill for any other, given the opportunity. 'Where are you living?'

'Haslemere. Bloody great barn of a place and nothing to fill it.'

For the first time in their conversation Hilary sensed traces of anger in Johnboy's words, or was it regret?

'Kids,' he said flatly. 'I love 'em, but can't have any.'

'You could adopt,' Hilary said, beginning to feel uncomfortable with the way the conversation was going. Should they be talking about such personal things? Wasn't this whole evening supposed to be superficial and on the level of merely comparing notes on what they had all achieved?

'Can you see Naomi with her hands anywhere near a nappy?'

'She might if given the chance,' Hilary said brightly.

'She only married me because she knew I wouldn't be able to get her pregnant and spoil that lovely body of hers.'

'I'm sure she didn't.'

He shook his head. 'You really haven't changed, have you, Hilary? You always did look on the bright side of things and see life through rose-tinted spectacles. What a wonderful way to be.'

The party broke up just after eleven. A few were heading off into town to a club but after Hilary had said her goodbyes she drove home, pondering on the evening. What had threatened to be a nightmare had actually turned out to be an enjoyable evening out. It had been fun catching up with all those people she hadn't thought of in years. What had surprised her most was that there had been no one-upmanship. Life had dealt each one of them a hand of cards which they had simply got on and played. It didn't seem to matter whether they had achieved incredible wealth, notoriety, or had been made redundant, got married or divorced, had children or not, they were simply living their lives as best they could – failure didn't come into it. What was it Johnboy had said when they'd been looking at the school photographs together? 'We're all monumental successes just to have got this far.'

He was right. And had he been right when he'd suggested it was time for her to start thinking about herself, now that the children were both at school? 'Go back to teaching,' he'd said, 'if that's what you're good at.'

Half an hour later, and still reflecting on the evening, it struck Hilary with force, as she drove along the main street of the village, that from now on David's affair was not going to make a failure of her. No longer would she allow her breaking heart to make her think her life was completely worthless. Skinny Lesley, Carrie Maxwell and Johnboy – especially Johnboy – had unwittingly helped her to see things more clearly.

She turned into Acacia Lane and, as the street-light on the corner lit up the interior of the car, she caught sight of her handbag on the passenger seat. She smiled as she thought of Johnboy's business card tucked inside her purse. He had insisted they exchange addresses. 'We must stay in touch,' he'd said. 'Who knows what might happen to us from this night on?'

'Who knows indeed?' Hilary said out loud, as she looked thoughtfully up at The Gables.

26

It was less than a week until Christmas and Hilary was rolling out a ragged oval of pastry to the sound of Johnny Mathis singing 'When a Child is Born'. For the first time ever, she was way behind with her festive preparations: the marzipan wasn't on the cake, the crackers weren't bought and she hadn't given a thought to the brandy butter.

She sprinkled more flour on to the worktop, glad at least that she'd ordered all the cards and wrapping-paper through one of those charity catalogues at school and that the children's presents were carefully hidden at the top of the airing cupboard – they'd been there since before . . . before she'd found out about David.

She'd lost count of how many weeks it was since her life had undergone such a dramatic change, but somewhere along the line, during the time that autumn had given way to winter, the impossible had happened: she had become accustomed to this new way of life. Only yesterday one of those current flavour-of the-month clerics on the radio had been saying that when people accept that their lives are about to change they are more able to cope with what lies ahead.

Hilary started pressing out small circles of pastry, knowing that it was all well and good acknowledging the changes being forced on to her by David but she was still struggling to accept the consequences.

She looked up from the cutter in her hand, remembering what Nick had said, that awful day at his cottage: '. . . our response determines the consequences'.

Her response, for the time being, was to stay quiet and put her mind to thinking about a new course of direction for her own life as Johnboy had said a few weeks ago: 'Go back to teaching.' Well, come the new year, she would make enquiries. If nothing else, a job would give her independence . . . independence she might well need.

The egg-shaped timer on the windowsill gave a loud shrill ring and, shaking the flour from her hands, she pulled on a pair of oven gloves and reached into the Aga for the fourth batch of mince pies she'd made that afternoon. She placed the hot tray on the draining board and wondered what David would buy her for Christmas. Probably the *Which? Guide to Divorce*. He'd want a quick economical divorce, wouldn't he?

Last year he'd bought her a daring négligé in a large box with a ribbon, and he'd been so embarrassed after the Queen's speech when everyone had insisted she open her present there and then in front of them all.

'Go on,' her mother had urged. 'Let's see what David's got for you.'

David's face had been a picture as he'd tried to deflect Louise with another glass of port. His own mother had tried to hide her shock at the transparency of the garment when, finally, the box had been opened. 'Very nice,' she had muttered, pretending to be more interested in the *Batman* film the children were watching on television.

Hilary placed the last of the hot mince pies on a cooling rack and was about to dust them with icing sugar when the doorbell rang.

It was Charlotte with Mabel. 'It's Tuesday, my day off from the shop, so how about a walk?'

'That sounds more like an ultimatum than an invitation,' Hilary said.

'You're right, it does. So get your coat and lock up.'

'But it's been raining all day, it'll be wet and—'

'It's stopped, now get a move on.'

They set off for the mere along the narrow footpath between All in the Mind and The White Cottage. Iris Braithwaite was in her back garden. She was wearing an old mac and a plastic rain-hood tied with a large bow under her chin. She was prodding at a reluctant bonfire with a long stick. 'Can't seem to get the wretched thing going,' she said, through the privet hedge. 'The leaves are too wet after all this rain.'

As Hilary and Charlotte carried on down the sheltered muddy path, a low pale sun burst through the parting clouds catching the drips of rain on the wet black branches of the trees either side of them and turning each droplet of water into a sparkling pearl. But when they reached the more exposed area overlooking the mere, where there was a large gap in the trees, an icy blast of wind swept across the water, rippling small waves as it did so.

Hilary buttoned her coat, right up to her chin. She watched Charlotte bend down to let Mabel off the lead. 'I feel like our roles have reversed,' she said unexpectedly.

Charlotte had never before credited Hilary with much intuition. Her sister had always blundered her way through any thought-provoking situation with as much mental agility and sensitivity as a charging bull. 'I know what you mean,' she said, slipping her arm through Hilary's. 'For once I do actually feel like I'm the eldest.'

'Ever since I can remember, I've always wanted to be the older sister. As a child I was maddened by our mother's ineffectualness and decided from an early age that if she didn't want to play the part of mother hen, then I would. And now—'

'And now you can't cope with supervising me because your well-ordered life has come to an end . . . just as mine did.'

They walked down the sloping bank to the water's edge. Hilary picked up a flat stone and sent it skimming across the water. 'One . . . two . . . three . . .'

she counted, before the stone disappeared from view. She turned and faced Charlotte. 'Do you think Peter would have ever had an affair?'

Charlotte suddenly laughed. 'Oh, Hilary, Peter had been having an affair almost from the day I met him, probably before as well.'

Hilary was shocked. 'But you never said anything. Who was it? Anyone you knew?'

Charlotte bent and picked up a stone. She angled her arm low and spun the stone away from her. It disappeared into the water at once. 'It was work with Peter. His career was his all-consuming mistress.'

'Well, that doesn't count,' Hilary said off-handedly. She reached for another stone.

'Oh yes it does. When a man implies to his wife that his job means more to him than his marriage, believe me, it counts. An affair with a career is just as damaging as a sexual one. So much so, on the morning Peter died, I . . . I had just asked him for a divorce.'

The stone in Hilary's hand dropped to the ground. 'Charlotte . . . I don't know what to say. Why didn't you tell me? Does Mother know about this?'

Charlotte shook her head. 'No, but I told Dad a few months ago.'

'I had no idea you were so unhappy. I wish I'd known – I could have helped in some way.'

'I didn't tell anyone . . . I didn't want people to know I'd failed.'

'Oh, God, that's just how I feel and Mother's the last person I'd want to know that I'd failed in my marriage.'

Charlotte went over to Hilary and hugged her. 'I can hear Mother's words now – "You girls are so careless with your husbands!" '

Hilary managed a laugh and they rejoined the path and began the circuit of the mere. In the distance they could see Mabel's furry white body moving in and out of the trees.

'What would you have done if you had discovered Peter was having an affair – I mean, a conventional bed-hopping type of affair?'

Charlotte thought for a moment. She tried to imagine Peter in bed with another woman but found it difficult even to picture his face. Unable to come up with a suitable image, she said, 'With hindsight I'd like to think I'd have wished him a small amount of happiness in his miserable existence. But that's with hindsight and with the safety of Alex in my life.'

'But what about before Alex? Say, two years ago.'

'I probably would have gone berserk and done the same as that woman in the paper last summer.'

Hilary almost smiled. 'What – cut off all the arms and legs from your husband's expensive suits?'

'Exactly, and probably a lot worse.'

'I smashed all David's expensive glasses from his mother,' Hilary admitted.

Charlotte laughed. 'Brilliant! And how very out of character.'

'I tried something even worse,' Hilary said, quietly. She pushed her cold hands into her jacket pockets, remembering with annoyance that she'd left her gloves on the oak chest in the hall.

'Go on,' Charlotte urged. 'What did you try?'

'I . . . I wanted to prove – Oh, Lord, I don't know how to say it.'

'It can't be all that bad.'

'I threw myself at another man,' she said, coming to a stop by a wooden bench that gave an uninterrupted view of the mere. She ran her fingers over the back of the seat. 'And not by chance. I planned it to happen.'

Charlotte raised her eyebrows.

'You see, you *are* shocked. I knew—'

'Calm down. Of course I'm shocked, but that's not to say I don't understand why.'

'Did you ever . . . well, you know . . . Were you ever unfaithful when you were so unhappy in Brussels?'

'No, I wasn't. Though who's to know what might have happened if I'd met Alex before Peter's death? But never mind me. What do you really feel about David? Do you love him or is it the tick-tock of your anniversary clock that keeps your marriage going?'

'I'm not sure of anything now. I thought I loved David and then, oh, I don't know, I just seem to be conscious of all his faults right now. Because of his affair I can't see anything good or attractive in him.'

The wind was bitingly cold as they stood still. Charlotte indicated that they should carry on walking and said, 'And what does Nick Bradshaw mean to you?'

Hilary looked up sharply. 'How do you know it was him?'

'A lucky guess. Probably it was his behaviour towards David at Derek and Cindy's party, and I'd also seen the two of you talking together earlier on in the evening.'

Hilary was shocked. 'You don't suppose anyone else will have thought the same, do you?'

'I doubt it.'

'Honestly, Charlotte, nothing's actually happened between us, I swear.' Hilary's face was earnest. 'I planned to make him seduce me, but he refused to play along. It was all rather humiliating.'

'Horrible man,' Charlotte said sympathetically. 'But why did you . . . why did you turn to him?'

Hilary thought back to the night at the restaurant with David and the moment when she'd made up her mind to ring Nick. She quickly swallowed back the hurt and anger that were rising in her throat. 'I wanted reassurance, I suppose.'

'Hardly surprising, given the circumstances.'

'And now I keep asking myself the same question: Is my marriage worth saving?' She gazed into the distance across to Bosley Cloud, looming high on the horizon, then turned back to her sister. 'I've decided to confront David after Christmas.'

Charlotte put her arm round Hilary's shoulders. 'I'm so proud of you. You're handling this far better than I would have done.'

'Common sense, I suppose. You always said I was the practical one.'

As the light began to fade and a hazy twilight blurred the water's edge, they completed the circuit of the mere and returned to the clearing in the pine trees. While Charlotte put Mabel on the lead, she reflected on how much closer she and Hilary had grown in the past few months. She hoped that when Hilary's life was back on an even keel they would never lose this new-found deeper level of understanding.

'We haven't even discussed your wedding on Saturday,' Hilary said, cutting into Charlotte's thoughts. 'I'm sure I should be doing more.'

'Rubbish!' Charlotte said, recognising that the time for shared disclosures and intimacy was over. 'You've got enough on your plate. But you are coming to the rehearsal tomorrow night, aren't you? Seven o'clock. Is that okay?'

'It's fine. Becky and I'll be there.' Suddenly Hilary's face broke into a frown.

'What's wrong?' Charlotte asked, concerned.

'The children,' Hilary said in a tightly controlled voice. 'What about the children? It's all very well us having this sophisticated grown-up talk about whether or not my marriage is worth keeping, but the bottom line is that a wrong decision on my part could destroy their lives.'

'That won't happen,' Charlotte said firmly, and with more assurance than she felt. 'Now, tell me how Becky looks in her bridesmaid's dress.'

'She looks beautiful,' Hilary said, accepting Charlotte's distraction, 'but she's refusing to wear it on Saturday.' Then, looking at her watch, she said, 'Goodness, we must hurry or I'll be late for Becky coming out of school.'

As Charlotte followed her sister along the footpath she had the terrible feeling that her big day wasn't going to go exactly as she and Alex had planned. She let Hilary's words go, preferring instead to live a little longer in hope and ignorance.

27

'Heureux anniversaire, Martina!'

Martina smiled round at the group. 'Merci,' she said.

'Maintenant les bougies,' Patricia instructed, glancing up from the scrap of paper in her hand with its selection of carefully thought-out phrases.

'Yes, blow them out so that we can get on and have something to eat, I'm starving,' Nick whispered in Hilary's ear.

Hilary had hoped that Nick might have missed this, their final French class of the term and small party to celebrate Martina's birthday. He hadn't turned up for the previous two lessons, since the embarrassing incident at his cottage, and now here he was standing next to her and reminding her only too well what a fool she'd made of herself.

She watched Martina cut the birthday cake which Patricia had made specially – the fondant icing was even coloured the same as the French tricolour. What a monumental creep, thought Hilary, as she stabbed a stick of celery into the Stilton and *crème fraîche* dip she'd made that afternoon after her walk with Charlotte.

Nick squeezed past her and helped himself to a stick of celery. She felt she ought to say something to him. But what? What on earth could she say to a man who, in a moment of madness, she had kissed in the hope of getting him to . . . ?

'I hope you're not going to ignore me.'

She crunched on her celery.

'I should be very disappointed in you, Hilary, if that's to be the case.'

She crunched some more.

'We can still be friends,' he persevered.

At the front of the classroom Patricia was fiddling with a ghetto-blaster and suddenly the room was filled with Edith Piaf's husky voice singing 'Non, Je Ne Regrette Rien'. 'Just to get us in the right mood for our little *soirée*,' Patricia called out.

Nick looked at Hilary and smiled. 'Come on, Hilary, we can't pretend it didn't happen, so let's not regret it either.'

'But I do,' she murmured.

'What embarrasses you most? The fact that we kissed or that we didn't make love?'

'Please,' she said desperately, 'keep your voice down.'

'Only if you answer the question.'

Hilary tried to think straight. Just what exactly was her honest answer? There was no doubt in her mind that she had enjoyed kissing Nick, just as she'd enjoyed Johnboy's attention at the school reunion a couple of weeks ago. Thinking of that night, she saw that what she'd hoped to get from Nick in a moment of madness she had, in fact, gained from Johnboy – and without making a fool of herself. In just a few short hours her old classmate had sufficiently raised her self-esteem so that she could imagine herself coping with the future.

'You two are very cosy together, aren't you?' Patricia interrupted, handing them each a slice of birthday cake on paper napkins. 'Quite the Romeo and Juliet of the group with your regular hushed *tête-à-têtes.*'

'Always willing to make it a threesome,' Nick said lightly.

Patricia eyed him. 'A *ménage à trois*, you mean?'

'No,' he said firmly. 'Technically that would mean that Hilary and I would have to be married.'

Patricia laughed. 'Now I think David might just have something to say about that.'

'And to think I used to like that awful woman,' Hilary said quietly, as they watched Patricia move on to dole out more of Martina's tricolour birthday cake.

'Perhaps you're becoming more discerning these days.'

She looked up at Nick and met his eyes. 'You know, I do believe I am. Since I discovered David's affair I've started thinking and acting quite differently. What used to matter to me no longer does. You're the expert, is that normal?'

'Whether it's normal or not, is irrelevant, it's what—'

'I wish you'd answer my questions with a simple yes or no.'

He took a bite of birthday cake and chewed it. 'Yes,' he said at last. 'Hilary, I pronounce you quite normal.'

'Thank goodness,' she said, biting into her piece of cake. 'Ugh! Cheap margarine and too much sugar.' She looked about her for a suitable hiding place for the rest of Patricia's baking disaster.

'Here, let me finish it for you,' Nick said, taking it from her. 'I'm obviously not as fussy as you, and while I eat you can tell me why you're learning French – I've never asked you that before.'

'No,' she said, handing him her slice of cake, 'you've been too busy prying into everything else in my life.'

He smiled. 'Sharper as well as more discerning. Go on, tell me why you're here.'

She helped herself to a handful of crisps. 'Just a boring case of the annual pilgrimage to France being backed up with the ability to do more than navigate one's way around a menu.' She shook her head and sighed. 'Ironic,

338

isn't it? At the rate things are going, a camping holiday in France *en famille* is the last thing I'll be doing next summer.'

'Who knows where we'll all be in a year's time?'

'Who knows?' she repeated, thoughtfully.

'Penny for them?'

She told him about the school reunion and what Johnboy had said to her.

'He's right, of course,' Nick said. 'This Johnboy character, he's not going to become a complication, is he?'

She shook her head. 'I shouldn't think so for one minute. So, why are you learning French?'

'Same reason as you. I love Brittany and go there each summer and last year I decided to put a stop to looking such an idiot every time I opened my mouth.'

'I don't think you could ever look an idiot.'

Nick laughed. 'Are you flirting with me?'

Hilary laughed, too, seeing for the first time that even in the depths of wretchedness there was always a degree of humour to be found.

From the other side of the room Patricia gave them both a long, hard stare.

Later that night Georgia's Jeep crept quietly along the deserted main street of the village. It stopped just outside Ted the Toup's, its engine still running. Three silent figures got out and went and huddled around the glass door of the shop. The smallest of the figures pushed open the letter-box; it made a loud grating noise.

'Ssh,' the tallest of the trio said.

The third person then inserted a polythene bag through the opening, turned the bag upside down and began to shake it.

Georgia smiled as the trio climbed back inside the Jeep. Once word got round, Ted would be lucky to sell a newspaper, never mind anything else he kept hidden under wraps at the back of his shop.

The shop was still in darkness when Ted came downstairs the next morning. He hated the winter months and having to get up in the cold to organise those militant newspaper boys and girls. They were always asking for more money or complaining that the bags were too heavy for them. Kids! Wimps, the whole lot of them. Nosy too. He'd caught that lad with the whiskers just showing through on his top lip having a good old rummage in the boxes of new gear he'd got out the back. It was expensive stuff, and he didn't need the likes of that lad's grubby hands fingering any of it.

He yawned, then pulled out a cigarette from the box in his cardigan pocket. He flicked at his lighter and walked over to the door to bring in the papers left there on the doorstep. He was looking forward to reading about that politician who was supposed to be doing it five times a night with his research assistant. No wonder the Government was making such a bloody mess of running the country, they were all too exhausted.

As he walked towards the door his shoes made a strange crunching sound. He looked down at the floor.

'Shit!' he yelled, jumping back in horror and knocking into one of the rotating racks of novels. Bonk-buster novels crashed to the floor, scattering a thousand wriggling white bodies yet further.

'Shit!' he shouted again, seeing his wig lying amongst what looked suspiciously like maggots.

A bang at the door made him jump again. It was the nosy lad with the whiskers. Ted let him in.

'Yuck,' the lad said, looking about him. 'Where've all these maggots come from?' He tried hard not to look at his employer's bald head.

'Bloody good question,' Ted said. He bent down, picked up his wig and waved it vigorously at arm's length. 'Well, don't just stand there. Get a broom and sweep up this mess.'

The lad shook his head. 'I'm a paper boy not a cleaner.'

Ted sucked so hard on his cigarette he almost bit it in two.

Within half an hour most of the village had heard from the paper boys and girls that Ted's shop was crawling with maggots. Within an hour, Iris Braithwaite had appeared and declared the shop a health hazard. And within two hours, a sharp-faced woman from the Environmental Health Department had arrived. While Ted tried to conceal his recently bought merchandise, the woman filled in a form, slapped it on the counter and announced that unless the shop was cleaner than an operating theatre by five o'clock that day it would be officially closed.

'I've been set up,' he said, 'this is all to try and prevent me—'

'Prevent you from what, Mr Cooper?' the sharp-faced woman asked, knowing full well of the raging debate currently going on in Hulme Welford.

'Nothing,' Ted muttered. He knew disapproval when he saw it and he was looking at it right now in the face of the representative from the Environmental Health Department.

'Either I or a colleague will be back later,' she said, her hand already pulling open the door. 'Oh, and by the way,' she added, 'I think you'll find you have a maggot crawling out from under your – I mean, crawling in your hair.'

As she closed the door behind her Ted snatched off his wig and hurled it across the shop.

28

While Ted the Toup grappled with a mop and a bucket of Jeyes fluid, the school gym, decorated in paper chains and depictions of the Three Wise Men, erupted with enthusiastic and relieved parental applause.

Flashbulbs sparked and video cameras rolled as the school nativity play came to the end of its one and only performance of the year to a packed house, and right in the front row of a cast of a dozen or more curtsying angels, Becky, with her lopsided wings and tinsel halo, waved energetically at her mother next to Georgia. Hilary discreetly waved back. Chloe, holding an upside-down plastic Jesus and dressed in expiation blue, was sulking in the back row along with a multitude of cotton-wool-bearded shepherds. She caught sight of her mother and scowled. Georgia stuck her fingers in her mouth and let out a piercing whistle.

'A way to go!' she yelled. She nudged Hilary and whispered, 'I'm only doing that to annoy Mesdames Longton and Hampton. That, and Chloe bet me I wouldn't have the nerve. That's a week's pocket money she owes me and just look at the smile on her face now.'

When the clapping finally subsided and Mr Atkinson, the headmaster, made his way to the front of the stage and stood alongside the stable, which looked more like an exotic pool-side bar than a ramshackle Judaean outbuilding, Hilary and Georgia got to their feet and crept along the row of applauding parents and associated grandparents. A few other mothers joined them. As members of the PTA, they knew from experience that the headmaster's vote of thanks would be sufficiently long-winded to give them ample time for any last-minute finishing touches required for the Christmas Fayre.

During lunch-break the PTA had decorated the classrooms in which the stalls were to be set up. The room where Hilary had her French lessons each week was to be home to 'Pin the Red Nose on Rudolf', while the surrounding classrooms were to have home-baked goods, refreshments, a bottle tombola, 'Throw the Angel's Halo Over the Crib' and the white elephant stall – where last year's unwanted Christmas presents were to be recycled.

Unable to get away from the nursery any earlier, Georgia had turned up at the last minute with her Jeep full of green foliage to decorate the classrooms, along with an armful of mistletoe. 'A wind-up for Chloe's benefit,' she'd said to Hilary as they unloaded the back of the Jeep.

While the headmaster got on with thanking his excellent and overworked staff, Georgia assembled the PTA in the largest of the classrooms, where alcoholic refreshments were to be served. 'Right,' she said briskly. 'Patricia, here's the money for each stall-holder's float, it's clearly marked, so go round all the classrooms and—'

'Yes, I'm well aware of the procedure,' Patricia said, reaching for the money-bags and snatching them out of Georgia's hands. 'I *have* done this before.'

'Look, chuck,' Georgia said, placing a hand on Patricia's arm, 'try making it easier on yourself. Okay?'

Patricia was horrified and shrugged away from Georgia's hand. 'Don't you ever, ever touch me again, you—'

Georgia laughed. 'Oh, you're beautiful when you're angry, Pattie babes!'

'Why do you do it?' Hilary asked, when they were left alone after Patricia had flounced off in a panic of potential defilement.

'I can't help myself,' Georgia replied, taking the lid off a large saucepan on a hot plate and giving the contents a stir. She popped in a few more slices of orange. 'She's such a sitting target. All that prejudice and middle-class crap all rolled up into one almighty time-bomb just waiting to go off.' She put the lid back on the mulled wine. 'Why are you looking at me like that?'

Hilary shook her head and sighed. She draped a garland of green tinsel along the front of a table covered in red crêpe paper. 'You're so sure of yourself, aren't you?'

'Arrogant, you mean?'

'No, not arrogant. I always get the feeling that you don't care what anyone thinks of you.'

'And you'd be right. Now stop jabbering on like this. Lost-His-Way Atkinson will be winding up any moment now and we've got all these cups to set out, and you know how everyone makes a bee-line for anything alcoholic after suffering one of his interminable speeches.'

Georgia was right. A flood of eye-rolling parents soon descended upon them, hands outstretched for a sedative cup of mulled wine. But the mood soon changed and with what sounded like Pinky and Perky singing 'O Come All Ye Faithful' on Patricia's ghetto-blaster, mothers who had stayed up late the night before running to earth a checked tea-towel for a shepherd's headdress, or who had knocked up a last-minute pair of wings, began to relax while their husbands, who were all playing hookey from work, stood around in groups jangling coins in their trouser pockets and comparing notes on the latest mileage allowances on their company cars.

As she took in the familiar scene Hilary felt angry that David wasn't there. At breakfast that morning he'd told her that he'd be unable to make it in time for the nativity play, something about a meeting with his accountant. Accountant, my foot, she'd thought afterwards as she'd stripped the children's beds and stuffed the sheets and duvet covers into the washing machine. Now he can't even spare an hour or so to see his own daughter on stage. Fired up with anger she had raced around the house with the vacuum cleaner, deliberately bashing into David's armchair in the sitting-room, then the desk in his study. But when she'd taken the washing outside to hang on the line, her anger had miraculously vanished. Sunlight was filtering through the naked branches of the cherry trees at the end of the garden, throwing long spindly shadows across the lawn, and she found herself smiling. As she pegged the first of the sheets on the line and breathed in the pleasant smell of washing powder, she wondered at the absurdity of her situation; that even in a moment of extreme anger and bewilderment she could derive enjoyment from something as simple as sunlight streaking across the lawn. Perhaps it was true, after all, that the ordinary could always outweigh the unexpected and traumatic.

'You're looking serious, Hilary.'

'Dad, what are you doing here?' she asked, surprised to see her father on the other side of the table holding out his hand for a cup of mulled wine.

'You didn't think I'd miss Becky's big performance, did you?'

She was touched. 'Oh, how sweet of you. Is Mother with you?'

He shook his head.

'Of course not,' Hilary said, her voice matter-of-fact as she handed him his drink. 'Busy at the shop.'

'Can't stop long myself.'

'Oh?'

'Things to do in the kitchen,' he replied. 'I've got the cake to ice.'

'I haven't done mine yet either.'

'I don't mean the Christmas cake, I'm talking about Charlotte and Alex's cake.'

Hilary felt a stab of jealousy. Charlotte's wedding cake. Just as she'd set about playing Cupid last year with Charlotte and Alex, so, too, she had fully intended to take care of the catering for her sister's big day. Now that pleasure was to be denied her. She had been usurped by – of all people – her father, who up until six months ago had done little more in the kitchen than stir his own low-calorie cocoa. Now here he was preparing a finger-food buffet for an army of guests, who were going to expect a darn sight more than a few pickled onions and bowls of crisps to pick over. She knew it was nasty of her but she couldn't help but wish that Neville had stuck to his lifelong hobby of gooseberry-growing. Why the sudden change?

But it wasn't only that she'd been upstaged by her father that was causing her to feel jealous. For years she'd known and accepted that she didn't mean as much to her father as Charlotte did; there was a closeness between them that she herself had never experienced. As a young child she'd been conscious of a gap between her and her father; a gap she'd never been able to bridge. It hadn't bothered her at the time – like all children, she had simply filled her life with the busyness of growing up. The intricacies of relationships are nothing to a ten-year-old girl intent on a life given over to choir practice and ballet lessons. That Charlotte had preferred their father's company to perfecting a *grand battement* had seemed slightly bizarre to Hilary, all those years ago. Often she had come home after an arduous ballet class and found Charlotte and Neville together in the garden bent over a gooseberry bush, each convincing the other that this was the bush which would yield a prize-winning berry.

Hilary watched her father take a sip of his wine as he cast his eyes about the room. Rarely did she take the time to regard him with anything more than a passing look of interest. She did so now and, to her surprise, was taken aback by what she saw and felt. There was a reassuring benignity to his face that made her throat tighten. She felt cheated. Why had he not bestowed more of that kindliness on her? Anger and hurt merged together inside her. She felt almost as badly betrayed by her father as she did by David – the two men in her life who should have loved her most had let her down. Why?

'See you,' Neville said, as he moved away from her.

'Yes,' she replied, filled with a sudden need to rush over to him and ask what terrible thing she had done. What crime had she committed to be on the receiving end of so little love?

'Mum!' It was Becky, now out of her angel costume and wearing her school uniform. In her hands was a large jar of Smarties. Chloe was by her side and she was holding a note-pad and pen. 'We're doing "Guess How Many Smarties in the Jar",' Becky said, her eyes wide as she looked down at the sweets.

'Lovely,' Hilary said, ladling out two cups of mulled wine for a customer and trying not to think of her father. 'Don't get in anyone's way, will you?'

'Fifty pence a go,' Chloe shouted above the music. 'Each Smartie represents an oppressed woman.'

'What's that, dearie?' asked one of the old ladies from the local nursing home who, each year, were treated to this extravaganza of entertainment. She was wearing a snowball of a hat and too much make-up; in one hand she held a plastic cup and in the other a half-eaten mince pie. She should have been having tea and biscuits in Class I with the rest of her group but she'd escaped, following her nose to something stronger than Typhoo.

'Fifty pence a go,' Chloe repeated, even louder. 'Each Smartie represents an oppressed woman.'

'They don't look overdressed to me, dearie,' the old woman said, giving the jar of sweets a long, hard stare.

'Oppressed!' shouted Chloe impatiently.

The old woman thought about this. Then, chucking Chloe under the chin, she said, 'And what will Santa be bringing you this year? A nice little dolly?'

Chloe looked as though she was about to bite the woman's hand off. 'No such thing as Father Christmas,' she said tersely. 'It's a silly myth invented by men to glorify their own self-image.'

'That'll do, Chloe,' Georgia intervened, catching the shocked expression on Becky's face. 'I'm sorry, Hilary, but I think you might have some bedtime explaining to do tonight.'

They watched Chloe and Becky move off to prey on an easier target.

'You were only joking, weren't you?' Hilary heard Becky asking Chloe.

Poor Becky, Hilary thought. This Christmas she would discover that Father Christmas was a sham . . . and who knew what she would discover about her own father?

As Pinky and Perky moved on to 'I Saw Mommy Kissing Santa Claus' a harassed-looking Patricia came towards them.

'We're running out of small change,' she said accusingly, a five-pound note in her hand. 'You didn't make up the floats properly. We always have—'

'No problem,' Georgia said, reaching for the petty-cash box under the table. 'What do you need?'

'Ten- and twenty-pence pieces. If you had done it the way we—'

Georgia handed over the money, and from behind her back she pulled out a sprig of mistletoe. She dangled it in front of Patricia. 'Give us a kiss, Pattie babes,' she said, with a leery grin.

'I thought I'd warned you to leave me alone,' Patricia said, in a loud, angry voice. Heads turned.

'Ah, why don't you do us all a big favour and ease up? You're up to your panty-line in repression.'

'How dare you!' shrieked Patricia. 'And while we're about it, let me tell you, I'm sick and tired of being the butt of your foul humour. In fact, I'd go as far as saying that we're all sick of your views. People like you are quite out of place in a respectable village like this. And, what's more, we all know it's you who's been terrorising poor Mr Cooper. I saw, with my own eyes, you and your Jeep outside my house when all those things were thrown at his shop.'

'Well, if I was outside your house it couldn't have been me terrorising that disgusting man, could it?'

'It *was* you!' persisted Patricia, her voice now reaching a piercing soprano pitch. She was sounding and looking for all the world like a petulant prima donna, with one hand on her hip and the other pointing a finger at Georgia.

'How dare you speak to Ms D'Arcy like that?' thundered a familiar contralto with all the force and impact of the 'Ride of the Valkyries'.

Patricia lowered her finger and began to tremble as Iris Braithwaite marched into the room.

'I've heard quite enough from you, young lady,' Iris went on. 'And I can assure you that Ms D'Arcy is not alone in her brave fight against Mr Cooper. On the morning to which you are referring I was present. I not only saw what took place, I instigated it. There, now, what do you say to that?'

A shock wave of surprise rippled around the room – and while nobody was looking, the old lady from the nursing home helped herself to another cup of mulled wine. She took a large gulp. 'Happy Christmas,' she said merrily, then spat out a small black clove.

29

'Now, Becky,' Malcolm Jackson said, in his extra-specially patient voice – the one he sometimes used with the more troublesome members of the PCC. 'You've got a very important job to do, haven't you?' He smiled encouragingly at Becky, hoping that now that she was centre stage of Charlotte and Alex's wedding rehearsal she would pay attention and stop banging her feet against the pew in front of her.

Becky jumped up and joined him. Malcolm carefully manoeuvred her behind Charlotte. 'There now,' he said, 'you pretend your Auntie Charlotte's got her beautiful dress—'

'I think dresses are silly,' Becky said importantly, 'I've given them up. Auntie Charlotte, can I wear jeans on Saturday?'

Wear anything you want, thought Charlotte, just so long as you're quiet long enough for Alex and I to say *we do*. 'You'll have to check with Mummy.'

'Mummy said I'd have to check with you.'

Hilary and Charlotte exchanged looks of *now what?*

'As I was saying,' Malcolm persevered, 'I'm sure Charlotte likes dresses and the one she'll be wearing for the wedding will probably have a long bit trailing the floor behind her—'

Charlotte shook her head vehemently. She had deliberately chosen a dress without a train. She had no intention of running the risk of having anything touching the ground with Becky walking behind her.

'Well, imagine there is,' Malcolm continued, thinking that Job had got off lightly, 'because you must keep your distance, Becky. We don't want you tripping the bride up by getting too close. Do you think you can remember that?'

'Easy-peasy!'

Charlotte suspected that this was about as likely as hell freezing over, given that her niece had the attention-span of a goldfish.

'But what about Gramps?' Becky asked. 'Shouldn't he be practising this with us?'

Malcolm looked at his watch. 'We'll try it once without Gramps, then with him.'

'You in a hurry to get home to watch *Brookside* like Mum?'

Malcolm smiled stiffly.

'It might be nice to catch the *News at Ten*, though,' Louise said, from the front pew. Neville was sitting next to her, his head drooping so low that his chin was almost touching the knot in his tie.

'Are you sure about wanting to marry into my family?' Charlotte called over to Alex, who was sitting alone on the opposite pew to Louise and Neville.

'So long as we only have the one wedding,' he answered.

'I don't understand why Auntie Charlotte's got to practise. This is her second wedding, isn't it?'

'Because she didn't get it right the first time,' suggested Louise.

'What did you do wrong, Auntie Charlotte?'

'She didn't do anything wrong,' Malcolm interrupted, hoping his wife would have the presence of mind to put the video recorder on. 'Neville, perhaps you'd like to come and join us, after all. Neville?'

'*Neville!*' Louise shouted in her husband's ear. 'You're wanted.'

'Sorry, everyone,' Neville apologised, as he got to his feet and staggered towards the group. 'Sorry, Charlotte, shan't do it on the big day.'

And as the trio at last began the walk up the aisle, to the sound of Louise singing 'Stately as a Galleon I Sail Across the Floor', Charlotte wondered whether it wasn't too late to call the whole thing off.

It was snowing when they finally got outside, with soft downy pillows of snow lying against shadowy tombstones. Becky whooped with delight and danced excitedly about the churchyard. She picked up a handful of snow and threw it at her mother. Light and powdery, the snowball disintegrated before it reached its target. Hilary laughed at her. She turned to Charlotte. 'Do you remember New Year's Eve, all those years ago, when you danced in the snow without your shoes?'

Charlotte smiled. 'I think I was showing off.'

'Fancy trying it now?' Alex said, slipping his arm through Charlotte's.

'What, and catch pneumonia just in time for Saturday? Second thoughts, maybe that's not such a stupid idea.'

'You're marrying me in three days' time and that's an end to it,' Alex said, 'or otherwise—' He bent down and scooped up a handful of snow.

'Oh no you don't!' shrieked Charlotte. She ran off along the whitened path and out through the lych-gate. Alex chased after her with Becky close behind, their feet crunching the snow.

'How about everyone coming back for a drink?' asked Hilary, thinking of the wall of silence at The Gables when she and Becky returned home.

'No,' Louise answered with a shiver. 'There's another one of those court-room dramas on the telly I want to see.' She pushed her hands into her sheepskin gloves and braced herself for the walk back up the hill.

Neville was disappointed. He would have liked to join in the fun. He kissed Hilary goodnight and followed in Louise's trail of footsteps.

With her parents' figures already little more than blurred outlines in the snowy darkness Hilary crossed the main street of the village alone. Ahead of her she could hear Becky's happy voice in the muffled silence of the snow-filled sky, and within the orangy glow of light cast from the lamp-post at the top of Acacia Lane snowflakes were falling in an easy, constant rhythm. It was a perfect Christmas card setting and reminded Hilary of the scene in *The Lion, the Witch and the Wardrobe* when Mr Tumnus first appears to Lucy. How perfect it had all seemed to Lucy until she found out the truth from the sad little faun.

She hurried on and soon caught up with Charlotte and Alex. It was then that Becky's scream rang out long and shrill, jarring terrifyingly with the quietness of Acacia Lane.

They rushed over to The White Cottage where Becky stood at the open gate staring down at the ground, her eyes wide and frightened. Beneath a blanket of snow lay a body, and at one end of it a small patch of snow was turning pink.

Alex knelt on the ground and quickly started brushing away at the thick covering of snow. 'My God,' he said, ripping off his coat and covering the body, 'it's Mrs Braithwaite!'

Hilary clutched at Charlotte's arm and Becky whispered, 'Is she dead?'

'She's only mildly concussed, but we'll keep her in overnight to be on the safe side,' the nurse told Charlotte and Alex. 'We've stitched and patched her up but, like most old people who are mugged, she's as mad as hell. It's their pride as much as anything that gets hurt. I'll let you see her for a few minutes, but only one of you, mind. She's had enough excitement for one night.'

Charlotte found Iris propped up in bed with several pillows behind her. Her bandaged head was sagging to one side as if she was asleep, but when Charlotte approached, her bruised and swollen eyes immediately flickered open.

'I just came to make sure you—'

'Spare me the pleasantries, Mrs Lawrence. The man who did this to me is going to be locked up.'

'Did you see who it was?'

'Of course I did. It was Ted Cooper.'

30

'Hi,' Tiffany said, as she saw Alex close the post-office door and start walking towards where she stood outside the baker's.

'No school today?' he asked, when he reached her after negotiating his way through the shovelled-up piles of snow on the pavement.

'Last day of term yesterday,' she answered. 'Barry comes home tomorrow. He said on the phone last night that the snow's been really bad in Leeds. I hope he makes it – I don't much fancy Christmas without him.'

'He'll make it,' Alex said, beginning to feel the cold – minus four had been given on the weather forecast earlier that morning, along with more snow. He stamped his boots on the pavement, shaking off the clumps of ice, while marvelling at Tiffany's ability, like most of her contemporaries, to brave the elements in little more than a skimpy black denim jacket and thin silky skirt.

'He better had, or I'll come and spend Christmas with you and Charlotte.'

'You're forgetting that Charlotte and I won't be there. We're getting married on Saturday.'

'Muffin 'ell, so you are. I wish you'd reminded me yesterday. I was late-night shopping in Manchester with Mum and Dad and could have bought you your wedding present. Now you'll have to make do with something local.' She glanced up and down the row of shops. 'What do you fancy? A pound of carrots or a bag of custard tarts?'

'Louise has got some rather nice Georgian silver candlesticks in her shop.'

'In your dreams! Either that or I'll have to go out and mug somebody.'

Alex flinched.

'What's wrong?'

'Haven't you heard about Iris Braithwaite?'

'Why, what's she done?'

Alex told Tiffany what had happened last night, how they had discovered the old lady lying unconscious in the snow and how they'd called an ambulance to take her to the hospital. 'It must have all been going on while you were coming back from Manchester.'

'Was it a burglar?'

'We're not sure yet—' but the rest of Alex's words were lost in the noise of a police car pulling up outside Ted Cooper's next to the baker's. Two uniformed officers got out and went inside.

'It's not about the maggots, is it?' Tiffany asked Alex. 'He's not prosecuting or anything daft like that, is he?'

Alex noticed the anxious look on Tiffany's face. 'I should think that's the least of his worries, right now. Mrs Braithwaite told Charlotte last night at the hospital that it was Ted who attacked her.'

'*What?*' And then it dawned on Tiffany. 'You mean revenge? He beat Mrs Braithwaite up because of the protest?'

Alex shook his head. 'I can't believe that he would do a thing like that. I know he's an old sleaze-bag, but to attack a woman he's known all these years and in a community like this ... Well, it just seems so unlikely.'

'Bloody men! You all stick together, don't you?'

'Tiffany, I'm just trying to be objective.'

'Shit you are!' She turned away angrily and pushed open the door of the bakery. From inside the shop she watched Alex walk back down the road.

'I'd like to squeeze the jam out of that one,' the younger of the two assistants said, as she arranged a tray of doughnuts in the window display and stared after Alex.

Tiffany cleared her throat noisily. 'A French stick and a large wholemeal, when you've got a moment.'

'Got one on you this morning, have you, Tiff?'

'No, I haven't,' she replied indignantly. 'But that Ted the Toup soon will have when the police have finished with him. They're next door, right now.' She leaned towards the counter. She knew that what she was doing was malicious, but she was so angry. 'He attacked Mrs Braithwaite last night. She's in hospital, in a really bad way.'

Tiffany watched their faces with satisfaction, handed over her money and left the shop, sure in the knowledge that, within the hour, practically everyone in the village would know that Ted Cooper wasn't just a pervy but a dangerous attacker of innocent women.

On her way home, she decided she'd give Georgia a ring. Perhaps they could visit Mrs Braithwaite. As she passed Charlotte's shop she saw Nick Bradshaw's car coming along the main street, his tyres churning the slush and ice on the road. He turned slowly into Daisy Bank. Immediately all thoughts of Mrs Braithwaite were put out of her mind. She tucked the French stick and wholemeal loaf under her arm and hurried home.

She arrived at All in the Mind just as Nick was reaching into the back of his car for his briefcase. 'Hi,' she said, trying to conceal that she was out of breath.

'Been running?' he asked.

Damn! 'Jogging,' she said, with an easy laugh.

'In the snow?'

'I have to keep fit, even in winter.' What was she doing? Why was it every time she wanted to talk to Nick she ended up sounding a right geek?

He slammed the car door shut and moved towards the house. 'You look fit enough to me,' he said over his shoulder.

She smiled. 'Do you think so? If you fancy a run, you could always come—'

'Never touch the stuff,' he said.

'What?'

'Exercise.' He pushed the door open. 'And something else I never touch, my employer's daughter, especially when she's young enough to be my own daughter.' He held the door and waited for her to go ahead of him.

She held back. 'Shit before the shovel,' she said. 'After you.'

Tiffany went inside and called Georgia on the mobile from her bedroom. 'You sound upset,' Georgia said. 'What's up?'

Tiffany threw a wet screwed-up tissue across the room. She told Georgia about Iris Braithwaite, which accounted for part of her anger, but she said nothing about Nick. 'Mrs Braithwaite says it was Ted Cooper who attacked her. The police are with him now.'

'The bastard!'

'You don't suppose we went too far and pushed him—'

'Look, Tiffany, shoving maggots through somebody's letter-box doesn't mean it's open season for beating up old ladies. How bad is Iris?'

'I don't know. Alex Hamilton only just told me ... Oh, God, Georgia, what have we done?'

'Hold tight, Tiffany. I'll ring the hospital.'

By the time Georgia had dialled the number for the hospital hot tears were pricking at her eyes. She rubbed them roughly with the heel of her hand, to the sound of Tiffany's words echoing accusingly in her head. *What have we done?*

'Come on, come on,' she said angrily into the mobile phone, as she paced the few available feet of space in the caravan. 'Answer the wretched thing!'

No answer came.

She pressed the off button, followed by redial. Still no answer. 'Bloody government cut-backs!' She cursed loudly and slammed the phone down on the table. She stared out at the snow-covered greenhouses and was suddenly struck by how very alone she was. There was no Gordon today – he and Winnie were Christmas-shopping in Macclesfield – and Chloe was at a friend's. She let out a long sigh and, resting her head against the flimsy wall of the caravan, she thought of the unimaginable horror Iris must have gone through ... alone. She clenched her fists, knowing that it was all her fault, it was down to *her* that this terrible thing had happened. She should never have got involved. She should have left the silly old woman to her ineffectual posters and clipboard. What right had she had to go stirring things up?

And just what the hell had she thought she was doing, getting herself involved with a woman like Iris? Nobody liked her. She was a pain. A nosy, interfering woman who irritated the hell out of everyone and who had even had the nerve to start butting in on her life – baking her cakes and sticking up for her against the likes of that bloody Longton woman. Bloody cheek!

She didn't need help like that. She could manage on her own. Life was about coping, managing and getting on with it. It wasn't about tins of cakes being delivered to the doorstep.

She tried to keep hold of this anger, forcing herself to rail against the image of someone who had tried to impose an unwanted presence on her life but, despite her anger and despite her defiance, a solitary stinging tear escaped and slowly made its way down her cheek. She let it go, surprised at the unexpected warmth of it against her cold skin. Another followed, and then another.

When Nick couldn't find anyone to help him pick out a Christmas tree, he knocked on the caravan door.

He found Georgia slumped on the floor, her head tucked hard against her drawn-up knees. She was shaking and crying so violently he could get no sense out of her. He picked her up and carried her over to the bungalow where he set her down on the sofa in the sitting-room and wrapped her in the throw-over from the back of a chair. He made no attempt to stop her tears but went to the kitchen to make a hot drink. When he took it through to her she had stopped sobbing but her frail body was still shuddering with uncontrollable spasms of what he took to be shock.

He held the mug of hot sweet tea against her chattering teeth and forced her to drink.

She took a sip, then looked at him through distant eyes and stammered, 'It's ... Iris. She really isn't the dragon everyone thinks she is.'

'If you say so,' he replied soothingly, pressing the mug against her mouth again and wondering whether he should call a doctor.

Cindy paused outside an empty seminar room, where earlier that morning Nick had given his class, 'Phone Home to Your Inner Self'. Peering through the glass panel she had watched a group of women lying on the floor. At first glance it could have been a fitness class from the days of In the Pink, except that these women hadn't formed a rainbow array of brightly coloured leotards and Lycra tights, they had been in their everyday clothes covered with a blanket and a pile of books under their heads – she kept meaning to ask Nick, why books? Why not a cushion? According to Nick, this supine position was a sure way to understanding your internal stress. Watching the women she had wondered how many of them lying there in front of Nick had anything remotely stressful going on in their lives. Most of them gave the impression of being completely at ease with life and here only to enjoy the attentions of their good-looking counsellor.

Nick had certainly turned out to be an asset to All in the Mind. Whether or not it had anything to do with his counselling skills Cindy wasn't entirely convinced. She suspected the popularity of his classes had more to do with the soft black curls at the nape of his neck; that and the tousled style of his dress caused most of the more mature women to want to take him in hand

and mother him. The younger ones probably had sex on their minds as they lay there submissively on the floor with their legs slightly apart.

To her shame she had actually pressed her ear to the door and tried to hear what he was saying. She'd caught snatches about energy systems and auras and a lot of other nonsense. Then he'd gone on to say, 'Now imagine yourself floating ... Does that give you a sense of freedom ... or does it make you feel helpless and vulnerable?'

Remembering how his question had made her feel like a monumental con merchant, Cindy moved along the corridor and on to the next seminar room. Through the open door she caught the unmistakable sound of Derek's laughter. She raised her hand to push the door further open but hesitated when she heard a woman laughing. A million and one past scenarios leapt into Cindy's mind, along with the conclusion that a leopard really couldn't change his spots.

She listened at the door.

'Rosie, you've got me all wrong.'

'Have I, I wonder?'

'Yes, you really couldn't be more wrong.'

'Derek, you must stop focusing on the negative. Now, come here and let me help you channel—'

'I need to get back to the office – Cindy will be expecting—'

'What are you afraid of, Derek?'

'Nothing.'

'You're afraid of me. I've sensed it for some time now.'

'Nonsense!'

'Are you sure I don't unnerve you because of my strong sexuality?'

'Rosie, I'm well aware of your—'

'Derek, I know you want me, I can see it in your eyes, but it's fear that keeps you from touching me, isn't it?'

'I've never been frightened of anyone in my life.'

'I don't believe you.'

'Certainly not of a woman.'

'Then touch me.'

'Rosie!'

'Yes, Derek.'

'This has gone far enough. Shouldn't you be preparing for your next seminar? What is it?'

' "When Heavenly and Earthly Bodies Collide".'

'I don't remember that being in the diary.'

'A change of plan. Why don't you come along? You could help me with the practical side of the session.'

'I'd love to only ... Rosie, what do you think you're doing? Get up!'

Cindy had heard enough. She stuffed a fist into her mouth, held her breath and ran as quickly and as quietly as she could to the office. She shut the door behind her and leaned against it. Tears began rolling down her cheeks as she laughed and laughed. Poor old Derek, he'd finally met his Waterloo.

She was still laughing when Derek, red-faced and sweating, came into the room.

'I'm not sure we chose exactly the right person when we took Rosie on.' He slumped over the desk, his head in his hands.

'Oh, do you really think so?' Cindy said, with only a trace of amusement in her voice. 'I thought you made an excellent choice.'

'She's a man-eater, Cindy!' He looked up at her and thumped his fist on the desk. 'You've got to help me!'

When Ted came back from the police station he couldn't believe his eyes. The front of his shop was daubed in graffiti. 'Vicious pervert' was scrawled across the window, and underneath in red letters were the words 'No scumbags in Hulme Welford'.

'Spot of bother?' the taxi driver asked, his hand outstretched.

Ted said nothing. He handed over his fare, then caught Jane and Brenda in the baker's staring at him. When he returned their gaze they both turned away. So did all their customers.

'I didn't do it!' he shouted at them. 'I didn't touch the silly old bag.'

31

From her fireside armchair Iris saw a third plate of mince pies being ushered into the kitchen. 'I've been viciously assaulted, not starved,' she shouted through to Hilary and Neville.

Hilary appeared in the doorway with a pretty blue and white china bowl of fragrant hyacinths – another gift from a well-wisher. She put the flowers on the table in front of Iris.

'Not so close, I can't abide the smell.'

Hilary moved over to the window and placed the bowl on the sill, behind a small, prim, artificial Christmas tree that had all the charm of a toilet brush. 'Now, are you sure you're warm enough?' She began straightening the tartan rug on Iris's lap. Iris pushed her hands away.

'I'm quite warm enough, thank you. It's thirst I'm dying of, not hypothermia.'

'I'll go and see if Dad's made the tea.'

'How's it going?' Neville asked, when she joined him in the kitchen.

'Nursing a scorpion suddenly has its attractions. Honestly, Dad, she's so ungrateful. No wonder she was let out of hospital so soon, they probably couldn't cope a moment longer with her.'

'I'll take her tea through. You take a break out here and see what you can rustle up for lunch.'

'Mince pies, by the looks of things,' Hilary muttered as her father disappeared and she viewed the doily-lined offerings of Mesdames Haslip and Bradley and the vicar's wife – a woman more known for her views on prisoners' rights than for parish pastry.

Hilary had had no intention of babysitting Iris Braithwaite when she came out of hospital that morning, but as the children had gone to friends for the day, and in the absence of anyone else being brave enough, she had volunteered. Then, surprisingly, Neville had stepped forward to collect the old lady from Macclesfield. Together they had brought her home and had put up with a constant barrage of orders and ill-temper, and now the task of pleasing her palate had fallen to Hilary. Oh, joy!

She opened the fridge and stared at the near-empty shelves: a packet of Lurpak, a couple of tomatoes – one that looked as swollen and as bruised as Iris's face – a plate of left-over cooked cabbage and a saucer of mashed potato, which had the beginnings of a fur coat. Two eggs in the door rack shone like beacons in a wasteland and Hilary picked them up and carried them carefully to the enamelled draining board. As she hunted for a small saucepan she found herself thinking of the cheerless contents of Iris's fridge – it was unseasonably empty, given that Christmas was only two days away. She had never before considered what Iris did over the festive period.

It was common knowledge that she never attended midnight mass on Christmas Eve – she had been quoted many times as saying that, over the years, the service had turned into nothing more than a drunken orgy of revellers, who on being tipped out of the Spinner found the warmed pews of St John's a welcome diversion from the bitter reproach they would expect to receive from their wives when they finally made it home.

As for Christmas Day itself, Hilary had no notion what Iris did. Friends, perhaps? Mrs Haslip or Mrs Bradley? Certainly Hilary couldn't recall any sightings in the village of anyone who could remotely be described as family coming to stay. So what did she do? Did Malcolm take pity on her and invite her into his home for the day?

Hilary had the uneasy feeling that, perhaps, everyone, including herself, had refused to think too deeply how Iris amused herself over the festive period so as not to court disaster on themselves. A pricked conscience was a painful thing to have for Christmas.

As the eggs began to boil Hilary turned the timer upside down and watched the trickle of sand pass from one glass balloon to the other. Reluctantly she knew what steps she would have to take if she was to avoid any feelings of guilt over the next few days. It would be a squash, what with David's parents arriving tomorrow for five days.

Five days! She closed her eyes, not wanting to think of the terror in store for her. Five whole days of listening to her mother-in-law's incessant praise of her only son – David, the blue-eyed wonderboy who could do no wrong.

Ah! Did she have news for them!

She brought the flat of her hand down on the draining board with a loud crack. Plates and cutlery rattled noisily in the plastic rack.

'Steady on there, Hilary.'

She turned round to her father. She suddenly felt furious and wanted more than anything to take her anger out on someone. And here was her father, good-natured Neville, whom everyone liked and respected. So why couldn't he see how upset she was? Why couldn't he put his arm around her and make it all better for her? Wasn't that what fathers did? Hug me! she wanted to scream at him. I'm your daughter. I may not be as interesting as Charlotte but I'm still your daughter.

'How's lunch coming along?' he asked, awkwardly.

She couldn't speak.

He glanced about the kitchen for some sign of food. 'Hilary? This isn't like you, what's wrong?'

She gulped. 'No. You're right, it's not like me at all.' And that's the problem, she thought miserably, reaching into the bread bin. Everyone thinks of me as good old Hilary, the born organiser. Want anything doing? Then give it to Hilary. Sunday school, PTA secretary, Christmas Fayre. Well, I don't want to play that part any more. I'm tired of being a pillar of the community. I'm crumbling and can't anyone see that?

'Hilary, how long has that egg-timer been like that?'

'Hell!'

Neville was startled. He'd never seen his younger daughter like this before. He watched her whip the saucepan off the heat and douse the eggs under the cold tap. She then moved about the kitchen in a fury of activity. Something was wrong, very wrong, and he had the uncomfortable feeling that he was somehow partly to blame.

'Hilary—'

'Not now, Dad,' she said briskly, loading a tray with the eggs and slices of bread and butter. She was battling to stay in control.

Neville could see that her eyes were moist with the threat of tears. 'Let me take that to Iris,' he said.

'I can manage,' she answered flatly, trying to push past him.

'Give it to me,' he said, surprising himself at how stern he sounded. Perhaps he should try that tone with Louise some time?

'*Two* boiled eggs?' Iris said, when Neville set the tray in front of her. 'Good gracious, Dr Archer, you and Mrs Archer may be able to afford to live the high life, but a woman in my position can't possibly—' She turned away from him, distracted by something moving outside. Neville sensed her nervousness.

The sound of the door knocker made them both jump. Hilary went to answer it.

It was Ted Cooper, a heavy dusting of snow on his overcoat, a frozen dewdrop on the end of his nose and a small poinsettia in his hands. 'I want to see her,' he said.

'Whoever it is, I'm not at home,' called Iris.

'I don't think it's a good idea,' Hilary whispered to Ted.

Only a matter of minutes after Ted had arrived home from the police station, word had gone round that he had been eliminated from their enquiries. A few in the village had received the news with shamefaced expressions, but Iris had not been convinced of his innocence. 'I saw him with my own eyes,' she had said in the car coming away from the hospital. 'I assure you, I'm not going senile,' she'd added. 'I know what I saw.'

'Please, Mrs Parker. I want her to know it wasn't me.'

'Is it that dreadful man, Mr Cooper?' Iris called. 'Tell him to go away or I shall telephone the police.'

'Calm down, Mrs Braithwaite,' Neville placated. 'Why don't you see him for a couple of seconds? What harm could—'

'What harm?' Iris repeated. 'You stand there with the state of my disfigured face before you and you have the gall to—'

'Please, Mrs Braithwaite, nothing is going to happen to you while I am in the room.' Neville was beginning to wonder at himself. Twice now in one afternoon he had taken charge.

Iris stared hard at him. 'You're getting very high and mighty these days, Dr Archer, I must say.' She waved a dismissive hand at him. 'Very well, let Mr Cooper in by all means, but be assured, the responsibility is all yours. Be it on your own head.'

Neville went and joined Hilary and Ted Cooper in the hall.

'You'd better take your shoes off,' Hilary warned Ted. She led him through to the sitting-room and watched Iris give him one of her notorious gimlet-eyed looks – black eyes or not, she was still capable of giving a good dressing-down.

Ted held out the sad little poinsettia. Iris made no attempt to take it from him and neither of them spoke.

There was something dreadfully pathetic about the scene – a grown man in his stockinged feet with a peace-offering and a proud woman with a face like a war victim. Hilary couldn't bear it. She stepped forward and took the plant from Ted. 'Hurry up, Mr Cooper,' she urged, 'Mrs Braithwaite needs to have her lunch.'

Ted steeled himself. 'Mrs Braithwaite,' he began, at the same time pushing his hands deep inside his coat pockets. He could feel his packet of cigarettes, his lighter, too. Automatically he started fingering the packet open, then remembered where he was and jerked his hand out. Light up at The White Cottage and die!

'Yes, Mr Cooper?'

'You and me—'

'You and I, Mr Cooper. If you are going to apologise, you might just as well be grammatically correct.'

'I'm not bloody well apologising—'

Iris tutted. 'Ever wondered why one's fingers are the shape they are, Mr Cooper?'

Ted shook his head, baffled.

'It's so that one can plug one's ears when one hears such disgusting language.' She promptly stuck both her forefingers in her ears.

Ted turned to Hilary and Neville. 'Now what?'

Neville shook his head at Iris and she slowly removed her fingers. 'Merely making a stand,' she said stoically. Hilary was reminded of Becky.

Ted took a deep breath. 'I may not be much of a bloke to you, Mrs Braithwaite, but I can tell you I'd no more hit a woman to the ground than—'

'How do you know I was hit to the ground if you weren't there?' retorted a triumphant Iris.

'Jeeze! It's common knowledge. It'll be in the paper next week.'

Iris raised her fingers to her ears again.

'I didn't do it,' Ted said impatiently. 'I was at the Spinner. They all saw me there. I'm innocent.'

'Well, somebody did this to me,' Iris said, pointing to her battered face. 'Somebody who looked a lot like you.'

'It wasn't me. You told the police it was somebody with a hat on. So it couldn't have been me because I never wear a hat on account of—'

'On account of what?' Iris asked.

'On account of my wig,' he replied, embarrassed. 'I can't wear a wig and a hat.'

'Piffle!'

'It's true and I'm very sorry you're hurt, Mrs Braithwaite, and I'm sorry too about all the fuss at the shop, and . . .'

'Go on.'

'And I want you to know that I've decided to get out of the clothing business. It's too much hassle.' He started shuffling towards the door. 'I've said my piece now so I'll show myself out.' He paused and then turned back to face Iris. 'By the way, you wouldn't happen to know anything about maggots would you, Mrs Braithwaite?'

'Nasty things, maggots, Mr Cooper.'

'Yes,' Ted said, scratching the skin under the front of his wig, recalling all too vividly just how nasty the little blighters were.

'That wasn't so bad, was it?' Hilary said, when Ted had slipped on his shoes and left The White Cottage.

Iris banged down her spoon on one of the boiled eggs. It made little impression. 'Hard and cold,' she replied, pushing the tray away from her. 'But, as you say, not too bad.'

Hilary was sure that beneath Iris's swollen lips there lurked a hint of a smile – a smile of victory.

As Ted plodded through the snow back to his shop, a smile hovered on his lips. Okay, so he'd given in to the old bat, but mail-order was the thing to get into anyway.

Georgia woke with a jolt, disoriented and heavy-headed. She caught sight of Nick reading a book in the chair opposite her and sat bolt upright. 'What the hell's going on?'

He closed the book and smiled at her. 'I was rather hoping you'd put me in the picture there.'

She pushed back the throw-over and got clumsily to her feet. This was her house, right? This was her sitting-room, right? 'Where's Chloe?' she demanded, trying to make sense of a situation that was all wrong.

'Relax. Somebody called Cas phoned and said they were going to watch a film and she'd drop Chloe off just after six. Is that okay?'

Georgia rubbed her hands over her face, the fog of confusion beginning to lift. She could remember Cas coming for Chloe early in the morning, then

Tiffany calling and sounding upset, and telling her something about Iris. Again she rubbed her face, forcing a further piece of the puzzle to appear. At last it did. Iris had been attacked . . . Iris was in hospital. She swallowed hard and slowly sank back on to the sofa, remembering now her reaction to the news. She raised her eyes to Nick.

'When I found you,' he said, in response to her unasked question, 'you were on the floor in the caravan. You were crying, very cold and shaking, like you were in a state of shock.'

She looked away.

'Do you want to tell me what had upset you so much?'

'No!'

'Fair enough.'

They sat in silence and, to Georgia's disbelief, Nick opened the book he'd been reading and started casually flicking through to find his page.

'And just how long do you intend to sit there?' she said suddenly.

'Until you've decided to tell me what happened,' he answered, without even looking up at her.

She scowled, leaned back against the sofa and crossed her arms in front of her.

He raised an eyebrow. 'You look just like you did the first time I met you at Hilary's.'

'Oh, this is ridiculous!'

'I agree.' He put the book down and shifted forward in his seat, somehow managing to appear as if he were almost touching her. 'Tell me, Georgia — may I call you Georgia?'

She nodded.

'Do you always cry so violently?'

'Don't be absurd, of course I don't. I never cry.' She stood up and walked over to the window, but the sight of the caravan at the other side of the car park brought back the pain she had felt earlier. She moved away.

'Never?'

'Never what?'

'Cry.'

'Well, obviously not completely never, as today's débâcle testifies to.'

'So when was the last time you were upset?'

She ran her hand through her hair. 'What the hell is this? Derek Rogers not got enough customers to keep you busy? Talking of which, I need to get outside and get on with some work — there'll be punters wanting Christmas trees.'

'There won't be,' Nick said quietly. 'I turned the sign round at the gate. I thought it best.'

'You did what?' Georgia turned on him. 'How dare you? You make yourself well and truly at home in my house, you read my books and have the cheek—'

'Yes,' he said, rising slowly from the chair. 'How dare I call in during my lunch-hour for a Christmas tree and find you all alone curled up on the floor howling like a baby, and how dare I carry you into the warm and make you a mug of tea, and how dare I have the bare-faced cheek to sit here with you for over two hours to make damn sure you're all right. By God, they don't come much worse than me, do they?'

'I . . .'

'Yes,' he said, standing over her, his face dark with fury.

'So masterful when you're angry,' she said, with just the hint of a smile.

He stared at her, his eyes blazing and she thought, for a moment, that he was going to retaliate with a further outburst. But he didn't. Instead, he reached for his coat and scarf from the back of the chair he'd been sitting in and said, 'I'll turn the sign round on my way out.'

As he pulled on his coat, she said, 'If you still want a Christmas tree you can have one for free, if you like,' her voice was conciliatory, 'seeing as I've put you to so much trouble.'

'Thank you.'

She helped him choose a tree, then watched him drive out of the snow-covered car park, the boot of his car wedged open with the last six inches of a Norway spruce poking out. She shivered in the freezing cold and looked at her watch. It was nearly three o'clock and the light was already beginning to fade. She'd lost the best part of the day and there was still so much to get done.

But first she had to find out about Iris, which she knew would mean she'd have to face up to why, today, she'd cried for the first time in three years.

Georgia found Iris alone, having eventually got through to the hospital only to be told that Mrs Braithwaite had been discharged just before lunch-time.

'Thank goodness you haven't brought any more wretched mince pies with you,' Iris said, slowly leading the way into the sitting-room after Georgia had removed her boots. She pointed to a chair for Georgia and settled herself in her own armchair, which was surrounded by a collection of small tables covered with an assortment of invalid requirements – tissues, boiled sweets, a Thermos flask, a cup and saucer, a glass of water, a bottle of aspirin, two magazines and an untouched plate of mince pies. 'Dr Archer and his daughter have spent the afternoon with me,' she said, pulling a tartan blanket over her legs, 'for which I'm very grateful, but they do fuss so.'

'What on earth happened, Iris?' Georgia asked, straight to the point, but doing her best not to stare at Iris's ghastly face. She was alert, though, to the tiredness in the older woman's voice, which made her wonder for the first time just how old she was. She had to be seventy-something, which was about how old she herself felt today. 'Tiffany said something about it being Ted Cooper who attacked you.'

'Apparently I was mistaken in thinking it was that shabby little man.'

'Oh.'

'Oh, indeed.' Iris stared back at Georgia. 'And what, may I ask, is troubling you, young lady? You look red-eyed and worn out.'

'You, you tiresome, bothersome old woman, that's what's troubling me,' Georgia answered, with a small smile. 'You've caused me no end of trouble today.'

'I have, have I? Well, perhaps you'd like to help me out with these mince pies and tell me what I'm supposed to have done.' She handed Georgia the plate. 'Go ahead, they're Hilary Parker's, so perfectly edible, not like Mrs Bradley's. I wouldn't offer you hers.'

'There you go again!' Georgia exclaimed loudly, pushing the plate away. 'You see, that's what you do to me. Nobody else tries it on. You're the only one. You're the only bloody person that's got the nerve. And don't you see what that does to me?' Suddenly she was leaning forward in her seat, her head in her hands, her shoulders shaking involuntarily just as she'd cried earlier that day. 'I don't want you being nice to me,' she sobbed. 'Be horrible or leave me alone.'

'Kindly blow your nose and stop that language. I simply won't have it, not even from you.'

And as if by magic Georgia's tears immediately stopped. Looking up she saw that Iris was holding out a box of Kleenex. She took a handful of tissues. 'I'm sorry,' she mumbled. 'It's so long since I've cried. It's all Rory's fault. When he started messing me about I was so angry and so upset I clamped a lid on anything I felt and vowed I'd never again let anyone screw me up like he did.'

'Which meant you had to stop anyone getting near you,' Iris suggested.

'Yes. And somehow, you, you silly old woman, managed to sneak under all my carefully erected barriers. How did you do it?' She started crying again. 'It's the bloody juxtaposition of how you appear to everyone else and then how you treat me,' she bawled. 'Why do you do it?'

'Ever thought that perhaps I like you, Georgia?'

Georgia blew her nose. 'No you don't, you don't like anyone.'

'And are you going to add that nobody likes me?'

'Everybody's terrified of you, you know that.'

'But not you? You're not scared of me, are you?' Iris asked softly.

'Too right I'm not.'

'And perhaps that's why I like you, Georgia. Mince pie?'

Georgia threw her pile of soggy tissues on the fire and laughed. 'Iris, you're the strangest and strongest woman I know.' She took a mince pie. 'Other than myself, of course.'

'Of course.'

Georgia bit into the pastry, sending up a small cloud of icing sugar into the air. She munched hungrily. She'd had nothing to eat since breakfast. When she'd finished, she said, 'Iris, can I ask you something?'

The old lady nodded.

'I know you've been widowed for years, but did you have . . . well, are there any Braithwaite juniors running amok somewhere?'

It was a while before Iris said anything. 'Sadly no,' she answered, her hands clasped together on her lap and her eyes staring dimly into the flickering fire. When at last she turned her attention back to Georgia, she said, 'I'm very tired now, would you mind . . . ?'

'Of course,' Georgia said, getting quickly to her feet. 'I shouldn't have kept you talking for so long. Is there anything I can—?'

'No, nothing.'

'I'll call you tomorrow, then.'

'Thank you, that would be kind.'

Georgia had the strongest of urges to hug Iris, but instead she patted the old woman's hand. She was surprised, though, when Iris took hold of hers and squeezed it gently.

32

'Come on, David old mate,' Derek yelled above 'I Wish It Could Be Christmas Every Day'. 'It's your round so dip your hand in that dusty old wallet you keep hidden and get the beers rolling.'

Alex noticed David's long face as he approached the crowded bar. For a man who was indulging in illicit sex he looked far from happy. From the moment Charlotte had told him that David was having an affair Alex had tried to equate his future brother-in-law – a man who had never before struck him as a risk-taker – with the concept of a man who was throwing all caution to the wind.

He watched David pull out his wallet and was shocked to see his hands shake slightly. Was that the result of his duplicity? Obviously David wasn't cut out for a life of extramarital spice.

'What's that serious expression for, Alex? Getting doubts for tomorrow?'

'No chance.' Alex turned away from David and faced his brother sitting next to him.

James cast his eyes about the public bar of the Spinner in amusement. The place was dripping with red and silver tinsel and gaudy paper chains that criss-crossed from one wall to another; from every light-fitting clusters of green baubles sparkled with glitter and dangled like swollen grapes. Over in the corner, by the entrance to the men's toilets, an old woman stood over a fruit machine, her loose false teeth sliding backwards and forwards as she stabbed with her fingers at the electronic buttons, her eyes lighting up with each spin of the drum. 'And to think we could have had your stag night in a smart little wine bar in Sloane Square,' James said, with a wry smile.

'And been bored to death.'

'You really have gone native, haven't you?'

Alex laughed. 'Come to my senses, more like it.'

'You always were an awkward bugger.'

'And still am, hopefully.'

James drained his glass of beer, then leaned back against a fake beam. 'How you found someone like Charlotte in a place like this I'll never know. But then maybe you're not the fool I thought you were.'

'So which fool does that make him?' Derek interrupted, as he handed out another round of drinks from the tray David was carrying.

Alex noticed that David still looked miserable. He watched him go over to the dart-board where Malcolm and Nick were challenging Barry and Stephen to a game.

The evening had been totally unplanned until last night when Derek had called round, saying, 'No neighbour of mine is getting married without proper respect for tradition.' His insistence had put paid to the decision that he and Charlotte had come to, which was to ignore convention and spend the evening with James and old friends, Stephen and Sally, who were coming over from Yorkshire for the wedding with their young deaf son Mark.

'Don't worry, Charlotte,' Derek had persisted. 'I've been to more last nights of freedom than there have been Conservative scandals. He'll be in safe hands with me.' Then, of course, had come the inevitable parting shot at the door. 'By the way, how do you like your kiss-o-grams, male or female?'

Over by the dart-board Alex could see Nick approaching David. He decided to join them – the last thing he wanted on his stag night was a repeat performance of Derek and Cindy's party.

'Muffin 'ell,' shouted Tiffany, springing forward in her seat and scattering peanuts over the floor. 'How can she say such a bloody stupid thing?' She mimicked Mia Farrow's thin, highly strung voice, ' ". . . That's the best thing a girl can be in this world, a beautiful little fool." '

'Quiet,' Cindy reprimanded, 'I can't hear what they're saying.'

Charlotte looked about the sitting-room and smiled. She was enjoying her 'girls' night' that Hilary had arranged. 'We must do *something*,' her sister had said, when she'd heard that Derek was organising an evening out for Alex. 'The men can't have it all their own way.'

Hilary had said more or less the same thing before her wedding with Peter and had put together a night out in Manchester. Now, nine years older, they had both decided that a night in with a good video and a meal would be preferable to an exhausting night out on the tiles. Charlotte had been touched by the polite, almost tiptoey way Hilary had gone about things – normally she would have taken charge of the whole event, steamrollering everybody into turning up at the appointed time whether they wanted to or not. But not tonight. Instead, she had been most solicitous to Charlotte's request for a fuss-free evening. But her thoughtfulness had not stopped there. Hilary had remembered that Charlotte's all-time favourite film was *The Great Gatsby* and had bought the video specially. Even now Charlotte could recall how as teenagers they had gone to the cinema together and had sat in the front row both quietly drooling over Robert Redford.

'I hope this film isn't about male dominance—'

'Ssh, Tiffany!' both Hilary and Charlotte said, each knowing that Gatsby was about to make his entrance.

'When are we eating?' Tiffany asked, in a bored voice, tilting her head back and dropping a handful of nuts into her mouth. She was sick of men, especially one in particular. Nick Bradshaw, the arrogant ratbag! As if she'd ever shown any interest in him. 'I said, when are we eating?'

'Ssh!'

Bob Evans, the landlord of the Spinner, brought out the last of the steak and chips. 'Started snowing again,' he said, setting the plates on the table. He began to collect up the empty glasses. 'Another round?'

'Same again,' repeated Derek. 'I'm spitting feathers.' He dropped a dollop of Colman's on the side of his plate and offered the jar to James. 'So what tales have you got on our Alex, then?'

James looked at his brother and laughed. 'I reckon I spent nearly all my time bailing this idiot out of trouble at school.'

Derek raised an eyebrow. 'Round here he gives the impression butter wouldn't melt. Tell us more.'

'Nothing to tell,' Alex said, quickly. He had the feeling that, despite himself, his brother was beginning to enjoy the evening.

'We'll be the judge of that,' Malcolm said. 'Go on, James, I could do with a bit more background information for the service tomorrow.'

'Butter wouldn't melt, eh? As I remember it, he hated being told what to do. He was full of all that anti-Establishment bunkum and with the right provocation he could make James Dean look like a beatific Noddy high on LSD.'

Alex stuck a chip in his mouth, let it hang like a cigarette, and squinted. 'How's my belligerence rating now?'

'About as high as Mother Teresa's!' answered Stephen, with a laugh.

'Ah, of course, the best man,' Derek said, turning to him. 'You were students together, weren't you? You must have a regular cache of titbits for us. Fire away.'

'More cheesecake, anyone?' Hilary asked, standing in front of Tiffany.

'I can't see,' Tiffany said, her head moving from side to side as she tried to keep her eyes on the television.

'Changed her tune, hasn't she?' Charlotte whispered to Cindy, who nodded and helped herself to a second portion of dessert. Charlotte had never seen Cindy eat so much. Nor had she seen her drink wine before. It was strange when people started acting out of character.

'Everything all right upstairs?' she asked Sally when she came back into the room and sat cross-legged on the floor beside her.

'Fine. Mark's fast asleep. Have they got to the bit in the film where Daisy—?'

'Ssh!' hissed Tiffany.

Charlotte smiled to herself and glanced across the room at her sister. Despite all the trauma and uncertainty in Hilary's life right now, she was looking surprisingly calm and assured. Perhaps she had always underestimated Hilary. Then, in the background of her thoughts, she heard Tom

Buchanan's arrogant voice, talking about people sneering at family life. She watched Hilary turn away from the screen, her eyes instantly dark with sadness. Like a swan, Charlotte thought, serene on the surface but paddling like crazy underneath.

Alex was almost disappointed in Derek. They were being tipped out of the Spinner and still nothing had happened. Where were the practical jokes? The cooking oil and feathers? The triple vodkas in the beer? The tart in nun's clothing? Perhaps Derek's behaviour had been tempered by having Barry with them for the evening – nothing like the presence of a child, even a grown-up one, to bring out the maturity in an adult.

'I'll be off home,' Malcolm said, peering out into the darkness at the snow-covered road. 'See you all tomorrow. Mind how you go.'

Shouldering each other to stay upright, they watched Malcolm trudge through the snow, which was coming down so fast that his footsteps were almost immediately covered up.

'I've got an idea,' Derek said suddenly.

'Dad?' warned Barry.

Derek grinned. 'Follow me.'

'What are we doing here?' David asked, when at last they'd staggered to a stop in the churchyard. He swayed slightly as though the wind had caught him.

'We're going to build a pair of snowmen,' Derek said, 'like the figures on Alex's wedding cake tomorrow.'

They laughed, then James said, 'I've got a better idea.' He was sitting on top of a tombstone dangling his legs like a small child. There was no mistaking how drunk he was. The mistake was that none of the others realised that they were equally inebriated.

33

Hilary looked at her daughter's implacable face and knew that it was the turd-in-the-potty syndrome all over again.

When Becky was sixteen months old she had, much to Hilary's delight and motherly pride, sat on Philip's old Thomas the Tank Engine potty and performed splendidly. Then, to a round of applause, Becky had stood up, seen what was behind her and had promptly burst into tears. She was horrified with what had come out of her tiny perfect body. From that moment, toilets and potties were no-go areas and served only to remind Becky that something ghastly had once happened to her. Until the age of two and a half she had clung tenaciously to her Pampers, her mind made up that she would never undergo a repeat performance of such abject humiliation. Hilary had tried all manner of chocolate-button bribery, together with persuasive arguments along the lines of, 'But everyone does it, Becky, even the Queen.' Such comments were sometimes met with quiet contempt but usually a full-blown Oscar-winning tantrum would be the response. Either way Becky would display a grim determination that she was not going to give in, or be taken in for that matter.

Hilary was face to face with that expression now. It was Christmas Eve, the morning of Charlotte and Alex's wedding and Becky, still in her pyjamas, was holding her bridesmaid's dress in one hand and a pair of kitchen scissors in the other.

'As a member of the Sisterhood I'd rather die than wear this dress.'

Becky's words were slow and well rehearsed and sounded more than a little absurd spoken by a seven-year-old. But Hilary knew her daughter well enough to understand that her words had the equivalent of a Herculean task force behind them. It was certain that Becky had no idea what Chloe was teaching her, but the whole thing was bound to appeal, given the club-membership perks on offer – immediate supremacy over her brother and the licence to rebel at will.

Hilary watched Becky flex open the kitchen scissors and decided that it was now or never to take control. She pounced on the dress, but Becky held on tightly, and the terrible but inevitable sound of ripping filled the gap between them. They stared in astonished silence at each other – Hilary because she didn't want to let herself believe her ears, and Becky because she was just beginning to wonder how much more courage she would need to remain Chloe's friend.

'So what do you suggest we do now, Becky?' Hilary asked, frighteningly calm.

Becky remained silent.

'Any ideas?' Hilary pushed on.

Still neither of them lowered their eyes, each lacking the courage to see just how much damage they had caused.

Becky opened her mouth to speak. She wanted to say sorry but she couldn't. Instead she could feel herself about to cry, like when she'd been told off at school last week for flooding the toilets. She had only meant to see what would happen when you unravelled a roll of toilet paper and stuffed it down the loo. How was she supposed to know that water would pour all over the floor? Mrs Wilson had been furious and had made her stand up in class the next morning and apologise to everyone. Mum didn't know about that ... but she did know about the dress. Then inspiration hit her. 'You shouldn't have tried to snatch it from me,' she said, in a clear loud voice. 'It's your fault I can't wear the dress. You'll have to tell Auntie Charlotte.'

Hilary stared in disbelief. Surely she had misheard. But no. There was Becky pushing the dress away and walking over to her unmade bed. She threw herself on top of the rumpled duvet and lay on her front, elbowing Peter Rabbit and Jemima Puddleduck out of the way as she opened and shut the scissors in her hands, snipping the air as though keeping in time to a piece of music.

The performance was breathtaking.

When and how had she gone so badly wrong? Hilary thought desperately. Then, as the satin fabric slipped through her fingers and dropped to the floor, she thought, To hell with that! Why did she always assume it was *she* who had gone wrong?

'I'm not sure I even want to be Auntie Charlotte's bridesmaid any more,' Becky said, tossing away the scissors and turning over on to her back. She kicked both legs in the air above her head and did a neat roly-poly. She faced her mother once more. 'Chloe says marriage is like a verruca, the more you pick it the worse it gets, and then one day it just disappears.'

Hilary breathed in deeply. 'Perhaps,' she said slowly, 'you'd like to go over the road and share your pearls of wisdom with your aunt. Then maybe you'd like to tell her what a spoiled brat of a niece she has.'

Becky pouted. Spoiled brat? Her mother had never called her that before. Precious. Special. Clever. Brilliant. Beautiful. Lovely. Perfect. That's what she'd always called her. Indignation made her jump off the bed. 'I'm not a spoiled brat!' she screeched.

'Oh yes you are!'

It was Philip. He came into the bedroom and stood by his mother.

'How long have you been standing there, Big Ears?' Becky shouted.

'Long enough to know you've got a vending machine of a gob.'

Becky scowled and moved back to the bed. She picked up Peter Rabbit and held him to her.

'Right,' said Hilary, finding she was gaining strength from Philip standing next to her. 'You've got a couple of hours to sort yourself out, madam. You've created the problem as to what you're going to wear for my sister's wedding, so you can resolve it.' She turned to go, but then added, 'And a word of warning. If you make yourself look ridiculous everybody will laugh at you.'

When she was alone Becky rushed to the door and slammed it shut. She picked up the silky dress from the floor and looked at it reproachfully. Tears began to trickle down her cheeks and she stuffed her face into the cool fabric. It wasn't fair.

She sat on the bed and hunched herself up against the pillows. She thought about running away. That would show them. She got off the bed and went over to the window. It was misted up with condensation and a small pool of water had gathered in the mildewy corner of the frame. She wrote her name on the glass then drew a Christmas tree with a large star on the top. She placed her eye to the star and peered through it. It was snowing again. Perhaps running away wasn't such a good idea . . . but she could hide for a while, couldn't she?

She quickly got dressed and wondered where nobody would think of looking for her.

34

Alex was up first. After he'd showered and shaved he made a large cafetière of strong coffee. He took it through to the small sitting room where James and Stephen were still on the floor in sleeping bags. They looked like two gigantic comatose caterpillars.

He drew the curtains and stared out at the garden. It reminded him of a Brueghel landscape. The trunks and branches of the trees, darkened by the effect of so much snow, were set against a pewter sky. Laurel bushes and rhododendrons, almost buried in deep snowdrifts, drooped beneath the weight of last night's blizzard, and in the distance a crow landed on a branch and created its own mini snowstorm.

Alex turned his attention to the two sleeping bodies at his feet and rattled a spoon against an empty coffee mug. There was no response. He bent down on one knee, held the mug next to his brother's ear and rattled the spoon again.

'Go easy with that bell, won't you?'

'Not a bell, James, just an empty mug which I'm about to fill with coffee for you.'

Stephen slowly surfaced. 'Somebody mention coffee?' he asked with a yawn. Then with a sudden burst of movement he stretched out his arms above his head and punched James in the eye.

Sally stopped tying Mark's shoe-laces. 'Am I imagining things, Charlotte, or did I just hear a scream from next door?'

Charlotte put her flowers down on the table and smiled. 'A scream followed by something quite rude is what I heard.'

'It didn't sound like Stephen?'

'Alex neither.'

'James, then,' Sally said, continuing with her son's shoe-laces. 'He's not at all like Alex, is he?'

The sound of crashing furniture and more outbursts of angry words made them turn towards the wall that backed on to 1a Ivy Cottage.

'Here,' Charlotte said, grabbing a glass and handing one to Sally. 'Let's have a proper listen.'

'Having fun, aren't they?' Sally said, as they jammed themselves up against the wall.

'What are you doing, Mummy?' asked a bemused Mark, who was unaware of the commotion next door.

Sally put down her glass and faced Mark so he could read her lips. 'We're listening to Daddy and Uncle Lex next door, they're having a fight.'

'A fight?' Mark looked worried.

'Not a real fight,' Charlotte said, kneeling in front of Mark, 'they're just being silly. Men are like that.'

She stood up, suddenly serious. 'Sally, you don't think it's all going to go disastrously wrong today, do you?'

Sally gave a loud laugh. 'Not disastrously wrong.' She put her glass against the wall again. 'But I have the sneaky feeling it could well be the funniest day of your life.'

As the bells rang out and the wedding guests arrived they were met by the sight of a six-foot fully erect penis against the west wall of St John's. It was quite complete in all its icy construction even down to a frozen ejaculatory spurt of semen.

'Busy last night, were you?' Malcolm greeted Alex's entourage when they made their appearance. They stared shamefaced at the sight of their handiwork – it looked bigger in daylight.

'Boys will be boys,' James said, sheepishly, from behind a pair of borrowed sunglasses.

'Hangover, or a bad case of snow blindness?' Malcolm enquired, looking at him. He also noticed that Alex was wearing a bandage on his left hand. Stephen, though, looked as if he'd come through the night unscathed. He led the way towards the front of the church. The gathering congregation were in buoyant mood, laughing over what they'd just seen outside. It struck Malcolm as odd, however, that they all looked so red in the face. Blushing? Surely not.

'I should watch yourselves,' Malcolm said, reaching out to Alex as he skidded slightly off balance. 'The floor seems a tad slippery today. Must be all this snow people are bringing in on their shoes.'

They paused at the front reserved pew just as James slid to a halt. He reached out to a long mahogany candle holder at the end of the pew and snapped it clean in two. It crashed on top of his head, knocking his sunglasses to the floor.

Malcolm flinched. 'Heck of a black eye you've got there. How—'

'Don't ask,' growled James, scrabbling on the floor for his sunglasses.

Malcolm picked up the broken candle holder. 'Right,' he said, 'seeing as you're the usher, James, I need you to come back to the porch with me.'

'Do I have to move? This aisle's like a bloody ice rink.'

Malcolm laughed. 'Come on. You can hang on to me if you like.'

'Bloody odd show you've got here,' grumbled James as he followed behind. 'Most unorthodox.'

'I assure you we're straightforward Anglican.'

'What the—!' This time there was nothing for James to reach out for. Malcolm helped him to his feet. 'I'm all right,' he said bad-humouredly. Red-faced, he dusted down his suit and inched his way towards what he hoped was the safety of the porch. 'If I'd known it was going to be like this I'd have brought snow chains,' he muttered.

Neville eased his gleaming Volvo carefully out of Charlotte's driveway. Everywhere was inches deep in snow with a treacherous layer of ice beneath, and he drove painfully slowly down Acacia Lane. At the end of the road he turned into Daisy Bank and glanced up to look in his rear-view mirror. He caught a glimpse of Charlotte in the back of the car. She looked beautiful.

'I wouldn't have minded walking,' said Becky, who was sitting next to Charlotte.

In the front passenger seat Hilary turned round. 'So that you could have worn wellington boots up the aisle, no doubt, just to finish off your attractive attire.'

'Becky looks fine,' Charlotte said, in an effort to keep the peace.

Becky took a sideways peek at her aunt. 'Do you really think so?'

'Yes,' Charlotte said, looking at Becky's wrinkled black leggings and oversized check shirt. She hadn't liked the dress Hilary had chosen in the first place.

'And is my hair okay?'

'Really suits you,' Charlotte answered truthfully. Becky had done her own hair and had tied it up into two stubby bunches either side of her head – she looked like a little devil complete with horns.

'You don't mind me not wearing—'

'I told you, you look great.'

Becky almost felt guilty about the ripped dress now. After she'd got dressed earlier in the morning she had come up with the perfect hiding-place. The only trouble was that no one had come to look for her and she'd got bored all on her own and had then gone home, only to find that nobody had missed her anyway. She'd stayed in her bedroom, then, and spent ages trying to decide what to wear and fiddling about with her hair. She was glad Auntie Charlotte liked it.

Neville slowly manoeuvred the car alongside the pavement on the north side of the church. A sudden tooting of a horn from behind made him slam his foot down hard on the brake pedal. But instead of the brake he hit the accelerator and lurched the car into the Volvo in front. 'Oh my God! Oh my God!' he panicked. 'What have I done?' His face was white with shock. He looked round to check his passengers.

'Calm down, Dad,' said Charlotte, picking up her posy of red and white carnations. 'We're all fine.'

'Hilary?'

Hilary turned to her father, and with a strange smile on her lips, said, 'That's David's car in front.'

Another toot from behind made them open the doors and start to get out. They were greeted by Barry coming towards them. 'You okay?'

'We're all fine,' Charlotte said calmly.

Barry went round to the front of the car and stopped to pick up a piece of smashed headlamp in the snow. 'I told Dad not to hit the horn.'

Tiffany came over, followed by Cindy, her face wreathed in concern. Derek, who was oblivious to what he had caused, sauntered towards them and let out a long whistle. 'Charlotte, have I ever told you how ravishing you—'

'Derek, this is certainly not the time or the place to be trying your luck.'

'Cindy, as if I would.' He faced Charlotte and grinned. 'Bit cheeky of you to go for white, don't you think?'

Charlotte laughed and pulled the fur-lined hood that formed part of the Cossack-style dress over her head. 'I'm freezing, can we get a move on?'

'Allow me,' said Derek, offering his arm.

'That's my job,' Neville said, and with his composure fully restored he pushed Derek's arm aside and, with all the grandeur he could muster, steered Charlotte towards the lych gate.

As the small party made its way up the path – their eyes to the ground as they picked their way through the snow – Charlotte let out a sudden laugh. She had just caught sight of the large penis. Her poor father stood still, his face white with shock again.

Derek stared appreciatively. 'Now that's what I call—'

'What is it, Mummy?' interrupted Becky.

'It's a . . .' Hilary looked around for help.

'Could be a bottle of champagne,' Barry suggested.

'Yes,' said Tiffany, smirking, 'it's just been opened, you can see the bubbles coming out of the end.'

'That's enough, you two,' said Cindy.

'Well, I think you're wrong,' Becky said, her voice matter-of-fact. 'It looks like an enormous willy to me.' She ran on ahead and waited for them in the porch.

Malcolm greeted Charlotte; he looked hot and flustered. 'Here at last,' he said, relieved. 'A word of warning, make sure you—'

But his words were lost as Mr Phelps, eager to get on, caught sight of Charlotte and started up with Mendelssohn's Bridal March.

'Oh, never mind,' muttered Malcolm, and he started to walk tentatively up the aisle. To Charlotte's surprise he almost fell over. Drunk? It would explain his red face. She watched him reach out to the back of the pew and saw that in front of him one of the decorative candle holders lay in pieces on the floor.

'I think we'd better sit down,' Hilary said to Cindy, 'or we'll spoil

Charlotte's big entrance. Let's hope David and Philip have saved us a pew.'
She turned to Becky. 'Now, you know what to do, don't you?'

'Go on,' urged Neville, 'leave her to us.'

Derek led the way and straight away found the going slippery. Miraculously they managed to reach the safety of a pew and, thinking that he was home and dry, Derek sat down and slid clean off the wooden seat, his knees firmly planted on a hassock.

'Say one for me while you're down there,' giggled Tiffany.

'I'm not bloody praying!' he hissed. 'Help me up, won't you? God, but it's hot in here, I'm sweating cobs.'

As Barry and Tiffany helped their father, Charlotte and Neville, followed by Becky, made their entrance. Someone from the congregation yelled out, 'Steady as you go, it's as slippery as hell out there.'

'And about as hot,' joined in somebody else.

By the time Charlotte stood beside Alex she was stiff with concentration and her face felt like cement with the effort of trying not to laugh. 'Okay?' he whispered.

She pushed back the hood of her dress. 'I feel like Maria Vetsera in this.'

'Just so long as I don't have to agree to a suicide pact. It's turning into a bit of a farce, isn't it?'

Charlotte looked at his bandaged hand and then at James on the other side of Stephen. 'What have you all been—'

'If you don't mind,' Malcolm interrupted, tiredly. He ran a finger round the inside of his collar, then wiped at the sweat that was beading on his forehead. 'It's Christmas tomorrow and I've still got my shopping to do, so can we get on?'

'Yes, Malcolm,' laughed Charlotte. She lifted her eyes up to the ceiling bosses and thanked God that Sally had been right – this was fast becoming the funniest day in her life.

As Malcolm started the ceremony she looked at Alex out of the corner of her eye and gave his hand a squeeze.

He winced and withdrew his bandaged hand.

35

'Goodness! I suppose you really are quite married? It was all such a fiasco it's hard to know.'

Alex handed his mother a glass of sweet sherry. 'I think it was when the boiler blew that I really felt things were getting a bit out of hand.'

'Out of hand,' his father repeated, eschewing the sherry and helping himself to a tumbler of Famous Grouse. 'It was wonderful. The whole thing was tremendous. Never seen anything like it. Not many wedding guests leave behind them a trail of devastation like we just have. I counted at least two twisted ankles, a platoon of firemen, not to mention a rather flaccid John Thomas.'

'I thought Malcolm was drunk when I saw him,' laughed Charlotte, 'he looked so flushed and then when I saw him nearly fall over—'

'It was the heat from the boiler,' Alex said, 'it was getting to us all.'

'And to your handiwork outside,' Charlotte said, with a grin. 'The boiler backs on to the west wall.'

'Doesn't explain why the floor was like a black run, though, does it?' Alex's father said. 'By the way, how did your brother get that shiner?'

'Yes, tell us what the three of you were getting up to this morning. Sally and I heard you through the wall, but couldn't for the life of us work out what was going on.'

'It was Stephen.'

'Not maliciously so,' said Stephen, coming over and stooping slightly to avoid one of the beams in Louise and Neville's sitting room, to where they'd all escaped for the reception, leaving poor Malcolm to sort out the mess at St John's.

'It was you who punched James in the eye then knocked the coffee all over my hand.'

Stephen shrugged his shoulders. 'Just as well I'm a doctor, then.'

'Thought I was going to need a doctor at the start of that service,' joined in Derek. He was carrying a plate piled high with cold meat and salad. 'My bum slipped off the pew that fast. What the hell do the good ladies of the parish use to polish those pews? T-Cut?' He bit into a large pickled onion and chomped noisily.

'Don't go blaming me for your inability to sit down properly,' Iris

Braithwaite called from an armchair by the log fire where she was comfortably settled in her fur coat with a pot of tea by her side. A wide-brimmed hat perched on her head gave her an elegant and superior air and went a long way to disguising her disfigured face. 'I can assure you Mrs Haslip and I have not polished those pews in over three months. Have you any idea of the price of beeswax, Mr Rogers? Perhaps if you contributed more to the running costs of St John's we—'

'Got your drift, Mrs B. I'll think on it,' Derek replied, poking out a piece of onion from between his front teeth. 'It did look like fate was determined to keep you two apart,' he said to Charlotte. 'Maybe the Big Fella up in heaven doesn't approve of your earthly match. I reckon it was a wrathful thunderbolt that made the boiler blow up.'

'Ignore him, Charlotte,' Barry said, over his father's shoulder.

Charlotte noticed the badge pinned to the lapel of Barry's suit: 'Without Jesus at Christmas You're a Dead Turkey.' She smiled at him and he winked at her. How he had changed. Just over a year away at university and he'd lost all his nervousness and was now completely at ease with himself and, Charlotte suspected, at ease with his father.

'I hope you're aware, Dad,' Barry said, 'that Malcolm thinks it was you who sabotaged the church and the service.'

'Now why on earth would Malcolm think I had anything to do with it? I mean, Charlotte's like a sister to me. Why would I want to spoil her big day?'

Alex laughed, and Charlotte said, 'Seriously, though, it was you, wasn't it, who turned up the heating too high, changed the hymn numbers and did heaven knows what to the floor to make it so dangerous?'

Derek shook his head. 'Hand on heart. Not guilty. The only crime I'll admit to is my share of the artwork outside St John's.' He gave Charlotte a nudge. 'Modelled on me, of course.'

'Don't you believe it.'

'Ah, Cindy,' Derek said, draping his arm loosely round her shoulder.

'Seen Tiffany?' she asked.

'She herded the children upstairs ten minutes ago to watch a video,' Barry answered.

'That's right,' Louise said, coming among them with a tray of chicken nuggets and chips. 'I'm on my way up there now with this little lot.'

'I didn't know you had a telly upstairs, Mother.'

'Lots you don't know about me, Charlotte. When your father's fallen asleep I need something to amuse me, so I bought myself a clever television with a natty little built-in video player. I saw one of those interesting Tarantino movies the other night. One has to get one's pleasure somehow.'

'You'll have to excuse my mother,' Charlotte said to Alex's parents, when Louise had disappeared. 'She has a strange sense of humour.' She was conscious that Peter's parents had always acted like 'Horrified of Aldershot' whenever the two families had got together. She wondered how last night had gone: her parents had offered to have Angela and Toby Hamilton to stay with them. She hoped her mother had behaved.

'She's an interesting and colourful woman,' Toby said, crinkling his eyes approvingly.

'You make her sound like a Jackson Pollock painting.'

'Language, Mrs Lawrence . . . I mean, Mrs Hamilton,' Iris called once again from the fireplace.

'So, then,' Angela said, slowly and deliberately, looking first at Charlotte then at Alex. 'Grandchildren.'

'Banging on the wrong door there, I shouldn't wonder,' Derek said, waving a cold sausage in Alex's direction.

'Derek!'

'Yes, Cindy?'

'I'd like a glass of wine.'

'But you don't drink wine,' he said, incredulously.

'I do now.'

Derek sloped off.

'Now, about these grandchildren,' Angela tried again.

Alex rolled his eyes.

'And we're banking on you, Charlotte, to get Alex back into a proper job. Children need a father who's bringing in a regular salary.'

'Attaboy, Dad,' agreed James, who was over by the window, talking to Hilary.

'You always could sniff out an argument, couldn't you?' Alex answered, good-humouredly.

James came over. 'Am I right in thinking, then, that Charlotte is pregnant and this is in fact a shotgun wedding?'

'No,' said Charlotte, her voice slightly raised. 'I am not pregnant.'

'Conceived out of wedlock but at least born within it,' chipped in Iris.

'No, Mrs Braithwaite,' Charlotte said, horrified, and in a loud voice she said as clearly as she could, 'I said I am *not* pregnant.'

'There there, Charlotte,' Derek said, reappearing with a glass of wine for Cindy and putting his arm round Charlotte. 'Don't take on so. If Alex can't cut the mustard I know a man who can.'

Cindy took a sausage roll from Derek's plate, stuffed it into his mouth, then dragged him over to talk to Hilary who was now standing all alone.

It had started snowing again when everyone gathered outside in the dark to see Charlotte and Alex off.

Becky stood in front of her mother and next to Mark. They had spent most of the afternoon together and, despite all Chloe's warnings about boys being stupid and growing up into selfish men, she had found herself enjoying the company of this quiet thoughtful boy. He had told her he was deaf and that if she spoke slowly he'd be able to read her lips and understand what she was saying. He'd even told her she was very good at it. It was then that she'd decided to tell him what she'd done. He had laughed and told her he thought she was very funny.

She was bursting now to tell somebody else.

She looked at her Auntie Charlotte through the open window of the car and, seeing her so happy, she stepped forward and said, 'You didn't mind about everything at the church, did you?'

Charlotte smiled back at her. 'I wouldn't have missed it for the world.'

'Good.'

Charlotte hesitated and then laughed. 'For a moment there, Becky, I had the craziest of feelings that maybe you had something to do with it.' She then stopped laughing. 'Becky, you didn't, did you?'

Becky beamed. 'It *was* me,' she said proudly. 'I went over to the church this morning because I was so cross with Mummy. I hid there, but then nobody came to look for me and I got bored and . . .'

Everybody around the car, including Hilary, was staring at Becky but, blissfully unaware, she carried on, '. . . and I went into that funny little room at the back and found some cans of polish. I started spraying one of the pews, then the floor . . . I thought it looked so dirty. Then I got cold and so I fiddled with the boiler . . . I've seen Mummy do it when she does the flowers . . . It was funny when it exploded, wasn't it?'

Nobody spoke, but when Charlotte saw the expression on David's face, she whispered to Alex, 'Start the engine before we get caught up in another explosion.'

Becky's confessional timing was perfect. As Charlotte and Alex drove slowly away, another car appeared. It was Nanna and Grandpa Parker. They had arrived too late for the wedding, but in time for Christmas.

36

The Parker Seniors followed the Parker Juniors back to Acacia Lane. Barbara and Jeffrey were listening to the closing moments of the afternoon play on Radio Four – a nineties inner-city interpretation of *The Little Match Girl* – and Hilary, David, Philip and Becky were listening hard to nothing in particular. Nobody seemed inclined to speak. Hilary wanted to but was terrified of laughing.

She tried to excuse herself on the grounds of too much wine and champagne that afternoon, but she knew that wasn't the real reason behind the bubble of mirth rising within her. Every time she recalled Charlotte and Alex standing at the altar and Malcolm pronouncing them man and wife she thought of the explosion that had come only seconds later from the boiler room next to the vestry. And trust old Derek to have his mobile phone with him so that they could call for the fire brigade.

The funny thing was that she didn't feel at all cross with Becky. By rights she should be punished and if David had his way she would be, but Hilary had no intention of taking her daughter to task. She couldn't remember a time when she had laughed more.

She felt her face breaking into a smile even now, and turned to look out of the window as they pulled up at The Gables. The children leapt out of the car at once, as if they were glad to escape the threatening silence, and started scooping up handfuls of snow. Inside The Gables the timer device had automatically switched on the lights, including the pretty fairy lights on the Christmas tree in the sitting-room and the house beckoned welcomingly.

It wasn't by any means the smartest or most attractive property in the village but Hilary had loved the beautifully proportioned Edwardian house from the moment they had viewed it and had wanted David to make an offer to the owners there and then. Six months later they had moved in – Philip had been five at the time and in his first term at school, and Becky had been a wobbly toddler just finding her feet.

'You love this house, don't you, Hilary?' David said, unexpectedly at her side.

She froze. What was he saying? That he was leaving her and they'd have to sell it? Was that it?

'What do you mean?' she said, turning slowly to face him. She was shocked to see how tired he seemed. There were lines around his eyes, shadows even. And had he lost weight? She couldn't remember the last time she had sat this close to him and looked at his face, *really* looked at it.

To her annoyance she found herself feeling sorry for him, but this was one emotion she didn't want and immediately she stamped on it. 'What do you mean?' she repeated, her voice hardened with resolve.

'I just meant . . .' He, too, now stared up at the house. 'Oh, nothing,' he said, and got out of the car to help his parents with their luggage.

'Oh, nothing to hell and back!' Hilary muttered as she unlocked the front door and walked through to the kitchen. Hadn't Cindy warned her that she might lose the house? She covered her face with her hands and leaned against the Aga. She felt miserable. And furious. Furious that her future lay so hopelessly in the hands of a man who no longer loved her.

She reached for the kettle, knowing that at any moment Barbara would come waddling into the house bringing with her half a dozen suitcases and enough edible 'contributions' to stock an entire corner shop. She turned on the tap and felt the familiar feelings of isolation and alienation she experienced whenever David's parents stayed with them. David was their only son and between them they never missed a chance to take the credit for having treated the world to such a splendid chap.

When Hilary had first met David's parents she had assumed that their comments towards their son and about him were heavily loaded with sarcasm – in those days she knew no other kind of parental affection, having been fed all her life a continuous diet of sarcasm by her mother. But then it had slowly dawned on Hilary that Barbara and Jeffrey were in earnest: in their eyes they had quite literally produced a Christ-like super-being.

She put the kettle on the Aga and noticed Becky's cut-out nativity scene tucked behind an open packet of shortbread and a tissue box. She smiled. There they were, the Parker clan – Barbara kneeling at the manger with Jeffrey standing dutifully behind, the pair of them gazing down at the world's Saviour in among the straw.

Well, by the end of this Christmas dear old Barbara and Jeffrey were in for one hell of a shock. They'd produced a Judas, not a Jesus. And just how would they come to terms with that?

Heavy footsteps told Hilary that Barbara was heading this way.

'Hilary, there you are. I've brought you some Darjeeling, I know how much you like it. And never mind that it's almost twice the cost of PG Tips.'

'Thank you, Barbara,' Hilary said, bracing herself for the rest of her mother-in-law's offerings from the large box she was carrying into the kitchen. She hated Darjeeling. It was Earl Grey she liked. She had told Barbara that a million and one times, but the simple message had never once penetrated those ghastly grey poodle-perm curls. She watched her lower the heavy box to the floor, her wide-skirted bottom sticking up in the air revealing a large area of dough-like flesh bulging over the top of a pair of brown pop-sox.

'Dates. I've brought you some stuffed dates. Just how David likes them.'

'Lovely.' Hilary took them and plonked them on the worktop.

'A pot of damson jam. Home-made, of course.'

'Naturally.'

'Mince pies. Reduced. I simply couldn't let them go in the supermarket this morning.'

'Super.' They'll go nicely with the four dozen in the freezer and the two dozen in the pantry.

'Lime marmalade. David's always had that on his toast ever since he was a boy. I know how fond he is of it.'

'Wonderful.' These days he has orange.

'Coffee. Real coffee beans. I thought I'd treat David. That decaff you give him is all very well, but it's got no taste.'

'How thoughtful.' Yes, why don't you go ahead and just poison him for me? Save us all a lot of trouble.

'Turkish Delight. Do you remember the Christmas when David ate so much he made himself—?'

'Yes, Barbara. I remember cleaning the bathroom afterwards.'

'Poor boy. He never did know when to say no.'

Oh, how true. 'Well, Barbara, how about I put all this away while you go upstairs and sort yourself out? You must be exhausted from your journey.' Come on, Hilary, show her whose house this is!

'A cup of tea while I'm in the bath would be most agreeable.'

'Good idea. You go ahead and I'll send David up with a—'

'No, no, no. The poor boy's exhausted. Let him have a glass of whisky in the drawing-room with Jeffrey. He must be so upset after Neville crashing into his car like that. How careless of your father. Don't forget the ice, will you?'

'Ice?'

'In their whisky.'

'Sure you wouldn't like one?'

Barbara let off a laugh that sounded as cheery as a fire bell. 'Hilary, I sometimes wonder about you. You know perfectly well that whisky's a man's drink.' Her foot already on the lower step of the stairs, she called back, 'Just the one sugar in my tea.'

'Man's drink indeed,' Hilary said, lifting the kettle off the Aga and filling the teapot. But, then, Barbara had always been obsessed with gender, especially one's femininity – this from a woman who had tufts of whiskers growing from a large mole on her cheek!

Hilary crept past the family bathroom where she could hear Barbara finally running the bathwater away – she'd been in there for over an hour, having consumed two cups of tea and a plate of Hobnobs.

Hilary held her breath until she was in her own bathroom and the door was firmly locked. She exhaled deeply, put the plug in the bath and ran the water.

She lay in it, cosseted by the knowledge that she was safe for at least the next twenty minutes. She had given David – the poor exhausted boy – strict instructions to keep an eye on the crown of lamb in the Aga and to put the new potatoes on in exactly twelve minutes' time. When she'd asked him to do this simple menial task she had been given the usual baleful-eye treatment by her father-in-law and had half expected him to say, 'She'd never have got away with that with me' – Hilary always awarded Jeffrey a broad Yorkshire accent when she imagined him speaking, it seemed so apt for his chauvinistic character, whereas in fact he was as clear-vowelled as any southerner she knew. What he had actually said as Hilary had handed him his second whisky was, 'Indispensable, David, that's what you are. You spoil Hilary, you really do. She's a lucky girl.'

Hilary sank deep into the water, her frilly shower hat clamped tightly on her head. 'Indispensable. Well, we'll soon see, won't we?'

At the end of the bath, among the baskets of toiletries and bottles of shampoo, Captain Scarlet and Mr Blobby stared back at her – they had been decamped from the family bathroom to make room for Barbara's armoury of Bronnley products. Captain Scarlet was down on one knee, his head twisted round so that he was staring over his shoulder at Hilary. Mr Blobby, with both his arms raised in the air, had lost the dot from one of his eyes and he looked as if he was winking salaciously at her. Hilary didn't like the way they were both eyeing her and slapped her knees together.

Stupid thing! she told herself with a smile. They're only bottles of bubble bath – anyone would think they were Derek or Nick sitting there.

She hadn't seen much of Nick recently and she wondered what he would be doing for Christmas and why she had just thought of him. She closed her eyes and for the sheer fun of it tried to imagine him kissing her again. Disappointed, she found she couldn't. His face eluded her, as did his lips. How unfair that she couldn't even fantasise adultery, whereas David was busy doing the real thing.

She glanced at her watch, in front of Mr Blobby's left foot. In two minutes' time poor exhausted David would have to stagger along to the kitchen. She reached for the bar of soap and began washing herself. She scrubbed her neck, shoulders and breasts hurriedly and uncaringly, her eyes staring straight ahead, unable even to view her own body for fear of coming to the dreadful conclusion that, perhaps, here lay the reason for David's rejection.

She tried to think of something different as she carried on washing. Charlotte and Alex. Had they arrived at their honeymoon destination yet? Everyone had tried to prise out of Alex where he was taking Charlotte, but he had parried their questions effortlessly. Louise had joked that he was taking her back to Brussels. How typical of their mother to make a joke in such poor taste.

There was a loud rap at the door.

'Hilary, you're needed in the kitchen.' It was Barbara.

'I told David what needed doing,' Hilary answered.

'We can't find the salt for the potatoes.'

'I never put salt in . . .' Oh, what was the point? She tugged on the plug chain and reached for a towel. 'Coming.'

Later that night, when supper had passed without incident and the children had gone to bed in a state of Christmas Eve fever, Hilary left David and his parents reminiscing on his days of glory as the most perfect child ever. She put on her warmest coat, donned a hat, scarf and gloves and escaped into the snow for midnight mass.

At the top of Daisy Bank she could see the village hall. Unusually for Christmas Eve it was brightly lit and she could make out people moving about inside. As she drew nearer she noticed a piece of paper stuck to the door. She went over and read it: 'St John's out of action – midnight mass here.'

Hilary stepped inside. Rows of chairs were set out with a small central aisle. Most seats were occupied and everyone was chattering and laughing. It was more like a party than a church service.

'Over here, Hilary.'

Hilary was surprised to see Georgia waving to her from a row of seats near the back. Next to her was Chloe – she was the only child there as far as Hilary could make out.

'Hello,' Hilary said, when she'd eventually squeezed along the row of knees.

Georgia kissed her on the cheek. 'And before you pop a shot at me, this is the one and only time I ever come to church because, as everyone knows, it doesn't really count. What's up? You look exhausted.'

'In-laws. They've arrived.'

'No worries. You'll lose them when you divorce David.'

Hilary looked shocked.

'Oops. Being too blunt, am I? Tell me what you think Santa's bringing you instead.'

Hilary turned her sapphire and diamond engagement ring round on her finger. The stones caught a beam of light from a fluorescent tube overhead and sparkled brightly. 'I suppose I'd rather like Santa to bring me a ready-made solution,' she said thoughtfully.

Georgia squeezed her hand. 'I hate to put a dampener on things but he can only bring you what you've asked him for.'

They heard a loud tut from further along the row. It was Patricia, leaning forward and staring in disgust at Georgia's hand covering Hilary's. They looked at one another and laughed loudly. Enjoying the unfamiliar sensation of knowing she was misbehaving, Hilary pulled a face and mimicked Patricia's admonishment. 'Tut-tut,' she clicked with her tongue. She then wondered if this was how Becky often felt.

It was strange, but when she really thought about the shenanigans Becky had got up to earlier that day she had to admit to a curious sense of pride in her daughter. When she had been Becky's age she had never done anything naughtier than sneak the raisins from the Whitworth's packet in the larder. Small-time compared to Becky's exploits. Singlehandedly, in one day, she had caused more mayhem at St John's than your average person would in a lifetime. Extraordinary. But how exciting and liberating to know that you alone had been responsible for so much. Oh, to be that rebellious, to have that freedom of self. Lucky Becky! And what if she herself was to be so cavalier? What would she do and to whom would she do it? Quick as a flash, Jeffrey and Barbara came into Hilary's mind. Odd that they should receive her first strike. Or was it? Wasn't it all their fault that David was the way he was – the sins of the father and all that?

She was just smiling to herself when the hall was plunged into darkness. 'Sorry!'

The lights immediately came back on. 'Sorry,' the voice repeated, 'caught it with my shoulder.'

Hilary looked up to see Derek by the light switches. He was holding the door open for his family. They came and sat behind Hilary and Georgia. Derek kissed Hilary and shook hands with Georgia. 'It was Bas's idea we came,' he said, by way of explanation. 'Cindy was all for an early night, but I said if my lad Bas wants us to go to midnight mass then the rumpy-pumpy will just have to go on hold.'

'A little louder, Dad.' Tiffany smirked. 'I don't think they heard at the front.'

Derek winked at his daughter, then put his arm round Cindy's shoulders.

How like Becky Derek was, Hilary reflected, as she turned to face the altar. Quite simply, the pair of them didn't give a damn.

'Good evening, everyone,' Malcolm greeted his congregation. He looked a lot less flustered than he had earlier, Hilary decided, as he stood behind his makeshift altar of two covered trestle tables. 'As you all know we had one or two surprises at St John's this afternoon, which is why we're assembled here.'

'What d'yer mean, surprises?' heckled Derek. 'We were fannying around doing more triple axels than Torvill and Dean.'

'Quite,' continued Malcolm, 'but I'd like us all to take this opportunity to pray for St John's to be back in action as soon as possible . . . and for the person responsible for the chaos to stay out of my way until I've had a chance to cool down.'

Hilary lowered her head, hoping to goodness that nobody from the wedding reception had had an opportunity to talk to Malcolm. She felt Derek nudging her from behind. 'You praying extra hard, Hilary?' he whispered.

The first carol was 'Hark! the Herald Angels Sing', and as the congregation let rip with merry gusto Hilary thought of Charlotte. It was her sister's favourite carol. Suddenly she felt sad. She wanted Charlotte here with her. It was quite likely that the next time she saw Charlotte her life would be very different. It was then that she knew with absolute certainty exactly what she wanted from Santa.

She wanted the courage to tell David that she'd had enough.

37

'Louise, happy Christmas!'

'You too, Barbara.'

The two women faced each other with all the warmth and enthusiasm of a pair of sumo wrestlers. Louise stepped over the threshold of The Gables and thought how fortunate she was that she and Neville had no cause to go to Peterborough and that Barbara's visits to Cheshire were limited to a minimum.

'Hilary's in the kitchen and I'm afraid to report that the turkey went in far too late.' Barbara's voice was low and confidential as if she was breaking the news that a loved one was at death's door with only minutes to live.

Here we go, Louise said to herself, rule-the-roost Babs telling tales again. But what poor, stupid Babs couldn't get into her tea-cosy of a head was that she didn't give a damn how inefficiently Hilary ran her life and The Gables. As far as Louise was concerned, Hilary could cavort naked in the kitchen partnering the turkey for a tango with a Christmas pudding shoved up its—

'David's absolutely shattered,' Barbara said, with a little wobble of her head. She took Louise's coat, then Neville's. 'I wonder whether you could have a word with Hilary,' she burbled from the depths of the under-stairs cupboard. 'Not exactly what you'd call spick and span in here,' she added.

'What do you want us to say to Hilary?' Louise asked, reaching out her hands as if to close the cupboard door on Barbara. Neville smiled and walked away.

Barbara finally emerged, a sticky cobweb clinging to a grey curl. Louise decided not to tell her it was there.

'I think Hilary expects too much from David,' Barbara said, smoothing out the creases in her new Christmas frock. She produced a neatly folded handkerchief from her sleeve and blew her nose. 'So much dust in there.' She blasted noisily a second time into the small square of embroidered linen.

'In what way, exactly?' Louise was intrigued.

'I'm sure you must have noticed how tired David's looking,' Barbara stepped closer to Louise and added, 'to say nothing of the atmosphere.'

Perhaps only since you arrived, Louise thought. 'To be honest I think it's Hilary who's worn out. Ever thought that your son might be expecting too much of his wife?' Louise had no grounds for suggesting such a thing, but why should dreary old Babs have it all her own way?

Barbara gave a dismissive laugh. 'Louise, dear. I've been here barely twenty-four hours, but grant me sufficient intelligence to detect which way the wind is blowing. Your Hilary is constantly asking David to do a never-ending number of jobs around the house. Little jobs that Hilary's quite capable of doing herself. Call me old-fashioned, but the kitchen really is the woman's domain.' She gave off another irritating laugh.

Louise wanted to grab the nearest object to hand.

'I think you've spoiled your girls,' Barbara went on. 'You taught them to expect too much.' She smiled, as though her opinion would be welcomed as an enormous act of kindness. 'Let's join the others for a glass of Christmas sherry. We've brought some of our favourite. Especially dry.'

'I'll have a gin and tonic,' Louise said, through clenched teeth. 'Especially strong, please.' Bloody queen bee, she scowled as she followed Barbara in her fluffy mules through to the kitchen. Why couldn't she just sting herself and have done with it?

'Mother,' said Hilary with a potato peeler in her hand and a harassed expression on her face. 'Happy Christmas.'

Louise embraced her and whispered in her ear, 'How long's the witch staying this time?'

'Five days,' Hilary whispered back.

'You poor devil,' Louise said, her arms uncharacteristically still round her daughter's shoulders. She then stepped back and in a louder voice, said, 'Goodness, all these guests staying and no one to help with the vegetables. Here, let me give you a hand.'

Both Hilary and Neville stared at Louise in surprise. Louise never offered to help in the kitchen, or anywhere else for that matter. 'Where's David and the children?' Neville asked, by way of conversation.

'Dear David's upstairs with Becky and Philip,' answered Barbara. 'He's loading a new game on to the computer. I think that's the correct expression, isn't it?' She looked around the kitchen as if waiting for a burst of applause. 'Ah, there you are, Jeffrey,' she said, as her husband appeared in the doorway with a tray of filled sherry glasses. He was dressed in a smart double-breasted grey suit and his shoes gleamed as if they'd been treated to a lick of black gloss paint. Neville fiddled with the top button of his old tweed jacket and rubbed one of his Hush Puppies on the back of his trouser leg.

'I thought it was about time for a sherry,' Jeffrey announced.

Barbara beamed. 'Call me old-fashioned but I do think a man should pour out the drinks, don't you? It's like carving the turkey. It's proper etiquette for the man of the house to carve.'

'Well, let's hope David won't be too exhausted to carry out that onerous task later on this afternoon,' Louise said, attacking a potato with a small knife. 'Though doubtless Jeffrey or Neville could step into the breach if one of us poor idiotic females couldn't manage it. Personally I love nothing better than carving up an old bird, especially a dumb old bird.'

Hilary joined her mother at the sink. Normally it was she who was on the end of her mother's tongue – it was good to hear somebody else coming in for a good lashing.

'I rather think Louise has been sleeping in the cutlery drawer again,' Barbara said with a patronising little laugh. She ran her hand over her sculptured hair and found the cobweb. She pulled a face.

Go on, Mother, Hilary silently urged, say something else. In the past she had always seen herself in the role of a peacemaker. Now to her surprise she found herself wanting to encourage her mother to fight on, but not only that: she found herself wishing that she could be more like her maverick mother. She cut a potato in half and plopped it into the saucepan on the draining board, thinking that only yesterday she had been wishing she was more like her daughter. She had never before thought that Becky was anything like Louise, but it was as plain as the nose on her face that Becky was exactly like Louise. And didn't Charlotte have that same rebellious streak of not wanting to conform? So why had she always been such a Goody Two Shoes? Why had she missed out on the genes of nonconformity? Or had they always been there but she had suppressed them?

With the sound of polite conversation in the background about the quality of the amontillado they were drinking, Hilary reached in front of her mother for another potato.

'Silly old witch,' Louise muttered. 'Does David really mean that much to you that you can put up with her?'

'No,' Hilary said, without thinking.

Her mother looked at her.

Hilary stared at the potato in her hand.

'Hilary?'

She looked up and met her mother's questioning gaze. 'I didn't mean—' she started to say, then she thought of her decision made during midnight mass and what lay ahead of her. 'I meant exactly what I just said,' she said. Her voice quiet but firm.

'I see,' was all Louise said. She turned the tap on and rinsed her hands. 'I suppose you'll eventually get around to telling me what's going on here.'

Barry was wearing another of his badges. Derek wondered how many more his son had. Today's was 'Stuff the Turkey, Not Jesus!' He smiled and looked down at his plate. An enormous half-eaten turkey leg stared back at him along with a lone sprout. He didn't know about the turkey but he felt pretty stuffed himself. He leaned back in his chair, picked up his glass of Hunter Valley red and took a large mouthful. Contentment flowed through him. He was one hell of a happy man.

He noticed that Cindy was staring at him. He noticed, too, the smile on her face as she twirled her wine glass round between her fingers. Strange that she should have suddenly taken to drinking wine . . . odd, also, the way she was looking at him. Self-conscious, he turned his attention to Tiffany on his right.

There she was, gorgeous, angry Tiffany. His little girl, all but grown-up now. He thought of all those years of confrontation with her. How the hell they'd survived he didn't have a clue, especially Cindy who had borne the brunt of Tiffany's toddler to teenager tantrums. He looked over to his wife and found she was still staring at him, and there was that smile again.

Bloody hell! Was she flirting with him?

He reached for the bottle of wine, refilled his glass and tried to remember when he'd last felt this good. To hell with that! When was the last time he'd felt this turned on at the family dinner table?

He tried to think of something else and turned to his left where Bas was sitting. He was chatting across the table to Tiffany and was telling her about some medical-school prank that had involved a jar of eyeballs. What a bloody neat son he was.

And what a bloody fantastic family they were.

He risked a quick look at his wife again and found she was *still* staring at him. 'A toast,' he said, raising his glass and crossing his legs.

They turned and looked at him.

'To my bloody neat family,' he said. 'I feel like the luckiest man alive.'

'Are you drunk?' Tiffany laughed.

'And what if I am?'

'Dad's right,' Barry said, 'we are pretty neat.' He and Tiffany raised their glasses against their father's.

'Cindy?' Derek waited for her to lift her glass. It was suddenly important to him to hear his wife's agreement, as though it would be the seal of approval to all he felt and had achieved over the past years, and more recently the creation of All in the Mind. But as he waited for her response, it occurred to him that what was also important to him was not just his own happiness . . . but Cindy's. Had he made Cindy happy?

Never before had Cindy felt herself to be the entire focus of her family. And right now she was. Tiffany, Barry, even Derek, they were all looking at her. She knew, too, what they wanted to hear from her. Ironic, that for what seemed for ever they had each pulled in different directions, each straining against the other.

'I've got something to say,' she said, sensing her family's disappointment. 'Barry, would you go and get me that large brown envelope with the red ribbon I showed you last night? It's at the bottom of the Christmas tree.'

'This what you want?' Barry asked, when he came back into the dining-room.

Cindy nodded. 'Thank you.' She took the envelope and pulled at the satin ribbon. 'I'm afraid you'll think this totally self-indulgent. It's a Christmas present to me, from me.' She met her husband's eyes as the ribbon slipped away from the envelope.

'I don't have a problem with that,' Derek said, watching Cindy's fingers playing with the ribbon. It reminded him of a strip-tease.

'You told me not so long ago that we've all got to find a niche in this life. Well, I've decided that you don't really need me here, Derek, so before it's too late I'm going to—'

'Mum, you're not . . . you can't—'

Cindy looked at her daughter. 'What, Tiffany?'

Tiffany turned to her father. 'Dad, don't let her do this. Do something. Say something.'

Derek was silent. All the joy and contentment he'd experienced only moments ago drained out of him. Dejected, he stared down at his dinner plate. He pushed it away. The idea was unthinkable.

Barry reached over to his mother. He touched her hand lightly and smiled. 'I think you'd better finish what you were going to say, Mum, and put them both out of their misery.'

Cindy smiled, embarrassed. 'I've got Barry to thank really,' she said, pulling a brochure out of the envelope in her hands. 'He's convinced me that I should go back to school, so I'm joining what's known as an access course for a year and then I'm going to have a go at studying . . . What is it?' she asked, seeing the look first on Tiffany's face and then on Derek's. 'Don't you think I can do it?'

Tiffany laughed. 'Muffin 'ell! 'Course you can do it, Mum.'

Derek slowly got to his feet. He went to Cindy and kissed her.

'What's that for?' she asked, genuinely surprised.

He swallowed hard. 'No reason,' he answered, his hand resting on her shoulder.

'Liar!' shouted Tiffany with a smile. 'You thought Mum was—'

Barry reached across the table and waved a cracker under his sister's nose. 'Pull a cracker with me and shut up, will you, Tiffany?'

'Anything I can do?' Iris asked for the third time from the quiet comfort of the sitting-room.

'You've done quite enough already,' Georgia called, from the chaos of the steam-filled kitchen. 'More than enough, in fact,' she muttered under her breath, as she drained off the fat from the meat juices in the roasting tin. Inviting Iris to spend Christmas Day with her and Chloe had turned out to be nothing more than a monumental battle of wills rather than a festive act of good cheer to all men.

The day after she had made a fool of herself in front of Iris she had phoned Hilary, who'd said she was just about to call on Iris to suggest she spend Christmas at The Gables. 'No,' Georgia had said. 'You've got enough on your plate with the dreaded in-laws coming, she can come to me.' Hilary's relief had been almost palpable but when the idea had been put to Iris she had refused point-blank even to consider the invitation.

'I couldn't possibly spend Christmas Day away from The White Cottage.'

By this stage Georgia was determined that if it was the last thing she ever did, it would be to get Iris away from that depressing little sitting-room for Christmas Day. By their third phone call Georgia lost her temper with the old woman and shouted down the line, 'I shall never speak to you again if you don't do this one simple thing for me.'

'What a pity,' Iris had responded, 'but so be it. Unless . . .'

'Unless what?' Georgia had asked, recognising a classic negotiating opening.

'Why don't you make more of an occasion of the day? Why not invite Nick Bradshaw as well?'

'No way!' she'd roared, when she'd regained the power of speech.

'I shall see you some other time then. Goodbye.'

'Don't you dare hang up on me, you meddling snake in the grass!'

A long silence had ensued between them until Iris had said craftily, 'So what time will you be expecting me? Perhaps Mr Bradshaw would be kind enough to give me a lift?'

Georgia had conceded the battle on the basis that the war would be won with Nick turning down such a ridiculous invitation. But she had been wrong. Nick had accepted and offered immediately to act as chauffeur for Iris and now here he was back in her house once again and in the sitting-room charming the thermal underwear off Iris and quoting Simone Weil to Chloe. God rest ye merry, gentlemen, indeed!

'I've set the table,' Nick announced, standing in the kitchen doorway. 'What else can I do?'

'You can pour some of that wine you brought, and quick, before I pass out.'

He filled two glasses and handed her one. 'Happy Christmas,' he said, chinking his glass against hers, 'and thanks.'

'Oh, no, you don't!' she said, taking a gulp of wine. 'Don't start on all that sincerity stuff about Christmas not being Christmas unless you're amongst friends and family. You're here because it was the only way I could get Madam in there to accept my invitation. Okay?'

'I'm flattered.'

'Yeah, well, don't let it go to your head. Now pass me that dish by your elbow – these sprouts are ready.'

As she stood by the sink and drained the vegetables, one hand holding the saucepan and the other holding the lid firmly against the pan, she felt Nick come up behind her. He kissed her neck lightly just below her ear. She was so taken aback at his sheer nerve that she almost dropped the saucepan. She put it on the draining board and then turned and faced him. 'What's that for?'

'I should think that's obvious.' He handed her the dish for the sprouts.

She stared at it for a moment and then at him. 'So why wait until my hands were full before kissing me?'

He smiled. 'It was the only way I could be sure of you not hitting me.'

Georgia laughed loudly.

'Everything under control out there?' enquired Iris.

'Oh, yes,' answered Georgia smiling, 'everything's completely under control.'

Lunch was noisy and fun, with Chloe in high spirits insisting on pulling crackers with everybody in turn – crackers that, late last night after coming back from midnight mass, Georgia had doctored by slipping some extra novelties inside the green and gold cylinders of card and crêpe paper. And now Nick at the opposite end of the table was wearing a false nose and Poirot-style moustache, with Chloe on his left sporting a pair of Mr Spock ears, while Iris was laughing and playing with a pair of clockwork false teeth, winding them up and then sending them chattering across the table. 'Perfectly disgusting,' she chortled, reaching out for them to set them off again.

'Come on, Mum,' Chloe said, 'it's your turn now to pull your cracker with me.' She grinned. 'And I know what's inside it.'

'You do, do you? Well, here goes.'

They both tugged hard, but it was Georgia who fell back against her chair the victor. 'What's this?' she asked, when a small silver brooch decorated with tiny sparkling marcasites tumbled out of the cracker and on to the table. She was expecting a plastic bleeding finger with a nail through it, not this exquisite piece of jewellery.

'Let me see,' Chloe said. 'Cool! It's great.'

'It certainly is,' Nick agreed, leaning over to have a closer look. 'Looks expensive as well.'

'But I only put silly things inside the crackers, not anything like—' She looked up and stared round the table, her eyes finally resting on Nick.

He shook his head. 'As much as I'd like to take the credit, it's got nothing to do with me.'

Iris cleared her throat. 'It was me,' she said. 'I put it there.'

'You! But when?'

'Don't look so surprised. I had plenty of time when you and Mr Bradshaw were busy in the kitchen.' She smiled and looked across the table. 'And Chloe was a willing accomplice by keeping a look-out for me.'

'But why?'

Iris swallowed. 'It's a present, and before you start with any of your nonsense I insist that you accept it. It belonged to my mother and I'd very much like you to have the pleasure of wearing—'

'Give over and give me a hug, you silly sentimental old woman.'

With eyes wet with tears they held on to each other tightly. Nick smiled to himself. He knew little about the strange relationship between Georgia and Iris but he could see only too well that they touched each other in a way that forced themselves to acknowledge some part deep within them that they had previously kept from anyone else. He winked at Chloe, hoping that one day she, too, would know that sometimes a risk was worth taking, especially where relationships were concerned.

'Nanna Parker?'

'Yes, Becky dear.'

'Why have you got that black thing with hairs growing out of it on your cheek?'

'Because she's a witch,' muttered Louise, helping herself to a dollop of brandy butter.

'I beg your pardon?'

'I asked why you had that black—'

'Not you, dear,' Barbara said, without looking at her granddaughter. 'Louise, what did you say?'

'I was just saying what a pretty dish this is,' Louise said, making a play of examining the bowl of brandy butter. 'Alfred Meakin, excellent condition.'

Barbara viewed Louise suspiciously with her pale grey eyes. 'I could have sworn I heard you—'

'So why have you, Nanna Parker? You'd look nicer without it.'

Barbara straightened the purple paper hat which she had swapped for David's so that he could have one to match the red tie she'd given him. 'Even if I put myself through the painful experience of having the mole removed,' she said, her voice matter-of-fact, 'I'd still be the same lovely old Nanna Parker, wouldn't I? Outward beauty is nothing compared to inner beauty.'

Louise snorted into her wine.

'I wonder how poor old Mrs Braithwaite is today,' Hilary ventured, desperate to avoid any bloodshed at the table. 'I had invited her to join us for the day but—'

'Yes, David mentioned that to me last night,' Barbara interrupted, seizing her opportunity. 'And I told him how wonderfully thoughtful he was to open his home to a lonely old neighbour on Christmas Day.'

'Apparently the police have caught the man who attacked her,' Louise said to Hilary, ignoring Barbara at the other end of the table. 'He was after Royal Doulton figurines, which is ironic because he wouldn't have found anything like that in Iris's house.'

'I knew a woman who had her entire collection stolen. The burglar came right into—'

'Any more takers for Christmas pudding?' asked Hilary, who couldn't bear the thought of Barbara clacking on a minute longer.

Everyone shook their heads. 'In that case perhaps you'd like to make some coffee, David, to go with our mince pies and cheese?'

'Hilary! There you go again.' Barbara looked triumphantly at Louise. 'You see what I mean? She just never leaves him alone.' Barbara reached out to her son. He looked on as though in numb sufferance; a sad and lonely figure at the head of the table surrounded by bits of spent crackers. Barbara patted his hand. 'You sit there, my love. Hilary and I'll make the coffee.'

'Can we get down now, please?'

'Yes, Philip,' Hilary said quickly. If something awful was about to happen amongst the adults she didn't care for her children to witness her mother wrestling Barbara to the floor.

'Tell you what, I'll make the coffee,' Neville said, helpfully, when the children had gone.

'Barbara always makes the coffee in our house,' Jeffrey asserted as Neville slipped out to the kitchen. 'Damn fine coffee maker she is too.'

'You make her sound like a percolator,' Louise said, acidly.

Barbara made a warning rattling noise in her throat. 'Tell me, Hilary, was that the recipe I gave you last year for the Christmas pudding?'

'No, it's Delia's—'

'I thought not,' Barbara said smugly, pulling the string on the light-up Santa brooch she was wearing.

'Okay, Babs. I've had enough. Are you going to spend the whole of Christmas criticising my daughter's cooking, or is there any hope of you keeping that rictus mouth of yours shut?'

Everyone gaped.

'You have always shown us, Louise dear, what a way with words you have. But you have to admit that leaving the bag of giblets in the plastic bag inside the turkey is certainly a novel way to serve the lunch. I wonder how David has survived Hilary's cooking all these years.'

'Perhaps he won't have to much longer,' Hilary said quietly.

'And what's that supposed to mean?' demanded Jeffrey.

Hilary, who had always been a little scared of her father-in-law, met his hostile gaze. She then looked at David at the opposite end of the table. He stared back at her unseeingly. His indifference was the final straw. She screwed her napkin into a tight ball and threw it at his face.

'Barbara and Jeffrey, there's something you should know,' she began in a determined voice. 'Your son is a cheat, a liar, and he's been having an affair for goodness knows how long. There, what do you say to that?'

38

Barbara kept her pale insipid eyes on Hilary, never once letting them drop or turn towards her son. She got to her feet slowly, as though she were about to deliver an after-dinner speech.

'If you had been a better wife he wouldn't have needed to look elsewhere. If you had appreciated what a wonderful and special—'

But Barbara's words were lost in the sound of crashing crockery and glass as David, in one single movement of his arm, swept his place setting on to the floor. He looked up at everyone around the table. 'I've lost everything!' he shouted.

'That's what happens when you play with fire,' Hilary screamed back at him, on her feet now and shaking with the awful truth hammering inside her that there was no going back. This was it.

Barbara moved towards David. She put her hand on his shoulder and stared defiantly at Louise. 'You see what you've brought upon your family.'

'Oh, shut up, you old trout,' Louise fired back.

'Shut up, the lot of you,' David roared.

'Well said—'

'Be quiet, Dad, and let me speak.' David looked at Hilary. 'I don't know where you've got this idea that I'm having—'

'You are!' she shouted. 'I know you are. Don't sit there denying it. After what I've been through at least have the decency to own up to what you've been doing.'

He got to his feet and moved towards her but she backed away, tears streaming down her cheeks.

'Hilary, I don't understand—'

'And what about all those nights when you said you were working late or at some Rotary meeting? You weren't there. I know you weren't.'

David's face darkened and he turned from her. 'I can explain—'

'I bet you can. But it's too late because I've had enough. I want a . . .' She clenched her fists and willed herself to say the dreaded words. 'I'm leaving you.' There! She had done it. She sobbed even louder and stumbled out of the room crashing into her father, who had been hiding outside in the hall. She grabbed her car keys and slammed the front door after her.

*

It was dark when she returned. Two hours of driving around on her own in the snow had left her feeling numb with exhaustion. She let herself in. The house was in darkness and behind her there was no sign of her parents' Volvo on the drive or of Barbara and Jeffrey's Rover. She stepped into the hall and reached for the light switch. She started.

David was on the bottom step of the stairs, slouched against the wall with an empty wine bottle next to him. He looked dreadful and as he blinked and tried to shield his eyes from the light he said, 'Hilary, please listen to me. I've got something to tell you.' He moved the empty bottle for her to sit next to him.

She stayed where she was. 'Where is everyone?'

'At your parents', I thought it best.'

'It's a bit late for your consideration,' she said flatly. She turned away from the sight of him and hung her keys on the hook by the telephone.

He stood up and came towards her. 'Hilary, I'm not having a bloody affair.' He took her by the shoulders and turned her round to face him. 'We're in a worse sodding mess than that!'

He sounded drunk and she recoiled from him. 'Mess?' she said angrily. 'What kind of mess?'

He stroked her hair gently, as though suddenly distracted. 'I've been seeing a new firm of accountants these past few months. The business is ... Oh, God, Hilary, I'm so sorry.' He lowered his eyes and moved back towards the stairs and leaned heavily against the banisters.

'David, what is it? Tell me.'

'I've lost it all.' He shrugged his shoulders, then covered his face with his hands, unable to speak.

She stared at him. Was he so drunk that he was saying the first thing that came into his head?

'I'm so sorry, Hilary,' he whispered, coming back to her. He held her hands. 'It's all been such a nightmare ... and the worst part was I couldn't tell you.'

Dear God, he was serious.

'I didn't want you to think I was a failure, that I couldn't ... I just didn't want you to find out, ever.'

'... *Hilary must never find out* ...' She felt sick. What had she done? 'Catherine!' she blurted out, clutching at the last remnants of what she'd thought was the truth. 'You've been seeing her. I know you have.'

He looked confused. 'My secretary? Or my new accountant? They're both called Catherine.'

Hilary swallowed. 'In your sleep ... you've been talking about Catherine ...' Her voice trailed away.

They stood in silence. Then David said, 'We might have to sell the house.'

She looked up at him, remembering his words in the car only yesterday – '*You love this house, don't you?*' 'And Philip ... his school fees?'

He shook his head. 'Hilary, I'm so sorry. It's the recession. I thought I could ride it out, I . . .'

In disbelief she shook her head and then slumped down on to the bottom step of the stairs. 'How? How's all this happened? Surely this doesn't happen to people like us?'

He sat next to her. 'Hundreds of small businesses are going to the wall. Rents are so high these days. I thought I could sell the business to a chain. That's what I've been trying to set up with Catherine these past few months. But then they discovered things weren't as good as I'd tried to make out. They lowered their offer by half just this week. They've told me to take it or leave it.'

Hilary raised her eyes. 'But you could stay on as manager, couldn't you?'

He shook his head. 'They want me out.'

'Oh, David. Isn't there anything else we can do?'

'If I refuse this offer, word will get out and I'll be lucky to get even as much from anybody else.'

'Well, then, there's nothing else for it, I'll have to get a job,' she said briskly. 'I'll go back to teaching. I always said I would.'

He stared at her, but she lowered her eyes, unable to bear the suffering in his face.

The phone rang and made them both jump. Hilary went to answer it, glad of the diversion.

'Charlotte! . . . Where are you? . . . Lake Coniston . . . Snowed in, I'm not surprised . . . We're all fine . . . Well, not really, David's just told me . . . No, not an affair, after all . . . It's the business, he's lost it . . . I've no idea. Yes, well, it does explain things. Yes, I'll give him your love. 'Bye.' She put the receiver down.

'My God,' David said, 'did you really think I was having an affair?'

She walked through to the kitchen and he followed her. 'Hilary, did you?' His words were clearer now, as though he had sobered up.

She chewed her lip and nodded. 'It's always been my worst nightmare, David, that you might leave me . . . I . . . I just jumped to the conclusion that—'

'But how the hell did you manage to carry on as if nothing was happening?'

'I could ask you the same thing. How did you hide all your problems from me?'

'And Charlotte, did she think—?'

Hilary nodded again.

David rubbed his chin with his hand. 'I thought she was distant, that somehow she didn't approve of me.'

Hilary began to cry. 'Oh, David, I'm so sorry . . . I feel dreadful that I thought the worst of you, when all the time you were going through hell and . . .'

He smiled. It was the first time in months that she could remember him smiling.

'It'll be all right, won't it?' she said, as she tentatively reached out to his hands. She wasn't sure just what she was really asking him, but she knew that losing the business was nothing compared to what she had thought she was going to lose.

39

Star Struck was busy with people wanting to escape Boxing Day turkey remains. Tony Farrand himself was resplendent in one of his sparkly seventies game-show-host suits. He greeted Hilary and David at the door in his usual flamboyant manner and stuck out his tongue at Becky and Philip.

'I love Christmas,' he said, as he showed them to a table. He held a chair for Hilary. 'One day of being polite with the miserable old relatives and everybody's here wanting to lap up my scintillating company. What can I get you to drink? Something lavish and expensive – champagne?'

'Yes,' said David, 'why not?'

'But, David,' Hilary said, when Tony went off to fetch a bottle, 'we mustn't, we can't afford—'

'Today we'll eat and drink exactly what we want—'

'And tomorrow?'

He smiled. 'We'll see.'

'Are we going to be really poor?' Becky asked, tipping over the salt pot and making a white trail. She dipped her finger in the salt and then licked it. She looked up when nobody answered her question.

'I don't know,' Hilary replied awkwardly. She didn't know what to say. It was all so bewildering. One minute she had thought David was having an affair and the next he was about to join the ranks of the unemployed.

Last night, after David had explained everything to her, she had telephoned her parents. Her father had been wonderful and had insisted that Barbara and Jeffrey stay the night with them. 'You and David need to be alone,' he'd said. 'The children can stay as well.' But Neville's suggestion had been met with a firm refusal from Barbara. They had set off for Peterborough immediately, saying that neither of them was prepared to stay under the same roof with a woman who had been so intolerably rude. When Hilary had apologised to David for her mother's behaviour he had laughed and said that it was about time somebody had taken his mother in hand.

'We'll be a lot better off than some,' David said, meeting Hilary's gaze.

'Chloe's poor, isn't she, Mummy?'

Hilary thought of Georgia's tiny bungalow and the coldness of the caravan that she and Chloe had lived in and how she herself had viewed it all with an air of 'I couldn't possibly live like this'. But then she thought of the closeness between Georgia and her daughter. 'No,' she said at last, 'no, Chloe isn't poor.'

'You're very quiet,' David said to Philip, who was next to him, his head hidden behind the menu. 'What are you going to eat?'

'I'm not hungry,' Philip answered, his head still lowered.

David leaned into his son. 'You don't have to be that stoic,' he said. 'You can eat exactly what you want tonight.'

Philip looked up. 'Will I have to change schools?'

David frowned and Hilary's heart went out to him. 'Let's not talk about that,' he said.

'Only I'd like to.'

Hilary and David both stared at Philip. 'Why?' they said together.

'No big deal.' He shrugged. 'I just don't like it very much.'

'But you're doing so well,' Hilary said, 'your report was excellent at the end of term and Mr Wells himself told me—'

'I keep being picked on.' Philip's words were almost lost in the noise of a large party at a nearby table suddenly cheering.

'You mean you're being bullied?'

Philip looked up at his father. 'Yes,' he said, his voice still quiet, his face a picture of misery.

'Why didn't you tell us?' Hilary asked, every ounce of her wanting to protect her child. 'You should have told us. We could have helped.'

Philip shrugged again. 'You can't go running home to your parents every time something goes wrong at school.'

Hilary was appalled. All this time she'd been so preoccupied with her own life that she'd been totally unaware of Philip's problems.

'Mum's right, you should have come to us,' David said, putting his arm round his son. 'But if you're anything like me,' he looked across the table at Hilary, 'or your mother, for that matter, you kept it to yourself because you thought you could sort it out on your own.'

Philip smiled awkwardly. 'So can I leave and go to the High where all my friends are?'

'We'll see.'

'I'll take that as a yes. Thanks, Dad.' His problems over, Philip picked up his menu and said, 'I'll have a pizza with everything on it and a large Coke.'

'I need the loo,' said Becky, who had now written her name in salt on the table in front of her.

'You'd better go with her, Philip,' laughed David.

As Philip shepherded his sister towards the toilets Tony Farrand arrived with their bottle of champagne. When he left, another waiter squeezed past their table with more customers.

Hilary felt a hand on her shoulder. 'Hello, Hilary.' It was Georgia with Chloe. 'Did Santa bring you what you wanted?' she asked, glancing at David.

'He brought a total surprise,' Hilary said. 'How about you?'

'The same, I guess,' she answered with a sly smile on her face. She turned away.

Hilary followed her gaze and saw Nick over by the door pulling off his overcoat and scarf and hanging them up. He came towards them.

'Hello,' he said, seeing Hilary and David. 'Happy Boxing Day.' He turned to Georgia. 'Have they kept our table for us?'

'Yes. You go on ahead with Chloe.' Georgia bent down and whispered in Hilary's ear, 'See you in the loos.'

'That all sounded rather cryptic,' David said, when they were alone.

Hilary laughed and, not giving any explanation, she said, 'I need the loo too. I'll have a pizza like Philip's.'

On her way to the toilets she crossed over with Becky and Philip and a couple of seconds after the door closed behind her it opened and in walked Georgia.

'Come on then, spill the beans.'

Hilary told her everything.

'Bloody hell and the stupid idiot couldn't bring himself to tell you because of his huge ego. It's the same old story, again and again.'

Hilary frowned. 'Don't be so hard on him.'

'I'm sorry. I didn't mean it quite like that. It's just that these poor fools are moulded into being super-beings and can't ever be seen to fail. I blame the parents.'

Hilary thought of David's parents. Georgia was right. She'd never thought of the pressure David must always have been under. All his life Barbara and Jeffrey had built him up to practically god-like status. She wondered now whether David in a strange way would feel relieved that he was no longer Mr Perfect, that no more would he have to stand precariously aloft the pedestal of his mother's making. She suddenly remembered what Nick had said to him the night of the bonfire when he'd asked him if he was frightened of not making the grade in some way. Poor David, no wonder he'd been so aggressive towards Nick. And no wonder there had been that scene at Derek and Cindy's.

'Aren't you going to ask me about Nick?' asked Georgia, looking at Hilary in the mirror.

Hilary smiled at the coincidence of their thoughts and delved into her handbag for her lipstick. 'Go on, then,' she said, through stretched lips. 'What have you been up to?'

'You were right about him being a good kisser. He's bloody good.'

Hilary laughed. 'Hypocrite!'

Georgia smiled. 'And, believe me, this is no meeting of the minds, this is purely physical. When I'm finished with him I'll send him on his way.'

'Will you, I wonder.'

'Oh, no, not you as well. Look, I'm having enough trouble in that department with Iris.'

'So how was Christmas with Iris?'

'Unbelievable! I've never known anyone to cheat so blatantly at Scrabble.'

'I get the feeling she's taken a liking to you,' Hilary said, with a smile. 'I think it's rather sweet.'

'And since when has there been anything wrong in a simple case of mutual respect?'

'I think there's more to it than that.'

'You do, do you?' Georgia replied, looking in the mirror and straightening one of her ear-rings. 'And so what if she's decided I'm the daughter she never had? I don't have a problem with that. In fact, like you just said, it's rather sweet. Now get a move on, I've got a mug out there offering to buy me supper.'

When Hilary returned to David he was alone. He said, 'Tony's taken the children off with Chloe to watch the pizzas being tossed about the kitchen.' He handed her a flute of champagne. 'Do you remember the last time we came here and Philip was asking me how I loved you?'

'Yes. He was talking about different ways of loving, wasn't he?' She reached for a breadstick and broke it in two. She offered David half.

'I can't remember which way round it was,' David continued, 'whether it was *agape* or *eros*, but – and I know I'm not very good at this romantic stuff – but I love you unconditionally, Hilary.' He clinked his glass against hers. 'And I'm sorry for mucking up our lives and spoiling everything.'

She leaned across the table and pressed a finger to his lips. 'Nonsense, I think we were ready for a change anyway.' Then she kissed him, happy in the sure knowledge that whatever the future held, it could never be anything like the hell they'd both just put themselves through.

'You sound like you're already rolling up your sleeves to sort this mess out.'

She squeezed his hand. 'It's easy when you know what you're up against. It's the not knowing that turns your world upside down.'

'Boxing Day,' wrote Iris in her diary, sitting by the fire, 'spent quietly and alone listening to the radio. Tomorrow, though, Georgia and Chloe are coming for tea. Must remember to order an extra pint of milk and bake a cake.'

She closed the diary then flipped it open again and re-read her entry for Christmas Day: 'Quite a departure from the norm. Spent the day with Georgia and Chloe and that nice man, Mr Bradshaw. I can't recall a happier time. A change certainly does one good!'

Airs & Graces

To Edward and Samuel
for their love and sense of fun . . .

Thanks to Big G for the belief, and to all those who answered my questions, no matter how personal.

Grateful thanks to Jonathan at Curtis Brown for being there for that crucial 'man to man' session.

Thank you, Jane, at Orion for the gentle words of encouragement and for almost convincing me I could do it.

And as ever, enormous thanks to Helena and Maureen for the never-ending supply of friendship and good times.

But my special gratitude must go to Alwyn for his supreme act of bravery on the M25 and A3, and for having a carrier bag to hand. Thank you.

PART ONE

April

The Song of the Lords-and-Ladies Fairy

Here's the song of Lords-and-Ladies
(in the damp and shade he grows):
I have neither bells nor petals,
like the foxglove or the rose.
Through the length and breadth of England,
many flowers you may see –
Petals, bells, and cups in plenty –
but there's no one else like me.

In the hot-house dwells my kinsman,
Arum-lily, white and fine;
I am not so tall and stately,
but the quaintest hood is mine;
And my glossy leaves are handsome;
I've a spike to make you stare;
And my berries are a glory in September.
(BUT BEWARE!)

Cicely Mary Barker

1

Crantsford was the last place in which Ellen expected to see a young teenage girl begging for money.

The prosperous small market town didn't lend itself easily to being a backdrop for the tired figure hovering outside the Patisserie. Its narrow, winding roads, some cobbled and lined either side with pretty Georgian bay windows displaying old-fashioned jars of humbugs, Jacques Vert separates and Lladro china, gave off an air of Easy Street; the young girl, on the other hand, smacked of Queer Street.

Ellen sensed that the girl hadn't much experience in what she was doing, and turned away at the uncomfortable sight of passers-by offering little more than stony disapproval at the sight of an outstretched hand in their midst. She cupped her own hands around her eyes and peered through the window of the travel agent's where Hermione was cruising the shelves for the holiday of a lifetime. She could see one of the assistants approaching her, ready no doubt to humour the old lady once more. They were quite used to her regular flights of fancy. Last month it had been talk of a trip on the Orient Express.

A few moments later Hermione came out onto the street with a bundle of glossy brochures. 'Egypt,' she said briskly, 'I rather fancy the look of the Nile.'

'And I rather fancy a cup of tea. Shall we?'

Ellen linked arms with her elderly friend, not because Hermione was in any way fragile and unable to cross a road alone, but out of love and gratitude – there had been times during the two years since Roger had left her when Ellen herself had been more than a little fragile and it had been Hermione who had been there for her, sure footed and rock solid.

They crossed the road and came upon the young girl. With nobody else on the pavement outside the Patisserie there was no avoiding what Ellen had tried earlier to ignore.

'Twenty pence?' the girl said, her voice unsure as if she knew she was pushing her luck.

Ellen reached into her bag. Excluding the money she had set aside for that morning's treat with Hermione, she knew she had only twelve pounds with her and that was to last until after the Easter Bank Holiday. She opened her wallet and pulled out a pound coin, but then hesitated. It suddenly felt too much. The girl would think her ostentatious, would probably thank her lucky stars to have stumbled across someone so gullible. Visions of the girl, later that day, high on some mind-altering drug flitted through Ellen's head. You read such stories, of children doped up to the eyeballs to simulate hunger and deprivation, when in reality . . .

Oh, to hell with reality!

She dropped the coin into the proffered hand and tried to smile in a sympathetic and understanding kind of way.

'Thank you,' the girl said, but there was no smile. Ellen felt annoyed, not with the girl for failing to show gratitude, but with herself for confirming the hypocrisy of charity. Sure, I'll give you money, but here's the deal – in return you have to make me feel good about it.

'Very commendable of you,' Hermione said as they pushed open the door to the Patisserie and waited for a waitress to come and show them to a table. 'Though it might have been of more use to the girl to have invited her in with us. She looked unspeakably hungry to me.'

'I've a table free now in the window,' a waitress greeted them importantly in a larger than necessary frilly pinny, the size of which Hermione and Ellen had long since decided denoted that this particular waitress was superior to the rest of the staff, who all wore tiny plain aprons. 'How many are you?' she asked Ellen.

Ellen hesitated. For most of her life she had rationalised and analysed to the point of what she thought was absolute certainty in any decision-making process and then more often than not had regretted the outcome. And since she had been on her own she had grown worse, analysing everything she and everyone else did and said; questioning motives, seeking out hidden agendas and exploring all possible means of justification. Hermione called it her 'rationalising to the point of inertia'. But just recently she had tried hard to act with more spontaneity. She thought of the pound coin she'd just given away and seized her moment.

'Three,' she answered quickly, and without risking a look at Hermione she turned and went back outside onto the street.

Hermione took her seat in the window and decided not to be put out at being deprived of Ellen's undivided attention. She watched Ellen approach the girl. She read the young girl's body language – surprise first, followed quite rightly by suspicion and then shoulder-shrugging submission as Ellen led the way. For all Ellen's dithering, when she made a decision there was no stopping her.

There was no danger of heads turning as the door opened, or of voices being subdued, for the girl in her ill-fitting clothes looked as badly dressed as most of the teenagers in Crantsford, if not better than some. And mercifully she seemed clean enough and had nothing skewered through her nose or eyebrows. Hermione picked up one of her glossy holiday brochures and shuddered at the thought of some of the youngsters in the town who apparently had more bodily parts pierced than a pin-cushion.

'This is Jo-Jo,' Ellen said brightly.

'Hi,' the girl said awkwardly. She looked older than she had outside, but paler.

Hermione lowered her brochure. 'Well, Jo-Jo,' she said, 'this would seem to be your lucky day. There are still plenty of meringues left on the trolley over there, I see.'

'I'm not big on meringues,' Jo-Jo said, stowing a large rucksack under the table and sitting on the edge of the chair – she had the look of being ready for flight, just in case.

Hermione raised an eyebrow. 'Correct me if I'm wrong, but in my day it was beggars who couldn't be choosy.'

'And even in your day I'm sure that beggars suffered from allergies. I get a rash from egg whites, if it's any business of yours.'

Hermione instantly warmed to Jo-Jo. She loved a dash of hostility and this girl had it in spades. That was the trouble with being old: too often you were treated with reverence and respect, nobody ever told you to shut up. It was amazing what you could get away with once you got past sixty. Ellen was one of the few people who wouldn't let her get away with too much nonsense. The same was true of Matthew, who had always been blunt and to the point. Last week he had been especially blunt. He'd called Hermione to ask how she was and when she had asked after his current girlfriend he'd replied tersely, 'Mind your own business, I don't want to talk about it.'

'Pot of tea for three?' asked the waitress with the pinny.

Both Hermione and Ellen looked at Jo-Jo, each suspecting, each dreading, that she would want something different – something more expensive.

'What?' she said, when she realised she was being stared at.

'Tea or coffee?' Ellen urged.

'Earl Grey would be great.'

'Expensive tastes for one so impoverished,' Hermione muttered. Both she and Ellen exchanged looks of concern. They only treated themselves once a month to this luxury of having morning tea in town, a luxury comprising a couple of cream meringues – justified on the grounds that they could not make them successfully at home – and a pot of the Patisserie's cheapest tea. Never did they squander money on the more expensive teas that the tearoom's proprietor, Miss Astley, kept in large Chinesy-looking tins on the glass shelf above the rows of cups and saucers. It was out of the question: neither had money to throw so recklessly down the drain.

'Normal tea will be fine,' Ellen told the waitress. If Jo-Jo was going to take her for a ride it would be a very cheap ride.

The order was completed with the addition of two meringues and a modest hot cross bun for Jo-Jo, and was brought to the white-clothed table with bustling speed and efficiency that spoke of Miss Astley having impressed upon her staff that time was money.

It was only when Jo-Jo had wolfed down her bun before Ellen and

Hermione had even reached for their pastry forks that Ellen realised quite how hungry the poor girl was.

'Would you like another one?' she asked, overcome with shame.

Jo-Jo nodded and then she fainted.

2

'I'm all right,' Jo-Jo mumbled weakly. 'I'm all right.'

'Sure you are,' responded Ellen, kneeling on the floor beside her. 'People go around fainting all the time.' She tried to ease the girl into a sitting position. 'Let's get you back onto your chair and do something about trying to get your head between your knees. I think that's what you're supposed to do.'

'No!' said Jo-Jo, her voice suddenly more forceful. She pushed Ellen's hands away from her. 'I told you, I'm fine. Now leave me alone.'

'Is anything the matter?' It was Miss Astley, a solid chunk of a woman with too much eye-liner and a short navy-blue skirt slightly concertinaed below the curve of her pot-bellied stomach. She was accompanied by the large pinny, who must have summoned the great lady from her den at the first sign of trouble. An audience of curious onlookers were casting surreptitious glances over their china cups towards the scene of the commotion.

'Nothing that a glass of water won't put right,' Hermione answered smoothly, straightening the tablecloth and picking up a knocked-over bowl of sugar cubes.

'Would that be still or carbonated?'

Hermione gave Miss Astley a withering stare. 'I think you'll find tap water is generally still.'

There was nothing else for Miss Astley to say and, giving Jo-Jo a reproachful look, she turned away and stretched her lips into the professional smile that she reserved for her less troublesome clientele.

'I really don't know why we bother coming here,' Hermione said huffily, in a voice designed to be heard some several yards away.

Ellen ignored Hermione's stage-managed attempt at pique. She was watching Jo-Jo retrieving her rucksack from under the table. 'What are you doing?' she asked, when the girl got to her feet.

'Look, you've done your bit for society and I've had something to eat, so that makes us quits and happy all round.' She moved towards the door. 'And thanks,' she added, sounding as if she meant it.

'But you can't go yet,' Ellen called after her. 'You need to have something else to eat, you need . . .'

413

'Let her go,' Hermione said. 'After all, what else do you want to do? Offer her a bed for the night?'

Ellen watched Jo-Jo step outside onto the street. She couldn't bear the thought of abandoning her and leaving her to the mercy of a way of life that would inevitably turn her into little more than a depressing statistic.

There but for the grace of God go I, she thought miserably.

The girl slung her bag over one shoulder, looked first to her left along the narrow road, which would take her to the bottom of Lower Market Street, and then to her right, which would lead her up the hill towards Church Walk and eventually onto the main road out of Crantsford. While she seemed to weigh up which road to take a group of women appeared and gathered round the tearoom window. They peered in through the small panes of glass to see if there were any free tables and when they finally pressed against the door and stepped inside Jo-Jo had gone.

'Perhaps now we can get on,' said Hermione, pushing her pastry fork into the crisp meringue in front of her. With one eye on her brochure, she said, 'Did you know that the temple at Abu Simbel was rescued from the floodwaters of—'

'Don't you care at all?'

'I care very much,' Hermione said slowly, her hooded eyes staring straight at Ellen. 'That's why—'

'I'm not talking about some rescued temple,' Ellen said sharply, 'and you know jolly well I'm not.'

'Whose is the glass of water?' the pinny said, once again at their table.

'You're too late!' Ellen said crossly.

The pinny looked confused. 'I'll leave it anyway, shall I?'

'Oh, do what you want.'

'My, you really are bothered by her, aren't you?' Hermione said, when the glass had been plonked down and they were left alone. 'The question is, why?'

Ellen said nothing and then she jabbed at her meringue. Small powdery chunks exploded off her plate and onto the tablecloth. 'I don't know,' she said at last. 'I really don't know. She just seemed so pathetic. And here I am, worried half out of my mind every time my bank statement slips through the letter-box, and yet compared to the Jo-Jos of this world I'm probably sickeningly well off.'

'Aha! Do I detect the first signs of some fledgling socialist tendencies coming to the fore? Tendencies which a stable marriage and comfortable middle-class background have kept at bay all these years?'

'Oh, be quiet!'

Hermione chuckled and looked affectionately at Ellen. 'Maybe the Jo-Jos of this world are a good influence on you. But I'd like to point out, though, that she didn't seem too impoverished. Her clothes were clean enough and there was nothing backward about her in her choice of tea.'

'Appearances can be deceiving.'

'Indeed they can,' Hermione said, casting an eye about the Patisserie.

They sat in companionable silence for a while. When they'd both finished eating, Ellen said, 'I'm fed up with having no money, I mean *really* fed up. And living here doesn't help.' She inclined her head towards Miss Astley's other customers, with their trim carrier bags of expensive goodies carefully positioned on the floor beside their chairs.

'I know,' Hermione said. She glanced down at her right hand, where up until a week ago her third finger had worn a ring that her father had given her for her twenty-first birthday. Now the heavy-knuckled finger was naked, its loose skin deeply channelled where the ring had once been. She placed her hand on her lap, out of sight, and tried to think positively: at least now there was sufficient money in the bank account to pay off the builder who had patched up the roof last month.

'So what are we to do?'

'Do, Ellen, my dear? Why, I only wish I knew. Perhaps we ought to take to the streets like our young friend. Or maybe we could set ourselves up in a knocking shop. I'm a little past my best, but heaven only knows there are enough strange men out there who might take some perverse pleasure in—'

'Don't flatter yourself.' Ellen laughed lightly, wishing that Hermione wouldn't be so flippant at times. 'But seriously, though, we have to find some way round the problem that doesn't include lying flat on our backs and thinking of England.'

'Was that what you did with Roger?'

Ellen kept her eyes down and folded her paper napkin neatly in four. There were times when Hermione had an irritating knack of aiming her arrow with unerring accuracy. Sex had certainly become a problem between her and Roger when towards the end of their marriage Roger had decided that he wanted to be more adventurous. Dressing up as a school-girl at the age of thirty-seven had not appealed to Ellen and with visions of having to perform this ritual regularly for her husband she had begun to go off the idea of sex altogether. Eventually Roger had got tired of her reluctance to play along with his flights of fantasy and had sought his pleasure elsewhere; secretly, of course, until one day he had simply announced over supper that he had met a woman who had literally made all his dreams come true. Shock and fear at losing her husband and their twenty-year marriage and the only life she'd known had driven Ellen to extraordinary limits, making her plunder the agony columns in magazines for help and advice, which all, to a single voice, urged any woman in her position to take her courage in both hands and play the tart in bed. For two miserable and agonising months she had tried it, only to find a note on the mantelpiece one morning after coming back from the supermarket. Roger had not only left her for the accommodating Charmaine, who worked as his dental nurse at the surgery, but they were leaving the country. The note had gone into considerable detail – she had always viewed that A4 piece of paper as not only a coward's way out, but as Roger's final confession – explaining that he was tired of their marriage and of capping teeth in Crantsford; he wanted a new life and was setting up home in Provence with Charmaine.

For the first six months after Roger had gone Ellen had been unable to stomach anything with a French connection. Irrationally she had blamed croissants, baguettes and Perrier water for the loss of her marriage. She also blamed Peter Mayle. For who else had planted the idea of Provence in Roger's confused brain? The writer's tales of fragrant lavender fields and garlic-smelling plumbers and good-for-nothing builders must surely have been responsible for seducing her husband away from her. But it wasn't long before she had realised that Peter Mayle and his charming come-right-in-the-end tales had had no more to do with the end of her marriage than she had.

'There's one very obvious answer to solving your financial problems,' Hermione said, sensing that she had set her friend off down the tortuous track of Memory Lane.

'Yes?' Ellen said, lifting her head to meet Hermione's faded blue eyes. 'So, what's your latest brainwave then?'

'Marry Duncan.'

Ellen prodded at the cubes of sugar in front of her with her unused teaspoon and smiled. 'I'm not so sure Duncan's the marrying kind.'

'Everyone's the marrying kind at some time or other. Have you considered him as a potential husband?'

Ellen laughed. 'Well, of course I have. He's ideal husband material. He's single, about my age and a respected solicitor with a reputation—'

'And loaded, up to his legal lawsuits,' interrupted Hermione, 'to say nothing of the gorgeous Queen Anne manor house he lives in.'

Ellen continued to play with the sugar cubes, stacking them on top of each other into a wobbly pyramid. Without looking up she said, 'Would you be very shocked if I told you that if I ever marry again it will be for money and not for love? . . . I tried the love thing and look where it got me.'

'Seems perfectly reasonable to me,' Hermione said. 'I just wish I could do the same. Do you think there's any chance of Duncan falling for you?'

'I don't know. He's so quiet it's difficult to know what he's thinking half the time.'

'I hope by quiet you don't mean dull?'

Ellen sighed. 'After what Roger put me through I'll settle for dull any day.' She reached for her bag. 'Come on,' she said. 'Time to pay and let our fertile imaginations cool down. Oh, what's this?' She picked up a pound coin from beside the plate that Jo-Jo had used.

'Should we think well of the girl, or put it down to carelessness?' asked Hermione.

Johnny Foreigner was hot and airless and Ellen and Hermione quickly wound down the windows. Johnny Foreigner was Ellen's car, and being unfortunate enough to be French – a Peugeot 205 – it had come in for its share of abuse after Roger had run off to France and had subsequently been renamed.

'We didn't get to discuss Egypt,' Hermione said, when Ellen had negotiated her way through the one-way traffic system and paused at the lights at the top of Church Walk. As they turned green and Ellen slipped into first gear she was conscious that anybody who didn't know Hermione well might wonder if the seventy-eight-year-old woman wasn't showing signs of senile dementia with all her talk of holidays that could never be. But it was harmless enough. Whereas some people dreamed of winning the Lottery each Saturday night and revelled in idle speculation as to how they would spend their winnings, Hermione simply let her mind wander from country to country, indulging herself in the harmless fantasy of exploring new territories from the safety of her armchair. Even Ellen had sometimes joined in with the game, allowing herself to be drawn into talk of a cruise for the pair of them around the Norwegian fjords. Hermione would speak of cocktail parties and sitting at the Captain's table for dinner, while Ellen contented herself with the happy thought of escaping the financial mess in which Roger had left her.

'Well, well, well,' Hermione said, with a ring of pleasure in her voice, 'and who do I spy pounding the road out of town with her thumb catching nothing but the wind?'

There was no mistaking the figure with the rucksack slung over its shoulder. The only difference now was that Jo-Jo had removed a layer of clothing and as she turned round at the sound of their approaching car a ripple of wind caught her thin white T-shirt and flattened the fabric against her young body. What Ellen had suspected earlier on the floor in the Patisserie when she had tried moving Jo-Jo was now confirmed. By her reckoning the girl had to be at least four months pregnant. She slowed the car and pulled over.

'Going our way, young lady?' Hermione asked through the open window.

Jo-Jo shifted her rucksack as though trying to hide behind it. 'I might be,' she said, pushing her long hair out of her eyes as the warm spring wind whipped it up from her shoulders.

'Well, hurry up and get in, and let's have no more nonsense from you. We'll sort out the details later, but if you play your cards right I'm sure my well-meaning friend here will provide you with a bed for the night.' Hermione turned and faced Ellen. 'That was what you had in mind, wasn't it?'

3

'Shall I drop you off?' Ellen asked Hermione, knowing full well the answer.

'There's no hurry,' the older woman replied. 'I'll toddle home later.'

Yes, thought Ellen, why go home now when things were just getting interesting?

'Is she your mother?' Jo-Jo asked Ellen, catching her eye in the mirror from the back of the car.

'You'd think so, wouldn't you?' Ellen said, with a sideways glance at Hermione.

Hermione humphed. 'What rubbish. I'm infinitely better than any mother. Have I ever made demands on you or made a nuisance of myself?'

'Never, thank goodness.' Ellen smiled. She indicated left to leave the main road. There were three signs at the top of the small unadopted road they turned into. The smallest one was a dead-end sign and beneath it was another – Beggarman's Lane. The irony of her address never failed to make Ellen wonder at the way her life had turned out. The most obvious sign was a large, well-positioned cream board with green lettering on it spelling out the words Spring Bank Dried Flowers, and in one corner there was a simple depiction of a jug containing an arrangement of blooms. The sign still looked brand new although it had been in position now for several months. For Ellen it was yet another reminder of the many changes she'd been forced to accept. Sometimes she resented the sign – that was on a bad day when her anger for Roger could not be stifled; on other days she would indulge in a little back-patting and allow herself the luxury of imagining herself as Businesswoman of the Year. The reality was quite different, of course: she had yet to reach a point where she could even pay herself a regular salary.

There had been no rain for over a week and as Johnny Foreigner bumped its way down the steep incline of the potholed lane a gauzy cloud of dust was left hanging in the air behind the car. The narrow lane curved gently round to the left and brought them to a tiny white-rendered cottage with a low, sloping roof and a front door that was painted black; either side of the door was a window and a matching pair above. It was the archetypal house painted by every primary-school child who had ever picked up a brush – all it needed to make it complete was a splodgy yellow sun wearing a smily face in the top right-hand corner.

Directly opposite the cottage was a grassy bank, dotted with daffodils, which fell away to a stream, and beyond this there were trees bordering the edge of a field where local people walked their dogs. On the face of it, it looked a dream hideaway cottage, but for Ellen there had been times when it had been more like a nightmare – the cottage from hell, she'd called it when she'd moved in and discovered just how damp and dilapidated the place was. Wet rot and dry rot abounded, but these were defects she could tolerate; they were small fry compared to the more obvious horrors that had demanded her immediate attention. She had spent weeks scraping off the mould from the kitchen walls and twice as long in ridding the entire cottage of the foul stench of urine, the source of which was the minuscule bathroom on the first floor. The previous occupant had been a man who had lived alone in the house – and died in it – for nearly half a century and whom Ellen was sure had never acquainted himself with even the most basic of household cleaning products. She had cursed him daily for his lack of hygiene, especially his inability to aim anything into the toilet, preferring instead, it seemed, to leave his mark like a tom cat on the filthy sodden green and yellow lino that partially covered the bathroom floor.

But at least all the cursing and constant elbow grease had taken her mind off Roger.

When Roger had done his disappearing act, Ellen had had no idea of the mess he'd left behind him. She'd been aware of the second mortgage that he had taken out on their home – had even been a party to it, as joint owner of Orchard House – understanding that the money borrowed from the bank was to enable Roger to expand his recently acquired dental practice. What she hadn't been aware of was that when she had signed the papers giving her agreement to this transaction she had also given him *carte blanche* to borrow further amounts of money. Within days of his disappearance she had discovered that over the previous year Roger had been spending money secretly like a drunken sailor home on leave. It was mind-boggling how much he'd spent on weekends away in Amsterdam and Paris with Charmaine. But worse was to come: Roger had developed a drug habit, which had not only drained away their savings to nothing but also the hope of making him responsible for the debts he'd left behind.

Ellen still didn't know what had shocked her more – that Roger had been leading a double life, or that she had been stupid enough to believe in all the dentistry conferences he had suddenly felt so compelled to attend.

And while trying to come to terms with the emotional trauma of the loss of her marriage, she was forced to sell her home – her lovely dream home – find a new one and a way of earning a living.

She parked the car alongside the barn where over a wide, studded door hung a similar sign to the one at the top of the lane – Spring Bank Dried Flowers.

'Here we are,' she said, unnecessarily.

Jo-Jo got out first. Ellen and Hermione watched her wander across the thin strip of road to the sloping bank. She dipped her hand in the water. 'It's freezing!' she yelled back at them, as if they were in some way to blame.

'Are you sure you know what you're doing?' Hermione asked Ellen, as they walked towards the cottage. 'She'll make a dreadful house guest.'

'I like that. It was you who invited her to come back with us.'

'I was only voicing what was already in your mind.'

Ellen ignored this truth and unlocked the cottage door. It was pleasantly cool inside and she hung her bag on the back of the door where she kept her coats – gone were the days of a cloakroom the size of a small bedroom. She mentally slapped her wrists: Orchard House was long gone and Spring Bank Cottage was her new home. She looked about her at what doubled as her sitting-room and dining-room. Hanging from the two beams that ran the length of the cramped room were enormous bunches of dried flowers – a clever device for covering up the ominous cracks in the ceiling. Either side of the fireplace were two armchairs she'd covered with yellow and blue fabric bought from the market in Crantsford – last year's colours but a classic in its own right, the stallholder had insisted. She'd made scatter cushions from contrasting fabric and used these to make a pretty feature of the window-seat that overlooked the front garden and the stream beyond. To the left of the window she'd managed to squeeze in one of the few remaining pieces of furniture from her marriage: a large dresser that had stood perfectly in the kitchen at Orchard House. Here it dominated the small room like a towering oak tree in a tiny walled garden. She should have sold it, along with the other pieces of furniture that had had to go, but sentiment had got the better of her. Opposite the fireplace and nestling against the wall was a chunky pine table; this was where she ate her meals, struggled with her paperwork and sometimes fell asleep.

'So what exactly do you intend doing with her?' Hermione asked, settling herself into one of the armchairs.

'Jo-Jo, you mean?'

'Who else?'

Ellen sat on the window-seat, and peered out through the square panes of glass. Jo-Jo was lying on the grassy bank, her trousers rolled up and the sleeves of her T-shirt pushed up to her armpits. She looked so at home lying among the daffodils; so childlike. Ellen suddenly longed for her own child.

At the age of nineteen Simon would hardly like to be described as a child, and coming to the end of his second term away at college he was now more of an adult than Ellen felt herself to be at times. They had always been close and if she let herself dwell on how much she missed him she felt wretched at the thought of being separated from him . . . She'd already lost so much.

'She's pregnant,' she said, returning her attention to Hermione.

'Does that make a difference?'

'Oh, Hermione, she's so young to have fouled up her life already.'

'So it's better to wait until you're older, is it?'

'You know what I mean.'

'I do, but it's only your opinion that she's made a mess of things. She might not think she has. How old were you when you had Simon?'

'That's different. I got married as soon as—'

'How old?'

Ellen shrugged. 'Twenty, as well you know.'

The point made, Hermione moved the conversation on. 'I suppose you'll keep her here for tonight and then persuade her to go to some kind of authority-run place tomorrow. Who do you think we should get in contact with?'

'Perhaps we should be trying to persuade her to go back to her parents.'

'Don't even think about it,' said an angry voice from the open doorway.

Ellen stood up awkwardly. 'Would you like a drink?'

Jo-Jo nodded and followed Ellen to the kitchen.

Ellen took a carton of orange juice down from a shelf beside the cooker and snipped off the corner with a pair of scissors. Juice spurted over the work surface.

'My gran was always doing that.' Jo-Jo laughed unexpectedly, her features instantly softening. She turned away and picked up a cookery book, *Easy Meals For One*.

Ellen wanted very much to pursue this tiny piece of accidentally offered information, but the expression on Jo-Jo's face told her that it would be an unwelcome intrusion. And, anyway, what right had she to pry into Jo-Jo's life? She would give her a bed for the night and tomorrow she'd set about organising a more permanent base for her and that would be that. By this time tomorrow she would have done what Jo-Jo had described at the Patisserie as her bit for society. She handed the girl her glass of orange juice. 'Would you like a biscuit?'

'I'd prefer a sandwich.'

'Of course.' How utterly stupid she was being. Here she was handing out well-meant crumbs of hospitality when what this girl really needed was a damn good meal inside her. The absurdity of what she'd instigated now hit her. Just what had she thought she was doing, acting like Lady Bountiful on the streets of Crantsford, offering food and then a bed for the night? Had she gone completely round the bend?

'Cheese and pickle okay?' She hoped it was. It was either that or a few sad-looking lettuce leaves and the tail end of an out-of-date cucumber.

'That'd be great and . . .'

Ellen waited for her to carry on. 'Yes?' she said, when the silence became uncomfortable.

Jo-Jo swallowed. 'I just wanted to say thank you. There's not many who'd do this. I mean, I could be a drug-crazed psycho for all you know.'

'You mean you're not?' called Hermione from the sitting-room, where she was flicking through her travel brochures. 'How very disappointing.'

Jo-Jo and Ellen looked at each and both smiled. 'Is she for real?' Jo-Jo whispered.

'And some.'

Ellen made two rounds of sandwiches for Jo-Jo and they joined Hermione in the sitting-room. While Jo-Jo ate, Hermione kept up a rapid fire of questions to which Jo-Jo either shrugged her shoulders in response or lied blatantly with an inscrutable expression on her face. When Hermione asked her where her family lived she made it obvious that she had had enough and in a bored voice said, 'I am not of this planet.'

To which Hermione replied, 'And just how do you go about getting yourself pregnant on your planet? The same way we earthlings do, with the tried and much-tested act of sexual intercourse?'

Jo-Jo froze. She looked accusingly at Ellen. 'I knew you'd guessed,' she said.

'So why the secrecy?' asked Ellen gently. 'In a matter of weeks you'll find it even more difficult to conceal the fact that you're pregnant. Is the baby the reason you've run away from home?'

'The baby's a way out,' she said, cramming the last of the sandwiches into her mouth. 'A blessing, you could say.'

'Well, I'm glad you've been blessed so abundantly,' Hermione said drily. 'Ellen, my dear, this could be the answer to all our problems. We'll get ourselves pregnant and then run away and all our troubles will be over. I don't know why the idea hadn't occurred to us before.'

Jo-Jo scowled and wondered why she'd allowed herself to be talked into accepting help from these two women. The younger one was okay but the older one had to be a head-case. Still, a proper bed for tonight would be better than another night spent in that churchyard. It felt like weeks since she'd slept in her own bed, whereas it was only yesterday that she'd left home. Her mother had discovered the pregnancy-test kit in her bedroom, which she'd forgotten to throw away, and then all hell had broken loose when her step-father had been told. She had known her mother would be too weak to stand up for her, she had expected that – two nervous breakdowns and a decade of tranquillisers had kept her firmly under her husband's thumb. Maybe when she got herself sorted she'd write to her mother, just to let her know she was okay. Or perhaps it would be better to ring when *he* was out at work. She felt sad at the thought of her mum in that miserable house all alone with nothing but the telly for company.

'You mustn't mind Hermione,' Ellen said softly. 'She's an old lady and we have to humour her.' She frowned at Hermione. Hermione frowned back and stuck out her tongue.

Jo-Jo laughed. 'You're a right pair, you really are.' After a few seconds she said, 'It's no big deal why I left home. I just don't get on with my step-dad, that's all. He likes to push people about. Mum isn't able to stand up to him, but I won't put up with it . . . and never will. I'm not going back.'

'He sounds a delightful man, your step-father,' Hermione said. 'Perhaps we should arm ourselves and plan a rescue attempt for your mother.'

Ellen ignored Hermione and leaned towards Jo-Jo. 'What about the baby's father? Does he even know that you're pregnant?'

'He knows all right, but he doesn't want anything to do with it, or me. It wasn't like we were together ... It wasn't serious.'

Hermione noted the twisted hands in the girl's lap and decided that, for now, enough questions had been asked.

An hour later, when Jo-Jo had wallowed in a bath and had been instructed by Ellen to take a nap in Simon's tiny bedroom, Hermione gathered up her holiday brochures and said it was time she was going.

'I'll run you back,' Ellen said, already reaching for her keys.

'You'll do no such thing. My legs are more than capable of making the short walk home. I'll give you a ring in the morning to see what you've decided to do with our young friend.'

A few minutes after Hermione had left, the phone rang.

'Ellen, it's me, Duncan.'

'Hello, Duncan.' She wanted to add, 'We were only talking about you earlier', but remembering what the conversation had been about she thought better of it. 'How are you?' she said instead.

'I'm fine. Look, I was wondering if you're not working tomorrow whether you'd like to come over for lunch.'

'Oh.'

'Is that a no?'

'No. I mean, yes. Yes, I'd love to. You just surprised me, that's all.' This was the first time Ellen had been invited *home* and the tempting picture of an elegant Queen Anne house shimmered enticingly before her eyes.

'We always like to have people round on Good Friday – it's a bit of a thing Mother has, roast lamb and a table of guests to share it with.'

The Queen Anne house instantly vaporised and was replaced with the far from pleasant image of the indomitable La Carter. 'What time shall I come?' Ellen asked, squeezing her eyes shut to block out the vision of Duncan's mother about whom she had heard so much from Hermione.

'It's twelve for twelve thirty, but don't worry about driving, I'll come and pick you up.'

Ellen replaced the receiver in its cradle and smiled. Of course Hermione had been right this morning in the Patisserie – she had done a darn sight more than merely consider Duncan as a potential husband. What fool wouldn't? But was there really any chance of winkling the eligible Duncan out of his tightly fitting bachelor shell?

4

As Hermione walked home the thought occurred to her that perhaps she shouldn't have left Ellen alone with a person they knew so little about, but crossing the main road to join the Crescent she dismissed this as absurd. Jo-Jo may have tried earlier to come across as bolshie and street-wise but there was a naïvety and overall honesty to her bearing that gave one no reason to suspect her capable of taking an axe to her good Samaritan and making off with the family silver and credit cards.

Much good it would do the girl anyway, for Hermione knew better than anyone how hard up Ellen was these days. Her dried-flower business was still in the early stages of getting off the ground and Hermione suspected that it would be a while before Ellen's financial position improved dramatically.

She was now halfway along the Crescent – a road that bore no resemblance to the shape suggested by its name, but which was a quiet through road and home to some of the largest and most interesting houses in Crantsford. Most of the properties had been built at the turn of the century for the wealthy local industrialists of the era, but nearer the main road where Hermione was now walking stood a few recent additions. Built to individual designs and constructed of Cheshire brick, the modern properties blended in with their surroundings pleasantly enough, and in Hermione's opinion they deserved nothing like the outrage that had greeted their arrival from some of the more conservative-minded inhabitants of the Crescent.

She slowed her step as she drew level with one of the newer homes on her right – Orchard House. She stood still and cursed Roger under her breath.

Ellen and Roger had moved into Orchard House a month after the builders had moved out. Hermione had seen the removal van arrive late in the afternoon when she had been on her way back from Crantsford – in those days she had thought nothing of walking into town for her shopping, but recently her legs and back had started to object and she now used the local bus service or relied upon Ellen's generosity to drive her to the shops. Which was how she had got to know Ellen. It had been raining one morning when Hermione had set off with her basket and umbrella and as she'd come to the end of the Crescent a small red car had pulled up alongside her. An attractive fair-haired woman had wound down her window and asked Hermione if she wanted a lift into Crantsford. 'I'm still finding my way around,' she'd said, as Hermione had climbed into the passenger seat, 'so shout if you think I'm going the wrong way.'

They had taken to each other instantly and had quickly settled into a comfortable routine of tea and cake while listening to the afternoon short story on the radio in Ellen's luxuriously fitted kitchen. Afterwards they would give their verdict on the writer's talent, or lack of it, until it was time for Ellen to start thinking about feeding the men in her life, Simon and Roger.

Simon was the kind of son for whom any mother would willingly suffer. Tall, fair, well-mannered and heartbreakingly good-looking, he was also the kind of boy for whom most girls would willingly suffer. Hermione was sure that Simon's father's absconding to France just as he was about to sit his A-levels, had upset him more than he would admit but, all credit to the lad, he'd not only kept his head and sailed through his exams but had been there for his mother in moments of crisis. For one so young he was particularly clear-sighted and self-possessed, but with none of the arrogance usually associated with these qualities. It was hard to imagine how any father could have turned his back on such a delightful son.

Hermione was not by nature a vindictive person, but she felt sure that she would never forgive Roger for what he had put Ellen and Simon through . . . or for the disruption to her own life. She missed Ellen now that she worked full time and lived just that little bit further away. Ellen usually had only one day off a week – Thursday – and it wasn't enough for Hermione. She wanted things how they used to be when she'd had Ellen all to herself. Damn Roger! He'd spoilt everything. And damn him for making her realise what a selfish person she was becoming in her old age.

She moved along the road until she came to the Lodge, set back some thirty or so yards from the pavement. Early-flowering cherry trees lined the curving driveway and Hermione could see that even though the blossom was barely a week old there was already a sprinkling of delicate pale pink petals lying on the lawn beside the smooth black tarmac – this, too, had only made its appearance last week and gave the impression of having been laid by an experienced carpet-fitter.

The Lodge was one of the oldest properties in the Crescent and during the past six months it had been the focus of much speculation. It was by far the largest and most elegant of the houses in the road and had stood empty for almost a year before a buyer was found. Now it was in the process of being transformed into what had been advertised in the local press as 'A retirement home of distinction for the distinguished'. Rumour had it that the alterations and building work were nearing an end, and certainly there had been far fewer comings and goings of noisy tradesmen's vehicles just lately which would support this theory. In more recent days there had been quieter visitors to the Lodge. Several spotlessly clean cars had made appearances, bearing men in suits and brightly coloured ties as well as a woman with a scarf tucked artfully around her neck. They all carried briefcases and were too engrossed in what they were discussing to notice Hermione peering through the hedge at them as they walked the grounds comparing notes and nodding energetically into their mobile phones. She had named them the Management.

When planning permission had been sought for the change of use of the house the residents in the Crescent had all been assured that they would not be affected or inconvenienced in any way. Hermione had often wondered in what way anyone would think they could possibly be inconvenienced. Was the Management worried that the residents of the Crescent would be offended by the sight of a dead body being removed from the Lodge, and were they even now devising some discreet method of disposal of their future clients when they were no longer a viable proposition?

She pressed on towards Laburnum House, turned into the gravelled driveway and automatically stooped to tug at a clump of dandelions. She flung them, roots and all, into a massive rhododendron bush, its swelling buds on the verge of unfurling and showing tantalising glimpses of brilliant pink flowers, peeping out from beneath their protecting wrappings. She carried on round the house, through the courtyard and to the back door where she let herself in.

The telephone was ringing, but by the time she'd made her way through the garden room – stepping round and over discarded wellington boots, secateurs and gardening gloves – before reaching the kitchen and finally the hall, the ringing had stopped. Perhaps she should sell another piece of jewellery and buy herself a mobile phone. She laughed at this improbable idea and went to look for Botticelli and Giotto.

She found them in the sitting-room, curled up in her favourite armchair, asleep in the sunlight flooding through the south-facing bay window. The large panes of glass were almost opaque with neglect. Neither of the cats stirred when Hermione approached, until she clicked her tongue at them. Giotto, black and white with a completely white face, opened his eyes and stretched out his front paws. Then Botticelli lifted his mackerel-striped face at the disturbance and he, too, stretched. Together they jumped to the floor and rubbed themselves against Hermione's legs, lifting the hem of her skirt with their heads, purring rhythmically.

'Good boys,' Hermione said, commandeering the armchair. She picked up the faded needlepoint cushion on which Giotto had been sleeping, and which she'd made almost twenty years ago, repositioned it into the small of her back and sank gratefully into the old chair. She was tired, and putting her exhaustion down to the surprisingly warm temperature of the day she closed her eyes and permitted herself a late-afternoon doze.

She dreamed of the Lodge next door and of rows of upright chairs that tilted forwards at the touch of a button, sending the occupiers sprawling to the floor.

Duncan dropped into second gear and approached Crantsford Hall carefully through elegant cast-iron gates, the spearhead tips of which were painted gold. He drove slowly along the cobbled driveway, brought the car to a stop alongside the garage block and hesitated a few moments before turning off the engine. He rested his head against the restraint and closed his eyes to concentrate better on Mahler's 'Kindertotenlieder'. He felt enormously happy. Not only did he have his new BMW at last – he'd waited patiently for more than three months for this particular model – but he had the prospect ahead of him of four days off work during which time he planned to play several rounds of golf and see Ellen.

When the CD came to an end he reluctantly opened his eyes, gathered up his briefcase and the evening paper from the passenger seat, locked the car, taking care to set the alarm, and strode over towards the house. He let himself in through the heavy oak door and walked across the stone-flagged floor.

'Is that you, Duncan?'

He ignored the question and placed his briefcase neatly beside a bow-fronted chest of drawers, straightened an out-of-place tulip in the vase on top, glanced briefly at the mail waiting for his attention on a large silver plate, then sought out his mother. He found her in the dining-room at the other end of the Georgian table apparently attending to the oak panelling with a feather duster.

'What on earth are you doing, Nadia?'

'Please don't you use that tone of voice with me, Duncan, not after the day I've had. I've been let down. Mrs Harmen hasn't been in today. Not so much as a phone call. Not a word. Nothing. I'm completely worn out and I've a good mind to cancel lunch tomorrow. It'll be a miracle if I can get out of bed in the morning after all the cleaning I've done today, never mind put a meal together. You'll have to ring round and explain to everybody. Tell them I'm ill. They might even send flowers.'

'Don't be ridiculous,' Duncan said, balling his fists behind his back. He was furious that his good mood had been so roughly taken away from him, and, recognising that his mother was playing the part of helpless-woman-gone-to-pieces, he said, 'I need a drink.' He turned away and marched to the drawing-room where he spun the top off the whisky bottle, poured himself a good measure and tossed it back. He didn't know which had angered him most, his mother or his near loss of control just now.

By the time Nadia joined him he'd drunk another glass of whisky and had calmed down sufficiently to say, 'Don't worry about tomorrow, everything will be fine. You can lie in and I'll see to lunch.'

She smiled. 'What would I do without you, Duncan?'

'What indeed?'

Hermione could hear ringing. A vague persistent ringing. After a while it stopped, but then it started up again by which time she was fully awake and aware that it was the telephone she could hear. She hurried out to the hall and picked up the receiver.

'Where on earth have you been?'

'Asleep, as a matter of fact.'

'What, all afternoon?'

'Matthew, is it really any of your business what I choose to do—'

'I'm sorry, I was concerned, that's all. I tried this morning and earlier this afternoon. Are you sure you're okay?'

Hermione smiled. 'I'm fine, really. In fact, I've had quite a day.'

'So what have you been up to? Ram-raiding the local post office?'

'Matthew, you really are one of the most irritating and rude men I have the misfortune of knowing.'

'It's your own fault. As my godmother you should have played a more active role in my upbringing.'

'Yes, forty-two years ago I should have drowned you in the font!'

Matthew laughed. 'So that's all the thanks I get for ringing to see how you are and to ask if I can come and stay with you on Saturday.'

'What, the day after tomorrow?'

'Is there a problem?'

'Well, I had thought I might go hot-air ballooning for the Easter weekend, but I suppose I could put it off until another time. Why are you coming?'

'To see you.'

'Rubbish. When you come to see me you never ring, you just arrive. Why is this visit different? Why the advance warning?'

'If you must know I've been asked to do a commission for some neighbours of yours, the Buchanans. What are they like?'

'I'll let you work him out for yourself, but she's sweet, a bit of a Dizzy Nora.'

Matthew groaned.

'And they've more money than you'd ever know what to do with. Now if you've nothing more to tell me I'm in dire need of the lavatory. Goodbye.'

'Hermione.'

'Yes.'

'Take care, won't you?'

'Matthew, the day I can't manage the loo is the day I shoot myself.'

'I didn't mean that, you silly old woman.'

'I know. I just don't like people being sentimental these days.'

'I'll see you on Saturday, then. Late, probably about ten. I'll eat on the way. 'Bye.'

5

When Ellen woke up she could hear music, a faint trickle of sound coming from downstairs. For a split second she thought that Simon must have arrived home in the middle of the night and that he was in the kitchen beneath her making himself a gigantic sandwich, the radio blaring beside him. 'It helps me concentrate,' he'd say, in his typical youthful fashion, whenever she turned the volume down in her typically parental way.

But realising that her bedroom floorboards weren't actually pulsating to the beat of something fast and furious, Ellen abandoned the idea that it was Simon downstairs and decided that Jo-Jo was up and about.

Ellen hadn't seen anything of Jo-Jo all yesterday evening. She'd slept right through from what was supposed to be a late-afternoon nap till now. The poor girl must have been exhausted to have slept so long.

Ellen pushed back the duvet, got out of bed and padded downstairs. She found Jo-Jo in the small narrow kitchen. She was already dressed, in the same clothes that she'd been wearing yesterday. She was getting herself something to eat while listening to the radio and swinging her narrow young hips. She looked as if she didn't have a care in the world.

'Hello.'

Jo-Jo started and turned round. 'I'm sorry,' she mumbled guiltily, her mouth full of what Ellen took to be toast and Marmite, judging from the things spread over the work surface and the smell from the toaster. 'Did I wake you?'

'You did, but I should have been up anyway. How are you? Did you sleep well?'

'I slept brilliantly and I feel great. Well, great for a pregnant runaway. I helped myself to some bread, do you mind?'

Ellen shook her head. 'Have another slice of toast while I make us some tea.'

'No,' Jo-Jo said. 'You go and sit down and I'll make you some breakfast.' She hesitated and then laughed. 'Bloody hell, I sound just like I do at home.'

'What do you mean?'

'It's what I have to do with Mum. Sometimes she's like a child and you just have to treat her like one.'

Ellen cleared the table in the sitting-room while Jo-Jo filled a tray of breakfast things and carried it through. 'You're very domesticated for your age,' Ellen said, slightly amused at the situation.

Jo-Jo shrugged. 'I've been doing it for years. Or, rather, I've been covering up for Mum for years. My step-father can't stand it if things aren't done the way he likes and Mum's so far gone she hasn't got a clue about organising a meal or the house. So when I finish school I pick up something from the shops and shove it in the oven and peel a few veg. Then all Mum has to do when he gets back from work is serve it up for him.'

Ellen was shocked. 'But how long has that been going on?'

'Ages. Well, for as long as I can remember.'

Ellen didn't have the nerve to ask how Jo-Jo thought her mother might be coping without her.

They ate in silence for a while until Jo-Jo said, 'I'll wash up for you when we've finished and then I'll get going, see if I can find a hostel or something.'

After a pause Ellen said, 'Yes. I suppose that would be best.'

Jo-Jo looked up at her. 'Best?' she repeated, disappointed. She had thought, had hoped, that maybe she could ... Oh, but what was the use? She'd got a bed for the night and something to eat, what more could she expect? This wasn't some fairy-tale where the poor little runaway lands on her feet in the land of plenty and ends up marrying a handsome prince – or even, to be politically correct as Alan would insist, ends up with a person of above-average means and well-enhanced looks.

Ellen dusted the crumbs of toast off her fingers and then pushed her plate away from her. 'Best all round,' she said at last, her voice firm and determined. 'After all, I've done my bit for society, I've contributed my two penn'orth to the kitty for the great unwashed. Nobody could accuse me of not having helped.' She didn't like the sound of the words coming out of her mouth, but she had to distance herself from Jo-Jo and her problems. She had enough of her own.

She started gathering up the mugs and plates, crashing them onto the tray. 'Well, what else can I do?' she asked, her eyes anywhere but on Jo-Jo's face.

'You could let me stay, until I get myself sorted?' Jo-Jo whispered, hardly daring to ask. 'I could help you. I – I can cook quite well.'

Ellen sank into her chair. 'But I can't afford to have you here. I can only just keep a roof over my own head and occasionally Simon's, never mind anyone else's.'

'How about just for the weekend?'

'Go home, Jo-Jo,' Ellen said, exasperated. 'Just go home and sort out this awful mess with your parents. Get social services involved, get—'

'Anyone so long as it's not you, is that it?'

'That's not fair.'

'No, but then, so they tell me, life isn't. Now if you don't mind I'd like to stick to my agreement. I'll wash up and then go, and you needn't ever think of me again.'

'Oh, don't be so dramatic.' Ellen relented. 'Put that tray down, and heaven help me for my stupidity.'

Jo-Jo did as she was told.

'You can stay here over the Easter weekend but then on Tuesday we're going to have to find you a more permanent place in which to live. Don't interrupt, I haven't finished yet. And I'll let you stay these next few days on the condition that you ring your mother and let her know you're safe. Agreed?'

Jo-Jo nodded.

'And perhaps you should see a doctor. I don't want you fainting on me again.'

Jo-Jo gave another little nod.

'Good. Now, get cracking with that washing-up!'

Ellen followed a smiling Jo-Jo to the kitchen.

The phone rang. It was Hermione.

'So how's our little runaway? Not left town with all the silver, I hope?'

'No,' replied Ellen, watching Jo-Jo squeeze a long thin yellow snake of economy washing-up liquid into the sink. 'Not so much!' she cried out, alarmed at the extravagance. 'Sorry, Hermione, what did you say?'

'I'm ringing to make sure you haven't been robbed in the night.'

'Only robbed of my senses. I've been emotionally blackmailed into letting her stop here over the weekend.'

Hermione cackled. 'Now tell me why that doesn't come as a surprise.'

'Because I'm emotionally weak, I suppose.'

'Don't be so absurd. You've got more about you than any of that weak, wishy-washy lot yesterday who walked straight past Jo-Jo pretending not to notice her.'

'I don't recall you giving her anything. Does that make you weak and wishy-washy?'

'No, merely as tight as Giotto's bottom. And I'm referring to my cat's hindquarters, not to the great Italian artist's derrière, which, given the age he lived in, doesn't bear thinking about.'

Ellen smiled, thinking that if Hermione ever went round the bend nobody would ever notice. 'Hermione,' she said, looking at her watch, 'I'm going to have to go as I'm going out in a couple of hours and I've got to get ready. Hair to wash and act to clean up.'

'Duncan, I presume?'

'Yep. He's invited me for lunch at no less a place than Crantsford Hall.'

Hermione whistled. 'Time to meet the folks, is it? Oh, oh. So what are you going to wear? Nothing too racy, I hope.'

'No fear, not with La Carter there.'

'Now, Ellen, don't blow it. Just sit at the table nodding your pretty little head like one of those awful toy dogs in the back of a car. And if you keep your mouth shut she'll like you even better. And don't, whatever you do, say you've been ill recently. Nobody's allowed to be ill except La Carter. Got that?'

Ellen laughed. 'How do you know so much about her?'

'Old money, Ellen. It's the *entrée* to most evils, especially an old witch like Nadia Carter, and I'm referring to the days when I did have more than two and six to my name. But never mind all that. Go and tart yourself up while I have a quick word with Jo-Jo. And, Ellen . . .'

'Yes?'

'Try not to think of Daniel and the lions' den.'

6

Duncan arrived early, just as Ellen had thought he might.

She'd learned that much about him during the time he'd acted for her during her divorce. He'd always been ready at least five minutes before any of their appointments in his neatly presented beamed office in Church Walk Mews and had been painstakingly conscientious in his dealings with her.

Her first visit to his office had been almost as unbearable as reading the note Roger had left on the mantelpiece. She had arrived far too early for her eleven o'clock appointment and, sitting in the small waiting room, she had watched a variety of smartly dressed men and women passing to and fro through an open door – the other partners who made up the practice of Church Walk Mews Solicitors, she had assumed. At five to eleven Duncan had come for her in the waiting room. 'Mrs Jacobs,' he'd said briskly, holding out his hand, 'Duncan Carter. Shall we get on?'

He was younger than she had expected, but she had only spoken briefly with him on the telephone a couple of days previously. From the sound of his voice she had anticipated someone in his early fifties with thinning hair and a tired suit with faint pinstripes and shiny creases. But in reality it was difficult to pin an exact age on Duncan Carter, for his thick black hair, neatly cut and swept to one side, gave him a youthful, boyish appearance, which was immediately at odds with the mannered style in which he spoke and moved about his office. His suit was fashionably single-breasted and fitted his tall slim body perfectly, and his shoes, classic lace-ups, were as black as his hair while the toe-caps had a lustre matched only by the polished desk behind which he positioned himself. He motioned to a comfortable chair, waited until she was sufficiently settled, then removed his jacket and spent a few seconds straightening it on the back of his own chair, before sitting down, picking up his fountain pen and finally facing her.

For almost an hour she had listened in numbed silence to explanations of maintenance orders, decree nisis and decree absolutes while watching him methodically run his thumb and forefinger slowly up and down the sides of his pen, again and again. 'It's going to be a bumpy road for you,' he said kindly, when at last he seemed to run out of things to say, 'but not an impossible one. Just remember, my job is to smooth out those bumps for you. Do you have any questions?'

'How much will all this cost me?' had been the only one.

'My fee is one hundred pounds an hour,' he'd answered, without batting an eyelid.

One hundred pounds an hour! 'In that case I'll have a cup of tea. Or is that extra?'

Tea in delicate bone-china cups appeared within minutes. 'Mrs Jacobs,' he said, when they were alone again and he had passed her a cup and saucer across his desk, 'forgive the impertinence, but please don't let the issue of money cloud your long-term view.'

Advice that fell on stony ground, for ever since Roger had left all she had thought about was money. Did she have enough that month to pay the electricity bill or fill the car with petrol? Could she afford to splash out on real chocolate digestives instead of making do with the red and green labelled biscuits in the barrels at the supermarket, which were always broken and covered with a curious brown substance masquerading as chocolate that stuck tenaciously to the roof of her mouth like gum?

From the window she watched Duncan park what appeared to be a new car alongside the barn. She remembered him saying some months ago that he'd ordered a BMW. She smiled to herself, realising now why he had offered to pick her up.

He came towards the cottage and she congratulated herself on picking out the right outfit – a pale pink linen skirt and jacket she'd had for years but which never failed to lift her spirits, and which she had felt sure would complement what Duncan would be wearing. She had second-guessed him well. He was dressed in smart grey flannels with a navy blazer, white shirt and tie, and she had to admit that together they made an attractive couple. She let him ring the bell – it wouldn't do to let him know she'd been pacing the room waiting for him – and then very quietly chanted to herself, 'One two three, give him time to wait for me,' before opening the door.

'Duncan,' she said, in a voice that she hoped contained just the right amount of pleasure at seeing him. 'Come on in while I find my bag. Would you like a drink?'

'No thank you,' he said politely. She watched him move awkwardly into the little room. It was the first time he'd stepped inside Spring Bank Cottage. On their previous evenings out together they had arranged to meet up at the restaurants Duncan had pre-booked for dinner – these invitations had only materialised once her divorce had been finalised: while she had still been a client and a married woman Duncan had not made the slightest hint of an advance towards her. He was clearly a man of principle.

'You've done this up very nicely, Ellen,' he said, stooping slightly to avoid knocking the arrangements of dried flowers hanging from the ceiling. 'It's charming. You've made it quite your own.'

'I'm still trying to get used to it,' she said, gathering up her bag and a large bunch of daffodils that she'd picked from along the river-bank earlier that morning, 'but after Orchard House this seems so—'

He raised his hand in the air. 'Ellen, I've told you before, the past is irrelevant. It's where you are now that's important and where you think you might be going.'

She thought of Crantsford Hall and smiled. 'Perhaps you're right, Duncan. Shall we go?'

As Duncan pulled out onto the main road at the top of Beggarman's Lane he glanced sideways at Ellen and thought how attractive she was looking today. He noticed, too, her long legs just inches away from the gear stick.

'What a lovely car,' Ellen said, conscious that Duncan was scrutinising her. 'It's new, isn't it?' she added, doing her best to inch her skirt down discreetly, but it was having none of it and seemed determined to stay right where it was.

He smiled and pressed his foot down on the accelerator a touch more. 'It arrived yesterday. Do you like it?'

'It's beautiful,' she answered. 'It must be wonderful to drive.'

'It is,' he agreed, and took a corner fast enough to feel the pull. He then had to brake sharply as he came up behind an ancient Allegro, flat out at twenty.

Ellen had a pretty good idea what was coming next – after all, Duncan had the perfect right to be a racing driver *manqué*, just like any other man with a new car. She held her breath as he swerved round the Allegro and then accelerated at such a rate that her head was forced back against the head restraint and kept there for some moments. As they came into the speed-restricted area at the top of Church Walk Duncan slowed down. He took the fork in the road that directed the traffic away from the town centre, headed in a north-easterly direction towards Mobberley and once they were clear of any speed restrictions his foot went down again. Within a matter of minutes they were in open countryside and he was slowing down to swing the car through a pair of cast-iron gates. They turned a bend in the cobbled driveway and Crantsford Hall stood before them, resplendent in the bright midday sunshine, slightly raised above a lawn planted out with clumps of yellow and white daffodils, their delicate heads bobbing in the gentle breeze.

'How long have you lived here?' Ellen asked.

'We moved here when I was ten, but I've had stints away of course – boarding school, college, a couple of years in London and then for a while I had my own place over in Alderley Edge.' He paused for a moment before adding, 'But when my father died so unexpectedly it made sense to move back here to keep an eye on Nadia.'

He parked the car next to a dusty Range Rover and a metallic grey Jaguar. 'Good,' he said, switching off the engine. 'Everyone else has arrived.'

They entered the house through a large oak door, which Duncan held open for her.

'Sounds like they're all in the drawing-room,' he said. And sure enough, as they passed a series of closed panelled doors and grim-looking oil paintings of what looked like eighteenth-century grandees, they came to a room where the other guests were standing around, glasses in hand, making noisy small-talk. Ellen didn't recognise any of them, but she recognised their type – the honkers and brayers, as Hermione called some of Crantsford's worthies.

An extremely large woman came forward. She wasn't fat, but everything about her seemed oversized, shoulders, hands, feet, even eyes. She was colossal. If Ellen wanted to be generous, and she wasn't sure she wanted to be, she would say the woman was big-boned – like a dinosaur! Ellen disliked her on sight.

'Nadia,' Duncan said, 'this is Ellen Jacobs. Ellen, this is my mother.'

'Well, get out of the way so I can see her,' Nadia said impatiently. She was anxious to view this guest of Duncan's, especially as he hadn't mentioned anything about inviting anybody else for lunch until a couple of hours ago. All legs and blonde hair, she thought dismissively, after paying the scantest of attention. Where *did* Duncan find them?

Ellen handed her hostess the large bunch of daffodils. 'Though having seen your garden I feel a little silly giving you these,' she said, with a light laugh.

'Delightful,' Nadia said, without even looking at them.

Sensing his mother's disapproval, Duncan intervened. 'Why don't you put those in water, Nadia, while I introduce Ellen to everyone?'

Reluctantly Nadia did as she was told. In the kitchen she threw the daffodils in the sink, took a gulp from the glass of sherry tucked behind the jars of herbs and spices in the alcove above the cooker and hurried back to the drawing-room, just in time to catch the last of the introductions being made. Henry and Cynthia Koval were having their glasses refilled and the Winstanleys – Maurice and Phyllis – were shaking hands with Ellen.

'Jacobs,' Henry said loudly, coming back towards Ellen. 'That name rings a bell. Bugger me if I can think why.'

'You always say that,' Cynthia drawled. 'Ignore him, Ellen. He thinks he knows everyone in Crantsford.'

'Do you play golf?' asked Maurice who, Ellen decided, had the look of a man who certainly knew his way round a clubhouse bar as well as a bag of clubs, if his weather-beaten face and purplish red hooter was anything to go by. 'Is that how you met Duncan?'

'No,' Ellen said, amused. 'I'm no golfer.'

'Ellen and I met in a professional capacity,' Duncan said, passing round a tray of olives and cashew nuts.

'Got you,' Maurice said. 'You're one of those clever types, aren't you? I knew it the moment you opened your mouth. I said to myself, she's not just a pretty popsie on legs. So you're in the legal profession as well, are you?'

Popsie! Any more talk like this and she'd pop him right in the eye! 'Actually,' Ellen said, straining to keep a polite smile on her face, 'Duncan was my solicitor. He acted for—'

'Come on, Maurice,' Duncan interrupted. 'You're not wearing a wig and gown today.'

'A wig and gown,' Ellen repeated, helping herself to a couple of olives. 'Does that mean you're a barrister or a transvestite?'

'Ellen, my dear,' Nadia said in a voice awash with condescension, 'Maurice is a judge. You must surely have heard of Judge Winstanley.'

And, as though to rub her nose in it even more, Nadia placed Ellen next to Maurice-the-red-nosed-judge for lunch, which was served in an enormous oak-panelled dining-room with a polished oak floor and stone fireplace the size of a single bed. The room must have been north-facing and was freezing, and Ellen stared reproachfully at the empty fireplace.

Conversation around the table fairly skipped along with talk of birdies and handicaps and, even more exciting, the Winstanleys weren't renewing their AA membership after being kept waiting for more than thirty minutes on the hard shoulder of the M6 in February when their Jaguar broke down. Ellen let their voices drone on while she contented herself with imagining how, as mistress of Crantsford Hall and with a limitless budget, she would bring this cheerless room to life. The drab, sludge-green curtains would be first to go and in their place she'd put up sumptuous drapes with plenty of warm tonal shades to the fabric, probably reds, golds, anything that would add some warmth to the room. Next she'd have a log fire crackling and everywhere there'd be flowers: armfuls of daffodils in the spring and in the summer masses of fragrant sweet peas and roses and anything else that would sweeten the leaden atmosphere.

'Jacobs!' roared Henry-bugger-me-Koval from the other side of the table.

Ellen jumped and sent a piece of roast lamb skidding across the table, followed by a splash of mint sauce.

'Bugger me if I haven't got it!' Henry beamed happily. 'I knew I'd get there in the end. There was that dentist chappie in Lower Market Street called Jacobs. Bugger of a dentist he was. I turned up for my appointment and he wasn't there. Buggered off to France with some totty. I ask you! I heard that he left behind him debts worse than the national borrowing rate of a third-world country and a pretty wife to pick up . . .' His words fizzled out as he looked at Ellen and saw the expression on her face. 'Oh, bugger!' he muttered, his discomfort as great as Ellen's.

Nadia saw her chance. 'Ellen, my dear. I had no idea you were *that* Mrs Jacobs.'

'Mother.'

'Don't you Mother me anything, Duncan. You really should have said something. It's unforgivable that you should have caused Henry to feel so embarrassed and to humiliate Ellen in this way. Why didn't you say that you had acted on her behalf for her divorce? Why all the secrecy?' Her enjoyment of the situation was undisguised.

'I didn't think it was anyone else's business,' Duncan said simply. He reached forward to retrieve Ellen's piece of meat from the tablecloth, slipped it onto his own plate and then carefully wiped his hands on his napkin.

'I don't feel at all humiliated,' lied Ellen, lifting her eyes from the congealed lamb in front of her. 'And, Henry, please don't worry on my account. Your description of my ex-husband is as apt as any I've heard.'

Henry mumbled something that passed for an apology, and Phyllis Winstanley said, 'Didn't you have to sell your lovely house in the Crescent?' She knew full well that this was indeed the case. She'd seen it for herself in the estate agent's window in Lower Market Street last year, and had also seen the asking price drop steadily.

Ellen nodded.

'I heard you'd recently set yourself up in your own little business,' Cynthia said. 'Terribly brave of you, and after everything you'd gone through.'

Ellen felt trapped. It was obvious that these two women knew everything there was to know about the infamous dentist, Roger Jacobs. The only missing piece to their jigsaw of gossip was that they hadn't known who Mrs Jacobs was, but now that they had the very woman herself in their midst they were clearly determined to squeeze every last detail out of her.

'What kind of business is it you do?' asked Nadia from the head of the table. 'Business lunches or interior design? I hear that's what a lot of young women are occupying themselves with these days.'

'Dried flowers,' replied Ellen, mustering what was left of her dignity. 'I have a barn in Beggarman's Lane where I sell them. I also take orders.' She glanced over to the fireplace. 'In the summer months when you're not using it, that fireplace would look wonderful with one of my arrangements.'

Nadia took this as a personal slight. 'I think you'll find that a fireplace which has a date stone of 1705 stands for itself and needs no artificial adornment.'

But Phyllis was more cunning. 'I'd love you to put something together for my sitting-room. Perhaps I could come along and see your barn. Beggarman's Lane, did you say?'

'What a good idea,' chimed in Cynthia. 'I'll join you. Nadia, you'll have to come as well. You're always saying how we should support local businesses.'

'I'm surprised you're not working today, Ellen,' Nadia said flatly. 'It's the Easter weekend, after all. I would have expected this to be one of your busiest times.'

'Mother,' Duncan said sharply, 'it's Good Friday and I'm sure you'll agree that Ellen's as entitled as the next person to take a holiday if she so chooses. I think it's time for our dessert now.'

Just desserts, Ellen wanted to add.

The plates were cleared away and Duncan brought in a large trifle and the customary noises of appreciation were made. 'Bugger me,' said Henry, who had now overcome his earlier blunder and resumed his normal self, 'that looks promising.'

The mood around the table lightened.

'You'll never guess what I saw in Crantsford yesterday,' said Cynthia. 'A girl begging! In Crantsford, of all places.'

Ellen stiffened. She kept her eyes firmly on her bowl, but beside her she felt Maurice-the-red-nosed-judge pull himself up onto his judgemental high horse.

'We're being overrun with them,' he said. 'Worse than vermin in my opinion.'

'Absolutely,' agreed his wife, Phyllis.

'I think I saw her as well,' said Duncan. 'She was trying her luck in Church Walk Mews.'

Ellen remained silent and hated herself for it. She thought of Jo-Jo and hoped that she was enjoying herself with Hermione, who had insisted that while Ellen was out for lunch the girl should go to her. Dear sweet Hermione, mad as a hatter but more in touch with the real world than any of this lot with their tired old clichés. Suddenly Ellen wanted very much to go home.

As it turned out she was first to leave.

'Let's go for a drive,' Duncan whispered to her, when everyone had started decamping to the drawing-room for coffee and he found her lagging behind the group. She nodded, and in the kind of voice that would brook no argument he said to his mother, 'Nadia, I'm taking Ellen home.'

Nadia made a token gesture of disappointment and everyone stood to say goodbye. Ellen thought she had better give a plausible excuse for her early departure. 'A headache,' she apologised, 'it'll soon go.' Too late, she remembered Hermione's warning.

'Headaches are nothing compared to migraines,' announced Nadia, 'nothing but an inconvenience that can be easily borne with the right mental attitude. But migraines are a completely different matter. When I have one of my sessions, I'm flat on my back for at least a week. Isn't that so, Duncan?'

Eventually they made it to the front door where they stood for a further five minutes while everyone insisted on waving Ellen off with promises made by both Cynthia and Phyllis that they would be calling on her in Beggarman's Lane before very long.

In the end Duncan took Ellen firmly by the arm and led her to his car. She felt like a bride being whisked away on her honeymoon and as they drove out of view of the house Duncan leaned over and kissed her cheek.

7

'Who's Duncan?' Jo-Jo asked.

Hermione looked up from the tray of sweet-pea seedlings she was potting on. She was dressed in one of her more eccentric gardening outfits – an old brown and cream kaftan with a fringe added onto the hem to give it extra length, except it didn't quite reach all the way round and there was a gap at the back. On her head was a large floppy hat that possessed a solitary pink feather, which had a habit of shifting position. Sometimes it was upright like an antenna and other times it drooped mournfully over the brim and tickled Hermione's face.

'Duncan is hopefully going to be Ellen's next husband,' she confided, with a smile.

'You make her sound like she collects them. How many has she had?'

Hermione laughed and returned her attention to the seedlings on the wooden table in front of her. 'Just the one,' she answered, making a small hole in a pot of compost with the end of a pencil. She carefully picked up a tender plant and settled it into its new home.

They were sitting on the terrace overlooking the garden, having eaten lunch, cleared away and then come outside to enjoy the afternoon sunshine. Her young companion had proved to be good company – a compulsive interrogator it turned out, which backed up the opinion Hermione had made of her yesterday, that despite the stupidity of her current predicament she was an intelligent girl with something to say for herself.

'So where's he now?'

'With any luck being driven mad by the brainless wonder he flitted off to France with.'

'You don't sound as if you liked him very much.'

Hermione thought about this. Had she liked Roger at all? Probably not, was the honest answer. More likely she had tolerated him, and only tolerated him because he was Ellen's husband. 'He was a dentist,' she replied. 'Nobody likes dentists.'

Jo-Jo laughed. 'You're just like my grandmother. She never answered my questions properly either.'

Hermione lifted out another sweet-pea plant and held it gently between her thumb and forefinger. 'No chance of this *doppelgänger* of mine taking care of you, is there?'

Jo-Jo rose from her chair and went and stood next to the low black wrought-iron railings that overlooked the rockery six feet below. 'No,' she said.

'I thought not.'

'But if she'd still been alive that's where I'd have gone.'

'I'm very pleased to hear it, and it only goes to confirm what I've long since thought – that we old folk certainly have our uses.'

Jo-Jo came and sat at the table again. She traced her finger in a mound of spilled compost on the table and formed the letter A. Hermione pretended not to notice. 'I can't always work out whether you're being sarcastic or just plain horrid,' Jo-Jo said, picking up a clay pot and obliterating what she'd just drawn.

'Don't fret yourself. You'll get the hang of it eventually.'

Jo-Jo doubted this, and decided to follow her earlier line of questioning. 'Why does Ellen want to get married again? Isn't she better off on her own?'

'Depends what you mean by better off.'

'You're not saying she wants this Duncan for his money, are you?'

'My dear Jo-Jo, you look quite prim. But whoever said that Duncan had money? I certainly didn't.'

Jo-Jo frowned. 'You implied that he did.'

'You don't want to listen to what a rambling old woman says. Especially one as daft as me.' She shook her hands free of compost. 'Come on, let's go for a wander. The rest of these sweet peas can wait till later.'

They left the terrace and took the small path of stone steps to the right of the rockery down to the area of lawn below. 'This used to be a tennis court,' Hermione said, 'but I stopped playing when Fred Perry bowed out. I lost heart in the game.'

'Who's he? An old boyfriend of yours?'

Hermione smiled. 'Oh, the ignorance of youth. What a joy to behold.'

To their right, and behind a straggly beech hedge, was a greenhouse, and to their left, tucked into the rhododendron bushes and surrounded by a mass of yellow daffodils and primroses was a wooden summer-house with an ornately tiled roof. But Hermione ignored both of these and continued further down the garden where there were two large yews which for the past thirty years she had clipped and bullied into resembling a pair of Christmas puddings. Between them were more steps and as Hermione walked on she stooped to pick a daffodil bent at a ninety-degree angle. She snapped it off and wiped the gooey thread of sap from the stem onto the step and handed the flower to Jo-Jo.

'Will you keep the baby?' she asked unexpectedly.

Jo-Jo was taken aback. 'I don't know,' she said.

Hermione gave her a long, hard stare. 'You must have thought about it, though. Is it too late for an abortion?' She lowered her eyes to Jo-Jo's stomach.

Jo-Jo didn't answer but she wrapped her slender arms in front of her and covered her stomach protectively.

'Much too late obviously,' Hermione said. 'But at least that narrows your options to just the two possibilities open to you. You either keep the baby, or give it up for adoption. Do you love the father?'

'For a daft rambling old woman, you're very direct, aren't you?'

Hermione didn't respond and started walking again. 'There's a seat further down,' she said. 'Let's go on, it'll be cooler in the shade.'

They crossed another lawn and went through an arch to the wild, unkempt patch of garden that Hermione rarely visited these days. There wasn't a path and their shoes all but disappeared into the thick layer of leaves as they made their way through the wilderness that had been left to fend for itself. Fallen branches obstructed the way, with brambles and stinging nettles.

Just as Jo-Jo was beginning to wonder if they shouldn't be heading back towards the house they came across a stone seat and a statue of a young woman with her hands in front of her holding an open book. Her face was turned up, as though something in the air had caught her attention, and even with the gathering moss and years of discoloration that had taken its toll, the features were still visible and Jo-Jo could make out a familiar smile.

'She looks so happy,' she said, going straight to the statue and touching the face. She brushed away some lichen and traced her fingers over the cheekbones and proud chin.

'The man who made it was a friend and he had that effect on . . .'

Jo-Jo glanced back at Hermione. 'Is it you, when you were young? Was he that Perry bloke you mentioned earlier?'

'Just as I was beginning to think you possessed half a brain you go and spoil it. Fred Perry was one of the most brilliant tennis players this country ever produced and sadly he was never a boyfriend of mine.' She turned away and sat down on the seat. Jo-Jo joined her.

'But the man who created that beautiful statue, he *was* a boyfriend of yours, wasn't he?' she persisted.

Hermione shrugged. 'It matters not what he was, he's no longer here. Now tell me about the baby's father. Do you love him and is that the reason you want to keep the child?'

Jo-Jo considered lying but what was the point? 'His name's Alan, I don't know how old he is but he's married with two children of his own and he's my English teacher, or rather he was. Are you shocked?'

'Now what do you really think?'

'I suppose not,' Jo-Jo said, with a smile. 'You're not the shockable type, are you?'

'Thank you, I'll take that as a compliment. But this Alan character, he sounds like he might be of the shockable variety.'

Jo-Jo thought about this. She recalled the look of horror on Alan's face when she'd told him. He was taking her home after she'd babysat his children while he'd been out for the evening with his wife. He'd stopped the car in the usual place down a quiet unlit road and had started kissing her and pulling at her clothes. It never took him long. And always afterwards he'd tell her how clever she was. He would stroke her hair and say how she was the best student he'd ever taught and that she was special. But he didn't that night. That night he told her she was stupid and that she should have known better. Banging his fist on the steering-wheel, he'd shouted, 'Haven't you listened to anything in school? The amount of curriculum time devoted to pastoral care and you still wind up pregnant!'

Two days later he'd spoken to her at school. 'Sorry about the other night,' he'd whispered. 'It was the shock. I'll get the money together and we'll arrange an abortion. You're not to worry about a thing.'

But the next day her mother had found the pregnancy-test kit in her bedroom and told her husband about it. Predictably he had ranted and raved about how much he'd done for her since taking her on from the age of six and what a disappointment she'd turned out – he made her sound like an employee caught with her hands in the till. And, just as predictably, she was told to leave the house. She had thrown some things into a bag, emptied the box in her drawer where she kept her babysitting money and then got a bus to the station, where she caught a train with the intention of going to Manchester. But she messed everything up and found herself on the wrong train heading for a place in Cheshire she'd never even heard of – Crantsford. As she had stepped down onto the empty platform, tears had filled her eyes: all she could think of was her mother's act of betrayal. Why had she told her step-father? After all the years of help she had given her mother, was this to be all the thanks she got?

She had phoned her mother earlier, just as Ellen had instructed, and again the betrayal was there. 'It's better this way,' her mother's pathetic voice had said. 'Better that you stay away.' It was as if she was pleading with her.

'Jo-Jo?'

She looked down to see Hermione's liver-spotted hand covering her own. Gran used to do that to her when she knew she was about to cry. She swallowed hard to loosen her constricted throat, but it didn't work. 'I only went with him because I was so lonely,' she murmured. 'I wanted somebody to love me in the way Gran used to love me. He said I was special, I . . . I wanted to believe him.'

Hermione took Jo-Jo in her arms and held her tightly. 'Oh, Jo-Jo, you poor sweet child, of course you're special.'

8

'Were you very bored?' Duncan asked, pulling up alongside Ellen's barn.

'Not in the slightest,' she lied glibly.

Duncan suspected that this was not the truth but he let it go, preferring instead to admire Ellen for her tact. 'I'm sorry about all that fuss with Henry at lunch,' he said. 'He can be a bit of a terrier. Once he gets hold of something he doesn't like to give it up.'

'No harm done.' Ellen thought that of all the people round the table who most resembled a terrier it was La Carter who fitted the bill. 'Would you like to come in for a drink?' she asked, sensing that they'd reached the tricky stage of still sitting in the car, the engine off, and each waiting for the other to determine what happened next. She wondered if Duncan was now regretting having kissed her when they'd sailed through the gates at Crantsford Hall. It had been so unexpected that it had rendered them both silent for the following few minutes – he silent with embarrassment, she fancied, and she silent with wishful thinking. She'd been mentally stuffing her belongings into packing cases and setting up home with Duncan ever since.

He looked at the clock on the walnut dashboard. 'I really ought to get back, but, well, all right, then, but just a soft drink.'

Not much chance of anything else, thought Ellen, as she let them into the cottage. She left Duncan prowling around the small sitting-room and went through to the kitchen. She opened the fridge and found the carton of orange juice she'd opened yesterday morning, but there was little more than a dribble left in it – Jo-Jo would have to be pointed in the direction of the tap for the remainder of her stay. 'Fizzy water okay?' she called out to Duncan.

'That would be fine,' he answered.

She reached into the door of the fridge and pulled out a near empty plastic bottle. She twisted the cap and, just as she had dreaded, it gave off a tired little hiss confirming her fears that the remains of the carbonated water were way past their best. She poured out what was left into a glass and then rummaged through the contents of the fridge. Not that there was much to rummage through, just a tub of margarine, a cling-film-wrapped nugget of cheese that had all the taste of a bar of soap, and a bag of carrots – carrots were a frequent stand-by at Spring Bank Cottage, they were good and cheap, especially if you bought the pre-packed inferior variety with splits running the length of them. Hiding behind the carrots she found what she was looking for. A plastic lemon. She squirted a shot of juice into Duncan's glass, added a couple of ice cubes and hoped for the best.

'Here we are,' she said, joining him in the sitting-room. She handed him his drink.

'You not joining me?'

'No,' she answered, and went and sat in the window-seat. She opened the small window behind her, hoping that the warm breeze blowing in through the window would somehow make her seem more alluring, but her efforts were wasted as Duncan continued to prowl round the room preferring to inspect her meagre possessions rather than her potential charm.

'That's a nice watercolour,' he said, pointing with his glass at the picture above the fireplace. After the dark foreboding paintings she'd just seen at Crantsford Hall, Ellen supposed that the light, airy depiction of a group of children playing on a beach would seem like a breath of fresh air to him.

'And you've some interesting china,' he continued, now addressing the assortment of jugs, plates, cups and saucers on the dresser. 'Very nice,' he added, ducking the hanging dried flowers as he moved across the room to take a closer look.

'All junk, I'm afraid,' Ellen said, getting up from the window-seat and settling herself in an armchair where perhaps her legs might be more noticeable. 'Just bits and bobs I've collected over the years, nothing of any value. I had to sell the good stuff.'

He came and sat opposite her and lifted his glass to his lips. The taste took him by surprise and he peered at the slightly cloudy water.

'It's a new variety I've just tried,' Ellen said, 'but I don't think I'll bother with it again. It's a touch too tangy for my taste.'

'Perhaps not,' Duncan said politely, waiting for his mouth to recover from being turned inside out.

'Would you prefer something else?'

He shook his head and bravely took another sip but instantly regretted this foolhardiness. He placed the glass on the hearth and smiled at Ellen. She smiled back and wondered how on earth to crank up the conversation. 'You must thank your mother for such a lovely lunch,' she said.

Duncan leaned back and crossed his legs. 'I will,' he said, and thought of the irony. He himself had cooked the meal while Nadia had lain in bed upstairs. It was easier that way. By keeping her out of the kitchen he could at least ensure that she wasn't troubling him. It also meant that she wouldn't drink as much. Even Nadia wouldn't drink in bed. For some time now he had taken to monitoring the quantity she got through and as long as he was able to do this he felt he was in control of the situation. That, of course, had been the main reason for his moving back to Crantsford Hall after his father had died. There had been no question of Nadia being allowed to live alone. With nobody there to check on her each day, there was no knowing the havoc she could cause.

'You must be very close to your mother,' Ellen said.

'What do you mean?' His tone was too sharp and at once he corrected this slip by adding lightheartedly, 'You're surely not insinuating something along the lines of an Oedipus complex?'

She laughed awkwardly. 'Heavens, no.'

But he was nettled, and not just by Ellen's comment. During lunch it was as if Nadia had gone out of her way to be as hostile towards Ellen as she could. To a lesser extent it had happened in the past, with previous girlfriends, but then it hadn't seemed important. With Ellen, it was different. He was genuinely fond of her. He didn't want this relationship spoiled.

'Ellen,' he said, suddenly understanding that if he hoped to further things with her there would have to be a degree of honesty between them. There were explanations to be made. Confidences to share. 'There's something I'd like to say to you.'

Ellen was all ears. A declaration of love, perhaps? 'Yes,' she said calmly, her mind already racing along to the nearest jewellery shop.

Duncan reached nervously for his drink. Just in time he remembered the last mouthful and lowered the glass. He cleared his throat. 'I've never actually told anyone this before,' he began.

Yes! cheered Ellen to herself. A declaration for sure – *Darling, I've never said this to anyone before, but I love you.* Not that she'd had much experience in that department. In fact, she couldn't remember Roger broaching the subject of love with her, even when she had made her feelings for him so obvious. She had loved him so much she had never once doubted that he didn't feel the same for her, and when she'd discovered that she was pregnant with Simon and they had married almost immediately, she couldn't have been happier.

'There's never been any real reason to tell anyone before,' Duncan carried on.

Yes, yes, Duncan, she silently encouraged him. You love me and want to spend the rest of your life by my side. She had chosen the ring and was tearing along the high street of matrimony towards the bridal shop.

'The thing is, I want to be honest with you, I feel it's important. And once you know, well, then I think you'll understand things better. You see ... Nadia isn't my natural mother.'

'Oh.'

'You sound disappointed.'

'No, not at all.' She was now plodding home empty-handed, exhausted and let down.

'Does it make the situation clearer?'

'Clearer?' she asked. 'In what way?'

He got to his feet and resumed his earlier prowling. He went over to the dresser and picked up a plate. He examined the back of it and then returned it to its place. 'My parents adopted me when I was three weeks old,' he said, as though the plate inspection had been a metaphorical gulp of Dutch courage, 'and I think, as can quite often be the way, Nadia as an adoptee parent has always veered towards over-protecting me, and in return I've always been slightly over-protective towards her. She's not a strong woman and sometimes she's in need of a little shoring up.'

Shoring up! Surely he wasn't referring to that Amazonian woman with shoulders Atlas would have given worlds for?

He sat down again, part horrified at what he'd just told Ellen and part relieved. Now at least she'd understand the relationship between him and Nadia.

'Well,' Ellen said, completely at a loss as to what to say next. Clearly what Duncan had just shared with her was of the utmost importance to him. Though why, she didn't know. She was desperately trying to think of something to add to the conversation when she was distracted by the sound of something moving outside the window.

'What is it?' he asked.

'I don't know.' She went to investigate. 'What the—'

Duncan joined her and found himself looking down on two strange figures crouching in the flower-bed beneath the window. One was a young girl, who appeared normal enough, but her companion was a different matter altogether. Was it a nightdress she was wearing? Or a pair of curtains? And as for that hat! He was about to launch into a polite 'Be off with you,' when he heard Ellen start to speak at his side.

'Duncan, I'd like you to meet some friends of mine. Hermione and Jo-Jo.'

Outwardly, Ellen was all smiles and nonchalance; inwardly she was screaming like a banshee and wishing Hermione a million miles away.

But Hermione was clearly enjoying herself and, stretching her hand through the open window, she smiled engagingly at Duncan. 'How do you do? I've heard so much about you.'

'How long have you been there?' he asked, suddenly mortified at the thought of his conversation with Ellen having been overheard.

Hermione shook her head and puffed at the feather on her hat, which was tickling the end of her nose. 'Matter of seconds.' She puffed again. 'No more than that. We thought we'd come and see if Ellen was back yet and when we saw a strange car parked by the barn and a window open, we thought, Aha, we'd best creep along in a stealth-like manner and check that all was well. One can never be too sure, can one?' She smiled sweetly at Duncan.

Duncan smiled back, but warily. Then he glanced at the young girl behind this strange elderly apparition and thought for a crazy moment that he recognised her. 'Do I know you?' he asked.

'I shouldn't think so,' she answered.

Duncan continued to stare at her. After a few seconds he said, 'I know who you are. You were begging in town yesterday, weren't you?'

'Begging's such an ugly word,' Hermione said serenely. 'I'm sure there must be a more politically correct phrase.'

'Yes – how about income-supplementing for the economically marginal-ised?' offered Jo-Jo. She turned her back on them all and sauntered over to the river-bank.

Ellen knew that there was no chance of getting rid of Hermione so easily. She had no choice but to invite her in. 'No, not through the window,' she cried. 'Use the door, and take off that silly hat. You're frightening the life out of Duncan with it.'

Hermione did as she was told and removed the offending article. 'Duncan, dear boy, please allow me to put your mind at rest. I am a perfectly respectable member of the community. In fact, I'd go so far as to say—'

'Enough, Hermione!'

Duncan, too, had had enough and Ellen watched him inch his way towards the open door to make his escape.

'I think it's time I was going,' he said.

'Yes, I suppose so,' she replied, resigned to the inevitable truth that this was the end of the road as far as she and Duncan were concerned. He'd have no more to do with her now, not after he'd met her lunatic of a friend. Without doubt she'd be tarred with the same brush. 'I'll walk you to your car,' she said gloomily.

Outside they saw Jo-Jo sitting by the river-bank. She was throwing pebbles into the water.

'Is she a relative of that strange woman?' asked Duncan, as he pulled his keys out of his jacket pocket.

'Not exactly,' Ellen said cautiously.

'Solicitors don't like phrases like that,' he said, unlocking his car.

'It's a long story, Duncan.'

He looked at her thoughtfully. 'Perhaps you'd like to tell it to me over dinner next week?'

All was not lost! 'Yes,' she said. 'Yes, I would.'

'Eight o'clock, Wednesday night. I'll pick you up.'

There was no goodbye kiss, but then Ellen didn't think there would be, not with Hermione gawping out of the window at the pair of them.

When Duncan's car was out of sight she marched back to the cottage. 'And just what the dickens did you think you were doing?' she shouted at Hermione. 'You very nearly blew everything, crouching there in the bushes like a couple of second-rate spies.'

'I thought it all went rather well.'

'Rather well?' repeated Ellen, stunned. 'What on earth do you mean?'

'The poor man will be hooked, Ellen. Simply hooked with the desire to rescue you from a life of poverty and batty old women peering in through your windows. Take my word for it, he'll be back. He won't be able to help himself.'

Ellen laughed and some of her anger subsided. 'Actually, he's just invited me for dinner next week.'

'Well, there you are!'

'So why's he so hung up about being adopted, then?' asked Jo-Jo, who was now leaning in through the window. 'Why's he never told anyone about that before? It's hardly a big deal, is it?'

'She's right,' said Ellen. 'There really isn't any stigma attached to being adopted, so why would he feel the need to keep it a secret?'

'You dunderheads, you're both missing the crucial point here,' Hermione said impatiently.

'Which is?'

'Which is, Ellen my dear, why Duncan has chosen to tell his most closely kept secret to *you*.'

9

'So,' Nadia said, as she came into the kitchen where Duncan was clearing up the mess from lunch.

He didn't bother looking up from the dishwasher he was stacking, but carried on carefully placing the less expensive pieces of crockery into the racks – the Wedgwood plates he'd wash by hand in a moment, along with the silver cutlery.

'So,' repeated Nadia.

'I heard you the first time,' he said, still not looking up. He had no need to. He knew only too well what the expression on Nadia's face would be. Yesterday she had played the part of helpless woman and today, like a chameleon adapting to its surroundings, she'd adopted her more usual role of imperious matriarch. He knew, too, that she'd had just the right level of alcohol throughout the day to buoy her sufficiently to be thoroughly disagreeable if she so chose.

He moved over to the sink where Ellen's bunch of daffodils still lay – one or two of the flower heads were crushed beneath a large saucepan. 'You were supposed to put these in water.'

'Daffodils,' muttered Nadia.

Duncan walked the length of the kitchen to the pantry where his mother kept a selection of vases. When he reappeared Nadia said, 'Cynthia and Phyllis brought me proper bouquets with ribbons and cards.'

He made no response but carefully removed the aluminium foil from the stems of Ellen's daffodils and put them in the vase he'd chosen. He held it under the tap for a few moments and passed the flowers to Nadia. 'Go and put these somewhere,' he said, 'and make sure it's somewhere nice.'

Nadia pursed her lips and left the kitchen. She stood in the large reception hall and glanced round at the oak-panelled walls and closed doors. Which room should she choose? The drawing-room? No, her 'proper flowers' were there. The dining-room? No, that rude Jacobs woman had implied there was something wrong with the fireplace. The games-room, then? No. Nobody ever went in there and there was no point in unnecessarily antagonising Duncan. Her own personal sitting-room was certainly out of the question, which left only Duncan's study. At least then she wouldn't have to look at the flowers and be reminded of that wretched woman. Transvestite indeed!

She opened the door and walked over to Duncan's leather-topped desk – a desk that had once belonged to her husband, as indeed had the book-lined room. It was strange but she hardly missed Donald, but maybe that was because Duncan was so like his father. There were times when it was as if she was face to face with Donald himself. Duncan may not have inherited any biological genes from his father but he'd acquired so much more that he had earned the right to be described as a real chip off the old block.

She dumped the vase on Duncan's tidy desk, sure in the knowledge that despite the designs Ellen might have on Duncan, her presence in their lives would be short-lived. She knew her son well enough to know that his sense of duty would come before anything else.

She had learned years ago that holding on to what was important was all a question of balance. All she had to do was make Duncan believe that he was in charge, and by appearing incapable at times and making herself out to be a loose cannon on deck, this was simplicity itself. She was secretly very proud of the loose cannon bit and had come up with the idea during Donald's funeral last year. Standing over the gaping hole in the cemetery, the rain lashing against their black umbrellas and with so many depressed-looking people surrounding her, she had found herself wanting to be anywhere but there. When they had all moved away to the cars and she was the only one still standing there over the hole, people had thought her consumed with typical widow's melancholy. Duncan, very correctly and dutifully, had come back for her and whispered that it was time to go. But what they hadn't realised was that she had lost track of where she was and had been imagining herself in the clubhouse bar overlooking the eighteenth tee and downing a large gin and tonic. It was then that she'd realised how easy it was to fool people.

And hiding bottles about the house had proved to be the perfect method of keeping Duncan on his toes. Poor Duncan, so concerned with keeping up the appropriate appearances of their position that he was horrified he might have an alcoholic for a mother. The truth, of course, was very different, but appealing to her son's sense of propriety had been her trump card in having him reinstated at Crantsford Hall.

She went back to the kitchen, where she found Duncan up to his elbows in hot soapy water and a pile of clean plates on the draining board.

'Where did you put them?' he asked.

'In your study.'

Clever, thought Duncan. Very clever.

'I thought they'd remind you of *her* when you're working late at night. Isn't that the kind of thing lovers like to do?'

'I wouldn't know,' he replied evenly. 'Ellen and I are not lovers.'

'What's her background?' she pursued. 'Apart from having been married to that appalling dentist fellow.'

'I really don't think it's fair to saddle Ellen with blame by association. It's hardly her fault her husband – her ex-husband – turned out the way he did.'

'Maybe she drove him to it,' Nadia said quietly.

Slowly Duncan turned round. 'I think you've said enough.'

'Perhaps so,' she agreed, but only for now. 'I only want what's best—'

'Please,' he interrupted, turning his back on her and submerging his hand under the soapy water where Nadia couldn't see that his fists were tightly clenched, 'just please don't say that. I've heard it too many times before.'

'But it's true.'

'Why don't you go and sit down and let me finish here?'

A few minutes later, while flicking through that month's issue of *Cheshire Life* in her sitting-room, Nadia made up her mind to get in touch with Phyllis and Cynthia first thing in the morning. A little trip to Spring Bank Cottage was called for.

Duncan pulled sharply on the plug and watched the water drain away from the sink. He pushed at the bits of food left behind and forced them down the plug-hole. The moment he'd decided to invite Ellen for lunch he'd known what the consequences would be. He thought now of his words at Ellen's when he'd tried to explain his relationship with his mother. He'd said that Nadia was over-protective towards him and how this had brought about a mirrored response from himself, but this wasn't the whole truth.

From as early as he could remember Nadia had brought him up to believe that he was special; special because he'd been adopted and had been picked out from all the other babies available to Nadia and Donald at the time. 'No ordinary baby would have done,' she'd told him. 'We were looking for the very best because we had the very best to offer.' He'd grown up with this belief deeply engrained in his whole being, that and the idea that everything he had he owed to his parents. He couldn't remember a time when he hadn't felt beholden to Donald and Nadia, especially Nadia. His entire childhood had been shaped around the one single thought: that without his parents, he was nothing. They hadn't just rescued him from being an unwanted child, they had re-created him. As a boy it had been a heavy load to carry and as he'd grown up he had come to know that instead of there being a bond of love between him and his adoptive parents a tough, impenetrable chain of duty linked them together.

Not long after his eighth birthday he had been sent away to school, and as he'd waved goodbye to Donald and Nadia he had made the decision that from that day on he wouldn't tell anyone that he was adopted. Even at that age he was tired of feeling 'special'. He wanted to be normal. He wanted to be like the other boys in his dormitory. But he found he couldn't. Quite simply, he didn't fit in. While his contemporaries laughed and joked about their parents, he had remained on the sidelines of companionship, appalled at this apparent display of disrespect. Inevitably the other boys found out that he was adopted and he became even more isolated. He also became a target for bullying. In a strange way it didn't bother him: at least it was some sort of connection with his peers; he wasn't totally ignored.

He thought now of what he'd shared with Ellen. He'd had no intention of telling her that Nadia was not his real mother, but sitting opposite her in her cramped sitting-room and hearing her words, 'You must be very close to your mother', he had suddenly felt overwhelmed with the desire to put the record straight. He was no Hamlet with some strange obsession with his mother. He was just an ordinary forty-one-year-old man who had been brought up with a deep sense of duty and loyalty and, as habits went, especially a lifelong habit, it was unlikely he'd be able to give it up.

He didn't regret telling Ellen, but he did regret her odd friends having been there to hear their discussion.

Ellen had always struck him as such a sensible woman, which was why he couldn't understand her having such unusual friends. Throughout her divorce she'd never once overreacted to any of the bad news that he'd had to deliver. It was one of the things that had attracted him to her. After Nadia it came as a refreshing tonic to find a woman who was calm and level-headed. During his first appointment with Ellen he'd realised straight away that she stood out from the rest of his clients – there had been no histrionics, no demands for vengeful letters to be written and mercifully no tears in his office. All in all she'd been a perfect client. And just lately he had begun to believe that she could also be the perfect wife.

But there were those weird friends to consider.

'So why exactly were you eavesdropping on my conversation with Duncan?' Ellen asked Hermione, as the old woman tried to catch her reflection in the picture glass above the fireplace. She was putting her hat on, getting ready to go home.

Hermione whipped round to face her. 'Perish the thought, dear Ellen, that I would ever be accused of eavesdropping.'

'What would you call it, then? Hunkering in the bushes checking the damp-proof course?'

'Ellen, you've become really quite assertive these past twenty-four hours. What can have come over you? Is it love? Has the sight of Crantsford Hall and all its booty made you tetchy with love for Duncan?'

'I thought you said this Duncan bloke didn't have money?' Jo-Jo joined in with the questioning.

'I neither said he had money nor hadn't any,' Hermione replied, regretting the conversation she and Jo-Jo had had earlier while out on the terrace at Laburnum House. She'd known at the time that the girl had wheedled out from her more than Ellen would approve of. And as she turned to readjust her hat in the reflection of the picture she caught the expression on Ellen's face, which confirmed her fears. It was one thing privately admitting to a good friend that one had plans to marry purely for money as a way out of being strapped for cash, but it was quite another making it common knowledge. 'As I told your beau earlier,' she said airily, 'we came to see if you were back and when I saw the ostentatious car parked over by the barn I made the assumption that it was Duncan's. I then thought it best to take the precautionary measure of listening at the window to check if I was right before barging in on your romantic tête-à-tête. There, now, does that satisfy you?'

'Not in the slightest,' Ellen said.

'So *is* Duncan loaded?' Jo-Jo persisted.

Ellen glared at Hermione.

'He obviously is,' Jo-Jo said at last, when nobody answered her question. She went over to the window-seat and joined Ellen. 'But you don't just like him for his money, do you?' Even to her own ears she sounded sanctimonious.

'Ellen, my dear,' cut in Hermione, wishing more than anything that Jo-Jo would drop the subject, 'my legs are worn out, would you mind driving me home?' Her legs were perfectly all right but the conversation needed finishing and she also wanted the opportunity to talk to Ellen alone, about Jo-Jo.

10

Only seconds after a middle-aged couple had left, carrying with them a large box containing an expensive garland arrangement, the barn door opened again and a young mother came in with a round-faced toddler dangling from her arm. 'Don't touch,' she said to the child, 'hands in pockets.'

Ellen watched the mother and child move about the barn. Whenever anyone came in she liked to see which arrangements caught their eye. She could see, though, that the small child wasn't interested in any of the flowers: his eyes were fixed firmly on the basket beside the till, which was filled with fluffy yellow chicks and tiny chocolate eggs. Yes, it was an exploitative trick guaranteed to have the punters slipping their hands deeper into their pockets, and yes, it was devious, but if it was good enough for all the other shops in town then it was downright good enough for her.

She'd started work just after nine that morning and so far this Easter Saturday was proving a busy one, and if trade kept up for the rest of the Bank Holiday weekend then she might be able to think about paying her telephone bill before the reminder made an untimely appearance through her letterbox. She might even go so far as to treat herself to a bottle of plonk from the supermarket that evening when she went into town for her weekly late-night shopping. She usually planned it so that she got there in time to catch the marked-down food items which in theory wouldn't last the weekend on the shelves of the chilled cabinets – heaven help her if the small family-run supermarket decided to open on a Sunday as bang would go her bargain buys.

'I can't find what I'm really looking for,' the young mother said, approaching the work-bench where Ellen was putting the finishing touches to a commission for a hall table.

'What have you got in mind?' Ellen hoped that this wasn't a customer wanting a twee little wheelbarrow or a rocking chair filled with gaudy flowers. She hated making these ornaments but for reasons known only to those who bought them they were a steady seller. If she wasn't so desperate for the money she wished she could put up a sign outside the barn saying, *No miniature wheelbarrows or rocking chairs sold here – tasteful arrangements only.*

'Well, I've got one of those pretty Victorian cast-iron fireplaces in my bedroom and I'm looking for something with shades of gold and russet to match the curtains.'

'No problem.' Ellen smiled, relieved. 'If you want to bring in some measurements and a sample of the fabric I can make one specially for you. I can have it done within a week.'

'As quick as that?'

Ellen nodded and handed her a small business card. To be sure of clinching the deal she leaned over the counter and gave the round-faced child a chocolate egg. He beamed up at her and began to peel away the gold foil.

When Ellen was left alone she thought how much she enjoyed running her own business. Hindsight was a marvellous thing and it told her she should have done this years ago. After Simon had been born she had revelled in the role of mother and home-maker, and even when her friends, with children more or less the same age as Simon, had started to drift back to work she had chosen to stay at home. She was content with her life the way it was, she told her friends, who were all claiming to be liberated and fulfilled now that they were back in the saddle of the workplace – no matter that they frequently complained of saddle-sores from trying to run a home and a career. The rewards far outweighed the disadvantages, they told Ellen repeatedly. And while she was surrounded by all these heroic women, she quietly told herself that they were doing their families no good, their children would grow up delinquents through neglect, and their marriages would suffer.

How self-righteous she had been. And how very wrong.

But the real reason behind her disinclination to join the great salaried workforce was not because she was some fossilised remnant from the fifties who believed that a woman's place was in the home, but because she was crippled by the thought that nagged at her constantly: she doubted her ability to get a job, and as the years went by the doubt grew bigger, as did the cover-up. 'Who in their right mind would want to employ me?' she'd laugh over the dinner table with friends, only to have Roger's quick-fired response, 'Certainly not anyone I know.' And so it became a running joke: 'The day hell freezes over is the day Ellen goes out to work.'

But then along had come Charmaine and Roger's one-way ticket to love in Provence – not quite hell freezing over, but just as unlikely – and suddenly Ellen had had to find a way of supporting herself.

Nearly two decades of home-making was hardly material to get the head-hunters' adrenaline pumping with eager anticipation; it was unlikely to have anyone beating a path to her door to help plan her all-important career move. Night after night she had lain awake in bed, trying to figure out what to do next. And never far from her mind was the thought that her current situation served her right. She should have got off her butt years ago. It was a deserved punishment for someone who had hidden behind a husband's ability to bring home the bacon.

'We suggest your client brush up on her existing skills,' had been the

phrase Roger's helpful solicitor had put forward in response to a maintenance proposal submitted by Duncan. Which had left her with precisely two
mind-boggling options: child-minding or cleaning.

It was Hermione who had suggested that Ellen try running her own
business. 'You're imaginative enough,' she'd said. 'Just look around your
own home and see how you've made it so attractive. Do it for other people
and charge them the earth.'

The idea of dried flowers had come to Ellen while spending a wet, weepy
weekend with her mother, who had a passion for I-told-you-so disaster
stories – she had known right from the start that Roger was a bad 'un but
had never had the heart to tell Ellen so – and visiting craft fairs. That
particular weekend a craft fair had been on at a nearby National Trust
property and when they entered the marquee with its array of stalls Ellen had
been struck by the amount of dried flowers for sale, but even more struck by
the quantity of customers each stall attracted. There was obviously money to
be made out of thistles and honesty, she had concluded.

She returned home and did her research. She drove around the
surrounding areas of Crantsford and found, to her amazement and delight,
that apart from one small shop selling the ubiquitous decorated wheelbarrows and rocking chairs the market was ready to be tapped. She borrowed all
the books on the subject with which the local library could supply her and
sent off for as many catalogues as were available.

Then Spring Bank Cottage with its run-down barn came on the market
and, fired up with enthusiasm – and Hermione telling her constantly that it
was fate (and never mind that the place was falling apart and that no one
with half an inch of common sense would touch the stench-ridden property)
– Ellen told her estate agent to pull her finger out and find her a buyer for
Orchard House. Within four months she had not only moved but was
enthusiastically opening the barn door of Spring Bank Flowers to the
inhabitants of Crantsford. She wasn't exactly rushed off her feet in the first
few weeks, in fact she was so demoralised with the lack of interest she almost
gave up. But gradually a few customers found their way to the barn and
things began to pick up.

By lunch-time Ellen had finished a second arrangement and boxed it up
ready to deliver – another service she offered. She had taken more money
that morning than the whole of last week put together. Hey ho, she might
even run to some decent loo paper instead of that scratchy cheap stuff with
the perforations that never quite worked.

There were no customers now and, taking the opportunity to grab herself
a break, she made a drink and went outside to sit in the sun on the bank by
the stream. She wondered if Jo-Jo was still asleep. Teenagers were like that –
given the opportunity, they'd sleep for ever.

When Ellen had driven Hermione home yesterday, not surprisingly
Hermione had confessed to having legs fit enough for a marathon and that
she wanted to talk to her about Jo-Jo. Ellen had listened to her friend repeat

what Jo-Jo had told her earlier that afternoon. Poor Jo-Jo. So mature and worldly wise on the one hand but so young and confused on the other.

They talked at length. Just how best could they help Jo-Jo? And what was the legal situation if she was under eighteen, as they suspected? Could they be accused of kidnapping? Would they be better off just informing the local authority, or whoever it was who dealt with things like this, and leaving them to sort out the rest of Jo-Jo's life?

Ellen sipped thoughtfully at her mug of tea, knowing very well that she could no more turn her back on Jo-Jo than she could welcome Roger home with a hug and a smile. Hermione had put forward the idea that Jo-Jo could move in with her. 'My house is far larger than yours,' she'd said. 'It makes sense for her to be with me,' and then she had added, 'Just until we get her sorted.'

'You're not going soft, are you?' Ellen had asked her with a smile.

'Don't be ridiculous, I'm going to get her signed up for some lucrative benefits and then insist she pays me rent.'

'Are we mad?' Ellen had asked Hermione, as her elderly friend levered herself out of Johnny Foreigner.

'I thought you'd given up rationalising.'

'I have or, rather, I'm still trying to.'

Ellen drained her mug of tea, lay back on the soft grass and wondered about this. The truth was she was still busy rationalising everything like mad, as how else would she be prepared to contemplate marrying a man – if the opportunity arose – whom she didn't love?

But perhaps love would come later.

Jo-Jo looked out of the bedroom window and saw Ellen sitting on the grass, but as a car came along the bumpy road Ellen immediately got to her feet and went back to the barn. Jo-Jo continued to stare out of the window beyond the stream and to the field the other side of the bank where she could see a woman walking an Irish setter.

She would miss this place when it was time to go, and she'd miss Ellen and that head-case Hermione even more. She'd only been here forty-eight hours but it seemed longer, longer because she felt so happy. It was as if she'd escaped to another world – there was no Mum to worry over, no step-father to put her down and no Alan. She breathed out . . . No Alan.

She thought of what she'd said to Hermione yesterday – *I wanted somebody to love me in the way Gran used to love me.* And she had. But Alan had never said he loved her. She'd offered so much of herself in the hope of him loving her. She covered her stomach with her hands. She had no idea what a baby inside you was supposed to feel like: all this felt like was a firm swelling. She tried to imagine the baby – *her* baby. Would she be able to love it? Would it love her?

She breathed out deeply again, turned away from the window and looked along the shelves of books above Ellen's son's bed. The selection was mainly science fiction, including a couple of *X-Files* books, but mostly the shelves were full of what she recognised as A-level set texts – *Mansfield Park*, *Howards End*, *Lady Windermere's Fan*, *Hamlet* and *Jane Eyre*. She picked out *Howards End* and opened it at random. There were neatly pencilled notes on either side of the printed text. She sat on the bed and started reading what Simon had written, enjoying his thoughts and comments, for she, too, had recently studied this book . . . with Alan.

Alan had joined the school last year, halfway through the autumn term after their previous English teacher had suddenly left without explanation. He'd insisted from the start that they call him by his Christian name, and sitting on his desk at the front of the class, his thin legs swinging backwards and forwards, he'd said to them, 'Now, tell me what you know about *Howards End*. For my money the ending's wrapped up too conveniently. It's a cop-out.'

At first nobody had known what to say. This wasn't the way they'd been taught by Mr Johnson. 'Come on,' he'd shouted, 'I want our lessons to be an open forum.'

Jo-Jo had taken up the challenge. 'I don't think the way the novel ends is important,' she'd said. 'It's the way he portrays human relationships that counts.'

'Oh, oh,' he'd responded, leaping from the desk and coming towards her. 'Would you care to expand?'

She snapped the book shut and returned it to its space on the shelf above Simon's bed. She got dressed and went downstairs, hungry.

She made herself some Marmite toast, cleared up and then wondered what she should do next. She decided she should earn her keep and when she'd found where the cleaning things were kept she set about surprising Ellen.

It was such a small house that she was soon finished, but all the while she was dusting and hoovering she kept thinking of the one aspect of her life that she'd left behind which she missed. Reading through Simon's notes upstairs had brought home to her how much she would miss her studies. Last night, on their way back from the supermarket, she'd told Ellen that before she'd found out she was pregnant she'd planned to go to university – it was to have been her escape. 'But now I've blown it,' she'd told Ellen.

'Just because you're pregnant,' Ellen had answered, 'don't think for one minute you've lost your brain.' She'd then added in a sombre voice, 'I made that mistake.'

Jo-Jo knew Ellen was right. But what was she to do? Drop out now and go to night school next year? Or could she sit the exams this summer anyway? She'd covered most of the syllabus already.

But it was all pointless. How could she do her exams when she had nowhere to live? And there was nothing that would make her go back home. Not now.

It was too late. She pushed the Hoover back into the space under the stairs in the sitting-room where she'd found it and drew the pretty curtain across that kept it out of sight. She felt miserable. She'd screwed up badly. She didn't know who she hated most, herself or Alan.

Ellen was delighted. She'd sold two more large fireplace arrangements and taken another commission and it was only two o'clock. Now there was just a fussy-looking woman, examining in minute detail the baskets of hydrangea, achillea and helichrysum. Ellen decided the woman was a definite case of the three Ps – the pick up, the put down and the push off. After a few minutes she was proved right, and the woman left empty-handed, but the door opened again almost immediately and Ellen, just in the process of wiring a rose head, nearly pierced her forefinger in shock at the sight of her next customers: La Carter, with Phyllis and Cynthia in tow. The three were dressed to kill and wearing sunglasses, which, given the subdued lighting in the barn, gave them a bizarre, comical appearance – the Spite Girls, thought Ellen, Crantsford's answer to the Spice Girls. 'Hello,' she said. 'I didn't expect to see you so soon.'

'We've come to prove we're as good as our word,' Phyllis said brightly, advancing towards the counter at breakneck speed. 'Isn't that right, Nadia?'

Nadia nodded. 'It's much smaller than I'd imagined,' she said. 'Darker, too.'

Try taking your sunglasses off, you ugly old harpy! 'Barns come in all sorts of sizes,' Ellen said demurely. 'Thank you for yesterday by the way,' she added. 'Lunch was lovely.'

'And your headache?'

'Headache?'

'Yes,' Nadia said, raising her sunglasses and moving off to make a full inspection of the shelves. 'You had a headache, don't you remember?'

'Oh, that – it was practically gone by the time Duncan got me home.'

They could go on sparring like this for ever, thought Ellen, it came as naturally as breathing. She returned her attention to pushing wires through the pile of rose heads on the work-bench behind her. Phyllis and Cynthia got the message and joined Nadia over by the shelves. When she heard the sound of the door scraping open she turned round, hoping to greet a *bona fide* customer. It was Jo-Jo.

'I've brought you a sandwich,' she said.

Ellen was touched. 'Thank you,' she said, aware that the Spite Girls were twittering at the other end of the barn. 'How long have you been up?' she asked. 'Not that I'm checking on you.'

'For ages. I read for a while and then I did a bit of tidying for you.'

'There's no need for you to do that.'

'But I might just as well, anyway. There's always the hope I can make myself indispensable. Is there anything I can do here for you?'

Ellen smiled. 'Not really, but how about you go and see Hermione? I think she has a proposition for you.'

When Jo-Jo closed the door behind her, Ellen saw Phyllis nudge Cynthia. 'Go on,' she heard Phyllis whisper, 'ask her.'

Ellen knew what was coming next.

'I hope you don't think we're being nosy, but wasn't that the girl . . . you know, the one we were talking about at lunch yester—'

'What Cynthia is trying to ask you,' interrupted Nadia, 'is whether that's the person she saw begging in town on Thursday. I've told her it can't possibly be the same girl, as what would a friend of Duncan's have to do with a good-for-nothing like that?'

'Which girl?' Ellen asked, knowing she sounded ridiculous and that her next line would have to be, 'Oh, you mean that girl.'

'The one you were talking to just now,' replied Nadia, with a look that said she knew when she was being led a merry dance.

'Oh, you mean that girl. Well, Nadia, I'm afraid you've got it totally wrong and, Cynthia, you're absolutely right. Jo-Jo is indeed the very same girl you saw in Crantsford on Thursday.'

'I knew I was right,' Cynthia said smugly. 'I never forget a face.'

'But what is she doing here?' asked Phyllis.

'She's got nowhere else to stay so she's stopping with me for a few days.'

'You mean, you took her in from off the street?' Cynthia shuddered. 'But, Ellen, what do you know about her?'

'Very little,' Ellen said, enjoying the look of shock on the three faces in front of her, 'but I'm sure the good Samaritan didn't wait to take up character references before he offered a helping hand.'

'But surely this is taking things too far,' said Phyllis, whose idea of a helping hand was buying a book of raffle tickets at a charity coffee morning in the hope of winning a bottle of champagne.

'I think you're a fool,' Nadia broke in. 'She'll take you for everything she can get and then move on to the next half-witted person who'll take her in.'

Half-witted! Ellen's face coloured and the wire she'd been about to push through one of the roses suddenly snapped in two and dug into the palm of her hand. She hoped it hadn't damaged her marriage line.

11

Hermione stepped into the pitch-dark greenhouse and shone the torch along the rows of sweet-pea pots on the wooden bench. She had never experienced motherhood but she had always supposed that this was the kind of thing mothers of newborn babies got up to: nocturnal visits to the nursery to check on their offspring for the slightest of reasons.

The young girl on the television had said the weather was going to turn cold that night with the likelihood of a heavy frost covering most parts of the country, which had had the effect of galvanising Hermione into ransacking the cluttered drawers in the garden room for the torch and then pulling on her boots.

She found some old sacking from further along the bench and carefully tucked it around the pots and, satisfied that this was as much protection as she could offer the plants, other than taking them to bed with her, she closed the badly fitting door as best she could. From further down the garden she heard a rustling sound. She flashed the torch over the black lumps of silhouetted bushes and saw the tail of something disappear out of sight. A fox, perhaps? Or one of the boys, Giotto or Botticelli?

On her way back up towards the house she paused on the steps between the two Christmas puddings and ran her hand over their shape, feeling for new growth. 'Soon be time for a short back and sides for you two,' she told them affectionately. She then walked across the lawn to the summerhouse where she sat in one of the wicker chairs. It rasped and creaked like arthritic joints under her weight, sounding loud and obtrusive in the still night air.

Hermione had never been scared of the dark. Even as a child when her elder sister had locked her in the musty-smelling wardrobe at the top of the house because she had given her measles, she had spent a couple of happy hours there asleep until their mother had instructed the maid to look for her. If Roberta hadn't been such an actress and made such a fuss of being ill, and if their mother hadn't been such a gorgeously flighty woman more intent on getting herself ready for a party that night, Roberta would have been punished. But she rarely was.

The summerhouse was built mostly of stone with vertical oak beams supporting an ornately tiled roof, and though it had been repaired many times over, it was, to all intents and purposes, the same summerhouse in which Hermione had secretly slept one hot summer night as a child. It was also where she'd first kissed Matthew's father.

She shone her torch at her watch. Nine o'clock. Matthew would soon be here. Matthew, the child she'd always considered her own. She breathed in deeply and felt the first signs of night coldness bite through her. She got up and went inside the house where she found Giotto and Botticelli curled up on the boiler in the garden room.

The room was a mess even to Hermione's indifferent eye. Like her mother, she had no inclination towards housework, but whereas her mother had lived in an era of cooks and housemaids Hermione did not. For most of her married life she had employed the services of a cleaner, and a handyman called Mutters – so-called because Hermione had never been able to understand a word he'd said – who had been a wonder with a fork and a barrow. But Mutters was long gone, as was the cleaner.

She wondered for all of three seconds about tidying up the garden room, but the sight of the overloaded shelves that sagged in the middle and the knowledge that all the cupboards and drawers were already stuffed full made her dispense with any good intentions. She placed the torch on top of a pile of seed packets sprawled over a stack of newspapers and went through to the kitchen, which was just as untidy.

Jo-Jo had commented on her untidiness earlier that afternoon when she'd called to see her. It was funny how some people just weren't comfortable in a room full of clutter. Jo-Jo was obviously one of them, for she had surreptitiously tried to move things into neat piles. 'Leave that alone!' Hermione had said, after ten minutes of sleight-of-hand movements. 'You're making me feel confused.'

'You mean I'm making you feel guilty,' Jo-Jo had responded.

'Sharp little minx,' Hermione threw back. 'Now come through to the sitting-room where there's nothing for you to fiddle with. I want to put something to you.'

Poor Jo-Jo had made the mistake of sitting in the armchair that smelled of lavender – put there to cover up the less fragrant aroma of forty-five years of active service – and had a tendency to take the unwary by surprise and swallow them whole.

'How would you like to stay here with me for a few days?' Hermione had asked. 'Just until you've got yourself organised. I wouldn't like you to go running off with the idea that you've got it made. Unlike Ellen I run a tight ship here.'

'I can see that.' Jo-Jo smiled as she tried to haul herself out from the depths of the chair.

'What do you say, then?'

Jo-Jo frowned. 'Why?' she said. 'Why are you and Ellen doing all this for me?' She stood up and paced the room. 'I mean, you don't know me. You meet me on the street, you give me something to eat—'

'Correction, Ellen gave you something to eat. I didn't.'

Jo-Jo stopped moving. 'Okay, but now *you* are offering me somewhere to live—'

'Only to stay.'

'To stay, then. But why?'

'Lawks! It's come to something when a truly altruistic person such as myself can't offer—'

'Be serious!'

'How do you know I'm not?'

Jo-Jo began pacing again. 'Because . . . because I don't believe in fairy-stories – or fairy godmothers for that matter. What is it you want from me?'

'Would you believe your company?'

'No. You're too independent for that.'

'Okay, then, I admit it. I'm after your money. It's a financial nightmare running this house and I want a cut of the benefits you must be entitled to.'

Jo-Jo leaned against a large bookcase and stared at her. 'Are you serious?'

After a few moments, Hermione shook her head and laughed. 'Jo-Jo, you're going to have to learn to trust me . . . just as I trust you.'

In the end Jo-Jo had agreed to move in but only on the understanding that she helped Hermione about the house.

'We'll see,' Hermione had told her.

Alone now in the kitchen, Hermione wondered about what she had said to Jo-Jo about wanting her to stay with her for her company. Like everybody else, Jo-Jo had assumed that she was too independent to want anybody else's company. It grieved her to admit it, but they were wrong. She did get lonely. Very lonely. She missed her lazy afternoons with Ellen. There was nobody else in the Crescent half as much fun as Ellen: they were all mostly executive types and not her sort of people at all. The Buchanans next door but one in Ellen's old house were civil enough, but with two young children to occupy them they were too busy to be much interested in her. She had the feeling that the rest of the neighbourhood had dubbed her as you-know-the-eccentric-one and were probably forming a committee in case she started going ga-ga and appeared in the Crescent in nothing but her wellington boots. She smiled. Who knows? One day she might do exactly that. But not just yet. Best wait till the threat of frost had passed.

She filled the kettle, plugged it in and looked at the clock on top of the fridge. Half an hour and Matthew would be here.

No more than ten minutes from Crantsford, Matthew's car headlights picked out an Audi estate on the grass verge ahead of him. He could see a woman standing beside a man and they were both staring at a flat tyre.

Matthew slowed his car and pulled up behind the Audi. He wound down his window. 'Need any help?'

The woman came over. She was smartly dressed with dark hair pushed back from her face with a black velvet hair-band, and within a fraction of a second Matthew could smell her perfume. 'You angel of a man,' she gushed.

'My husband's a genius with a woman flat on her back but an absolute ninny when it comes to anything mechanical. Please do help us.'

Matthew got out of his car and followed the woman and her trail of perfume.

'Hi,' the genius-cum-ninny said. 'I'm afraid my wife's absolutely right. I know this is a flat tyre, but what the devil I do with it is anybody's guess. Any ideas?'

This had to be a wind-up. These people just couldn't be for real.

'Why have we stopped, Daddy?' came a faint, sleepy voice from the back of the Audi. 'This doesn't look like home.'

'Go back to sleep, Floss, there's a good girl, we'll be home soon.'

'I think you should get your children out of the car,' Matthew instructed, resigned to rolling up his sleeves, at the same time wondering whether there shouldn't be a law against incapable twits like this being allowed out to drive, let alone to procreate.

'Oh, do you think it's really necessary?' implored the wife. 'There's only the two of them and they're both so light, barely an ounce on them. I'm on at them every day to eat more.'

'Okay.' Matthew gave in. 'But you'll need to get me the spare tyre.'

The genius-cum-ninny, whom Matthew had decided bore an uncanny likeness to a young Terry-Thomas, looked first at his wife and then back at Matthew. 'That'll be where exactly?'

When Matthew was tightening the last of the nuts on the wheel, the woman said, 'We're so enormously grateful to you. Are you local? Perhaps you'd like to call in for a drink one evening?'

'No, I'm not local,' Matthew said, straining to unwind the jack. 'I'm just visiting Crantsford.' He removed it, stood up and handed it to Terry-Thomas.

'Well, I really insist that you call in on us so that we can thank you properly. Bonkers, darling, have you got one of our cards?'

Bonkers? Nobody, but nobody, could be called Bonkers!

'Sorry, they're in my other jacket, but we're easy to find – Orchard House, the Crescent.'

Matthew stopped in his tracks. 'The Crescent,' he repeated.

'That's right. Do you know it?'

Matthew nodded, realisation and horror dawning on him. 'I'm Matthew Collins, and you must be Susie Buchanan. We spoke on the phone.'

Bonkers looked on, confused, but his wife trilled delightedly, 'Ah, ah, ah. Too extraordinary. Just too extraordinary.'

She was right and the prospect of working in the same household as this extraordinary couple filled Matthew with dread as he followed the red Audi for the rest of the journey. Why hadn't Hermione warned him? And why hadn't he himself realised what he was getting into when he'd spoken to Susie Buchanan on the phone earlier in the week? Perhaps his judgement was going. Maybe this commission was going to be a complete disaster. They were probably expecting him to paint cartoon characters all over the children's bedrooms.

When they reached the Crescent, the Buchanans – with much tooting of the car horn and hands waving out of the windows – turned into their drive. Matthew waved back politely and drove on until he pulled into Hermione's. It was well after ten but there were still lights on. He smiled, pleased that Hermione had waited up for him, and pleased also to have arrived. Laburnum House was like a second home to him.

He found Hermione in the sitting-room. The curtains were drawn, the room was lit by a single lamp and in the corner a man and a woman were making love, noisily and energetically. Matthew switched off the television and went over to Hermione, who was fast asleep, her head slumped almost to her shoulder. She smelled of 4711 cologne and Matthew could see the distinctive glass bottle tucked into the side of the armchair.

'You daft old thing,' he whispered affectionately. As a young boy he'd often given her a bottle of 4711 at Christmas and now each time he came to see her she would make a point of wearing the fragrance. He knelt and kissed her soft cheek.

She started.

'It's okay, it's me, Matthew.'

She straightened up. 'What time is it?'

'Twenty past ten.'

'You're late,' she rebuked him, and looking across the room she said, 'what's happened to the television?'

'I switched it off.'

She tutted. 'There was a film I wanted to see, one of those ones they warn you about.'

'I think you've missed the best bit.' He laughed.

She sighed and shook her head. 'That's what will be written on my gravestone – "Here lies Hermione Rowlands, sadly she missed the best bits".'

'If you think for one moment I've come all this way to listen to your self-pitying drivel you can forget it. Now, be quiet and stand up so I can hug you properly.'

'Only if you've brought me a present.'

'You're a hard woman, Hermione Rowlands.'

'That's what your father always said.'

12

Bonkers was not a pretty sight first thing in the morning, and as much as Susie loved him there was no getting away from the fact that he benefited enormously from a shower followed by a shave. And only after he'd cleaned his teeth would she entertain the idea of kissing him. She could hear him now, the tap running and the sound of him intermittently brushing his teeth and singing 'I Am the Monarch of the Sea' from *HMS Pinafore*.

She sat up, positioned the pillow behind her head and glanced about the bedroom. Their suitcases lay open in front of the wardrobes that ran the length of the room and she thought of all the washing waiting for her. They'd only been away for a couple of days to the cottage in Abersoch but seemingly they'd used more clothes in those few days than they'd normally have worn in a week. She closed her eyes to the thought of filling and emptying the washing machine for the rest of day.

Bonkers had now moved on to 'Three Little Maids From School Are We'. Bless him, the man was a complete butterfly brain, switching from one operetta to another. But there again, the way the poor darling sang, the songs all ended up sounding the same anyhow.

When the bathroom went quiet she opened her eyes and saw that Bonkers was standing in the doorway. He had a small towel wrapped around his waist and was rubbing his hair with another. 'I've been thinking,' he said, peering out from beneath the towel. 'How about a party?'

'What sort of a party?'

'Just drinks and nibbles. Nothing too over-the-top. I thought we could invite a few people from work, some of the neighbours and maybe one or two parents from school. What do you think?'

'I think you're a genius.'

He came over to her and smiled. 'That's not what you told that artist chappie last night.'

She laughed and reached out to him. 'You weren't listening properly. I told him you were a genius with a woman flat on her back.' She loosened his towel and pulled him into bed. 'And so you are.'

'Sweetie, I can't find my trousers,' Bonkers said, an hour later, turning over the contents of his suitcase.

Susie smiled the smile of a woman who'd just enjoyed great sex and who was prepared to forgive her husband anything so long as he continued to please her in the way he just had. She often joked with friends that marriage to a consultant gynaecologist and obstetrician had a lot going for it – Bonkers knew exactly where everything was and what it was supposed to do. Sadly, though, his consummate skill as a lover wasn't much use when he needed to get dressed.

'Darling,' she called through to him, from the bathroom, 'there are plenty of clean pairs in the wardrobe.' She carried on brushing her hair and wondered who to invite to their drinks party. Bonkers could sort out his work colleagues, but she would choose the rest of the guests.

She went downstairs, leaving Bonkers still wandering around the bedroom in his boxer shorts, and found the girls in the kitchen. The Frosties packet was on the worktop and a trail of cereal led from it to the far end of the kitchen where the children were sitting at the table. 'Good morning,' she said, kissing them both on the top of the head, which was a bit difficult in Millie's case as she was wearing an Easter bonnet she'd made at school in the last week of term.

Floss, the elder, aged ten and the spitting image of her mother, though her hair was less dark, glanced up from her cereal bowl. 'It was Millie who made the mess.'

'You did it as well,' Millie shot back. Three years younger than her sister, she was always convinced she got the worst of everything.

'Not in the mood, girls. Simply not in the mood. You can both tidy up the mess or there'll be no Easter eggs for either of you.'

They pulled faces at one another and carried on eating in silence until their father drifted into the kitchen. He was still in his boxer shorts, but had managed to find a polo shirt and a pair of slippers.

'Daddy, what happened to the car last night?' asked Millie. 'Floss says we broke down. I don't remember that happening. Is she lying?'

Bonkers groaned dramatically. 'It was ghastly, Millie. We had a wretched flat tyre and, luckily for you, you were fast asleep and didn't wake up until we reached home.' He crunched his way across the kitchen floor, oblivious to the Frosties and the look on Susie's face.

'See, I told you!' Floss said triumphantly, then, turning to her father, she said, 'And who was that man who helped you?'

Bonkers's face was a blank. 'Damned if I can remember his name. Your mother knows all about him, though.' He went over to Susie and encircled her in his arms. 'Please, sweetie,' he whispered in her ear, 'find me some trousers.'

She laughed and shrugged him off. 'Remember we told you we were having a special painting done?' she said to the children.

They nodded.

'Well, he's the artist who's going to paint it and his name's Matthew.'

Millie frowned. 'Will he wear one of those floppy hats when he comes here?'

'Good Lord, of course he will,' exclaimed Bonkers. 'He'll wear a large brown velvet one or he shan't be paid a penny. I want a proper artist, not some fly-by-night Johnny in jeans who flicks paint at a bicycle and calls it art.'

Matthew pulled on his jeans and pushed back the faded curtains. For the first time in ages he'd had a decent night's sleep. Usually he slept for little more than a couple of hours, four at most, but Laburnum House had always had a good effect on him. He should visit more often, he told himself ruefully, if not for the pleasure of seeing Hermione, for his sanity.

He was slightly ashamed of himself for not having been to see his godmother for so long – his last few visits had been one-night stopovers *en route* for London.

He stared out over the garden below and caught sight of Hermione. She was dressed in wellington boots and a fur coat over her nightdress and was walking across the frost-covered lawn. He watched her go into the greenhouse and then lost sight of her behind the dirty panes of glass.

As a young boy he had practically lived in that greenhouse with Hermione. When everybody else was busy playing tennis or croquet the pair of them would escape to the humid atmosphere and smell of compost and tomato plants and anything else Hermione was growing. He had hidden in there once when his mother had been cross with him. He couldn't recall what he'd done wrong, but he could remember Hermione shouting at his mother, 'Leave the boy alone, or you'll lose him for ever.' He hadn't understood what she had meant at the time for he'd only been six years old, but her words had held a prophetic significance.

He finished dressing and climbed the stairs to the top of the house, to the boxroom directly above the room he'd slept in which also overlooked the garden. But it wasn't the view that he was interested in. Directly opposite the window and behind a couple of dust-covered small tables and a battered trunk with bits of old clothes poking out was a large wall covered in the first mural Matthew had ever painted. In style it was reminiscent of the reading books Hermione had given him as a small boy, and it was for her that he had painted it. He'd painted animals for her, lots of them: rabbits, squirrels, cats and an owl tucked into a tall oak tree that had a winding staircase leading upwards. There were frogs and ducks in a meandering stream, a dragonfly hovering above it, and in the distance, far away beyond the perfect arches of a bridge and a tiny train puffing out clouds of steam, there were specks of cows.

It was an idyllic scene and made all the more interesting by the depiction of three different characters in varying stages of their lives. In the middle of the picture was a baby in the arms of a young woman in a pale blue coat, her hair tied back and her face happy and smiling. To her right there was a small dark-haired boy pushing along a toy donkey on wheels, and in the foreground this same boy, though several years older, was crouched in the grass and peering into the water at his reflection. To the left of an oak tree was an older woman staring straight out of the picture. As a portrait it was the most interesting part of the whole painting and showed a woman confident and at ease, and smiling more for her own pleasure than for anyone else's. To her right and the other side of the tree was a man. He was tall, serious, and looked awkward with himself, his hands in his pockets, his face half turned towards the woman the other side of the tree. This same figure appeared elsewhere in the painting, older, greyer but still undeniably the same man.

Matthew had been fifteen when he'd painted the mural while staying with Hermione during the long school summer holidays. She had asked him to paint a set of portraits: of Kit, himself and of her. But when he'd said he had something better in mind, she had given him free range to do as he pleased. He'd cleared out the old boxroom and set up his paints, telling her she couldn't go in the room until he'd finished. Working mostly from memory, and with the help of a couple of photographs he always kept with him, he managed to create a picture that captured the Hermione he'd grown up with, as well as his father who had made the mistake of not marrying the woman he loved. In many ways it was a sad painting, but one that he'd never regretted carrying out.

His talent for painting had come from his father, a man who had never had the opportunity to explore his own creative talents to the extent he would have liked. Kit had been an intense man of duty, but also a solitary man who had never been happier than when he'd been allowed to be alone. Matthew's mother had never understood that. Roberta had been a woman who couldn't bear to be alone and who only felt alive when she was surrounded by a gathering, the larger the better.

Matthew supposed he was the same as Kit. Now that Bridget had gone, his own company had become more important to him. He'd grown tired of trying to make the right impression on people and he was aware that these days he was becoming increasingly less tolerant of those around him.

The Buchanans came into his mind and he wondered how on earth he was going to survive them for the duration of the commission.

He returned his attention to the mural in front of him, smiled back at his father, then at Hermione, and left the room. As he went downstairs he noticed how much sadder and more down-at-heel the house had become since his last visit. On the top landing large areas of wallpaper were beginning to peel away from the walls and ominous patches of damp had appeared. Downstairs in the hall there were holes in the plasterwork. He couldn't bear to think of Laburnum House deteriorating any further, but he knew that Hermione could no longer afford to run the old place and he suspected they both knew what the solution was. He wished he had the money to help Hermione, but he hadn't.

*

He found Hermione in the kitchen, still in her fur coat. She turned round at the sound of his footsteps on the quarry-tiled floor.

'Is that coat for my benefit?' he asked.

'You flatter yourself, dear boy. I'm afraid my dressing gown didn't survive the rigours of the washing machine the last time I washed it, but so long as I go no further than the confines of Laburnum House I think that I shall be safe from the egg-throwing populace. And, talking of eggs, what would you like for breakfast? Kedgeree, scrambled eggs or kidneys on toast?'

He smiled. He'd seen the contents of Hermione's fridge last night and knew what was really on offer. 'How about some toast?'

They ate in the kitchen.

After a few minutes of watching him closely, Hermione said, 'You're very quiet. Why don't you tell me about you and Bridget.'

'Nosy old devil.' He reached for another slice of toast.

'Am I to presume she's given you the heave-ho and that's why you're behaving like a—'

'Actually it wasn't like that. It was me who said it was better we ended it.'

'Oh?'

'Because . . .' He twisted the top off a jar of damson jam and pulled a face at the sight and smell of a thick layer of mould growing inside. He screwed the lid back on tightly. 'Because I could see things going just the way they did with Kit and Roberta. I could see this awful pattern repeating itself.'

Hermione stared hard at Matthew. One of the great joys in her life was that he was so like his father. He had the same tall, angular body that tended to look constrained in anything other than a casual shirt and jeans. He had the same dark hair, which was just beginning to show signs of grey, and the same penetrating hazel eyes and lopsided smile that had made Hermione's heart lurch when Kit had spoken to her that special night in the summerhouse. But there was another similarity, and perhaps a more worrying one: like his father, Matthew, it seemed, had a growing need for solitude.

She had only met Bridget once – two years ago at Roberta's funeral – but that one occasion had been enough for Hermione to realise that Bridget in her extravagant black hat and high heels and endless talk of her job as a PR consultant was no more the right woman for Matthew than Roberta had been right for Kit.

'So what attracted you to her in the first place?' she said at last.

Matthew shrugged. 'Her mind?'

'You mean, you thought she'd be great in bed. And was she?'

'Mind your own business.'

Hermione laughed. 'So, you got rid of her before she drove you mad with her incessant chatter.'

'Surely it's better this way? If we'd stayed together I would have turned her into a sad, bitter woman, just like—'

'Just like your mother?'

They sat in silence for a while until Hermione said, 'My sister should never have married your father. They were totally ill-suited. Kit should have married a woman more—'

'The only woman my father should have married was you, and we both know that.'

Hermione stood up abruptly and went and looked out of the window. She watched Giotto slink across the herb garden and shake his tail at the bay tree. Matthew came and joined her.

'I'm glad you got rid of Bridget,' she said. 'I'd have never forgiven you if you'd married her.'

13

Ellen had never before seen herself as a neurotic person but in all honesty she could think of no other word to describe her current state of mind. She looked at the phone once more and willed herself to tap in the numbers that would either result in the sound of Duncan's reassuring voice speaking to her or La Carter's strident tones hammering in her ear.

It was eleven thirty in the morning and she'd already had the barn open for more than two hours and had managed to sell nothing but a measly selection of pink and white rhodanthe daisies. And all the while the phone hanging on the wall above the work-bench had been giving her the come-on – Ring Duncan, it urged her, ring Duncan . . . just for a chat, pretend you want to discuss Jo-Jo's legal position. But each time she reached for the receiver she pictured La Carter snatching it up at Crantsford Hall and immediately she backed away.

Cowardice was pathetic in other people but perfectly excusable in oneself and she had made up logical reason after logical reason why she shouldn't dial Duncan's number. He'll be playing golf. He'll be busy working in his study. He'll be busy, full stop!

And just why did she want to speak to him anyway? She was seeing him in a few days' time. What was the hurry?

The hurry was that somebody else might get to him before her. Somebody else might already have designs on Duncan, someone whom she knew nothing about. For all she knew, Duncan might have a string of lady friends he alternated between. Maybe that was why he wasn't married: he was too busy enjoying himself bouncing from one woman to another.

But then she thought of the Duncan she had come to know. Straightforward, uncompromising Duncan. A man who sat behind his desk soothing the troubled waters of so many divorces. This picture did nothing to help matters, though, for in her mind's eye she pictured countless distraught women rolling their tearful eyes at Duncan and he reaching forward with a handkerchief, a decree absolute and an invitation for dinner.

No! she told herself. Duncan was not a man to be swayed by tears. He was a man of detail who dealt in hard facts. If he was capable of falling for a weeping, wronged woman he would have married one years ago.

The phone suddenly rang, loud and shrill, barely inches away from her, and all at once she imagined a telepathic Duncan at the other end of the line declaring that he was missing her and that he couldn't wait until Wednesday, he had to see her now, there was something he wanted to discuss with her – how did she feel about a wedding ceremony in St Lucia?

This wildness of thought took all of two seconds and was squashed in less time by the sound of Simon's voice. 'Just thought I'd ring to say happy Easter,' he said, through the hiss and crackle of a bad line. 'I tried the cottage but you weren't there. Who's the girl?'

Ellen told him.

'Should I be worried?' he asked.

'What do you mean?'

He laughed. 'You're not about to turn into a crusading middle-aged hippie mother, are you?'

'Less of the middle-aged.' She laughed. 'So, when are you coming home?'

'The weather looks like it's going to break tomorrow, so we thought we'd give Buttermere a miss and drive back on Tuesday. Will there still be a bed for me?'

She explained about Jo-Jo going to Hermione's and then, hearing the sound of a car outside, she said, 'Look, I'm going to have to go. It's a customer. See you tomorrow. Drive carefully, now. 'Bye.'

Susie had meant many times to come and see where the previous owner of Orchard House had set herself up in business, but the hectic life she led had deprived her of satisfying her curiosity.

After breakfast, when she had been sorting through the mail that had come during their short stay away at the cottage, she had discovered a letter from France addressed to Mrs E. Jacobs – please forward. Delivering it by hand seemed the perfect excuse for leaving the pile of dirty clothes on the utility-room floor.

She pushed against the heavy door and stepped inside. She was immediately impressed with what she saw, and glad that she had brought her handbag with her. 'Hello,' she said, as she approached the counter. 'Do you remember me? I'm Susie Buchanan. My husband and I bought your house.'

'Yes,' Ellen responded with a stab of jealousy, remembering all too well who this woman was. 'Nothing wrong with the house, I hope,' she added, secretly hoping that the gable-end wall was cracking in two and that the foundations were slipping on a bed of sand.

'Oh, no, nothing wrong at all. The house is fine and we just love it. But we told you that when we looked round it the first time. It was definitely a case of love at first sight.'

Ellen recalled the Buchanans wandering rapturously about Orchard House – 'Darling, do look at this . . . Ooh, isn't this hall wonderful? . . . Ooh, isn't this window sweet?'

'I've brought you this,' Susie continued. She opened her bag and pulled out the envelope.

Ellen made no effort to take it but watched it being pushed across the counter. 'Thank you,' she said reluctantly. She recognised the handwriting and knew perfectly well who it was from. She had no desire even to touch it, never mind read it.

'I suppose you're all settled in now, aren't you?' Susie said. 'I know we are. It feels like we've always lived at Orchard House.'

'Good,' Ellen said flatly.

Susie looked at her, awkwardly. She knew the reasons behind Orchard House being sold – the estate agent had furnished her with diplomatic hints of divorce – but never had the previous owner openly discussed her situation, and being new to the area, moving up from London, Susie hadn't been privy to any local gossip. During the negotiations for buying the house she had been full of admiration for Ellen Jacobs. She couldn't imagine herself being that calm if Bonkers ever did the unthinkable, and she had clung to the image of Ellen Jacobs being a strong and capable woman rising above the ashes because she hadn't liked the idea of turning anyone out of a home they so obviously loved. 'Spring Bank Cottage is terribly sweet,' she said, with a smile. 'It must have been so snug and warm in the winter.' She nearly added, and cheap to run, but stopped herself in time.

'I'm sorry,' Ellen said, 'I probably seem rude and churlish, I didn't mean to—'

'Gracious me, you didn't sound anything of the kind,' Susie said, 'and now I'm going to have a look at all your gorgeous dried flowers. You're terribly clever to have done this. I'd be hopeless trying to run a business. I'm bad enough trying to organise my own family. Takes all my concentration to bring in the milk each morning!'

Ellen watched her move away to the area where the most expensive arrangements were displayed – perhaps out of charity she might buy one.

After ten minutes of browsing Susie returned to the counter with a large red and black stained rattan basket filled with a mass of red sterlingia and lagurus. 'For the dining-room,' she said. 'We've stacks of mahogany inherited from the old rellies and I've just had the most fabulous curtains made out of the heaviest brocade you've ever seen.'

'Sounds wonderful.' Ellen smiled generously, eyeing the price tag on the basket.

Susie started to delve in her bag for her wallet. 'I say,' she said, looking up with a credit card in her hand, 'I don't suppose you'd make up an arrangement specially for me, would you? I'd love a really big one for the fireplace in the sitting-room to go with the new sofas we've bought.'

'If you bring in a sample of the fabric I'd gladly do it.'

'Oh.' Susie's face dropped. 'No can do, I'm afraid. I haven't any spare material and no cushions either.' Then her expression changed and she smiled appealingly. 'Gosh, I don't suppose you'd call round and see for yourself, would you?'

Ellen opened her mouth to say no, and no with a capital N, but Susie went on enthusiastically, 'I've had an even better idea. We're giving a little drinks party next weekend. Why don't you come then? Do say yes. I'd love you to see the house and all that we've done. Oh, excuse me.' She opened her bag and retrieved a bleeping mobile phone. 'Bonkers, darling, what is it?'

Ellen turned away tactfully and started to cut some of the rhodanthe daisies to the length she required for the arrangement she planned to do next, but there was no avoiding Susie's loud voice or, she suspected, the invitation to Orchard House.

'Darling, calm down. I'll be back in two ticks. I'm still at Ellen Jacobs's place and I've invited her to our party. Yes, I thought it was a good idea too. Now you'd better put a video on for the girls and then clear up the worst of the mess. But don't, whatever you do, scrub at it. Just pat gently. 'Byee.' She put the phone away and rolled her eyes heavenwards. 'Bless him, he does try.'

14

Easter was over, and predictably the Bank Holiday had been true to form and offered up a ritualistic downpour as its contribution to the end of Holy Week.

It was Tuesday morning and still the rain hadn't let up. From her bedroom window Hermione watched the rain trampling on the drooping daffodils in the waterlogged garden below. She looked anxiously at the greenhouse. It was a wonder any of its panes were still intact.

She moved away from the window and went back to making the bed. She patted and smoothed the faded silky green eiderdown into place, gently, so as not to force any feathers through the many holes. But despite her care a tiny feather did break free. It floated upwards before it finally settled on the pillow. Hermione picked it up between her thumb and forefinger and slowly stroked it against her cheek, backwards and forwards, conjuring up the memory of a similar wet day when Kit had held her and softly caressed her cheek and kissed her. But eagle-eyed Roberta had seen them in the summerhouse and later she told Hermione that she meant to have Kit for herself.

'Are you okay?'

She dropped the feather and turned to face Jo-Jo. 'You shouldn't creep up on old ladies, it's bad for their hearts.'

'I'm sorry, I didn't think—'

Hermione smiled. 'You really must stop taking everything I say so literally. What is it you youngsters tell one another? Stay cool, get a life.'

'That's the trouble,' Jo-Jo said, coming further into the room and running her hand over her stomach, 'I did.'

'Oh dear, we've gone all deep and profound, have we? Well, I have just the tonic for that.' She flung open the doors of an ugly, cumbersome wardrobe and stood back. 'I've decided to have a sort-out,' she declared. 'You can help me if you like and by the time you've cringed and laughed at some of my clothes you'll have stopped feeling sorry for yourself.'

Hermione was right. Within a couple of minutes of seeing the old lady parade around the bedroom in a mishmash of dusty old clothes Jo-Jo was joining in the fun. She wrapped a pink feather boa around her neck, slapped a mauve hat the shape of a flying saucer on her head and struck up a silly pose in front of the mirror with Hermione.

'We look like a regular couple of old trouts.' Hermione laughed delightedly.

'As good as that?' It was Matthew, leaning against the door frame and staring in at them. There was a hint of a smile on his face.

Embarrassed, Jo-Jo tugged at the feather boa. She hadn't yet worked out whether Matthew was friend or foe. It wasn't that he was unpleasant to her, it was just that he seemed so stern. She had wondered whether he was jealous of her being here with Hermione or, worse still, suspected her of taking advantage of the old lady.

When she'd arrived yesterday afternoon he'd greeted her and her rucksack with politeness, but nothing more, disappearing upstairs within minutes of Hermione introducing her. Hermione was obviously very fond of him and Jo-Jo sensed that despite his aloofness he was fond of Hermione.

'Don't stare like that, Matthew,' Hermione said. 'You're making poor Jo-Jo nervous.'

'I'd be nervous in that hat.'

Jo-Jo had forgotten the flying saucer and she snatched it off quickly. 'I'm helping Hermione sort out her clothes,' she said, by way of explanation.

He ignored her. 'I've made some lunch, if anybody's interested.'

'How marvellous it is to have guests staying,' Hermione said, still in her dusty ensemble, as she and Jo-Jo followed Matthew downstairs to the kitchen, 'especially the helpful variety. And, my word,' she exclaimed when they saw the table, 'what a spread.' There were wholemeal rolls, pâté, slices of ham, a selection of cheeses and a bowl of salad, shiny with mustard dressing.

'I decided you hadn't anything worth eating in the house,' Matthew said, pouring out glasses of wine for Hermione and himself, 'and stocked up at the supermarket. You'll find I've thrown away your antique collection of tins from the larder and replaced them with stuff which should take you into the next century without too much risk to your health.' He handed Jo-Jo a glass of orange juice.

Hermione pulled a face at the sight of the juice. 'Matthew,' she said, 'this is most thoughtful of you, but Jo-Jo is technically an adult, so stop being so stuffy and let her have some wine with us.'

'She's also technically pregnant, so orange juice it is.' He got up from his chair and went over to a small carrier bag on the draining board. He handed it to Jo-Jo. 'I thought this lot might be a good idea.'

She peered into the bag.

'Vitamins and an iron supplement,' he said, in answer to her surprised expression. 'The woman in the chemist's recommended them.'

Both Hermione and Jo-Jo stared at him. Jo-Jo tried to assert herself. 'How do you know I'm not already taking –' she glanced inside the bag again '– folic acid and—'

'Call it intuition.'

'My, you have been a busy boy this morning,' Hermione said. 'You're quite the patriarch all of a sudden.'

Matthew cut himself a wedge of Cheddar. 'And what about a doctor?' he asked. 'Have you even had so much as a check-up yet?'

'Oh, do stop fussing, she's perfectly all right, anyone can see that.'

'Hermione, she needs to register with a doctor,' Matthew said firmly. 'There are scans, blood tests and heaven knows what else she has to do. You can't just take her in off the street and forget about the fact that she's pregnant. What if something goes wrong? Don't touch that!'

Hermione started and Jo-Jo stopped in her tracks.

'I'm sorry,' Matthew apologised to Jo-Jo, 'but you're not supposed to have any soft cheese, or pâté for that matter.'

'Why on earth not?' Jo-Jo asked, disappointed, her hand and knife still poised over the triangle of ripe Brie.

'You see?' Matthew said, raising his hands in the air. 'Neither of you have got a clue about pregnancy. Haven't you heard of listeria?'

'No,' Hermione said, with a smile, 'but I've heard of hysteria.'

Jo-Jo sniggered and Matthew gave up. Why bother? It really wasn't his problem. His problems, he suspected, were waiting for him at Orchard House where he was going after lunch.

From the road Matthew couldn't see much of Orchard House: it was set back and discreetly hidden by a large imposing brick wall, which was newly built like the house itself and stuck out, in his opinion, as stark and ostentatious. It wasn't until he was standing between an unnecessarily large pair of wrought-iron gates that he caught his first glimpse of the house and, walking up the herringbone brickwork drive in the pouring rain, he was surprised to find that he actually quite liked its exterior design, despite the architect's propensity to mock Tudor, especially in brown and white. There was a symmetry to the front aspect of the house that appealed to him, that and a tall thin Gothic window in the middle that he decided must light the hall and landing beautifully. Already his painter's eye was sizing up this area of the house as a potential canvas.

He rang the bell and almost immediately the door opened. He found himself staring down at a dark-haired girl with large inquisitive eyes – shrewd, inquisitive eyes, he decided. She said nothing, but an excited voice behind her whispered, 'Is he wearing a hat?'

The question was ignored and the shrewd-eyed girl said in an authoritative voice, 'Mummy's on the telephone.' She sounded as though she was perfectly at ease with the situation, which was more than Matthew was.

'Right,' he said. Children were strange beings to him and he rarely felt comfortable with them, especially the quiet, noncommittal, staring ones. He shifted the bag on his shoulder, turned away and looked out over the sodden lawn with its perfectly mown stripes. Thoughts of abandoning this particular commission flitted through his head. It wasn't as though he was desperate for the money. He had enough for his modest lifestyle and now that he no longer had a mortgage hanging over him, which meant that his small Lakeland cottage was secure, all he had to do was earn enough to get by, and he could do that on the paintings he sold effortlessly and regularly to the tourists who poured into the Lake District each year.

So why the hell was he standing here in the rain being scrutinised by some devil child?

'Oh, I'm terribly sorry to have kept you waiting,' Susie's voice sang out loudly from behind him, accompanied by a rattle of gold bangles from one of her wrists. 'Do come in. And thank you again for your help the other night. Come on, girls, make way for our very own Michelangelo.'

Matthew smiled politely – he suspected he'd be doing a lot of that while he was here. He stepped inside and wiped his feet on the *Welcome* doormat. He took in his surroundings. The hall was large – large enough to accommodate the beautiful grand piano facing him, a grandfather clock, several other items of furniture and about an acre of cream carpet between himself and any of these objects. Behind him was the window he'd noticed from outside: it stretched elegantly up to the floor above them, and if the sun had been shining the hall would have been filled with light. In place of natural light several large lamps illuminated the space.

'I thought you said his name was Matthew,' whispered a voice from behind Little Miss Shrewd Eyes.

'Millie, come on now, don't be shy.' Susie looked up at Matthew. 'She's been so excited about you coming to see us. She loves drawing, don't you, Millie, darling? I'm sure Matthew would like to see your pictures in the playroom.' She smiled encouragingly at him.

Matthew could relate to shyness – he'd been painfully shy as a young boy himself. He offered a smile to the small girl now peering cautiously at him from behind her more confident sister.

'Ignore her,' said Little Miss Shrewd Eyes. 'She's only attention-seeking.'

Susie laughed. 'Just listen to Floss, only ten years old but going on eighteen. I don't know what I'd do without her. She's truly the only sane member in our family. Bonkers and I very nearly didn't have children. There's madness in the family. No, honestly, mad as hatters some of them!'

Matthew could well believe it.

Coffee was suggested and served in tiny china cups and saucers along with gold-edged paper napkins decorated with cherubs. They sat in a large conservatory filled with the sickly smell of pot-pourri. Draped from a central point above their heads, and hanging in four white columns against the glass, were yards and yards of muslin – it was like being in a four-poster bed. Millie hadn't ever fully materialised and had apparently disappeared upstairs to her bedroom. Little Miss Shrewd Eyes, on the other hand, chose now to tackle her music practice.

'Fifteen minutes a day – her music teacher insists,' Susie told Matthew, and, leaning forward, her gold bangles clanking against her coffee cup, she added in a lowered voice, 'and honestly, it's the longest fifteen minutes of every day.'

Again Matthew could believe this as he listened to something completely unrecognisable.

'It's called "Mexican Melody",' Susie whispered helpfully.

'No, it's not,' came an indignant voice from the hall, 'it's "The Emperor's March".'

Matthew placed his cup and saucer and unused napkin on the glass-topped table in front of him. It was time to get things moving. 'Perhaps I could have a look at the room now.'

'Ah, yes,' Susie said slowly, making no move to get up.

Matthew inwardly sighed. He knew what was coming next.

'Thing is –'

Thing is, we've changed our minds. Yes, yes, he'd heard it all before. On one occasion the client had even changed her mind halfway through the commission.

'We've been having a think or, rather, *I've* been having a think.'

'No problem,' he said, getting determinedly to his feet. 'Just show me the wall and we'll take it from there.'

'Gosh, you must think me awfully stupid.'

As if! 'Of course not.' Unable to think of anything else to say, he picked up his bag of notebooks, pencils and photographs and started towards the door. He knew he made a wretched salesman and had always been grateful that he personally didn't have to sell his paintings back up in Coniston and the surrounding areas. These days all he had to do was deliver the pictures to the gallery owners and let them do the hard work. It was a cinch compared to this.

Still Susie made no attempt to move. 'Actually,' she said, 'it's this room I've decided on. Don't you think that wall would look absolutely sweet with one of your murals?'

Sweet! He didn't do sweet. He lowered his bag and stared hard at the wall Susie was pointing at and which was behind the chair he'd been sitting in. He walked up to it, backed away and then went over to the other side of the conservatory where Susie was sitting. He didn't need to consider the wall a moment longer.

'What do you think?' Susie asked anxiously. He was a strange man. Almost friendly, but not quite, which was a pity if he was going to be working here over the next few weeks. Not only that, but she'd had high hopes of showing him off among her new friends in Crantsford. She'd heard about him not long after moving into Orchard House while reading a copy of *Homes and Gardens.* A house in the Lake District had been featured and in particular it showed the owners' dining-room and its mural painted by a local artist called Matthew Collins, who had cleverly depicted all the members of the family at different stages in their lives. Bonkers had been all for it, saying that he never intended moving house again and wanted his family immortalised for ever – 'our own little bit of history', he'd called it.

Susie wondered if Matthew hadn't heard her, or whether this was all part and parcel of the floppy-velvet-hat syndrome; you could be as rude as you liked and make people pay for the pleasure of your wobbly ego. She cleared her throat in the silence that had been created now that Floss's fifteen minutes of piano practice had come to an end. 'What do you think?' she repeated.

'It's perfect,' he answered, at last wrenching his eyes away from the wall. 'Have you got all the photographs I asked for?'

'I thought maybe you could have a look through the albums yourself, that way—'

'Fine,' he interrupted. Now he'd have to suffer endless holiday snaps and all those meaningless 'special moments' caught on camera that meant nothing to anyone except those involved. 'But I'll have to take the albums away with me so I can study them. I need to get to know you all as a family.'

'Heavens, you'll end up as mad as us!'

More than likely, thought Matthew. More than likely.

Ellen was just locking the barn door when she heard the sound of a car coming down Beggarman's Lane. I'm not opening up, she told herself firmly, I don't care how much money they've got stuffed in their pockets. I'm all done in. They're too late.

All the same she held back from turning the last of the locks. But when a horn the volume of the *QE2* berthing in dock sounded she hurriedly turned the key and went to greet Simon and his rusting Fiat Uno.

She waited for him to unfurl himself from the small car, then kissed his stubbly cheek before he stood up completely and was beyond her reach. 'You smell,' she said, in the way only a mother can get away with.

'And so would you if you'd been cooped up in this car for the past three hours with Craig and Dave the Delhi Belly.'

Ellen groaned. Dave the Delhi Belly was one of Simon's oldest friends and was famous for two things: misquoting any and all of the great poets and eating kamikaze curries with life-threatening consequences for those around him.

Simon opened the boot and hauled out a backpack the size of a wheelie bin, hoisted it onto his shoulder, locked the car and followed Ellen into the cottage. After he'd showered, unearthed the horrors within the backpack and shoved them straight into the washing machine, he joined his mother in the sitting-room. She was perched on the window-seat, her chin resting on her drawn-up knees. She looked worried. Instinctively he knew she had something to tell him.

'I've poured you a lager,' she said. 'It's there on the table. And, by the way, your father's written.' She watched his freshly scrubbed and shaved face closely as he picked up the glass and sat opposite her, one leg hanging over the side of the chair.

'And?'

'And . . . and I haven't had the courage to open his letter.' She carried on watching him and noticed that the hanging leg had started to bounce up and down ever so slightly.

'Do you want me to read it?'

'Do you want to?'

The leg was bouncing more vigorously now.

'Not really.'

'Why do you suppose he's written?' Ellen had asked herself the question so many times since Susie Buchanan had delivered the letter to her on Sunday. It was the first piece of personal correspondence she had received from Roger since his mantelpiece confession. Why had he written to her now? Had he put together a letter that he hoped would atone for everything he had done, as though a few cheery words could make everything right? Or was he in trouble? Had his money run out and was he coming cap in hand to her? Oh, the irony! Or maybe the sexual pleasures so willingly provided by Charmaine had palled.

But all these possibilities came nowhere near what she really hoped lay behind Roger's putting pen to paper. It was dreadful of her, but she truly wished him the very worst. A letter explaining that he was dying a slow, agonising death would just about make amends for what he'd put her through.

'I couldn't give a shit why he's written,' Simon said, his leg now perfectly still. 'And I don't think you should. He chose to go his own way, which certainly didn't include either of us, so it can stay that way for all I care.'

'He is your father,' Ellen said tentatively.

'Yeah, and Elvis was King. So what?'

Ellen gave up on the text-book ideology – phrases like 'It's me your father's divorced, not you', never went down well with Simon. She got up and walked through to the kitchen. She was hungry and tired. Since Roger's letter had arrived she had spent hour after hour reliving the past events, turning over in her mind everything Roger had said and done . . . and everything that perhaps *she* should have said and done. It had been an exhausting couple of days.

Simon came into the kitchen. They looked silently at each other for a moment, both stinging with unresolved hurt and anger.

'Come on,' she said, acknowledging that they were both a long way off yet from making a full recovery from what Roger had done. 'I'll make us some supper while you tell me something disgusting about Dave the Delhi Belly.'

Simon shook his head. 'No way, I've had enough of that bloke.' He raised himself up onto the work surface, banged the heels of his bare feet noisily on the cupboard below and took an apple from the china bowl beside the earthenware pot of wooden spoons. 'Besides, I want you to tell me what's been going on here.'

'Well, you already know about Jo-Jo,' Ellen said as she filled a saucepan with water. She placed it on the hob and reached up to a shelf of jars where she hoped she had enough pasta shells for the pair of them. She was in luck. 'But something else has happened,' she said, opening a can of tuna and wondering how Simon might take the news, but feeling she should broach the subject before tomorrow night when Duncan would be picking her up for dinner. 'You could say there's possibly a man in the picture.'

'Anyone I know?'

'Kind of. It's Duncan Carter.'

Simon whistled.

'Is that approval or shock?'

'It's whatever you want it to be.'

She flicked a pasta shell at him. 'Clever Dick!'

15

'I've decided to get a job.'

'Just like that?'

'Yes,' replied Jo-Jo. She picked up a handful of tarnished silver-plated forks from the draining board and began to dry them. 'There must be loads of places in Crantsford where I can get work. Like that posh set-up where I met you and Ellen.'

Hermione rinsed a small cracked jug under the hot tap and smiled at the thought of the hideously pretentious Miss Astley being approached by a pregnant runaway looking for work.

'What's up? Why are you smiling like that?'

'No reason.'

Jo-Jo clunked the forks into the cutlery drawer, one by one. 'I'm surprised you haven't died of poisoning from the state of these knives and forks,' she said.

'I like to live dangerously,' Hermione said, tipping the dirty water out of the washing-up bowl and discovering the ubiquitous teaspoon hiding at the bottom. 'Are you serious about getting a job?'

'Yes. I have to do something. I can't stay here for ever just sitting about doing nothing.'

'I'd hardly say you've sat about the place doing nothing. Since the moment you arrived you've all but turned the house upside down.'

It was true. Jo-Jo had stuck to her guns and in return for her free board and lodgings she had tidied, cleaned and polished almost non-stop.

'I can't help it,' Jo-Jo said, hanging the tea towel up on a hook beside the old Electrolux fridge and returning to the sink where she proceeded to squeeze out the dish-cloth Hermione had left sopping wet behind the mixer taps. 'I've been doing it for Mum for so long it's second nature. By the way, this stinks, it needs bleaching.' She held up the cloth for Hermione's inspection, then opened the cupboard under the sink where she had already marshalled the barely touched cleaning products into an organised fashion, throwing away anything that didn't seem to bear any resemblance to the nineteen nineties.

'Does it, indeed? But have you thought that being pregnant might make you a tad unemployable?'

'I shan't let on.'

'And what about your studies?'

Jo-Jo stopped what she was doing. 'You sound as if you don't want me to get a job.'

Hermione thought about this. Jo-Jo was right, she didn't. This was a disquieting realisation. Was she really turning into a selfish old woman who, when it suited her, wanted to monopolise another person? First with Ellen and now Jo-Jo, a young girl whom she hardly knew. Was she so desperate for companionship that she was prepared to hold another person back, to thwart their plans?

'Of course you must get a job, Jo-Jo,' she said in a clipped voice. 'That way you'll soon be able to get yourself sorted and leave me to get back to my old untidy ways. This was always just a temporary situation until you got yourself on your feet.'

Jo-Jo watched Hermione go through to the garden room and then outside. Puzzled, she carried on filling the sink with water and then added some bleach. She dropped the grey dishcloth into the water and with the end of the mop prodded at the bubbles of air trapped by the stringy square of fabric.

'I shouldn't worry too much about Hermione, if I were you.'

She spun round to see Matthew coming into the kitchen. 'Do you have to keep creeping up on me?' she said, the annoyance in her voice undisguised.

'I wasn't aware that I was creeping up on you, or ever had been,' he replied. He opened the fridge and helped himself to a glass of orange juice. 'Hermione enjoys having you around,' he added, after he'd emptied the glass and set it down on the draining board.

Which is more than I do with you, thought Jo-Jo. Honestly, the man was so quiet. One minute there was no sign of him, and the next, there he was. She decided to be bold. 'Hermione likes having me here, but you don't, right?'

He stared at her closely. 'Why do you think that?'

She shrugged. 'You don't. You hardly ever speak to me and when you do you seem so disapproving . . . as though you don't trust me.'

'I'm afraid that's just the way I am.'

'So I'm right, you don't trust me.'

He smiled. 'And how many people do you trust, Jo-Jo?'

'I . . . I trust Hermione.'

'Snap. Which means that what you've just said about me is rubbish. Coffee?'

'Hang on,' she said, confused, 'I don't get what you mean.'

'I meant simply that I would put money on Hermione being a good judge of character. Now, do you want any coffee? I bought a jar of decaffeinated, which is better for the baby.'

For the first time Jo-Jo felt herself relax in Matthew's company. 'So how come you know so much about pregnancy?'

'Open any women's magazine and it's all there for any man to discover all he needs to know about women, everything from episiotomies to erogenous zones.'

'Apeasy-whats?'

'I think the sooner you see a doctor the better.'

Hermione was cross with herself.

Damn the girl!

She lifted the galvanised watering can over the pots of sweet peas and then cursed again at the sight of the tender young plants suddenly flooded under inches of water.

'I'm becoming a nasty, curmudgeonly, selfish old woman,' she said bitterly, and lowering the watering can to the ground she sat herself in her brown and orange flowered deck chair, which she kept permanently in the greenhouse.

Anger was an infrequent visitor to her door, but there was no getting away from it, right now she was furious. Manipulative was the word that kept coming into her mind and she was ashamed and disgusted with herself. What right did she have to question what Jo-Jo intended doing with her life? If the girl wanted to fly to the moon and back, what did it have to do with an old has-been like herself? It was Jo-Jo's life and she had only offered her accommodation, not interference of the *in loco parentis* variety.

Later she'd go back inside the house, apologise and perhaps start helping Jo-Jo to find a job.

No!

No, she wouldn't do anything of the kind. She would apologise for her churlish behaviour and let Jo-Jo go about finding her own job. She was not to involve herself so much ... even if she did think the girl was wrong.

She breathed in deeply and then exhaled slowly and assuredly. 'There, now,' she said calmly, and getting to her feet, she smiled at the sweet peas. 'No need to worry,' she told them. 'The danger of any more flash floods has passed.'

When she had finished pottering in the greenhouse she wandered down to the lower level of the garden, to the area where she had taken Jo-Jo on Good Friday. The grass was still wet from all the rain and her boots made a satisfying squelchy noise with each step she took. When she reached the stone seat she found it perfectly dry from having had the sun shining on it all morning. She sat down and breathed in the smell of moistened earth. It was a wholesome smell, like freshly baked bread or washing hung out to dry, and it lifted her spirits. She breathed in some more, letting her eyes linger over the statue ... Kit's statue.

How delighted she had been when he had asked her to pose for him, and how very cross Roberta had been when she had discovered what Kit was working on. Torn apart with jealousy, Hermione's sister had even threatened to smash the statue when it was finished.

She smiled and started to hum, quietly at first, just snatches of popular melodies, but then she moved on to one of Kit's favourite pieces of music, 'Ode to Joy'. He once said that it was the only piece of music that sounded truly joyous. She hadn't fully understood what he'd meant at the time, she'd been so young, but as the years had passed and she'd grown older, she had come to know exactly what he'd meant. There was a vastness to the great choral piece that could not be ignored, its composition as rich and as full as life itself should be, with each swell of the music singing out the joy and celebration of being alive.

Not long before he'd died Kit had told her that during his lifetime he'd only known pure joy because he'd experienced its antithesis.

She had cried when he'd said that, only too aware of the truth of his words.

'Hello there.'

Startled, Hermione swivelled her head and looked about her but she could see no one. She hoped this wasn't the beginning of the end – *voices in the head.*

'Over here.'

There it was again. Nearer this time and accompanied by a definite swishing of undergrowth. Did one hear swishing noises at the onset of senility? Voices, yes, but swishing? She stood up and went to investigate the *leylandii* hedge, which formed the boundary with the Lodge next door.

'That's right, over here. Left a bit, ah, there you are.' The voice was cheery and Hermione eventually found its source coming through a porthole-sized gap in the hedge. 'You hum very nicely. I was within a whisker of joining in, da dee da da—'

'Well, I can quite see what held you back,' Hermione interrupted. 'You're as sharp as a Bramley.'

The man laughed and then disappeared from view, leaving behind him the dreadful sound of coughing, followed by a wheezing that scraped at Hermione's own chest. A couple of seconds passed and then the face reappeared. 'Bloody pneumonia, never a dull moment. How do you do, by the way? I'm Bernard Malloy, but you can call me Bernie and I'm your new neighbour. I saw you from my window and thought I'd come and introduce myself.' A chubby hand with a chipolata of a little finger wearing a gold and diamond signet ring popped through the hole in the hedge.

'Hermione Rowlands,' she said, shaking the proffered hand, 'and I presume you're a newly recruited inmate at the Lodge. Do you intend on being a lifer?'

'I certainly hope so. It's like the Ritz here – red carpets, oak panelling, chandeliers, and a wine cellar to die for. I have great plans to drink myself to death on some of the finest wines available. And the best part is the totty.'

'The totty?'

'Practically throwing themselves at me during lunch, they were. One at a time I had to tell them, Bernie's not as young as he was.'

'Mr Malloy, you're obviously a pathological fibber of the highest order and

I sincerely hope I have the pleasure of many more such conversations through the hedge, but if I'm not mistaken there's somebody calling for you. Time for your enema?'

He laughed, turned away, then reappeared. 'It's the totty I was telling you about, I've promised them a game of croquet. Ta-ta.'

Croquet, mused Hermione, as she made her way back up to the house. She hadn't played for years. She wondered where her old set was. It was probably little more than a pile of woodwormy dust, she reflected with regret.

'It's just the right temperature, isn't it?'

'Sorry?'

'The champagne,' Duncan said, taking a sip from his fluted glass.

'Oh, yes,' she said, kicking herself for having let her mind wander. When Duncan had ordered the bottle of Moët & Chandon from the wine waiter she had immediately leaped to the conclusion that they were about to slip into celebration mode. Certain things came in pairs – baths and tide-marks, ornaments and dust, cars and traffic jams, proposals and champagne. And okay, yes, she was jumping the gun, and probably by a long way, but she was now so set on the idea of marrying Duncan that she couldn't believe that his mind wasn't working on the same wavelength as hers. She was conscious, though, that certain crucial elements were missing from their relationship.

Romance was one of them.

If she was honest with herself there was a worrying lack of schmaltz to their potential alliance, but then you couldn't have everything and champagne would do very well instead.

'Now, tell me again about this girl. What did you say her name was? And what on earth possessed you to get involved with her in the first place?'

For a ghastly moment Ellen was reminded of Roger. '*Why on earth did you do that? What were you thinking of?*' These had been some of his stock-in-trade questions; an interrogating technique she'd been unaware of until it was no longer there. It was strange and frightening what you became used to.

'Why are you so against her?' she asked defensively. 'There's nothing wrong with her. Jo-Jo's the same as you or me.'

Duncan snorted. 'I've never looked for hand-outs on the street.'

Then you should think yourself lucky you've never needed to, Ellen wanted to say, but instead she drained her glass and said pleasantly, 'Goodness, I'm so hungry I could eat a horse between two mattresses.'

'I think you'll have to make do with something a little more refined from La Maison d'Or.' Duncan smiled.

When he had called earlier to say where he'd booked for dinner, Ellen had been delighted – La Maison d'Or was one of the most expensive restaurants in Crantsford.

'Pulling out all the stops, is he?' Simon had said, when she'd put down the phone.

'I certainly hope so,' she'd answered, brushing her hair while kneeling on the floor in front of her bedroom mirror, which she still hadn't got round to hanging on the wall. 'I think I deserve a little pampering.'

Simon had opened the door to Duncan when he'd arrived and Ellen had watched the two men watching each other. The sitting-room had suddenly seemed perilously small and several times she had asked them to sit down, but her words went unheard as they shifted their way to the right and then to the left as if performing a little dance. The conversation had been polite, Duncan opening predictably with, 'And how's the world of academia these days?'

Ellen had flinched, but if Simon had found Duncan's question pompous he showed no sign of it and, sounding every inch a clean-cut American preppy, he'd answered, 'Fine, sir, though probably very different from when you were there.'

They talked at length about Oxbridge – Simon was at Brasenose College, Oxford, and Duncan had read law at Trinity, Cambridge – and when Ellen had heard enough she stared pointedly at Simon and made the slightest of movements towards the front door. Instantly both men had done what was expected of them – Simon had wished them a good evening and Duncan had reached into his pocket for his car keys.

Ellen wondered now what was expected of her as she considered Duncan from behind her menu. Just what did he want from her? Marriage? Or one of those platonic friendships that you only read about? If he was attracted to her, and she couldn't really be sure that he was, he kept it very much to himself.

She had been attracted to him almost from the first moment, well, in that simple multiple-choice question-and-answer way: If presented with Duncan Carter, would you (a) prefer a bout of flu to an evening out with him? or (b) imagine yourself capable of fancying him?

Sitting in his office for her second appointment the thought had crossed her mind that her solicitor was a very attractive man. So why wasn't he married? had followed, lightning-fast. She had tried to ignore these distracting thoughts and forced herself to concentrate on what Duncan was explaining, only to find herself drifting back to his well-manicured hands playing with his fountain pen on his desk and his pressed shirt and silk tie perfectly knotted below a smooth clean-shaven chin. His eyes, always glancing from the papers on his desk to her face, were as impassive as any she'd seen, but concealed, she was convinced, hidden depths, but of exactly what she wasn't sure.

And she still wasn't sure what those pale greyish-blue eyes across the table conveyed. She watched him read his menu. He looked up suddenly and met her gaze. One of us should say something, she thought, something romantic, or at least clever and witty. But unable to think of anything remotely along these lines herself, other than to start enacting *that* scene from *When Harry Met Sally*, she lowered her head and returned her attention to choosing her meal. She was surprised, though, to feel her menu being pulled away and Duncan covering one of her hands with his own.

16

If Hermione had suspected herself of being manipulative earlier that day she now knew with certainty that this was exactly what she was.

She dialled Ellen's telephone number, knowing full well that her friend was out with Duncan, but it wasn't Ellen she wanted to speak to. It was Simon. She hoped he was in. It seemed an age before she heard his voice at the other end of the line.

'Simon,' she said, relieved, 'it's Hermione. How do you see yourself in the role of great wise one and mentor?'

'It'd make a change from Simple Simon.'

Within minutes she had his agreement.

The idea had come to her while she was sitting in the greenhouse after tea and reflecting on Jo-Jo who, once again, had been talking about finding herself a job.

'I could join an agency and clean for people,' she'd said. 'At least that's one thing I know I'm good at.'

Hermione had kept quiet and sought refuge in the greenhouse, and despite her resolution to leave Jo-Jo to make her own mistakes, she was determined that someone had to take charge and talk some sense into the girl. Taking the first job that came along was not the answer to Jo-Jo's problems. Someone had to persuade her to go home and return to school.

At first she had thought that Matthew might be the one to reason with Jo-Jo, but then she'd remembered Ellen mentioning on the phone after breakfast that Simon was back from the Lake District for a few days before returning to Oxford. Simon, she'd realised, was the ideal choice. He was more or less the same age as Jo-Jo and if anyone could convince her that she should return home and do her exams this summer it was him, for he was one of the most strong-minded young men she had come across. He knew exactly what he wanted from life and how to go about getting it.

Simon rang the front-door bell but when it made no discernible sound he walked round to the side of Laburnum House where he found his charge in the enclosed courtyard in the dusky half-light of early evening. She was unpegging a row of washing from a drooping clothes-line.

'Hi,' he said, 'you must be Jo-Jo.'

She peered at him over the top of an enormous bundle of washing in her arms. 'And you must be Simon,' she said, after a few moments. 'I recognise you from your mother's photographs. If you're looking for Hermione she's inside watching *Inspector Morse*.'

'Actually it's you I came to see.'

'Me?'

'Here, let me help you.' He took part of the pile of washing from her. 'Hermione thought you'd appreciate some younger company. How do you fancy a drink?'

They walked the short distance into Crantsford. It was almost dark when they reached Church Walk and the narrow street was picturesquely illuminated by replica Victorian street lamps painted black with fiddly gold bits. Most of the shop windows were lit and the shop nearest to them was a jeweller's with a minimalist display of modern pieces in chunks of silver.

They moved further along Church Walk and as they passed even more tempting shop windows Jo-Jo was reminded of the time when, as a small child, her grandmother had taken her to see *Dick Whittington* as a Boxing Day treat. She had never been to a theatre before and had sat spellbound in her squeaking, tilting seat, one hand clutching her bag of sweets and the other tucked in her gran's while taking in the lights and the sounds and the amazement of being transported from the world she knew to a strange and magical one.

Crantsford was a bit like that theatrically created wonderworld. The streets weren't exactly paved with gold, but there was plenty of conspicuous wealth about the place, including a good many flashy cars parked outside the town's numerous restaurants, whose doors were wide open on this warm spring evening with upbeat music beckoning customers inside. Jo-Jo could see people sitting at the tables, their faces cheerfully intent on enjoying themselves, while efficient waiters and waitresses carried large trays high above their shoulders.

'Crantsford's an extravagant place in which to live, isn't it?' Simon said, breaking into her thoughts.

'I suppose it is,' she said. She wanted to say that actually she quite liked it, but wasn't sure whether it was the right thing to say. She suddenly felt very young and naïve. Though Simon wasn't much older than her, he seemed so much more sure of himself. Was that what going away to university did for you?

'Let's try this one,' he said, coming to a stop outside a small pub with neat window-boxes and a row of polished brass lanterns hanging overhead. Inside the public bar Simon ordered a pint of local beer for himself and, remembering Matthew's stern face at the lunch table yesterday, Jo-Jo asked for a Britvic orange juice. They found themselves a small table and a couple of low stools.

'It's stupid,' she said, with a sigh, 'but I was just thinking how young I feel and here I am reinforcing that feeling by drinking orange juice.' She poked at the cubes of ice in the glass with her finger and then sucked it dry. 'And the irony is that in a few months' time I'm going to be a mother. What a joke.'

Simon raised his beer and took a mouthful. He lowered the glass and wiped the traces of froth from his top lip. 'How do you feel about becoming a mother?'

'The truth?'

'What else?'

'At first I thought it was the answer. A way out. But now I can see it isn't.' She fiddled with a beer mat. 'This might sound selfish but I want the old me back . . . Well, some of the old me.'

'Mum said something about home not being ideal.'

Jo-Jo shook her head. 'What a huge understatement, but that's definitely the part I can do without.'

'So which bits do appeal?'

She thought for a moment. 'I want what you've got. I want to go to university and do something for *me*. I could never harm this baby but I'm not convinced I could be the mother it deserves.' She lowered her gaze and stared into her drink. 'You probably think I'm a selfish cow.'

'Sorry to disappoint you, but no. To a certain degree we've all got the same attitude of what's in it for me? We might manage to persuade ourselves that we're being altruistic, but mostly we do things because *we* want to do those things.'

'That doesn't sound at all politically correct.'

He laughed. 'Whoever said it was?'

'Alan always . . .' She hesitated.

'Is that the baby's father?'

She nodded. 'Alan was obsessed with being politically correct.'

'To the point of not believing in contraception, I suppose?'

A tiny seed of annoyance flared within her. She had known all along that she shouldn't have relied on Alan so heavily, she should have gone on the pill, but she hadn't. And because of her stupidity she had inadvertently gambled away her future.

'Haven't you ever taken a risk?' she asked bitterly.

'Not in that department,' he answered, without even having to consider the question. He drained his glass in one long gulp. 'You see before you *el supremo* when it comes to the art of self-preservation. I worked my arse off to get to Oxford, and what with the sacrifices Mum's made to help finance me, I'm not about to let a quick moment of pleasure get in the way of my future.'

'Which is?'

'Aha, you'll have to wait and see. Another drink?'

Jo-Jo watched Simon walk over to the bar. He was much taller than any of the other men either side of him and a darn sight better-looking. She hadn't realised until now how attractive he was and as he stood with his back to her she noticed how a group of girls wearing short skirts and tiny cropped tops in the opposite corner were leaning into each other and eyeing him up and down. A few moments ago she had felt young and naïve, but looking at these girls with their minuscule midriffs and giggly made-up faces she felt ancient, like she'd lived several lives already.

When Simon returned she said, 'So what would you do in my place?'

'The truth?'

'As you said earlier, what else?'

'Okay. When's the baby due?'

'September.'

'That's easy, then. I'd go home, no matter how awful it was, and sit my exams. I'd wait for my results, have the baby, give it up for adoption and then take up my place at college. How's that?'

'That's easy for you to say because—'

'Yeah, yeah, because I'm a bloke and I don't feel the same way about—'

'No, not that. I just don't know what I'll find if I go home. You might not have noticed but nobody's come looking for me.'

'Stuff that. You'll only be there for a few months. They'll just have to put up with you and you with them. The important thing is to get yourself back to school when your term begins in a couple of weeks' time. That way you won't miss any crucial work before your exams start.'

Jo-Jo frowned. 'Are you always this bloody sure of everything?'

'Yep. It's the only way. Go for it, Jo-Jo. And, besides, what have you got to lose?'

17

Much to Botticelli's annoyance, Hermione stopped rubbing his chin. She'd just caught a glimpse of Ellen's fair hair passing by the kitchen window. A couple of seconds later she appeared in the doorway between the garden room and the kitchen.

'I know it's early, but can I come in?'

'Ellen, it's barely eight o'clock. Has something terrible happened?'

Ellen's face broke into an enormous smile. 'Quite the opposite,' she said happily. She came and sat at the table, directly opposite Hermione. Botticelli, sensing either that he was no longer the centre of attraction or that there was no likelihood of him being fed, now begrudgingly leaped off Hermione's lap and disappeared out of the kitchen to go in search of something edible in the garden.

'So it's good news, is it?' Hermione said, straightening out her rumpled nightdress and fur coat. 'I'm so glad, because I've got something exciting to tell you as well.'

'Oh?' Ellen was put out. She hadn't bargained on having to wait her turn.

'Yes, while you were out ensnaring the hapless Duncan, things were happening here. Jo-Jo's decided to do the sensible thing and go home. She phoned her mother late last night and it's all arranged.'

'So your deviousness with Simon actually came off?' Ellen tried to sound genuinely pleased, but she felt childishly piqued. She had barely slept last night, going over what Duncan had said during dinner, and she had been bursting to tell Hermione ever since. He hadn't exactly proposed but their relationship had definitely moved on. There had even been a hint of romance in the car. As kissing went it had been a little hurried, but she suspected that had been down to Duncan trying to keep his eyes firmly on the cottage. Poor man, he'd probably been terrified of an over-protective son coming out and banging on the car window, demanding what the devil he thought he was doing with his mother.

'So Simon told you of the plan I'd hatched, did he?'

'Yes,' Ellen said, dragging her mind back to Jo-Jo. 'He told me when Duncan dropped me off late last night. I must say I hadn't expected it to work. She seemed so adamant about not going home.'

'Your son's a smooth operator, Ellen.'

'Evidently.' She heard the sarcasm in her voice and was mortified. Was she *that* annoyed with Hermione for not letting her share her good news first?

'Now all we've got to do is organise Jo-Jo's travel arrangements for getting back home.' Hermione had caught Ellen's sharp tone but had decided to get to the bottom of that when she had resolved the more pressing item on her agenda. 'It's your day off today, isn't it? Do you think Johnny Foreigner's up to the journey?'

'Today?' Ellen's heart sank. Two disappointments now. She had hoped to spend the day with Simon. She saw so little of her son that she had been determined to set aside her one day off to be with him. There was also still the matter of Roger's letter to deal with and she wanted Simon's help with that, especially as he'd told her yesterday afternoon that he wanted to get back to Oxford as soon as possible to make a start on some work before the summer term got under way. As far as the letter went, it was today or never.

Hermione saw the unhappy expression on her friend's face. 'Have you made plans already?'

She shook her head. 'No, not really.'

'You're lying, Ellen, I can see it written all over your face. Is it Duncan? Is it another command performance at Crantsford Hall?'

'No! And you wouldn't be asking me that if you'd let me get a word in edgeways!'

'Goodness, Ellen, whatever is the matter? I've never seen you like this before. He hasn't rumbled you, has he? Is that what you came here to tell me?'

'No!' cried Ellen. 'No! No! *No!*' She jumped up from the table. 'I just wanted to spend the day with Simon, if you must know, but to please you I'll agree to drive to Pluto and back if it will only shut you up and give me the opportunity to speak!'

Hermione was amused. Clearly Ellen was in danger of injuring herself if she wasn't allowed her two penn'orth, and soon. But a few moments longer wouldn't do any harm. 'How very kind of you, but I think Sheffield will be as far as we need go. And as to being deprived of Simon's company, that's easily remedied. Why don't we invite him along as well? We could make a day of it. We could put a picnic together and stop off on the way. It could be like a Jane Austen excursion, except we'd have to carry all our own hampers and whatnot. Do you remember when we went to see *Emma* and they all climbed up Box Hill with an army of Sherpas? What do you think? Shall we get out our Empire lines and heaving bosoms and a selection of frilly parasols?'

Ellen plonked herself back into the chair. Hermione was a formidable player in the art of prevarication and it was really quite futile to try to score any points against her. 'The trouble with picnics in novels,' she said, in a tired voice, 'is that they're quite often turning points.'

'What profundity for so early in the morning.'

'Jane Austen and E. M. Forster were always making a drama out of a day in the country with a hamper.' And I'm going slowly mad, thought Ellen.

Slowly, but ever so surely, I'm becoming as mad as Hermione. I only came to say that Duncan is making definite overtures towards me and here I am expounding on the English novel. She picked up an ancient, badly stained cork mat from the table and fiddled with the crumbling edge. She caught the blank expression on Hermione's face. 'Oh, never mind,' she muttered. 'Just forget I ever said anything. The idea's fine by me. I'll have a word with Simon.'

'Ellen, my dear, you seem quite *distrait*.' It was time to put her friend out of her misery. She had teased her long enough. 'Would I be right in thinking that you have news of earth-shattering importance to share with me?'

'You know jolly well I have. Whoops. Sorry.' Ellen pushed the cork mat away from her. It now had a hole where she'd poked her finger right through the middle.

Hermione smiled. 'Come on,' she said, 'tell me that your seductive skills have thoroughly charmed Duncan and that you're about to become the grand lady of the manor. I insist on being your matron of honour for the big day, by the way, and a regular house guest thereafter so that we can get back to afternoon tea and cake while listening to the short story on the radio.'

'If you don't be quiet you'll never hear another story again in your life,' laughed Ellen, glad to have her friend's undivided attention at last. 'Make some tea and I'll fill you in.'

Hermione did as she was told, held the kettle under the tap and then plugged it in. 'You won't miss the best bits out, will you?' she asked, picking up two mugs from the draining board.

'Best bits?'

'Well, I presume there was more than just prawn cocktail on the menu last night.'

'Duncan isn't like that,' Ellen answered, and, conscious that she sounded both defensive and prim, she added, 'he's too much of a gentleman.'

'Either that or he's impotent, or worse still he's—'

'Hermione!'

'I hope you're not discussing me.'

Hermione greeted Matthew with a broad smile. 'Good morning,' she said, and handed him the warmed teapot. 'You're just in time to make us a pot of tea, and, no, we weren't discussing you but Ellen's future husband. Have you met Ellen before? I can't remember.'

'No,' Matthew said, uninterestedly, and immediately turned his attention to seeing to the tea.

'She's a very dear friend of mine and used to live in Orchard House where the Buchanans now live. Ellen, you'll have to excuse my godson's appalling manners but he lives alone and has lost touch with the niceties of life. I think it's an air he affects to put other people at a disadvantage and keep them at arm's length. Take no notice of him.'

Ellen had forgotten that Hermione had told her about Matthew coming to stay, and from the way in which her friend had described him throughout their friendship she had expected someone quite different. She'd had in mind someone older, someone pale and thin with an earnest face – this was based on the sensitively painted watercolours dotted about Laburnum House, which she'd always admired. But from the little she had seen of him so far she could see that she had got him totally wrong. She certainly hadn't expected such a total lack of manners. While his back was to her she took the opportunity to size him up. He was tall – but not as tall as Duncan – and he had a square pair of shoulders beneath a white T-shirt and a loose-fitting denim shirt tucked into a pair of jeans. His feet were bare. She decided he had the kind of build that would look all wrong in a suit, and that *casual* was probably what he favoured most. His hair, though, was really quite smart and looked as if it had been recently cut. It was dark brown and very fine, with a hint of grey just beginning at the temples.

Matthew brought the tea to the table. He didn't sit down as if to join them but instead leaned on the back of a chair and stared first at Hermione and then at Ellen. She turned away. It was obviously his turn to size her up.

The only thought that flashed through Matthew's mind was that Hermione's attractive friend would be a terrible waste on an impotent husband.

'When's the big day?' he asked.

Ellen looked blankly at him.

'When are you getting married?'

Ellen coloured. 'I'm not, well, not yet, nothing's definite. You know how it is.' Floundering hopelessly, she looked to Hermione for help.

But Hermione chose not to notice. 'Ellen's just being discreet, Matthew. But before you came in she was about to tell me how her skill as a Mata Hari beguiled Duncan into proposing last night.'

'I never said that,' Ellen protested. Honestly, there was no trusting Hermione to behave with any tact at times.

'Perhaps I should go and leave you to your gossip,' Matthew said.

'There's no need,' Ellen said, suddenly rising to her feet and scraping her chair on the quarry-tiled floor. 'It's me who should go.' Addressing Hermione, she added, 'If we're going to have this picnic I'd better start making some sandwiches. What time are we setting off?'

Hermione smiled. 'Tell you what, why don't we invite Matthew to come with us as well? Do you think we can squeeze one more into Johnny Foreigner?'

'What picnic and what Johnny Foreigner?'

'Matthew, you sound almost as peppery as Ellen. We're taking Jo-Jo home to Sheffield and stopping on the way to break the journey, and Johnny Foreigner is what Ellen calls her little car.'

'We could take mine if you want. It's a decrepit old wreck, but it's got plenty of room. How many are going?'

Hermione did a quick mental head-count, wagging her forefinger in the air. 'I make that four of us, no, I'm wrong, I was forgetting Ellen's son, Simon.'

Matthew suddenly regretted his rash offer. Being cooped up in a car with a child who, no doubt, would insist on chattering the whole journey or, worse still, want to play stupid I-spy games was not his idea of fun. But it was either that or spend the day going through the Buchanans' photo albums. It was a peach of a dilemma.

Ellen walked home, down in the dumps. She was thoroughly out of sorts and thoroughly peeved with Hermione and that rude godson of hers. Between them they had spoilt her day. If Hermione hadn't rabbited on so much, and if *he* hadn't come into the kitchen when he had she would have been able to share with Hermione all about Duncan telling her how fond he was of her. 'I want you to know that you've become very important to me,' he'd said, his hand stretched out across the table and squeezing her own, 'and that there's nobody else I'd rather be with.'

She smiled happily to herself. Dear, sweet Duncan. He was so old-fashioned at times but, then, perhaps that was what she found so attractive about him. After the demands put upon her by Roger, Duncan's courteous approach to their relationship was so welcome that it made her feel safe and at ease. She was even beginning to wonder if she wasn't falling in love with him.

Everyone, even Jo-Jo, was in good spirits as Matthew headed out onto the Macclesfield road to Buxton, which would eventually take them on to Jo-Jo's home town of Sheffield. The sun had climbed high in the sky and was already hot and it made the dusty interior of the car warm and slightly smelly. There were strange and not very pleasant pongs coming from the back, which Ellen put down to Matthew's tools of the trade. She didn't know much about painting, but she presumed the cardboard boxes behind her were full of manky tubes of paint and filthy rags covered in turps, or was it linseed oil artists used? She wound down her window for some fresh air and thought that it was a shame Matthew wasn't a writer. Pens and paper were far less offensive.

In the front, next to Matthew, was Hermione. She was supposed to be in charge of map reading but she was more occupied with sorting out the position of her seat – she kept sliding it backwards and forwards, oblivious to Simon's long legs behind her. Jo-Jo was between Simon and Ellen, and with her head turned to the open window, Ellen was conscious that she was beginning to feel anxious.

Before they had set off from Laburnum House Ellen had taken Jo-Jo aside and asked her if this was really what she wanted. A part of her was worried that if Jo-Jo returned home and something ghastly happened to her it would be all their fault – it was like returning a rescued and cared-for animal to the wild, then having to trust the forces of nature. It was hard not to play God and intervene.

'Oh, yes,' Jo-Jo had answered. 'I think I knew all along what I should be doing, only I didn't have the nerve to admit it. I kept thinking what I thought would be expected of me. I tried to convince myself that I'd be happy having the baby and living off what I could, but deep down I knew it was wrong for me . . . and the baby. Simon really made me see things clearly.'

'Well, so long as you're sure. But what about your step-father? He won't have changed just because you can see things more clearly.'

'I'll just have to keep out of his way. Like Simon says, I've only got to put up with him for a few months.'

Simon says, thought Ellen, and tilting her head forwards slightly she looked across to her son. He was chatting to Jo-Jo about a book he'd read recently. She had never thought about it before but Simon was that rare person who only offered his opinion when it was asked for; mostly people were only too quick to give their advice. It was strange, though, that in the aftermath of Roger's disappearance she had never once asked Simon directly what he thought she should do. She wondered what his advice would have been, had she sought it. Come to that, what did he really think of Duncan? But did it really matter? Surely what mattered most was what *she* felt, and right now she decided she was close to falling in love with Duncan. She smiled contentedly and closed her eyes, but then wondered if it was possible to be consciously *close to falling in love*. Wasn't it more like being pregnant? You either were or you weren't? Oh, what the heck! What difference did it make anyway?

She opened her eyes to see where they were, only to find Matthew glancing at her in the mirror.

They drove through Dove Holes, past Sparrowpit and then onto the spectacularly steep and rocky gorge of Winnats Pass. A few minutes later Hermione gave the word and they left the car. Carrying between them an assortment of travel rugs, baskets and Hermione's deck chair from the greenhouse, they walked on until they found a secluded, sheltered spot among the gritstone boulders. Ellen spread out a blanket for the baskets and Matthew tried to position the deck chair for Hermione.

'No, not there,' she told him. 'I think here would be better – that way I can enjoy the splendid views across to Mam Tor.'

Then he offered her a travel rug for her legs but she shook her head and pushed it away.

'I haven't been here in years,' she said happily, taking an old pair of field-glasses from a mould-spotted leather case and peering through them like Jack Hawkins in *The Cruel Sea*. It was a wonder she could see anything at the speed she was sweeping the binoculars along the horizon, thought Ellen, as she settled herself on the blanket beside one of the baskets. She started lifting out the plastic boxes of food, at the same time watching Simon and Jo-Jo. They had wandered away to a large rock. Simon was leaning back against it: with one hand he was pointing out something in the distance, and with the other he was pushing his wind-blown hair out of his eyes.

From nowhere Ellen was reminded of Roger. She turned away, unable to cope with her son's unintentional betrayal. People had always said how alike she and Simon were; rarely, even as a baby, had anyone suggested that there was any of Roger in him, but of course there was, and in that simple gesture of raising his hand to his eyes she had witnessed father and son as one. Roger had always been running his hand through his hair. Angry, she hoped that he was now bald and didn't have any hair to run his hand through. She hoped that life in Provence had made it all fall out. *All of it, every last strand!*

'Good idea,' said Matthew, kneeling beside her to help open the boxes of sandwiches. 'I'm starving.'

She quickly dispelled a bald Roger from her mind and held up a large greaseproof-paper parcel tied with string. She called over to Hermione, 'What's in here?'

'Spam and chutney. I found a vintage jar knocking about. It's one of the few items to survive Matthew's ruthless desire to ethnically cleanse my larder.'

'And just how old is this vintage chutney?' Matthew asked. 'Roughly – to the nearest decade will do.'

'I know exactly when I made it,' retorted Hermione. 'Do you remember when you came to stay and broke your arm while mending the summer-house roof—'

'But that was *years* ago—'

'Oh, do stop making a drama out of everything, Matthew, you're getting as bad as Ellen. Now, pass me a sandwich and let me get on with enjoying myself.'

Reluctantly, Matthew handed Hermione her parcel then turned to Ellen. 'Let me have something you've made, and explain why you're being accused of making a drama out of everything.'

'Search me,' she said. 'I haven't a clue what she's on about.'

'You should have heard her earlier this morning,' Hermione said, waving a doorstep and a half of a sandwich in the air. 'She was like some harbinger of doom wittering on with some such nonsense about picnics being turning points.'

'A turning point doesn't necessarily mean a change for the worse,' Simon called over. He and Jo-Jo came and joined them. 'It's actually a moment when a decisive change occurs,' he added, helping himself to something to eat.

'He's right,' Jo-Jo said. 'Like last night when I decided I had to go back home.'

'Oh,' said Hermione craftily, 'so is that what happened with you and Duncan, Ellen? Was that what you came to tell me about this morning?'

'Behave yourself, Hermione,' Matthew said, sensing Ellen's discomfort. He delved into one of the other baskets for his contribution to their lunch: a bottle of white wine picked up on the way from the off-licence in Crantsford. He deftly pulled out the cork with a penknife from his trouser pocket and poured the wine. He handed the mugs round and gave Jo-Jo the one with the smallest amount in, 'So that you don't feel left out.'

'Here's to Jo-Jo's turning point,' Hermione said, raising her mug.

'You'll keep in touch, won't you?' Ellen asked, when they'd all toasted Jo-Jo.

'She'll be too busy climbing the ladder of success,' Simon said, with a proud smile.

When everything had been eaten – except for the spam and chutney, which had been universally condemned by all except Hermione – Ellen went for a walk on her own. She was sad. During lunch she had realised that Hermione was now the last person in whom she could confide about Duncan. Her dear friend was never going to believe that over the last few days Duncan had come to mean more to her than just a meal ticket.

With a heavy heart she wandered further away from the group until she came to a high drystone wall. She leaned against it and stared out at the uncompromising beauty of the Dark Peak. With its gritstone terrace of moorland it was more sombre and bleaker than the White Peak of undulating limestone lying to the south, but its hardness appealed to Ellen. She was no walker, no rambler of the highways and byways, but she was suddenly filled with an inexplicable urge to scramble over the wall and to walk as far as she could, on and on, basking in all that freedom and space. She wondered whether Duncan would enjoy doing the same. She tried to imagine the pair of them hand in hand, dressed in cagoules, woolly hats and sturdy walking boots.

But she couldn't.

She couldn't prise Duncan away from his BMW or his leather-topped office desk.

She heard footsteps and turned to see Matthew coming towards her. He drew level and he, too, leaned against the drystone wall. He said nothing, but kept his gaze firmly ahead of him.

'Beautiful, isn't it?' she said at last, when the silence grew uncomfortable for her.

He turned and faced her. 'No,' he said flatly. 'You're wrong. It's majestic, savage, benign, challenging and a whole lot more.'

'But not beautiful?'

He shook his head.

'Well, I disagree with you. I think it is.'

They remained in silent disharmony, each looking in separate directions until Matthew said, 'Does this Duncan know how lucky he is?'

'I beg your pardon?'

He suddenly turned, contemplated her for a moment, then as if it was the most reasonable thing in the world, held her face in his hands and kissed her on the lips.

And before she knew what she was doing she was kissing him back.

This is crazy, she thought, feeling the roughness of the wall behind her pressing into her back.

This is crazier still, she told herself, when he had wrapped his arms around her shoulders and had drawn her closer.

But she didn't care and for the sheer hell of it she sank deeper into the pleasure of him – it was as if she had climbed over the wall and was running free.

He pulled away abruptly.

'Is that how you kiss Duncan?' he asked, his voice low, and undeniably tinged with cynicism.

She could have slapped him!

And she would have, had she not caught sight of something even more alarming than the strange expression on his face.

Back at the picnic site, there was no sign of Simon and Jo-Jo. But Hermione was still there. She was alone, and sitting bolt upright in her deck chair, her binoculars glued to her eyes, she was looking straight at Ellen and Matthew.

18

The car was very quiet as they headed towards Sheffield.

Too quiet.

Even for Matthew.

He could never be described as a loquacious man – nowadays he spent most of his time alone and had come to value the peace of mind that he derived from his solitary way of life. The sound of meaningless chit-chat was abhorrent to him, he had no mind for it – but right now he'd give anything to be able to light the touch-paper of small-talk. He badly wanted someone to speak – even a facile comment about the weather would be welcome. He even wished that Ellen's son had turned out to be the young irritating chatter-box of a child he'd earlier imagined, and not the full-blown adult now sitting quietly in the back of the car reading *The Ballad of Reading Gaol*. But it seemed as though everyone was happy to sit in silence, either reading or staring out through the windows at the passing scenery.

He desperately needed someone to speak in the belief that it would break the spell of what he'd just done. He'd done some pretty dumb things in his life, but what had just taken place took some beating.

What the hell had he thought he was doing? Auditioning for the part of Rhett Butler in *Gone With the Wind*? If he wanted to play a romantic lead he should join an amateur dramatic society and not take it into his head to go behaving in such a foolish and juvenile manner. For the love of God he was forty-two years old and had just made a complete idiot of himself. What was worse, and much more worrying, was that he had no idea what had possessed him to do it. It was as if for a few seconds he'd lost control of his senses.

He would have to apologise. But how? Judging from the way Ellen had acted after discovering that Hermione had been secretly watching them through her binoculars, the possibility of speaking to her again, and alone, seemed about as likely as . . . as likely as Hermione pretending she hadn't seen them.

They had tidied up the picnic in silence – even Hermione had been rendered speechless and had turned her attention to trying to collapse her deck chair. He suspected that she would be saving up something special to say for when they were alone later that evening. As they'd walked back to the car, having called out to Simon and Jo-Jo that they were off, Ellen had kept as far away from him as possible, lagging behind on the pretext of either admiring the view or stooping to retie a shoelace. And in the car she'd practically glued herself to the window rather than risk so much as a glance in his direction.

'I shall miss you all.'

Matthew inwardly sighed. At last, somebody had spoken.

'I will, honestly. I'm not just saying that.'

'And we shall miss you, Jo-Jo, my dear,' Hermione said fondly, looking up from the map on her lap at which she'd been staring through unseeing eyes for the past thirty minutes. 'Isn't that right, Ellen? After all, it was you who set this particular ball rolling.'

Ellen prised her head away from the window and smiled at Jo-Jo. She caught Matthew's eye in the mirror. 'You can always come and see us again – you're more than welcome.'

Jo-Jo smiled. 'Tell you what, I'll come back for your wedding.'

Simon laughed loudly. 'I didn't know the fabulously wealthy Duncan had even proposed. Tell me more, Mum.'

'He hasn't,' she said, 'and I think you've all got hold of the wrong end of the stick. Duncan hasn't asked me to marry him. Okay?' She put her head back where it had been against the window and stared dejectedly out at the lacklustre terraced houses that now lined both sides of the road as they entered the city of Sheffield.

'Yet,' said Simon, with a laugh.

Ellen didn't respond. Her mood was as dark and as joyless as the streets they were passing through.

Mrs Clarke had been waiting for them since nine o'clock that morning. She looked hopeless and exhausted, red-eyed and taut with nervous anxiety, her arms as tightly wrapped around her wire-thin body as if they were a strait-jacket. The air in the sitting-room was blue and thick with smoke and an ashtray on the coffee table in front of the sofa was almost buried beneath a pile of ash and half-smoked stubbed-out cigarettes. There was no welcome hug for her daughter, no sign that her only child had even been missed. Ellen wanted to snatch Jo-Jo away. She wanted to bundle her into the car and drive her back to Crantsford. This woman didn't deserve Jo-Jo.

'I've been waiting so long for you to come,' Mrs Clarke whined.

Ellen watched the poor woman lower herself into the cushions of the Dralon-covered sofa – it was like watching a heavy wet sponge sink in the bath. Ellen moved towards the bay window that overlooked the surrounding houses and the road, where Matthew and Simon were sitting in the car. It was a good residential area made up of nineteen-thirties detached properties, each separated from its neighbour by a wide garden and a strip of driveway enabling the inhabitants to keep themselves to themselves – so that the likes of Jo-Jo and her mother could go unnoticed.

'I thought you'd be here hours ago,' Mrs Clarke complained again. 'I put the kettle on, but you never came. And I was so thirsty. I kept flicking the switch on the kettle ... I think it's broken now.'

Ellen wanted to offer sympathy to the woman before her, but she couldn't. All she could see was a worn-down woman who was obsessed with one thing, and that was herself. So consumed was she by her own struggle with life that even the trivial – such as the making of a drink – had become an insurmountable task, way beyond her capabilities. Clearly Jo-Jo and her problems wouldn't get a look-in.

'And you didn't say anything about bringing people with you.' Mrs Clarke looked accusingly at Jo-Jo, then at Ellen and Hermione. 'You're not social workers, are you? My husband won't like it if he finds out—'

'Come on, Mum,' Jo-Jo said patiently, 'I explained everything on the phone. I'll make you a cup of coffee, shall I?'

Ellen motioned to Hermione to stay with Mrs Clarke while she escaped to the kitchen with Jo-Jo. She closed the door behind them. 'Jo-Jo,' she whispered, 'are you sure you're doing the right thing by coming back?'

Jo-Jo smiled. 'This is Mum on a good day.'

When it was time to leave, Mrs Clarke remained in the sitting-room, lighting yet another cigarette. Jo-Jo led her friends to the front door. It was an awkward moment, standing there in the narrow hall. Behind them, a long thin mirror reflected their unsmiling faces.

'Come on,' said Hermione, 'we'd better get this over with.' She embraced Jo-Jo and slipped a folded ten-pound note into her hand. 'In case you feel like running away again.'

Ellen saw Jo-Jo's lips beginning to tremble and, frightened that if Jo-Jo cried so would she, she hurriedly threw her arms round the girl and hugged her tightly. 'You'll phone if there's anything you need, won't you? Promise?' She opened her bag and pulled out a phone card. 'Here, you'd better have this.'

Hermione and Ellen joined Matthew and Simon in the car. They waved goodbye, watched Jo-Jo close the front door and then drove away.

'I can't bear it,' murmured Ellen, her voice thick with emotion. 'I didn't think it would be so bad. Surely she would have been better off staying with us?' She suddenly turned on Hermione. 'It's all your fault!' she cried. 'You shouldn't have meddled.'

'Hey, Mum, that's not fair,' Simon said. 'It was Jo-Jo's decision to go home.'

'She was coerced!' she said defiantly, staring him in the eye.

Very calmly he said, 'How's that exactly?'

Ellen turned away. Deep down she knew that Simon was right. Nobody but Jo-Jo had taken the final step in deciding what she was going to do. 'I'm sorry,' she said with a sniff. She began hunting through her bag for a tissue. 'I'm behaving irrationally I suppose. Just ignore me.'

'I think it's been that kind of a day,' Matthew said quietly. He passed a tissue through to the back of the car for Ellen.

Forgetting herself she looked up and met his gaze in the mirror. 'Thank you,' she mumbled, then hid her face in the tissue.

'And the worst of it,' Hermione said, noting the small exchange between Ellen and Matthew, 'was that Jo-Jo's mother accused *me* of being a social worker! Imagine!'

19

Duncan parked in the office car park and wrenched on the handbrake. His mind was made up. He was going to do it. He'd been a fool to wait this long.

Late last night in his study Nadia had pushed him too far and he'd come within an inch of losing his temper with her. Their argument had started predictably enough with Nadia accusing Ellen of being nothing but a cheap gold-digger – an appalling cliché to have used – and further suggesting that he was a sitting target for such a woman.

'You know nothing about Ellen,' he'd responded calmly, 'other than what you and your gossiping friends have put together. So kindly keep your slanderous comments to yourselves.'

'But, Duncan—'

'Let me continue, I haven't finished. The very idea that you think me stupid enough to fall for such a scheme is utterly absurd. Credit me with sufficient perspicacity to recognise such a ploy!'

'Your fine words don't impress me,' she had said flatly. 'Everyone knows men are complete fools when it comes to sex. It makes them blind to what's really going on.'

He had been so annoyed that his relationship with Ellen had been debased and vulgarised in this offhand manner that he'd said, 'I think we should stop this conversation right now, before we both say things we'll regret in the morning.'

But Nadia, as ever, had been determined to have the last word and her parting shot had been, 'I should be very careful if I were you, Duncan. Sex can incite recklessness in the best of people. After all, you're the result of somebody's recklessness.'

Furious, he had leaped from his chair. But Nadia had sailed out of his study with nothing more to say. For some moments he had paced the room, expecting to be able to marshal his unruly emotions back into line, but he couldn't: he found that the confines of his study only added to the constraint he was experiencing. He had poured himself a large brandy from the decanter in the walnut bureau, opened the French windows in front of his desk and strolled out onto the terrace. Staring out into the chilly dark night sky he had tried hard to rationalise his reaction to his mother's words.

In the course of his work it was his job to use the law as a device for achieving the best possible outcome for his client; to this end he had to scrutinise, analyse and double-check everything pertaining to that case. To be a good solicitor one had to be highly attuned to motives and hidden agendas, and he considered himself to be as proficient at this as anyone could be. But at analysing his own behavioural patterns he was a non-starter. Introspection had never appealed: in his opinion, self-analysis could only be flawed. But right then, in that moment beneath the dark night sky, the question had to be asked, and answered: Why was he so furious?

The level of his anger was deplorable and disgraceful, and way beyond anything he had previously dealt with. He'd long since discovered the art of untangling himself from Nadia's grip of protection and arming himself against her possessiveness, but she'd caught him with his guard down. Never before had she referred to his illegitimacy in so cruel a fashion and her words had struck a blow so hard that he had been within an inch of striking her.

Even admitting the thought had filled him with horror. He had gone back inside the house, into his study, and had locked the French windows, knowing it was time for him to act.

And now, the following morning, he let himself into the office, fully prepared to. He was first to arrive, as he was most days. At this time in the morning the rest of the partners were either wiping regurgitated lumps of baby food off their ties or were caught up in the school run – an activity which was made to sound like an Olympic event when they finally made it into the office.

In comparison his own life seemed infinitely more agreeable, with the prospect of it becoming even more so. He picked up the mail from the mat and took it through to his office, where he placed the pile to one side of his tidy desk. Taking his fountain pen from his breast pocket, he sat down and pulled a pad of paper towards him. He began to write a list. First he wrote, *Visit florist*, followed by, *Woodward's the Jeweller's*. He was about to replace the cap on his pen when he hesitated. After a few seconds he began writing again: *Travel Agent's*. Well, why not? If a job was worth doing, it was worth doing properly.

Ellen still hadn't managed to shake off her gloomy mood from yesterday. She couldn't rid herself of the picture of poor Jo-Jo's face as they'd said goodbye. Jo-Jo deserved better.

The sound of an approaching car interrupted her thoughts. At first she thought it might be Simon but then remembered that his old Fiat made far more noise and, anyway, he'd said at breakfast he wouldn't be back until late and it was only one o'clock. Curiosity and the desire to sell something worthwhile made her want to peer out of the window to weigh up the potential customer, but knowing that there was nothing worse than an over-keen salesperson, she carried on organising the display of garlands she'd finished making late last night.

Even when the door opened she played it cool – *one two three, give them time to wait for me* – and only when she heard the sound of the door closing did she turn round with her best smile in place.

'Duncan!'

He came towards her at a surprising speed, managing in his haste to kick over a large basket in front of the main display area. 'Ellen,' he said, quickly settling the basket back into its correct position, 'I'm not a man given over to acts of impetuosity, but I want you to come with me. Now.'

'Now?' she repeated, astonished. This was not the Duncan she knew. 'Why, what's happened?'

'Please. Just lock up and I'll explain in the car.'

'Heavens, Duncan, if this isn't impetuous I don't know what is.' She flipped the Closed sign over, turned the key in the lock and hurried after Duncan, who was already standing by his car holding the door open for her.

He drove fast and in complete silence, ignoring all her questions. She sensed that he was nervous. When he brought the car to a halt in a quiet picnic spot he unbuckled his seat belt. 'I want you to close your eyes,' was all he said.

She wanted to laugh. It was all so bizarre. 'You're not trying to kidnap me, are you?' she called to him, as he got out and went round to the boot.

Still he didn't answer her. 'Don't open your eyes, not until I say so. I've got something for you.'

She did as she was told, but recalled Roger's words one night in bed. '*Close your eyes, I've got something for you.*' He'd disappeared out of the bedroom and when she'd been allowed to look she'd seen, just inches away from her face, two beady eyes staring at her through a terrifying black-leather mask. She'd screamed and leaped out of the bed and almost knocked herself unconscious tripping over a pair of shoes and banging her head on the dressing table. Playful eroticism, Roger had called it. Downright lethal, she'd described it, coming home from Casualty in the early hours of the morning with concussion and a couple of stitches to boot.

'There,' said Duncan. 'Now you can open them.'

She did. On her lap was the largest bouquet of red roses she'd ever seen. It was so large she could barely see over the top of the flowers. 'Duncan, they're beautiful.' She breathed in deeply, hoping the roses would smell. They did. The fragrance was heavenly, sweet and redolent of a perfect summer's day. 'They're wonderful,' she said.

'And so are you.' He slipped his hand into his pocket and pulled out a small square box. 'Ellen,' he said, his expression suddenly earnest, 'I . . . I want you to marry me.' He slowly opened the box and, like the roses, the ring was exquisite. 'Shall we see if it fits?'

Ellen was in shock. It had happened. It had *really* happened. Duncan had proposed. He had actually asked her to marry him. Oh, how she had hoped for this moment, and oh, how much mental effort she had put into rehearsing him till he was word perfect. It was too good to be true.

You're right, whispered a voice in her head, *it is too good to be true. And the sad truth is, you're not worthy to be this man's wife because you've planned it all along. And you can't plan love.*

She chewed her lip and squeezed her eyes shut. This was not what she wanted to hear.

'Ellen? Are you all right?'

She opened her eyes. 'Oh, Duncan,' she said, 'I don't know what to say. I . . .'

'Say yes. It's as simple as that.'

You're not worthy of him, hissed the voice in her head.

'Yes, I am!'

Duncan's solemn face broke into a tentative smile. 'Is that yes, you will marry me?'

'No! I mean, oh . . .' What was she doing? Of course she wanted to marry him. So why the hell was she letting some imaginary smooth-talking voice, otherwise known as her guilty conscience, push her around like this? She took a deep breath. 'Oh, Duncan,' she said, hoping to appease her high-minded conscience, 'you deserve someone so much better than me.'

Well, it's a start, but how about telling him the truth, eh? We could open with how attractive his bank balance is and then casually throw in yesterday's soap-opera scene when you were snogging a complete stranger among the rocks and boulders while supposedly admiring the view!

'Ellen. This is the first time I've ever proposed to anyone. Am I to understand that there's a level of prevarication to get through before I have my answer?'

His voice was bordering on the stern and had the immediate effect of stirring Ellen into action. Without giving another thought to the pestering of her inner voice, she waved it *adios* and said, 'Duncan, of course I'll marry you. Just name the day!' She reached out to kiss him, but he smiled and gently pushed her away.

'I'm not finished yet,' he said. He leaned through to the back of the car and picked up a large envelope from the seat. He handed it to her. 'I thought a honeymoon in Florence might be fun.'

She gazed ecstatically at the brochure. 'You've thought of everything, haven't you?'

'That's the kind of man I am – but, then, you knew that already. Now where's that kiss?'

They drove back to the barn at a less reckless speed. Ellen presumed Duncan's nerves were now fully restored to their usual composure, but hers were not. She felt sick and she was trembling inside with the sheer unadulterated excitement of what lay ahead.

She glanced down at the roses and beautiful ring Duncan had chosen for her and thought again how organised and methodical he was. She smiled. How wonderful he was, and how wonderful her life would be from now on.

No more dried flowers! No more cheap broken biscuits! No more tiny damp cottage! No more worries! Oh, what joy!

'Where shall we live?' she blurted out, having just pictured them flying back from their honeymoon and trying to squeeze Duncan and all his belongings into Spring Bank Cottage.

'I thought initially we'd live at Crantsford Hall,' he said, parking the car alongside Johnny Foreigner. They both looked up at the tiny cottage. 'I thought you might like that,' he added.

He was right. Oh, boy, he was right! She leaned across and kissed him.

'It is okay, isn't it? I mean . . . I know Nadia can be a bit much, but there's plenty of room for us all until we find a place of our own.'

She kissed him again. 'It'll be fine, don't worry. By the way, how does Nadia feel about me becoming her daughter-in-law?'

His expression changed. 'Ah—'

'Duncan?'

'I wanted you to be the first to know,' he said, quite reasonably. 'But why don't you come over tonight for a drink and we'll tell her together?'

'Good idea. Oh, but I can't. I've been invited to a party – and by, of all people, the Buchanans who bought Orchard House.'

'Well, ring them up and tell them you can't come. But don't say why. I don't want everyone else knowing before we've told Nadia.'

She frowned. 'But I've sort of promised. She wants me to do an arrangement for the sitting room and I need to see—'

'Darling,' Duncan said, patting her hand, 'you don't have to worry about all of that now. Once we're married you can give up toiling away here. Now, out you get. I must get on, I've a client in half an hour.'

Ellen smiled and opened the car door. 'Poor you,' she said. 'Another ghastly divorce to get through.'

'Now don't forget, ring this Buchanan woman and put her off, and I'll see you tonight at eight.'

She watched Duncan turn the car round. She waved goodbye, unlocked the barn door and went inside. She placed the roses on the work-bench and rushed to the phone, not to ring Susie Buchanan, but Hermione. She wanted to tell Hermione the news. She squeezed the receiver tightly in her hand, willing her friend to answer it, but it kept on ringing. She waited for what seemed an age before accepting that Hermione was probably pottering in the greenhouse and would no more hear the phone that far away from the house than she would notice if it was burning down.

Disappointed, she replaced the receiver, then remembered she was supposed to be ringing Susie Buchanan. But how stupid, she didn't have the number. Oh, well, she'd close the barn for the rest of the day and call round. What did a few lost customers mean now?

Susie was on the telephone and emptying the dishwasher at the same time. 'I don't know if he'll come, Janey,' she whispered into the portable phone.

'He's a bit Heathcliffy. You know, impossibly grumpy one minute as though I've just said completely the wrong thing and at other times he can be quite charming. I think he's got a soft spot for Millie, though. Anyway, must dash, I'm up to my elbows in sun-dried tomatoes. See you tonight, 'byee. And don't worry, of course I'll introduce you.'

She put down the phone and tiptoed through to the conservatory, which was now bereft of all its muslin drapes, plants and furniture. She could see Matthew bent over a selection of photographs and a large piece of paper with a roughly drawn sketch of what was going to be their family mural.

'Cup of coffee?' she offered. He didn't hear her. 'Coffee?' she repeated, this time louder. Still he didn't hear. She rolled her eyes and wondered why she'd just spent ten minutes whispering into the phone to Janey about a man who couldn't hear her voice when she was only a few feet away from him. She turned to leave him to it.

'Thank you,' he said, raising his head from the large piece of paper, 'that would be great.'

'How's it going?' she asked, venturing a little nearer. She had hoped for at least a few daubs of paint to be on the wall in time for the party that night, but as yet all there was to show for his work were a few pencilled outlines that bore little relation to anyone she knew, let alone her nearest and dearest.

'Okay.'

'And have you thought any more about coming tonight? I've got lots of people dying to meet you.'

He shook his head. 'I really don't think—' he started to say but was interrupted by the sound of the doorbell. Susie excused herself.

Matthew returned to the safety of his work, preferring to keep as low a profile as he could if this was another of Susie's many friends who was *simply dying* to meet him. So far there'd been three who'd been at death's door. He could hear Susie's voice out in the hall. 'Come on in,' she was saying, 'no, not interrupting at all. Stay and have a chat and I'll put the kettle on.'

Through the open door of the conservatory he saw Susie ushering her guest into the kitchen and immediately he picked up his pencil and climbed up the step-ladder against the wall he was working on.

'As you can see, we've barely touched the kitchen,' he could hear Susie saying, 'so I suppose it looks much the same as when you lived here.'

He stopped what he was doing. Hadn't Hermione said that Ellen had been the previous owner? He turned his head slightly and saw Ellen with her back to him. Funny, he hadn't got her down as Susie's type.

'I won't stop long,' he heard Ellen say. 'I'm afraid I've come to apologise. I can't make it tonight, after all.'

'Oh, that's too bad,' Susie said, disappointed, but added good-naturedly, 'have you had a better offer?'

Ellen laughed. 'You could say.'

'Oh, do tell. And if it's really good you'll be excused.'

Ellen hesitated. Duncan had asked her not to say anything, but . . . oh, but nothing, she had to tell somebody. You couldn't keep something like this a secret. 'Actually I'm getting married.'

'What, tonight?'

A crash, followed by a stifled cry, had Susie and Ellen rushing to the conservatory. They found Matthew lying on the floor among the step-ladders.

'Hi,' he said, slowly getting to his feet and rubbing himself down. 'So you finally got him to propose, did you? Congratulations.'

'How long have you known him?' Susie whispered, when they were back in the kitchen making coffee, having been reassured by Matthew that there were no broken bones and that he'd survived worse accidents. 'Matthew, that is.'

'Only since yesterday, though I've heard Hermione talk about him occasionally.'

'What do you make of him? No, don't answer me now, let me take his coffee to him while you go through to the sitting-room, it's the second door on the ... Oh, but you know that, don't you? How silly of me.'

Ellen smiled and wandered out to the hall of what had once been her dream home. She let herself into the sitting-room and braced herself. This room had been her favourite: south-facing with a wide door opening onto a patio and a landscaped terraced garden. She went over to look at the garden. She had spent weeks planting out hundreds of spring bulbs in the first few months of living in the house and she could see how Susie was reaping the benefits of her hard work. But there were tulips as well now, in neat small wooden barrels on the patio. She'd never liked tulips, they were too orderly and precise for her taste.

Turning away from the garden she felt pleasantly surprised at her reaction on being back in Orchard House. There was a marked absence of sadness or pain, no sense of regret, no thoughts of petty jealousy. It was easy to figure out why. She was on the verge of becoming Mrs Duncan Carter and her future sparkled as brightly as the diamonds on her finger.

Susie came into the room and found Ellen standing by the patio door, holding her left hand up to the light. 'May I see?' she asked, placing the tray of coffee on a polished table and coming over.

Ellen showed her.

Susie was impressed. 'How *sweet*. Now, tell me all about this divine man you're going to marry. What's his name?'

Ellen told her.

'Duncan Carter!' exclaimed Susie. 'As in Church Walk Mews Solicitors?'

'Yes, that's him. Do you know Duncan?'

'Oh, yes. Well, know of him in truth. Clever old you to have snapped him up. Sugar?'

Ellen shook her head and took the proffered cup and saucer. 'So how do you know of Duncan?'

'The mother of one of Floss's friends at school works with him. We had dinner with her and her husband just the other night and she was joking that there weren't many men left in the world like Duncan. He comes highly recommended, if you believe everything Miriam says. Apparently the dumped wives absolutely flock to the office for his charming desk-side manner. Miriam says that for years they've joked that the reason he's never married is that he's been waiting for the perfect woman to walk through his office door. Gosh, just think where that leaves you – Mrs Perfect! How awesome.'

'I don't think it's a matter of me being perfect—'

'I think you'll find it is. Biscuit? Not home-made, I'm afraid, but the next best thing, Marks and Spencer's.' She passed Ellen a plate of shortbread and a pretty napkin. 'All I can say is that I'm only too grateful I don't have to live up to any expectations like that,' Susie continued. 'When Bonkers proposed to me he knew exactly what he was getting into. "Darling," I told him, "what you see, is what you get." He knew right from the start there were no hidden extras. More coffee?'

Ellen held out her cup and hoped that another piece of shortbread was in the offing. She couldn't remember the last time she'd bought biscuits from Marks and Spencer.

'Please, help yourself,' Susie said, pouring the coffee from a cafetière, 'you mustn't stand on ceremony here. Just make yourself at home . . .' She lowered the coffee pot and covered her mouth with her hand. 'Oh, I'm terribly sorry,' she said. 'I keep putting my foot in it, don't I? What must you think of me?'

'Don't worry,' Ellen laughed kindly. 'It doesn't bother me. This is your house now. You must forget I ever lived here.' How easy it was to be magnanimous when all was right with the world!

'Oh, but I could slap myself for my stupidity.'

'Well, don't, you've done nothing to hurt my feelings. And, anyway, it's me who should be apologising for letting you down tonight.'

'Are you sure you can't come?'

'Duncan wants me with him when he tells Nadia about our engagement.'

'I bet he does! Oh, there I go again. Me and my big mouth.'

Ellen smiled. Whoever this Miriam was, she had the greater part of Duncan's private life pretty well sewn up.

'I'm afraid I've said too much,' Susie apologised. She nibbled on a sliver of shortbread in silence for a few moments. Then she smiled. 'I tell you what, why don't you and Duncan come here after you've been to see his mother? Do say yes, it'll be such fun to see you both. And you can tell Duncan that Miriam will be here, so at least there'll be one guest he'll know.'

Ellen hesitated. Maybe it wasn't such a bad idea. That way she and Duncan wouldn't have to hang around Crantsford Hall after they'd broken the news to Nadia, especially if she took it the way Ellen suspected she might. 'Okay,' she said. 'I'll ask Duncan and see what he says.'

'Wonderful! Now all I've got to do is convince Matthew to come.' She inclined her head towards the hall and conservatory beyond. 'Bonkers's sister, Janey, is coming tonight and she's absolutely *dying* to meet him.' She lowered her voice. 'She's on the prowl for a mate . . . been on her own for too long . . . if you know what I mean. She's a lovely girl, just a bit highly strung. I think they'd hit it off marvellously well, if only I could get him to accept the invitation.'

'I'm sure you're right,' Ellen said, thinking that she wouldn't mind witnessing the spectacle of Matthew being chased around Orchard House by the frustrated Janey! An idea occurred to her. 'If you really want him to come, invite Hermione to the party. That way I'd put money on Matthew turning up to keep her company.' Ah! That would teach him not to use that sarky tone of voice with her again – *So you finally got him to propose, did you? Ah!*

'Ellen, you're an absolute marvel. How clever you are. Now what about my flower arrangement? Shall we sort that out now, rather than later? That way tonight will be all pleasure for you and no business.'

It certainly will, thought Ellen.

20

Hermione was enjoying herself. When Bernie had popped his head through the *leylandii* hedge earlier that morning and asked if she was on for a spot of ravishing, she'd told him to come back after lunch by which time she would have finished cleaning out the water butt.

There'd been no ravishing but they'd drunk nearly the entire contents of a delightful bottle of claret Bernie had brought with him. They were sitting in the greenhouse and Bernie was telling her another of his colourful stories. She couldn't recall anyone ever telling her such lurid jokes. Her background was old school, which meant that when she'd grown up young ladies such as herself were warned about the likes of Bernie Malloy. Her headmistress had repeatedly instructed Hermione and her classmates on the perils of the bantam cock who with his crowing and fine feathers would familiarise himself with their *bodily functions* and as a consequence send them all to hell. It was a confusing message, and it was years before Hermione realised that she needn't be afraid of farmyards.

Things didn't improve much, even when she married Arthur – the *bodily functions* were explored, but they weren't up for discussion. Arthur was very clear on that point. Perhaps if they had talked more they might have managed to produce at least one child. As it was, she miscarried so many times that poor Arthur grew terrified of even touching her. He was so formal, so paralysed by his inbred chivalry that he practically asked her permission before he kissed her goodnight.

They had met at a difficult time in both their lives, indeed it was a difficult time for the entire country. Britain was at war and Hermione's parents had recently died in a car accident … and Roberta had married Kit.

After her parents' funeral, the family solicitor, a dandy of a man with a penchant for hats and cigars, explained to Hermione that her father had made several unsound investments during the past five years and, while not wishing to cause alarm, he wanted to advise her that there were sufficient funds for her to live off for the next few years if she was careful, but ultimately his professional advice was to sell Laburnum House. 'Either that or marry someone exceedingly wealthy,' he'd joked. With equal humour, even at so young an age – she was only twenty-two – she had asked him how much money he earned and would he be interested in applying for the position of her husband?

Very politely, he had declined.

Later that year, and in response to Ernest Bevan urging the female population of the country to join in with the war effort, Hermione started work in a silk factory that had been given over to producing woven cloth for parachutes. It was while she was 'doing her bit' that she had met Arthur. As a child he had suffered prolonged bouts of tuberculosis and, declared unfit to fight for King and country, he had been forced to remain at home and help his father run the family business. Hermione first noticed him when he had been staring at her through the glass window of his office, which overlooked the factory line. She had smiled at him and the following night he had emerged from his office and pretended to inspect the loom she was operating. They were married within six months and were as content as most young couples living through the fear and hardship of a war.

But Hermione had always felt as though she'd cheated Arthur: not only had she been unable to give him the son he desired but, worse, she hadn't loved him as she should have. He was a kind, decent man who had willingly solved her financial difficulties and had insisted they live where she was happiest, which was, of course, Laburnum House. He died of pneumonia, not long after his fiftieth birthday, and she suspected that he had passed away knowing that there had been a part of her that she had deliberately withheld from him. Only a small part, mind.

Her heart.

'You've got that look in your eye again, haven't you, my little Hermaseta? You're thinking, I wish that Bernie would shut up and make with the foreplay.'

'If you really want to know, I was wondering what the poor doddery folk at the Lodge make of you,' she lied.

He poured the rest of the wine into her glass and laughed. 'You reckon I don't fit in with them, don't you? That I'm not lah-di-dah enough. That it?'

'Frankly, yes, that's exactly what I think.'

He laughed again, so much so that his large round belly wobbled over the top of his trousers, but his chest got the better of him and he coughed loudly, then spluttered to catch his breath. He didn't sound at all well and Hermione was reminded again of Arthur. She wondered just how ill Bernie really was.

'It's the sex that does it,' he wheezed, reaching into his jacket pocket. He pulled out an inhaler and held it to his mouth. 'Three times a day is too much I keep telling them, but they won't listen.'

'Oh, shut up, you silly old sod.'

'Hermaseta, my little sweet,' he said, when at last he'd caught his breath, 'I'm shocked. Such language, and from one who considers me too vulgar to be socially acceptable.'

'You haven't answered my question,' she said, ignoring his look of mock horror. 'How do they view you next door?'

'How I've always been viewed.'

'Which is?'

'They throw themselves at me.'

Hermione gave up. 'Does anyone ever get any sense out of you?'

'Not if I can help it. Now, why don't you ask me some less serious questions?'

'Like what exactly?'

'Like, what shall we do tonight?'

'That's easy. While I'm enjoying an evening with Matthew, you'll be forced into eating puréed carrots before being strapped into your plastic-covered chair in the communal lounge to watch a television screen with the sound up too loud.'

He started to laugh again.

'No. Don't laugh any more,' she said. 'I don't want you dying in my greenhouse.'

'For your information,' he said, 'tonight I was planning on having prawn roulade followed by noisettes of lamb and a crème caramel to finish up with. And after dinner I had in mind a game or two of snooker. There are plastic chairs but they're out on the terrace and to my knowledge they don't have straps.'

Hermione humphed and stared at him beneath her hooded eyelids. 'Bully for you,' she said quietly.

'On the other hand, you could join me. We're allowed guests.'

'What? And give you the opportunity to show me off as some new piece of totty?'

He slapped his forehead with the palm of his hand. 'Heavens to Betsy, I've been rumbled!'

'Come on,' she said, 'let's go up to the house. I'm in need of a cup of tea – that red wine's completely dried me out.'

When they reached the garden room they met Ellen coming into the small courtyard. Hermione took one look at the expression on Ellen's face and knew what her friend had come to tell her. But instead of being delighted for her, she felt her heart sink. She suddenly had no desire for Ellen to get married, because if she did, it would mean having to share her. Or, worse still, Duncan would monopolise her to the extent that Ellen would have no time for her old friend. Appalled at her selfishness, she hurriedly introduced Bernie and led the way inside.

'Well,' she said, when she knew she had to listen to Ellen's news, 'I can see from that ridiculous smile on your face that you've got something to tell me.'

Ellen didn't speak, but she held out her hand.

Hermione whistled and Bernie leaned forward to take a look as well.

'Bernie,' Hermione said sternly, 'I suggest you keep your mouth closed while Ellen's here. She won't want to hear any of your dirty jokes, not now that she's going to be moving up in the world. She's marrying money, and lots of it.'

'Congratulations,' Bernie said, 'you're a woman after my own heart. Marrying for money is the only way to true happiness, in my opinion.'

'I'm not marrying for money,' Ellen protested. Why did Hermione have to keep telling people that she was? She wished she'd never confided in her now. 'Duncan's a lovely man,' she continued, 'he's—'

'I'm sure he is,' Bernie cut in, 'but I bet the old oncers make him even lovelier!'

Hermione and Bernie laughed complicitly. Ellen felt annoyed and left out. She wished she hadn't come now. She refused a drink and went home to put Duncan's roses in water.

Susie tiptoed into the conservatory.

'I'm just popping out,' she said to Matthew. 'The girls are in the playroom – could you be a real sweetie and listen out for them while I'm gone? I'll be less than two ticks.' She didn't wait for a reply.

As soon as the front door closed Floss appeared in the conservatory with Millie in tow. For several minutes they stood and stared up at Matthew. From the top of the ladder he stared back at them. He tried a smile but their faces remained blank. 'No school?' he asked.

'We're still on holiday,' Little Miss Shrewd Eyes informed him, and in a tone of voice that suggested he should know this. 'We go back on Monday. You haven't done very much, have you? Dad says you'd better make a good job of it or he'll make you do it again.'

Matthew came down the ladder and moved it along a few feet. 'And I suppose your father considers himself an expert,' he muttered under his breath.

'Dad's a special kind of doctor,' Little Miss Shrewd Eyes continued.

'Yes, I know,' Matthew said, climbing back up the ladder.

'Do you know what he does?'

'I think so.'

'What, then?'

Matthew gripped his pencil and wondered how much longer Susie would be.

'Shall I tell you?'

'Do I have a choice?'

'He looks up ladies' bottoms.'

'A fascinating job in anyone's book. Isn't there anything on the television you want to watch?'

'We're only allowed to watch the television if Mum says we can. She's very strict like that.'

Not strict enough, in Matthew's opinion. 'What about your music practice?' he asked, anxious to be left alone. 'Have you done that yet?'

Floss considered this. 'Okay,' she said. And as though a satisfactory agreement had been reached she turned and left the conservatory.

Millie remained where she was. She took a step closer to the wall Matthew was working on.

'This is me, isn't it?' she said quietly, pointing to a sketched outline of a girl holding a toy rabbit in her hands.

'Yes,' Matthew answered. He came and stood beside her. 'Do you like it?'

Her small serious face looked up at him, her eyes large and solemn. 'Yes,' she nodded, 'I really like the way you've drawn Bobtail. Could you do him on a piece of paper for me? Please.'

He smiled and said he would. From the hall the unmistakable sound of 'The Emperor's March' filled the house. Matthew wondered again how much longer their mother would be.

Susie was delighted. Hermione had accepted the invitation and was bringing with her that jolly man who had been in the kitchen when she'd arrived at Laburnum House. She didn't know what Bonkers would say to all these extra guests, but he would think it was worth it if they could get poor old Janey fixed up. She just had to hope that Ellen had been right when she'd said that if Hermione was invited Matthew would agree to come.

21

Duncan glanced at his watch.

She was late. She had never been late before, so why now, and on such an important night? He'd told her in the car to be here at eight, there could have been no confusion. Even on the phone earlier when she had called to say that they'd both been invited to the Buchanans' he had reminded her what time to arrive.

His bedroom overlooked the lawn that straddled the long strip of driveway. He went over to the small leaded window, lifted the latch, leaned out and watched for Ellen's car headlamps. But there was no sign of her. He shut the window, went over to the mahogany wardrobe and inspected himself in the mirror. He pulled at his tie, trying to straighten it, then noticed a tiny stain in the silk fabric. He yanked it off, threw it on the floor and opened the wardrobe to choose another. Lifting his shirt collar he slipped the replacement tie round his neck and carefully began to knot it.

There were to be no hitches tonight. Everything had to be exactly right. So where the hell was Ellen?

The sooner she came, the sooner they could get this over and done with.

Downstairs in her sitting-room Nadia was pouring herself a glass of Croft's pale cream sherry from the tray on the Pembroke table behind the sofa.

'Cheers,' she said, raising her glass to her reflection in the gilt-framed mirror above the mantelpiece. She drained the glass in one and poured herself another.

In a strange way she was looking forward to the evening. 'I've invited Ellen for a drink tonight,' Duncan had told her on the phone late that afternoon, calling from his office. 'I thought it would make a pleasant evening, just the three of us,' he'd added.

She raised her glass and scoffed at the idea. Pleasant for whom?

Ellen was about to leave the house when the phone rang.

'Hi, Ellen, it's me, Jo-Jo.'

'Everything's all right, isn't it?' Ellen asked, immediately concerned, her mind flitting through a list of atrocities that might have happened to Jo-Jo since yesterday, and before Jo-Jo even had a chance to reply, Ellen had the step-father banged to rights.

'Yeah, don't worry. I'm fine, apart from being treated as a social leper by you-know-who, but I'm managing pretty well to keep out of his way.'

'And your mother? How are you coping with her?'

'The same as ever.'

'How about seeing a doctor? Have you arranged an appointment yet?'

'Way ahead of you. I had an antenatal check-up today and I'm seeing someone at an adoption agency in a couple of weeks' time. I start back at school on Monday. I can't say I'm looking forward to seeing Alan again.'

'Don't give him a thought,' Ellen told her. 'Just think about yourself. Now, take care. I've got to dash, I'm seeing Duncan and I'm already late. Oh, Simon's just walked in, do you want a word?'

She passed the phone to her son, mouthed to him that she'd see him later, grabbed her bag and rushed out of the cottage, nearly missing her footing in the dark as she hurried over to Johnny Foreigner. She drove like the wind, at the same time skidding some lipstick across her lips and smoothing down her hair. Twenty minutes late, she turned into the cobbled drive of Crantsford Hall. She'd never been late for Duncan before and, given the importance of the evening, this was probably the one time when he wouldn't make allowances for her. This thought did nothing to calm her already lurching stomach.

It had been easy to say to Duncan, in the excitement of the moment earlier that afternoon, that it would be fine living with La Carter, but there was no doubt in her mind that in reality it would be quite the opposite – a padded cell and a strait-jacket held more appeal right now. She parked Johnny Foreigner alongside Duncan's BMW and gazed up at the house.

In the dark, Crantsford Hall seemed large, looming, sinister and not at all welcoming as it had in the sunshine on Good Friday. A flicker of movement at a window on the first floor of the house caught her eye. She smiled. The situation was fast becoming a scene out of a Gothic novel: any minute now Duncan would appear in riding breeches surrounded by a pack of snarling dogs, with a wild, haunted look on his face.

She was just locking the car when the front door opened, spilling light across to where she stood.

'What happened? I was worried.'

'I'm sorry, Duncan,' she said, hurrying over to him. 'The phone rang just as I was—'

'Oh, well, never mind all that. At least you're here now. Come on inside and let's get this over with.'

So, Duncan was as nervous as she was. But instead of feeling comforted by this, Ellen was disappointed. Following him up the steps and into the house she felt let down – her lion-hearted Sir Galahad wasn't supposed to be frightened of his mother.

When Ellen and Duncan came into the room Nadia didn't bother getting up from her chair. This was her house and she would do as she pleased.

'Ellen,' she said, 'how good to see you again. This is the third time in just over a week.'

Ellen laughed and, settling in for a sparring session, began, 'Yes, it's as if I'm part of the family, isn't it?'

Duncan rattled his throat and Nadia looked on stonily. She shot a glance at Duncan. 'Another sherry for me and I'm sure you'll know what Ellen's tipple is.'

'White wine?' he offered.

If she didn't feel so sorry for Duncan being caught in the crossfire she'd ask for a cocktail, something outrageous and along the lines of a Long Hard Screw, but it was an old joke and she thought better of it. 'White wine would be fine,' she answered decorously, and as no one asked her to sit down she stood awkwardly by a handsome satinwood secretaire, ornately decorated with large marquetry flowers. She examined it for a few seconds then watched Duncan pour the drinks.

The room was silent and, in Ellen's opinion, looked as if it had been pre-set. The only light was cast from two lamps placed either side of Nadia in the corner where she was sitting: it was as if she was meant to be the focal point. If this was the case, it was working a treat. There was no avoiding the incredible big-boned hulk.

Duncan handed Nadia her sherry and then came over to Ellen. 'Please,' he said, 'sit down.'

They perched on a sofa together, directly opposite Nadia who had already finished her sherry. Like a fish, thought Ellen, watching Nadia place the empty glass on the table beside her.

'Well, this is *pleasant*,' Nadia said, her tone implying that it was anything but. 'We should do this more often, but Duncan has so little time for socialising. I pity the poor woman who ever marries him.' She laughed without humour. 'She'd see precious little of him, what with the hours he works, and then there's the golf course that takes up so much of his weekends. No. It would have to be a very stupid woman willing to put up with that, don't you think, Ellen?'

'A patient and understanding woman, perhaps,' Ellen said with a smile, willing Duncan to take his cue. Come on, Duncan, she wanted to say, get on and tell the wicked old witch!

'I think you're exaggerating, Mother,' Duncan said quietly, leaning back, crossing his legs and turning the stem of his wine glass round in his fingers. 'I don't work absurdly long hours and on average I play just one game of golf a week.'

Nadia waved aside his words with a huge hand. 'Whatever you say. Another drink, Ellen?'

Ellen had barely touched her wine – her stomach wasn't up to it. 'No, thank you,' she said politely.

'I think I'll have another sherry,' Nadia said. She looked pointedly at Duncan but he made no move. 'I said, I think I'll—'

Reluctantly he got to his feet.

Nadia frowned when he handed her glass to her. 'Are we on short measures tonight?' she asked. He topped up the glass and Ellen was sure she heard him muttering to himself.

'Duncan, you can be so churlish when you want to be,' Nadia scolded, as he stood beside her. 'A few glasses of sherry won't do me any harm.' She held the glass to her lips and drained it in one long swig.

Ellen watched, mesmerised. She wouldn't be a bit surprised if the ghastly woman didn't drag the back of her hand across her mouth and bang the empty glass down on the table and demand another – *Line 'em up, bartender!* When this didn't happen, Ellen shifted her gaze to Duncan. She was alarmed at what she saw. His whole body had turned rigid with fury, his jaw was tightly clenched in a grim, hard line and a muscle at his temple was ticking worryingly.

This was no way to announce an engagement, thought Ellen. What they needed was a diversion.

She let her glass slip between her fingers. 'Oh, I'm so sorry!' she cried. 'How careless of me.'

'Duncan, fetch a cloth,' Nadia ordered, not making a move herself.

Duncan didn't move either. His eyes were fixed on Nadia. 'No, not until you've heard what I've got to say.'

'The carpet, Duncan. It'll be ruined.'

'To hell with the sodding carpet!' he exploded. 'Ellen and I are getting married.'

They arrived at Orchard House to find that the only parking spaces available were further up the Crescent beyond Laburnum House. Duncan got out of the car and came round to Ellen's side. He hadn't spoken a word since they'd left Nadia gulping like a fish and reaching for another fix of Croft's pale cream.

Ellen couldn't get over La Carter and all that sherry. It was truly the last thing in the world she had expected and it was probably a family secret that Duncan would have preferred to stay that way. She was saddened, though, that he was so ashamed of his mother's behaviour that he had been unable to share it with her.

Susie opened the door to them. She was dressed simply in a black dress that hugged her slim body perfectly.

'Ellen!' she exclaimed, her voice in party mode, high and shrill. 'You made it, and this must be the gorgeous Duncan I've heard so much about. Bad news, I'm afraid. Miriam and Charlie have cried off, little one's got a tummy bug.'

'Darling,' came a voice from another room and, above the sound of a sudden burst of laughter, 'any more bubbly? We're running low, getting through it at a terrifying rate!'

'I'm out here, sweetie. Ellen's just arrived,' Susie called back.

Bonkers appeared in the hall with an empty bottle in his hand. He was wearing a paisley silk bow tie with a matching waistcoat and a helpless look on his face. 'I can't find any more of this stuff. Where've you hidden it?'

'Don't be so rude, Bonkers. Say hello to our guests. You remember Ellen, don't you? And this is her fiancé, Duncan. You take them through to the party and I'll find some more champagne.'

Bonkers led the way to the sitting-room where he unexpectedly clapped his hands together. 'Attention everyone,' he yelled, 'this is Ellen and Duncan. Be nice to them.'

Ellen wanted to slink under the nearest piece of furniture. This was just how she used to feel when as a small child she had been deposited at a birthday party. She wondered what Duncan was thinking, and when Bonkers was called away to the other side of the room she glanced sideways at him.

He didn't look happy.

Was he still cross with Nadia or was he regretting coming here? Something told her they wouldn't be staying long. He caught her staring at him.

'How did she know we were engaged?' he asked, in a low voice.

Ellen frowned. 'I told her this afternoon ... I didn't think you'd—'

'I told you not to tell anyone, not until we'd told Nadia.'

'I'm sorry, Duncan,' she said, taken aback at the sight of his clenched jaw again, 'I didn't think it really mattered.'

He stared at her incomprehensibly. 'Mattered,' he repeated. 'That it mattered is simply not the point.'

'Duncan, what's got into you?'

He seemed to consider this question for a moment, and then shook his head. 'You're right,' he said. 'It doesn't matter at all, and I'm sorry I snapped at you. Forgive me, darling?'

'Of course,' she said, relieved to see his face now returning to its normal composure. 'Let's get a drink and mingle, seeing as we've been left to our own devices.'

It wasn't long before Ellen recognised Janey, or a woman whom she took to be Janey. Duncan had found himself a hospital administrator to talk to and, bored with the conversation, she had wandered away and noticed a self-conscious-looking woman standing alone with an empty glass in her hand. She had a mass of dyed chestnut hair piled on top of her head with what looked like a stick pushed through it. From the way she was shifting her weight from one foot to the other she was either very nervous or desperate for the loo.

'Hello,' Ellen said, going over to her. 'Are you by any chance Susie's sister-in-law, Janey?'

'Yes,' she said, instantly on her guard, her eyes darting anxiously through several layers of mascara and eye-liner, 'how did you know?' She tried drinking from her empty glass.

'A lucky guess.' Ellen introduced herself.

'Oh, right, you're the woman Susie and Bonkers bought the house from. Nice place. What've you gone to – something even bigger and better?'

'I traded down,' Ellen replied noncommittally, and was glad when Janey didn't pursue the subject but said, 'I expect you know everyone here. Susie's told me about this gorgeous artist she's got working for her. Have you met him?'

'Yes, I have.'

'What's he like?' whispered Janey, moving in closer and wobbling slightly.

Ellen thought about this. It was a good question. Matthew Collins was really a bit of an enigma. He was strange, unlike most men she'd ever met. 'I'm afraid I don't know him well enough to say.'

'First impressions, then.'

Ellen laughed. 'Those are always dangerous.'

'But usually the best ones.'

Ellen's immediate opinion of Matthew was that he could be taciturn and brusque to the point of rudeness and that Hermione was right when she had said it was an air he affected to make himself superior. She was about to say this when she remembered his response to her suggestion that the Dark Peak was beautiful. 'I'd say he was a passionate man,' she said, 'the kind of man who when he feels something he feels it strongly.' She then recalled him kissing her for no apparent reason. 'He's also a bit on the spontaneous side.'

'He sounds a dream. Hey, we're not in competition, are we? I mean, you don't want him for yourself, do you?'

'Good grief, no.' Ellen laughed. She held up her hand. 'Look, I've just got engaged today.'

Janey admired the ring. 'It's an omen,' she said, suddenly sounding like Mystic Meg and staring into the distance. 'I can feel it. You're going to bring me luck tonight.' She tried another hopeful sip at her empty glass.

Only Hermione could make arriving at a party an event in itself, thought Ellen, when the Laburnum House trio eventually turned up. She was like the Queen Mother, standing in the hall for an age, escorted on one side by Matthew and her new neighbour Bernie on the other, as if waiting for all the guests to be lined up in front of her. She was dressed in a pastel floaty chiffon number – more echoes of the Queen Mum – and once she'd moved on from the hall she was determined to meet as many of Susie and Bonkers's friends as she could. 'Gracious,' Ellen heard her say after being introduced to yet another of Bonkers's work colleagues, 'and just how many gynaecologists have we here tonight, and is there a collective noun for such a gathering?'

'How about a handful?' suggested Bonkers, his bow tie now hanging limply round his neck like a string of sausages.

'Or a wombful,' put forward Bernie.

'Isn't that the strange woman I met at your cottage last week?' asked Duncan, coming over to join Ellen who was now on her own.

'Yes.' Ellen smiled. 'That's our Hermione, working the room like a real pro. Star quality or what?'

'But is she quite the full shilling, I find myself asking?'

'Oh, I doubt that. But she's been a wonderful friend to me since Roger left.'

He squeezed her hand. 'And now you've got me, darling.'

She leaned into him and kissed his cheek. 'So I have.'

'I'll go and get us another drink, shall I?'

Ellen watched Duncan go in search of the kitchen, where no doubt the bottles would be lined up on the granite worktops that she had spent weeks deliberating over when she had had the kitchen designed. It was strange being at a party in a house where she had once been the hostess. It was difficult not to rush about offering drinks and plates of food.

'You look deep in thought.' It was Matthew.

'Just remembering days gone by,' she said, when he came and stood beside her.

'In the circumstances, I think you're pretty brave coming here at all.'

'Not as brave as you.'

He stared at her, puzzled. 'What do you mean?'

'Oh, nothing.'

'Liar.'

'All right, I'll tell you. Susie's got someone lined up for you to meet. I've just met her. She's interesting in a—'

'Oh, hell!'

'There's always a chance you might like her.'

'Yeah, and I'm a Chinaman. Do me a favour and don't leave me alone with her.'

She laughed. 'You're a big boy, Matthew, you can look after yourself.'

He scowled. 'I bet it's the usual scenario. She's divorced and hunting for a new husband and Susie's told her I'm single.'

'And if you stay as obnoxious and as arrogant as that you'll end up single for the rest of your life and you'll deserve what you get.'

'Enlighten me. What will I get?'

'A lonely, miserable old age.'

He laughed cynically. 'While you, Ellen, will be a happy kept woman. Oh, yes,' he carried on, seeing the look of anger on her face, 'Hermione's told me all about your little ploy to catch yourself a rich husband. You must be very pleased with yourself, though how you'll feel in a few years' time when you realise your mistake is anybody's guess. Perhaps it will be you who's lonely and miserable.'

Ellen was livid. 'I don't think there's anything else I want to say to you. Goodbye.' She started to walk away from him.

'The truth always hurts,' he called after her.

She came back. 'The truth,' she hissed at him, 'is that you don't know what you're talking about. Duncan and I love each other and we're—'

'Love! Don't make me laugh! I've met your precious Duncan just now in the kitchen and he looks no more capable of loving another person than he is of climbing Everest.'

'And I suppose you're an expert on both counts, are you?'

Matthew opened his mouth to reply but then thought of all the disastrous relationships in his life. 'I've climbed Helvellyn,' he said, with a slow lopsided smile spreading over his face.

Despite herself, Ellen couldn't help but return it.

'I'm sorry,' he said. 'I shouldn't have sounded off at you like that. It's been one of those days. I don't find it easy working here, it's all the interruptions. Then when you said about Susie having got somebody lined up to meet me, it was the last straw.'

'Forget it,' Ellen said, her anger beginning to subside.

'Seeing as I've made one apology, there's – there's something else I should make amends for. I, um . . .' He hesitated and his eyes wavered from her face. He suddenly looked overcome with embarrassment.

Ellen guessed what was coming next and was curious to see how he was going to explain himself. 'Yes?' she said, helpfully.

He cleared his throat. 'You could try to make this easier for me.'

Ellen opened her eyes wide. 'How so?' she asked innocently. 'I don't know what you're talking about.'

'Yes, you bloody well do,' he growled. He pushed up the sleeves on his denim shirt then folded his arms across his chest and stared down at his shoes, his tall frame slightly hunched.

She smiled, touched by his awkwardness. 'Is it something to do with yesterday?'

'Well, of course it is. What else could it be to do with?'

'For someone making an apology you don't seem very penitent. Is this a new phenomenon for you?'

'Ye gods! You're the most infuriating woman I've ever met.'

'You should get out more.'

He rolled his eyes. 'Will you just shut up and let me get this over with. When I kissed you, I . . .' He unfolded his arms, pushed his hands into his jeans pockets and tried again. 'I don't know what came over me and I want you to know that I don't normally go around behaving like that.' He ran his hand over his chin and finally met her gaze. 'Is there anything I can do to make amends for what I did?'

'Yes,' she said, seeing Duncan coming towards them, 'don't mention it ever again.'

'Darling, sorry I've been so long, here's your wine. Drink up and let's get going, I'm bored with all this medical talk.'

'Matthew's not a doctor,' she said lightly. 'Try talking to him.'

Duncan gave Matthew a cursory glance. 'Have we met?'

'A few moments ago in the kitchen.'

Ellen saw the expression on Matthew's face. 'Matthew's a painter,' she said hurriedly. 'He's doing a job for Susie and Bonkers.'

'Wouldn't have thought Orchard House needed much decorating,' Duncan said.

Matthew had heard enough. 'I'll see you, Ellen.' He turned and collided with a woman who had a ridiculous bird's nest stuck on her head. 'Sorry,' he muttered, without even stopping. But she came after him.

'Matthew Collins?' she asked. 'Susie's artist?'

He froze. Was this the woman so keen to meet him? 'No,' he said, 'you've got the wrong man, I'm not Susie's anything.'

He walked out of the room and out of Orchard House.

22

When Ellen and Duncan went in search of Susie and Bonkers to say goodbye they found them in the kitchen with Janey who was clearly upset and hugging a box of Kleenex to her chest.

'Anything we can do?' Ellen offered hesitantly. She had witnessed the brief exchange between Matthew and Janey only a few moments ago and had also seen Janey literally disintegrate before her eyes and then stumble away in the direction of the kitchen. What *could* Matthew have said?

'Family problems are best left to those personally involved,' Duncan said, holding Ellen firmly by the arm and edging her back towards the door.

'She told me he was passionate,' came a reproachful voice from behind Bonkers as Ellen allowed herself to be propelled out of the kitchen. 'She said he was spontaneous.'

Remembering her manners Susie quickly followed them. 'Gosh,' she said, when they were out in the hall, 'I don't know what to say. Poor Janey, she's always been highly strung and she was so hurt when Matthew refused to talk to her. Apparently he was quite rude. I've no idea where he is now, have you?'

Ellen shook her head. 'Sorry, I haven't got a clue. Will she be all right?'

'Oh, heavens, yes. A good dose of black coffee and she'll be as right as rain. She really shouldn't drink so much. And Bonkers is too soft with her, of course. It's as plain as the nose on my face that he needs to take a firmer line, but you know what men are like with their families – duty and the desire to hush everything up turns them into complete jelly babies every time.'

Ellen felt Duncan stiffen at her side and, conscious that Susie was unintentionally tweaking a raw nerve in him, she inched towards the front door and raised her hand. 'It's been lovely, Susie,' she said, 'but it's been a long day for us and we ought to be off. Tell Hermione I'll catch up with her tomorrow. Goodnight.'

As Duncan drove the short distance to Spring Bank Cottage, Ellen thought that the evening had been anything but lovely. Poor Duncan, he must have had an awful night. First Nadia and her coldness towards him and then a party at which he'd obviously felt out of place.

'I shan't come in,' he said, bringing the car to a stop outside the cottage and alongside Johnny Foreigner, which Ellen had left there after she'd driven back from Crantsford Hall with Duncan following behind. 'Like you said to your friend, it's been a long day.' He leaned over and pecked her lightly on the cheek. 'Goodnight, darling. I'll ring you in the morning.'

Duncan didn't go straight home – he knew exactly what would be waiting for him when he did get back. He wanted some time on his own, so he drove through Crantsford and then out onto the dual carriageway. It was late enough for there to be barely any traffic on the road. He turned up the volume on Mahler's 'Das Lied von der Erde' and pressed his foot on the accelerator. He felt the surge of the engine and his spirits lifted.

Cruising at a hundred and twenty-five he caught sight of a flashing blue light in his rear-view mirror. He jerked his foot off the accelerator and hoped that he'd seen the police car before his speed had been registered. There was always the chance that they weren't interested in him anyway and that they were on their way to deal with something more worthwhile than his Highway Code misdemeanour.

He was wrong. The police car slowed behind him and flashed its lights for him to pull over into the nearest lay-by.

Two officers got out of the Ford Sierra and sauntered towards him. 'Good evening,' one of them said when Duncan activated the electric window; the other was already making a note of the number plate. 'I shan't insult your intelligence by asking if you were in a hurry, sir, but do you have any idea just how fast you were—?'

'Oh, spare me the niceties and just get on with it, will you?'

The two officers looked at each other. 'It'll be a pleasure.'

Matthew wasn't sure what had rattled him most – Ellen's gross stupidity or Duncan's patronising manner.

'What a complete and utter jerk!' he said out loud. 'And with more airs and graces than you could shake a stick at.'

He threw himself into an armchair in Hermione's sitting-room and kicked off his shoes. 'What the hell does she see in him anyway?' He poked his finger into a hole in the heel of one of his Wallace and Gromit socks – a Christmas present from Bridget last year.

It had been a waste of an evening and it was the last time he'd allow himself to be talked into doing something he didn't want to do. He'd had enough of that with Bridget. 'Parties are important,' she would say in the face of his apathy. 'It's how you build up an effective network; it's how you get on in life.' He would then be forced into spending a mind-numbing evening being bored to death by sharp-faced young men in city suits, ever more convinced that if there was one thing he didn't want, it was to get on in life. He would never be so stupid as to say that he was ambivalent about money because he wasn't – he'd had enough lean times in his chosen profession to appreciate the benefits of a steady income – but he could think of nothing worse than sacrificing oneself on the high altar of success and ambition for fear of being considered an also-ran.

It was crazy that he'd got involved with Bridget in the first place. It hadn't really been the age difference that had made them incompatible towards the end – she'd been twelve years younger than him – so much as the difference in their lifestyles. But he had come to realise that for Bridget that had all been part of the attraction. For a smart City girl based in London, a boyfriend who was not only an artist but who was older and lived in what she referred to as Melvyn Bragg country was as much a turn-on as a bit of rough for a middle-class housewife. He smiled at this comparison and at the knowledge that in the early stages of their relationship it had flattered his ego that someone like Bridget had been interested in him at all.

He heard the sound of laughter coming from the hall and then footsteps. Hermione came into the room, followed by Bernie. Matthew was struck by how comfortable they looked together: it was as if he had seen Hermione and Bernie come through that door a million times before.

'There you are, Matthew,' exclaimed Hermione, settling herself on the sofa and covering most of it with her chiffon dress. Bernie squeezed in next to her. 'You wouldn't believe the kerfuffle you've caused next door. What on earth did you do to the poor girl?'

Matthew shrugged. 'I don't know what you mean. She was perfectly all right when I left her. In fact, I even apologised.'

'Well, it couldn't have been much of an apology. The idiotic wretch was quite beside herself.'

'If you ask me,' joined in Bernie, 'she's a sandwich short of a loaf.' He and Hermione laughed.

Matthew was puzzled at Hermione's rudeness towards Ellen. It wasn't like her to be disloyal to those she was fond of. 'I wouldn't have expected you to describe Ellen as an idiotic wretch,' he said.

'Good heavens, we're not talking about Ellen,' exclaimed Hermione.

'Then who, for crying out loud?'

'Bonkers's sister, of course. Janey.'

'I didn't even know he had one,' Matthew said dismissively, 'and I've certainly never met her.'

'But you must have. She said you were beastly to her.'

'Then she's got the wrong man, either that or she's off her head.'

Bernie chuckled. 'My money's on the latter.'

Matthew frowned. 'Is this some kind of wind-up, or have you both been drinking too much next door?'

'Neither,' Hermione said firmly. 'In fact, Bonkers is so cross he's talking about withdrawing the commission.'

'What?' Matthew said, exasperated. He wasn't bothered about losing the work but he was bothered by what people were saying about him. 'I was there less than half an hour and the only woman I spoke to was Ellen.'

'Not a woman with lots of hair piled up on top of her head?'

'There was a woman like that,' Matthew said slowly. 'She wanted to know who I was . . .'

'And?'

'I lied. I said I wasn't Matthew Collins. But that was all. Then I came home. From the way you're talking, anyone would think I'd attacked her.'

'She'd probably have made less fuss if you had!' joked Bernie.

Matthew stood up. He pushed his hands inside his trouser pockets and hunched his shoulders. 'Well, that's her problem. I'm off to bed.'

'Time I was going as well,' said Bernie, getting to his feet.

'Yes,' yawned Hermione, 'you'd better rush back in time for Matron to tuck you into bed.'

'Now there's an idea.'

After Bernie had left, Matthew offered to lock up and bring Hermione a mug of warmed milk. He knocked on her bedroom door and went in. She was in bed with an old Aran cardigan draped over her shoulders and she was brushing her long white hair. He was so used to seeing it pinned up on her head that he was surprised at how long it really was. She looked older, though, and slightly diminished, not the Hermione he knew.

'You're staring at me,' she said, putting the brush on the bedside table and taking the mug from him.

'Sorry.' He sat on the edge of her bed.

'Something on your mind?' she asked.

'No, not especially.'

'You sure?'

'Drink your milk and mind your own business.'

She raised the mug to her lips and stared at him over the rim. 'So what did you apologise to Ellen for?'

He stood up and walked over to the chest of drawers opposite the bed. It was covered in bits and bobs of cheap jewellery and old pots of cream and powder. A thick layer of dust dulled everything to the same peppery hue, except for the necklace Hermione had been wearing for the party. He picked up the string of amber beads. It had been a present to her from his father and she usually kept it hidden in a drawer because, as she had told him years ago, it was the only thing in the house of any real value – sentimental value, that was. He had teased her at the time that she thought so little of his paintings at Laburnum House.

'Did it have anything to do with you kissing Ellen during the picnic?' Hermione asked, catching his eye in the mirror above the chest of drawers.

This was the first time Hermione had referred to what she'd seen through her binoculars and the wonder was that it had taken her this long to get round to quizzing him. He came back to the bed and sat down.

'Maybe,' he said.

She humphed. 'And what's that supposed to mean?'

'I said some other things to her as well . . . I think I went too far.'

They gazed at each other for a moment. 'Well, go on, then,' Hermione said. 'Tell me what you said or I shall never sleep tonight.'

'I . . . Now, just a moment, Hermione,' he said, getting to his feet again, 'I'm not some silly schoolboy having to report my every move.'

'Then stop acting like one. If you fancy yourself in love with Ellen, do something about it and do it before it's too late.'

He scowled and went and stood at the end of the bed. He rested his hands on the brass rail. 'Who said anything about love?'

Hermione smiled at him beneath her hooded eyes. 'I saw you, Matthew, through my binoculars. I saw the way you held Ellen and the way you kissed her. I don't know what Ellen thought about it but I've a pretty good idea what was going through your mind at the time. Now, come back here and sit by me. We need to discuss what you're going to do.'

He banged his hand on the bedstead. 'Nothing!' he exploded. 'I'm going to do absolutely nothing because she's determined to marry that prat of a solicitor and live out the rest of her life in hypocritical splendour!'

'Don't be such a defeatist, Matthew.'

'But it's true. You told me yourself that her intention was to marry for money and that's exactly what Duncan can offer her.'

'Then make her realise that it would be better to marry for love.'

He shook his head violently. 'Love be damned! It's ready cash she wants.'

'No, Matthew,' Hermione said. 'Ellen isn't as mercenary as that. It's security she's looking for, and she truly believes Duncan will provide her with that.'

'Then she's a bloody fool.'

Hermione smiled. 'Quite possibly, but before you condemn her completely why don't you calm down and let me tell you what Ellen has gone through. Then maybe you'll understand why she's so keen to marry Duncan.'

23

Janey was all contrition. 'I'm sorry,' she croaked, concentrating all her efforts on lowering her cup of black coffee. When the cup was safely installed in its saucer she risked a bleary-eyed glance at Susie across the breakfast table. 'I'm sorry,' she repeated.

Susie carried on reading about the average niacin intake from a bowl of Raisin Wheats.

'What more can I say?'

Susie raised her eyes from the cereal packet. 'But it's not as though it's the first time, is it?' she said. She was trying to be stern, but it wasn't easy. She and Bonkers had discussed Janey for some time when they'd eventually collapsed into bed, just after three in the morning, hours after the last of their guests had left but only minutes after Janey had finally calmed down. Bonkers had agreed that something had to be done, but he hadn't come up with any solutions to the problem.

According to Bonkers, Janey had always been one for the dramatics. At the age of eleven she had been sent away to school in the mistaken belief that life as a boarder would be a great leveller. In Susie's opinion boarding school helped only those who were already level-minded, like herself: she'd thoroughly enjoyed her time away from home as a child. But sending a crackpot like Janey off to a school hundreds of miles from home might be convenient for those left behind breathing continuous sighs of relief, but for the poor soul in question – and not to mention the poor souls cooped up with said crackpot – life had been bound to be anything but a bed of roses. Bonkers's stories of Janey away at school were legionary. There were tales of Janey running away, tales of Janey smuggling a pet rabbit into the dormitory, only to forget about it tucked away in her trunk and then discover it days later, stiff and smelly. There were tales of Janey starving herself and, the worst of the lot, was the story of Janey making herself sick by drinking a glass of salty water before breakfast every day and pretending that she was suffering from morning sickness.

Susie knew as well as the next person that these acts of insubordination had all been cries for help and she felt genuinely sorry for her sister-in-law but, really, it could not go on. Janey was twenty-nine years old, and it was time for her to start acting in a responsible adult manner.

'Janey,' she said firmly, 'you're a dear sweet girl and you know how fond Bonkers and I are of you, Millie and Floss too, but last night was the final straw. Bonkers agrees with me. You need help in sorting out your muddled life.'

'What kind of help?' Janey whispered. 'Men in white coats?'

'There you go again, Janey, overreacting.'

'Well, what do you mean?'

'Ever thought that you might be ... well, you know –?'

Janey looked blankly back at Susie. 'Might be what?'

Oh Lord, how did one go about this bit? How did one tactfully suggest that one's sister-in-law was a touch barmy, that she was about as stable as a two-legged stool. 'Look, Janey,' she said, steeling herself, 'have you ever considered some kind of counselling?'

Janey's face crumpled. 'You think I'm doolally, don't you?' And seeing Bonkers coming into the kitchen, she struggled to her feet and went to him. She was crying now.

'Susie thinks I'm crazy,' she bawled into the shoulder of his dressing gown.

'Of course you're not,' he said, patting her reassuringly on the back.

Bonkers gave Susie a helpless stare and Susie returned it with a but-you-agreed-we-had-to-do-something expression.

An hour later Janey had packed her overnight bag and was preparing to drive home to her flat in Chester, where she said Dionysus would be waiting for her with nothing more accusing to strike her with than his slightly smelly litter tray.

The atmosphere in the hall when the goodbyes were being said was cold and unforgiving, and when Janey had gone Bonkers followed Susie into the kitchen. They had been so occupied with Janey last night that the clearing up from the party was still waiting to be done. Empty bottles jostled for space with plates and dishes of uneaten party food, and everywhere they looked there were screwed-up napkins and dirty glasses, hundreds of them.

The breakfast dishes were now adding to the chaos, and Susie pushed up her sleeves ready to tackle the mess. She was cross, though. Very cross. Rarely was she ever seriously angry with Bonkers, but today she was. She sensed him standing behind her.

'You could help,' she said, bending down to open the bin. Well, why shouldn't he? It was his sister's fault that this lot was still here this morning.

'What shall I do, sweetie?'

She banged the lid down on the bin. 'You can stop calling me sweetie for a start!'

Bonkers took a step back. 'Susie, whatever is the matter?'

She turned on him. 'It's you. You and your silly sister. I was just getting through to her when you walked in and totally undermined me.' She mimicked his voice, ' "*Of course you're not.*" Well, pardon me, but I don't share that opinion and you agreed in bed that it was time we did something. You agreed and then reneged just at the crucial moment.'

Bonkers laughed. 'I say, Susie, you don't think you're taking this whole thing a touch too seriously, do you?'

'It's not funny!'

'Yes, it is.' He came over and hugged her. 'Dear sweet little Susie. I've never seen you so uptight before. Why don't you go into town and cheer yourself up and let me sort out this mess?'

Susie contemplated this proposition. Trusting Bonkers to do anything in the kitchen was something she seldom did but, on the other hand, some new shoes would be nice.

Simon had finished packing up his car and Ellen watched him coming towards the barn.

'All done?' she asked, as he came in.

'Yep, including all the things you said I'd forget.'

She smiled. 'So when will I get to see you again? Not that I'm putting any pressure on you.'

'That's one thing you never do, Mum. But I guess it won't be for some time. It's going to be a hectic term.'

'Mm . . . All those summer balls and fun and games on the Cherwell, no doubt.'

'I was talking about work, Mum.'

'Come on.' She laughed. 'Let's get you on your way.'

They walked over to the bursting Fiat in the warm sunshine. It had rained in the night but now the clouds were little more than fluffy specks in the sky and a bright sun shone down, picking out the wisps of golden weeping willow trailing the surface of the stream.

'I suppose you'll be putting this on the market soon, won't you?' Simon said, gazing around him.

'I guess so,' she said.

'Shame.'

'Simon?'

'Nothing.' He opened the car door.

'Oh, no, you don't,' Ellen said. 'You're not leaving until you've explained what you meant just now.'

'It's no big deal.' He shrugged. 'I just quite like this place. It's got something about it.'

'You're right,' she agreed. 'Wet rot, dry rot and any other crumbling-house disease you'd care to mention.'

'Come on, Mum, where's your soul?'

'Oh, I'm all out of that.'

'Well, don't be. And just because you're marrying some rich bloke who can give you anything you want, don't go thinking that the things for free in life don't matter any more.'

She stared at him, shocked. 'Simon, is that how you see me?'

'It happens to the best of people.'

'But—'

'Cheerio, Mum. I'll give you a ring some time next week.'

Ellen watched him drive off and wondered how it was that some of the most important things people had to say were often relayed as postscripts to a conversation. Had Simon done it deliberately? Had he kept back his heavily weighted statements for when it was too late to discuss them properly?

He hadn't said all that much about her marrying Duncan. She'd tried to get him to talk about it late last night when Duncan had dropped her off after the party at Orchard House, but all she'd managed to get out of him was that he hoped she would be happy.

This noncommittal response worried her. It wasn't so much that she needed Simon's approval to go ahead, it was more that she couldn't bear his indifference, which in her opinion was the next best thing to disapproval.

'It's your life, Mum,' he'd told her. 'If he's the right man for you, then go for it.'

But that wasn't what she wanted to hear. She wanted him to say, 'Duncan's a really great bloke and I can see how much he loves you.' That was the confirmation and reassurance she was after, not this go-ahead-you're-a-grown-woman-free-to-make-your-own-decisions routine.

It was most frustrating.

Going back into the barn she heard footsteps on the gravel beyond the cottage. She turned to see Matthew coming along the lane. When he saw her he waved. She wondered what he wanted. After their conversation at Orchard House last night she thought they'd said all they were ever likely to say to each other. To her surprise she found she was pleased that this was not the case. There was something comfortably familiar about the sight of him as he strolled across the car park. She supposed it was the casual way in which he dressed. As on other occasions when she'd seen him he was wearing faded jeans and a loose-fitting shirt tucked in at the waist with the sleeves rolled up to his elbows.

'I met the postman at the top of the lane and thought I'd save him a trip,' he said, when he drew level. He handed her a bundle of mail.

'Thank you.' She watched him stare over towards the cottage, and then at the bank and the stream. He seemed lost in his own thoughts.

When he returned his attention to her he said simply, 'It's a nice spot here.'

What was this? First Simon and now Matthew going on about what a bijou residence she had.

He caught the expression on her face. 'But I suppose you'd prefer to be back at Orchard House, right? May I see inside the barn?'

'Feel free.' She stepped aside to let him pass. She followed him inside and went over to the bench where she was preparing a garland of herbs and dried flowers for a customer's kitchen. She flicked through the pile of letters

Matthew had just handed her and was about to condemn them all as bills when the last one showed itself as another letter from France – Roger must have found out her address.

She stared at the letter, unprepared for this second assault from Provence. The first still lay unopened on the kitchen windowsill: she had never got round to summoning up the courage to read it. Now it would have a companion.

'Not all bills, I hope,' Matthew said, coming over to her.

'No,' she replied. 'Though I wish they were.'

'Bad news?'

She bit her lip. 'Probably.' She tapped the offending envelope on the counter. 'It's from my ex-husband.'

'Oh.' Matthew wasn't sure what to say. After his conversation last night with Hermione, when she'd told him all about Roger, he'd come here this morning with the sole intention of trying to make his peace with Ellen and prove to her that he wasn't the curmudgeonly devil – Hermione's words – he had so far made himself out to be. The last thing he'd expected to happen was that he'd end up acting as a messenger boy for her ex-husband. 'What do you think he wants?'

'I've no idea.'

'Open it and see.'

She frowned.

'Come on, what's the worst it could say?'

'That he's sorry and wants to come back,' she almost whispered.

'And is that an option you'd consider?' He held his breath. It was bad enough knowing that he was competing against Duncan the Incredibly Wealthy One, without having the complication of an ex-husband also vying for a position in Ellen's heart.

'Of course not,' she snapped. 'I never want to see Roger again as long as I live.'

'Brilliant!'

She looked at him.

'I mean, it's good that you know your own mind so clearly. So why not simply get it over with and see what the letter says?'

'Trouble is, there's another in the kitchen. It came a few days ago.'

'And you've not read that either?'

She shook her head. 'I wanted Simon to do it for me but it got forgotten, what with Duncan and our engagement, and now he's gone.'

Matthew thought about what Ellen had just said. If she'd asked Simon to read the first letter it probably meant she didn't want to bother Duncan with it. Was this his chance to absolve himself by stepping in and offering his services? 'Would it help for a stranger to read the letters for you?'

She raised her eyes from the envelope in her hand. 'Meaning you?'

'Why not?'

'I wouldn't describe you as a stranger exactly.'

'What would you describe me as?' *Shit!* He couldn't believe he'd just said that. Just what the hell was happening to him that he was going around talking like some clever-arsed character out of a book?

'I don't know,' she answered, with a cautious smile. 'You don't seem a stranger exactly, not now, but you are strange. You do odd things like kiss women whom you've only just met.' She expected him to turn away embarrassed and to hunch his shoulders and fold his arms like he had at Orchard House. But he didn't.

'If you think I'm going to apologise again for that, you're wrong,' he said. 'It's not something I make a habit of.'

'The kissing bit, or the apologising?'

His face broke into his lopsided smile. 'Both,' he said.

'I seem to remember you saying last night that I was the most infuriating woman you'd ever met, so why the sudden desire to help me?'

'And if you recall our conversation correctly I also asked if there was anything I could do to make amends. I'd like to help you . . . if you'll let me.'

Ellen considered his offer. She lowered her eyes to the envelope in her hand. She was tempted. Very tempted. It would at least get it over and done with. All he had to do was read through the sheets of paper and tell her there was nothing to worry about. Except she knew in her heart that it wouldn't be as simple as that.

'You could always ask Duncan?' Matthew said, sensing her indecision and deciding to test her.

'No,' she said briskly. 'I don't want to bother Duncan, he's far too busy. And anyway it wouldn't be right, would it? Not my fiancé reading my ex-husband's letters.'

'I suppose not.'

'I need someone objective, someone . . . someone detached from me.'

Matthew hesitated. Her words were uncomfortably reminiscent of a conversation between him and Bridget one night in bed. 'I never feel I'm with the real you when we make love,' she'd said. 'You keep yourself so private at times, even at the most intimate of moments. It isn't good to be this detached. You must learn to give something of yourself.' She'd been quite right in her little lecture. He doubted whether he'd ever revealed the real him when he had been with her.

'I think you'll find me suitably detached,' he said, his voice perfectly neutral.

Ellen ran her hand through her hair. It was make-your-mind-up time. 'Oh, come on, then,' she said, remembering that these days her life was supposed to be spontaneous and free of self-doubt. 'Let's go over to the cottage right now and you can help me sort out Roger once and for all. And then you can laugh at me for my stupidity.'

24

Ellen watched Matthew's face intently, scrutinising his every eye movement for clues to what Roger had to say for himself. Of course, it would have been easier to have read the letters herself, but that would have taken more courage than she possessed right now. Coward that she was, she didn't even have the nerve to see how many lines Roger had scribbled.

'Well?' she asked at last, aware that Matthew had gone very quiet. 'What does he say? Has he run out of money?'

Matthew composed his face. 'It would seem so,' he said simply.

'And?'

He lowered his eyes and started folding the letter with great care.

'That can't be all. Surely there's more.'

'There is, but I don't think you should bother yourself with it.'

'He's not coming back, is he?'

Matthew shook his head.

'Has he asked for money?'

'Like I said, don't even think about it.'

It was no good. She had to know. 'How much? How much is he asking for?'

'Does it make any difference if he's asking for ten pounds or a thousand pounds?'

She didn't answer at first, but went over to the window-seat and straightened the cushions. 'Does he say why he needs the money? Is he ill? Is that it?'

Matthew's face hardened. 'Yes, I'd say he was ill, quite sick in fact.'

Ellen thought of all the times she'd wished for Roger to fall victim to some incurable disease. 'On a scale of one to ten, how ill would you say?'

Matthew stared at her. He was at a complete loss as to what to say or do. All he knew was that through the need to ingratiate himself with Ellen he now found himself in an impossible situation. He should never have come here this morning. He should have thrown some things into a bag while he was not wanted at Orchard House over the weekend, gone for a drive and found himself an interesting view to paint. But no! He'd been arrogant enough to think that all he had to do was show a little sympathy towards Ellen and she'd be bowled over by him. Whereas the truth of the matter was that he was now caught up in something he was sure she would rather he knew nothing about. He glanced down at the letter in his hand. If only he could get rid of it without Ellen reading the contents. But how? And there was the other letter as well.

'What's wrong, Matthew? He's . . . he's not dying, is he?'

'If you want my opinion, you should have a ceremonial bonfire,' he waved the letter in his hand along with the unopened one, 'and then forget about him.' He tried to sound casual, flippant, even.

'But you haven't answered my question,' Ellen persisted. She was beginning to be slightly annoyed by Matthew's evasiveness. 'Is he or is he not dying?' Having wanted Roger dead it was unnerving to consider the possibility that her wish might come true. She remembered Hermione telling her that the danger about wishing for something was that sometimes that wish was granted – 'Careful what you wish for,' she'd said in the past.

Matthew still hadn't answered her.

'Oh, this is hopeless,' she said. 'Give it to me and let me see what he's got to say for himself.'

'No!' But he wasn't quick enough. Ellen snatched the letter out of his hands.

'I just need to know,' she said. 'Then I can put this behind—' But her voice broke off as she began to read Roger's familiar handwriting and took in his message.

Matthew saw the disbelief on Ellen's face, then the horror and finally the humiliation. Last came the realisation that he, too, had read the same offensive words. She slowly screwed up the letter into a tight ball. She didn't look at him.

'He must have been drunk when he wrote it,' Matthew said pragmatically. Still she didn't look at him.

'Or, like I said, he's sick. Sick in the head.' He placed the second letter on the dresser behind him and reached out to Ellen. He touched her shoulder lightly. She stiffened. 'Forget him,' he said gently. 'He's just trying it on. You have to be strong and ignore the letter. Blackmail only works when the victim is weak.'

'But why?' she murmured, turning her head away from him, unable to look him in the eye. 'Why's he doing this to me? Hasn't he done enough already?' She began to cry. 'He took everything I had,' she sobbed, 'he humiliated me and threw me away . . . and now this.' She covered her face with her hands. 'Why?'

Unable to bear the sight of her suffering, Matthew took her in his arms to comfort her. It was an instinctive response and he didn't think twice about it. He held her tightly, willing her hurt to pass. He knew, though, that it wouldn't be as easy as that. Roger must have hurt Ellen badly in the past and from what his vile letter said he had every intention of continuing to do so. Matthew's heart went out to her, every inch of him wanting to protect her. Without thinking what he was doing he stroked her shoulders, slowly, reassuringly, gradually working his hands up towards her neck and then running his fingers through her fine hair. But suddenly he was conscious of his heart slamming inside his ribcage. He caught his breath and swallowed and with the greatest of effort kept his hands from moving any further. Very slowly, though, Ellen lifted her head from his chest. Don't do that, he thought, just don't look at me. Not now.

Oblivious to his unspoken words she gazed into his face. He swallowed again but knew he was trapped, held by the expression in her sad misty blue eyes and by his desire for her. He recalled now the moment a few days ago when he'd quite literally lost his wits and kissed her. It was the same now. He was no more in control of his emotions today than he had been that day of the picnic. He lowered his head to her lovely upturned face and kissed her fleetingly on the mouth. Finding no resistance he kissed her again, gently parting her lips with his tongue, and when she kissed him back and he felt the pressure of her hands linked around his neck and the sway of her body moving against his, he dared to dream that she might feel for him just a fraction of what he felt for her. He wanted to make love to her and he could think of nothing but the joy that their love-making would bring him and when Ellen started unbuttoning his shirt he knew with certainty it was what she wanted too.

They didn't speak and they didn't stop kissing, not even when they fumbled to get out of their clothes and slipped breathlessly to the floor clutching each other. Their love-making was clumsy and frantic and at one stage they were both helpless with laughter as they bumped their heads on the leg of a chair. Afterwards Matthew realised that never before in his life had he been so consumed with the act of simply loving a woman ... and never before had he given so much of himself. But when he turned to look at Ellen there were tears in her eyes.

They both heard the sound of an approaching car but it was Ellen who reacted first.

Immediately she was up on her feet and scrambling into her clothes. With one leg in her jeans she hopped over to the window.

'I don't believe it,' she cried, 'it's La Carter! Quick, get dressed and get out of here. No, second thoughts, stay where you are and don't move, not until I get back.'

If it wasn't such an anticlimax to what had just taken place Matthew would have laughed. Disappointed, though, he watched Ellen finish dressing and then launch herself out of the cottage. He pulled on his trousers and wandered through to the kitchen. He made himself some coffee and, while waiting for the kettle to boil, threw Roger's letters in the bin and wondered what would happen next between him and Ellen.

If he was honest it didn't bear thinking about.

Taking his cup of coffee with him he went upstairs to see if there was any chance of a shower.

*

Ellen was struggling to keep her composure while Nadia hurled one heavily loaded statement at her after another.

'*When* you marry Duncan,' she was saying, 'you must realise that you're not just marrying any old man. Duncan has his peculiarities.'

'Yes,' Ellen said, barely listening. She was too preoccupied with peering out of the window over to the cottage to be bothered with what Nadia had to say – there were also one or two thoughts running through her head demanding her attention, her immediate attention!

She couldn't believe what had just happened. She would have to talk to Matthew, and talk to him seriously. It was madness what they'd just done. It was a heat-of-the-moment thing. These things happen.

But never to her!

Oh, in heaven's name, never to her!

She snapped her eyes shut and tried not to think of the expression on Matthew's face when his hands had lingered over her body. She blamed herself entirely. He'd only been trying to comfort her but the effect of his arms around her had been so potent that suddenly every bit of her had ached to be touched. It had been so long since anyone had held her, really held her. When he'd kissed her she had been staggered at the intensity of her reaction. All her senses had been thrown into disarray and she'd wanted nothing but to make love with him. She had never before experienced a need so acute. Sex with Roger had been a very serious business and had always been planned precisely around his needs. Even in the early stages of their marriage it had never been a spontaneous act of love where they'd collapsed to the floor clamouring for each other. And towards the end of their life together his desire and passion had been squashed altogether by obsession and fantasy as he'd concentrated on forcing her to conform to the current role he fancied.

She chewed her lip, bringing to mind Roger's letter. She had forgotten about the photographs he'd taken of her and now he was threatening to send them to Duncan if she didn't send him the money he wanted.

'Ellen, you're not listening to me, are you?'

She turned and faced her future mother-in-law. She offered a conciliatory smile. 'I'm sorry, it's just that it's been a busy morning.'

Nadia gave the empty barn a contemptible stare. 'I see no customers, Ellen.'

'I've got a lot of orders to be getting on with,' Ellen parried.

Again the same stare but this time it was aimed at Ellen.

It hadn't passed Nadia's notice that Ellen was looking decidedly dishevelled. Her face was flushed and her hair didn't look as if it had been brushed since she had got out of bed, and her shirt was creased as though somebody had been sitting on it, and worse still the buttons had been done up incorrectly and one side was longer than the other.

Then it dawned on Nadia. *That* was why she had seen Ellen tearing out of the cottage and racing across to the barn to meet her. She had been otherwise engaged.

So Duncan had lied. He'd said he was going to be playing golf this morning, whereas in fact he had been coming here to get up to heaven knows what with Ellen. Well, she'd teach the pair of them a lesson.

'Oh!' she cried, putting her hand to her forehead. 'I feel quite faint. It must be the lack of air in here. I don't suppose I could rest for a few moments in your lovely little cottage?'

'No!' Ellen almost screeched.

Aha! thought Nadia. It was just as she suspected. She reached out to the counter for support. 'I think it's one of my migraines.'

Ellen was horrified. 'Perhaps if you go outside for some fresh air you'll feel better.'

She led Nadia to the door and the awaiting cure. Immediately Nadia said that the sun was too strong. 'Just let me sit in the cool of your sweet little cottage,' she implored. 'And maybe a glass of water would help.'

Ellen felt like Snow White. 'Sure you're not trying to palm off a juicy red apple?' she wanted to ask. 'Why don't you go and sit on the bank and I'll bring you some water,' she said, with a flash of inspiration.

'I don't think so,' Nadia said pithily, giving Ellen a baleful expression and smoothing away an imaginary crease in her expensive Jaeger skirt. She then set off towards the cottage at a surprisingly brisk pace for one so faint.

Ellen dashed after her, glancing up at the cottage windows for any sign of Matthew. 'It's such a lovely day, isn't it?' she said loudly, hoping to alert Matthew. 'Really beautiful,' she shouted.

Nadia smiled to herself. This was fun. The look of panic on Ellen's face was a picture and no doubt the expression on Duncan's face when she routed him out would be equally interesting.

'Oh, look,' she exclaimed, pushing against the front door, 'it's not locked. You really should be more careful, Ellen, you never know who might come calling.'

Oh, how true!

The sitting-room was empty and the relief showed only too plainly on Ellen's face. Nadia quickly sized up the interior of the cottage. The only other room downstairs was the kitchen and she could see from where she was standing that it was empty, which left upstairs. 'May I use the bathroom?' she asked.

Ellen could feel herself sweating. She was pretty sure she was hyperventilating as well. Any more of this and she'd pass out. 'How about that glass of water?' she tried.

'Ellen,' Nadia said in a voice that clearly indicated that she would brook no argument, 'I think I'm going to be sick, I need the bathroom *now*!'

Ellen had no choice but to lead the way upstairs. Perhaps Matthew had hidden himself up there when he'd heard their approaching voices. Oh, please, let him be hiding under a bed, or in a wardrobe, anywhere but the bathroom.

It was when they were standing on the tiny landing directly in front of the bathroom that Ellen heard a sound so distinctive that she nearly toppled back down the stairs.

Somebody had just pulled the plug out of the bath!

She gripped the banister beside her, but Nadia smiled triumphantly and reached out to open the door.

25

While Ellen gulped and Nadia clutched at the silk scarf knotted at her neck, Matthew reached for a towel and tied it around his waist.

'This is Duncan's mother,' Ellen squeaked.

He nodded at Nadia, then flashed one of his lopsided smiles at Ellen.

'It was good of you to offer the use of your bathroom while Hermione's is out of action,' he said. 'Are you having problems with your plumbing as well?' he asked Nadia.

Ellen smiled inanely but Nadia had steam practically coming out of her ears and was already stomping off down the stairs. Hurriedly Ellen followed. When she caught up with her in the sitting-room Nadia turned on her.

'Don't think for one moment that I'm taken in by that little charade,' she hissed. 'I shall tell Duncan what's been going on here the minute I see him.' She moved to the front door and glared at Ellen one more time. 'I knew you were up to no good the moment I set eyes on you. I warned Duncan, but he wouldn't listen and now he'll have to.' This was said with great satisfaction.

'Nice woman,' Matthew said, coming downstairs and joining Ellen in the sitting-room when the front door had been slammed shut and the china on the dresser had stopped rattling. He was fully dressed now and bracing himself for an angry outburst from Ellen. She would have to take it out on someone and it might just as well be him.

But she didn't turn on him. Instead she moved across the small room to the window-seat where she dropped down and stared forlornly out through the panes of glass at Nadia's car disappearing along the lane.

'I knew it was too good to be true,' she said gloomily, resting her head against the window and drawing her knees under her chin. 'And now I'm stuck here for ever. No money. No future. And no bloody Marks and Spencer's shortbread! He was my escape from all of this,' she cried. 'Now I'm going to end up a lonely old lady shuffling around Woolie's with a plastic mac and one of those horrible string shopping bags.'

'Oh, stop exaggerating. Of course you're not going to end up like that.'

She turned and faced him, her eyes tinged with a dark hue. He realised too late that he'd been too sharp with her.

'And what would you know?' she said angrily.

He moved across the room. 'Look,' he said gently, kneeling beside her, 'why do you think you have to escape? What you've got here is—'

She pushed him aside and walked away. 'You wouldn't understand, you don't know anything about me.'

'I think I do,' he said. 'Hermione told me how difficult it's been for you since you've been on your own.'

'So,' she said hotly, the colour rising in her face, 'Hermione's been gossiping about me, has she?'

'Hermione doesn't gossip,' he snapped defensively. 'She was trying to make me understand why you had decided to marry Duncan. That was all.'

'I'm marrying Duncan—' She broke off. 'Correction, I *was* marrying Duncan because I . . . because I . . .'

'You can't say it, can you?' he challenged, crossing the room to her. 'You can't bring yourself to say that you love Duncan because you don't.'

'What rubbish! Of course I love Duncan. There, I've said it.'

He scowled and pushed his hands into his pockets.

Weariness got the better of Ellen. 'What does it matter, anyway? Nadia's probably already told Duncan about you being here in my house.'

He looked up at her. 'And what about me, Ellen?' he said softly.

'You?'

'Yes,' he replied evenly. 'Shouldn't we talk about us and what we just did? Or have you decided to block that out conveniently?'

'No!' she cried. 'No, I don't want to talk about us.' Anger now replaced her weariness. 'It's all your fault that I'm not marrying Duncan. If you hadn't come here this morning none of this would have happened. I should never have let you read Roger's letter.'

'But you did.' He reached out to touch her. 'Look, Ellen, I want you to know—' But he got no further.

'And where's Roger's other letter?' she demanded. 'Where have you put them?'

'I put them both in the bin,' he said firmly, 'where they belong.'

She marched out to the kitchen and he saw her flip off the lid. He watched her tear open the envelope and slide out a sheet of writing paper. He caught a glimpse of a photograph, but turned away to allow Ellen the privacy she deserved. He heard the sound of ripping followed by a stifled moan. He went to her, but she pushed him away.

'No!' she shouted, tears streaming down her cheeks. 'Don't touch me! Just leave me alone. I wish you'd never come! Can't you see the harm you've done already? If you hadn't interfered over those awful letters we wouldn't have . . . Oh, please, just get out!'

He knew it would be useless to argue with her – anger and hurt were making her irrational – so he did as she asked.

When he reached Orchard House in the Crescent he paused and considered the comparison between this house and the one in which Ellen now lived. He knew which he preferred, but he could well understand how difficult it must have been for Ellen to leave this large, elegant house for something so much smaller, especially when it was through no fault of her own. He thought of the man to whom she had once been married. Surely Roger couldn't always have been such a bastard, for how else would Ellen have stayed with him for so long? He tried to comprehend what must be going through Roger's mind to make him turn on someone whom he must have loved once. Or perhaps he hadn't ever loved Ellen. People married for the strangest of reasons. Like his own father. He had never understood what had possessed a man like Kit to marry a woman like Roberta. They were as different as ... as different as Ellen and Duncan.

Hell, the woman had lousy taste in picking husbands!

He was still standing in front of Orchard House when he heard the sound of his name being called out. It was that wretched Bonkers.

This he did not need. A bollocking from a ranting Terry-Thomas, whose sister he had supposedly insulted, was the last thing he was prepared to put up with right now.

'Now, look here,' Bonkers said, slapping towards him in a pair of flip-flops, 'I think we need to have a word or two.'

Matthew fixed him with a long, hard stare. 'Yes,' he said savagely, seized with the urge to add, '*go ahead, punk, make my day.*'

Bonkers cleared his throat. 'It really won't do,' he said. 'I can't possibly let you go around offending a member of my—'

'You're right.'

'Don't interrupt, please. I simply can't allow you to get away with—'

'You're absolutely right.'

'Now, look here. I wish you'd let a chap get his words out. I'm trying to tell you that—'

'Yeah, and I'm trying to tell you that I agree with you. I'm obviously – and to use your tiresome vernacular – a bounder of the worst order and shouldn't darken your door again. Which is fine by me, so I won't. And to make everything all right I won't even charge you for wasting my time. How's that? Reasonable enough, *old thing*?'

Bonkers's jaw was dangling somewhere on a level with his collar-bone. He struggled to speak but all that came out of his gaping mouth was a croaked, 'Yah. Thanks.'

'Don't mention it,' Matthew said, through clenched teeth. He turned and went.

Bonkers slapped his way back inside Orchard House with a feeling of dread. He had the feeling that when Susie got back from town there would be hell to pay. He had only meant to extract an apology from the fellow and bluster a few threats of disbanding the commission – just to show who was boss, that kind of thing – but now this had happened and Susie would be so disappointed not to have her painting.

He stood in the kitchen and looked at all the mess from last night, which he still hadn't got round to clearing up – he'd been having a doze in the sitting-room while the girls were playing upstairs. He'd better get on or Susie would be doubly furious with him.

Laburnum House was empty. Matthew went outside to the garden to find Hermione. But there was no sign of her stooped figure pottering among the overgrown herbaceous borders. Nor was she in the greenhouse.

He sat in the summerhouse in an old wicker chair and stretched out his long legs in front of him. Coming away from Orchard House he'd made up his mind what he was going to do. There was no point in him hanging around any longer. He'd lost the Buchanan commission, and despite what he felt for Ellen, there really didn't seem much to be gained from staying on in the hope she would calm down and see sense. No, he might just as well push off home before he made an even bigger fool of himself. When Hermione turned up from wherever she was he'd tell her he was going and then get on his way.

He tried to comfort himself with the thought that he could be home by early evening, and if the weather held up for tomorrow he'd have a day painting from his boat on Coniston Water. And with a bit of luck Coniston would be relatively peaceful with most of the tourists chasing daffodils up at Dora's Field.

Hermione had just thrashed Bernie at croquet and she was now relaxing comfortably on a sun-lounger on the terrace at the Lodge. Apart from one or two residents who weren't up to the trip, the rest had been taken into Manchester to see a matinée performance of the hit show *Grease* at the Palace Theatre.

'Not such a bad place, after all, is it, my little Hermaseta?' commented Bernie, picking a slice of orange from his tall glass and sucking the juice out of it.

'If you like that kind of thing,' she conceded. As much as it pained her, Hermione had to admit that she was impressed with the Lodge. The Management had transformed what had once been a large, scruffy, rambling old house into a magnificent property. There was an atmosphere of ease and elegant country home about the place that reminded Hermione of a lifetime ago when Laburnum House had had money lavished freely on it.

Bernie had insisted on giving her a guided tour when he'd invited her over for a game of croquet and she had wandered through the rooms aghast at the opulence of so many crystal chandeliers hanging from the high ceilings. She was impressed by the quantity of antique furniture everywhere and the delicate side tables dotted about the place offering an assortment of magazines and pretty glass bowls of wrapped sweets. There was even a library, which would have delighted the heart of any avid reader, and a snooker room that was already suitably stamped with the smell of cigars and brandy. And housed in a new extension was an indoor heated pool in the shape of a kidney – admittedly it was small and Hermione didn't much care for the look of some of the hoisting tackle hanging from the ceiling – but it was a pool all the same. There were several Jacuzzis – in which she could well imagine Bernie with a female resident for company – and everywhere there was the smell of lavender polish as well as the more luxurious fragrance of cut flowers beautifully arranged in expensive vases.

It was stylish. It was wholesome. It was comfortable. And it was a million miles away from the image Hermione had had in her mind of what the Lodge would be like.

Where was the whiff of disinfectant to cover up the sad smell of urine-soaked chairs and mattresses? Where was the pong of institutional cabbage and poached cod? And where, she wanted to know, was the hum of death and decay? Surely that should be lurking somewhere among the sumptuous brocade curtains and ankle-deep carpets? But try as she might – just to prove that she'd been right all along – Hermione could not find fault with the Lodge. Even the annexe, which had once been the stable block and which was now the medical wing, didn't look too sinister. Bernie had caught her eyeing a couple of oxygen tanks and he'd joked that they were for the Monday-morning scuba-diving lessons.

Joking apart, the Lodge had a lot going for it.

'How much does it cost?' she asked, staring out at the well-kept lawn and croquet hoops. 'To live here, that is. How much gelt?'

Bernie chuckled. 'Thinking of shacking up with me?'

She turned her gaze on him. 'I could do a lot worse.'

He laughed again and rattled his chest. 'They don't take any old codger,' he wheezed.

'They took you!'

It was late afternoon and a low sun was casting beams of soft light through the small windows of the barn; dust motes danced in the rays.

Ellen was waiting for the phone to ring, as she was convinced it would. Surely Nadia must have spilled her poisonous beans to Duncan by now. So why hadn't he phoned? Or was he, perhaps, never going to speak to her again? Was she to be consigned to the silent-reproach treatment and never given the opportunity to say that she was sorry? Because she was, and sorrier than she could say.

It had been a sad, depressing afternoon, despite there having been a steady flow of customers, none of whom had left empty-handed. On any other day she would have been delighted with the amount of money deposited in the till, but today it meant nothing to her. She wanted Duncan and the life she'd thought they would have together, not this life that had been thrust upon her.

At last the phone rang. She reached out to it straight away. Please let it be Duncan, please, oh, please, let it be Duncan. But she hesitated. What if it was? What was she going to say to him? How was she going to deny what his mother had seen with her own eyes? A naked man in her bathroom!

The phone carried on ringing, loud and shrill, demanding her attention. She snatched it up.

'Spring Bank Dried Flowers,' she said, trying to sound normal, even businesslike.

'Ellen?'

It *was* him!

'Ellen?'

She swallowed hard. 'Yes, Duncan, it's me.'

'You're very faint, you're going to have to speak up.'

She struggled to say something. Anything. 'How are you?'

'I'm fine. Now look, I'm on my mobile in the car. Can I come and see you? There's something we need to discuss.'

Her legs buckled beneath her. So Nadia *had* told him and he was playing it cool right to the end. He was coming to watch her squirm while she confessed her sins. How ironic, the solicitor who had once acted for her was now to be her judge and jury.

'Can't you . . .' her voice broke, 'can't you tell me on the phone?'

'No. I want to speak to you properly. It's important. I'm at the lights at the top of Church Walk, I'll be with you in less than two minutes.'

She was shaking when she saw his car appear in the lane. She watched him lock the car methodically and activate the alarm. The BMW pipped and winked its lights behind his back as he strode over to the barn. Her throat was dry and she had no idea how she was even going to speak to him let alone what she was going to say. She stayed on her side of the counter and pretended to be counting the money from the till.

'You look upset, Ellen,' he said, when he came in and stood opposite her. 'And I would imagine it has something to do with Nadia coming to see you this morning. Am I right?'

She nodded, wishing he'd just get on with it. Any minute now he'd pull out a barrister's wig and lean his elbows on the counter and make a proper job of cross-examining her.

And how did she plead?

Guilty. She was as guilty as hell. She didn't know what had possessed her, but yes, that morning, in a crazy moment she'd ripped off her clothes and made love on the floor with someone other than her fiancé.

'Ellen,' he said, reaching out to take her hands in his, 'I'm so sorry for what my mother's put you through today. She obviously came here with the sole intention of causing trouble between us. I know what she's up to and I want you to know that it's not going to stop me marrying you. Not ever. My mind's quite made up.'

Ellen didn't know whether she was hearing right. But hang on. Was this some subtle courtroom trick for catching out the defendant?

'Nadia told me some ridiculous story about finding a naked man in your bathroom this morning.' He shook his head disparagingly. 'I know she's against me ever marrying but to sink to these depths is so unseemly and, to be honest, she's to be pitied. But you saw what she was like last night. And in a way I'm glad you know what I have to put up with. I've given her a good telling-off and she's under clear instructions to stay away from you.' He came round to her side of the counter and slipped his arm around her waist. 'Darling,' he said, 'I want you to know that there's no danger of Nadia ever coming between us.'

PART TWO

August

The Song of the Nightshade Fairy

My name is Nightshade, also Bittersweet;
Ah, little folk, be wise!
Hide you your hands behind you when we meet,
Turn you away your eyes.
My flowers you shall not pick, nor berries eat,
For in them poison lies.

Cicely Mary Barker

26

The estate agent – Call-Me-Trudi from Harker and Company – walked purposefully from room to room. Every now and then she would stop and nod. 'Delightful,' she would say. Often this was followed by an enthusiastic reference to a *charming double aspect* or *an interesting recessed fireplace.* An *airy outlook* was another favourite expression, as was *flexible accommodation.* And as for the *tremendous potential,* well, there seemed no end to it. But when the young woman, with her clipped voice and matching suit, started talking about the old Belfast sink with its wooden drainer in the garden room as though it was a national treasure, Hermione wondered whether the pudding wasn't being over-egged. In her opinion the old sink was only fit to be ripped out, put in the garden and used as a trough for alpine plants. Highly sought after, my foot!

Hermione let Call-Me-Trudi climb the stairs alone to the top of the house. It was not that she lacked the energy to follow the young woman, it was more that she didn't want to see the look of recrimination on Kit's and Matthew's faces staring back at her accusingly from the wall in Matthew's attic room.

Once she had made the decision to sell Laburnum House, she had known it was the right thing to do, although it had taken the best part of the summer to take the plunge. Her accountant had greeted the news by getting to work on something he called a spread-sheet, which would outline how the proceeds from the sale could best be allocated to enable Hermione to meet the cost of the next stage in her life. She had kept her plans to herself, confiding only in Bernie, and the Management of the Lodge, who had discreetly pointed out that they couldn't guarantee a space for her just yet as they were currently full.

'So the bottom line is that I have to wait until somebody dies,' she had said bluntly to Bernie, very much to the point after speaking to the Management. This was a chilling thought, and brought home to her just what the Lodge was all about. And while driving into town in his ancient Jag for an afternoon treat of tea and scones at the Patisserie she told Bernie that she'd changed her mind. 'I have no intention of waiting for somebody to die so that I can merely fill their space. Talk about dead men's slippers!'

'You're being morbid,' Bernie had said. 'We're all going to snuff it,' he went on, placatingly. 'Look at me. It's only the sex, drugs and croquet that keeps me going.'

During the summer months, Bernie had proved an ideal companion, encouraging her to spend less time talking to her sweet peas, which were now climbing the wigwam of canes in the garden and flowering rampantly, and more with him. He was honest and direct with her, which were qualities to which she had always warmed, and he told her on numerous occasions that she was clearly round the bend to live out the remainder of her life permanently worrying about maintaining Laburnum House.

'Sell the bloody place and live a little!' he shouted at her, late one starry night while they were sitting in the summerhouse drinking a bottle of claret from the Lodge's wine cellar. 'It's controlling you, sucking you dry of every last penny. Never mind all that sentimental tosh about your life being wrapped up in it, it's a whacking great investment just waiting to be used for a better purpose than keeping you here in solitary confinement. Sell the place and go off on one of those holidays of a lifetime you keep reading about.'

She had known he was talking sense and as she'd stared back at the pale disc of moon above their heads she'd thought how odd it was that she had indeed lived such a solitary life. She had never intended it to be that way.

Not so long ago, when Jo-Jo had stayed with her, she had admitted to herself for the first time that she was lonely. The feeling had crept up on her over the years and it wasn't until Ellen had moved in next door and then moved out that she had realised how much she valued another person's company.

And now dear Ellen, who had been so much a part of her life, had practically disappeared. Nowadays all her spare time was spent with Duncan. Hermione suspected that Duncan didn't like the idea of his future wife having a life other than the one he wanted for her. But so be it. So often that was what marriage was like. Her own brush with matrimony had been much the same. Even poor Arthur had wanted to shape and direct her life, and to a certain extent she had willingly gone along with him – in the hope of easing her conscience. Sadly, it hadn't worked. The plain truth of the matter was that she should never have married Arthur. She had only accepted his proposal because Kit had married Roberta and she couldn't bear the idea of being alone.

There had also been an element of wanting to hurt Kit, to prove to him that she could live quite happily without him. She had been wrong.

In the summer of 1940, he had appeared at Laburnum House one sunny day. He was on leave, his face ashen and clouded with the reality of war, his body aching with exhaustion. He'd greeted her parents in the garden with a stiff formality that she hadn't recognised, and right away she sensed that something was wrong. All the excitement and anticipation that had been building up within her, since he had telegraphed the previous evening to say that he would be calling on his way up to Cumberland, vanished and was replaced with a heart-stopping fear that something dreadful was about to happen. They had sat around a white-clothed table on the lawn, politely drinking tea and passing plates of sandwiches to one another, a warm summer breeze gently ruffling their hair and clothes. They had spoken in stilted tones of the Nazi swastika now flying from the Eiffel Tower and of the two million Parisians fleeing the city. But Hermione had known that there was worse to come in the hesitant flow of conversation. On one side of her was Kit, his melancholy hazel eyes lowered – not once did they meet her own – his slim body nervously taut, his hands occupied with the buttons on his uniform. On her right was Roberta, cool, languid and relaxed, with a contented smile stretched right across her face.

By the time Kit had left Laburnum House later that afternoon to resume his journey further north, their combined futures were set. Roberta was two months pregnant and was to marry Kit just as soon as he was able to request more leave. That night, just before bedtime, Roberta had taunted Hermione. 'Do you remember that day when I caught the pair of you in the summerhouse?' she said. 'I told you then that I intended to have him for myself. Aren't you jealous?'

Jealousy didn't come into it. Hermione was heartbroken. She had fallen in love with Kit and believed that in his quiet, undemonstrative way he loved her. When and *how* had he made love to Roberta?

Four months after Roberta married Kit she gave birth to a stillborn daughter. In the following year Hermione married Arthur.

'My word but it's hot up there,' exclaimed Call-me-Trudi, coming back down the stairs and fanning herself with her file.

Hermione smiled sympathetically. At this time of year it was as hot as stink in the attic rooms and that part of the house was a haven for bad-tempered flies that buzzed and crashed against the windows and at anyone who came near. 'How about we get down to business?' she said briskly. 'How much will I get for the house and what's your commission?'

'Well, now,' the young woman said, her hand resting on the balustrade, 'I haven't seen the garden properly, but you mentioned on the phone that in all it covers nearly two acres. That will have to be verified, of course, but I think we can safely say we're in a ball park of around four hundred and fifty thousand. Was that about what you had in mind?'

'Call it four hundred and fifty-five,' Hermione said. She had done her homework earlier that week, trawling Crantsford for its numerous estate agents who had all valued the house at roughly the same figure. But now was the clincher. 'And what ball park are we in for your commission?'

'We normally charge—'

'You can sell it for one and a quarter per cent,' Hermione said impatiently, not wanting to hear the same old spiel again, 'and naturally that's on a no-sale-no-fee basis.'

'Naturally.'

Hermione led the way back downstairs. Call-me-Trudi retrieved her briefcase from the kitchen table and handed Hermione her card. 'I'll go back to the office and put all this in writing. And don't worry, we'll have it sold in no time. In fact I can think of one particular buyer who'll snap your hand off the moment I let him know this is available.'

Actually, Trudi thought, unlocking her car door and slipping her slim body in behind the wheel, she'd be glad to get rid of that particular buyer. He was always on the phone pestering for anything new on the market and nothing was ever to his liking. Well, this one would be ideal. It was in one of the most sought-after areas in Crantsford and would suit him down to the ground.

Duncan closed the file on Conley versus Conley and placed it on the shelf behind him. He was nearing the end of that battle. It had been one of the more enjoyable cases because Mr Conley had stupidly thought that he could tuck away his money and plead poverty. The majority of people were too thick to hide large amounts of money successfully as any financial transaction left behind it an incriminating paper trail. It was a satisfying feeling, knowing that he had outmanoeuvred Mr Conley.

When he left law college he had not intended to specialise in divorce work, but had soon discovered he had a flair for it. One of the more pleasing aspects of his work was watching the way a case progressed. When a client initially approached him – and nine times out of ten the client was a woman – they would be lost and bewildered by the situation in which they found themselves and would come to him not just for legal advice but for emotional support. It wasn't a matter of simply steering his clients through the complexities of the latest divorce laws, it was more a case of enabling that person to realise that there really was life after divorce. Rarely did he fail.

Yes. All in all it was satisfying work, which was just as well for the past few months had been more trying than he could have believed. Nadia had always been a difficult woman, with her childlike way of playing games with him, but since his engagement to Ellen she had become impossible to live with, which was why it was so important for him and Ellen to find a place of their own. He had quite sensibly ruled out their living at Crantsford Hall with Nadia, understanding that no matter how short a time it might be, he would not risk his marriage getting off on the wrong foot.

Years of working with the detailed precision of the law had made him a patient, methodical man, but for the first time in his life he was impatient to get on. He wanted to marry Ellen but he would not do so until he had found the right house. He wanted their new life together to be exactly right. There would be no half measures.

He reached for another file – Moss versus Moss – and wondered whether things would have been different had his father not died so precipitately. One thing was for sure, the old man would have approved of Ellen. He'd had a fondness for pretty blonde women, which probably explained why Nadia had taken such a dislike to Ellen. He wondered if it was a genetic thing that he favoured fair-headed women but then checked himself. His father had *not* been his father.

It wasn't often that he caught himself out in this way and he slammed Moss versus Moss down on his desk. The file knocked over a cup and saucer beside the telephone and a puddle of cold tea spread towards the papers. He leaped to his feet, grabbed the file and began to mop up the mess with his handkerchief. He cursed loudly and threw the tea-stained square of dripping linen into the waste-paper bin. Too angry now to focus his mind on the proposed maintenance order for Mrs Moss, he pushed back his shirt cuff and looked at his watch. It was almost lunch-time.

On the way out of the office he left instructions with his secretary that he'd be back in time for his two-thirty appointment. He drove out of the car park and joined the queue of traffic at the top of Church Walk where the road was being dug up for the second time that year. The weather was hot, very hot, and the busy pavements were full of sun-tanned bodies in skimpy T-shirts and shorts. A mother stepped out in front of his car and steered a heavily laden pushchair across the road. Among the carrier bags of shopping hanging from the handles Duncan caught sight of a small red-faced child wearing a pair of silly sunglasses and holding a dribbling ice lolly. Further up the road, one of the workmen, the one with the pneumatic drill, stopped what he was doing and mopped his brow. He was shirtless and his sunburned body glistened with sweat.

Duncan turned away and switched on the air-conditioning. He drummed his fingers on the steering-wheel, turned on the radio for the *News at One* and tried to dispel his anger. After getting caught speeding back in April he'd been conscious that never again was he to allow his temper to get the better of him when he was behind the wheel of his car. But it wasn't easy, what with Nadia being so unreasonable and not being able to find exactly the right house. It had been a difficult few months.

He pressed the horn. Surely the silly old duffer of a driver in the Metro in front could see that the lights had changed to green. He sounded the horn again and as the Metro inched forward he revved the BMW's engine, waited for the road to widen and then overtook.

His mood swings were on the increase and they worried him. He knew it was the pressure he was under, not only in his private life but in his work – they were a partner down in the office due to an extended maternity leave – and the only remedy, it seemed, was Ellen. She was the one person upon whom he could depend. He could turn up at her place no matter what time of day and she would be there for him. He counted himself a lucky man. Not a day passed without him thinking how fortunate he was to have Ellen in his life. They were so right for each other, so compatible. In everything.

Even when it came to sex.

Sex could be so divisive and, in his experience, was more often than not the main cause of marital breakdown – most of the clients for whom he acted bore the scars of their partner's adultery. He was well aware of the myriad pleasures derived from this one simple act of desire, but he was even more sensible to what a powerful and dangerous weapon sex could be.

At first he'd been wary of taking this all-important step with Ellen because . . . because if he was painfully honest he didn't think he was much good at it. It was a shaming thing to have to admit, but it was the one area in his life in which he lacked confidence. Which was probably why he hadn't put much effort into prolonging any relationship in the past. Sex had never been a priority for him and over the years it had become little more than a perfunctory act. He had no way of knowing if Ellen minded his lack of bedroom zeal for they hadn't ever discussed their love-making – a post-mortem on his performance was the last thing he wanted to encourage – but he sensed that, like himself, she had no inclination towards entering a sexual marathon each time they went to bed.

He swung the car into Beggarman's Lane where at the top of the road a For Sale board was nailed to a tree. He bumped slowly along the dusty, potholed road and pulled into the car park. Straight away he saw that Ellen's Peugeot wasn't there. He locked the car and went over to the barn. There was no sign of Ellen. Next he tried the cottage. He crashed the knocker against the door. But there was no response and the sound reverberated loudly in the emptiness of the hot, still afternoon.

Annoyed and let down, he drove back to the office. A message was waiting for him on his desk. He rang the number and asked to speak to Trudi Jennings.

27

Crantsford station was busy. The one forty-five train from Manchester was due in at any minute, and waiting for it was a party of foreign-exchange schoolchildren, who were occupying the four wooden benches that lined the platform with its pretty hanging baskets of geraniums, petunias and tumbling nasturtiums. The children were French, noisy, exuberant and slightly intimidating, and despite the continuing heatwave, which was now into its second week, they were all dressed in jeans, thick-soled boots and sweatshirts. Ellen found herself wondering if they were from Provence and that maybe they found an English summer's day chilly in comparison to the dry heat of home.

She moved along the platform to find a quieter space and chided herself for thinking of Provence. Provence meant one thing and one thing only: Roger.

Since April she had received a further three letters from Roger and she had paid him over five hundred pounds – five hundred pounds she could ill afford. She knew it was cowardice on her part for giving in to him but what else could she do? She had to keep it from Duncan. She didn't want him knowing what had gone on before in her life – she wanted nothing from her past to sully her future. What she had with Duncan was so different to her life with Roger. Duncan was devoted to her; he was dependable and sincere, but most of all, being with him brought her the sense of reassurance and security she so badly craved. He made everything seem right and the very fact that his restrained approach to their sleeping together was the complete antithesis to Roger's made her even more convinced of their compatibility.

She smiled, thinking that there would be some who would view Duncan's temperance towards sex as being odd . . . somebody like Matthew perhaps.

The smile disappeared from her face. She hadn't heard anything from Matthew since that dreadful day back in April when she'd lost her head after reading Roger's vile letter. He'd disappeared back to the Lake District that evening and for that she was eternally grateful – seeing him again after what they'd done would have been intolerable. She had wondered whether he'd ring her or even write, but there had been no communication, none at all. Again she was glad. And again she knew that this was cowardice on her part. The thought of Matthew knowing what Roger had made her do filled her with shame. Oh, it was all very well saying that what people got up to in the privacy of their bedrooms was their own business and perfectly acceptable, and that was true . . . when it was between two people who both wanted it, but she hadn't. She had only done it to try to secure the love of her husband. And now he was throwing all the pain and humiliation of that episode back at her.

She glanced down at her hands and saw that they were clenched, the knuckles showing through her skin, sharp and white. How ugly they looked. She felt ugly too. She relaxed her fingers and heard the sound of an approaching train. Jo-Jo's train.

The phone had rung early that morning, forcing her to get out of bed before seven o'clock on her one day off and making her sound grumpy as she spoke into the receiver. But the moment she heard Jo-Jo's voice her mood changed.

'Is everything okay?' she'd asked anxiously.

'Not really,' Jo-Jo had replied tightly. 'Mum's been taken into hospital, a psychiatric ward. Nobody knows how long she's going to be there. She tried to kill herself . . . I only went out for a short while and when I got back she was . . . Oh, Ellen, she was in the bath and there was so much blood.'

'Who's there with you?' Ellen asked firmly. 'Who's looking after *you*?'

'No one. And I don't need looking after. I'm fine.'

Ellen had heard Jo-Jo speak like this before, at the Patisserie when her brave words had covered up a cry for help. 'Right,' she said. 'Have you still got that money Hermione gave you?'

'Yes, but—'

'Pack yourself a bag and get on the next train to Manchester. Give me a ring from there when you know what time you'll be arriving at Crantsford. Got that?'

'But, Ellen, I can't leave her like this. It doesn't seem right.'

'Your mother's in good hands for now, Jo-Jo,' Ellen said gently, 'and for a few days I think you deserve the same.'

Although Jo-Jo didn't speak, Ellen could feel the relief flooding down the line.

'And remember to leave a note to let people know where you are,' she continued. 'You're not running away this time, you're staying with friends.'

The train pulled into the station. The group of French children surged forward and Ellen stayed where she was. Doors began opening, passengers stepped down and pushed their way through the noisy mêlée. Ellen saw Jo-Jo struggling to get through the crowd and went to her. They hugged and when Ellen pulled away Jo-Jo was close to tears.

'Come on,' Ellen said, 'let's get out of here.'

Johnny Foreigner was waiting for them in the station car park and Ellen opened the door for Jo-Jo to get in. She was astonished to see how enormous

Jo-Jo was and she tried to remind herself that it must only be a matter of weeks before the baby would be born.

Jo-Jo noticed Ellen staring at her. 'I'm huge, aren't I?' she said, with an embarrassed smile.

'That's pregnancy for you.' Ellen laughed lightly. 'How many weeks have you got?'

'Four, but I don't think I'll last that long. I feel ready to explode here and now.'

At Spring Bank Cottage they sat on the bank in the shade of the willow tree. The grass beneath them was parched dry and only a trickle of water remained of the stream where shiny pebbles glinted in the dappled sunlight. A dragonfly skimmed across the water and on the other side of the stream hogweed, waist high with flower heads the size of dinner plates, towered over ferns and nettles and deadly nightshade. Jo-Jo fanned herself with a large dock leaf. It was good to be back.

'Heavens above,' exclaimed Susie, from the sun-lounger on which she was lying. She was flicking through last Sunday's colour supplement, which she hadn't had time to read until now. She clicked the chair into a vertical position and sat upright.

'What is it, Mummy?' asked Millie, raising her eyes from the picture she was drawing of the back of the house.

'It's Matthew,' Susie said, showing her daughter the magazine. 'Look, two whole pages about him. Come and see.'

Millie came and stood by her mother. Her reading wasn't up to the large blocks of tiny print but she smiled when she recognised Matthew's face staring back at her. 'Is he famous now?' she asked.

'I don't know, but he's probably very much in demand.'

Millie didn't know what her mother meant by *very much in demand* but she continued to stare at Matthew's face. She remembered how she had liked the way he smiled, not that he'd smiled very often. He wasn't smiling now either. He looked rather cross. 'Why didn't he ever finish our painting?' she asked. 'Didn't he like us?'

'It wasn't that exactly,' Susie said absent-mindedly, recalling how she'd come back from the shops that day back in April and not only found the kitchen in as big a mess as she'd left it but that Bonkers had taken it upon himself – and to use his words – to relieve Matthew of his duties. Their very first full-blown argument had followed, with Bonkers sticking to his guns and saying that there was no way he'd let the man back into *his* house. She had sulked a good deal for the rest of the day and had even given him the cold shoulder in bed that night.

'Why don't we ask him to come back?'

Susie lowered the magazine and smiled at her younger daughter. 'Would you like that?'

Millie nodded, her eyes large and appealing. 'He was nice. If he came back he might draw Bobtail for me. He said he would.'

'I'm afraid your father will need some convincing on that score,' Susie said doubtfully, but all the same she couldn't help wondering what the consequences would be if she contacted Matthew herself and then presented the whole thing to Bonkers as a *fait accompli*. Would he really be able to turn down the opportunity of owning a work of art that would be so well thought of, not to mention highly admired and the envy of all their friends? She glanced back at the magazine and carried on reading the article, reassuring herself of Matthew's worth.

When she finished the piece she began to wonder whether there was any real chance of tempting Matthew back to Crantsford.

Matthew had always thought that Coniston Water was the most striking of all the sixteen lakes in the Lake District. The surrounding wooded fells, lush and green, came right down to the water's edge and were backed by gentle moorland – it was a sight that never failed to inspire him in his work.

Along the eastern shore was Fir Island together with Peel Island, which had been the setting for Arthur Ransome's *Swallows and Amazons*, but the main focal point of the landscape was the Old Man of Coniston, a peak deeply scarred with quarries and mines, and it was this that Matthew was painting from his old wooden dinghy.

It was said of his work that he captured the spirit and serenity of the Lake District and while he had no pretentious views about painting, and in particular of his own ability to paint, he believed he had a natural affinity with the landscape that enabled him to reflect on paper and canvas what was there for all to see. Completely self-taught, he was a great advocate of teaching oneself to observe with the greatest of accuracy – 'To see clearly is poetry, prophecy and religion – all in one,' John Ruskin had written, and over the years this had been like a creed to Matthew.

For a moment he put down his paintbrush and turned his head to view the impressive house behind him. It was Brantwood, where Ruskin had made his home for the last twenty-nine years of his life and where Matthew often lingered over the sketches and watercolours that had inspired him so much as a young boy.

He returned to his painting, giving all his concentration to it. His hand moved deftly, not once did he hesitate. Occasionally he would look up and shield his eyes against the glare of the sun on the water and focus on some part of the massive fell. He would hold the image in his mind, then lower his gaze and simply allow the paint from his brush to reproduce what was in front of him.

He worked quickly and was soon finished. He packed up his box of paints and brushes, then pulled out a bottle of beer from the small cool-box in the bow of the clinker-built dinghy. He snapped off the bottle top with his penknife and drank half of the beer in one long gulp. He had been so absorbed in his work that he'd forgotten how hot it was. He looked at his arms, where the sun had deepened the colour of his already tanned skin to a dark mahogany, and caught sight of his watch. It was nearly six o'clock and, looking across the water, he saw that apart from one or two sailing dinghies further up the lake and a man walking a dog along the shore, he was alone. He finished his beer and stared up at the empty blue sky and listened to the water lapping gently against the hull of the boat.

It was a mistake, for in that moment when his body relaxed and his mind had nothing on which to focus, his thoughts immediately strayed to Ellen.

For four months now he'd spent each day trying to get her out of his mind. He'd deliberately not even phoned Hermione for fear of the temptation of asking how Ellen was – he didn't want to hear that she was now married ... that she was happy. What right did she have to be happy when she'd made his life such hell?

He tidied away his things and started rowing for the shore, pulling hard on the oars to rid himself of any lingering thoughts of Ellen.

When he'd left Crantsford he'd had no idea of what lay ahead. He'd had no comprehension of the misery in store for him. He had stupidly thought that by running back to Coniston his problems would be left in Cheshire, but he of all people should have known that this wouldn't be the case. When he'd unloaded his car and opened the door to his Lakeland slate cottage he had merely brought his own personal damnation with him. He couldn't sleep that night, couldn't rid himself of the memory of making love with Ellen, and after lying awake for most of the night he'd padded downstairs to his studio and sketched her face – he could see her in his mind's eye as clearly as if she was sitting with him in his studio. He'd finally turned out the light, just as the first signs of an apricot dawn began to creep over the sky, and had gone back upstairs to bed leaving his studio littered with a dozen or so frustrated attempts at capturing the woman he loved.

Love? He must be mad.

How could it have happened? How could his life have been so dramatically turned upside down by a woman he barely knew? And how the bloody hell had he allowed it to happen?

When he reached the shore he rolled up his jeans, slipped off his canvas shoes, stepped into the cool water and began to haul the small boat across the shingle. He tied it to a stubby wooden post where his nearest neighbours kept their own rather grander vessel, gathered up his things and started for home.

Several messages were waiting for him on his answerphone.

'Hi, this is Joy Reynolds from the Cumbrian Tourist Board. We'd like to discuss the possibility of you doing a range of postcards of the area. I'll call back some time tomorrow.'

The second was from one of the gallery owners in Windermere.

And the third was from Susie Buchanan.

He glowered over the machine and listened to what she had to say.

28

Hermione opened the door.

When Call-me-Trudi had telephoned just a few hours after leaving Laburnum House to say that she had a client who was keen to view the property that very evening, she had been taken by surprise, not just by the woman's apparent efficiency but by the name of the client. Duncan Carter.

Ever since the night of the Buchanans' party Hermione had wanted to sit down with Ellen and do some serious talking with her. But the chance had never presented itself. Ellen was either busy at the barn or she was with Duncan, and as it was Duncan Hermione wanted to discuss it hardly seemed appropriate to invite them both round for a drink in order to tell her friend that she thought she was making a monumental mistake.

It irked Hermione that she had encouraged Ellen to set her sights on Duncan. How flippant she had been that day at the Patisserie when they had discussed him as the means of solving Ellen's financial difficulties. It was bad enough suspecting that he was the wrong man for Ellen, but quite another accepting that part of the responsibility for the match going ahead lay fairly and squarely at her door.

It wasn't just that Hermione had taken a dislike to Duncan. It was more basic than that. If she wanted Ellen to marry anyone, she would prefer her to marry Matthew.

In the early stages of Ellen's divorce, it had never occurred to Hermione to consider Ellen and Matthew as a potential couple. She supposed it was because she had been convinced that Matthew was going to repeat history and make the terrible mistake of marrying the wrong woman – Bridget. It had been a case of her worst fears coming true. Hadn't she dreaded Roberta's siren-like charms luring Kit away from her, and hadn't it happened?

She had no idea what Matthew was up to now but she knew him well enough to realise that his sudden disappearance from Crantsford was nothing to do with a pressing engagement as he'd made out. 'Pressing engagement, my foot,' she'd told him. 'You're running away.' He hadn't risen to the bait but had carried on slinging his few pieces of luggage into the back of his car. 'I'll ring you,' he'd said. Another lie. There had been no calls, none of his usual weekly check-ups on her well-being, just a silence that spoke volumes. Damn the boy.

And damn Duncan Carter and all his money.

'Mrs Rowlands?'

Hermione brought herself back to the present and stared at the lofty figure standing in the doorway. He was holding out his hand.

'Duncan Carter, we have met before, it was some months ago at—'

'Good evening,' she said curtly. She was disappointed to see that he was alone – she had hoped that Ellen might come as well. Then it crossed her mind to have some fun. Just a little sport. She would play the part of eccentric old lady.

'I'm so glad you could come,' she said, adopting the voice of Dame Edith Evans playing the monstrous Lady Bracknell. 'It's this way, come on through. Have you left your bag of tools in the car? But how clever of you to think that you could manage without.'

Duncan tilted his head to one side. 'I beg your pardon?'

She hauled him over the threshold and tutted. 'No, no, dear boy, this won't do at all. You'll have to hurry along or else I shall miss this evening's episode of *Dixon of Dock Green*, I do so like that bit when he says, "Evening, all." ' She bent her knees accordingly and pretended to lose her balance. She reached out to Duncan for support.

'Perhaps I've called at a bad time,' he suggested, doing his best to release himself from Hermione's surprisingly firm grasp as she began to propel him at speed through the house. Barking! She was completely barking! He'd thought so the first time he'd met her.

They came to a stop in what he took to be the dining-room. He tried to concentrate on the reason why he was there in the first place and started checking out the size of the room and then its architectural features, such as original plaster cornices and the like. His eyes came to rest on an interesting watercolour above the fireplace, a landscape of water and softly rolling hills in the gloomy half-light of dusk, but before he had a chance to take a really good look he found himself being dragged across the room.

'There, now, just look at the shocking picture on that. You can't see a thing, can you? I don't understand it, it was fine last night.'

He followed the old woman's gaze to a sturdy chest of drawers. Good grief! Clearly she was so ga-ga she thought this was a television.

'Well, go on then, have a twiddle with those knobs and see what you can do.'

'Look,' he said, trying to gain control of a situation that was fast slipping away from him, 'I think you've made a mistake. I'm not a television repair man, I'm—'

'Aren't you? But you certainly have the look of one, dear boy.' She saw him bristle. 'Why not have a go for me anyway? I'm sure all you've got to do is play around with those knobby things.' She forced him nearer and made him bend down. 'There, now,' she said. 'You twiddle away to your heart's content while I stand back and tell you when the picture is clear.'

There was nothing else for it but to do as she said.

Behind his back Hermione was struggling to keep a straight face as she watched Duncan in his expensive suit get down on his hands and knees and start turning one of the loose wooden knobs on the old chest of drawers. 'Try left,' she said, just managing to choke back a snigger, 'yes, that's it, oh, that's much better. How clever of you. If you're not a television repair man then I really do think you should give some serious thought to a career move.'

Duncan got to his feet and considered the possibility that this woman's madness might just work to his advantage if he decided to make an offer on the house. That's if he ever managed to see round it.

'I'll show you out now,' Hermione said mischievously. She was watching Duncan's face closely, and could see him wondering how best to proceed.

'If there's nothing else for me to fix, Mrs Rowlands, I'd like to view the house. That's why I've come.'

Ten out of ten, she thought. Most men would have been only too ready to make their escape. Credit where credit was due. 'Well, why on earth didn't you say so in the first place?'

She saw him relax.

But she wasn't finished yet. 'Let's start at the top of the house,' she suggested, thinking of all the flies. 'Now, tell me, what did you say your name was?'

'Duncan Carter, I'm engaged to a friend of yours—'

'You're not Duncan as in Ellen's *Duncan*, are you?' She smiled engagingly. Gone was Lady Bracknell, now she was everybody's favourite sweet old auntie with a jelly for a brain.

He nodded.

'But we've met already, haven't we?' She giggled. 'At Ellen's little cottage, and at the Buchanans' party. How silly of you to have forgotten.'

As they climbed the stairs to the top of the house Duncan loosened his tie. He noted the damp patches, the cracks in the plaster, the peeling wallpaper and the general state of neglect, and for each negative point he notched up he mentally knocked five thousand pounds off the asking price. He'd soon have it down to a more realistic figure.

As soon as the estate agent had given him the address of the property he'd known that no matter how bad a state the house was in, it would be right for him and Ellen. But he was no fool. He was more than aware of the colossal amount of money it would take to turn Laburnum House into the home he desired.

'It must be quite a drain on your resources, keeping a great big old house like this going,' he said sympathetically, hoping to appeal to an old lady's emotions as well as opening up the way for future wranglings. He ducked out of the way of an angry bluebottle as they entered the first of the junk-filled attic rooms.

'Terrible,' she answered. 'Shockingly expensive. You wouldn't credit how much it costs. I wouldn't recommend anyone to buy this old barn of a place.'

He laughed politely and swiped the air as another fly buzzed at him. He moved towards the escape route. 'Shall we?' he said, his hand on the doorknob.

He found the other attic rooms just as disgusting as the first: dusty, crammed full of boxes and large pieces of ugly furniture, and yet more flies. 'You've a lot of memories stored up here,' he said tactfully.

'Rubbish,' she said.

He looked at her.

'I mean, it's all rubbish waiting to be turfed out.' She started for the stairs.

'What about that room?' He pointed to a door, which was closed.

'Oh, it's full of junk just like the other ones. There's no need to go in there.'

'I think I ought to see all the rooms, don't you? I'm really quite interested in the property.'

'Surely not?'

'I'm sorry?'

Just as Hermione had made up her mind at the front door to have some fun at Duncan's expense, the past rose to her mind and she knew she could not, *would not*, sell her beloved home to – of all people – Duncan Carter. And under no circumstances was she going to allow him to pry into the one room of the house that meant so much to her; a room that would mean absolutely nothing to him. He'd probably wallpaper over Matthew's painting the moment completion took place.

'What does Ellen think about living here?' she asked.

'I haven't discussed it with Ellen yet,' he said, wanting to add, if it's any of your business. After he'd left Spring Bank Cottage and gone back to the office and made his call to the estate agent, he'd been too busy to ring Ellen and had decided in the end to view Laburnum House on his own and surprise her with the news that he'd found the perfect home for them.

Hermione stared at him, her eyes small, dark and piercing. He shifted uncomfortably beneath her gaze.

'I can't imagine that Ellen would want to live so close to Orchard House,' she said. 'Don't you think it would be a little insensitive to expect that of her?'

'Ellen's not a woman to be swayed by sentiment,' he said firmly. 'Now, if we could get on, I'd like to see the rest of the house.'

'I've changed my mind,' she said, her voice brisk and businesslike. 'I don't want to sell it.'

Duncan breathed in deeply and took a step towards Hermione. 'But *I* want to buy it,' he said slowly.

Hermione noticed Duncan's hand gripping the newel post of the handrail. She also caught a look of something in his face that she didn't much care for. She turned away from him and started going down the stairs to the next floor. 'Then I'm sorry to have wasted your time,' she said over her shoulder, glad to have put some distance between the two of them,' 'but I'm sure you'll find something much more to your taste, maybe even to Ellen's.'

She held open the front door for him and as he crunched his way across the gravel to where he'd parked his car she called after him, 'Oh, and by the way, thank you so much for fixing the television for me.'

Duncan drove the short distance from Laburnum House to Spring Bank Cottage. 'Bloody stupid old woman!' he swore, as he turned into Beggarman's Lane. 'How dare she make a fool of me?'

It was when she had stared at him through those hooded eyelids on the top landing that he'd realised that, far from being round the bend, Hermione Rowlands was as astute as any person he knew. Television repair man indeed!

He saw Ellen sitting in a deck chair in the front garden of her cottage, but she wasn't alone.

'How long is *she* staying?' he asked Ellen, when they'd gone inside the house leaving Jo-Jo stretched out on a blanket enjoying the last rays of the evening sun.

'I'm not really sure,' Ellen said, disconcerted. Duncan was clearly angry and, while she had become adept at soothing his temper, she sensed that it would take more effort than usual to pacify him. 'What is it?' she ventured. 'A problem at work?'

'No.' He turned and faced her. 'I've just been to see a property which I thought would be ideal for us, but the owner was inexcusably rude and for no good reason suddenly decided that the house was no longer for sale.'

'Oh,' was all Ellen said. Duncan had viewed dozens of properties over the past few months and none of them had been to his liking. They had either been too small or in the wrong area, or worse still, in terms of adding to his frustration, had been snapped up by some other purchaser.

'And the worst thing is she's a friend of yours,' he said accusingly. 'It was that dotty Hermione Rowlands.'

Ellen was stunned. 'But I didn't even know she'd put her house on the market. Where is she thinking of moving to?' As she heard herself speak, her conscience pricked. How long was it since she'd spent any time with Hermione? Hermione, who had been so kind and loving after Roger had left her.

'That's not the point,' Duncan said. 'She was rude to me.'

Ellen frowned. 'She has a strange sense of humour, she's what you'd call fey—'

'I don't think you're listening to me, darling.'

'Okay, okay,' she said soothingly. 'I'll have a word with her.'

'And while you're about it make sure you convince her that I'm serious about the house.'

'But, Duncan, is it really what we want?' Ellen didn't think it was. Quite apart from what lay next door but one, she couldn't see herself living in

Hermione's house. She would feel like an intruder. 'It's going to take a lot of putting right,' she said.

'I know,' he said, and seeing the unsure look on Ellen's face he said, 'darling, it'll be perfect for us and the sooner we can exchange contracts the sooner we can get married. Don't you want that?' He kissed her on the forehead. 'Why don't you go and see the batty old dear and work your charms on her? I want Laburnum House for *us*, darling, and soon.'

'I wouldn't call Hermione a "batty old dear",' said a cross voice from the doorway. It was Jo-Jo and, coming into the sitting-room, she gave Duncan a chilling stare.

'You have quite a habit of listening in to other people's conversations, don't you?' Duncan said, his voice as cool as the look he gave Jo-Jo.

The phone rang and Ellen went into the kitchen to answer it. She threw an anxious look over her shoulder at Jo-Jo and Duncan.

'What brings you back to Crantsford?' Duncan said. He moved across the room and made himself at home in an armchair beside the fireplace. He didn't look at Jo-Jo: for some strange reason he found the sight of her large, swelling body unpleasant.

'Ellen invited me to stay with her, if it's any concern of yours.'

'Ellen is very much my concern,' he said, resting his elbows on the arms of the chair and steepling his fingers in front of him.

Jo-Jo didn't reply. She was busy trying to work out why she disliked Duncan so much.

'So why are you here? The father-to-be giving you a hard time?'

She looked him directly in the eye. 'If you must know, my mother just tried to kill herself.'

'Oh,' he said, taken aback, 'I'm sorry.' But then he went on, 'So why are you here? Surely, in the circumstances, a daughter should stay with her mother and not go rushing off—'

'Look,' she said angrily, 'butt out of my life, will you? You know nothing about me, so just—'

'That was my mother on the phone,' Ellen interrupted, coming back into the sitting-room. 'She wants us to go and see her at the weekend, Duncan. She's suggesting Sunday.'

'I'm playing golf,' Duncan answered. 'It'll have to be another time.'

'Oh,' Ellen said, disappointed, and aware of the tension between Jo-Jo and Duncan she wondered how to resolve it. 'I thought I'd do some fish kebabs for supper. Why don't you join us, Duncan?'

'No, thanks,' he said, suddenly springing to his feet. 'I wouldn't want to be in the way here.'

She walked him to his car. 'You could have stayed,' she said. 'You wouldn't be in the way.'

He shook his head. 'I don't think your pregnant tearaway likes me very much.'

'She's not a tearaway, and I have the impression that you're not so keen on her.'

He placed a finger on her lips. 'Nonsense.' He smiled. 'I just don't like having to share you. I want you all for myself. It's a weakness I have.'

She kissed him, pleased that his good mood was fully restored.

He got into his car and lowered the window. 'Now don't forget to go and see that woman about Laburnum House,' he said. 'If anyone can talk her round you can.'

Ellen waved him off.

From the sitting-room window Jo-Jo watched Duncan's car bump along the track. When Ellen came back into the cottage she was still wondering what it was about Duncan that made her feel so uncomfortable.

Bonkers couldn't believe his ears. He threw down his Jeffrey Archer novel. 'You've done what?'

'Oh, don't get all steamed up and overreact. I'm doing this for all of us. Surely you can see that?'

Bonkers goggled. 'That's a good one! How do you make that out?'

'Now you're just being churlish.'

'No, I'm not!'

Susie came over and joined him in bed. 'It's an investment.'

'Pah! And what happens to our investment if we move from here?'

'You said yourself you didn't ever want to move again. If I remember your words correctly, you said, "I'd rather have my testicles..."'

'On the spur of the moment one says these things.'

'Yes, and on the spur of the moment I've invited Matthew to come back and finish the mural.'

'Then you can pay for it yourself!'

Susie smiled at him.

'I'm serious,' he said, picking up Jeffrey Archer from the folds of the duvet and finding his page. 'If you want that ill-bred chap here in this house, you can jolly well pay for it yourself! You can have a scaled-down version of the Sistine Chapel for all I care, just so long as you don't expect me to hand over any money to that hoodwinking fellow.'

'But how? Works of art don't come cheap and I don't earn any money.'

'Well, then, sweetie, there lies your dilemma.'

'That's not fair!'

Bonkers smiled. 'You sound just like Floss.'

Matthew said goodnight to Hermione. He put down the phone and went and sat outside in the garden. It was dark, but still visible in the inky night sky was the blurred outline of the Old Man of Coniston. He lit the two large candles on the wooden table and poured himself another glass of red wine from the bottle he'd opened earlier.

He knew that the decision he'd come to a few hours ago with a delighted

Susie was a foolish one. It was the decision made by a man no longer in control of his senses. The moment he'd heard the sound of Susie's tinkling voice at the other end of the line he'd waved goodbye to reason and had made mindless chit-chat in order to ask the one question he'd dared not put to anyone before.

'And how's Ellen?'

'Gosh, to be honest I don't really know. I've not seen her for weeks, she seems to have disappeared.'

'Too wrapped up in married life, perhaps?'

'Oh, no,' Susie had said. 'She's not married yet. Though to be honest with you, and this is strictly *entre* the *nous* of us, I hear that it's Duncan who's dragging his feet because he's such a fuss-pot and can't find the right house in which to set up home.'

Matthew was so delighted with the news that he had wanted to blow Susie a kiss down the phone, but instead he'd said, 'When shall I come and start work? Day after tomorrow?'

'Golly, that would be wonderful. And I know this is terribly cheeky, but you couldn't possibly stay next door with your godmother again, could you? Only I don't think Bonkers—'

'Don't worry, I'll ring Hermione and square it with her.'

The squaring of which had just been completed. Hermione had greeted the news of his visit with her usual aplomb. 'Didn't you find enough of the family silver to filch on your last stay with me?'

'I'm hoping to come away with gold this time,' he'd replied ambiguously.

Hellfire! What a crass thing to have said, he thought now, as he sipped his wine and stared through the flickering candlelight into the darkness. If that was what love did to you, then surely he was better off without it!

He drained his glass and set his mind to figuring out how best to convince Ellen that she was marrying the wrong man.

29

Ellen awoke to the sweet smell of honeysuckle.

All spring and summer long the determined shrub had been steadily climbing its way up the front of the little cottage, stretching its tendrils and fragrant flowers towards Ellen's bedroom window. It was now sending out exploratory leafy shoots to investigate her alarm clock on the windowsill as well as the framed photograph of Simon as a baby.

With only a cotton sheet covering her, Ellen raised herself up. She parted the cream lace curtains, leaned against the sill of the tiny open window and breathed in the luscious fragrance.

It was a wonderful way to wake up and for once she didn't curse the fact that her bedroom was so small that the bed was jammed up against the wall – she had meant to get rid of the double bed when she moved out of Orchard House but the idea of sleeping in a single had seemed such a retrograde step that she'd hung on to it, despite the nuisance it had made of itself by taking up most of the space in the tiny room.

She looked at the alarm clock by her elbow. It was only half past seven but already the early-morning sun was hinting at another scorching summer's day. She leaned a little further out of the window, allowing the sheet to slip away from her. She plucked a pink and yellow flower from the honeysuckle and breathed in its scent. It was heavenly and for the first time in months she felt a strange sense of calm come over her.

Life was good.

Really good.

She smiled, lay back on the bed and twirled the flower between her thumb and forefinger. But as she closed her eyes a completely different sensation began to creep over her. Words like yearning and longing and passion came into her mind. She shivered – though she was far from cold – and her stomach took a flying leap as she turned the page of her sensory diagnosis and moved on to a more down-to-earth description of how she felt.

A woman has her needs, was her conclusion.

She smiled. It was some weeks since she and Duncan had slept together and even longer since she'd experienced the truly spontaneous desire to make love; she was unprepared for her body to take things into its own hands and invite her erogenous zones out to play.

Except it wasn't so long, was it? There had been that crazy moment downstairs on the floor with Matthew.

But she refused to dwell on this memory and turned her thoughts to wondering if she was beginning to recover from what she had allowed Roger to do to her.

For a time she had been convinced that the shame and humiliation Roger had bequeathed her might stay with her permanently. She wondered now if the aftermath of his sexual predilections would have been less painful if she had had the courage to share it with somebody. But she hadn't. She had told no one, because no matter what all the magazines and tabloids had to say about sex, it was still taboo among people to talk about what they *really* got up to in their bedrooms.

As far as Ellen was aware, her friends and acquaintances were more than willing to discuss size, quality and quantity but not one had ever shared anything of a more intimate nature. Over the years there had been the usual jokes around the dinner table about men always wanting *it* and women preferring freshly laundered bedlinen and a good book. There had been tales of *coitus interruptus* with the appearance of curious small children in the bedroom, or even stories of the family Dalmatian appearing under the duvet and poking its cold wet nose where it wasn't wanted. But not once had there been any shared confidences of a husband wanting his wife to dress up on a nightly basis like something out of St Trinian's.

But no, she mustn't think of Roger, she really mustn't keep reminding herself of the past. She was now an intelligent woman who listened frequently to *Woman's Hour* and knew about the liberating joy of sex and all its equal opportunities.

It was just a shame that Roger hadn't had his surgery radio tuned in to Radio Four and listened to Jenni Murray while tinkering with his patients' mouths, because maybe then he wouldn't have been so selfish or treated her as some object for his own gratification.

The real shame, though, was that she hadn't stood up to him.

Ellen and Jo-Jo had breakfast in the garden, and sitting in a deck chair with a plate of toast balanced on her huge stomach Jo-Jo was relaxed and happy. She sipped her orange juice thoughtfully and watched a pair of young sparrows having a mud bath in the lane.

'I love it here,' she said. 'It's so simple and uncomplicated. Do you know what I mean?'

Ellen thought about this and decided there was an element of truth in what Jo-Jo had said. 'You mean, there are no frills? What you see is what you get?' She pulled a face.

'What's up?'

Ellen shook her head. 'Somebody said that to me recently. I wish I could remember who it was and in what context.'

'It was probably Duncan.'

Ellen caught the tone of sarcasm in Jo-Jo's voice. 'You don't like Duncan very much, do you?'

Jo-Jo turned away and looked at a robin perched on the sagging wire fence on the other side of the stream. 'Not particularly,' she said.

'Why?'

Jo-Jo returned her gaze to Ellen. 'Because he doesn't like me.'

'That sounds petty for someone as smart as you.'

Jo-Jo shrugged and bent forward to put her empty plate on the little table beside her. She suddenly winced. She straightened her back and rubbed her stomach. 'I keep forgetting I can't do things like that any more.'

Ellen looked at Jo-Jo's swollen body. 'You've barely spoken a word about the baby since you arrived.'

'That's because there's nothing to say. It's all arranged. Everything with the adoption agency is set up, all I've got to do is grow even fatter and somehow find the energy to give birth. Do you know? They even try to match the parents-to-be with what they think the baby will look like. Amazing.'

'So you've not had any second thoughts, no doubts?'

Jo-Jo shook her head. 'None. I know what I'm doing is right, and when you know that, you don't have any doubts.' She watched Ellen's face closely. 'I suppose that's how you feel about marrying Duncan, isn't it? You know that it's the right thing to do.'

'I hadn't really thought of it in those terms, but, yes, I suppose it is like that.'

'And is that because you think he can give you the security Roger took away?'

Ellen sucked in her breath. She carefully placed her empty cereal bowl on the small table between her and Jo-Jo and poured herself some more orange juice. 'As one grows older security becomes more important,' she answered, in a measured voice, 'your priorities change. But I wouldn't expect you to understand that, not at your age.'

Jo-Jo decided to try a different tack. 'What does Simon think about Duncan?'

'They get on well enough.' Ellen had the uncomfortable feeling that Jo-Jo was building up to something.

'And Hermione?'

'Look, Jo-Jo, it's me who's marrying Duncan, not Simon, and certainly not Hermione. Okay?'

'Okay, okay.' Jo-Jo returned her gaze to the wire fence and the robin who was still surveying the scene.

Ellen got to her feet and picked up the breakfast things. 'I need to get on,' she said. 'I want to see Hermione before I open the barn. I'll tell her you're here, I'm sure she'd like to see you.'

Jo-Jo watched Ellen go back inside the cottage. If she didn't feel so grateful to her for inviting her to stay she would have been honest with her just now when they were discussing Duncan.

In bed last night she had finally worked out what it was that she didn't like about Ellen's fiancé.

She didn't trust him.

The water butt was empty and, despite the ban, Hermione was screwing the end of her old hose pipe onto the outside tap. She looked up when Ellen came round the corner of the courtyard.

'Long time no see,' she said. But instead of being delighted at seeing Ellen, she felt cross with her friend for having stayed away so long. She felt childishly put out, as if she wanted to pay Ellen back. 'But I'm afraid I can't stop,' she said, 'I have to water these tomato plants or there'll be no chutney this year to take us into the millennium.'

Ellen took in Hermione's slightly frosty welcome as well as her wellington boots beneath a faded cotton summer dress and a straw hat that was beginning to unravel itself. 'How are you?' she asked.

'Well enough. And you?'

'Fine. I hear you've put your house on the market.'

Hermione turned on the tap and fired a jet of water at the first of the tomato plants. Its tender leaves trembled beneath the ferocious downpour and a clutch of small red tomatoes dropped to the ground. Hermione tried to adjust the nozzle on the end of the hose but only managed to soak herself in the process.

'I didn't know you wanted to move,' Ellen continued, making sure that she kept a safe distance between her and the hose.

Hermione gave up on watering the tomatoes. 'Well, you wouldn't, would you?' she said curtly. She turned off the tap.

Ellen was mortified. Hermione was so cross with her. Where had their friendship gone? The last thing in the world she wanted was this cold hostility from her dear friend.

'Hermione, I know I've been busy all this—' she started to say, but she got no further.

'I need to wash my hands,' Hermione interrupted.

Ellen felt nothing but sadness as she followed Hermione inside the house. She watched the old lady wash her hands at the sink in the garden room.

'You look troubled, Ellen,' Hermione said, drying her hands on the sides of her dress. 'Like you've got something to say, which is probably what brought you here in the first place.'

'I have, as a matter of fact.' There was so much to say, but Ellen was so saddened and choked with guilt for having neglected Hermione all these weeks that she found herself unable to articulate what she really felt. She badly wanted to apologise but the thought of a rebuff from Hermione was too much, so she decided to take the coward's way out. 'It's about the house,' she said, in a small voice. 'Duncan's really serious about making an offer.'

Hermione narrowed her eyes. 'And he's sent you here to make me change my mind, has he? To soften me up? Is that it?'

Ellen picked up a clay pot from an overcrowded shelf and smoothed away some dried-on soil from its discoloured surface. 'He said you were rude to him.'

'I suppose I was.'

They stared at each other.

'Why?'

'I'm not sure why,' Hermione lied. 'It just struck me as an amusing thing to do at the time. Did he tell you about the television?'

Ellen looked puzzled. 'What television?'

Hermione suddenly laughed. 'No, I don't suppose he would have. Come on, let's go and sit in the garden and I'll tell you what I did to your darling Duncan. It was terribly amusing.'

It was just like old times.

Except it wasn't.

'I haven't got much time,' Ellen replied stiffly. 'I've got to get back to open the barn.' She replaced the clay pot on the shelf. If Hermione had been making fun of Duncan it was her job to make Hermione know that it wasn't on. And if there was any apologising to be done, it was quite obvious that it was down to Hermione.

'Oh, Ellen,' cried Hermione, 'just listen to yourself. What on earth has happened to you? You used to be so much fun, but now you've turned into as boring and stuck-up a person as that fool of a man you intend to marry!'

'He's not a fool, and he's not boring!'

'But you agree he's stuck-up?'

'Oh, you're impossible!'

They glared at each other defiantly. Then Ellen turned to leave. There seemed nothing else to say. It was only when she reached home that she remembered she'd forgotten to tell Hermione that Jo-Jo was back in Crantsford.

Hermione was more upset than she cared to admit. She hated the idea that Ellen had only visited her to carry out Duncan's bidding, and when Bernie popped round a short while later he could see that she was very much out of sorts.

'Well, my little recalcitrant Hermaseta, are you going to tell old Bernie what's troubling you, or are you going to sulk for the rest of the day?'

'Nothing's troubling me,' Hermione said, pushing him out of the way to peg out the washing.

'What a temper you have on you this morning, Grandmama.' He chuckled. 'And what attractive undies you have.' He flicked at a pair of her sturdiest knickers on the line.

'Oh, go back to your harem and leave me alone.'

'Not until I've had the truth from you.'

Hermione pursed her lips and carried on with what she was doing.

Bernie went inside the house and ransacked the kitchen for something cold to drink. He found nothing so went back outside to Hermione. 'Get your wellies off and come with me.'

'Why?'

'Because I've asked you to.'

'No!'

'Hermione Rowlands, if I was twenty years younger and you were three stone lighter I'd put you over my knee. Now do as you're told and come along.'

Hermione compromised. She went next door to the Lodge but kept her boots on. Bernie took her up to his suite, forced her to sit in the comfortable chair overlooking the croquet lawn, fetched an ice-cold can of lager from the fridge in his neat kitchenette and waited for her to speak.

He waited a long time.

'I've just lost a friend,' she eventually capitulated in a small voice, 'a very good friend.'

'Who?'

'Ellen. It was awful. She came to see me and we were both so horrible to one another.' She sniffed and hunted for a tissue in her pocket. 'It's that wretched Duncan,' she continued. 'Ever since they've been engaged it's been a case of divide and conquer. It's terrible to see someone change so dramatically. She's going to end up just like him. He's not at all the right man for her.'

'And what precisely is wrong with him?'

'Don't you remember him at Susie and Bonkers's party?'

He shook his head. 'Not particularly. Should I?'

'He's a bloody great snob and he wants to buy my house.' She told him about last night.

Bernie laughed and nearly risked his chest when she described how she'd made Duncan get down on his hands and knees and retune the chest of drawers.

'That wasn't at all kind of you.' He chortled.

'But that's the sort of man he is, he brings out the worst in me.'

'Oh, Hermione, whatever shall I do with you?'

'Don't patronise me,' she snapped.

'But you won't cut off your nose to spite your lovely old wrinkled face, will you?' Bernie asked, the laughter in his voice now gone. 'If he offers you a fair price, you will accept it, won't you?'

'Must I?'

Bernie took her hands and placed them between his own. 'Oh, yes, Hermione,' he said softly. 'Indeed you must.'

30

Susie knew that Bonkers would have forgotten that it was his sister's birthday the day after next and as she herself had only remembered that morning she decided she'd have to go into Crantsford and choose something.

'Girls,' she called through to the playroom, 'we've got to go shopping.'

Floss's predictably scowling face appeared at the door. 'It's too hot to go out,' she said.

'It's too hot to do *anything*,' Susie said, 'but we need to buy a present for Auntie Janey. It's her birthday on Sunday. So hurry up and find your sandals. I want to get on.'

'I'm not going out,' Floss said. 'Shopping's boring.'

'Only because you make it so by constantly moaning.'

'*I* don't moan,' joined in Millie, appearing in the hall with her sandals in her hands and sensing that for once she might be better at something than her elder sister. '*I* like shopping.'

'Well, I don't. And I'm not going out!'

Susie was determined not to lose her temper. 'I know,' she said. 'How about we go to Spring Bank Dried Flowers and choose something for Janey there? We could walk and maybe Ellen will let you paddle in the stream. What do you think?'

Within no time at all they were crossing the main road that went into Crantsford and walking along Beggarman's Lane. The road was dry and dusty and it was lined on either side with an out-of-control hawthorn hedge. Grass had grown almost shoulder high in places and it was interspersed with hogweed, and buttercups, stinging nettles and daisies, bindweed and the occasional spiky pink foxglove. The girls paused for a moment and played with the bindweed, pressing the base of the snowy-white trumpet-shaped blooms between their fingers and firing the delicate flowers at one another.

There were quite a few cars in the car park and the door of the barn was wide open. It was welcomingly cool inside. Susie caught sight of Ellen behind the counter with a queue of people waiting to be served. She waved discreetly and moved about the shelves trying to find something suitable for her sister-in-law.

'This is pretty, Mummy,' said Millie, pointing at an enormous arrangement. 'Would Auntie Janey like that?'

'I was thinking of something a little smaller,' Susie said – cheaper, too.

'It's boring in here. I'm going outside,' Floss announced. 'Coming, Millie?'

'Stay together,' Susie called after them. 'No wandering off.' She returned her attention to a small arrangement of red roses in a dear little earthenware pot. She couldn't really imagine Janey with something quite as sophisticated as this in her flat – she was more into a couple of twigs stuck in an empty wine bottle – but even so, a present had to be bought so it might just as well be this. And, besides, it wasn't too expensive.

Ever since Bonkers had told her that she personally would have to foot Matthew's bill she had been racking her brains as to how to go about this. The first thing she had decided was to economise on certain items, secretly, of course, and siphon off the money saved to go towards paying Matthew. She would cut back on brand names, maybe even stop buying the fillet steaks they liked so much. Their nightly bottle of wine would have to stop, as would those expensive dips with ready washed and chopped crudités. She would have to convince Bonkers that they needed to watch their weight and that she had devised a diet for them. But even so, a few little economies here and there wouldn't go anywhere near the full cost of Matthew's bill. What she needed was a job. Something part time and not too taxing, which would pay her lots of money. She couldn't really go back to being a secretary, which was what she had done before she'd had Floss, as she'd need to do some kind of refresher course and there wasn't time for that. It was *now* that she needed money, not in six months' time.

'Hello, Susie.'

Susie looked up from the pot of roses in her hands and saw that the barn was empty. 'Ellen,' she said, going over to the counter, 'how are you? Business looks like it's picked up nicely for you.'

'It certainly has,' Ellen agreed. 'It's been like this for some weeks. I'm so busy on the counter I haven't got enough time for making the arrangements, and if I don't make them I've nothing to sell. Ironic, isn't it? Just when it seems I don't need to work, the business is booming. I've even been approached to supply arrangements for the show houses on that new estate being built over at Holmes Chapel.'

Susie was impressed. 'And have you had much interest from anyone to buy the business?'

Ellen shook her head. 'No. I don't understand it. I thought there'd be any number of women in Crantsford who might see this as a bit of a hobby for them. But, then, I suppose buying the cottage as well isn't that attractive a proposition.'

'Why don't you sell it separately?'

'I probably will in the end, but to begin with Duncan thought we'd try our luck selling it as one. Do you want to buy that?'

'Please.' Susie put the pot of roses on the counter. 'It's for Janey. I'm not sure it's really her, if you know what I mean.'

Ellen smiled and saw Millie and Floss come in through the open door.

'Can we have an ice cream, Mummy?' asked Millie.

'Sorry, darling, you'll have to wait until we get home. There's a couple of Feasts in the freezer if you haven't eaten them already.'

'I'm thirsty,' added Floss.

Susie turned back to Ellen, handed over a ten-pound note and waited for her change. 'You know, that wouldn't be a bad idea,' she said.

'What wouldn't?'

'Selling refreshments – teas and coffees, sticky buns and all that stuff.'

'And ice cream.' Millie smiled over her shoulder and went outside again with her sister.

'You'd do a roaring trade here,' continued Susie. 'You could have tables and chairs with pretty umbrellas overlooking the stream. I can just see it, it would be perfect. You'd become a tourist attraction with coach parties—'

Ellen laughed. 'I can't quite see a coach managing to negotiate Beggarman's Lane.'

'Well, maybe not, but it's worth considering, don't you think?'

'But you're forgetting, I'm selling up.'

'Oh, yes,' Susie said absent-mindedly. She was turning over the glimmer of an idea. 'You won't be bored, then, when you give up work?'

'I shouldn't think so,' Ellen replied, though she did have to admit that now she had been working so hard for the past year she couldn't imagine herself sitting around in a large, empty house twiddling her thumbs, waiting for Duncan to come home. 'I expect there'll be plenty for me to do when Duncan and I are married. Setting up home can be pretty time-consuming.'

Susie looked about the barn and at the depleted shelves, and decided to give the glimmer of an idea an airing.

'Ellen,' she said, 'I don't suppose you'd consider taking somebody on to help you out over the next few months, just until you've found a buyer?'

Ellen listened to what Susie had to say. Frankly she wasn't sure. Hadn't Susie once said it took all her concentration to bring in the milk? 'But why, Susie, why do you want a job?'

'Why does anyone want a job? I need the money.'

Ellen was startled. Susie and Bonkers had always given the impression of being very comfortably off – they certainly hadn't made any attempt at haggling over the asking price of Orchard House. And dressed in her Versace jeans and Lacoste polo shirt, with Ray-Ban sunglasses pushed back on the top of her head, Susie looked the least likely person to be saying that she was strapped for cash, unless . . . unless she'd got herself into a pickle with her credit cards and didn't want Bonkers to find out.

'I'd love to help,' she said, 'but there doesn't seem much point with the business being up for sale.'

Susie was desperate. With the chance of earning some real money so very nearly to hand, she wasn't going to give up easily. 'Just keep me on until a buyer turns up. You said yourself a few minutes ago how busy you've been, and if I work here just a couple of days a week you might even be able to take a bit more time off to get yourself ready for your wedding.'

Ellen was tempted. But would it work? Susie and her working *together*?

'But what about the girls? How will you manage with them?'

'Easy. Mummy only lives over in Plumley, she'd love to have them. Oh, please, say yes. It is for a good cause.' She decided to tell Ellen exactly why she needed the money. 'I really want Matthew to finish that painting for us, and it would serve Bonkers right and show him I'm a force to be reckoned with.'

'Well,' Ellen laughed, 'I suppose we women must stick together. When do you want to start?'

'I'll have a word with Mummy as soon as I get home and then I'll ring you back. Golly! I can't wait to see the expression on Bonkers's face.'

Ellen watched Susie rounding up Floss and Millie from the stream and hoped she wouldn't regret the decision she'd just made.

Though what she might regret even more was seeing Matthew again.

If he was going to be at Hermione's for the next couple of weeks, as Susie had just told her, she couldn't imagine there not being at least one occasion when they would meet. It also meant that his being back in Crantsford would force her to confront what they had done that day in April. When he had disappeared so suddenly he had taken with him the guilt of her betrayal of Duncan, but now he was returning he would be bringing it back for her to face.

She suddenly wished wholeheartedly that she and Duncan were married. At least then she'd feel safe, because if there was one thing Matthew made her feel it was completely *un*safe. There was a recklessness about him that seemed to rub off on her.

'I've heard tell that there's a man in your life.'

Nadia lowered the dented EPNS silver teapot and fixed Phyllis Winstanley across the table at the Patisserie with a long hard stare.

'Is that so?' she remarked.

Phyllis exchanged a smile with Cynthia Kovel.

'Come on, then, Nadia,' Cynthia urged. 'You can tell us. What's he like?'

Nadia resumed pouring her tea. 'I should think you know well enough as I've no doubt you've thoroughly researched the entire subject and exhausted all sources of likely information, namely Crantsford Golf Club.'

'As if!' laughed Phyllis, helping herself to another macaroon from the tiered cake-stand.

Nadia laughed too. She had wondered how long it would be before her *little secret* would be out. To summarise: Nigel Wade was new to Crantsford; he was a sixty-five-year-old widower who had taken up golf late in life and was, according to him, trying to make up for lost time. They had met after a ladies' tournament – which Nadia had easily won – and during the presentation she had found herself standing next to him in the bar. The club membership secretary, Magnus Jefferson, had made the introductions and had left them to their gin and tonic while he went to deal with a telephone call. The following week they played a round of golf together and several weeks on they played again and had lunch afterwards in the clubhouse. Nigel was a retired businessman who led a busy life with his large family – four children and a horde of grandchildren – and was frequently away on what he called 'loose ends of business' down in London. That was all she knew about him.

'And what does Duncan make of—'

'Duncan doesn't know,' Nadia interrupted Cynthia.

'But why ever—'

'There's absolutely no reason why I should report my every move to my son,' Nadia asserted. 'Just because he lives in *my* house it doesn't make him my keeper.'

'Well, of course not,' Phyllis said, backing off from what was obviously a sensitive issue. She and Cynthia had often remarked on the strange relationship Nadia had with her son. 'A bit love–hateish, I'd say,' she'd often commented to Cynthia, 'especially now that he's decided after all these years to get married. I expect she's taking it a bit hard. Feelings of rejection and betrayal are probably near the surface in that rambling old house.' She and Cynthia had spent many conversations speculating on Nadia's future after Duncan's marriage. Would she sell Crantsford Hall? Would she heal the rift between her and Duncan? Would she ever consider marrying again?

'Why don't we have a dinner party?' Cynthia suggested, thinking that this would be the perfect way to smoke out Nadia's friendship with Nigel Wade. 'We haven't had a get-together for ages. Come on, girls, fish out your diaries and let's fix a date here and now. Nadia, you could bring Nigel along.'

Nadia raised an eyebrow. 'You know what I like about you, Cynthia?' she said, reaching for her handbag. 'It's the way you approach everything so honestly and directly. There's not an ounce of guile in you, is there?'

Matthew was stunned by the For Sale board.

When they had spoken on the phone last night Hermione hadn't mentioned anything about putting Laburnum House on the market. When had she taken this important step, and what had made her do it? Had her health deteriorated in the last couple of months and the house finally become too much for her? Or were her finances in a worse state than he'd imagined? He cursed himself for not having kept in touch throughout the summer.

He slammed the boot of his car and carried his luggage round to the courtyard where he found Hermione watering a row of tomato plants.

'You're early,' she said.

'And you're breaking the law.' He kissed her and went to turn off the tap. 'Come inside and tell me what's going on.'

'I'm not sure I like the tone of your voice, Matthew,' she said tetchily, 'especially as you're the second man to try pushing me about today. I'm not some silly child who –'

'Then stop acting like one and give me a break. Why didn't you tell me you were selling Laburnum House?'

'How could I?' she flung back at him. 'You haven't phoned me all summer. And anyway it's my house and I'll sell it if I want to.'

She sounded tired. Reproachful, even. And standing in her old boots in the corner of the courtyard with a limp hose in her hand and the low evening sun glinting off the puddles she'd created, she looked like a small defeated child. To his horror Matthew saw her eyes fill with tears. He went to her and put his arms around her shoulders.

'I'm sorry,' he said. 'I didn't mean to sound off at you like that. It was the shock of seeing the For Sale board. Please, come and tell me all about it.'

He led her slowly round to the back of the house, down the steps and across the lawn to the greenhouse where they had always gone when there had been anything serious to deal with. It was where they'd gone when Kit had died. They'd spent nearly all night in there consoling each other.

The sun had moved round and the greenhouse was in full shade, but even so, it was still warm and muggy inside. Matthew sat Hermione in her old deck chair and he opened as many windows as possible – some were beyond it, so rotten was the wood.

'Looks like you've had quite a party in here,' he said, eyeing a row of wine bottles under one of the slatted benches. He held one up. 'Pouilly Fumé,' he read from a label. 'I'm impressed.'

'It's Bernie,' she said, 'he's leading me astray.'

'And is it Bernie who's encouraged you to sell Laburnum House?'

'In part, but only because I've finally had enough of it all. I'm an old woman, Matthew. I want a rest. Is that so much of a crime?'

He came and sat next to her. 'It's nothing of the sort. So what are you planning on doing?'

She told him about the Lodge.

'Makes good sense to me,' Matthew said, after listening to her, 'but I don't think it's selling Laburnum House that's upset you, is it? You seem quite clear on that. What else has happened?'

She explained about Duncan coming to view the house and what she'd made him do and then how she'd refused to sell to him. 'I think I may have been a little cruel to him,' she conceded.

Matthew laughed. 'What I wouldn't have given to see that! You're priceless, Hermione, really you are.'

'But it's the consequences of what I did that are so appalling. Oh, Matthew, if you'd seen how Ellen and I treated one another this morning. We were like strangers. And I'm sure she only came here on Duncan's say-so to try and make me change my mind. I haven't seen her all summer, and then hey presto! here she is on my doorstep telling me off for being rude to Duncan.' Hermione shook her head and tears filled her eyes again. 'And what

I'm most cross about is that I'm to blame. I encouraged her, Matthew. I as good as said, "Go and prostitute yourself for an easy life of riches." I just wish I could undo all the harm I've done. I've spent most of today thinking about going to see her and making her understand what a mistake Duncan is. Because he is, I know it.'

Matthew leaned back in his deck chair. He sat thoughtfully for a few moments before speaking. 'I've given Ellen a lot of thought since April—' He broke off and shook his head. 'You can't imagine what an understatement that is.'

She reached out and squeezed his hand. 'I think I can.'

'Anyway, the only conclusion I've reached is that I don't think anyone but Ellen herself can decide whether or not she marries Duncan. If you or I point out why Duncan isn't right for her she'll dig her heels in even more. Remember when I was ten and I wanted to climb that old apple tree at the bottom of the garden beyond Kit's statue and you kept telling me how dangerous it was and that I wasn't to go anywhere near it? Well, you made me want to climb it all the more.'

'Yes,' she smiled, 'and a branch gave way just as I said it would and you nearly broke your neck. I remember only too well. Roberta never stopped blaming me for that.'

'The thing is, I don't think we ever grow out of that childish desire to prove our independence,' Matthew continued, 'and it will be the same with Ellen.'

'So what can we do? I don't want her to break her neck, Matthew.'

'She won't . . . I'll see to that. But first of all, and for your own peace of mind, I think you should go and apologise to Ellen, Duncan as well if you can bear it. At least then you'll have your friendship back, and that's what's really upset you, isn't it?'

She nodded. 'But what about you and Ellen?'

He sighed and ran his hand through his hair. 'I'm giving it one more shot. That's why I'm here.'

'I thought so. Or, rather, I hoped so.'

'I must be out of my mind. I don't know what it is about her but she's driven me almost insane this summer.' He explained why he'd left so unexpectedly on his last visit. He told her about Roger's letters and him and Ellen making love and then Nadia Carter arriving on the scene.

Hermione was shocked. 'Why did she never tell me about what Roger had done?'

'I don't think it's an easy subject to bring up when you've been made to feel so utterly ashamed of yourself.'

'Poor Ellen. Poor confused Ellen. No wonder she's so desperate to marry Duncan. She wants to build as big a barrier as she can to keep that blasted Roger out of her life. I see now why she agrees with everything her new lord and master says. She came so close to losing him back in April that now she'll do anything to keep him sweet.'

'That's right,' Matthew agreed. 'There's nothing like the threat of losing something to make you value it more highly . . . even if it isn't worth hanging on to.'

'So what should I do about Laburnum House? If Duncan makes an offer, should I turn it down?'

'Please don't think about sacrificing your own happiness on my account,' Matthew said firmly, 'I'd never forgive myself if you did that.' He caught an odd faraway expression in Hermione's face. 'What is it?' he asked.

'I'm not sure, really. I was just remembering Duncan's face when I told him I'd changed my mind about selling the house. There was something in his eyes that was quite disturbing.' She gazed at Matthew. 'I'm not easily scared, but in that split second of a moment I was.'

Matthew knew that Hermione was not a woman given over to flights of fancy and this description of Duncan worried him.

It was late and outside Jo-Jo's bedroom the faintest of breezes was blowing gently through the trees, rustling leaves and making the gingham curtains slide to and fro above the windowsill at the end of her bed.

She had done nothing all day but sleep, and with only a few weeks left of her pregnancy she knew she was growing ever more tired. The worry of her mother's attempted suicide had also added to her exhaustion. She had phoned the hospital after breakfast when Ellen had gone to see Hermione and she had spoken to the nurse who had been on duty when her mother had been admitted. Her mother was now in a ward with two other women of about her own age and who, for their own differing reasons, had reached a similar point in their lives. And they were probably all married to monsters like her step-father, Jo-Jo concluded. What was it with men who felt the need to dominate those closest to them? Did they do it because their wives and girlfriends were such easy targets? She felt the baby move inside her, so strongly that she had a picture in her mind of the baby being a girl and punching the air with a small defiant fist in response to her thoughts. That's right, Jo-Jo told the baby, don't make yourself an easy target . . . not like me.

Initially when she'd returned to school, Alan – who during the Easter holidays had decided to start wearing his hair in a weedy little pony-tail – had ignored her, which was an amazing feat in itself, since he was her English tutor and she had lessons with him in small groups of twelve several times a week. Then, after nearly a fortnight when he had avoided her at all costs, he'd approached her in the corridor and said that if she had any plans to blackmail him he would simply deny everything, call her home life into question and reason that she was a born trouble-maker with an unstable background.

'Oh, very politically correct,' she'd thrown back at him. 'Worried about the Child Support Agency knocking on your door and waking your wife up to what a sad loser you are?'

From that day on the man had walked about the school in dread of bumping into her. Surprisingly enough, the rest of the staff, including the headmaster, had been sympathetic towards her. She had anticipated being turned away from school, with allegations flung at her from all directions that she was a bad role model for the younger children, but not a word had been said. Even her classmates, whom she had dropped when she and Alan had been seeing one another, drew near again. They were curious. What was it like having *something* growing inside you? And who was the father? She had joked that she'd been abducted by aliens and had had sex with an Agent Mulder lookalike. Which, with hindsight, would have been more fun than what had really happened.

She closed her eyes ready for sleep and then remembered that her A-level results were due out on Monday. She fell asleep with her fingers crossed.

31

Susie had told Matthew not to turn up until she called him. 'Bonkers won't be leaving the house until ten-thirty,' she'd whispered on the telephone yesterday evening, 'but just in case he's running late, or we've had a drama over breakfast, best come when I've given you a little tinkle. The girls are so looking forward to seeing you again.'

As Matthew rang the doorbell he somehow doubted that Little Miss Shrewd Eyes was waiting with bated breath for his reappearance at Orchard House.

He heard somebody on the other side of the door struggling with the lock. When the door opened Millie stood before him. She smiled shyly, her toy rabbit, Bobtail, in her hand.

'Hello,' she whispered, 'Mummy's on the phone.'

Was she ever off it?

'Have you brought all your paints?'

'Of course he has,' answered Little Miss Shrewd Eyes from behind her sister. 'Or why would he be here? Let him in, then.'

They took him through to the conservatory.

It was like an inferno. The French windows were wide open but there still wasn't enough air; a fiercely hot sun was blazing through the glass. Matthew thought of the stifling day ahead of him. Already he was sweating. He began to set out his things on the floor and stared up at the wall. He was relieved to see that his sketches were still intact – at least that idiot Bonkers hadn't defaced his work, or taken a pot of paint to it. He smiled to himself, doubting that Bonkers would be capable of doing even that much.

'Matthew, you're here!' exclaimed Susie, joining him at last. 'Oh, what a treasure you are! Sorry about all that subterfuge. But it's rather exciting, really, isn't it? I suppose this is how people having affairs feel. Gosh, not that I'm suggesting anything. But, honestly, I thought Bonkers would never get on and leave this morning. He only has to do the occasional Saturday at the hospital and I thought for one ghastly moment that perhaps I'd got the dates wrong.' She paused for breath. 'Shall I just leave you to it?'

'Yes, that would probably be the best thing,' he said quickly.

She came back ten minutes later. 'You'll be needing these, won't you?' She gave him the step-ladders.

Half an hour later she reappeared again. 'You must be dying of thirst.' She handed him a glass of mineral water.

And then it was lunchtime.

Within twenty minutes of getting back to work after a chicken sandwich and a can of lager, she popped her head round the door once more. 'You will say if you need anything.'

It was hopeless. Completely hopeless! Would he never be left alone?

Oh, Ellen, you'd better be worth all this!

Hermione kicked off her boots and slipped her hot feet into an ancient pair of leather sandals; one of the straps was hanging by a thread and it looked as if it would be lucky to see the summer through. She glanced in the mirror above the sink in the garden room and smoothed back her hair, then noticed that her hands were muddy from pulling up new potatoes. She turned on the tap and started washing herself. If she was going to call on Ellen then the least she could do was look clean and tidy.

The phone rang.

'Mrs Rowlands? Hi. It's Trudi . . . Trudi from Harker and Company.'

'Hello,' Hermione responded, a little cautiously. She was half expecting a ticking off for having frightened away a potential buyer.

'The good news is we've received an offer.'

'And the bad news?'

'I'm afraid the offer is well below the asking price.'

'And, um . . . who's made the offer?'

'Mr Carter. He's just called into the office.' At the other end of the line Trudi crossed her legs and her fingers. 'He mentioned something about a little awkwardness between the two of you on Thursday evening when he viewed the property. Something about you having changed your mind and not wanting to sell.' She held her breath. Please, God, don't let this be true. Let it be some stupid mix-up. She gripped the phone tightly, as well as the thought of the one and a quarter per cent commission so very nearly in the bank.

Remembering Bernie's insistence that she mustn't cut off her nose to spite her face and what Matthew had told her in the greenhouse, she said, 'Gracious! What can the silly man have been talking about? Of course I want to sell. How much is he offering?'

Trudi let out her breath, uncrossed her fingers and legs and leaned back in her chair. 'Now, we have to bear in mind the sluggish state of the market—'

'That's not what I heard on the news a couple of weeks ago. More houses were sold last month than in any previous—'

'But national averages don't really give the full picture when it comes to specific county—'

'Just tell me what he's trying to rip me off for, will you?'

'He's offering three hundred.'

'And what?'

'No, that's it. Three hundred thousand.'

Hermione's derisive laughter filled Laburnum House, as well as the purple-and-green-carpeted offices of Harker and Company.

'What do you want me to tell him, Mrs Rowlands?'

'You're a sweet young girl,' Hermione said drily, 'and I don't think you're up to the message I'd like to pass on to Mr Carter.'

'I don't think we want to be too hasty,' Trudi said patiently, leaning forward in her chair – elderly clients really were the most awkward, they had no idea how to play the market. 'We've got him hooked so let's try and nudge him up to a more suitable figure, shall we?'

'Nudge him! The man needs spearing with a harpoon!'

'Shall I tell him that—'

'You can tell him to increase his offer to a more realistic figure or not bother. Goodbye.'

Hermione put the phone down and decided she'd better hurry along to Ellen and see if she could make peace before Call-Me-Trudi had a chance to report back to Duncan and he had had an opportunity to whinge at Ellen.

She was halfway down Beggarman's Lane, and just pausing to admire a Red Admiral quivering its beautiful wings on a bindweed bloom, when she saw a familiar figure lumbering slowly towards her.

'Jo-Jo! What are you doing here? And, my word, just look at the size of you!'

Jo-Jo smiled and ran her hand over her thin cotton dungarees. 'Fit to burst, eh?'

Hermione kissed her. 'When did you arrive?'

'The day before yesterday.' She told Hermione about her mother and Ellen inviting her to stay. 'I didn't fancy being on my own with my step-father. I couldn't face the idea of all those silent, resentful stares.'

Hermione's heart warmed towards Ellen. She may have got herself wedged under Duncan's thumb, but at least she'd done the right thing by Jo-Jo. A shame she hadn't seen fit to let her know their young friend was back in Crantsford, though.

As if picking up on her thoughts, Jo-Jo said, 'What's up between you and Ellen? She came back dead miserable after seeing you yesterday.'

'It's a little complicated, but I've come here to apologise to Ellen. We've had a small disagreement.'

'Would it have anything to do with Duncan?'

'How very perceptive of you. Now, come along, it's far too hot to stand here gossiping. Where are you off to?'

'I was on my way to see you, so you've saved me a trip.'

They walked towards the barn. Several cars were parked outside.

'Oh dear,' said Hermione. 'I had hoped to catch Ellen on her own. I can hardly eat humble pie in front of a lot of strangers.'

'Don't worry.' Jo-Jo laughed. 'I'll mind things while you two patch up your differences out here.'

'Perhaps you could go inside and tell Ellen I'm here. Would you?'

When Ellen came out she smiled hesitantly at Hermione. 'Jo-Jo says you want to talk to me. Shall we go over to the cottage?'

Hermione shook her head. 'The bank looks as though it would be agreeably cool.'

They sat in the shade of the willow tree. At first neither seemed to know what to say. Ellen played with a long piece of grass, while Hermione fiddled with the strap on her sandal, like a small child worrying at a loose tooth. Then it came away suddenly in her hand.

'Oh dear, now I'll have to pay a visit to Oxfam.'

Ellen raised her eyes from the blade of grass. 'We used to love our rummages in Oxfam, didn't we?'

Hermione smiled at Ellen. 'Do you remember when I bought that handbag and we found a ten-pound note in it?'

'Yes, we went straight out and blew it on tea and cakes at the Patisserie.'

They fell silent again.

'I'm sorry, Ellen,' Hermione said at last. 'I'm sorry I was rude about Duncan and that I made a fool of him.'

'And I'm sorry too. I've neglected you badly these past few months, and that's unforgivable.'

Hermione shook her head. 'Nothing's that bad, Ellen.'

'I know you don't really like Duncan,' Ellen said, 'and I know he can appear a little prosaic, but it's just his way. He's what you'd call a man of form and order. I don't think he's used to people making a joke at his expense. And things are difficult at the moment between him and Nadia, she's making it very awkward for him. That's why he's so desperate to find the right house so we can get married.'

Hermione was finding it hard not to speak her mind. More than anything she wanted to shout at Ellen that Duncan was no more the right man for her than Donald Duck was. But she'd promised Matthew she'd play it his way, which meant she had to keep her mouth shut.

'Ellen,' she said, 'did you know that Duncan has made an offer on my house this morning?'

'No,' she answered. 'No, I didn't.'

'The thing is, it's too low, so . . . so I've turned it down.'

'Oh.'

'You have to see it from my point of view. I need to get as much as I can because I'm hoping to move into the Lodge.'

'The Lodge? But I thought you hated the idea of old people's homes. You've always been so rude about them.'

'Believe me, this is no ordinary nursing home. This is de luxe retirement accommodation. And it's not something I'm rushing into. I've thought about it all summer.' She flicked at an ant crawling up her bare ankle. 'I'm tired of carrying the burden of Laburnum House on my shoulders. I want a rest and after all these years of making do with buttons I think I've earned the right to a bit of pampering.'

'Does Duncan know you've refused his offer?'

Hermione looked at her watch. An hour had passed since Call-Me-Trudi had phoned. 'Probably by now, yes,' she said.

Ellen sighed. She wasn't looking forward to her next conversation with Duncan.

32

'I shan't be able to make it,' Duncan said from the pantry, where he was supposed to be looking for a new jar of coffee. Instead he was checking up on Nadia's cache of sherry bottles. To his surprise he'd drawn a blank, which meant that she was probably getting sneakier and was hiding them somewhere other than behind the old flour bin on the top shelf.

He emerged from the pantry and found his mother sitting at the refectory table reading the *Daily Telegraph*.

'You've forgotten the coffee,' she said, glancing up from the sports page and looking at his empty hands.

'We've run out,' he said.

'Don't be ridiculous. Of course we haven't.' She got up from her chair and went to the pantry. 'What did I tell you?' she said, reappearing almost immediately with a new jar of Nescafé. She handed it to him and returned her attention to her newspaper and an American lady golfer with a sun visor and a mouthful of large, immaculate teeth. 'I'll have mine black, please.'

'Black?'

'Yes, that's what I said, Duncan. Your hearing going as well as your eyesight? Oh, and only one spoonful of sugar.'

Duncan placed the jar of coffee on the work surface beside the kettle. If he didn't know better he'd say that Nadia was on some kind of diet. She had taken to eating just half a grapefruit for breakfast each morning instead of her usual two slices of toast and large bowl of Fruit 'n' Fibre. There was also an alarming amount of rabbit fodder in the fridge.

'You haven't answered my question,' Nadia said, raising her eyes. 'Why can't you make dinner next Saturday at the Kovels'? Cynthia has gone to the trouble of inviting Ellen.'

He unscrewed the lid from the Nescafé jar, then took a knife from the cutlery drawer and stabbed at the seal. 'I've got a Law Society dinner in Manchester,' he said.

'No, you haven't. I've already checked with your secretary.'

He flung down the knife and faced her. 'You really have no right to pry into my private life.'

'And does that work both ways?' she asked. She gave him a curious look.

'I don't know what you mean.'

'I think you do.' And, in a voice Duncan didn't recognise as his mother's, she went on, 'There's a special reason why I'd like you to go to the Kovels' on Saturday. I want you to meet a friend of mine. His name's Nigel.'

It was a few seconds before Duncan had taken in this information. 'What do you mean, a *friend*?'

'I should think I've made myself quite clear. Nigel and I have struck up a relationship, if you must know.'

Duncan moved away and stood at the head of the table where he normally sat. He rested his hands on the back of his chair. 'Nigel,' he repeated, 'and just who on earth is he? Sounds like some kind of car salesman with a name like that.'

At the other end of the table Nadia carefully smoothed out her newspaper. She closed it, folded it in half and then in half again. When she'd finished she said, 'If you want to know anything about Nigel I suggest you come to Cynthia's next Saturday.' She got to her feet. 'And on second thoughts I shan't bother with that cup of coffee, it's later than I thought. I'll be out for most of the day.'

'Why? Where are you going?'

'I'm having my hair done.'

'Again? You only went the other day.'

'Well, I'm having it done again.'

'What time will you be back?'

'When I'm ready.'

She swept out of the kitchen and Duncan considered the potential consequences of what his mother had just told him.

The idea of Nadia remarrying had never occurred to him. Not in his wildest dreams had he thought it a possibility.

He barely had time to gather his wits before the phone rang.

His mood was not improved by the news from the estate agent. Hermione Rowlands had turned down his offer.

For the next hour he mooched angrily about the house. He knew there was no point in going to see Ellen. It was Saturday afternoon and she'd be far too busy to talk to him, so he went into his study and took out his temper on the errant Mr Yates of Yates versus Yates by dictating a stinging broadside on the dictaphone for his secretary to type up first thing on Monday morning. He rattled off a further series of letters and at six o'clock he rang Ellen at the cottage, but all he got was her belligerent house guest.

'Is Ellen there?' he asked.

'Yes.'

'Well?'

'Well, what?'

'Can I speak to her?'

'Don't you mean, *may* I speak to her?'

'Are you doing this deliberately?'

'Doing what deliberately?'

'Oh, for goodness' sake, just tell Ellen I want to speak to her.'

A few minutes passed and then he heard Ellen's voice.

'Hello, Duncan,' she said brightly.

'I want to come and see you. I'll be there in about a quarter of an hour.'

Ellen thought it best, given the mood she suspected Duncan was in, if Jo-Jo wasn't around when he arrived.

'Why don't you go and see Hermione?' she said, going through to the kitchen where Jo-Jo was in the middle of one of her cleaning sessions. 'I'm sure she'd love to see you again.'

Jo-Jo stopped what she was doing and put down the dishcloth. 'Is it *him*? Is he coming here?'

Ellen nodded. 'I think he's a bit upset about Hermione refusing his offer, and it might be best if I see him alone. Do you mind?'

'Course not.'

Not long after Jo-Jo had left the cottage, Duncan's car appeared in the lane. Ellen braced herself. If only she could persuade him to buy a different house.

She plied him with a glass of wine from a bottle she'd stuck in the small freezer compartment of the fridge as soon as she'd put the phone down and hoped it was sufficiently cold to mask the fact that it was cheap and not what he would normally favour. She tried to tempt him to sit outside in the garden, but he declined.

'No, I'd rather stay inside.'

While he paced the floor she settled herself on the window-seat, grateful for the slight breeze that blew in from the open window. She waited for him to speak.

'I just can't believe she's done this. I thought you were going to have a word with her. Didn't you go and see her?'

They were off.

'I did, Duncan,' she said calmly. 'In fact, I've seen Hermione twice since we spoke, but I can't make her do something she doesn't want to do. Nobody can. Can't you increase your offer?'

'But I've offered her far more than the house is worth, she won't get a better—'

'Then perhaps we should look elsewhere.'

He stopped pacing and came and stood in front of her. 'Ellen, I don't understand you. Don't you want Laburnum House?'

She reached out to him. 'Not really,' she said in a quiet voice.

He stared at her, stunned. 'Why ever not?'

'Because . . . because it just doesn't seem right. It's Hermione's house and always will be.'

'Well, I disagree. I think it's perfect and I'm not going to back down just because you've got some silly sentimental notion about it. Besides, I want to get married. I'm tired of waiting. Just think, we could be man and wife and living in our own house in a matter of months. Don't you want that?'

She smiled and thought how lovely it would be to have everything sorted out, to be rid of all this conflict and for Duncan to be back to his old self. 'Of course I do. More than anything.'

'So why don't we both go and see the old lady? Let's ring her now and see if she'll play ball. Come on, Ellen.'

Ellen did as he asked.

'What a good idea,' Hermione exclaimed, at the other end of the line, when Ellen put Duncan's proposition to her. 'And there's no time like the present. Why don't you pop round in about an hour's time? Bernie's here, so is Jo-Jo, but then you know that – oh, and Matthew's here as well. We'll have a little party, shall we?'

When she put Hermione's idea to him Ellen knew it wasn't quite what Duncan had in mind.

'Is nothing ever straightforward with that damned woman?' he asked.

She laughed and found herself looking forward to the rest of the evening.

Ellen took Duncan round to the courtyard at the side of Laburnum House where they were confronted with two lines of washing drying in the low evening sun. As they tried to slip underneath, Duncan caught a blazer button on an item of Hermione's underclothing, the peg flipped off and the bra hung suggestively from his sleeve just as Matthew appeared.

'Hi,' Matthew said, noting the embarrassment on Duncan's face. 'You look well, Ellen.' He didn't attempt to kiss her, as she'd suspected he would, and he even kept his hands firmly by his sides – it was as if he was keeping any physical contact between them to an absolute minimum, as though he was as reluctant as she to repeat what had gone before.

'Hermione will be down shortly,' Matthew said, 'she's just changing.' Then he turned to Duncan, who had now dealt with the offending piece of washing. They shook hands.

'Do you remember me this time?' Matthew asked.

Ellen caught the edge to Matthew's voice, but Duncan seemed unaware of the sarcasm. 'Didn't we meet at the Buchanans'?' he replied.

'Brilliant memory you've got,' Matthew said generously, giving Duncan a matey slap on the shoulder. 'Why don't you come on down to the garden?' he said to them both. 'Bernie and Jo-Jo are just warming up.'

'Warming up?' repeated Duncan warily, as Matthew led the way.

'We've decided to hold a croquet party. Any good at the game, Duncan?'

Duncan relaxed and smiled. 'As a matter of fact I used to be. I played for my college.'

Matthew smiled as well. 'I thought as much.'

They found Jo-Jo and Bernie sitting either side of a large covered drinks table in front of the summerhouse, and further down the garden the croquet hoops were ready and waiting. Jo-Jo was sipping orange juice while Bernie was mixing himself a Pimm's. He was wearing cream-coloured trousers and a cream shirt with the sleeves rolled up, and looked very much the part, even down to the cravat at his neck.

'Ellen,' Bernie exclaimed, 'how lovely to see you again and how very beautiful you're looking. I'm so looking forward to roqueting you into the bushes.'

Duncan rolled his eyes. But then he caught sight of Hermione coming across the lawn from the house. She was wearing a lime green shell suit with matching sweatband around her head and large trainers.

'Isn't this fun?' she called out, with a happy smile on her face. 'I thought I'd dress up, as we're having a sporting party.'

Ellen smiled back, recognising the shell suit as one of Hermione's impulse buys in Oxfam last year, along with the trainers.

'It was Matthew's idea,' Hermione carried on enthusiastically. 'He came across my old croquet set in one of the attic rooms and suggested we gave it an airing. Now, how's everyone for drinks? Bernie, how many of those have you had?'

'Not enough, my little Hermaseta.' He chuckled and started to pour two more tall glasses of Pimm's, one for Ellen and one for Duncan.

Duncan waved his aside. 'I'll stick to soft drinks for the evening, I'm driving.'

'Not staying at Ellen's for a night of passion, then?'

'Hermione!' warned Matthew.

Hermione looked innocently about her. 'My dears, I'm so sorry, but a natural assumption to make in this day and age, don't you think? Shall we partner up and get on?'

Duncan took a step closer to Ellen.

'Oh, no,' said Hermione, with a laugh. 'Duncan, you're going to play with me – that way we can mix business with pleasure. Ellen, you go with Matthew, if you can bear to be parted from your beau, and Bernie, you and Jo-Jo will make a delightful pair of rotundities together, Tweedledum and Tweedledee.'

'What sort of game are we going to play with six?' Duncan enquired. 'I've only ever played association croquet.'

'Oh, how dull for you, Duncan,' said Hermione, 'but it's never too late to learn something new. Now, come along with me while I explain the house rules.'

Everyone put down their glasses, fell in step behind Hermione and Duncan and wandered over to the starting hoop where they picked up their mallets and chose their colours.

'But these aren't the proper colours,' Duncan said, mystified. 'We should have only four balls, red, black, yellow and blue. This is most unorthodox. I've never seen a purple or an orange ball in play before.'

'I agree,' replied Hermione, 'it is unorthodox, but then that's how we do things at Laburnum House. This way we all get a ball each. It's much more fun than having to leave people out.'

'Well, seeing as you're the expert, Duncan, why don't you go first?' suggested Matthew.

'I wouldn't say expert, exactly.' He bent down and placed his black wooden ball the required distance from the hoop. He spent an inordinate length of time flattening out the dried grass and lining himself up, then taking several little practice swings.

Matthew had to fight back the urge to laugh.

'It's years since I've played,' Duncan said, after hitting the ball clean through the hoop. It ended up halfway to the next, perfectly placed, and he marched after it to take his next shot.

'I've picked myself the ideal partner, haven't I?' commented Hermione. 'You next, Ellen.'

Ellen missed.

So did Jo-Jo.

Matthew and Bernie also missed the target, but Hermione cleared it easily and moved on to join Duncan.

Duncan took his next shot. The ball shot through the hoop. 'Amazing how it all comes back,' he called, to the small group still huddled around the first hoop.

Seeing Duncan happy for the first time among her friends, Ellen began to relax a little. It didn't help her game, though. Jo-Jo and Bernie were now chasing after Duncan and Hermione and she and Matthew were left behind.

'Shall we cheat?' he whispered.

She laughed. 'It's rather humiliating, isn't it, when you can't get beyond first base?'

'Tell me about it!' he muttered, thinking of him and Ellen, and with a surreptitious nudge of his foot he lined up her red ball for her. 'Go on,' he said, 'nobody will ever know.'

She tapped the ball and smiled happily when it passed through the metal hoop. She took her next shot and waited for Matthew to do the same. They stood side by side and watched across the lawn as Duncan took a vicious stab at his ball and sent it crashing into Jo-Jo's.

'Do you think Hermione will reconsider Duncan's offer?' Ellen asked Matthew.

'Do you think he'll increase it?'

'He might, though don't let on I said so. It's just that I know he wants the house so badly.'

'And do you?'

She pretended to practise her swing.

'Ellen?'

She raised her eyes. 'No,' she said, 'not really. But if it's what Duncan wants ... if it will make him happy—'

'And what about your happiness?'

'But I am happy.'

'Come on, you two,' shouted Jo-Jo, from the other side of the second hoop. 'It's your turn, Ellen.'

Ellen stood astride and began to make a small swinging movement with the mallet in preparation for hitting the ball with as much force as she could. She held her breath to help her concentrate. She sensed Matthew moving behind her. 'Keep still,' she said.

He moved again.

'You're putting me off.'

He came and stood beside her. 'Ellen, will you marry me?'

Ellen's red ball shot off at an angle and went hurtling under the drinks table, out the other side and straight into the summerhouse.

'Ellen, please—'

'I heard you the first time,' she said faintly, already moving away to retrieve her ball.

'Matthew, it's your go,' called Bernie, leaning nonchalantly on his mallet.

Without any finesse Matthew whacked his ball in the direction of the summerhouse.

'Not having much luck over there, are you?' shouted Duncan, who was nearing the third hoop.

'How right you are,' muttered Matthew. 'Well,' he said when he'd caught Ellen up, 'aren't you going to answer me?'

'You know very well that I'm marrying Duncan, so why are you doing this?'

She got down on her hands and knees at the furthest end of the summerhouse and began hunting for her ball among the chaos of seed trays and broken flowerpots and old gardening tools. She found it under a wicker chair alongside Matthew's.

'Here,' she said, rolling his ball to him as he crouched next to her.

He ignored it and taking her hand he raised it to his lips and kissed her palm.

'Stop it, people will see.'

'Let them, I don't care.'

'Well, I do. I've got everything to lose if we're seen.'

'And I've got everything to gain.'

She tried to snatch her hand away from him, but he held on tightly and kissed her palm again, brushing his lips against her skin. Her heart began to pound and a spark of something shot from her hand all the way up her arm.

'Please don't do that.'

He did it again.

'Matthew, stop it.' She was horrified at the effect he was having on her body – it was going to be the sitting-room floor all over again if she didn't do something. And fast.

'No. Not until I've convinced you that I've asked you to marry me because I love you.'

His face was merely inches away from her own and as she gazed into the darkening depths of his hazel eyes she saw such an intense expression of love in his face she knew he meant what he said.

'I'm marrying Duncan,' she whispered, desperate to hang on to what reason she still had.

'Ellen, I can't let you do that. I can't stand back and see you marry somebody else. Can't you see how much I care for you?'

The look in his face was too much for her and, frightened at what he might see in her own face, she summoned all her strength and lowered her gaze. She slowly withdrew her hand from his. 'Please, Matthew, don't do this to me ... or yourself.'

'I don't seem to be able to help myself,' he muttered despondently. 'You make things bloody difficult for me.'

'I'm sorry, but it's not my intention.' She handed him his ball. 'I think we should get back to the others.'

'Yes, and pretend to everybody else that none of this has happened, like we've pretended so well that we never made love on the floor in your—'

She raised her hand to stop him. 'Matthew, please. It was a mistake. I'm not proud of what I did.'

'You should be. You were quite beautiful that day.'

She looked away, embarrassed. 'You won't make trouble, will you?'

His face darkened. 'I'll be the model of discretion, Ellen. Don't you worry about that.'

'Good.'

'Well, that's that, then,' he said flatly.

'So, there'll be no more proposals of marriage?'

He shook his head.

'No more kissing?'

'Stop torturing me, Ellen. I've made a big enough idiot of myself without you rubbing it in. And if you dare to suggest we be friends, God help me, I'll kill Duncan with my own bare hands and enjoy the moment.'

Ellen smiled, and in the ensuing silence they both heard the crack of wood against wood and the sound of Duncan's triumphant voice saying, 'I think that makes me the overall winner!'

It was late when they walked back to the cottage. The sky was dark and the air was thick and warm; insects hovered over the stream and several bats circled the barn.

Duncan was happier than Ellen had seen him in a long while, but he had every reason to be pleased. Not only had he won all three games of croquet that evening but Hermione Rowlands had agreed to his revised offer on Laburnum House.

'Now there's nothing to stop us from marrying,' he said, when Jo-Jo went on ahead and let herself into the cottage.

'No, nothing at all,' she murmured, staring out into the darkness.

33

Monday morning and Duncan was back in control.

It was as if the greatest of weights had been lifted from his shoulders since Saturday night and already one of the younger partners had the conveyancing of Laburnum House well in hand and Howard, an old friend, was arranging to carry out a full structural survey on the property. If all went well there was no reason why they couldn't exchange contracts within the month, which meant that within the month he and Ellen could be married.

They had decided to have a registry office wedding as neither wanted any fuss, or the complication of finding a vicar prepared to marry a divorcée. Naturally Nadia had opposed the idea when he had first mentioned their plans back in April, but just recently, he now realised, she had barely opened her mouth about his forthcoming marriage. Knowing his mother as well as he did, he'd put down her attitude to her having decided to play things from a different tack – he'd been the recipient of her silent disapproval several times. But now he saw how wrong he'd been. Nadia hadn't been rude about him and Ellen for the past few weeks because she was no longer interested in what he was doing. She was much too preoccupied with Nigel – *Nigel!* – to meddle in his affairs.

He gave a short laugh. No wonder there had been such a propensity of lettuce and grapefruit in the fridge at Crantsford Hall, as well as so much time spent at the hairdresser's. He'd even caught Nadia preening herself in front of the mirror in her sitting-room yesterday afternoon.

It was laughable.

And, quite frankly, next Saturday couldn't come soon enough. He had decided to accept the Kovels' invitation for dinner next weekend as, really, it was too good an opportunity to miss. He'd even suggested that Nigel should come for drinks before they all set off to Henry and Cynthia's, so at least then he'd get a good sighting of the man who most surely planned to shuffle his feet under the table at Crantsford Hall.

He'd tried doing a bit of detective work at the golf club yesterday lunchtime but had only unearthed what Nadia had already told him: that Nigel Wade was a widower, had recently moved to the area and had joined the club to start a new life for himself. Magnus Jefferson had hinted that he doubted whether there would be any bother over club fees being paid. 'Pretty comfortably off, I should think,' he had said confidentially in the bar, 'judging from that car he's got. Would you believe there's a nine-month waiting list for that model?'

Duncan knew all about waiting lists – he'd waited three months for his BMW, whereas Magnus drove an off-the-forecourt Toyota Corolla.

His thoughts were interrupted by his secretary bringing in some letters for him to sign. He read through the first one – Yates versus Yates, the one he'd dictated on Saturday afternoon.

'This can't possibly go out, Gail,' he said sharply. 'It'll have to be done again.'

He screwed it up and threw it into the bin, furious that he had allowed his professionalism to be jeopardised by his private life.

While waiting for Susie to turn up on her first morning at the barn Ellen thought of Duncan and how pleased he was with himself.

She thought also how downhearted she was.

She had tried to put it down to tiredness, that and the pressure she and Duncan had been under these past few months, but she knew that this wasn't entirely the case. Her low spirits were directly attributable to the purchase of Laburnum House. She didn't want to live there.

But Duncan did.

They'd spent yesterday evening together at a restaurant in town and he'd spoken eagerly about the plans he had in mind for Laburnum House.

'If we knock through from the garden room to the kitchen we'll be able to create a decent-sized room more like the kitchen at Crantsford Hall. And one of the first things to go will be that decrepit summerhouse. Honestly, darling, it's a disaster waiting to happen. Did you notice how the tiles are practically ready to slide off? Catch one of those on your head and you'll surely know about it.'

'I rather like Hermione's old summerhouse,' she'd said.

'Oh, Ellen, we'll replace it with a much smarter one.' He'd reached out across the table and patted her hand. 'Now what about our honeymoon? I thought a week in Florence followed by a few days in Venice, or Rome. I've always wanted to see the Vatican and the Sistine Chapel. Maybe we could even go along to the Scrovegni Chapel in Padua and see those Giotto frescos the art historians are making all the fuss about. I like real art, not this pretence at it that we're bombarded with these days. What's that Matthew's stuff like?'

She had thought of the simply drawn sketches and evocative watercolours dotted about Laburnum House, and of the precocious but sensitively painted mural upstairs in the attic that Hermione had shown her one day. 'He's good,' was all she'd said, reluctant to say any more about a man who, the previous evening, had said that he loved her.

But now, as she waited for Susie, Ellen allowed herself to think of Matthew.

Several months ago Susie's sister-in-law had asked her what she thought of Matthew. At the time she had described him as passionate and spontaneous. Well, he was certainly both those things, she hadn't been wrong there. But there was something else about him which she'd never encountered in anyone before. When you were with him, you were *with him* and nobody else. It was as if he had an overwhelming presence that demanded your attention. And certainly after she'd spent any time with him she always came away feeling as though she'd been mentally mugged. He was much too much of a demanding character for her, and deep down she had the sneaky suspicion that perhaps he went around falling in love with women all the time. Maybe it was all part of his nature to make grand gestures of love like the one he'd made to her on Saturday night.

She was sure that when Matthew spoke of love he had passion in mind. Wildness, too. And lust and abandonment. But love for her had to be something much more contained. It had to be safe. It had to be secure. It had to be contentment and certainty.

That was why she was marrying Duncan.

Any woman who married Matthew would have to cope with a daily routine of ups and downs. It would be a lifetime of uncertainty and she'd had enough of that. More than enough.

'Gosh, late on my first day, sorry, Ellen.'

It was Susie and she was dressed for action in a smart pinstripe suit with a nipped-in waist that Ellen would have died for. She looked as if she'd be quite at home behind a large black desk with a day of hiring and firing ahead of her.

'Is the suit okay?' Susie asked, noticing Ellen's gaze.

'It's fine. I'm envious, it puts my T-shirt and jeans to shame.'

'Oh, I wouldn't say that. Now, what do you want me to do?'

'Let's start with the till, shall we?'

Susie was a surprisingly fast learner and by mid-afternoon she had mastered the complexities of the till and had most of the customers eating out of her hand. Secretly Ellen had thought she would turn out to be a dead loss and that she'd be bored within an hour, but she had been proved wrong, and could see only too well what an asset Susie might turn out to be. She had a real talent for convincing people that they couldn't possibly leave the shop empty-handed, and while she was selling coals to Newcastle Ellen was able to catch up on the backlog of orders that had been steadily growing in number.

Ellen also had to admit that it was quite fun having somebody to work with in the barn.

Matthew had Orchard House to himself. Susie had explained to him about her new job, starting at Ellen's barn, just as she was flying out of the door with Floss and Millie. 'I've got to get the girls to Mummy's,' she said. 'Just help yourself to anything you need. 'Byee.'

Never had Orchard House felt so good.

He opened the French windows in the conservatory, stared thoughtfully up at the mural and decided to start work on Bonkers. It would have been the easiest thing in the world to caricature him as a bumbling fool but Matthew knew better than to do that.

He rolled up his shirtsleeves, set out his brushes, prepared his palette and started work, his eyes occasionally flicking from the photographs of Bonkers to the wall.

By three o'clock Matthew's neck and shoulders had almost seized up from standing in the same position for so long. He was also hungry. It was time to stop for a break. He put down his palette, opened his rucksack and pulled out a foil-wrapped package of sandwiches. He munched hungrily and wandered from the conservatory out into the garden.

There was a comfortable-looking sun-lounger on the patio but he ignored this and went and stretched out on the grass. He stared up at the Wedgwood blue sky, then closed his eyes. Straight away he flicked them open. He hadn't slept for the last two nights and he knew if he stayed there a moment longer on the grass he'd fall asleep.

He got to his feet and reluctantly went back inside the house to the stuffy heat of the conservatory. His sandwiches finished, he went in search of a cold drink from the fridge in the kitchen. He found a bottle of still mineral water, poured himself a glass and returned to the conservatory to start work again. It was best that way – it was only when he was working that he didn't think of Ellen.

He hadn't intended to say any of the things he'd said to her on Saturday, but after four months of agonising over whether he would ever see her again he had been unable to stop himself from telling her he loved her.

But it was over now, that was abundantly clear. He'd done everything he could to convince her of his feelings. Maybe she did love Duncan, after all, and he'd been wrong all along, arrogance had got the better of him and turned him into the kind of bare-chested medallion man who thought he was too good an opportunity to pass up.

Hermione and Jo-Jo were sitting on the terrace. Hermione was doing her best to coax her young friend to go inside the house and ring her school.

'But I'm too scared,' Jo-Jo said. 'What if I've failed? What will I do then?'

'You'll simply do the exams again. Now come on, there's no point in putting it off. The sooner you know your results, the sooner you'll have a smile back on that lovely face, which is tanning by the minute in all this sun.'

'Will you come inside with me?'

'I'll even hold your hand.'

Hermione watched Jo-Jo dial the number from the pad of paper in her shaking hand. It was a while before she was put through to the right person. As they waited Hermione was almost as nervous as Jo-Jo.

'Yes, this is Jo-Jo Clarke, I'm ringing about my A-level results ... Yes, I'll wait ... Hold on, I've dropped my pencil.'

Hermione handed it back to her and then watched Jo-Jo scribble across the paper.

They were both crying and dancing a little jig about the kitchen when Bernie knocked on the back door. 'Steady on, you two, you'll do yourselves a mischief.'

Jo-Jo couldn't speak. Hermione gave him the news. 'It's her A-level results. An A and two Bs! Isn't she brilliant?' Hermione hugged her again. 'I'm so proud of you.'

Jo-Jo gasped and suddenly clutched her stomach. She collapsed onto the nearest chair. 'Oh dear, I think this is too much excitement for the baby.'

Immediately Hermione was concerned. 'It's not started, has it?'

'Don't be silly,' Jo-Jo said, breathing deeply. 'I've got three weeks to go yet.'

'Even so, it might have decided to come early. Perhaps you should—'

'Shut up! I'm fine.'

'Do as the little lady says, Hermione, and calm down. If she is about to produce this child the last thing she needs is you fussing like a mother hen.'

'Will you both shut up!' shouted Jo-Jo. 'I am not in labour!' She laughed and waved the pad of paper with her results scribbled on it. 'But I am free,' she said happily. 'This is my ticket to the rest of my life.'

'And talking of which,' Bernie turned to Hermione, 'have you instructed your solicitor about the sale of your house?'

'Yes, yes, yes,' Hermione said impatiently. She didn't want to think of that right now. Jo-Jo's good news was a welcome diversion from dwelling on what lay ahead.

She had decided to sell to Duncan on Saturday night because she knew that if she wanted to take the step of moving out of Laburnum House and into the Lodge she had to think only of herself. It was too bad that by accepting Duncan's revised offer she was condoning a marriage of which she strongly disapproved. But, as Matthew had said, it was down to Ellen herself to realise that.

'I can't believe we've taken so much money,' Susie said, goggling at the day's takings neatly set out on the counter, ready to be bagged up and taken to the night safe in town.

Ellen thought how strange it was that Susie of all people should be saying this. Surely this, to her, was petty cash?

'It never used to be as good as this,' Ellen said, slipping the rows of pound coins into a money bag. 'When I first started out I was lucky to make this amount in a week.'

'Well, I think you're brilliant,' Susie said. 'You should be proud of yourself to have achieved so much. And if it was me I wouldn't give it up just because

I was getting married. I'd want to keep it as a symbol of my independence. Give me my time again and I'd jolly well make sure I had a decent education instead of all that silly stuff I was force-fed at the school I went to. Do you know? Mummy admitted recently that she and Daddy only sent me there and then to the Swiss finishing school to equip me to find the right kind of husband.'

'I thought that attitude went out with the dinosaurs.'

Susie laughed. 'Heavens, no.'

'So what about Floss and Millie? What kind of future have you in mind for them?'

'Not the same, that's for sure. Floss is sharp enough to be a politician, and Millie, well, Millie is the dreamer of dreamers and never happier than when she's got a pencil in her hand and is drawing. Which reminds me, if we've finished here I should get on home. Mummy said she'd drop the girls off and I want to see how much Matthew's done of the painting.'

'Yes, that's fine. I'm practically finished myself. I've just got to take this lot into Crantsford and then I'm going to see Hermione.'

'I'll give you a lift if you like.'

They locked up, deposited the money in the night safe, then headed back towards the Crescent. When Susie had parked her car outside Orchard House she invited Ellen in.

'Why don't you come and have a peep at the painting?'

They found Matthew in the conservatory. He was halfway up the step-ladder and staring hard at a section of blue sky that he was working on in the top right-hand corner of the wall.

'Matthew!' exclaimed Susie loudly, which made him start. 'Just look how much you've done! It's beautiful, truly it is.'

He turned and faced her.

Then he saw Ellen. He quickly returned his attention to the wall.

'What do you think, Ellen?' Susie asked. 'Isn't he just the most divine person imaginable to have created this? And, golly, there's Bonkers ... and there's me!' She rushed forward to take a closer look. 'You've got Bonkers's expression just right, as well as making him even more handsome. Clever you.'

While Susie carried on admiring the picture Matthew came down the ladder.

'Susie's right,' she murmured. 'It is lovely.'

'Thanks,' he said, and at a loss to say anything else he started packing up his things.

'Mind if I take a look at the garden?' Ellen asked Susie.

'Of course, go ahead.'

Matthew watched Ellen go outside. He wanted to follow her but he forced himself to stay where he was. He could hear Susie chattering on but all his thoughts were wrapped up in Ellen.

'I hope we won't become like a pair of Dorian Grays.' Susie laughed.

'Oh, I expect so,' Matthew replied absent-mindedly, wiping his hands on a piece of cloth sticking out from his jeans pocket.

Susie frowned and turned to face him. He was staring through the open French windows and there was an expression of such longing on his face that she did a double take and followed his gaze.

Well, well, well, she thought.

34

The following Saturday, while Jo-Jo was having tea in the garden at Laburnum House, Matthew offered to take her to see a film. 'Come on,' he said, flicking through the local paper for the entertainments' page, 'we're the only ones not doing anything tonight. What shall we go and see?'

Jo-Jo leaned over his shoulder and read what the cinema in Crantsford had to offer. 'How about that?' She pointed to what was described as *the* summer box-office hit starring Sandra Bullock.

'A romantic comedy,' said Matthew in disgust, 'you've got to be joking.'

Hermione glanced up from the holiday brochure she was reading. 'Isn't there something more along the lines of *Death of an Extremely Dull and Pretentious Solicitor?*'

Jo-Jo looked first at Hermione then at Matthew, who immediately turned away.

It had occurred to her back in April that Matthew had the hots for Ellen – it was the way he'd stared at her during the picnic that had made her wonder, and also the way he'd kept trying to get a look at her in his rear-view mirror when they were in the car later – but what she hadn't been able to work out was whether or not Ellen was aware of this.

She decided to tackle Matthew later that evening when they were alone. She might even have a word with Ellen. She shifted in her seat as the baby did what felt like a pirouette inside her. She breathed out deeply and closed her eyes.

'You okay?' Matthew asked.

She nodded. 'But I reckon I'll have to go back home pretty soon. I want the baby to be born at the hospital I'm booked in at.'

'And have you got somebody who's going to be there with you?' Hermione asked.

Jo-Jo gave her a blank look.

'I think it's called a birthing partner,' Matthew said helpfully.

Jo-Jo gave a snort of derision and fanned herself with one of Hermione's brochures.

'But you must,' Hermione said emphatically. 'You simply can't go through this alone. If need be, one of us will be there with you.'

'Give over, will you? From what the midwives have told me there's no chance of being alone anyway. There'll be that many people fussing around me the last thing I'll need is somebody else getting in the way.'

Hermione wasn't convinced and she gave Matthew a something-will-have-to-be-done look.

Duncan was amused at his mother's reluctance to tell him anything about Nigel Wade, other than to say that he was fond of crushed ice and a slice of lime in his gin and tonic.

Well, *Nigel*, thought Duncan, as he cut through the middle of a small shrivelled lime, all is about to be revealed.

He looked at his watch and saw that it was exactly ten minutes past seven, which meant that not only was his mother's fancy man late but so was Ellen – Ellen he could forgive, but not a man who had such affected drinking habits.

The doorbell rang, but before he'd had a chance to wipe his hands Nadia had beaten him to it. He joined her in the hall just as she was opening the door to both Ellen and Nigel, who had arrived at the same time.

This was the first time since April that Nadia had seen or even spoken to Ellen, and Duncan had warned his mother to behave. He watched her face closely as their guests stepped over the threshold. He also weighed up N. Wade, Esquire.

He'd half expected to see an inferior version of his moustachioed military-bearing father, but the man before him couldn't have been further from his expectations. Nigel Wade was small – doubtless he had an ego like Napoleon or Hitler – excessively tanned, wearing much too much aftershave, which went hand in hand with his crushed ice and lime, and – sin upon sin – he was wearing an open-necked shirt.

Duncan thought he looked exactly like the kind of man who would go on a golfing holiday in the Algarve.

He held out his hand. 'Good evening,' he said. 'I'm Duncan and you seem to have met my fiancée, Ellen, already.' He gave Ellen a discreet peck on the cheek.

'Indeed I have, Duncan, and what delightful taste in women you have. A beautiful girlfriend and a charming mother. What a fortunate young man you are.'

Duncan cringed and watched in disbelief as his mother was kissed smack on the lips. She metamorphosed into a giggling schoolgirl, slipping her arm through Nigel's and taking him through the house and out into the rose garden where earlier that afternoon she had instructed Duncan to set out the table and chairs.

'What a lovely man,' whispered Ellen. 'How long's that been going on?'

'A darn sight too long, in my opinion,' Duncan replied drily, his mind even more set on turning up what he could about this midget-sized Romeo.

By the time they had joined the others in the rose garden, Nigel was already very much at home, pouring drinks for him and Nadia and discussing Nick Faldo's latest run of bad luck.

Bernie arrived at Laburnum House just as Hermione had finished watering the tomato plants. She was dressed in her best going-out-for-dinner skirt and blouse with Kit's necklace and her faithful old wellington boots. When she saw Bernie she turned off the hose.

'You look tired,' she said critically. 'What have you been up to?'

'A day given over to the pleasures of the flesh takes its toll,' he replied. He kissed her cheek.

'You don't fool me,' she said. 'You look pale and about ten years older since yesterday.'

'Pining for you, my little Hermaseta, that's what it is. Now hurry up and get out of those bloody awful boots and let me take you into Crantsford for an evening of good food and my scintillating company.'

They drove into town and after spending nearly fifteen minutes chasing a parking space they eventually reached La Maison d'Or where Bernie had booked a table. They were greeted in a manner that made Hermione wish she still had on her rubber boots.

'Why have you brought me here?' she hissed, when they were placed like ornaments at their table.

'Behave yourself or while you're having your coffee I'll sneak out through the Gents' window and leave you with the bill to pay.'

'And I shall simply pretend to have a heart attack and I'll be carried out in style.'

Bernie laughed but his face suddenly contorted with an expression of acute pain as he tried to catch his breath. He slipped his hand into his jacket pocket and pulled out his inhaler.

'How often are you having to use that now?' Hermione demanded.

'Mind your own business,' he gasped.

'Very well. And when you've finished dying I'll have the lobster with brandied mayonnaise followed by the fillet of pork parcel.'

'More mange-tout and baby corn, Ellen?'

Ellen declined and carefully placed her knife and fork together on her plate. 'That was beautiful, Cynthia,' she said diplomatically, having just forced herself to eat a slab of overcooked rump steak. She was cross with herself for having been too cowardly to admit that she no longer ate beef. Another principle bites the dust, she thought gloomily.

'I hope you have room for dessert. Nadia, how about you? Any more?'

Nadia also refused.

'Nadia's watching her weight now,' laughed Phyllis, casting her eyes across the dinner table at Nigel. She was still trying to disguise her shock at her friend's apparent pulling power. On the face of things, Nigel was quite a catch. He was still pretty good-looking for a man of his age, which she surmised was slightly younger than Nadia, and he had more hair than Maurice and Henry had between them and it was silvery white in a way that complemented his tanned face. For a widower he even had good dress sense, though if she were to be at all critical he was perhaps a little on the casual side. There was, of course, the matter of him being a touch small, but what he lacked in physical stature he certainly made up for in his charming manner – in that department he was a giant. But for the life of her she couldn't understand what he saw in Nadia. A man such as he would be quite able to attract a young woman half his age. One saw it all the time in the wine bars and restaurants in town: white-haired man in open-necked shirt with a blonde piece propping him up.

'Or maybe she's lost her appetite altogether. Love does that,' smirked Cynthia from the other end of the table, interrupting Phyllis's thoughts.

Ellen almost felt sorry for La Carter, but she needn't have, for Nadia stepped in to scotch any further mischief from her friends.

'Cynthia,' she said, in a dangerously silky voice, 'you have something in your right nostril that needs attending to.'

Cynthia's embarrassed face disappeared behind a napkin. She then scuttled from the dining-room on the pretext of fetching another bottle of wine and an awkward silence fell upon the diners.

Ellen found herself wishing she was at home, stretched out in a deck chair in her little front garden with a glass of wine in her hand, watching the sun slowly sink away. Then she reminded herself that Laburnum House would soon be home, and imagined sitting in Hermione's charming old summer-house. She had determined that she would have to convince Duncan that nothing should be done to spoil it in any way. She looked to her right where Duncan was sitting next to her. He was staring across the table at Nigel, who was trying gamely to crank up the conversation around the table.

Henry-bugger-me-Kovel, who was under orders from his wife to undertake a proper sounding-out of Nadia's new golfing partner, responded with, 'So how long have you been living here in Crantsford?'

'Ooh, it must be getting on for nearly six months now,' Nigel replied.

'Bugger me, six months and our paths haven't crossed at the club. Who'd have thought it possible?'

'But I haven't been a member for as long as that.'

'So what's your line of business?'

Yes, thought Duncan, visibly leaning forward in his chair. Just what is your business? Other than digging out a suitably wealthy replacement for your dead wife. He had been most disappointed that before coming here to the Kovels for supper all he'd managed to glean from their drinks in the rose garden was that Nigel Wade seemed little more than a monumental golf bore.

'Oh, I've done nothing more than dabble,' Nigel said, with a light laugh, and taking a sip of his wine he reached out and patted Nadia's hand beside his. 'Ask Nadia,' he added. 'She'll tell you what a dull fellow I am.'

Despite themselves, everyone looked expectantly at Nadia, except Duncan, who kept his eyes firmly on the hand still covering his mother's. He was sickened by the display of cheap and easy affection in front of him and, worse, he knew a prevaricator when he saw one. He'd dealt with enough wrigglers from the truth in his time as a solicitor to know precisely which way the wind was blowing tonight, and this one was practically gale force in its obviousness.

'Dabbling,' he repeated coolly. 'You're not giving us much to go on.'

Ellen was surprised at the way Duncan was treating Nigel, especially as the man might turn out to be a godsend by taking Nadia off their backs.

'I think Nigel's just being modest,' she intervened.

'Quite possibly,' Duncan said coldly.

The two men stared at each other across the table. Then suddenly Nigel threw back his head and laughed robustly. 'Nadia, what a wonderful job you've done raising this fine young man. See how he's got your interests so close to his heart. He views me as nothing but a scheming bounty-hunter.'

Nadia started to laugh and soon everybody around the table joined in, except Duncan. Cynthia reappeared in the dining-room, bringing with her another bottle of wine.

'Have I missed something?' she asked, rubbing the end of her nose nervously.

'Yes,' answered Maurice-the-red-nosed-judge, 'young Duncan's been putting Nigel here in the witness box.'

Again everybody laughed.

Duncan forced a smile to his lips but Ellen sensed him tense and hostile beside her. She wished somebody would change the subject, but the others were warming to it.

'Go on, then,' encouraged Maurice good-humouredly. 'You'll have to put us all out of our misery.'

'Bugger me, yes,' agreed Henry, 'especially Duncan. The poor boy needs to know if his mother's safe in your hands.'

Nigel smiled and, very slowly, drained his glass. Then, just as slowly, he said simply, 'Well, Duncan will have to wait and see, won't he?'

Hermione was lightheaded from too much wine and as she unlocked the garden-room door and let her and Bernie in she had no desire for the evening to end.

'Brandy?' she said, as Bernie followed behind her.

'Are you trying to get me drunk and seduce me?' he asked, catching her wrist and turning her round to face him.

'And there was I thinking that that was what you were up to with me.'

He held her close to him. 'I wish I'd met you sixty years ago, my little Hermaseta.'

She rested her head against his shoulder and sighed. 'Sixty years ago I wouldn't have looked twice at you.'

'Oh,' he said, lifting her face up to his, 'so who was the lucky man? Your husband or some other undeserving wretch?'

She slipped out of his arms. 'It's a long story, but come upstairs with me and I'll tell you all about it.'

'Now there's an offer I can't turn down.'

They took a small bottle of brandy and two glasses to the top of the house. Bernie struggled for breath when they reached Matthew's attic room. He puffed on his inhaler and sank gratefully into the old leather sofa opposite the painting. Hermione watched him closely and resigned herself to the uncomfortable truth that Bernie's health was deteriorating. She felt annoyed with him. Why couldn't he be honest with her? Why keep up the silly pretence? Pride, she supposed, as she poured the brandy and took the glasses over to the sofa and sat next to him. When it came down to it she was no different herself. All these years she'd lived alone, battling to keep Laburnum House and her independence, believing these things to be more important than anything else, to the point of excluding life itself.

'You've gone quiet on me,' Bernie said, raising his glass to Hermione's. 'Care to explain why you've dragged a poor old man up two flights of stairs?'

'So suddenly you're a poor old man?'

He grinned. 'I thought I'd try appealing to your sympathetic nature in the hope of eventually luring you into bed. That's if I can manage the stairs back down again.'

'I don't suppose there's any chance of you being honest with me, is there?'

'Heavens to Betsy, no!'

'I thought not.'

A few moments passed before Bernie said, 'Was there something specific you had in mind, in the honesty department, that is?'

She shrugged and sipped her brandy.

Bernie watched her. 'And have you thought any more about the proposal I put to you over dinner?'

'You proposed a lot of things to me over dinner.'

'You know what I'm talking about.'

'I do?'

'You do,' he said firmly.

She smiled. 'As a matter of fact, I have.'

'And?'

She lifted her head and met his gaze. 'I'd love to. The answer's yes.'

Bernie chuckled. 'I must be going deaf as well as infirm. I could have sworn I heard you say yes.'

'You heard all right.'

'Well, bless me. But is there a catch? Will the heavenly Hermione declare that—'

'Bernie Malloy, will you kindly shut up. I've merely agreed to accompany you on a cruise on the Nile the minute that twit Duncan Carter has paid up my money and—'

'Oh, be quiet yourself and give me a kiss. I've waited long enough.'

They finished the bottle of brandy and leaned companionably against each other and, while staring bleary-eyed at the painting in front of them, Hermione told Bernie about Kit.

She told him everything, how they'd met one summer when one of Roberta's many boyfriends down from Oxford brought him to the house one day. There had been an instant but shy attraction between them. They had become friends – not lovers – enjoying each other's company, knowing there was a rare level of understanding between them. There were times they were together when they barely spoke to each other, simply because there was no need. They would go for long walks up on the Edge where Kit would paint the hedgerows of gorse and red campion and delicate pink dog roses. On one occasion they drove out to Winnats Pass with a picnic and the heavens opened up and they were forced to take shelter among the rocks with a travel rug over their heads for more than an hour before finally making a run for the car.

It had been an idyllic summer.

But the following year war had broken out, bringing with it the end of Hermione's dreams. She hadn't seen Kit again until another year had passed, which was when he and Roberta announced unexpectedly that they were getting married. Years later Kit had told Hermione that he had met Roberta in London just twice when he was home on leave. The first time had been quite by chance, but the second had been by design, on Roberta's part, when they met at a party where a lot of people had been drunk, including Kit. He and Roberta spent the night together and when she told him she was pregnant, seven weeks later, he had immediately offered to do what was expected of him.

It had been a night of excesses for which he paid dearly, he admitted to Hermione in a letter a short while after Matthew's birth in the mid-fifties.

It was a long time before Hermione was able to forgive Kit, or Roberta, for what they'd done, but gradually the pain lessened until she allowed herself the luxury of enjoying the love she still felt for Kit, and the love he had for her, even though she was now married to Arthur and a different life was expected of her.

As the years slipped by, Roberta became more and more highly strung and unpredictable and despite the unhappiness of her marriage was determined never to give it up. She saw her marriage as a possession and she viewed Kit and Matthew in the same way – though Matthew she was prepared to share. 'You can never have Kit,' she told Hermione one day, 'but I will let you have Matthew when it suits me. You can be his godmother. He can be a reminder of what you missed out on.' Cruel words, and Hermione was never sure whether they were a reference to her inability to have children or a jibe at her being allowed to lavish love on her godson but not on his father.

When Kit finally asked Roberta for a divorce, not long after Arthur had died, she refused to listen to him and tried to kill herself. Afterwards Kit was desperate with guilt and so was Hermione. From that moment on they both knew they could never be together; neither of them wanted Roberta's death on their conscience.

'I think that's the saddest thing I've ever heard,' Bernie said, when Hermione fell quiet.

'Please don't tease me.'

'But I'm not.'

'You mean for once you're being serious? Good grief, Bernie Malloy, the shock's too much for me, I need the loo!' She got to her feet with a smile. 'Bladders just aren't what they used to be.'

'Speak for your own.' Bernie snorted. 'Mine's fine.' He settled himself back into the sofa, yawned and watched her leave the room.

Hermione slowly tottered her way downstairs. She really shouldn't have drunk so much. She went into the bathroom and fumbled for the light pull. Afterwards she went down the next flight of stairs to the kitchen and made some coffee. Better sober the old fool up before I send him next door, she thought.

'Sorry I was so long,' she said, when she had climbed the stairs again and pushed open the attic-room door with the edge of the tray.

'Bernie!'

She put the tray down on an old trunk and rushed to him. He was slumped to one side of the sofa, his face contorted with pain, his eyes wide, bulging, but unseeing. One of his hands was tightly fisted and was held close to his chest, the other was gripped around his inhaler. His breathing was terrifyingly laboured and the sound of his lungs fighting for oxygen filled the small room. Hermione pushed the inhaler to his mouth. She pressed on the top as she'd seen him do so many times. She waited for his breathing to slow, but it didn't. She squeezed the inhaler again and started pulling at his tie and the top button on his shirt. But it made no difference.

'An ambulance. I must call for an ambulance.'

At the sound of her words Bernie's eyes focused on her and, as though summoning the last ounce of energy that was left in his body, he tried to move his pale lips. He was trying to tell her something. She moved nearer to him, her face almost touching his.

'Yes, Bernie, what is it?'

His voice was barely audible, little more than a whisper above the painful scraping sound of his worn-out chest. 'I think it's goodbye time,' he whispered hoarsely.

Hermione covered her face with her hands. 'No,' she murmured, 'please no.' But even as she spoke the room went quiet and Bernie's pain-racked body relaxed. He closed his eyes and very slowly his head tilted backwards.

Tears streamed down Hermione's cheeks. She brushed them away, but more tears came and splashed onto her hands now clasped tightly round Bernie's. She began to shake.

'No!' she cried in anguish. 'You can't do this, Bernie. You can't die. Don't leave me. You mustn't! Please don't leave me all alone.'

But it was no good, her dear sweet friend could no longer hear her. Bernie was dead.

She knelt on the floor beside him and sobbed.

35

Matthew dropped Jo-Jo off outside Ellen's cottage and waited for her to go inside before he turned the car round and drove back to Laburnum House.

There was no sign of Hermione and, assuming she must have gone straight to bed after her meal out with Bernie, he went upstairs to check on her. When he reached the first floor he saw that lights were on at the top of the house. He climbed the second flight of stairs, two at a time, his pace quickening with the uneasy feeling that something was wrong.

He found Hermione in the attic room on the floor, her body motionless, her head resting against Bernie's knees, but as she turned to look at him, he saw the sadness in her face and understood straight away what had happened. He gently raised her to her feet and steered her away from Bernie and held her to him.

'He's dead,' she murmured. 'He died just over an hour ago.' She looked up into Matthew's face, her own wet with tears. 'He was in such pain and I couldn't do anything for him. I only left him for a few moments, and when I came back he was . . .'

'Hush, hush,' he soothed, gently stroking her wrinkled cheek. He knew there was nothing he could say, all his words would be futile in the face of such grief; the best thing he could do was comfort Hermione with love and tenderness, just as he'd done once before.

'I'm going to put you to bed next and then call a doctor,' he said softly. 'Do you think you can manage the stairs?'

She nodded and moved stiffly from his arms. 'You'd better speak to somebody at the Lodge, they'll need to know what's happened.'

'Don't worry, I'll see to everything.'

Matthew woke early. It was a little after five.

Sunlight streamed through the large bay window in his room – he had forgotten to draw the curtains when he'd finally got to bed after dealing with poor Bernie. The doctor had given Hermione a sleeping pill and she had fallen asleep almost immediately, but he himself had lain awake for most of the night recalling his father's death nearly twenty years ago in the very same attic room in which Bernie had died.

In the autumn of 1978 Kit had asked Hermione if he could come and stay with her while Roberta was away on one of her bridge holidays. But what none of them knew was that Kit was ill. He was dying. He had been told six months previously that he had cancer of the liver and that with the right treatment he might just manage to see the year out. But Kit told no one of this. He kept his fate to himself – until he arrived at Laburnum House in October to stay with Hermione. Even to this day Matthew had no idea how Hermione had taken the news, for it was something she had never shared with him, but she did tell him that for two wonderful days she and Kit were able to live as they'd always wanted to, as man and wife. Then they had called Matthew and asked if he would come and spend a few days with them, they had something to tell him.

How shocked he'd been when he had found out that his father was dying.

'But why didn't you tell me sooner?' he'd asked Kit, deeply hurt that he'd been kept in ignorance.

There had been no answer for him and Kit had died the following evening while hunting for some old photographs in the attic room.

They discovered later, in a letter his father had left for Hermione, that Kit had deliberately stopped taking the medication that had been helping to prolong his life so that he could die in the way he wanted to, and when. 'It will be the best way to go,' he'd written, 'to be with the two people in the world I love most.'

Poor Hermione, thought Matthew as he got out of bed and went over to the window. He hoped the shock of Bernie's death wouldn't stop her from selling up and moving into the Lodge. If anything, she needed even more to be rid of Laburnum House: it held far too many memories for one person to carry alone.

Leaning on the windowsill he stared out onto the garden below and caught a flash of movement in the greenhouse.

So Hermione was up already.

Jo-Jo couldn't sleep. It was as if her body was too small now for the baby, which seemed to be wriggling and pushing her insides about as if it was trying to make more room for itself.

She was hot too.

She kicked back the sheet on the bed, raised herself to a sitting position and lowered her feet to the floor. She breathed in deeply and then exhaled slowly. She did this several times before standing up – it was what she did each morning to stop herself from feeling dizzy. She went over to the window and stretched her back and shoulders. She rubbed her stomach through her oversized T-shirt and wondered how much longer it would be before her body would be her own again. Maybe it was selfish of her, but she longed for the baby to be born and for her new life to start.

She went carefully down the narrow stairs to get herself a drink and found Ellen hunched up on the window-seat. She was looking out over the garden through the open window.

'Can't sleep either?' she said, as Ellen turned to face her.

'Nope,' Ellen said. 'I was too hot. There's some tea in the pot. Shall I pour you a cup?'

'That's okay, I'll do it.'

When she went back into the sitting-room she joined Ellen by the window.

'I've decided to go home tomorrow,' she said. 'I think I ought to, don't you? I don't want to risk going into labour here.'

'You're probably right. But can you hang on until the evening? That way I can drive you home and you won't have to mess about with the train.'

'Sure. That would be great.'

'So how was the film last night?' Ellen asked. 'You were sound asleep when I got back.'

'Not bad. It was one of those romantic comedies. Not really Matthew's kind of film.'

Ellen smiled. 'How was he?'

'To be honest I might just as well have gone on my own. He barely opened his mouth all evening and had a face on him as miserable as sin. He wasn't a lot of fun to be with.'

The truth was she'd wound him up good and proper. During the short drive into Crantsford she'd started pumping Matthew for a reaction to Ellen, dangling her name in front of him in just about every other sentence, until finally he brought the car to a halt in the car park at the back of the cinema, snatched on the handbrake and asked her what the hell she thought she was up to. She'd felt like a small child being told off and had meekly got out of the car and queued in silence with him for their tickets in the foyer of the cinema. But one thing she was sure of: if she'd rattled him to that extent then she'd been right in her suspicions that he did fancy Ellen.

'He's a moody so and so, isn't he?' Ellen laughed. 'It must be the creative genius in him.'

'Or maybe it's because . . .' But Jo-Jo lost her nerve when Ellen's eyes met hers.

'Or maybe it's what?' Ellen said slowly.

Oh, what the hell! 'Perhaps he's miserable because the woman he's got the hots for doesn't fancy him.'

'What makes you say that?' Ellen asked warily. She rose from the window-seat and went into the kitchen.

Jo-Jo followed her. She decided to press the point. What did it matter anyway? She was going home tomorrow and had nothing to lose. 'The funny part is I reckon it's you he's mad about. What do you think?'

Ellen spun round. 'That's not funny, that's just plain stupid.'

'Do you really think so?' asked Jo-Jo thoughtfully. She could see from the expression on Ellen's face that she had struck a chord. Maybe Ellen had known all along about Matthew, and maybe Ellen felt the same, only . . . only there was Duncan to consider.

'I think the stupid bit in all of this is you marrying Duncan,' she said, deciding to seize the moment, 'especially as nobody in their right mind would love a sad effort like Duncan, not when there's somebody else who's so much more—'

'That's enough!' cried Ellen. 'Jo-Jo, you've no right to talk about Duncan like that.'

'Why not?'

But Ellen's response was interrupted by a knock at the door. She went to answer it, relieved that the heated discussion between her and Jo-Jo had been brought to such a timely end. But when she opened the door she stepped back, not just in surprise, but in sheer unadulterated horror.

It was Roger.

36

If this had been a Victorian melodrama she would be clutching her bosom and slipping gracefully to the floor, and right now that didn't seem a bad way to avoid the shocking sight of her ex-husband standing on the doorstep.

Scruffy and unshaven, gaunt and hollow-cheeked with eyes darkly rimmed, he was dressed in creased jeans and a grimy shirt with sleeves tightly rolled up to the elbows. He was barely recognisable as the man with whom she'd spent nearly twenty years of her life; the man whom she had once loved and who had always cared so deeply about his appearance.

'Well,' he said, 'aren't you going to say anything? No long-time-no-see clichés?' He took a step forward and came into the cottage.

His intrusion had the instant effect of bringing Ellen to her senses. Here was the man who was the cause of everything wrong in her life; this was the man she had learned to hate.

'Out!' she shouted at him, appalled at his arrogance in thinking that he could just barge into her home like this. 'I don't want you here. Ever.'

'Oh, come on,' he said, with an easy smile that incensed her even more, 'there's no need to overreact, especially since you've been so generous to me, these last few months. I really did expect more of a welcome. Who's your friend?'

Ellen had forgotten that Jo-Jo was standing behind her. Jo-Jo came forward and, in a heavily loaded voice, said, 'Much more to the point, who the hell are you?'

She spoke with all the conviction of a soap-opera actor, which was how Ellen was beginning to view this whole thing.

It was unreal, Roger turning up here so unexpectedly. It was as if the situation was being manipulated by some omnipotent scriptwriter who was burning the midnight oil and playing God with his characters, moving them off-stage at the stroke of his pen, only to have them come back on when it was time to turn up the pace and move the plot along.

And there was more to come.

Behind Roger and through the open door she stared in disbelief at the sight of yet another character making his appearance. It was Matthew!

With the slightest of movements she shook her head at him, hoping he'd interpret the gesture as a polite way of her saying, 'Get lost, I've got enough on my hands as it is, without you adding to the mayhem.'

From beside her Jo-Jo directed another question at Roger.

'It sounds like Ellen doesn't want you here, so why don't you push off back to the stone you crawled out from?'

Roger smirked. 'Ellen's just surprised,' he said lightly. He came further into the room. 'A drink would be nice. How about it, Ellen? You used to make great coffee. Some breakfast wouldn't go amiss either.'

Jo-Jo looked wide-eyed at Ellen. The penny had dropped. 'Tell me this isn't Roger,' she said, horrified.

Ellen nodded helplessly. She was at a loss as to what to do, now that Roger was inside the cottage. 'Please, Roger,' she said, 'you've done so much already, why can't you leave me alone?'

Roger shrugged. 'I'll think about it.' Casting his eyes about the cottage, he said, 'Small but cosy, and you've even got your own little business. You've done better than I have out of the divorce. But hey, guess what, Charmaine's pregnant, I'm going to be a father all over again.'

'Simon will be delighted,' Ellen said acidly.

There was a flicker of something in his face. Remorse, perhaps?

'How is Simon?'

'What would you care? You just dumped us both and ran.'

'Shit, Ellen, can't you let the past go? Do you have to keep positioning everything? Things happen. Lives change.'

'Mine certainly has,' she threw back at him. 'And while we're on the subject, my *new* life doesn't include an ex-husband turning up unexpectedly and demanding a welcome cup of coffee.'

'You're right, Ellen. You're so right. So why don't we cut to the chase and I'll tell you what I've come for and then you'll see no more of me? How about it? Have we got a deal?'

Ellen gazed at him disbelievingly. Not only did he not look like the Roger she knew but he didn't sound like him either. Who was this stranger, sounding for all the world as though the only company he now kept was with boardroom hustlers?

Jo-Jo said, 'Don't listen to him, Ellen, he's going to ask you for money, it's written all over his face.'

'Bright friend you've got.'

'I know that, Roger. And the answer is no. I'm not giving you any more money. You've had all you're going to get out of me.'

'Now that's so disappointing.' He smiled and went over to the dresser. 'I remember this.' He picked up a willow-pattern plate, tossed it in the air and then caught it. 'Funny how things stay with you.'

'But there's nothing particularly funny about you, is there?'

It was Matthew. He came straight into the room, took the plate out of Roger's hands and placed it carefully on the dresser. He glanced across to Ellen. 'Everything okay?' he asked.

But before she had a chance to reply, Roger let out a loud, caustic laugh. 'And this must be Duncan Carter, the husband-to-be.'

Ellen opened her mouth to correct him, but Matthew held up his hand and stopped her. 'Jo-Jo,' he said, 'would you go upstairs, please. I want to have a private word with Roger ... if that's all right with you, Ellen?'

Jo-Jo disappeared to the tiny landing upstairs where she hovered on the top step, hoping to hear what Matthew was going to say.

Roger spoke first.

'So, Duncan,' he said, 'what is it you want to talk to me about?' He settled himself in an armchair and waited expectantly. 'How can I help you? Do you want to know what marriage to Ellen will be like, is that it? But if you don't mind me saying so, that's not very gallant of you.'

Matthew ignored Roger and sat himself in the armchair opposite him. 'I'll come straight to the point,' he said. 'I know all about the disgusting letters you've written to Ellen. In fact, I've read them and I've seen the photographs, and as a solicitor I think you'll find me more than ready to take the necessary action in preventing you from causing my future wife any further unhappiness. I presume that's why you've turned up here, to see what you could extract from her. Am I right?'

Ellen held her breath and Roger squirmed in his seat. One of his eyelids began to twitch and no longer did he look the cocky chancer he had a few moments ago. Beads of sweat were gathering on his forehead and he licked his dry lips nervously. He stood up abruptly and ran his hand over his stubbly chin. 'I don't need much. Just enough to—'

'Forget it.'

'What's a few thousand to you? I know you can afford it. You're loaded, you and your mother.'

'Whether I can afford it is immaterial. You're not scrounging off me or Ellen. Is that clear?'

Roger appealed to Ellen. 'How about it, Ellen? Couldn't you find it in your heart to lend me a bit of cash, just until I've—'

Matthew leaped to his feet. 'Don't even think about it! You've had everything you're ever likely to get from Ellen. Now, get out of here.'

'Picked yourself a regular champion, Ellen, haven't you?' Roger said, with a sneer. 'Well, I suppose there's nothing for it but to be on my way. But who knows? I might be back.'

As he started to move towards the door, Ellen said, 'Before you go, Roger, tell me how you knew about Duncan and me?'

'What's it worth?'

'It's worth you getting out of here with both arms resembling their current state,' Matthew said.

Roger laughed. 'That's really not the kind of talk I'd expect to hear from a solicitor. But it just goes to show that beneath all that well-polished veneer of respectability you and your mother affect you're just as vulgar and yobbish as the next man.'

'Just tell me,' Ellen said.

'Well, why not? You've a spy in the camp up at Crantsford Hall, Duncan. Your cleaner has an easy tongue when it comes to tittle-tattle and has unwittingly shared your daily goings-on with any number of folk in Crantsford – Charmaine's sister for one. By the way, how's your mother's drinking these days?'

Roger's exit was as sudden as his arrival. Ellen watched him walk along the lane away from the cottage.

'I don't know what to say,' she said, when he was completely out of sight. 'I can't get over how changed he is. He looked so pathetic. So wasted.' Her face suddenly brightened with a radiant smile. 'But you were wonderful, Matthew. I couldn't believe it when you pretended to be Duncan. Thank you. I mean it, really.'

'That's okay.' He went over to the mantelpiece and picked up a framed photograph of Ellen and Simon. He stared at it for a few moments, then put it down. 'I hope he doesn't bother you again but, out of interest, how much have you given him so far?'

She turned away, embarrassed.

'Look, Ellen, I don't want to pry, but when I was outside I heard you say you wouldn't give him any more, which means you must have given in to his blackmail. Why, in God's name?'

'I didn't know what else to do.'

He swung her round to face him. 'Why didn't you just tell Duncan? He's a solicitor, he would have dealt with it.'

'I didn't want Duncan knowing about ... well, you know. It's ... it's something we don't discuss.'

A creak of floorboards above their heads reminded them both that Jo-Jo was still upstairs on the landing and that she was probably listening to their conversation.

'I think we need to talk privately,' Matthew said. He took Ellen by the elbow and led her outside, to the bank, where he made her sit down. 'Now, explain to me exactly why you didn't tell Duncan about Roger's letters.'

'Matthew, do you have to be so high-handed? I'm very grateful for you helping me just now with Roger, but this is really none of your business.'

'I disagree.'

'How can you say that?'

'Ellen, anyone who cares about you would say it was their business to help you.'

'Oh, please, don't start all that up again.'

'Start what up?'

'You know.'

'No, I don't, you'd better spell it out for me.'

'Don't be obtuse.'

He smiled. 'Does it really bother you so much that I care for you?'

She plucked a long stem of grass and chewed it.

'I'll take that as a yes, shall I?'

They sat in silence and Ellen was reminded of the day when she had first met Matthew and the moment when they'd stood side by side in silence as they'd leaned against the drystone wall. Except now she no longer felt awkward in his company. There was even an element of enjoyment creeping into their conversations, as though every exchange between them was like a verbal game of ping-pong with their wits acting as bats driving the points home. She braced herself ready for the challenge ahead and served the ball to start the match.

'You said you'd behave.'

'So I did. But if I promise to make an extra effort at curbing myself will you talk to me as . . . as a friend?'

'I thought you didn't want to be friends.'

'I've changed my mind.'

'So what kind of friend do you want to be?'

'How about you forget that I'd willingly hurl myself under a stampede of wildebeest for the chance of gaining your love and talk to me like – like you would with Hermione?'

She smiled. 'You don't know what you're saying. A conversation with Hermione is like dancing with a snake.'

They both laughed and Ellen turned over on to her front and stretched out on the grass. Matthew lay alongside her. After a few moments he said, 'What did you mean when you said it's something we don't discuss?'

She inclined her head towards him but didn't answer him.

'Is sex a problem between you? You know, actually doing—'

She smiled.

'What's so funny?'

'I don't know.'

'Yes, you do. Tell me.'

'I suppose I'm finding it slightly amusing that you should be interested in, of all things, my sex life with Duncan.'

'Given a choice I'd rather discuss *our* sex life.'

She smiled again. 'I'm sure you would.'

'Can I ask you a question?'

'You've done nothing else.'

'One more, then?'

She nodded.

'Why did you cry when we made love?'

'I didn't.'

He reached out and stroked her arm. 'You did and I want to know why.'

She shifted her arm away from him. 'It was probably because I knew it was wrong, what we'd just done.' Which wasn't exactly true. She had cried because what had passed between them had been so exquisite – she had never known a more fulfilling moment. It had made her realise that all her married life she had put up with something that had been so utterly second rate.

'I suppose it was . . . if you really loved Duncan.'

'But I do.'

'Then prove it to me. Since I've known you I've not seen any evidence that you love the man.'

'I don't know how you carry on when you're in love but not every relationship has to be chock-full of grand gestures and stomach-churning sugary sentiment.'

'I agree, but then I didn't have in mind silly *Love Is* cartoons or messages left on the fridge. Am I allowed another question?'

She sighed. 'Go on.'

'It's quite a personal one.'

'And the others weren't?'

'Did you *ever* have a good, loving sex life with Roger?'

'Heavens, you're obsessed!'

'Well?' Matthew pressed.

'Is this the objective friend wanting to know, or the flattened body under the wildebeest?'

'The objective friend,' he lied.

'Then I suppose the answer is no,' she said simply. 'No, I didn't. And isn't it obvious? Isn't that why all men are unfaithful? If they can't get what they want at home they look elsewhere.'

'I wouldn't know, I've never been unfaithful.'

'Well, Roger was and he went off because he found someone able to satisfy him in a way I was unable to. I . . . I wasn't enough for him, I suppose. I didn't enjoy sex when it was make-believe, when I had to be something I wasn't. It just didn't feel right.' She looked up at him. 'He made me feel so inadequate.'

'Believe me, Ellen, there's nothing inadequate about you. The problem was all Roger's, not yours.'

She thought about this. How easy it was to accept blame when it was so freely thrust upon one. Not once had she questioned Roger's ability to perform in bed, only her own. 'I think I'm just beginning to realise that.'

'Good, because whatever it was that Roger felt towards you it wasn't love. How could it have been? When somebody really cares for a person the last thing they want to do is hurt or humiliate them. Now answer me this, and tell me the truth. Are you marrying Duncan because sex isn't all that important to him and you think that with him you'll be spared any further humiliation?'

She lifted her head. 'Why on earth should I answer a question like that?'

'Try it and see.'

'You're an arrogant swine, aren't you?'

He smiled. 'I did just save you from a fate worse than death.'

She shook her head. Why the hell shouldn't she tell him the truth? There was no shame in it. 'Okay, then,' she said, 'I'll admit it. I'm marrying Duncan because he's not obsessed with sex and never in a million years will he hurt me in the way Roger did. Satisfied now?'

'So you see him as safe?'

'Yes,' she agreed. 'He's wonderfully safe ... unlike you.'

He raised an eyebrow. 'If by safe you mean dispassionate and cold and lacking the desire to make love to the woman I adore, then certainly I agree, I'm not safe.' He reached out and gently traced his hand along the line of her jaw. 'You know exactly how I feel about you, Ellen, so there's no point in repeating myself, but if Duncan wasn't around and I asked you to marry me, would you then?'

'No.'

He looked hurt. 'Am I really that bad?'

She pursed her lips and turned away from him. 'You've broken your promise. You're no longer behaving yourself.' She got to her feet. 'And I've got work to do. I need to open the barn.'

He stood up too. 'In that case I'd better get on and give you the bad news, which is why I came here so early in the first place. Bernie died last night, and I hoped you and Jo-Jo might be able to spare some time to be with Hermione. She's more upset than she's letting on.'

Susie was more than delighted to take charge for the morning. 'Gosh! Me in charge, just imagine,' she said happily. 'Of course you must go off and look after dear old Mrs Rowlands, I'll be fine here.'

Ellen hoped she was right: Sunday was usually the busiest day of the week.

By eleven thirty the day was hot, sticky and airless, the same as it had been for some days. Ellen and Jo-Jo took the steep incline of Beggarman's Lane at a slow pace. They crossed the busy Crantsford road and then walked along the Crescent in the shade of the chestnut trees. It had been hot for so many weeks now that the leaves had started to drop and lay scattered on the pavement, crisp and yellow.

'I was lucky,' Ellen said. 'When I was expecting Simon we had a lousy summer. This heat must be awful for you.'

Jo-Jo paused for a moment. 'You're right,' she puffed, 'it is, and why on earth women put themselves through this time and time again I'll never know. I can see why you only had Simon.'

They passed Orchard House where they saw Bonkers herding Floss and Millie into the car. He waved to Ellen and promptly dropped his keys.

The back door was open at Laburnum House and Hermione was throwing a pile of old newspapers into a large dustbin.

'Time to start clearing the decks ready for you and Duncan,' she said flatly, when Ellen and Jo-Jo stepped into the garden room. She hurriedly brushed away her tears. 'Goodness, Jo-Jo,' she said, in a more concerned voice, 'you look worn out. Come into the kitchen at once and sit down.'

'Don't start fussing,' Jo-Jo warned, wiping the sweat from her forehead, 'I'm fine. It's just this dreadful heat. I feel like I'm being cooked alive.'

Despite Jo-Jo's remonstrations Hermione made her sit in the kitchen where it was relatively cool. She fetched her a glass of water. 'Now don't move, not until I say so. I'm sure I've got some ice somewhere in the freezer.'

'Why don't you let me do that?' Ellen said kindly.

'Just because Bernie's died and I'm upset, don't go thinking I've lost all my capabilities,' Hermione snapped. She covered her face with her hands. 'I'm sorry,' she said, 'it's just that—'

Ellen went to her. 'It's all right,' she said, wrapping her arms around Hermione, 'I know how fond you were of him. He was a lovely man and you've every right to be sad.'

Hermione leaned into Ellen. 'He was stupid and rude and he said the silliest of things, but I miss the old rascal already. He made me laugh . . . and he gave me the courage to question things I'd long since thought I had the answer for. Oh, Ellen, I shall miss him so much, he was one in a million. Truly he was.'

Duncan received the news with a mixture of annoyance and pleasure.

'Thanks, Howard,' he said, into the phone. 'I really appreciate you doing the survey so promptly and letting me know on a Sunday how you got on.'

'No problem, I'll get the typed report to you by Tuesday. Best of luck. I'm off for a round of golf now.'

'What – in this heat? You're mad.'

'Just think of the tan I'll have. See you.'

After he'd put down the phone Duncan looked at the notes he'd made. He contemplated the first four points: replace roof, replumb and rewire throughout, employ a specialist firm to eradicate wet and dry rot. There were a further ten points but they were of a secondary nature. Howard had suggested that, by the time the shouting was over, he'd be looking at a repair bill in excess of forty thousand pounds.

He leaned back in his chair and swivelled it round to gaze out of the window. The lawns at Crantsford looked worse than he'd ever seen them – there was barely a hint of green. He wondered how long it would take for the dusty grass to recover from the drought. The forecast had given rain later that day with severe storms predicted for most of the country, bringing an end to the humid muggy atmosphere they'd been suffering for over a week now. And according to Maurice, at the golf club last night, there was even a danger of flash floods.

But the weather was of little importance to Duncan right now. His two main priorities were to sort out Laburnum House and his mother.

What a ghastly little man that Nigel Wade was. And what an opportunist. Question was, where would it leave him if Nadia was stupid enough to marry the man?

Shortly after Donald had died, Nadia had made a will but she had never revealed its contents and had had it drawn up by a rival firm of solicitors in town. He could only guess at what she'd decided to do with the house and all her money. But now that *Nige* was on the scene, it was just possible that things could change.

He had no ready answers for this particular problem so he decided to shelve it until he was in a better position to do something about it – he'd always been of the belief that if sufficient information was not to hand, the right solution would never be found.

Instead he turned his thoughts back to Laburnum House and decided to call Hermione Rowlands directly, rather than leaving it to the estate agent to tell her that he was lowering his offer.

He dialled the number. Matthew answered.

'Hello, this is Duncan Carter. Is Mrs Rowlands there, please?'

Matthew recognised Duncan's voice immediately. 'She is, but I'm afraid she's not available.' This wasn't exactly the truth but he didn't want Hermione bothered by the likes of Duncan when she was so upset.

'Oh.'

'Perhaps I can help you, Duncan, this is Matthew.'

Duncan thought for a moment. It was always best to negotiate directly, but really there wasn't much time. Everything was now set for him and Ellen to be married on the twelfth of September, which was exactly three and a half weeks away. But even so, just because they had set a date he wasn't going to lose out financially. He had to hope that the Rowlands woman was keener to sell than he was to buy.

'Is it about the house?' prompted Matthew.

Duncan took the plunge. 'As a matter of fact, yes. Perhaps you'd like to pass a message on to Mrs Rowlands. It's bad news, I'm afraid. The survey report has been rather damning and the list of repairs is extensive and runs into tens of thousands, and . . . and in view of this I need to review my offer.'

'How many tens of thousands?'

'Approximately sixty,' lied Duncan.

'Approximately,' repeated Matthew derisively. 'What would you say *exactly*?'

'Sixty-five,' Duncan said coolly, doodling a picture of a house on the bottom of his note-pad.

'Go to hell!'

The phone went dead and Duncan's fountain pen skidded across the sheet of paper neatly dividing his house in two.

'Who was that?'

'I thought you were in the garden, Hermione,' Matthew said, straightening the receiver in its cradle.

'I was, but I came in for another glass of water for Jo-Jo. Was it Duncan?'

'How did you guess?'

She smiled. 'It must have been the friendly way you said goodbye to him. What did he want, apart from the woman you love?'

Matthew pushed his hands into his trouser pockets. 'Hell, Hermione, do you have to be so direct?'

'I'm sorry.'

'Oh, forget it. Ellen's delightful fiancé is trying to lower his offer by sixty-five thousand.'

Hermione whistled. 'Is he, by Jove?'

'I did the right thing, didn't I?'

'You most certainly did. Now come and join us outside. We're in the summerhouse in the shade.' She tucked her arm through his. 'And I want to thank you for bringing in the cavalry to cheer me up. Ellen's been telling me all about Roger's appearance at the cottage this morning. Fancy you pretending to be Duncan. Pardon the expression but it sounds to me like you were quite the rooster.'

37

By late that afternoon the air was as thick as treacle and the sky was as black. Threatening storm clouds had gathered and they were casting an eerie darkness over the garden of Laburnum House.

Hermione's earlier rush of energy and settled mind had evaporated and now she felt weary and overcome with sadness again. Ellen had hinted several times already that she needed to get back to the barn, but each time she mentioned relieving Susie, Hermione insisted that she stay just a little longer.

'Please don't go yet,' she said gloomily, sitting back in her wicker chair in the summerhouse. 'It's like old times having you here. It's like it used to be, before . . .' But her voice trailed away.

'Before what?' asked Ellen gently.

'Before everything, before Roger and Duncan . . . and Bernie. Why don't you give Susie a ring and see if she can cope another hour without you?'

'I've got a better idea,' Jo-Jo said. 'I want to go back to the cottage for a shower so I could check on Susie and if there's a problem I'll get her to ring you.'

Although Hermione was reluctant to part with anyone's company, she saw that if she let Jo-Jo go she could at least keep Ellen with her for a few hours more.

'Do you want a lift back?' Matthew asked from behind his easel a few yards away, where he was working on a painting of the summerhouse.

'Don't be daft,' Jo-Jo said, struggling to her feet and smoothing down her cotton dungarees, which had ridden up between her legs. 'It's only ten minutes, if that.'

'But it's so hot,' Hermione implored. 'Why not let Matthew—'

'I'd rather walk. I feel like my body's seizing up.'

Ellen walked up to the house with her. 'Tell Susie to close the barn, will you?' she said when they reached the courtyard, and she handed over the keys of the cottage. 'I feel awful that I've left her alone practically all day. Just get her to lock up and I'll sort everything out in the morning. Are you sure you're okay?'

Jo-Jo tutted. 'Stop fussing. I'll see you later.'

When Jo-Jo reached the barn her whole body was wet with sweat: she could feel it trickling between her swollen breasts. She was also conscious of a persistent dull ache in the lower part of her back, which had been with her since breakfast-time. She supposed it was the baby getting into position for the big event shortly to come. It didn't cross her mind that she might be in labour.

She passed on Ellen's message to Susie and then puffed her way over to the cottage where she gratefully let herself in and slowly climbed the stairs. As she started running the shower and stripped off her clothes, a loud crack of thunder boomed overhead and rattled the small window in its rotting frame. She opened it. A large fat drop of rain splashed on the end of her nose. Rain at last to clear the air, she thought. Suddenly the sombre sky was lit up as a dramatic flash of lightning streaked angrily across it like a magical piece of graffiti. A few seconds later more thunder crashed and rumbled overhead.

Jo-Jo closed the window and stepped into the shower. The water was cool and refreshing, but while the storm gathered momentum outside the pain in her back steadily increased.

Duncan thought his timing would be perfect as he swept out through the gates at Crantsford Hall. Ellen would be just locking up the barn and he'd be able to talk to her about Laburnum House. He needed to make her realise that it was now down to her to convince Hermione Rowlands that what he was offering for her property was a fair price. Nobody in their right mind would be stupid enough to buy Laburnum House at anything more than he was offering. The trouble was, as he well knew, he wanted the house too much. Everything about it was perfect for him and Ellen – apart from the neglect and the current owner – which meant, of course, that he was at a disadvantage in terms of sitting round the negotiating table. It would be so much easier if he could simply walk away. But he couldn't. His mind was set and he was determined that nobody, least of all an old woman, was going to get the better of him. He would outmanoeuvre her if it was the last thing he did.

Another crack of thunder roared overhead and the rain increased. Duncan flicked the wiper blades on full and they dashed frantically to and fro across the windscreen in a futile attempt to keep it clear. The car in front had now slowed to a snail's pace and would have been invisible, had it not been for its rear lights, which glowed faintly red like hot coals, in the deluge of torrential rain pelting down and making Duncan's expensive car sound horribly like a tin can.

He pulled off the main Crantsford road and turned into the potholed Beggarman's Lane. Amazed, he saw that it barely resembled a road any longer, it was more like a river. Muddy water was gushing down the small hill, cascading into the stream at the bottom, which for the past few weeks had almost run dry. He bumped and splashed his way to the car park and, seeing no sign of light or movement over in the barn, made a dash to the cottage. He cursed it for not having a porch and he hammered on the door.

'Ellen,' he shouted, 'it's me, Duncan, let me in.'

He thumped on the door and called out again, but his voice was swallowed up by the crash of yet more thunder. Within seconds he was drenched. He bent down and pushed open the letter-box.

'Ellen,' he yelled, 'are you there?'

He saw a figure coming towards him wrapped in a towel. He breathed a sigh of relief. She must have been having a bath or a shower, that's why she hadn't heard him. But when the door opened he saw his mistake.

'Oh,' he said, when he saw Jo-Jo clutching a towel around her. 'Well, let me in,' he went on, 'I'm getting soaked standing out here.' He pushed past her. 'Where's Ellen?'

'She's not here.' Jo-Jo slammed the door shut.

He swung round. 'So where is she?'

'She's at Hermione's.'

'And?'

'And what?'

'When will she be back?' he demanded.

'I've no idea.'

'Then I'll wait.'

'I'd rather you didn't.'

'I beg your pardon?'

'You heard.'

Duncan stared at Jo-Jo, then turned away from the sight of her. He went and stood by the fireplace. He ran his hand over his wet face. 'I don't know how you've wormed your way into Ellen's life, but let's get one thing entirely straight between us. When I marry Ellen next month she'll never see you again. Is that clear?'

'Isn't that for Ellen to decide?'

'No,' he said, his eyes dark and steely. 'Ellen's too good-natured to see you for what you really are. Now get me a towel, I'm wet through.' He began pulling at his shirt and unbuttoning it. 'Well, go on! What are you still standing there for?'

She took a step nearer to him. 'Two things. First, you don't ever tell me what to do, okay? And second, you can stop treating me as though I'm nothing more than a pile of shit.'

He laughed at her. 'But that's exactly what you are.'

'The hell I am!' She lashed out at him with her hand, but he caught hold of her wrist. He stood for a moment contemplating her and all at once her open hostility towards him made him question himself. Why not just let his anger go? Why not, just for once, say and do what he really felt? Why should he have to keep struggling to control himself?

'Let go of me, you bastard!'

At first he didn't hear her, but then, very slowly, her words sank in. 'What did you say?'

'You heard me, you bastard, now let go of me.'

He gripped her wrist even harder. 'Apologise!'

'No!' She kicked out at him and somehow managed to break free. She crossed the room and clutched her towel around her. She stood behind one of the armchairs, frightened at what he might do next. She could see that both his hands were tightly clenched. He started moving towards her.

'Apologise for what you just called me,' he said, in a dangerously low voice.

'Okay, okay,' she said nervously, 'I'm sorry.'

He stood still. But her apology wasn't enough to stop what was happening inside him. The resentment he'd experienced as a child for being different – for being unwanted – had finally broken free and suddenly *it* was in control. The misery of being bullied at school because he'd been a misfit swam before his eyes. He felt the terrible burden of it and wanted to be rid of it, once and for all. He moved towards Jo-Jo.

'You're a tart, Jo-Jo, aren't you?'

She gripped the back of the armchair.

'Answer me.'

'No! No, I'm not.'

'Yes, you are. You're a waste of space.' He was standing beside her now. 'Look at you, still a child and pregnant. I bet you don't even know who the father is, do you?' He prodded at her shoulder.

She wanted to get away from him but he was too close. She was trapped. He prodded her again and his touch sent a sharp pain searing through her body. She gasped and clutched her stomach.

'How many did you sleep with? And what does it feel like knowing you're producing a child without any chance of a future?'

'It will have a future!' she shouted at him.

At the sound of her words the room lit up with an explosive flash of lightning followed by a spontaneous clap of thunder and her body tightened with the most excruciating pain. It was so awful she wanted to fall to the floor, to curl herself into a tiny safe ball. But she wouldn't let him see her weaken. She had to stay strong.

He pushed his face closer to her and laughed derisively. 'And tell me, what kind of future can *you* offer *it*?'

'I'm giving the baby up for adoption,' she managed to say. Then as swiftly as the pain had consumed her body it went, leaving her with the strength to fight back. 'You're adopted, aren't you, Duncan?' she said, her voice level and quite calm.

He drew away from her but didn't speak.

'Yeah,' she said, seeing a way to get the better of her tormentor. 'I'd forgotten that you were adopted. And I reckon you don't like it, do you? Because maybe, just maybe your natural mother was how you see me, and where does that leave you, Duncan? I'll tell you, Mr Airs and bloody Graces, it makes you nothing but a bastard!'

Too late she realised her mistake. Instead of making Duncan back off, her words had the opposite effect. She had totally misjudged him.

She felt the blinding crack of his hand against the side of her face and then nothing.

Duncan stumbled out of the cottage and ran wildly through the rain to his car. He crashed the gears and rocketed away, but the car stalled just as he reached the steepest and narrowest part of the lane. He cursed and turned the key. Nothing, just a weak apology of the engine stuttering to spring into life, and with the torrent of water still gushing down the lane the car began to slide slowly backwards. He snatched on the handbrake and then tried the engine again. Nothing. He thumped the steering-wheel again and again, and then, looking back towards the cottage, he began to shake.

What in God's name had he done?

He was horrified at the anger that had unleashed itself in that small room. Horrified that he, of all people, had been unable to check it. It was like a Jekyll and Hyde experience. One minute he'd been in control and the next he'd lost it. Shame overcame him and he bent his head over the steering-wheel and wept.

When eventually he pulled himself together he realised he couldn't stay where he was. He had to get away.

He abandoned the car and by the time he had staggered up the hill to the main road and reached Church Walk Mews and let himself into the office, he had managed to re-create in his mind the events that had just taken place.

The girl had provoked him.

They had had words.

She had attacked him.

He had merely defended himself.

She had been fine when he left her.

Hermione's eyes sparkled.

'I can't remember a thunderstorm like it,' she said, gazing out of the sitting-room window and over the water-logged garden.

Ellen didn't share Hermione's enthusiasm for the weather. She was worried about Jo-Jo. They had tried ringing the cottage to make sure she was okay only to find that the lines were down.

'I'm going to see if Jo-Jo's all right.'

Hermione came away from the window. 'Good idea, Ellen, I'll come with you.'

'Don't be ridiculous, Hermione,' Matthew said. 'I'm not having you out there in this weather. I'll go with Ellen.'

Hermione pulled a face. 'I always miss out on the fun.'

'I'd hardly call this fun,' Matthew said, when he opened the back door in the garden room. As he stepped outside, the ancient cast-iron guttering above the doorway gave way and an ocean of water poured over him.

Ellen laughed but Matthew caught hold of her hand and pulled her under the broken piece of guttering so that she, too, ended up soaked to the skin.

'You pig,' she spluttered, pushing back her wet hair from her face.

He smiled. 'It's called a baptism by fire. Now it doesn't matter how much it rains, we can't get any wetter.'

They found Duncan's abandoned car near the top of Beggarman's Lane. They pressed on and knocked at the door of the cottage. There was no answer. They pushed against the door but it was shut.

'Well, unless she opens the door we can't get in,' Ellen shouted above the boom of more thunder. 'I gave her my keys and the other set's hanging up in the kitchen.' She pounded on the door again. 'Maybe she's having a nap.'

Matthew peered through the sitting-room window.

'Oh, no, she's not, Ellen, she's on the floor!'

They smashed one of the small panes of glass and climbed in through the window.

Jo-Jo was unconscious. Her right cheek was swollen and bruised and blood was beginning to congeal in the corner of her mouth.

'Jo-Jo,' Ellen said loudly, down on her knees beside her. 'Jo-Jo, can you hear me?'

Jo-Jo could hear her name being called. It was a distant voice. A voice she hadn't heard in years. She could barely hear it from where she was playing at the bottom of the garden. But there it was again. It was Gran and she was calling her in for tea. She was standing on the back step, her arms outstretched, waiting for her best little girl to run to her. She ran all the way up the garden but when she got to the house it was Hermione waiting for her. 'There now,' Hermione said, 'come inside and wash your hands, your tea's on the table.'

But now somebody else was calling her name. Over and over.

Jo-Jo . . . Jo-Jo . . . Jo-Jo.

She forced her eyes open. A pink blob swam before her. 'Hermione?'

'No, it's me, Ellen.'

'Ellen?'

'Yes, and Matthew's here as well. Can you tell us what happened?'

'I . . . I don't know, I was in the garden with Gran. No, I wasn't. I was here . . . and so was Duncan, he was—' But she broke off and her face twisted with pain. She let out a loud cry and drew her knees up then slowly released them, taking small shallow breaths.

'I don't believe it,' muttered Matthew, standing behind Ellen. 'She's in labour!'

The contraction passed and a faint smile spread over Jo-Jo's face. 'I'm glad you told me that, Matthew, I would never have guessed.'

'Right,' said Ellen purposefully, doing her best to disguise the panic rising within her. 'Do you think you can move?'

'Yeah, sure,' Jo-Jo replied, 'no problem.' She lifted her head but the room started to spin. 'Er . . . actually, no, I don't think I can.'

'Okay,' Ellen said. 'Just stay there and don't do anything.' She got to her feet and motioned for Matthew to join her in the kitchen. 'I think we'd better call for an ambulance.'

'You're forgetting, the lines are down.'

She grabbed the phone from the wall. It made no sound. 'Damn! Now what?'

'We'll use your car to drive her to the hospital.'

She shook her head. 'Not with Duncan's car in the way, we won't. Oh, Matthew, what are we going to do?'

'Right,' he said, breathing out deeply and trying to keep calm, 'there has to be a way.' He ran his hands through his hair and paced the floor in the tiny kitchen. 'Okay. This is what we'll do. You stay here and look after Jo-Jo, and I'll go and see if I can get into Duncan's car to let the handbrake off. With a bit of luck I'll be able to roll it back down the lane. Then we'll drive her to hospital.'

But when Matthew went out into the pelting rain he found the car locked. Undaunted, and even taking a certain sense of pleasure in what he did next, he picked up a large stone from the muddy ground and smashed the driver's window. He reached in to open the car door. Immediately an alarm went off, loud and piercing, and as soon as he sat in the car and released the handbrake and tried to move the steering wheel he realised it was no good. The wheel had locked and the angle at which the tyres were pointing meant that the car would only move a few inches before it hit a tree, which would still leave the lane impassable.

He darted back to the cottage.

'It's no good,' he whispered to Ellen in the kitchen. 'I can't move the car. How long do you think we've got? Labour can go on for hours, can't it?'

Ellen chewed on her lip. 'I wouldn't like to say. The contractions are coming quite fast.'

Matthew groaned.

'I know!' she said, her face instantly brightening. 'Bonkers! Run up to Orchard House and get him to come here.'

'But what use would that fool be?'

'Don't be so bloody dense, Matthew. He's a gynaecologist. He knows more about delivering babies than we'll ever know. Now go and fetch him. And be quick.'

38

When Bonkers opened the front door at Orchard House Matthew's relief was profound. He would never have imagined it possible to be so relieved at the sight of a man whom previously he had written off as an idiotic buffoon.

It was a while before he could speak – his running days had long since passed him by – and while trying to regain his breath he stood in the hall of Orchard House dripping water onto the cream carpet, while Bonkers looked anxiously at the rapidly developing puddle.

'We need your help,' he managed to say at last. 'It's Jo-Jo, a friend of Ellen's, she's in labour and we can't get her to a hospital and . . . and we don't know what to do. Please will you come?' He could hear the desperation in his voice, but then as if by magic he saw the man before him undergo a complete character change. Superman couldn't have whizzed into his underpants any faster.

Explanations were made quickly to Susie, who was busy with the girls in the kitchen gathering candles in case the power went, and a call was put through to the emergency services on her mobile. They were out of the house within minutes, with Matthew unable to keep up with Bonkers who was sprinting effortlessly towards Beggarman's Lane, his medical case in his hand. When Matthew managed to catch up with him, Bonkers, who wasn't even out of breath, said, 'Can you talk me through what's happened so far?'

Matthew couldn't have talked his way through anything right at that moment. 'Ask Ellen when we get there,' he panted.

Ellen let them in. Bonkers went straight over to Jo-Jo and knelt on the floor beside her. Her head was now on a pillow and she was covered with a blanket which Ellen had fetched from upstairs. 'Can you fill me in?'

'I think she's got concussion. She keeps complaining of dizziness and she's been sick a few times.'

'And the contractions?'

'Every few minutes.'

He opened his case. 'It's too dark in here, I need more light.'

Ellen and Matthew jumped to attention and crashed into each other as they moved about the room switching on lamps.

'Now, Jo-Jo,' Bonkers said, in a lighter tone, 'do you think I might possibly take a peep to see how everything's getting along?'

She nodded and then grimaced.

'Another contraction?'

She squeezed her eyes shut.

'In that case, we'll wait a few moments, shall we? Hold my hand and squeeze as hard as you can. That's it, Jo-Jo, well done. Now keep the breathing going, nice and slowly, you're doing fine. There now, you handled that splendidly.' He released his hand from her slackened grip. 'Sure you haven't done this kind of thing before? No? You do surprise me, but while we've got a moment, shall I have a quick shufti?'

Ellen and Matthew were mesmerised. Bonkers was marvellous. His words had a wonderfully hypnotic quality to them, which meant that not only was Jo-Jo more relaxed now, so were they. Matthew had the feeling that at some time in the not too distant future he might even apologise to Bonkers for having misjudged him.

Jo-Jo gave birth to a wailing girl just minutes before there was a knock at the door announcing the arrival of the ambulance, which was waiting for them at the top of the lane. A stretcher was brought to the cottage and it was only when Matthew, Ellen and Bonkers walked alongside Jo-Jo that they realised the storm had passed.

'Did it rain much?' Jo-Jo asked, sleepily, as the ambulance crew tried hard not to lose their balance on the muddy sloping path where Duncan's car was still in the way.

'Can't say I noticed,' Matthew said, with a laugh. 'How about you, Ellen?'

But Ellen wasn't listening. She was lost in her own thoughts. She was thinking of Duncan and what Jo-Jo had told her while Matthew was fetching Bonkers.

Later that evening Ellen drove over to Crantsford Hall.

'I'm afraid Duncan isn't here,' Nadia said. 'I thought he was with you,' she added. 'He left here hours ago just as the storm started up.'

Ellen explained about Duncan's abandoned car in Beggarman's Lane. 'And there's something else I'd like to discuss with you.'

'In that case you'd better come in.'

Ellen followed Nadia through the house and to a small, light room that overlooked the sunken rose garden where only last night she had sat with Duncan drinking gin and tonic – the memory appalled her now. Through the French windows she could see that the roses had taken a beating from the torrential downpour and only the tightest buds remained intact. The rest of the blooms formed a scarlet carpet on the sodden flower bed. Tiny pools of water had gathered in the petals and they glistened in the low evening sun that was filtering through the last remaining storm clouds.

'Sit down,' Nadia said. 'So what is it you have to tell me?'

Ellen wished that there was a drink on offer, but in the absence of any Dutch courage she was forced to rely on her own.

'Does it sound feasible to you that your son has a darker side to his nature?' In view of what Jo-Jo had told her at the cottage, this question was absurd and it was as much as Ellen could do to restrain herself from resorting to the same level of violence on Nadia that her son had used on Jo-Jo.

Nadia tilted her head and considered Ellen's words, her eyes keenly alert. Very slowly she leaned back in her chair. 'Get to the point.'

Ellen did. She told her what Duncan had done to Jo-Jo. 'He left her lying on the floor, Mrs Carter, unconscious and bleeding.'

Nadia's face remained impassive.

'And I suppose as his mother you'll defend him, and even convince yourself that Jo-Jo is lying. Well, let me tell you,' Ellen rose to her feet, 'the hospital will testify to the injuries inflicted on her.'

Nadia cleared her throat. 'Am I allowed to speak?'

'There's nothing you can say. It's probably down to you that he's turned out the way he has. If you hadn't bullied him he'd—'

'Sit down and let me have my say,' Nadia intoned. 'Duncan's behaviour is not my responsibility. Do you understand? I am not answerable for his character defects.'

'Then who the hell is?'

'He is, of course, and his natural parents.'

'His natural parents? You can't be serious.'

Nadia leaned forwards. 'Donald and I gave Duncan everything we possibly could. He wanted for nothing—'

'Except your love, perhaps,' Ellen said.

Nadia waved this comment aside with one of her large hands. 'That's just the kind of predictable, facile conclusion I would have expected from someone like you. But let me ask you this, was it love *you* were offering Duncan?'

Ellen hesitated. 'I . . . I would have given him what he needed.'

Nadia laughed nastily. 'As I thought. And now, I suppose, you're breaking off the engagement. That's the thing with your kind of love, easy come, easy go. Will this girl go to the police?'

'That's up to her,' Ellen responded coolly.

'But you could persuade her not to?'

'Never! Duncan deserves what he gets.'

'If it goes to court Duncan will run rings around her. He's a respected man of position, it'll be her word against his.'

Ellen sprang to her feet. 'He's nothing but a bully and so are you! And what the hell that nice man Nigel sees in you I'll never know.'

Nadia also stood up. A strange smile spread over her face. 'I thought I gave rather a convincing performance with that pathetic little man. It certainly took you all in – Cynthia, Phyllis, you and Duncan. Especially Duncan.'

'I don't understand.'

'Nigel Wade was merely to serve a purpose. I wanted to prove a point to my son.'

Ellen frowned. 'You mean you wanted to make him jealous?'

'No. I wanted to show him how easy it was to attract the wrong sort of admirer.' She gave Ellen a pointed look.

For a split second Ellen experienced a wave of sympathy towards Duncan. If she had grown up with this twisted, loathsome woman, who possessed all the love and warmth of Medea, she would have been driven to violence years ago. 'I think I should go now,' she said.

'I agree. I'll see you out.'

They stood at the front door in the hall, where it felt dark and dismal. Ellen couldn't get out of the house fast enough. She opened the door herself.

'Just one thing more,' Nadia said. 'You came here this evening full of self-righteousness, but you have to remember that I know exactly what I saw in your cottage that day back in April. You successfully fooled Duncan, but not me. I'd just like you to know that.'

PART THREE

September

The Song of the Hawthorn Fairy

These thorny branches bore the May
So many months ago,
That when the scattered petals lay
Like drifts of fallen snow,
'This is the story's end,' you said;
But O, not half was told!
For see, my haws are here instead,
And hungry birdies shall be fed
On these when days are cold.

Cicely Mary Barker

39

Ellen locked the barn and wandered down to the stream. It was something she usually did at this time of day, finding it a relaxing way to finish work, and now that the summer was gradually drawing to a close she was determined to make the most of the remaining opportunities to sit outside.

It was nearly four weeks since the storm and all its associated drama, and during that time Ellen had neither heard from Duncan nor seen him. She had certainly made no effort to get in touch with him, other than to return his ring in a small Jiffy bag – there was no accompanying note.

The day after the storm she had taken the cottage and Spring Bank Dried Flowers off the market and thrown herself into her work, ensuring that there would be no time for her to reflect on her relationship with Duncan. For the first few days, she worked day and night, extending the number of hours the barn was open and even working into the early hours of the morning, assembling all manner of arrangements in the hope that by the time she collapsed into bed she would be too tired to interrogate herself. It worked. Physical and mental exhaustion kept the thought police at bay.

Until the day of Bernie's funeral, when in the quiet of the church she had found herself unable to avoid the list of questions waiting to be answered.

By the time of the funeral Jo-Jo had been discharged from hospital, had returned to Sheffield and soon after had parted with her daughter. They had spoken on the phone just hours after Jo-Jo had said goodbye to the grateful couple, and not surprisingly Ellen had detected a strained wistfulness to Jo-Jo's voice.

'They've called her Emily,' she said, 'and they're going to send me photographs on her birthday each year. They say they want her to grow up knowing who I am.'

'And how do you feel about that?' Ellen had asked.

'Confused, if I'm honest,' she'd said, 'but I'm still sure those people can offer her more than I can right now.'

How clearly Jo-Jo saw things.

Which was what Ellen had ended up doing while sitting next to Hermione in Crantsford's parish church. There were few empty pews. Bernie had been an immensely popular man and there were mourners from all over the country. All the residents of the Lodge, including the Management, had been there to show their respect and fondness for the old rascal.

But most of the words of the service had floated over Ellen's head while she had absent-mindedly flicked through her hymn book and thought of Duncan.

How could she have been so blind? had been the question uppermost in her mind. The answer was glaringly obvious. She had been fully determined to see Duncan in only one light – as her saviour. And that, together with her guilt for what she and Matthew had done, had made her incapable of ever questioning him. Through her own weakness and stupidity she had exalted and ennobled Duncan. Time and time again she had defended him, to Jo-Jo, to Hermione, to Simon and to Matthew, and all because she had so very badly wanted him to be her knight in shining armour. How pathetic she had been.

She was thoroughly ashamed of herself.

Matthew had asked her once why she thought she needed to escape. At the time she had refused to listen to him but, blast the man, he'd been right, she could see that so clearly now.

Now she swivelled her head and gazed proudly up at her little cottage and at the barn – her home and her business. She sighed. She had been so busy complaining and manipulating that she hadn't been aware of just what she really had.

During Bernie's funeral service one of his oldest friends had stood up to say a few words about the man he'd known since he was a small boy. He had quoted from Dante's *Divine Comedy* – 'No greater sorrow than to recall in our misery the time when we were happy.' It was the only part of the service that she could remember because it had echoed exactly what she had been doing ever since Roger had left her. All her energy had been focused on trying to achieve the lifestyle she'd led before. Her anger and resentment at what Roger had done had blinkered her to the point that, in her mind, a different life had meant a worse life.

She smiled. She was glad that she had resolved at least one piece of self-deception. Her life was certainly different from how she had once envisaged it but on the whole she had to admit that it was much more fulfilling, these days. She had plans too. She had given a lot of thought to Susie's idea about providing refreshments for customers. She would have to see about planning permission to extend the barn as well as approach the bank for a loan, and goodness knows what other obstacles she would have to overcome, but no matter, she was convinced it was something worth pursuing. As was taking on extra staff, and maybe even a few outworkers to help with making the arrangements.

Susie had turned out an absolute godsend, especially now that the girls were back at school, and Ellen didn't know how she'd managed without her.

Susie had also come to Hermione's rescue by taking care of Giotto and Botticelli.

She shivered and realised that the sun had long since slipped away. She got to her feet and walked over to the cottage. She gazed fondly at it. The honeysuckle around the door had now climbed past her bedroom window and was creeping along the guttering. It was beginning to lose its scent, but there was still just enough sweet fragrance left in the flowers to greet her as she unlocked the cottage door.

She made herself a cup of tea and prepared to sit down in her favourite seat by the window with a novel she'd picked up last week. Just as she'd opened the book and found her page the phone rang. It was Hermione.

'We're having lamb ragoût tonight. Care to join me?'

Ellen knew that the offer wasn't made out of loneliness – Hermione had made lots of friends since she'd moved into the Lodge.

'Try and stop me. What time?'

'Same as last time, about seven.'

It was out of sheer practicality, rather than giving themselves airs, that the gong was always sounded at the Lodge before meals. Ellen arrived just in time to catch the benefit of it. Hermione was there to greet her in the entrance hall and she took her through to the dining-room. They had a table to themselves, though Hermione usually shared a larger table with a few of the other residents.

'No need to ask how you are.' Hermione smiled, flapping open her napkin and settling it on her lap. 'You're looking well.'

'You too,' Ellen said. 'I only saw you a few days ago but I swear you've put on weight?'

'A few pounds,' Hermione admitted.

'It suits you.'

A waiter brought their soup to the table. 'Cream of chicken,' he announced cheerfully, then left them.

'I had a phone call from Jo-Jo this morning,' Hermione said, shaking an elegant silver pepper pot over her soup bowl.

'How is she?'

'Desperate to get off to university. She can't wait. And she's going to see Simon before term starts. I think she sees him as a bit of a guru.'

Ellen laughed. 'And how about her mother?'

'Getting better by the day.'

'And her step-father?'

'No mention of him, but she did refer to Duncan.'

'Oh?' Ellen looked up from her soup.

'She's decided not to press charges.'

Ellen frowned. 'But she should!'

Hermione shook her head. 'Look at it from her point of view. She wants to put the past year behind her. By going to the police everything about her would be dragged up. It can't have been easy for her, what with her mother and then getting pregnant. You have to admire her. At least she's not bitter.

She's got the courage to pick up her skirts and make a dash for the next stage in her life.'

'And is there a little message in there for me?' Ellen asked, with a smile.

Hermione scraped up the last of her soup. 'Maybe,' she said.

'Maybe, my foot! And for your information I've already reached that conclusion myself.'

'What, all on your own? My word, Ellen, you're coming on nicely.'

'Sarky madam. But I still don't like the idea of Duncan getting away with it.'

'What is it that you dislike most about the episode? Jo-Jo getting hurt or your judgement of the man?'

'That's a terrible thing to ask.'

'I agree, but then it's never been my intention to have the merest hint of a saintly quality to my nature, though it's an admirable state of affairs to expect in others.'

'Ah, but it's our expectations that usually let us down.'

Hermione wiped her mouth with her napkin. 'Quite. But are we talking generally now, or specifically?'

Ellen drank some wine. 'I suppose my expectations of Duncan were way off the mark, weren't they?'

'He fooled us all to begin with.'

'When did he stop fooling you?'

'I can't say that it was any one moment. It was a combination of things. I can remember thinking that I didn't want you to marry him because if you did I knew I'd lose your friendship. I think that had a lot to do with colouring my view of him. But the real moment of concern was when he came to view the house.'

'What? When you made out you were away with the fairies?'

Hermione smiled. 'Yes. It was upstairs when he was insisting that I sell to him. There was such a look in his face. I could see that beneath all that poise and courteous behaviour there was a side to him none of us had seen.'

Ellen thought about this. 'I saw flashes of his temper but didn't want to acknowledge them. I tried desperately to ignore his faults, even though I found them worrying. I kept making excuses for him.' She shook her head. 'I made the same mistake with Roger. There were warning signs for years but I chose not to act on them. Why the hell do we do that?'

'Because we're frightened of the consequences, should we acknowledge that all is not well.'

'And another thing. Why do we refuse to listen to trusted friends who can see only too well what's going on?'

'You're not paying me a compliment, are you, Ellen?'

'Don't be ridiculous,' Ellen responded with a smile. 'But, seriously, when I think of Duncan now, I see him as a time bomb just waiting to go off . . . and poor Jo-Jo was unlucky enough to hit the detonator.'

'I would hazard a guess that his upbringing is mostly responsible.'

'Nadia, you mean?'

'In part.'

'You never told me how you knew La Carter. What was your connection?'

'It was more a connection with her dead husband, Donald. Have you ever wondered how the Carter family made their money?'

Ellen shook her head. 'Duncan never mentioned anything.'

'No, he probably wouldn't. Duncan would have preferred his father to have made his wealth out of something solid and respectable like slavery, but the bulk of the money was made through the silk industry. His father owned several small factories over in Macclesfield where they made dresses, handkerchiefs, scarves and underwear. Some said that Donald Carter was an astute businessman, but there were others who thought he was a hard-nosed scoundrel who later managed to make more money out of the war than was decent producing silk parachutes.'

Ellen considered this. 'Didn't you tell me that you and Arthur were once in the silk trade?'

'I'm impressed, Ellen. That means you actually listen to me from time to time. But you're right. When Arthur died I was left to run the family business but, like so many factories at the time, we weren't gaining orders and we were losing out to the foreign markets. I struggled on for a number of years and then Donald Carter made an offer to buy me out and I threw in the towel. I'd had enough.'

'Do you suppose Duncan ever made the connection between you and his father?'

'I shouldn't think so. Donald got out of the industry not long after I did and he became a man of considerable leisure. Duncan was only a boy at the time.'

'It must have been particularly galling for you when Carter Junior came along waving his wad of notes, determined to wrest Laburnum House from you.'

Hermione smiled. 'There was a touch of *déjà vu* to the situation, I'll admit.'

'Why did you never tell me about this when Duncan and I became engaged?'

'Would it have made a difference? Would it have made you any more able to dissuade Duncan from his chosen course?'

Ellen shrugged. 'Probably not.'

'It would have made me seem like a petty old woman with a score to settle. And, besides, it was all in the past and there's really only so much of that that is worth hanging on to. That's why I'm here.'

'And it was the right decision, leaving Laburnum House?'

'I can't tell you how wonderful it is to wake up in the morning and know that the day is mine. I feel like I'm on holiday for the rest of my life.'

The waiter came and took away their empty soup bowls. A few minutes later he returned with the main course.

'Have the builders started work on Laburnum House yet?' asked Ellen, helping Hermione to the vegetables.

On the same day that Ellen had taken Spring Bank Cottage off the market Duncan had withdrawn his offer on Laburnum House, which had surprised no one. But what had come as a surprise was that the Management at the Lodge had approached Hermione, and within the week a figure was agreed upon and a contract drawn up.

'You wouldn't believe how quickly these people move when they get going,' Hermione said. 'The site manager gave me a guided tour yesterday. The place is barely recognisable, walls knocked down and great holes here, there and everywhere.'

'Bet it looks tidier,' grinned Ellen.

Hermione humphed. 'That's as may be. But now that you've insulted me I shan't mind asking you for a favour.'

'I always knew there was no such thing as a free meal. Go on, what do you want me to do?'

'Is there any chance you could get away from the barn for a few days?'

'I'd have to check with Susie. Why?'

Johnny Foreigner was making heavy weather of the hill. 'Come on,' Ellen urged the car, 'it's not as though this is Kilimanjaro.'

'Perhaps you ought to speak to it in French,' suggested Hermione.

'Any more from you and you'll be out and pushing,' Ellen replied, above the whining scream of the struggling engine.

'Is that any way to talk to a frail old lady?'

'Cut the lip, Grannybags, and keep your eyes on the directions and tell me where we are.'

Hermione tutted. 'Is this bolshiness anything to do with being nervous?'

Ellen kept her eyes on the road. 'Look,' she said, 'there's a signpost. What does it say?'

'It says A593 to Coniston to the left.'

'And is that what we want?'

Hermione flipped the piece of paper over in her hands. 'Yes,' she said, 'and then after a mile and a half there should be a narrow road off to the left.'

They found it and began a gradual climb upwards. Johnny Foreigner started protesting again.

'The car sounds as nervous as you,' Hermione fished again.

'If you're not careful I'll turn round and drive you straight back to Crantsford.'

'There's not room,' Hermione said, seeing the close proximity of the stone walls either side of the car. 'And, besides, you wouldn't deprive an old lady of a few days with her godson, would you?'

Ellen pushed the gear lever into first and wondered how she'd let herself be talked into this trip to Coniston.

'I haven't had a holiday in twelve years,' Hermione had said craftily over supper that evening at the Lodge. 'I could catch the train, I suppose, but there would be so many changes I would be sure to end up lost and possibly even mugged.'

Of course, she could have just refused to drive Hermione but then her sneaky friend would have sulked and, worse still, would have asked her why she didn't want to go and stay with Matthew.

Matthew had finished work on Susie and Bonkers's painting not long after Bernie's funeral and had returned home before the paint had even dried. In the end Bonkers had been so pleased with the results that he'd paid Matthew himself, which was what Ellen had suspected would happen anyway.

'There's his cottage,' exclaimed Hermione excitedly.

Ellen parked Johnny Foreigner alongside Matthew's old wreck and went round to Hermione's side to help her out. Behind her she heard a door open but she gave all her concentration to Hermione, wanting at all costs to avoid looking into Matthew's face and seeing, written large and pointedly, the words *I told you so.*

She didn't need to be told that she'd made a complete fool of herself, and if Matthew thought for one moment she was going to put up with any gloating nonsense from him she'd abandon Hermione and drive straight back home. If she had learned one thing from the past few months it was that she was going to take control of her life and stand on her own two feet, which included ignoring what anyone else had to say about what she should or should not do. It was she who called the shots now!

Oh, really, said a smug little voice inside her head. *Is that why you put your foot down with Hermione and refused to come?*

She watched Matthew kiss Hermione, went round to the back of the car and busied herself with hauling out their luggage. And if there was going to be any romantic nonsense from him she would have to stamp on that as well.

Yeah, sure! I really believe you.

'Hi, Ellen,' he said, coming towards her. 'Here, let me help you with that.'

'I can manage.'

He smiled his wretchedly handsome lopsided smile and she felt her stomach lurch. Damn the man! Couldn't he at least have the decency not to look so . . . so bloody desirable?

There! What did I tell you? Putty in his hands.

'I know you can manage,' he said. 'I'm just trying to be helpful.'

'Well, it'll take more than a few suitcases to convince me of that.' The sharpness of her voice surprised her, even the voice inside her head.

Not bad. Almost convincing.

He raised an eyebrow. 'Bad journey?'

'Yes. Look who my travelling companion was.'

Hermione laughed. 'Matthew, what dear Ellen needs is a big glass of wine and a good lunch inside her to sweeten her up. She's in the most terrible mood. I can't think why.'

I can.

*

Although it was mid-September it was still warm enough to sit outside for lunch. They sat at a big wooden table looking directly over the lake and an enormous hill that Matthew referred to as the Old Man of Coniston. Ellen noticed he was relaxed and jovial, in a way she'd never seen him before. He was handing round glasses of perfectly chilled wine and serving an assortment of cheeses and pâté with crusty rolls. Ellen didn't know whether it was the effect of the wine on an empty stomach or that she had been working so hard recently but with nothing to do but sit back and relax she found herself mentally unwinding. She listened to Hermione and Matthew chatting about the Lodge and stared out at the lake. It was heavenly.

After lunch they went for a short walk down to the water's edge. But Hermione said she was tired and fancied a nap so they went back to the cottage and while Matthew settled her into the spare room Ellen decided to take a look in his studio.

It was unbelievably tidy, with everything neatly pigeonholed. Shelves were clearly labelled with what was supposed to be stored there – jars of charcoal, boxes of palette knives, bottles of turpentine, hundreds of tubes of paint and just as many brushes. Several easels bore half-finished canvases, and beneath a window that overlooked the spot where they'd just eaten lunch was a massive bench. On this, and in isolation it seemed, was a large portfolio. Curiosity made her open it and when she'd had a chance to take in what it contained she found Matthew standing behind her.

'Fancy a row on the lake?' he asked, ignoring the startled expression on her face.

They took off their shoes, rolled up their trousers to their knees and dragged the boat across the shingle to where it was deep enough to launch it.

'You get in,' he said, 'and I'll give it a shove.'

The water was calm and the setting was tranquil.

'Is it always as beautiful as this?' she asked, trailing a hand in the water as Matthew pulled at the oars.

'You're seeing it at its best,' he answered. 'Most of the tourists have gone.'

Within a short while they were in the middle of the lake and Matthew's cottage was small and distant, partially hidden behind a clump of trees. They seemed very alone.

'That's Brantwood,' Matthew said, pausing with the oars and pointing to a large white house. 'It's where Ruskin lived, and over there is where Donald Campbell—'

'I'm not sure I want a guided tour,' Ellen said, thinking of the portfolio in Matthew's studio and all the sketches he had made of her. Did he really love her that much? And could she go on pretending that she didn't feel anything for him? While she had been engaged to Duncan she had tried hard to convince herself that he meant nothing to her, but now there was nothing to stop her from admitting what she really felt: that there had always been an attraction.

Except there was the small matter of the voice inside her head, whose name was Pride.

Her pride told her that just because Duncan was no longer in the picture it didn't mean she could automatically turn to Matthew. It was too obvious. He would think she was using him and he would sneer at her and accuse her of all sorts of unpleasant things. Oh, it was useless. She was a victim of her own making.

She looked up and found him staring at her.

'If you don't want a guided tour, Ellen, what do you want?'

She met his gaze and for a moment they were silent.

You dare! hissed Pride.

'A go at rowing,' she said, lowering her eyes.

The following afternoon after lunch Matthew took Ellen out in his boat again. It was even warmer than yesterday and Ellen could feel the comforting rays of the autumn sun lingering on her skin as she turned her face upwards. She breathed in contentedly.

'You like it here, don't you?' Matthew said.

'Yes,' she said. 'Why do you ask?'

He stopped rowing. 'No reason.'

She smiled. 'You never ask me anything without there being a reason. Go on, tell me.'

'Maybe later,' he said. 'How have you been, since . . . ?'

'Since what?'

'Since that . . . since that spineless jerk vanished from your life.'

She leaned over the side of the boat and dipped her hand in the cool water. 'Which one do you mean? Roger or Duncan?'

'Which do you think?'

She laughed. It was back to playing verbal ping-pong. 'Oh, Matthew, I'd forgotten how much I enjoyed our chats. But if this is the moment when you say *I told you so*, I shall be very angry.'

'I wouldn't waste my breath or insult your intelligence.'

'Good.' She flicked some water at him. 'And how have you been since you left Crantsford?'

He shrugged. 'You know how it is. Still waiting for that herd of wildebeest.' He watched her face closely, keeping his own perfectly composed.

'You wouldn't be much use to me if you went and got yourself flattened,' she said, with a smile.

This was too much for Pride. It began leaping up and down inside her head. *See? See what I said? I was right all along. You're flirting with him. You've no shame!*

He swallowed. 'So what did you have in mind for me?'

I can't bear it. You're going to say something really stupid now, aren't you?

'Will you let me row again?'

Oh, a tease as well as a shameless hussy!

They changed places and when the boat had stopped rocking Ellen began to pull on the oars.

'You're very good,' he said, approvingly.

'Any reason why I shouldn't be?'

'None at all. You haven't answered my question, by the way.'

'Which one was that?'

'Dear God, Ellen! Have you been taking lessons from Hermione? I'm asking you what possible use you might have in mind for me?'

She ignored his question – and the voice of Pride. She squashed it flat with honesty and desire.

'Have you ever made love in this boat? Do you suppose it would capsize if we tried?'

He stared at her, unsure whether to trust his ears. But she gazed steadily back at him. He then shook his head and burst out laughing. 'It didn't cross my mind to bring either life-jackets or condoms!' Suddenly he leaned forward and kissed her.

She kissed him back, as she had on the first day they met.

When they finally stopped Matthew took the oars and rowed them to a sheltered spot further up the lake. They lay in the sun, wrapped in each other's arms. They talked. They kissed. And they talked some more. There was so much they needed to say to each other.

'I'm not on the rebound,' Ellen said, 'or, rather, I don't think I am.'

'I know you're not.'

'And I'm not using you as a replacement.'

'I know that as well.'

She raised herself up on her elbow and looked into his face. 'How can you be so sure?'

'Because I'm an arrogant swine. You told me that yourself.'

'Be serious.'

'As if I'm ever anything but serious.'

'Look, this is not the time to play one of our verbal games. Tell me how you can be so sure that what I feel for you is love? Maybe it's lust. Perhaps it's only your body I'm in need of.'

He raised an eyebrow. 'I'm hoping it's a bit of both.'

'Matthew, I need to be sure that you're sure, if you see what I mean.'

'Okay,' he said. 'It was because you cried that day we made love in your cottage. It was the one moment when you were incapable of covering up how you felt. There were other times, like the night of the croquet party, when I suspected you cared for me, but you were less vulnerable then and more able to disguise your feelings, but that day at the cottage I saw the real you.'

She thought about this, then lay back in his arms and laughed. 'It was a close thing that night in the summerhouse, I can tell you. If you'd carried on kissing my hand I dread to think what might have happened.'

'Shall I have a go now?'

It was late afternoon when they reached the shore and tied the boat to its mooring post.

'Do you have any doubts, Ellen?'

She squeezed his hand. 'A few. But I don't care. I'm going to be reckless. I've no idea how we're going to make things work, not when you live here and I live in Cheshire.'

'You make it sound like we live in different countries. We're little more than two hours apart.' He drew her into his arms. 'I want you to know I don't ever want to force you into something you don't want to do. You've worked so hard building up your own business – nobody has the right to take that away from you.'

'You've read too many magazines,' she said, with a smile. 'You're too word perfect. And another thing—'

'Dear God! Do you never give up?'

'We barely know each other. We've spent little more than a few days together.'

He laughed and held her tightly. 'I know all I need to know. Now come on. Stop worrying. It won't be a conventional marriage, not with us living in two different homes, but it'll be wonderfully—'

She released herself from his hold. 'I haven't agreed to marry you.'

'I know,' he said. 'It's that tedious routine of one day at a time.' He kissed her tenderly. 'But I can live in hope.'

They walked back towards the cottage arm in arm.

'Do you think Hermione will be surprised when we tell her?' Ellen asked.

'Are you joking? If there's one thing you can rely on, it's Hermione always being one step ahead of everybody else.'

From the spare bedroom, Hermione peered through the window with her trusty old binoculars, which she'd thoughtfully brought with her. A satisfied smile spread over her face. Then she placed the glasses carefully in their leather case and went downstairs to offer her congratulations.